D1058616

The Story of King Arthur and His Knights

The Story of King Arthur and His Knights

HOWARD PYLE

FALL RIVER PRESS

New York

FALL RIVER PRESS

New York

An Imprint of Sterling Publishing
387 Park Avenue South
New York, NY 10016

FALL RIVER PRESS and the distinctive Fall River Press logo
are registered trademarks of Barnes & Noble, Inc.

This compilation © 2014 by Fall River Press
The Story of King Arthur and His Knights was first published in 1903.
The Story of the Champions of the Round Table was first published in 1905.

All rights reserved. No part of this publication may be reproduced,
stored in a retrieval system, or transmitted in any form or by any means
(including electronic, mechanical, photocopying, recording, or otherwise)
without prior written permission from the publisher.

The Fell Types are digitally reproduced by Igino Marini. www.iginomarini.com

ISBN 978-1-4351-5298-4

Manufactured in the United States of America

2 4 6 8 10 9 7 5 3 1

www.sterlingpublishing.com

Contents

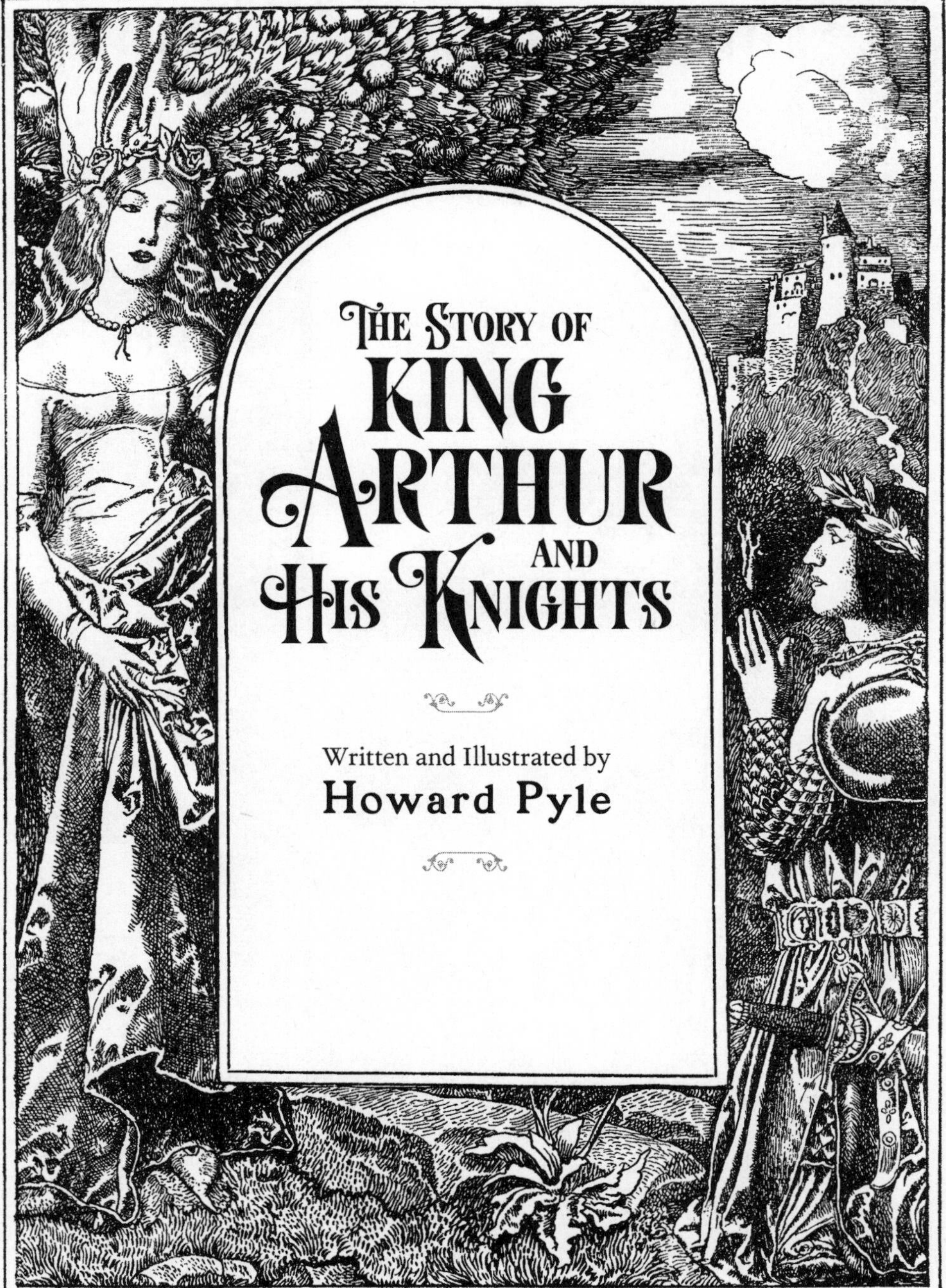
The Story of
King
Arthur
and
His Knights
Written and Illustrated by
Howard Pyle

ing Arthur of Britain.

Foreword

After several years of contemplation and of thought upon the matter herein contained, it has at last come about, by the Grace of God, that I have been able to write this work with such pleasure of spirit that, if it gives to you but a part of the joy that it hath afforded me, I shall be very well content with what I have done.

For when, in pursuing this history, I have come to consider the high nobility of spirit that moved these excellent men to act as they did, I have felt that they have afforded such a perfect example of courage and humility that anyone might do exceedingly well to follow after their manner of behavior in such measure as he is able to do.

For I believe that King Arthur was the most honorable, gentle Knight who ever lived in all the world. And those who were his fellows of the Round Table—taking him as their looking-glass of chivalry—made, altogether, such a company of noble knights that it is hardly to be supposed that their like will ever be seen again in this world. Wherefore it is that I have had such extraordinary pleasure in beholding how those famous knights behaved whenever circumstances called upon them to perform their endeavor.

So in the year of grace one thousand nine hundred and two I began to write this history of King Arthur and his Knights of the Round Table and, if I am able so to do, I shall endeavor, with love of that task, to finish the same at some other time in another book and to the satisfaction of whosoever may care to read the story thereof.

Contents

The Book of King Arthur

PART I

The Book of Three Worthies

PART I

PAX·CVM·JVSTICIÆ

✠ List of Illustrations ✠

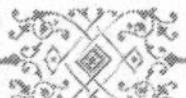

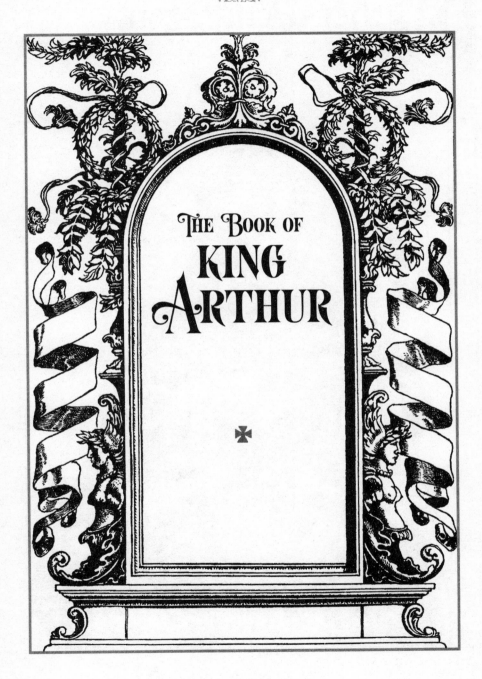

THE BOOK OF KING ARTHUR

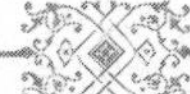

Uther-Pendragon.

Prologue

In ancient days there lived a very noble King, named Uther-Pendragon, and he became Overlord of all of Britain. This King was very greatly aided unto the achievement of the Pendragonship of the realm by the help of two men, who rendered him great assistance in all that he did. The one of these men was a certain very powerful enchanter and sometime prophet known to men as Merlin the Wise; and he gave very good counsel unto Uther-Pendragon. The other man was an excellent noble and renowned knight, hight Ulfius (who was thought by many to be the greatest leader in war of any man then alive); and he gave Uther-Pendragon aid and advice in battle. So, with the help of Merlin and Sir Ulfius, Uther-Pendragon was able to overcome all of his enemies and to become King of the entire realm.

After Uther-Pendragon had ruled his kingdom for a number of years he took to wife a certain beautiful and gentle lady, hight Igraine. This noble dame was the widow of Gerlois, the Duke of Tintegal; by which prince she had two daughters—one of whom was named Margaise and the other Morgana le Fay. And Morgana le Fay was a famous sorceress. These daughters the Queen brought with her to the

Uther-Pendragon taketh to wife Lady Igraine.

Court of Uther-Pendragon after she had married that puissant King, and there Margaise was wedded to King Urien of Gore, and Morgana le Fay was wedded to King Lot of Orkney.

Now after awhile Uther-Pendragon and Queen Igraine had a son born unto them, and he was very beautiful and of great size and strength of bone. And whilst the child still lay wrapped in his swaddling clothes and lying in a cradle of gold and ultramarine, Merlin came to Uther-Pendragon with a spirit of prophecy strong upon him (for such was often the case with him), and, speaking in that spirit of prophecy, he said, "Lord, it is given unto me to foresee that thou shalt shortly fall sick of a fever and that thou shalt maybe die of a violent sweat that will follow thereon. Now, should such a dolorous thing befall us all, this young child (who is, certes, the hope of all this realm) will be in very great danger of his life; for many enemies will assuredly rise up with design to seize upon him for the sake of his inheritance, and either he will be slain or else he will be held in captivity from which he shall hardly hope to escape. Wherefore, I do beseech thee, Lord, that thou wilt permit Sir Ulfius and myself to presently convey the child away unto some place of safe refuge, where he may be hidden in secret until he groweth to manhood and is able to guard himself from such dangers as may threaten him."

Concerning the birth and perils of the young child.

When Merlin had made an end of speaking thus, Uther-Pendragon made reply with a very steadfast countenance in this wise: "Merlin, so far as my death is concerned—when my time cometh to die I believe God will give me grace to meet my end with entire cheerfulness; for, certes, my lot is in that wise no different from that of any other man who hath been born of woman. But touching the matter of this young child, if thy prophecy be true, then his danger is very great, and it would be well that he should be conveyed hence to some place of safe harborage as thou dost advise. Wherefore, I pray thee to perform thy will in this affair, bearing in thy heart the consideration that the child is the most precious inheritance which I shall leave unto this land."

All this, as was said, Uther-Pendragon spake with great calmness and equanimity of spirit. And Merlin did as he had advised, and he and Sir Ulfius conveyed the child away by night, and no one but they wist whither the babe had been taken. And shortly afterward Uther-Pendragon was seized with the sickness as Merlin had foretold, and he died exactly as Merlin had feared that he would die; wherefore it was very well that the child had been taken to a place of safety.

King Uther dieth according to the prophecy of Merlin.

And after Uther-Pendragon had departed from this life, it was likewise as Merlin had feared, for all the realm fell into great disorder. For each lesser king contended against his fellow for overlordship, and wicked knights and barons harried the highways as they listed and there levied toll with great cruelty upon helpless wayfarers. For some such travellers they took prisoners and held for ransom, whiles others they slew because they had no ransom to pay. So it was a very common sight to see a dead man lying by the roadside, if you should venture to make a journey upon some business or other. Thus it befell that, after awhile, all that dolorous land groaned with the trouble that lay upon it.

Thus there passed nearly eighteen years in such great affliction, and then one day the Archbishop of Canterbury summoned Merlin to him and bespake him in this wise: "Merlin, men say that thou art the wisest man in all the world. Canst thou not find some means to heal the distractions of this woeful realm? Bend thou thy wisdom to this matter and choose thou a king who shall be a fit overlord for us, so that we may enjoy happiness of life once more as we did in the days of Uther-Pendragon."

The Archbishop of Canterbury advises with Merlin.

Then Merlin lifted up his countenance upon the Archbishop, and spake in this wise: "My lord, the spirit of prophecy that lieth upon me sometimes moveth me now to say that I do perceive that this country is soon to have a king who shall be wiser and greater and more worthy of praise than was even Uther-Pendragon. And he shall bring order and peace where is now disorder and war. Moreover, I may tell you that this King shall be of Uther-Pendragon's own full blood-royal."

To this the Archbishop said: "What thou tellest me, Merlin, is a wonderfully strange thing. But in this spirit of prophecy canst thou not foretell when this King is to come? And canst thou tell how we shall know him when he appeareth amongst us? For many lesser kings there are who would fain be overlord of this land, and many such there are who deem themselves fit to rule over all the others. How then shall we know the real King from those who may proclaim themselves to be the rightful king?"

Merlin prepares a test of Kinghood.

"My lord Archbishop," quoth Merlin, "if I have thy leave for to exert my magic I shall set an adventure which, if any man achieve it, all the world shall straightway know that he is the rightful King and overlord of this realm." And to this the Archbishop said, "Merlin, I bid thee do whatsoever may seem to thee to be right in this affair." And Merlin said, "I will do so."

So Merlin caused by magic that a huge marble stone, four square, should suddenly appear in an open place before the cathedral door. And upon this block of marble he caused it to be that there should stand an anvil and into the anvil he caused it that there should be thrust a great naked sword midway deep of the blade. And this sword was the most wonderful that any man had ever seen, for the blade was of blue steel and extraordinarily bright and glistering. And the hilt was of gold, chased and carved with marvellous cunning, and inlaid with a great number of precious stones, so that it shone with wonderful brightness in the sunlight. And about the sword were written these words in letters of gold:—

Whoso Pulleth Out this Sword from the Anvil
That same is Rightwise King-Born of England.

So a great many people came and gazed upon that sword and marvelled at it exceedingly, for its like had never before been beheld upon the earth.

Then, when Merlin had accomplished this miracle, he bade the Archbishop to call together all the chief people of that land upon Christmastide; and he bade the Archbishop to command that every man should make assay to draw out the sword, for that he who should succeed in drawing it forth out of the anvil should be rightwise King of Britain.

So the Archbishop did according as Merlin said; and this was the marvel of the marble stone and the anvil, of which same anyone may easily read for himself in that book written a very long while ago by Robert de Boron, which is called Le Roman de Merlin.

Now when the mandate of the Lord Archbishop went forth, summoning all the chief people of the land to the assay of that miracle (for, indeed, it was a miracle to draw forth a sword-blade out of an anvil of solid iron), all the realm became immediately cast into a great ferment, so that each man asked his fellow, "Who shall draw forth that sword, and who shall be our King?" Some thought it would be King Lot and others thought it would be King Urien of Gore (these being the sons-in-law unto Uther-Pendragon); some thought that it would be King Leodegrance of Camiliard, and others that it would be King Ryence of North Wales; some thought it would be this king and others that it would be that king; for all the world was divided into different parties who thought according to their liking.

Then, as Christmastide drew nigh, it presently appeared as though the entire world was wending its way to London Town, for the highways and the by-ways became filled with wayfarers—kings and lords and knights and ladies and esquires and pages and men-at-arms—all betaking their way whither the assay was to be made of that adventure of the sword and the anvil. Every inn and castle was filled so full of travellers that it was a marvel how so many folk could be contained within their compass, and everywhere were tents and pavilions pitched along the wayside for the accommodation of those who could not find shelter within doors.

But when the Archbishop beheld the multitudes that were assembling, he said to Merlin, "Indeed, Merlin, it would be a very singular thing if among all these great kings and noble, honorable lords we should not find some one worthy of being the King of this realm."

Unto which the Merlin smiled and said, "Marvel not, my lord, if among all those who appear to be so extraordinarily worthy there shall not be found one who is worthy; and marvel not if, among all those who are unknown, there shall arise one who shall approve himself to be entirely worthy."

And the Archbishop pondered Merlin's words, and so beginneth this story.

PART I
THE WINNING OF KINGHOOD

Here beginneth the story of the sword, the anvil, and the marble stone, and of how that sword was first achieved by an unknown youth, until then of no renown, whether in arms or of estate.

So hearken unto that which I have hereinafter written.

ir Kay breaketh his sword, at ye Tournament.

CHAPTER FIRST

How Sir Kay did Combat in a Great Tournament at London Town and of How He Brake His Sword. Likewise How Arthur Found a New Sword For Him.

IT HAPPENED THAT AMONG THOSE WORTHIES WHO WERE SUMMONED UNTO London Town by the mandate of the Archbishop as above recounted, there was a certain knight, very honorable and of high estate, by name Sir Ector of Bonmaison—surnamed the Trustworthy Knight, because of the fidelity with which he kept the counsel of those who confided in him, and because he always performed unto all men, whether of high or low degree, that which he promised to undertake, without defalcation as to the same. So this noble and excellent knight was held in great regard by all those who knew him; for not only was he thus honorable in conduct but he was, besides, of very high estate, being possessed of seven castles in Wales and in the adjoining country north thereof, and likewise of certain fruitful tracts of land with villages appertaining thereunto, and also of sundry forests of great extent, both in the north country and the west. This very noble knight had two sons; the elder of these was Sir Kay, a young

Of Sir Ector, the trustworthy Knight.

knight of great valor and promise, and already well renowned in the Courts of Chivalry because of several very honorable deeds of worthy achievement in arms which he had performed; the other was a young lad of eighteen years of age, by name Arthur, who at that time was serving with good repute as Sir Kay's esquire-at-arms.

Now when Sir Ector of Bonmaison received by messenger the mandate of the Archbishop, he immediately summoned these two sons unto him and bade them to prepare straightway for to go with him to London Town, and they did so. And in the same manner he bade a great number of retainers and esquires and pages for to make them ready, and they likewise did so. Thus, with a very considerable array at arms and with great show of circumstance, Sir Ector of Bonmaison betook his way unto London Town in obedience to the commands of the Archbishop.

So, when he had come thither he took up his inn in a certain field where many other noble knights and puissant lords had already established themselves, and there he set up a very fair pavilion of green silk, and erected his banner emblazoned with the device of his house; to wit, a gryphon, black, upon a field of green.

And upon this field were a great multitude of other pavilions of many different colors, and over above each pavilion was the pennant and the banner of that puissant lord to whom the pavilion belonged. Wherefore, because of the multitude of these pennants and banners the sky was at places well-nigh hidden with the gaudy colors of the fluttering flags.

Among the great lords who had come thither in pursuance to the Archbishop's summons were many very famous kings and queens and noblemen of high degree. For there was King Lot of Orkney, who had taken to wife a step-daughter of Uther-Pendragon, and there was King Uriens of Gore, who had taken to wife another step-daughter of that great king, and there was King Ban, and King Bors, and King Ryance, and King Leodegrance and many others of like degree, for there were no less than twelve kings and seven dukes, so that, what with their court of lords and ladies and esquires and pages in attendance, the town of London had hardly ever seen the like before that day.

Now the Archbishop of Canterbury, having in mind the extraordinary state of the occasion that had brought so many kings and dukes and high lords unto that adventure of the sword and the anvil, had commanded that there should be a very stately and noble tournament proclaimed. Likewise he commanded that this contest at arms should be held in a certain field nigh to the great cathedral, three days before that assay should be made of the sword and the anvil (which same was to be undertaken, as

The Archbishop declares a tournament.

aforesaid, upon Christmas day). To this tournament were bidden all knights who were of sufficient birth, condition, and quality for to fit them to take part therein. Accordingly, very many exalted knights made application for admission, and that in such numbers that three heralds were kept very busy looking into their pretensions unto the right of battle. For these heralds examined the escutcheons and the rolls of lineage of all applicants with great care and circumspection.

Now when Sir Kay received news of this tournament he went to where his father was, and when he stood before his face he spake in this wise: "Sire, being thy son and of such very high condition both as to birth and estate as I have inherited from thee, I find that I have an extraordinary desire to imperil my body in this tourney. Accordingly, if so be I may approve my quality as to knighthood before this college of heralds, it will maybe be to thy great honor and credit, and to the honor and credit of our house if I should undertake this adventure. Wherefore I do crave thy leave to do as I have a mind."

Sir Kay asks permission to attend the tournament.

Unto these Sir Ector made reply: "My son, thou hast my leave for to enter this honorable contest, and I do hope that God will give thee a great deal of strength, and likewise such grace of spirit that thou mayst achieve honor to thyself and credit to us who are of thy blood."

So Sir Kay departed with very great joy and immediately went to that congress of heralds and submitted his pretensions unto them. And, after they had duly examined into his claims to knighthood, they entered his name as a knight-contestant according to his desire; and at this Sir Kay was filled with great content and joy of heart.

So, when his name had been enrolled upon the list of combatants, Sir Kay chose his young brother Arthur for to be his esquire-at-arms and to carry his spear and pennant before him into the field of battle, and Arthur was also made exceedingly glad because of the honor that had befallen him and his brother.

Now, the day having arrived when this tourney was to be held, a very huge concourse of people gathered together to witness that noble and courtly assault at arms. For at that time London was, as aforesaid, extraordinarily full of nobility and knighthood, wherefore it was reckoned that not less than twenty thousand lords and ladies (besides those twelve kings and their courts and seven dukes and their courts) were assembled in the lists circumadjacent to the field of battle for to witness the performance of those chosen knights. And those noble people sat so close together, and so filled the seats and benches assigned to them, that it appeared as though an entirely solid wall of human souls surrounded that meadow where the battle was to be fought. And, indeed, any knight might well be moved to do his uttermost upon such a great occasion with the eyes of so many beautiful dames and noble lords gazing upon his performances. Wherefore the hearts of all the knights attendant were greatly expanded with emulation to overturn their enemies into the dust.

In the centre of this wonderful court of lords and ladies there was erected the stall and the throne of the lord Archbishop himself. Above the throne was a canopy of purple cloth emblazoned with silver lilies, and the throne itself was hung all about with purple cloth of velvet, embroidered, alternately, with the figure of St. George in gold, and with silver crosses of St. George surrounded by golden halos. Here the lord Archbishop himself sat in great estate and pomp, being surrounded by a very exalted court of clerks of high degree and also of knights of honorable estate, so that all that centre of the field glistered with the splendor of gold and silver embroidery, and was made beautiful by various colors of rich apparel and bright with fine armor of excellent workmanship. And, indeed, such was the stateliness of all these circumstances that very few who were there had ever seen so noble a preparation for battle as that which they then beheld.

Now, when all that great assembly were in their places and everything had been prepared in due wise, an herald came and stood forth before the enstalled throne of the Archbishop and blew a very strong, loud blast upon a trumpet. At that signal the turnpikes of the lists were immediately opened and two parties of knights-contestant entered therein—the one party at the northern extremity of the meadow of battle and the other party at the southern extremity thereof. Then immediately all that lone field was a-glitter with the bright-shining splendor of the sunlight upon polished armor and accoutrements. So these two parties took up their station, each at such a place as had been assigned unto them—the one to the north and the other to the south.

Now the party with which Sir Kay had cast his lot was at the north of the field, and that company was fourscore and thirteen in number; and the other party stood at the south end of the field, and that company was fourscore and sixteen in number.

Sir Kay takes hand in the lists.

But though the party with whom Sir Kay had attached himself numbered less by three than the other party, yet was it the stronger by some degree because that there were a number of knights of great strength and renown in that company. Indeed it may be here mentioned that two of those knights afterward became companions in very good credit of the round table—to wit: Sir Mador de la Porte, and Sir Bedevere—which latter was the last who saw King Arthur alive upon this earth.

So, when all was prepared according to the ordination of the tournament, and when those knights-contestant had made themselves ready in all ways that were necessary, and when they had dressed their spears and their shields in such a manner as befitted knights about to enter serious battle, the herald set his trumpet to his lips a second time and blew upon it with might and main. Then, having sounded this blast, he waited for a while and then he blew upon the trumpet again.

And, upon that blast, each of those parties of knights quitted its station and rushed forth in great tumult against the other party, and that with such noise and fury that the whole earth groaned beneath the feet of the war-horses, and trembled and shook as with an earthquake.

So those two companies met, the one against the other, in the midst of the field, and the roar of breaking lances was so terrible that those who heard it were astonished and appalled at the sound. For several fair dames swooned away with terror of the noise, and others shrieked aloud; for not only was there that great uproar, but the air was altogether filled with the splinters of ash wood that flew about.

In that famous assault threescore and ten very noble and honorable knights were overthrown, many of them being trampled beneath the hoofs of the horses; wherefore, when the two companies withdrew in retreat each to his station the ground was beheld to be covered all over with broken fragments of lances and with cantels of armor, and many knights were seen to be wofully lying in the midst of all that wreck. And some of these champions strove to arise and could not, while others lay altogether quiet as though in death. To these ran divers esquires and pages in great numbers, and lifted up the fallen men and bare them away to places of safe harborage. And likewise attendants ran and gathered up the cantels of armor and the broken spears, and bare them away to the barriers, so that, by and by, the field was altogether cleared once more.

Then all those who gazed down upon that meadow gave loud acclaim with great joyousness of heart, for such a noble and glorious contest at arms in friendly assay had hardly ever been beheld in all that realm before.

Now turn we unto Sir Kay; for in this assault he had conducted himself with such credit that no knight who was there had done better than he, and maybe no one had done so well as he. For, though two opponents at once had directed their spears against him, yet he had successfully resisted their assault. And one of those two he smote so violently in the midst of his defences that he had lifted that assailant entirely over the crupper of the horse which he rode, and had flung him down to the distance of half a

Sir Kay bears himself well in the encounter.

spear's length behind his steed, so that the fallen knight had rolled thrice over in the dust ere he ceased to fall.

And when those of Sir Kay's party who were nigh to him beheld what he did, they gave him loud and vehement acclaim, and that in such measure that Sir Kay was wonderfully well satisfied and pleased at heart.

And, indeed, it is to be said that at that time there was hardly any knight in all the world who was so excellent in deeds of arms as Sir Kay. And though there afterward came knights of much greater renown and of more glorious achievement (as shall be hereinafter recorded in good season), yet at that time Sir Kay was reckoned by many to be one of the most wonderfully puissant knights (whether errant or in battle) in all of that realm.

So was that course of the combat run to the great pleasure and satisfaction of all who beheld it, and more especially of Sir Kay and his friends. And after it had been completed the two parties in array returned each to its assigned station once more.

And when they had come there, each knight delivered up his spear unto his esquire. For the assault which was next to be made was to be undertaken with swords, wherefore all lances and other weapons were to be put away; such being the order of that courteous and gentle bout at arms.

Accordingly, when the herald again blew upon his trumpet, each knight drew his weapon with such readiness for battle that there was a great splendor of blades all flashing in the air at once. And when the herald blew a second time each party pushed forward to the contest with great nobleness of heart and eagerness of spirit, every knight being moved with intent to engage his oppugnant with all the might and main that lay in him.

Of the contest with swords.

Then immediately began so fierce a battle that if those knights had been very enemies of long standing instead of friendly contestants, the blows which they delivered the one upon the other could not have been more vehement as to strength or more astonishing to gaze upon.

And in this affair likewise Sir Kay approved himself to be so extraordinary a champion that his like was nowhere to be seen in all that field; for he violently smote down five knights, the one after the other, ere he was stayed in his advance.

Wherefore, beholding him to be doing work of such a sort, several of the knights of the other party endeavored to come at him with intent to meet him in his advance.

Amongst these was a certain knight, hight Sir Balamorgineas, who was so huge of frame that he rode head and shoulders above any other knight. And he was possessed of such extraordinary strength that it was believed that he could successfully withstand the assault of three ordinary knights at one time. Wherefore when this knight beheld the work that Sir Kay did, he cried out to him, "Ho! ho! Sir Knight of the black gryphon, turn thou hitherward and do a battle with me!"

Now when Sir Kay beheld Sir Balamorgineas to be minded to come against him in that wise—very threateningly and minded to do him battle—he turned him toward his enemy with great cheerfulness of spirit. For at that time Sir Kay was very full of youthful fire and reckoned nothing of assaulting any enemy who might demand battle of him.

Sir Kay contests with Sir Balamorgineas.

(So it was at that time. But it after befell, when he became Seneschal, and when other and mightier knights appeared at the court of the King, that he would sometimes avoid an encounter with such a knight as Sir Launcelot, or Sir Pellias, or Sir Marhaus, or Sir Gawaine, if he might do so with credit to his honor.)

So, being very full of the spirit of youth, he turned him with great lustiness of heart, altogether inflamed with the eagerness and fury of battle. And he cried out in a great voice, "Very well, I will do battle with thee, and I will cast thee down like thy fellows!" And therewith he smote with wonderful fierceness at Sir Balamorgineas, and that with all his might. And Sir Balamorgineas received the stroke upon his helmet and was altogether bewildered by the fury thereof, for he had never felt its like before that time. Wherefore his brains swam so light that it was necessary for him to hold to the horn of his saddle to save himself from falling.

But it was a great pity for Sir Kay that, with the fierceness of the blow, his sword-blade snapped short at the haft, flying so high in the air that it appeared to overtop the turrets of the cathedral in its flight. Yet so it happened, and thus it befell that Sir Kay was left without any weapon. Yet it was thought that, because of that stroke, he had Sir Balamorgineas entirely at his mercy, and that if he could have struck another blow with his sword he might easily have overcome him.

Sir Kay breaketh his sword.

But as it was, Sir Balamorgineas presently so far recovered himself that he perceived his enemy to be altogether at his mercy; wherefore, being filled beyond measure with rage because of the blow he had received, he pushed against Sir Kay with intent to smite him down in a violent assault.

In this pass it would maybe have gone very ill with Sir Kay but that three of his companions in arms, perceiving the extreme peril in which he lay, thrust in betwixt him and Sir Balamorgineas with intent to take upon themselves the assault of that knight and so to save Sir Kay from overthrow. This they did with such success that Sir Kay was able to push out from the press and to escape to the barriers without suffering any further harm at the hands of his enemies.

Now when he reached the barrier, his esquire, young Arthur, came running to him with a goblet of spiced wine. And Sir Kay opened the umbril of his helmet for to drink, for he was athirst beyond measure. And, lo! his face was all covered over with blood and sweat, and he was so a-drought with battle that his tongue clave to the roof of his mouth and he could not speak. But when he had drunk of the draught that Arthur gave him, his tongue was loosened and he cried out to the young man in a loud and violent voice: "Ho! ho! Brother, get me another sword for to do battle, for I am assuredly winning for our house much glory this day!" And Arthur said, "Where shall I get thee a sword?" And Kay said, "Make haste unto our father's pavilion and fetch me thence another sword, for this which I have is broken." And Arthur said, "I will do so with all speed," and thereupon he set hand to the barrier and leaped over it into the alleyway beyond. And he ran down the alleyway with all the speed that he was able with intent to fulfil that task which his brother had bidden him to undertake; and with like speed he ran to that pavilion that his father had set up in the meadows.

Sir Kay bids Arthur get him a sword.

But when he came to the pavilion of Sir Ector he found no one there, for all the attendants had betaken themselves unto the tournament. And neither could he find any sword fit for his brother's handling, wherefore he was put to a great pass to know what to do in that matter.

In this extremity he bethought him of that sword that stood thrust into the anvil before the cathedral, and it appeared to him that such a sword as that would suit his brother's purposes very well. Wherefore he said to himself, "I will go thither and get that sword if I am able to do so, for it will assuredly do very well for my brother for to finish his battle withal." Whereupon he ran with all speed to the cathedral. And when he had come there he discovered that no one was there upon guard at the block of marble, as had heretofore been the case, for all who had been upon guard had betaken themselves unto the contest of arms that was toward. And the anvil and the sword stood where he could reach them. So, there being no one to stay young Arthur, he leaped up upon the block of marble and laid his hands unto the hilt of the sword. And he bent his body and drew upon the sword very strongly, and, lo! it came forth from the anvil with wonderful smoothness and ease, and he held the sword in his hand, and it was his.

Arthur draweth the sword from the anvil.

And when he had got the sword in that way, he wrapped it in his cloak so that no one might see (for it shone with an exceeding brightness and splendor) and he leaped down from the block of marble stone and hastened with it unto the field of battle.

Now when Arthur had entered into that meadow once more, he found Sir Kay awaiting his coming with great impatience of spirit. And when Sir Kay saw him he cried out, very vehemently, "Hast thou got a sword?" And Arthur said, "Yea, I have one here." Thereupon he opened his cloak and showed Sir Kay what sword it was he had brought.

Now when Sir Kay beheld the sword he immediately knew it, and he wist not what to think or what to say, wherefore he stood for a while, like one turned into a stone, looking upon that sword. Then in awhile he said, in a very strange voice "Where got ye that sword?" And Arthur looked upon his brother and he beheld that his countenance was greatly disturbed, and that his face was altogether as white as wax. And he said, "Brother, what ails thee that thou lookest so strangely. I will tell the entire truth. I could find no sword in our father's pavilion, wherefore I bethought me of that sword that stood in the anvil upon the marble cube before the cathedral. So I went thither and made assay for to draw it forth, and it came forth with wonderful ease. So, when I had drawn it out, I wrapped it in my cloak and brought it hither unto thee as thou beholdest."

Then Sir Kay turned his thoughts inward and communed with himself in this wise, "Lo! my brother Arthur is as yet hardly more than a child. And he is, moreover, exceedingly innocent. Therefore he knoweth not what he hath done in this nor what the doing thereof signifieth. Now, since he hath achieved this weapon, why should I not myself lay claim to that achievement, and so obtain the glory which it signifieth." Whereupon he presently aroused himself, and he said to Arthur, "Give the sword and the cloak to me," and Arthur did as his brother commanded. And when he had done so Sir Kay said to him, "Tell no man of this but keep it privy in thine own heart. Meantime go thou to our father where he sits at the lists and bid him come straightway unto the pavilion where we have taken up our inn."

Sir Kay keepeth the sword for his own.

And Arthur did as Sir Kay commanded him, greatly possessed with wonder that his brother should be so disturbed in spirit as he had appeared to be. For he wist not what he had done in drawing out that sword from the anvil, nor did he know of what great things should arise from that little thing, for so it is in this world that a man sometimes approves himself to be worthy of such a great trust as that, and yet, in lowliness of spirit, he is yet altogether unaware that he is worthy thereof. And so it was with young Arthur at that time.

Sir Kay showeth the mystic Sword unto Sir Ector.

CHAPTER SECOND

How Arthur Twice Performed the Miracle of the Sword Before Sir Ector and of How His Birthright Was Discovered Unto Him.

So Arthur made haste to that part of the lists where Sir Ector sat with the people of his household. And he stood before his father and said, "Sire, my brother Kay hath sent me hitherward for to bid thee come straightway unto the pavilion where we have taken up our inn. And, truly, I think something very extraordinary hath befallen, for my brother Kay hath such a countenance as I never saw him wear."

Then Sir Ector marvelled very greatly what it was that should cause Sir Kay to quit that battle and to summon him at such a time, wherefore he arose from where he sat and went with Arthur. And they went to the pavilion, and when he had come there, behold! Sir Kay was standing in the midst of the pavilion. And Sir Ector saw that his face was as white as ashes of wood and that his eyes shone with a wonderful brightness. And Sir Ector said, "My son, what ails thee?" whereunto Sir Kay made reply, "Sire, here is a very wonderful matter." Therewith he took his father by the hand and brought him to the table that stood in the pavilion. And upon the table there lay a cloak and there was something within the cloak. Then Sir Kay opened the cloak and, lo! there lay the sword of the anvil, and the hilt thereof and the blade thereof glistered with exceeding splendor.

Sir Ector beholdeth the sword.

And Sir Ector immediately knew that sword and whence it came. Wherefore he was filled with such astonishment that he wist not what to do. And for a while his tongue refused to speak, and after a while he found speech and cried out aloud in a great voice, "What is this that mine eyes behold!"

To this Sir Kay made reply, "Sire. I have that sword which stood a while since embedded in the anvil that stands upon the cube of marble stone before the great cathedral. Wherefore I demand that thou tellest me what this may foretend?"

Then Sir Ector said, "How came you by that sword?"

And for a while Sir Kay was silent, but after a while he said, "Sire, I brake my sword in that battle which of late I fought, whereupon I found me this sword in its stead."

Then Sir Ector was altogether bemazed and knew not whether to believe what his ears heard. And after awhile he said, "If so be that thou didst draw forth this sword from the anvil, then it must also be that thou art rightwise King of Britain, for so the saying of the sword proclaimeth. But if thou didst indeed draw it forth from the anvil, then it will be that thou shalt as easily be able for to thrust it back again into that place from whence thou didst take it."

At this a great trouble of spirit fell upon Sir Kay, and he cried out in a very loud voice, "Who may do such a thing as that, and who could perform so great a miracle as to thrust a sword into solid iron." Whereunto Sir Ector made reply, "Such a miracle is no greater than the miracle that thou hast performed in drawing it out from its embedment. For who ever heard that a man could draw forth a sword from a place and yet would not thrust it back whence he drew it?"

Then Sir Kay wist not what to say to his father, and he greatly feared that he should not be able to perform that miracle. But, nevertheless, he took what comfort to himself he was able, saying, "If my young brother Arthur was able to perform this miracle why should I not do a miracle of a like sort, for, assuredly, I am not less worthy than he. Wherefore if he drew the sword forth with such ease, it may be that I with equal ease shall be able to thrust it back into its place again." Accordingly he took such comfort to himself in these thoughts as he was able.

So he wrapped the sword in the cloak again, and when he had done so he and Sir Ector went forth from the pavilion and betook their way unto where was the marble stone and the anvil before the cathedral. And Arthur went with his father and his brother and they forebade him not. And when they had come to that place where the sword had been, Sir Kay mounted upon the cube of marble stone and beheld the face of the anvil And lo! the face of the anvil was altogether smooth and without a scratch or scar of any sort. And Sir Kay said to himself, "What is this my father would have me do! What man is there in life who could thrust a sword-blade into a solid anvil of iron?" But, ne'theless, he could not withdraw from that impossible undertaking, but was constrained to assay that miracle, wherefore he set the point of the sword to the iron and bore upon it with all his strength. But it was impossible for him to accomplish that thing, and though he endeavored with all his might with the sword against the face of the anvil, yet did he not pierce the iron even to the breadth of a hair.

Sir Kay assays to put back the sword but faileth.

So, after he had thus assayed for a great while, he at last ceased what he did and came down from where he stood. And he said to his father, "Sire, no man in life may perform that miracle."

Unto this Sir Ector made reply, "How is it possible then that thou couldst have drawn out that sword as thou sayst and yet cannot put it back again?"

Then young Arthur lifted up his voice and said, "My father, have I thy leave to speak?" And Sir Ector said, "Speak, my son." And Arthur said, "I would that I might assay to handle that sword?" Whereunto Sir Ector replied, "By what authority wouldst thou handle that sword?" And Arthur said, "Because it was I who drew that sword forth from the anvil for my brother. Wherefore, as thou sayest, to draw it forth is not more difficult than to thrust it back again. So I believe that I shall be able to set it back into the iron whence I drew it."

Then Sir Ector gazed upon young Arthur in such a strange manner that Arthur wist not why he looked at him in that wise. Wherefore he cried out, "Sire, why dost thou gaze so strangely upon me? Has thou anger against me?" Whereunto Sir Ector made reply, "In the sight of God, my son, I have no anger against thee." Then he said, "If thou hast a desire to handle the sword, thou mayst assuredly make assay of that miracle."

So Arthur took the sword from his brother Kay and he leaped up upon the marble stone. And he set the point of the sword upon the anvil and bare very strongly upon it and lo! the sword penetrated very smoothly into the centre of the anvil until it stood midway deep therein, and there it stood fast. And after he had performed that miracle he drew the sword forth again very swiftly and easily, and then thrust it back again once more as he had done before.

Arthur performeth the miracle of the sword and the anvil.

But when Sir Ector beheld what Arthur did, he cried out in a voice of exceeding loudness, "Lord! Lord! what is the miracle mine eyes behold!" And when Arthur came down from the cube of marble stone, Sir Ector kneeled down before him and set his hands together, palm to palm.

But when Arthur beheld what his father did, he cried out aloud like one in a great measure of pain; and he said, "My father! my father! why dost thou kneel down to me?"

To him Sir Ector made reply, "I am not thy father, and now it is made manifest that thou art assuredly of very exalted race and that the blood of kings flows in thy veins, else thou couldst not have handled that sword as thou hast done."

Then Arthur fell a-weeping beyond all measure and he cried out as with great agony of spirit, "Father! father! what is this thou sayst? I beseech thee to arise and not to kneel unto me."

So Sir Ector arose from his knees and stood before the face of Arthur, and he said, "Arthur, why dost thou weep?" And Arthur said, "Because I am afeard."

Now all this while Sir Kay had stood near by and he could neither move nor speak, but stood like one entranced, and he said to himself, "What is this? Is my brother a King?"

Then Sir Ector spake, saying, "Arthur, the time hath come for thee to know thyself, for the true circumstances of thy life have, heretofore, been altogether hidden from thee.

"Now I do confess everything to thee in this wise: that eighteen years ago there came to me a certain man very wise and high in favor with Uther-Pendragon and that man was the Enchanter Merlin. And Merlin showed me the signet ring of Uther-Pendragon and he commanded me by virtue of that ring that I should be at a certain assigned place at a particular time which he nominated; and the place which he assigned was the postern gate of Uther-Pendragon's castle; and the time which he named was midnight of that very day.

Sir Ector telleth Arthur the circumstances of his infancy.

"And he bade me tell no man aught concerning those things which he communicated to me, and so I kept his counsel as he desired me to do.

"So I went to that postern gate at midnight as Merlin had commanded, and at that place there came unto me Merlin and another man, and the other man was Sir Ulfius, who was the chief knight of Uther-Pendragon's household. And I tell thee that these two worthies stood nigher unto Uther-Pendragon than any other men in all of the world.

"Now when those two came unto me, I perceived that Merlin bare in his arms a certain thing wrapped in a scarlet mantle of fine texture. And he opened the folds of the mantle and, lo! I beheld a child not long born and wrapped in swaddling clothes. And I saw the child in the light of a lanthorn which Sir Ulfius bare, and I perceived that he was very fair of face and large of bone—and thou wert that child.

"Then Merlin commanded me in this wise: that I was to take that child and that I should rear him as mine own; and he said that the child was to be called by the name of Arthur; and he said that no one in all the world was to know otherwise than that the child was mine own. And I told Merlin that I would do as he would have me, whereupon I took the child and bare it away with me. And I proclaimed that the child was mine own, and all over the world believed my words, wherefore no one ever knew otherwise than that thou wert mine own son. And that lady who was my wife, when she died she took that secret with her unto Paradise, and since then until now no one in all the world knew aught of this matter but I and those two aforementioned worthies.

"Nor have I until now ever known aught of who was thy father; but now I do suspect who he was and that thou hast in thy veins very high and kingly blood. And I do have in mind that perhaps thy father was Uther-Pendragon himself. For who but the son of Uther-Pendragon could have drawn forth that sword from out of the anvil as thou hast done?"

Then, when Arthur heard that saying of his father's, he cried out in a very loud and vehement voice, "Woe! Woe! Woe!"—saying that word three times. And Sir Ector said, "Arthur, why are thou woful?" And Arthur said, "Because I have lost my father, for I would rather have my father than be a King!"

Now as these things passed, there came unto that place two men, very tall and of a wonderfully noble and haughty appearance. And when these two men had come nigh to where they were, Arthur and Sir Ector and Sir Kay perceived that one of them was the Enchanter Merlin and that the other was Sir Ulfius—for those two men were very famous and well known unto all the world. And when those two had come to where were the three, Merlin spake, saying, "What cheer?" And Sir Ector made answer, "Here is cheer of a very wonderful sort; for, behold, Merlin! this is that child that thou didst bring unto me eighteen years ago, and, lo! thou seest he hath grown unto manhood."

Merlin and Sir Ulfius appear to the three.

Then Merlin said, "Sir Ector, I know very well who is this youth, for I have kept diligent watch over him for all this time. And I know that in him lieth the hope of Britain. Moreover, I tell thee that even to-day within the surface of an enchanted looking-glass I have beheld all that he hath done since the morning; and I know how he drew forth the sword from the anvil, and how he thrust it back again; and I know how he drew it forth and thrust it back a second time. And I know all that thou hast been saying unto him this while; wherefore I also do now avouch that thou hast told him the very truth. And, lo! the spirit of prophecy is upon me and I do foresee into the future that thou, Arthur, shall become the greatest and most famous King that ever lived in Britain; and I do foresee that many knights of extraordinary excellence shall gather about thee and that men shall tell of their marvellous deeds as long as this land shall continue, and I do foresee that through these knights thy reign shall be full of splendor and glory; and I do foresee that the most marvellous adventure of the Holy Grail shall be achieved by three of the knights of thy Court, and that to thy lasting renown, who shall be the King under whose reign the holy cup shall be achieved. All these things I foresee; and, lo! the time is now at hand when the glory of thy House shall again be made manifest unto the world, and all the people of this land shall rejoice in thee and thy kinghood. Wherefore, Sir Ector, for these three days to come, I do charge it upon thee that thou do guard this young man as the apple of thine eye, for in him doth lie the hope and salvation of all this realm."

Then Sir Ector lifted up his voice and cried unto Arthur, "A boon! a boon!" And Arthur said, "Alas! how is this? Dost thou, my father, ask a boon of me who may have all in the world that is mine to give? Ask what thou wilt and it is thine!" Then Sir Ector said, "I do beseech this of thee: that when thou art King thy brother Kay may be Seneschal of all this realm." And Arthur said, "It shall be as thou dost ask." And he said, "As for thee, it shall be still better with thee, for thou shalt be my father unto the end!" Whereupon so saying, he took Sir Ector's head into his hands and he kissed Sir Ector upon the forehead and upon the cheeks, and so sealed his plighted word.

Sir Ector craveth a boon of Arthur.

But all this while Sir Kay had stood like unto one struck by thunder, and he wist not whether to be uplifted unto the skies or to be cast down into the depths, that his young brother should thus have been passed by him and exalted unto that extraordinary altitude of fortune. Wherefore he stood like to one bereft of life and motion.

And let it here be said that Arthur fulfilled all that he had thus promised to his father—for, in after times, he made Sir Kay his Seneschal, and Sir Ector was to him a father until the day of his death, which same befell five years from that time.

Thus I have told you how the royalty of Arthur was first discovered. And now, if you will listen, ye shall hear how it was confirmed before all the world.

JVSTISSIMVS·REX·

How Arthur drew forth $\overset{e}{y}$ Sword.

CHAPTER THIRD

How Several Kings and High Dukes Assayed to Draw the Sword Out of the Anvil and How They Failed. Likewise How Arthur Made the Assay and Succeeded Therein.

So when the morning of Christmas day had come, many thousands of folk of all qualities, both gentle and simple, gathered together in front of the cathedral for to behold the assay of that sword.

Now there had been a canopy of embroidered cloth of divers colors spread above the sword and the anvil, and a platform had been built around about the cube of marble stone. And nigh unto that place there had been a throne for the Archbishop established; for the Archbishop was to overlook that assay and to see that every circumstance was fulfilled with due equity and circumspection.

So, when the morning was half gone by, the Archbishop himself came with great pomp of estate and took his seat upon the high throne that had been placed for him, and all his court of clerks and knights gathered about him, so that he presented a very proud and excellent appearance of courtliness.

Now unto that assay there had gathered nineteen kings and sixteen dukes, and each of these was of such noble and exalted estate that he entertained high hopes that he would that day be approved before the world to be the right king and overlord of all Britain. Wherefore after the Archbishop had established himself upon his throne, there came several of these and made demand that he should straightway put that matter to the test. So the Archbishop commanded his herald for to sound a trumpet, and to bid all who had the right to make assay of the sword to come unto that adventure, and the herald did according as the Archbishop ordered.

And when the herald had sounded his trumpet there immediately appeared the first of those kings to make trial of the sword, and he who came was King Lot of Orkney and the Isles. With King Lot there came eleven knights and five esquires, so that he appeared in very noble estate before the eyes of all. And when King Lot had arrived at that place, he mounted the platform. And first he saluted the Archbishop, and then he laid his hands to the pommel of the sword in the sight of all. And he bent his body and drew upon the sword with great strength, but he could not move the blade in the anvil even so much as the breadth of a hair, for it stood as fast as the iron in which it was planted. And after that first assay he tried three times more, but still he was altogether unable to move the blade in the iron. Then, after that he had thus four times made assay, he ceased his endeavor and came down from that place. And he was filled with great anger and indignation that he had not succeeded in his endeavor.

King Lot of Orkney maketh assay of the sword and faileth.

And after King Lot there came his brother-in-law, King Urien of Gore, and he also made assay in the same wise as King Lot had done. But neither did he succeed any better than that other king. And after King Urien there came King Fion of Scotland, and after King Fion there came King Mark of Cornwall, and after King Mark there came King Ryence of North Wales, and after King Ryence there came King Leodegrance of Cameliard, and after him came all those other kings and dukes before numerated, and not one of all these was able to move the blade. And some of these high and mighty lords were filled with anger and indignation that they had not succeeded, and others were ashamed that they had failed in that undertaking before the eyes of all those who looked upon them. But whether they were angry or whether they were ashamed it in no wise helped their case.

Sundry others make assay and fail.

Now when all the kings and dukes had thus failed in that adventure, the people who were there were very much astonished, and they said to one another, "How is this? If all those kings and dukes of very exalted estate have failed to achieve that adventure, who then may hope to succeed? For here have been all those who were most worthy of that high honor, and all have tried to draw that sword and all have failed. Who then is there now to come after these who may hope to succeed?"

And, likewise, those kings and dukes spoke together in the same manner. And by and by there came six of the most worthy—to wit, King Lot, King Urien, King Pellinore, King Ban, King Ryence, and Duke Clarence of Northumberland—and these stood before the throne of the Archbishop and spake to him in this wise: "Sir, here have all the kings and dukes of this realm striven before you for to draw forth that sword, and lo! not one of all those who have undertaken that thing hath succeeded in his undertaking. What, then, may we understand but that the enchanter Merlin hath set this adventure for to bring shame and discredit upon all of us who are here, and upon you, who are the head of the church in this realm? For who in all the world may hope to draw forth a sword-blade out from a bed of solid iron? Behold! it is beyond the power of any man. Now, therefore, lest all this great congregation should have been called here in vain, we do beseech you of your wisdom that you presently choose the one from among the kings here gathered, who may be best fitted to be overlord of this realm. And when ye shall have chosen him, we will promise to obey him in all things whatsoever he may ordain. Verily, such a choice as that will be better worth while than to spend time in this foolish task of striving to draw forth a sword out of an anvil which no man in all the world may draw forth."

The kings and dukes are discontented.

Then was the Archbishop much troubled in spirit, for he said to himself, "Can it be sooth that Merlin hath deceived me, and hath made a mock of me and of all these kings and lordly folk? Surely this cannot be. For Merlin is passing wise, and he would not make a mock of all the realm for the sake of so sorry a jest as this would be. Certes he hath some intent in this of which we know naught, being of less wisdom than he—wherefore I will be patient for a while longer." Accordingly, having communed thus within himself, he spake aloud in this wise to those seven high lords: "Messires," he said, "I have yet faith that Merlin hath not deceived us, wherefore I pray your patience for one little while longer. For, if in the time a man may count five hundred twice over, no one cometh forward to perform this task, then will I, at your behest, proceed to choose one from amongst you and will proclaim him King and Overlord of all." For the Archbishop had faith that Merlin was about to immediately declare a king before them all.

Now leave we these and turn we unto Arthur and his father and brother.

For Merlin had bidden those three to abide in their pavilion until such time as he thought would be fit for them to come out thence. And that time being now come, Merlin and Sir Ulfius went to the pavilion of Sir Ector, and Merlin said, "Arthur, arise and come forth, for now the hour is come for thee to assay before the whole world that miracle which thou didst of late execute in privacy." So Arthur did as Merlin bade him to do, and he came forth from the pavilion with his father and his brother, and, lo! he was like one who walked in a dream.

So they five went down from thence toward the cathedral and unto that place of assay. And when they had come to the congregation there assembled, the people made way for them, greatly marvelling and saying to one another, "Who are these with the Enchanter Merlin and Sir Ulfius, and whence come they?" For all the world knew Merlin and Sir Ulfius, and they wist that here was something very extraordinary about to happen.

Merlin bringeth Arthur to the assay.

And Arthur was clad all in flame-colored raiment embroidered with threads of silver, so that others of the people said, "Certes, that youth is very fair for to look upon; now who may he be?"

But Merlin said no word to any man, but he brought Arthur through the press unto that place where the Archbishop sat; and the press made way for him so that he was not stayed in his going. And when the Archbishop beheld Merlin come thus with those others, he arose and said, "Merlin, who are these whom thou bringest unto us, and what is their business here?" And Merlin said, "Lord, here is one come to make the assay of yonder sword." And the Archbishop said, "Which one is he?" and Merlin said, "This is he," and he laid his hand upon Arthur.

Then the Archbishop looked upon Arthur and he beheld that the youth was very comely of face, wherefore his heart went out unto Arthur and he loved him a very great deal. And the Archbishop said, "Merlin, by what right doth this young man come hither?" And Merlin made reply, "Lord, he cometh hither by the best right that there is in the world; for he who standeth before thee clad in red is the true son of Uther-Pendragon and of his lawful wife, Queen Igraine."

Merlin proclaimeth the royalty of Arthur.

Then the Archbishop cried out aloud in great amazement and those who stood nigh and who heard what Merlin said were so astonished that they wist not what to think. And the Archbishop said, "Merlin, what is this that thou tellest me? For who, until now, in all the world hath ever heard that Uther-Pendragon had a son?"

Unto this Merlin made reply: "No one hath ever known of such a thing until now, only a very few. For it was in this wise: When this child was born the spirit of prophecy lay upon me and I foresaw that Uther-Pendragon would die before a very great while. Wherefore I feared that the enemies of the King would lay violent hands upon the young child for the sake of his inheritance. So, at the King's behest, I and another took the young child from his mother and gave him unto a third, and that man received the kingly child and maintained him ever since as his own son. And as to the truth of these things there are others here who may attest the verity of them—for he who was with me when the young child was taken from his mother was Sir Ulfius, and he to whom he was entrusted was Sir Ector of Bonmaison—and those two witnesses, who are without any reproach, will avouch to the verity of that which I have asserted, for here they stand before thee to certify unto what I have said."

And Sir Ulfius and Sir Ector said, "All that Merlin hath spoken is true, and thereunto we do pledge our most faithful and sacred word of honor."

Then the Archbishop said, "Who is there may doubt the word of such honorable witnesses?" And he looked upon Arthur and smiled upon him.

Then Arthur said, "Have I then thy leave, Lord, to handle yonder sword?" And the Archbishop said, "Thou hast my leave, and may the grace of God go with thee to do thy endeavor."

Thereupon Arthur went to the cube of marble stone and he laid his hands upon the haft of the sword that was thrust into the anvil. And he bent his body and drew very strongly and, lo! the sword came forth with great ease and very smoothly. And when he had got the sword into his hands, he swung it about his head so that it flashed like lightning. And after he had swung it thus thrice about his head, he set the point thereof against the face of the anvil and bore upon it very strongly, and, behold! the sword slid very smoothly back again into that place where it had aforetime stood; and when it was there, midway deep, it stood fast where it was. And thus did Arthur successfully accomplish that marvellous miracle of the sword in the eyes of all the world.

Arthur draweth forth the sword.

Now when the people who were congregated at that place beheld this miracle performed before their faces, they lifted up their voices all together, and shouted so vehemently and with so huge a tumult of outcry that it was as though the whole earth rocked and trembled with the sound of their shouting.

And whiles they so shouted Arthur took hold of the sword again and drew it forth and swung it again, and again drave it back into the anvil. And when he had done that he drew it forth a third time and did the same thing as before. Thus it was that all those who were there beheld that miracle performed three times over.

And all the kings and dukes who were there were filled with great amazement, and they wist not what to think or to say when they beheld one who was little more than a boy perform that undertaking in which the best of them had failed. And some of them, seeing that miracle, were willing to acknowledge Arthur because of it, but others would not acknowledge him. These withdrew themselves and stood aloof; and as they stood thus apart, they said among themselves: "What is this and who can accredit such a thing that a beardless boy should be set before us all and should be made King and overlord of this great realm for to govern us. Nay! nay! we will have none of him for our King." And others said, "Is it not apparent that Merlin and Sir Ulfius are thus exalting this unknown boy so that they may elevate themselves along with him?" Thus these discontented kings spake among themselves, and of all of them the most bitter were King Lot and King Urien, who were brothers by marriage with Arthur.

Several of the kings and dukes are angry.

Now when the Archbishop perceived the discontent of these kings and dukes, he said to them, "How now, Messires! Are ye not satisfied?" And they said, "We are not satisfied." And the Archbishop said, "What would ye have?" And they said, "We would have another sort of king for Britain than a beardless boy of whom no one knoweth and of whose birthright there are only three men to attest." And the Archbishop said, "What of that? Hath he not performed the miracle that ye yourselves assayed and failed to perform?"

But these high and mighty lords would not be satisfied, but with angry and averted faces they went away from that place, filled with wrath and indignation.

Certain kings and dukes accept Arthur.

But others of these kings and dukes came and saluted Arthur and paid him court, giving him joy of that which he had achieved; and the chiefest of those who came thus unto him in friendliness was King Leodegrance of Cameliard. And all the multitude acknowledged him and crowded around that place shouting so that it sounded like to the noise of thunder.

Now all this while Sir Ector and Sir Kay had stood upon one side. And they were greatly weighed down by sorrow; for it appeared to them that Arthur had, of a sudden, been uplifted so far from their estate that they might never hope to approach him more. For now he was of kingly consequence and they but common knights. And, after awhile, Arthur beheld them where they stood with downcast looks, whereupon he straightway went to them and took first one and then the other by the hand and kissed each upon the cheek. Thereupon they were again very glad at being thus uplifted upon him.

And when Arthur departed from that place, great crowds of people followed after him so that the streets were altogether filled with the press of people. And the multitude continually gave him loud acclaim as the chosen King of England, and those who were nearest to him sought to touch the hem of his garments; wherefore the heart of Arthur was exceedingly uplifted with great joy and gladness, so that his soul took wing and flew like a bird into the sky.

Thus Arthur achieved the adventure of the sword that day and entered into his birthright of royalty. Wherefore, may God grant His Grace unto you all that ye too may likewise succeed in your undertakings. For any man may be a king in that life in which he is placed if so be he may draw forth the sword of success from out of the iron of circumstance. Wherefore when your time of assay cometh, I do hope it may be with you as it was with Arthur that day, and that ye too may achieve success with entire satisfaction unto yourself and to your great glory and perfect happiness. Amen.

Conclusion

Now after these things had happened there was much talk among men and great confusion and tumult. For while some of the kings and nearly all the multitude said, "Lo! here is a king come to us, as it were, from out of Heaven for to bring peace unto our distracted land," yet other kings (and they were of greater number) said, "Who is this beardless boy who cometh with a claim to be High King of Britain? Who ever heard of him before? We will have none of him except upon further trial and upon greater avouchment." So, for the sake of peace, the Archbishop ordained that another assay of the sword should be made at Candlemas; and here again all those who endeavored to draw forth the sword failed thereat, but Arthur drew it forth several times, very easily, in the sight of all. And after that a third trial was made at Easter and after that a fourth trial was made at Pentecost. And at all these trials Arthur repeatedly drew out the sword from the anvil, and no one but he could draw it forth.

Arthur maketh sundry other assays of the sword and succeeds at all times.

And, after that fourth trial, sundry of the kings and many of the lesser barons and knights and all of the commons cried out that these were trials enough, and that Arthur had assuredly approved himself to be rightwise King; wherefore they demanded that he should be made King indeed so that he might rule over them. For it had come to pass that withersoever Arthur went great crowds followed after him hailing him as the true son of Uther-Pendragon, and rightwise overlord of Britain. Wherefore, the Archbishop (seeing how the people loved Arthur and how greatly they desired him for their King) ordained that he should be anointed and crowned unto royal estate; and so it was done at the great Cathedral. And some say that that Cathedral was St. Paul's and some say that it was not.

Arthur is crowned King of Britain.

But when Arthur had thus been crowned, all those who were opposed unto his Kingship withdrew themselves in great anger, and immediately set about to prepare war against him. But the people were with Arthur and joined with him, and so also did several Kings and many of the lesser barons and knights. And, with the advice of

Arthur overcometh his enemies.

Merlin, Arthur made friends and allies of sundry other kings and they and he fought two great wars with his enemies and won both of these wars. And in the second war was fought a very famous battle nigh to the Forest of Bedegraine (wherefore it was called the Battle of Bedegraine), and in that battle Arthur overthrew his enemies so entirely that it was not possible for them ever to hope to unite in war against him again.

And of King Lot, his brother-in-law, King Arthur brought two of his sons to Court for to dwell there and to serve as hostages of peace thereafter. And these two were Gawaine and Geharris and they became, after awhile, very famous and accomplished knights. And of King Urien, his other brother-in-law, Arthur brought unto Court his one son, Ewaine, for to hold as an hostage of peace; and he also became in time a very famous and accomplished knight. And because of these hostages there was peace thereafter betwixt those three kingly brothers for all time. And a certain very famous king and knight hight King Pellinore (who was one of his enemies) Arthur drove out of his possessions and away from the habitations of men and into the forest. And King Ryence (who was another of his enemies) he drave into the mountains of North Wales. And other kings who were his enemies he subjugated to his will, so that all the land was at such peace that it had not enjoyed the like since the days of Uther-Pendragon.

Arthur bringeth his nephews to court.

And King Arthur made Sir Kay his Seneschal as he had promised to do; and he made Sir Ulfius his Chamberlain; and Merlin he made his Counsellor; and Sir Bodwain of Britain he made his Constable. And these men were all of such a sort as greatly enhanced the glory and renown of his reign and established him upon his throne with entire security.

Now when the reign of King Arthur became thus entirely established, and when the renown of his greatness began to be known in the world, many men of noble souls and of large spirit and of high knightly prowess—knights who desired above all things to achieve glory at arms in Courts of Chivalry—perceived that great credit and exaltation of estate were likely to be won under such a king. So it fell out that, from all parts, by little and little, there began to gather together such a Court of noble, honorable knights about King Arthur as men never beheld before that time, and shall haply never behold again.

For even to this day the history of these good knights is known to the greater part of mankind. Yea; the names of many kings and emperors have passed away and have been forgotten, but the names of Sir Galahad, and of Sir Launcelot of the Lake, and of Sir Tristram of Lyonesse, and of Sir Percival of Gales, and of Sir Gawaine, and of

Sir Ewaine, and of Sir Bors de Ganis, and of many others of that noble household of worthy brotherhood, is still remembered by men. Wherefore, I think that it is very likely that so long as words shall be written, the performances of these worthies shall be remembered.

So in this history yet to be written, I have set it for my task to inform him who reads this book of many of these adventures, telling him, besides, such several circumstances as I do not believe are known unto everybody. And by and by, when I shall tell of the establishment of the Round Table, I shall set forth a tabulated list of a number of those worthies who at this time assembled at the Court of Arthur as men chosen to found that order of the Round Table, and who, for that reason, were entitled "The Ancient and Honorable Companions of the Round Table."

For though this entire history chiefly concerneth King Arthur, yet the glory of these great honorable knights was his glory, and his glory was their glory, wherefore one cannot tell of the glory of King Arthur without also telling of the glory of those noble gentlemen aforesaid.

PART II
THE WINNING OF A SWORD

Here beginneth the story of certain adventures of Arthur after that he had become King, wherein it is told how, with great knightly courage and prowess, he fought a very fierce and bloody battle with a certain Sable Knight. Likewise, it is told how he achieved, in consequence of that battle, a certain Sword so famous and glorious that its renown shall last as long as our speech shall be spoken. For the like of that sword was never seen in all the world before that time, and it hath never been beheld since then; and its name was Excalibur.

So, if it please you to read this story, I believe it will afford you excellent entertainment, and will, without doubt, greatly exalt your spirit because of the remarkable courage which those two famous and worthy knights displayed when they fought together that famous battle. Likewise you shall find great cheer in reading therein of the wonderful marvellousness of a certain land of Faerie into which King Arthur wandered, and where he found a Lake of Enchantment and held converse with a mild and beautiful lady of that land who directed him how to obtain that renowned sword of aforementioned.

For it hath given me such pleasure to write these things that my heart would, at times, be diluted as with a pure joy, wherefore, I entertain great hopes that you also may find much pleasure in them as I have already done. So I pray you to listen unto what follows.

In the Valley of Delight.

CHAPTER FIRST

How There Came a Certain Wounded Knight Unto the Court of King Arthur, How a Young Knight of the King's Court Sought to Avenge Him and Failed and How the King Thereupon Took That Assay Upon Himself.

Now it fell upon a certain pleasant time in the Springtide season that King Arthur and his Court were making a royal progression through that part of Britain which lieth close to the Forests of the Usk. At that time the weather was exceedingly warm, and so the King and Court made pause within the forest under the trees in the cool and pleasant shade that the place afforded, and there the King rested for a while upon a couch of rushes spread with scarlet cloth.

How King Arthur abided in the Forest of Usk.

And the knights then present at that Court were, Sir Gawaine, and Sir Ewaine, and Sir Kay, and Sir Pellias, and Sir Bedevere, and Sir Caradoc, and Sir Geraint, and Sir Bodwin of Britain and Sir Constantine of Cornwall, and Sir Brandiles and Sir Mador de la Porte, and there was not to be found anywhere in the world a company of such noble and exalted knights as these.

Now as the King lay drowsing and as these worthies sat holding cheerful converse together at that place, there came, of a sudden, a considerable bustle and stir upon the outskirts of the Court, and presently there appeared a very sad and woful sight. For there came thitherward a knight, sore wounded, and upheld upon his horse by a golden-haired page, clad in an apparel of white and azure. And, likewise, the knight's apparel and the trappings of his horse were of white and azure, and upon his shield he bore the emblazonment of a single lily flower of silver upon a ground of pure azure.

How the wounded knight cometh into the forest.

But the knight was in a very woful plight. For his face was as pale as wax and hung down upon his breast. And his eyes were glazed and saw naught that passed around him, and his fair apparel of white and blue was all red with the blood of life that ran from a great wound in his side. And, as they came upon their way, the young page lamented in such wise that it wrung the heart for to hear him.

Now, as these approached, King Arthur aroused cried out, "Alas! what doleful spectacle is that which I behold? Now hasten, ye my lords, and bring succor to yonder knight; and do thou, Sir Kay, go quickly and bring that fair young page hither that we may presently hear from his lips what mishap hath befallen his lord."

So certain of those knights hastened at the King's bidding and gave all succor to the wounded knight, and conveyed him to King Arthur's own pavilion, which had been pitched at a little distance. And when he had come there the King's chirurgeon presently attended upon him—albeit his wounds were of such a sort he might not hope to live for a very long while.

Meantime, Sir Kay brought that fair young page before the King, where he sat, and the King thought that he had hardly ever seen a more beautiful countenance. And the King said, "I prithee tell me, Sir Page, who is thy master, and how came he in such a sad and pitiable condition as that which we have just now beheld."

"That will I so, Lord," said the youth. "Know that my master is entitled Sir Myles of the White Fountain, and that he cometh from the country north of where we are and at a considerable distance from this. In that country he is the Lord of seven castles and several noble estates, wherefore, as thou mayst see, he is of considerable consequence. A fortnight ago (being doubtless moved thereunto by the lustiness of the Springtime), he set forth with only me for his esquire, for he had a mind to seek adventure in such manner as beseemed a good knight who would be errant. And we had several adventures, and in all of them my lord was entirely successful; for he overcame six knights at various places and sent them all to his castle for to attest his valor unto his lady.

The page telleth the story of the wounded knight.

"At last, this morning, coming to a certain place situated at a considerable distance from this, we came upon a fair castle of the forest, which stood in a valley surrounded by open spaces of level lawn, bedight with many flowers of divers sorts. There we beheld three fair damsels who tossed a golden ball from one to another, and the damsels were clad all in flame-colored satin, and their hair was of the color of gold. And as we drew nigh to them they stinted their play, and she who was the chief of those damsels called out to my lord, demanding of him whither he went and what was his errand.

"To her my lord made answer that he was errant and in search of adventure, and upon this, the three damsels laughed, and she who had first spoken said, 'An thou art in search of adventure, Sir Knight, happily I may be able to help thee to one that shall satisfy thee to thy heart's content.'

"Unto this my master made reply 'I prithee, fair damsel, tell me what that adventure may be so that I may presently assay it.'

"Thereupon this lady bade my master to take a certain path, and to follow the same for the distance of a league or a little more, and that he would then come to a bridge of stone that crossed a violent stream, and she assured him that there he might find adventure enough for to satisfy any man.

"So my master and I wended thitherward as that damoiselle had directed, and, by and by, we came unto the bridge whereof she had spoken. And, lo! beyond the bridge was a lonesome castle with a tall straight tower, and before the castle was a wide and level lawn of well-trimmed grass. And immediately beyond the bridge was an apple-tree hung over with a multitude of shields. And midway upon the bridge was a single shield, entirely of black; and beside it hung a hammer of brass; and beneath the shield was written these words in letters of red:

Whoso Smiteth This Shield
Doeth So At his Peril.

"Now, my master, Sir Myles, when he read those words went straightway to the shield and, seizing the hammer that hung beside it, he smote upon it a blow so that it rang like thunder.

"Thereupon, as in answer, the portcullis of the castle was let fall, and there immediately came forth a knight, clad all from head to foot in sable armor. And his apparel and the trappings of his horse and all the appointments thereof were likewise entirely of sable.

"Now when that Sable Knight perceived my master he came riding swiftly across the meadow and so to the other end of the bridge. And when he had come there he drew rein and saluted my master and cried out, 'Sir Knight, I demand of thee why thou didst smite that shield. Now let me tell thee, because of thy boldness, I shall take away from thee thine own shield, and shall hang it upon yonder apple-tree, where thou beholdest all those other shields to be hanging.' Unto this my master made reply. 'That thou shalt not do unless thou mayst overcome me, as knight to knight.' And thereupon, immediately, he dressed his shield and put himself into array for an assault at arms.

The page telleth of the Sable Knight.

"So my master and this Sable Knight, having made themselves ready for that encounter, presently drave together with might and main. And they met in the middle of the course, where my master's spear burst into splinters. But the spear of the Sable Knight held and it pierced through Sir Myles, his shield, and it penetrated his side, so that both he and his horse were overthrown violently into the dust; he being wounded so grievously that he could not arise again from the ground whereon he lay.

"Then the Sable Knight took my master's shield and hung it up in the branches of the apple-tree where the other shields were hanging, and, thereupon, without paying further heed to my master, or inquiring as to his hurt, he rode away into his castle again, whereof the portcullis was immediately closed behind him.

"So, after that he had gone, I got my master to his horse with great labor, and straightway took him thence, not knowing where I might find harborage for him, until I came to this place. And that, my lord King, is the true story of how my master came by that mortal hurt which he hath suffered."

"Ha! By the glory of Paradise!" cried King Arthur, "I do consider it great shame that in my Kingdom and so near to my Court strangers should be so discourteously treated as Sir Myles hath been served. For it is certainly a discourtesy for to leave a fallen knight upon the ground, without tarrying to inquire as to his hurt how grievous it may be. And still more discourteous is it for to take away the shield of a fallen knight who hath done good battle."

And so did all the knights of the King's Court exclaim against the discourtesy of that Sable Knight.

Griflet craveth a boon.

Then there came forth a certain esquire attendant upon the King's person, by name Griflet, who was much beloved by his Royal Master, and he kneeled before the King and cried out in a loud voice: "I crave a boon of thee, my lord King! and do beseech thee that thou wilt grant it unto me!"

Then King Arthur uplifted his countenance upon the youth as he knelt before him and he said, "Ask, Griflet, and thy boon shall be granted unto thee."

Thereupon Griflet said, "It is this that I would ask—I crave that thou wilt make me straightway knight, and that thou wilt let me go forth and endeavor to punish this unkindly knight, by overthrowing him, and so redeeming those shields which he hath hung upon that apple-tree."

Then was King Arthur much troubled in his spirit, for Griflet was as yet only an esquire and altogether untried in arms. So he said, "Behold, thou art yet too young to have to do with so potent a knight as this sable champion must be, who has thus overthrown so many knights without himself suffering any mishap. I prithee, dear Griflet, consider and ask some other boon."

But young Griflet only cried the more, "A boon! A boon! and thou hast granted it unto me."

Thereupon King Arthur said, "Thou shalt have thy boon, though my heart much misgiveth me that thou wilt suffer great ill and misfortune from this adventure."

King Arthur makes Griflet a knight.

So that night Griflet kept watch upon his armor in a chapel of the forest, and, in the morning, having received the Sacrament, he was created a knight by the hand of King Arthur—and it was not possible for any knight to have greater honor than that. Then King Arthur fastened the golden spurs to Sir Griflet's heels with his own hand.

So Griflet was made a knight, and having mounted his charger, he rode straightway upon his adventure, much rejoicing and singing for pure pleasure.

And it was at this time that Sir Myles died of his hurt, for it is often so that death and misfortune befall some, while others laugh and sing for hope and joy, as though such grievous things as sorrow and death could never happen in the world wherein they live.

Now that afternoon King Arthur sat waiting with great anxiety for word of that young knight, but there was no word until toward evening, when there came hurrying to him certain of his attendants, proclaiming that Sir Griflet was returning, but without his shield, and in such guise that it seemed as though a great misfortune had befallen him. And straightway thereafter came Sir Griflet himself, sustained upon his horse on the one hand by Sir Constantine and upon the other by Sir Brandiles. And, lo! Sir Griflet's head hung down upon his breast, and his fair new armor was all broken and stained with blood and dust. And so woful was he of appearance that King Arthur's heart was contracted with sorrow to behold that young knight in so pitiable a condition.

So, at King Arthur's bidding, they conducted Sir Griflet to the Royal Pavilion, and there they laid him down upon a soft couch. Then the King's chirurgeon searched his wounds and found that the head of a spear and a part of the shaft thereof were still piercing Sir Griflet's side, so that he was in most woful and grievous pain.

And when King Arthur beheld in what a parlous state Sir Griflet lay he cried out, "Alas! my dear young knight, what hath happened thee to bring thee unto such a woful condition as this which I behold?"

Then Sir Griflet, speaking in a very weak voice, told King Arthur how he had fared. And he said that he had proceeded through the forest, until he had discovered the three beautiful damsels whereof the page of Sir Myles had spoken. And he said that these damsels had directed him as to the manner in which he should pursue his adventure. And he said that he had found the bridge whereon hung the shield and the brazen mall, and that he had there beheld the apple-tree hung full of shields; and he said that he smote the shield of the Sable Knight with the brazen mall, and that the Sable Knight had thereupon come riding out against him. And he said that this knight did not appear of a mind to fight with him; instead, he cried out to him with a great deal of nobleness that he was too young and too untried in arms to have to do with a seasoned knight; wherefore he advised Sir Griflet to withdraw him from that adventure ere it was too late. But, notwithstanding this advice, Sir Griflet would not withdraw but declared that he would certainly have to do with that other knight in sable. Now at the very first onset Sir Griflet's spear had burst into pieces, but the spear of the Sable Knight had held and had pierced through Sir Griflet's shield and into his side, causing him this grievous wound whereof he suffered. And Sir Griflet said that the Sable Knight had then, most courteously, uplifted him upon his horse again (albeit he had kept Sir Griflet's shield and had hung it upon the tree with those others that hung there) and had then directed him upon his way, so that he had made shift to ride thither, though with great pain and dole.

Sir Griflet telleth how he was hurt.

Then was King Arthur very wode and greatly disturbed in his mind, for indeed he loved Sir Griflet exceedingly well. Wherefore he declared that he himself would now go forth for to punish that Sable Knight, and for to humble him with his own hand. And, though the knights of his Court strove to dissuade him from that adventure, yet he declared that he with his own hand would accomplish that proud knight's humiliation, and that he would undertake the adventure, with God His Grace, upon the very next day.

King Arthur is very angry.

And so disturbed was he that he could scarce eat his food that evening for vexation, nor would he go to his couch to sleep, but, having inquired very narrowly of Sir Griflet where he might find that valley of flowers and those three damsels, he spent the night in walking up and down his pavilion, awaiting for the dawning of the day.

Now, as soon as the birds first began to chirp and the east to brighten with the coming of the daylight, King Arthur summoned his two esquires, and, having with their aid donned his armor and mounted a milk-white war-horse, he presently took his departure upon that adventure which he had determined upon.

And, indeed it is a very pleasant thing for to ride forth in the dawning of a Springtime day. For then the little birds do sing their sweetest song, all joining in one joyous medley, whereof one may scarce tell one note from another, so multitudinous is that pretty roundelay; then do the growing things of the earth smell the sweetest in the freshness of the early daytime—the fair flowers, the shrubs, and the blossoms upon the trees; then doth the dew bespangle all the sward as with an incredible multitude of jewels of various colors; then is all the world sweet and clean and new, as though it had been fresh created for him who came to roam abroad so early in the morning.

King Arthur sets forth upon his adventure.

So King Arthur's heart expanded with great joy, and he chanted a quaint song as he rode through the forest upon the quest of that knightly adventure.

So, about noon-tide, he came to that part of the forest lands whereof he had heard those several times before. For of a sudden, he discovered before him a wide and gently sloping valley, a-down which ran a stream as bright as silver. And, lo! the valley was strewn all over with an infinite multitude of fair and fragrant flowers of divers sorts. And in the midst of the valley there stood a comely castle, with tall red roofs and many bright windows, so that it seemed to King Arthur that it was a very fine castle indeed. And upon a smooth green lawn he perceived those three damoiselles clad in flame-colored satin of whom the page of Sir Myles and Sir Griflet had spoken. And they played at ball with a golden ball, and the hair of each was of the hue of gold, and it seemed to King Arthur, as he drew nigh, that they were the most beautiful damoiselles that he had ever beheld in all of his life.

King Arthur cometh to the Valley of Delight.

Now as King Arthur came unto them the three ceased tossing the ball, and she who was the fairest of all damoiselles demanded of him whither he went and upon what errand he was bound.

Then King Arthur made reply: "Ha! fair lady! whither should a belted knight ride upon such a day as this, and upon what business, other than the search of adventure such as beseemeth a knight of a proper strength of heart and frame who would be errant?"

Then the three damoiselles smiled upon the King, for he was exceedingly comely of face and they liked him very well. "Alas, Sir Knight!" said she who had before spoken, "I prithee be in no such haste to undertake a dangerous adventure, but rather tarry with us for a day or two or three, for to feast and make merry with us. For surely good cheer doth greatly enlarge the heart, and we would fain enjoy the company of so gallant a knight as thou appearest to be. Yonder castle is ours and all this gay valley is ours, and those who have visited it are pleased, because of its joyousness, to call it the Valley of Delight. So tarry with us for a little and be not in such haste to go forward."

The damoiselles greet King Arthur.

"Nay," said King Arthur, "I may not tarry with ye, fair ladies, for I am bent upon an adventure of which ye may wot right well, when I tell ye that I seek that Sable Knight, who hath overcome so many other knights and hath taken away their shields. So I do pray ye of your grace for to tell me where I may find him."

"Grace of Heaven!" cried she who spake for the others, "this is certainly a sorry adventure which ye seek, Sir Knight! For already, in these two days, have two knights assayed with that knight, and both have fallen into great pain and disregard. Ne'theless, an thou wilt undertake this peril, yet shalt thou not go until thou hast eaten and refreshed thyself." So saying, she lifted a little ivory whistle that hung from her neck by a chain of gold, and blew upon it very shrilly.

In answer to this summons there came forth from the castle three fair young pages, clad all in flame-colored raiment, bearing among them a silver table covered with a white napkin. And after them came five other pages of the same appearance, bearing flagons of white wine and red, dried fruits and comfits and manchets of white fair bread.

King Arthur eats and drinks in the Valley of Delight.

Then King Arthur descended from his war-horse with great gladness, for he was both hungry and athirst, and, seating himself at the table with the damsels beside him, he ate with great enjoyment, discoursing pleasantly the while with those fair ladies, who listened to him with great cheerfulness of spirit. Yet he told them not who he was, though they greatly marvelled who might be the noble warrior who had come thus into that place.

So, having satisfied his hunger and his thirst, King Arthur mounted his steed again, and the three damsels conducted him across the valley a little way—he riding upon his horse and they walking beside him. So, by and by, he perceived where was a dark pathway that led into the farther side of the forest land; and when he had come thither the lady who had addressed him before said to him, "Yonder is the way that thou must take an thou wouldst enter upon this adventure. So fare thee well, and may good hap go with thee, for, certes, thou art the Knight most pleasant of address who hath come hitherward for this long time."

Thereupon King Arthur, having saluted those ladies right courteously, rode away with very great joy of that pleasant adventure through which he had thus passed.

Now when King Arthur had gone some ways he came, by and by, to a certain place where charcoal burners plied their trade. For here were many mounds of earth, all a-smoke with the smouldering logs within, whilst all the air was filled with the smell of the dampened fires.

As the King approached this spot, he presently beheld that something was toward that was sadly amiss. For, in the open clearing, he beheld three sooty fellows with long knives in their hands, who pursued one old man, whose beard was as white as snow. And he beheld that the reverend old man, who was clad richly in black, and whose horse stood at a little distance, was running hither and thither, as though to escape from those wicked men, and he appeared to be very hard pressed and in great danger of his life.

"Pardee!" quoth the young King to himself, "here, certes, is one in sore need of succor." Whereupon he cried out in a great voice, "Hold, villains! What would you be at!" and therewith set spurs to his horse and dropped his spear into rest and drove down upon them with a noise like to thunder for loudness.

But when the three wicked fellows beheld the armed Knight thus thundering down upon them, they straightway dropped their knives and, with loud outcries of fear, ran away hither and thither until they had escaped into the thickets of the forest, where one upon a horse might not hope to pursue them.

Whereupon, having driven away those wicked fellows, King Arthur rode up to him whom he had succored, thinking to offer him condolence. And behold! when he had come nigh to him, he perceived that the old man was the Enchanter Merlin. Yet whence he had so suddenly come, who had only a little while before been at the King's

King Arthur rescues Merlin from the three villains.

Court at Carleon, and what he did in that place, the King could in no wise understand. Wherefore he bespoke the Enchanter in this wise, "Ha! Merlin, it seemeth to me that I have saved thy life. For, surely, thou hadst not escaped from the hands of those wicked men had I not happened to come hitherward at this time."

"Dost thou think so, Lord?" said Merlin. "Now let me tell thee that I did maybe appear to be in danger, yet I might have saved myself very easily had I been of a mind to do so. But, as thou sawst me in this seeming peril, so may thou know that a real peril, far greater than this, lieth before thee, and there will be no errant knight to succor thee from it. Wherefore, I pray thee, Lord, for to take me with thee upon this adventure that thou art set upon, for I do tell thee that thou shalt certainly suffer great dole and pain therein."

"Merlin," said King Arthur, "even an I were to face my death, yet would I not turn back from this adventure. But touching the advice thou givest me, meseems it will be very well to take thee with me if such peril lieth before me as thou sayest."

And Merlin said, "Yea, it would be very well for thee to do so."

So Merlin mounted upon his palfrey, and King Arthur and he betook their way from that place in pursuit of that adventure which the King had undertaken to perform.

JVSTISSIMVS·REX·

The Battle with the Sable Knight.

CHAPTER SECOND

How King Arthur Fought With the Sable Knight and How He Was Sorely Wounded. Likewise How Merlin Brought Him Safe Away From the Field of Battle.

So King Arthur and Merlin rode together through the forest for a considerable while, until they perceived that they must be approaching nigh to the place where dwelt the Sable Knight whom the King sought so diligently. For the forest, which had till then been altogether a wilderness, very deep and mossy, began to show an aspect more thin and open, as though a dwelling-place of mankind was close at hand.

And, after a little, they beheld before them a violent stream of water, that rushed through a dark and dismal glen. And, likewise, they perceived that across this stream of water there was a bridge of stone, and that upon the other side of the bridge there was a smooth and level lawn of green grass, whereon Knights-contestants might joust very well. And beyond this lawn they beheld a tall and forbidding castle, with smooth walls and a straight tower; and this castle was built upon the rocks so that it appeared to be altogether a part of the stone. So they wist that this must be the castle whereof the page and Sir Griflet had spoken.

For, midway upon the bridge, they beheld that there hung a sable shield and a brass mall exactly as the page and Sir Griflet had said; and that upon the farther side of the stream was an apple-tree, amid the leaves of which hung a very great many shields of various devices, exactly as those two had reported: and they beheld that some of those shields were clean and fair, and that some were foul and stained with blood, and that some were smooth and unbroken, and that some were cleft as though by battle of knight with knight. And all those shields were the shields of different knights whom the Sable Knight, who dwelt within the castle, had overthrown in combat with his own hand.

King Arthur cometh to the castle of the Sable Knight.

"Splendor of Paradise!" quoth King Arthur, "that must, indeed, be a right valiant knight who, with his own single strength, hath overthrown and cast down so many other knights. For, indeed, Merlin, there must be an hundred shields hanging in yonder tree!"

Unto this Merlin made reply, "And thou, Lord, mayst be very happy an thy shield, too, hangeth not there ere the sun goeth down this even-tide."

"That," said King Arthur, with a very steadfast countenance, "shall be as God willeth. For, certes, I have a greater mind than ever for to try my power against yonder knight. For, consider, what especial honor would fall to me should I overcome so valiant a warrior as this same Sable Champion appeareth to be, seeing that he hath been victorious over so many other good knights."

Thereupon, having so spoken his mind, King Arthur immediately pushed forward his horse and so, coming upon the bridge, he clearly read that challenge writ in letters of red beneath the shield:

Whoso Smiteth This Shield
Doeth So At his Peril.

King Arthur challenges the Sable Knight.

Upon reading these words, the King seized the brazen mall, and smote that shield so violent a blow that the sound thereof echoed back from the smooth walls of the castle, and from the rocks whereon it stood, and from the skirts of the forest around about, as though twelve other shields had been struck in those several places.

And in answer to that sound, the portcullis of the castle was immediately let fall, and there issued forth a knight, very huge of frame, and clad all in sable armor. And, likewise, all of his apparel and all the trappings of his horse were entirely of sable, so that he presented a most grim and forbidding aspect. And this Sable Knight came across that level meadow of smooth grass with a very stately and honorable gait; for neither did he ride in haste, nor did he ride slowly, but with great pride and haughtiness of mien, as became a champion who, haply, had never yet been overcome in battle. So, reaching the bridge-head, he drew rein and saluted King Arthur with great dignity, and also right haughtily. "Ha! Sir Knight!" quoth he, "why didst thou, having read those words yonder inscribed, smite upon my shield? Now I do tell thee that, for thy discourtesy, I shall presently take thy shield away from thee, and shall hang it up upon yonder apple-tree where thou beholdest all those other shields to be hanging. Wherefore, either deliver thou thy shield unto me without more ado or else prepare for to defend it with thy person—in the which event thou shalt certainly suffer great pain and discomfort to thy body."

"Gramercy for the choice thou grantest me," said King Arthur. "But as for taking away my shield—I do believe that that shall be as Heaven willeth, and not as thou willest. Know, thou unkind knight, that I have come hither for no other purpose than to do battle with thee and so to endeavor for to redeem with my person all those shields that hang yonder upon that apple-tree. So make thou ready straightway that I may have to do with thee, maybe to thy great disadvantage."

"That will I so," replied the Sable Knight. And thereupon he turned his horse's head and, riding back a certain distance across the level lawn, he took stand in such place as appeared to him to be convenient. And so did King Arthur ride forth also upon that lawn, and take his station as seemed to him to be convenient.

Then each knight dressed his spear and his shield for the encounter, and, having thus made ready for the assault, each shouted to his war-horse and drave his spurs deep into its flank.

Then those two steeds rushed forth like lightning, coursing across the ground with such violent speed that the earth trembled and shook beneath them, an it were by cause of an earthquake. So those two knights met fairly in the midst of the centre of the field, crashing together like a thunderbolt. And so violently did they smite the one against the other that the spears burst into splinters, even unto the guard and the truncheon thereof, and the horses of the riders staggered back from the onset, so that only because of the extraordinary address of the knights-rider did they recover from falling before that shock of meeting.

King Arthur contests with the Sable Knight.

But, with great spirit, these two knights uplifted each his horse with his own spirit, and so completed his course in safety.

And indeed King Arthur was very much amazed that he had not overthrown his opponent, for, at that time, as aforesaid, he was considered to be the very best knight and the one best approved in deeds of arms that lived in all of Britain. Wherefore he marvelled at the power and the address of that knight against whom he had driven, that he had not been overthrown by the greatness of the blow that had been delivered against his defences. So, when they met again in the midst of the field, King Arthur gave that knight greeting, and bespoke him with great courtesy, addressing him in this wise: "Sir Knight, I know not who thou art, but I do pledge my knightly word that thou art the most potent knight that ever I have met in all of my life. Now I do bid thee get down straightway from thy horse, and let us two fight this battle with sword and upon foot, for it were pity to let it end in this way."

"Not so," quoth the Sable Knight—"not so, nor until one of us twain be overthrown will I so contest this battle upon foot." And upon this he shouted, "Ho! Ho!" in a very loud voice, and straightway thereupon the gateway of the castle opened and there came running forth two tall esquires clad all in black, pied with crimson. And each of these esquires bare in his hand a great spear of ash-wood, new and well-seasoned, and never yet strained in battle.

So King Arthur chose one of these spears and the Sable Knight took the other, and thereupon each returned to that station wherefrom he had before essayed the encounter.

Then once again each knight rushed his steed to the assault, and once again did each smite so fairly in the midst of the defence of the other that the spears were splintered, so that only the guard and the truncheon thereof remained in the grasp of the knight who held it.

The knights break lances a second time.

Then, as before, King Arthur would have fought the battle out with swords and upon foot, but again the Sable Knight would not have it so, but called aloud upon those within the castle, whereupon there immediately came forth two other esquires with fresh, new spears of ash-wood. So each knight again took him a spear, and having armed himself therewith, chose each his station upon that fair, level lawn of grass.

And now, for the third time, having thus prepared themselves thereof assault, those two excellent knights hurled themselves together in furious assault. And now, as twice before, did King Arthur strike the Sable Knight so fairly in the centre of his defence that the spear which he held was burst into splinters. But this time, the spear of the Sable Knight did not so break in that manner, but held; and so violent was the blow that he delivered upon King Arthur's shield that he pierced through the centre of it. Then the girths of the King's saddle burst apart by that great, powerful blow, and both he and his steed were cast violently backward. So King Arthur might have

King Arthur is overthrown.

been overcast, had he not voided his saddle with extraordinary skill and knightly address, wherefore, though his horse was overthrown, he himself still held his footing and did not fall into the dust. Ne'theless, so violent was the blow that he received that, for a little space, he was altogether bereft of his senses so that everything whirled around before his eyes.

But when his sight returned to him he was filled with an anger so vehement that it appeared to him as though all the blood in his heart rushed into his brains so that he saw naught but red, as of blood, before his eyes. And when this also had passed he perceived the Sable Knight that he sat his horse at no great distance. Then immediately King Arthur ran to him and catching the bridle-rein of his horse, he cried out aloud unto that Sable Knight with great violence: "Come down, thou black knight! and fight me upon foot and with thy sword."

"That will I not do," said the Sable Knight, "for, lo! I have overthrown thee. Wherefore deliver thou to me thy shield, that I may hang it upon yonder apple-tree, and go thy way as others have done before thee."

"That will I not!" cried King Arthur, with exceeding passion, "neither will I yield myself nor go hence until either thou or I have altogether conquered the other." Thereupon he thrust the horse of the Sable Knight backward by the bridle-rein so vehemently, that the other was constrained to void his saddle to save himself from being overthrown upon the ground.

And now each knight was entirely furious as the other, wherefore, each drew his sword and dressed his shield, and thereupon rushed together like two wild bulls in battle. They foined, they smote, they traced, they parried, they struck again and again, and the sound of their blows, crashing and clashing the one upon the other, filled the entire surrounding space with an extraordinary uproar. Nor may any man altogether conceive of the entire fury of that encounter, for, because of the violence of the blows which the one delivered upon the other, whole cantels of armor were hewn from their bodies and many deep and grievous wounds were given and received, so that the armor of each was altogether stained with red because of the blood that flowed down upon it.

The knights fight with swords upon foot.

At last King Arthur, waxing, as it were, entirely mad, struck so fierce a blow that no armor could have withstood that stroke had it fallen fairly upon it. But it befell with that stroke that his sword broke at the hilt and the blade thereof flew into three several pieces into the air. Yet was the stroke so wonderfully fierce that the Sable Knight groaned, and staggered, and ran about in a circle as though he had gone blind and knew not whither to direct his steps.

But presently he recovered himself again, and perceiving King Arthur standing near by, and not knowing that his enemy had now no sword for to defend himself withal, he cast aside his shield and took his own sword into both hands, and therewith smote so dolorous a stroke that he clave through King Arthur's shield and through his helmet and even to the bone of his brain-pan.

Then King Arthur thought that he had received his death-wound, for his brains swam like water, his thighs trembled exceedingly, and he sank down to his knees,

King Arthur is sorely wounded.

whilst the blood and sweat, commingled together in the darkness of his helmet, flowed down into his eyes in a lather and blinded him. Thereupon, seeing him thus grievously hurt, the Sable Knight called upon him with great vehemence for to yield himself and to surrender his shield, because he was now too sorely wounded for to fight any more.

But King Arthur would not yield himself, but catching the other by the sword-belt, he lifted himself to his feet. Then, being in a manner recovered from his amazement, he embraced the other with both arms, and placing his knee behind the thigh of the Sable Knight, he cast him backward down upon the ground so violently that the sound of the fall was astounding to hear. And with that fall the Sable Knight was, awhile, entirely bereft of consciousness. Then King Arthur straightway unlaced the helm of the Sable Knight and so beheld his face, and he knew him in spite of the blood that still ran down his own countenance in great quantities, and he knew that knight was King Pellinore, aforenamed in this history, who had twice warred against King Arthur. (It hath already been said how King Arthur had driven that other king from the habitations of men and into the forests, so that now he dwelt in this poor gloomy castle whence he waged war against all the knights who came unto that place.)

Now when King Arthur beheld whom it was against whom he had done battle, he cried out aloud, "Ha! Pellinore, is it then thou? Now yield thee to me, for thou art entirely at my mercy." And upon this he drew his misericordia and set the point thereof at King Pellinore's throat.

But by now King Pellinore had greatly recovered from his fall, and perceiving that the blood was flowing down in great measure from out his enemy's helmet, he wist that that other must have been very sorely wounded by the blow which he had just now received. Wherefore he catched King Arthur's wrist in his hand and directed the point of the dagger away from his own throat so that no great danger threatened there from.

And, indeed, what with his sore wound and with the loss of blood, King Arthur was now fallen exceedingly sick and faint, so that it appeared to him that he was nigh to death. Accordingly, it was with no very great ado that King Pellinore suddenly heaved himself up from the ground and so overthrew his enemy that King Arthur was now underneath his knees.

And by this King Pellinore was exceedingly mad with the fury of the sore battle he had fought. For he was so enraged that his eyes were all beshot with blood like those of a wild boar, and a froth, like the champings of a wild boar, stood in the beard

King Pellinore makes to kill King Arthur.

about his lips. Wherefore he wrenched the dagger out of his enemy's hand, and immediately began to unlace his helm, with intent to slay him where he lay. But at this moment Merlin came in great haste, crying out, "Stay! stay! Sir Pellinore; what would you be at? Stay your sacrilegious hand! For he who lieth beneath you is none other than Arthur, King of all this realm!"

At this King Pellinore was astonished beyond measure. And for a little he was silent, and then after awhile he cried out in a very loud voice, "Say you so, old man? Then verily your words have doomed this man unto death. For no one in all this world hath ever suffered such ill and such wrongs as I have suffered at his hands. For, lo! he hath taken from me power, and kingship, and honors, and estates, and hath left me only this gloomy, dismal castle of the forest as an abiding-place. Wherefore, seeing that he is thus in my power, he shall now presently die; if for no other reason than because if I now let him go free, he will certainly revenge himself when he shall have recovered from all the ill he hath suffered at my hands."

Merlin lays a spell upon King Pellinore.

Then Merlin said, "Not so! He shall not die at thy hands, for I, myself, shall save him." Whereupon he uplifted his staff and smote King Pellinore across the shoulders. Then immediately King Pellinore fell down and lay upon the ground on his face like one who had suddenly gone dead.

Upon this, King Arthur uplifted himself upon his elbow and beheld his enemy lying there as though dead, and he cried out, "Ha! Merlin! what is this that thou hast done? I am very sorry, for I do perceive that thou, by thy arts of magic, hath slain one of the best knights in all the world."

"Not so, my lord King!" said Merlin; "for, in sooth, I tell thee that thou art far nigher to thy death than he. For he is but in sleep and will soon awaken; but thou art in such a case that it would take only a very little for to cause thee to die."

And indeed King Arthur was exceeding sick, even to the heart, with the sore wound he had received, so that it was only with much ado that Merlin could help him up upon his horse. Having done the which and having hung the King's shield upon the horn of his saddle, Merlin straightway conveyed the wounded man thence across the bridge, and, leading the horse by the bridle, so took him away into the forest.

Now I must tell you that there was in that part of the forest a certain hermit so holy that the wild birds of the woodland would come and rest upon his hand whiles he read his breviary; and so sanctified was he in gentleness that the wild does would come even to the door of his hermitage, and there stand whilst he milked them for his refreshment. And this hermit dwelt in that part of the forest so remote from the habitations of man that when he rang the bell for matins or for vespers, there was hardly ever anyone to hear the sound thereof excepting the wild creatures that dwelt thereabout. Yet, ne'theless, to this remote and lonely place royal folk and others of high degree would sometimes come, as though on a pilgrimage, because of the hermit's exceeding saintliness.

So Merlin conveyed King Arthur unto this sanctuary, and, having reached that place, he and the hermit lifted the wounded man down from his saddle—the hermit giving many words of pity and sorrow—and together they conveyed him into the holy man's cell. There they laid him upon a couch of moss and unlaced his armor and searched his wounds and bathed them with pure water and dressed his hurts, for that hermit was a very skillful leech. So for all that day and part of the next, King Arthur lay upon the hermit's pallet like one about to die; for he beheld all things about him as though through thin water, and the breath hung upon his lips and fluttered, and he could not even lift his head from the pallet because of the weakness that lay upon him.

Merlin bringeth King Arthur to the cell of a lonely hermit.

Now upon the afternoon of the second day there fell a great noise and tumult in that part of the forest. For it happened that the Lady Guinevere of Cameliard, together with her Court, both of ladies and of knights, had come upon a pilgrimage to that holy man, the fame of whose saintliness had reached even unto the place where she dwelt. For that lady had a favorite page who was very sick of a fever, and she trusted that the holy man might give her some charm or amulet by the virtue of which he might haply be cured. Wherefore she had come to that place with her entire Court so that all that part of the forest was made gay with fine raiment and the silence thereof was made merry with the sound of talk and laughter and the singing of songs and the chattering of many voices and the neighing of horses. And the Lady Guinevere rode in the midst of her damsels and her Court, and her beauty outshone the beauty of her damsels as the splendor of the morning star outshines that of all the lesser stars that surround it. For then and afterward she was held by all the Courts of Chivalry to be the most beautiful lady in the world.

The Lady Guinevere consults with the priest.

Now when the Lady Guinevere had come to that place, she perceived the milk-white war-horse of King Arthur where it stood cropping the green grass of the open glade nigh to the hermitage. And likewise she perceived Merlin, where he stood beside the door of the cell. So of him she demanded whose was that noble war-horse that stood browsing upon the grass at that lonely place, and who was it that lay within that cell. And unto her Merlin made answer, "Lady, he who lieth within is a knight, very sorely wounded, so that he is sick nigh unto death!"

"Pity of Heaven!" cried the Lady Guinevere. "What a sad thing is this that thou tellest me! Now I do beseech thee to lead me presently unto that knight that I may behold him. For I have in my Court a very skilful leech, who is well used to the cure of hurts such as knights receive in battle."

So Merlin brought the lady into the cell, and there she beheld King Arthur where he lay stretched upon the pallet. And she wist not who he was. Yet it appeared to her that in all her life she had not beheld so noble appearing a knight as he who lay sorely wounded in that lonely place. And King Arthur cast his looks upward to where she stood beside his bed of pain, surrounded by her maidens, and in the great weakness that lay upon him he wist not whether she whom he beheld was a mortal lady or whether she was not rather some tall straight angel who had descended from one of the Lordly Courts of Paradise for to visit him in his pain and distresses. And the Lady Guinevere was filled with a great pity at beholding King Arthur's sorrowful estate. Wherefore she called to her that skilful leech who was with her Court. And she bade him bring a certain alabaster box of exceedingly precious balsam. And she commanded him for to search that knight's wounds and to anoint them with the balsam, so that he might be healed of his hurts with all despatch.

The Lady Guinevere biddeth her leech for to heal King Arthur.

So that wise and skilful leech did according to the Lady Guinevere's commands, and immediately King Arthur felt entire ease of all his aches and great content of spirit. And when the Lady and her Court had departed, he found himself much uplifted in heart, and three days thereafter he was entirely healed and was as well and strong and lusty as ever he had been in all of his life.

And this was the first time that King Arthur ever beheld that beautiful lady, the Lady Guinevere of Cameliard, and from that time forth he never forgot her, but she was almost always present in his thoughts. Wherefore, when he was recovered he said thus to himself: "I will forget that I am a king and I will cherish the thought of this lady and will serve her faithfully as a good knight may serve his chosen dame."

And so he did, as ye shall hear later in this book.

xcalibur the Sword.

CHAPTER THIRD

How King Arthur Found a Noble Sword In a Very Wonderful Manner. And How He Again Fought With It and Won That Battle.

Now, as soon as King Arthur had, by means of that extraordinary balsam, been thus healed of those grievous wounds which he had received in his battle with King Pellinore, he found himself to be moved by a most vehement desire to meet his enemy again for to try issue of battle with him once more, and so recover the credit which he had lost in that combat. Now, upon the morning of the fourth day, being entirely cured, and having broken his fast, he walked for refreshment beside the skirts of the forest, listening the while to the cheerful sound of the woodbirds singing their matins, all with might and main. And Merlin walked beside him, and King Arthur spake his mind to Merlin concerning his intent to engage once more in knightly contest with King Pellinore. And he said, "Merlin, it doth vex me very sorely for to have come off so ill in my late encounter with king Pellinore. Certes, he is the very best knight in all the world whom I have ever yet encountered. Ne'theless, it might have fared differently with me had I not broken my sword, and so left myself altogether defenceless in that respect. Howsoever that may be, I am of a mind for to assay this adventure once more, and so will I do as immediately as may be."

King Arthur desireth to renew his battle.

Thereunto Merlin made reply, "Thou art, assuredly, a very brave man to have so much appetite for battle, seeing how nigh thou camest unto thy death not even four days ago. Yet how mayst thou hope to undertake this adventure without due preparation? For, lo! thou hast no sword, nor hast thou a spear, nor hast thou even thy misericordia for to do battle withal. How then mayst thou hope for to assay this adventure?"

And King Arthur said, "That I know not, nevertheless I will presently seek for some weapon as soon as may be. For, even an I have no better weapon than an oaken cudgel, yet would I assay this battle again with so poor a tool as that."

"Ha! Lord," said Merlin, "I do perceive that thou art altogether fixed in thy purpose for to renew this quarrel. Wherefore, I will not seek to stay thee therefrom, but will do all that in me lies for to aid thee in thy desires. Now to this end I must tell thee that in one part of this forest (which is, indeed, a very strange place) there is a certain woodland sometimes called Arroy, and other times called the Forest of Adventure. For no knight ever entereth therein but some adventure befalleth him. And close to Arroy is a land of enchantment which has several times been seen. And that is a very wonderful land, for there is in it a wide and considerable lake, which is also of enchantment. And in the centre of that lake there hath for some time been seen the appearance as of a woman's arm—exceedingly beautiful and clad in white samite, and the hand of this arm holdeth a sword of such exceeding excellence and beauty that no eye hath ever beheld its like. And the name of this sword is Excalibur—it being so named by those who have beheld it because of its marvellous brightness and beauty. For it hath come to pass that several knights have already seen that sword and have endeavored to obtain it for their own, but, heretofore, no one hath been able to touch it, and many have lost their lives in that adventure. For when any man draweth near unto it, either he sinks into the lake, or else the arm disappeareth entirely, or else it is withdrawn beneath the lake; wherefore no man hath ever been able to obtain the possession of that sword. Now I am able to conduct thee unto that Lake of Enchantment, and there thou mayst see Excalibur with thine own eyes. Then when thou hast seen him thou mayst, haply, have the desire to obtain him; which, an thou art able to do, thou wilt have a sword very fitted for to do battle with."

Merlin telleth King Arthur of Excalibur.

"Merlin," quoth the King, "this is a very strange thing which thou tellest me. Now I am desirous beyond measure for to attempt to obtain this sword for mine own, wherefore I do beseech thee to lead me with all despatch to this enchanted lake whereof thou tellest me." And Merlin said, "I will do so."

So that morning King Arthur and Merlin took leave of that holy hermit (the King having kneeled in the grass to receive his benediction), and so, departing from that place, they entered the deeper forest once more, betaking their way to that part which was known as Arroy.

And after awhile they came to Arroy, and it was about noon-tide. And when they had entered into those woodlands they came to a certain little open place, and in that place they beheld a white doe with a golden collar about its neck. And King Arthur said, "Look, Merlin, yonder is a wonderful sight." And Merlin said, "Let us follow that doe." And upon this the doe turned and they followed it. And by and by in following it they came to an opening in the trees where was a little lawn of sweet soft grass. Here they beheld a bower and before the bower was a table spread with a fair snow-white cloth, and set with refreshments of white bread, wine, and meats of several sorts. And at the door of this bower there stood a page, clad all in green, and his hair was as black as ebony, and his eyes as black as jet and exceeding bright. And when this page beheld King Arthur and Merlin, he gave them greeting, and welcomed the King very pleasantly saying, "Ha! King Arthur, thou art welcome to this place. Now I prithee dismount and refresh thyself before going farther."

Merlin and King Arthur follow a white doe.

Then was King Arthur a-doubt as to whether there might not be some enchantment in this for to work him an ill, for he was astonished that that page in the deep forest should know him so well. But Merlin bade him have good cheer, and he said, "Indeed, Lord, thou mayst freely partake of that refreshment which, I may tell thee, was prepared especially for thee. Moreover in this thou mayst foretell a very happy issue unto this adventure."

So King Arthur sat down to the table with great comfort of heart (for he was an hungered) and that page and another like unto him ministered unto his needs, serving him all the food upon silver plates, and all the wine is golden goblets as he was used to being served in his own court—only that those things were much more cunningly wrought and fashioned, and were more beautiful than the table furniture of the King's court.

Then, after he had eaten his fill and had washed his hands from a silver basin which the first page offered to him, and had wiped his hands upon a fine linen napkin which the other page brought unto him, and after Merlin had also refreshed himself, they went their way, greatly rejoicing at this pleasant adventure, which, it seemed to the King, could not but betoken a very good issue to his undertaking.

King Arthur is refreshed in a mysterious manner.

Now about the middle of the afternoon King Arthur and Merlin came, of a sudden, out from the forest and upon a fair and level plain, bedight all over with such a number of flowers that no man could conceive of their quantity nor of the beauty thereof.

And this was a very wonderful land, for, lo! all the air appeared as it were to be as of gold—so bright was it and so singularly radiant. And here and there upon that plain were sundry trees all in blossom; and the fragrance of the blossoms was so sweet that the King had never smelt any fragrance like to it. And in the branches of those trees were a multitude of birds of many colors, and the melody of their singing ravished the

King Arthur cometh to a strange land.

heart of the hearer. And midway in the plain was a lake of water as bright as silver, and all around the borders of the lake were incredible numbers of lilies and of daffodils. Yet, although this place was so exceedingly fair, there was, nevertheless, nowhere about it a single sign of human life of any sort, but it appeared altogether as lonely as the hollow sky upon a day of summer. So, because of all the marvellous beauty of this place, and because of its strangeness and its entire solitude, King Arthur perceived that he must have come into a land of powerful enchantment where, happily, dwelt a fairy of very exalted quality; wherefore his spirit was enwrapped in a manner of fear, as he pushed his great milk-white war-horse through that long fair grass, all bedight with flowers, and he wist not what strange things were about to befall him.

So when he had come unto the margin of the lake he beheld there the miracle that Merlin had told him of aforetime. For, lo! in the midst of the expanse of water there was the appearance of a fair and beautiful arm, as of a woman, clad all in white samite. And the arm was encircled with several bracelets of wrought gold; and the hand held a sword of marvellous workmanship aloft in the air above the surface of the water; and neither the arm nor the sword moved so much as a hair's-breadth, but were motionless like to a carven image upon the surface of the lake. And, behold! the sun of that strange land shone down upon the hilt of the sword, and it was of pure gold beset with jewels of several sorts, so that the hilt of the sword and the bracelets that encircled the arm glistered in the midst of the lake like to some singular star of exceeding splendor. And King Arthur sat upon his war-horse and gazed from a distance at the arm and the sword, and he greatly marvelled thereat; yet he wist not how he might come at that sword, for the lake was wonderfully wide and deep, wherefore he knew not how he might come thereunto for to make it his own. And as he sat pondering this thing within himself, he was suddenly aware of a strange lady, who approached him through those tall flowers that bloomed along the margin of the lake. And when he perceived her coming toward him he quickly dismounted from his war-horse and he went forward for to meet her with the bridle-rein over his arm. And when he had come nigh to her, he perceived that she was extraordinarily beautiful, and that her face was like wax for clearness, and that her eyes were perfectly black, and that they were as bright and glistening as though they were two jewels set in ivory. And he perceived that her hair was like silk and as black as it was possible to be, and so long that it reached unto the ground as she walked. And the lady was clad all in green—only that a fine cord of crimson and gold was interwoven into the plaits of her hair. And around her neck

King Arthur seeth Excalibur.

King Arthur meeteth the Lady of the Lake.

there hung a very beautiful necklace of several strands of opal stones and emeralds, set in cunningly wrought gold; and around her wrists were bracelets of the like sort—of opal stones and emeralds set into gold. So when King Arthur beheld her wonderful appearance, that it was like to an ivory statue of exceeding beauty clad all in green, he immediately kneeled before her in the midst of all those flowers as he said, "Lady, I do certainly perceive that thou art no mortal damoiselle, but that thou art Fay. Also that this place, because of its extraordinary beauty, can be no other than some land of Faerie into which I have entered."

And the Lady replied, "King Arthur, thou sayest soothly, for I am indeed Faerie. Moreover, I may tell thee that my name is Nymue, and that I am the chiefest of those Ladies of the Lake of whom thou mayst have heard people speak. Also thou art to know that what thou beholdest yonder as a wide lake is, in truth, a plain like unto this, all bedight with flowers. And likewise thou art to know that in the midst of that plain there standeth a castle of white marble and of ultramarine illuminated with gold. But, lest mortal eyes should behold our dwelling-place, my sisters and I have caused it to be that this appearance as of a lake should extend all over that castle so that it is entirely hidden from sight. Nor may any mortal man cross that lake, saving in one way—otherwise he shall certainly perish therein."

"Lady," said King Arthur, "that which thou tellest me causes me to wonder a very great deal. And, indeed, I am afraid that in coming hitherward I have been doing amiss for to intrude upon the solitude of your dwelling-place."

"Nay, not so, King Arthur," said the Lady of the Lake, "for, in truth, thou art very welcome hereunto. Moreover, I may tell thee that I have a greater friendliness for thee and those noble knights of thy court than thou canst easily wot of. But I do beseech thee of thy courtesy for to tell me what it is that brings thee to our land?"

"Lady," quoth the King, "I will tell thee the entire truth. I fought of late a battle with a certain sable knight, in the which I was sorely and grievously wounded, and wherein I burst my spear and snapped my sword and lost even my misericordia, so that I had not a single thing left me by way of a weapon. In this extremity Merlin, here, told me of Excalibur, and of how he is continually upheld by an arm in the midst of this magical lake. So I came hither and, behold, I find it even as he hath said. Now, Lady, an it be possible, I would fain achieve that excellent sword, that, by means of it I might fight my battle to its entire end."

"Ha! my lord King," said the Lady of the Lake, "that sword is no easy thing for to achieve, and, moreover, I may tell thee that several knights have lost their lives by attempting that which thou hast a mind to do. For, in sooth, no man may win yonder sword unless he be without fear and without reproach."

"Alas, Lady!" quoth King Arthur, "that is indeed a sad saying for me. For, though I may not lack in knightly courage, yet, in truth, there be many things wherewith I do reproach myself withal. Ne'theless, I would fain attempt this thing, even an it be to my great endangerment. Wherefore, I prithee tell me how I may best undertake this adventure."

"King Arthur," said the Lady of the Lake, "I will do what I say to aid thee in thy wishes in this matter." Whereupon she lifted a single emerald that hung by a small chain of gold at her girdle and, lo! the emerald was cunningly carved into the form of a whistle. And she set the whistle to her lips and blew upon it very shrilly. Then straightway there appeared upon the water, a great way off, a certain thing that shone very brightly. And this drew near with great speed, and as it came nigh, behold! it was a boat all of carven brass. And the prow of the boat was carved into the form of a head of a beautiful woman, and upon either side were wings like the wings of a swan. And the boat moved upon the water like a swan—very swiftly—so that long lines, like to silver threads, stretched far away behind, across the face of the water, which otherwise was like unto glass for smoothness. And when the brazen boat had reached the bank it rested there and moved no more.

The Lady of the Lake summoneth a boat.

Then the Lady of the Lake bade King Arthur to enter the boat, and so he entered it. And immediately he had done so, the boat moved away from the bank as swiftly as it had come thither. And Merlin and the Lady of the Lake stood upon the margin of the water, and gazed after King Arthur and the brazen boat.

And King Arthur beheld that the boat floated swiftly across the lake to where was the arm uplifting the sword, and that the arm and the sword moved not but remained where they were.

King Arthur obtaineth Excalibur.

Then King Arthur reached forth and took the sword in his hand, and immediately the arm disappeared beneath the water, and King Arthur held the sword and the scabbard thereof and the belt thereof in his hand and, lo! they were his own.

Then verily his heart swelled with joy an it would burst within his bosom, for Excalibur was an hundred times more beautiful than he had thought possible. Wherefore his heart was nigh breaking for pure joy at having obtained that magic sword.

Then the brazen boat bore him very quickly back to the land again and he stepped ashore where stood the Lady of the Lake and Merlin. And when he stood upon the shore, he gave the Lady great thanks beyond measure for all that she had done for to aid him in his great undertaking; and she gave him cheerful and pleasing words in reply.

Then King Arthur saluted the lady, as became him, and, having mounted his war-horse, and Merlin having mounted his palfrey, they rode away thence upon their business—the King's heart still greatly expanded with pure delight at having for his own that beautiful sword—the most beautiful and the most famous sword in all the world.

That night King Arthur and Merlin abided with the holy hermit at the forest sanctuary, and when the next morning had come (the King having bathed himself in the ice-cold forest fountain, and being exceedingly refreshed thereby) they took their departure, offering thanks to that saintly man for the harborage he had given them.

Anon, about noon-tide, they reached the valley of the Sable Knight, and there were all things appointed exactly as when King Arthur had been there before: to wit, that gloomy castle, the lawn of smooth grass, the apple-tree covered over with shields, and the bridge whereon hung that single shield of sable.

"Now, Merlin," quoth King Arthur, "I do this time most strictly forbid thee for to interfere in this quarrel. Nor shalt thou, under pain of my displeasure, exert any of thy arts of magic in my behalf. So hearken thou to what I say, and heed it with all possible diligence."

Thereupon, straightway, the King rode forth upon the bridge and, seizing the brazen mall, he smote upon the sable shield with all his might and main. Immediately the portcullis of the castle was let fall as afore told, and, in the same manner as that other time, the Sable Knight rode forth therefrom, already bedight and equipped for the encounter. So he came to the bridge-head and there King Arthur spake to him in this wise: "Sir Pellinore, we do now know one another entirely well, and each doth judge that he hath cause of quarrel with the other: thou, that I, for mine own reasons as seemed to me to be fit, have taken away from thee thy kingly estate, and have driven thee into this forest solitude: I, that thou has set thyself up here for to do injury and affront to knights and lords and other people of this kingdom of mine. Wherefore, seeing that I am here as an errant Knight, I do challenge thee for to fight with me, man to man, until either thou or I have conquered the other."

King Arthur challenges King Pellinore to battle again.

Unto this speech King Pellinore bowed his head in obedience, and thereupon he wheeled his horse, and, riding to some little distance, took his place where he had afore stood. And King Arthur also rode to some little distance, and took his station where he had afore stood. At the same time there came forth from the castle one of those tall pages clad all in sable, pied with crimson, and gave to King Arthur a good, stout spear of ash-wood, well seasoned and untried in battle; and when the two Knights were duly prepared, they shouted and drave their horses together, the one smiting the other so fairly in the midst of his defences that the spears shivered in the hand of each, bursting all into small splinters as they had aforetime done.

Then each of these two knights immediately voided his horse with great skill and address, and drew each his sword. And thereupon they fell to at a combat, so furious and so violent, that two wild bulls upon the mountains could not have engaged in a more desperate encounter.

But now, having Excalibur for to aid him in his battle, King Arthur soon overcame his enemy. For he gave him several wounds and yet received none himself, nor did he shed a single drop of blood in all that fight, though his enemy's armor was in a little while all stained with crimson. And at last King Arthur delivered so vehement a stroke that King Pellinore was entirely benumbed thereby, wherefore his sword and his shield fell down from their defence, his thighs trembled beneath him and he sank unto his knees upon the ground, Then he called upon King Arthur to have mercy, saying, "Spare my life and I will yield myself unto thee."

King Arthur overcometh King Pellinore.

And King Arthur said, "I will spare thee and I will do more than that. For now that thou hast yielded thyself unto me, lo! I will restore unto thee thy power and estate. For I bear no ill-will toward thee, Pellinore, ne'theless, I can brook no rebels against my power in this realm. For, as God judges me, I do declare that I hold singly in my sight the good of the people of my kingdom. Wherefore, he who is against me is also against them, and he who is against them is also against me. But now that thou hast acknowledged me I will take thee into my favor. Only as a pledge of thy good faith toward me in the future, I shall require it of thee that thou shalt send me as hostage of thy good-will, thy two eldest sons, to wit: Sir Aglaval and Sir Lamorack. Thy young son, Dornar, thou mayest keep with thee for thy comfort."

King Arthur demands two of the sons of King Pellinore for hostages.

So those two young knights above mentioned came to the Court of King Arthur, and they became very famous knights, and by and by were made fellows in great honor of the Round Table.

And King Arthur and King Pellinore went together into the castle of King Pellinore, and there King Pellinore's wounds were dressed and he was made comfortable. That night King Arthur abode in the castle of King Pellinore, and when the next morning had come, he and Merlin returned unto the Court of the King, where it awaited him in the forest at that place where he had established it.

Now King Arthur took very great pleasure unto himself as he and Merlin rode together in return through that forest; for it was the leafiest time of all the year, what time the woodlands decked themselves in their best apparel of clear, bright green. Each bosky dell and dingle was full of the perfume of the thickets, and in every tangled depth the small bird sang with all his might and main, and as though he would burst his little throat with the melody of his singing. And the ground beneath the horses' feet was so soft with fragrant moss that the ear could not hear any sound of hoof-beats upon the earth. And the bright yellow sunlight came down through the leaves so that all the ground was scattered over with a great multitude of trembling circles as of pure yellow gold. And, anon, that sunlight would fall down upon the armed knight as he rode, so that every little while his armor appeared to catch fire with a great glory, shining like a sudden bright star amid the dark shadows of the woodland.

How King Arthur rode through the forest with great joy and delight.

So it was that King Arthur took great joy in that forest land, for he was without ache or pain of any sort and his heart was very greatly elated with the wonderfulness of the success of that adventure into which he had entered. For in that adventure he had not only won a very bitter enemy into a friend who should be of great usefulness and satisfaction to him, but likewise, he had obtained for himself a sword, the like of which the world had never before beheld. And whenever he would think of that singularly splendid sword which now hung by his side, and whenever he remembered that land of Faëry into which he had wandered, and of that which had befallen him therein, his heart would become so greatly elated with pure joyousness that he hardly knew how to contain himself because of the great delight that filled his entire bosom.

And, indeed, I know of no greater good that I could wish for you in all of your life than to have you enjoy such happiness as cometh to one when he hath done his best endeavor and hath succeeded with great entirety in his undertaking. For then all the world appears to be filled as with a bright shining light, and the body seemeth to become so elated that the feet are uplifted from heaviness and touch the earth very lightly because of the lightness of the spirit within. Wherefore, it is, that if I could have it in my power to give you the very best that the world hath to give, I would wish that you might win your battle as King Arthur won his battle at that time, and that you might ride homeward in such triumph and joyousness as filled him that day, and that the sunlight might shine around you as it shone around him, and that the breezes might blow and that all the little birds might sing with might and main as they sang for him, and that your heart also might sing its song of rejoicing in the pleasantness of the world in which you live.

Now as they rode thus through the forest together, Merlin said to the King: "Lord, which wouldst thou rather have, Excalibur, or the sheath that holds him?" To which King Arthur replied, "Ten thousand times would I rather have Excalibur than his sheath." "In that thou art wrong, my Lord," said Merlin, "for let me tell thee, that though Excalibur is of so great a temper that he may cut in twain either a feather or a bar of iron, yet is his sheath of such a sort that he who wears it can suffer no wound in battle, neither may he lose a single drop of blood. In witness whereof, thou mayst remember that, in thy late battle with King Pellinore, thou didst suffer no wound, neither didst thou lose any blood."

Merlin tells King Arthur of the virtues of Excalibur, his sheath.

Then King Arthur directed a countenance of great displeasure upon his companion and he said, "Now, Merlin, I do declare that thou hast taken from me the entire glory of that battle which I have lately fought. For what credit may there be to any knight who fights his enemy by means of enchantment such as thou tellest me of? And, indeed, I am minded to take this glorious sword back to that magic lake and to cast it therein where it belongeth; for I believe that a knight should fight by means of his own strength, and not by means of magic."

"My Lord," said Merlin, "assuredly thou art entirely right in what thou holdest. But thou must bear in mind that thou art not as an ordinary errant knight, but that thou art a King, and that thy life belongeth not unto thee, but unto thy people. Accordingly thou hast no right to imperil it, but shouldst do all that lieth in thy power for to preserve it. Wherefore thou shouldst keep that sword so that it may safeguard thy life."

Then King Arthur meditated that saying for a long while in silence; and when he spake it was in this wise: "Merlin, thou art right in what thou sayest, and, for the sake of my people, I will keep both Excalibur for to fight for them, and likewise his sheath for to preserve my life for their sake. Ne'theless, I will never use him again saving in serious battle." And King Arthur held to that saying, so that thereafter he did no battle in sport excepting with lance and a-horseback.

King Arthur kept Excalibur as the chiefest treasure of all his possessions. For he said to himself, "Such a sword as this is fit for a king above other kings and a lord above other lords. Now, as God hath seen fit for to intrust that sword into my keeping in so marvellous a manner as fell about, so must He mean that I am to be His servant for to do unusual things. Wherefore I will treasure this noble weapon not more for its excellent worth than because it shall be unto me as a sign of those great things that God, in His mercy, hath evidently ordained for me to perform for to do Him service."

So King Arthur had made for Excalibur a strong chest or coffer, bound around with many bands of wrought iron, studded all over with great nails of iron, and locked with three great padlocks. In this strong-box he kept Excalibur lying upon a cushion of crimson silk and wrapped in swathings of fine linen, and very few people ever beheld the sword in its glory excepting when it shone like a sudden flame in the uproar of battle.

For when the time came for King Arthur to defend his realm or his subjects from their enemies, then he would take out the sword, and fasten it upon the side of his body; and when he did so he was like unto a hero of God girt with a blade of shining lightning. Yea; at such times Excalibur shone with so terrible a brightness that the very sight thereof would shake the spirits of every wrong-doer with such great fear that he would, in a manner, suffer the pangs of death ere ever the edge of the blade had touched his flesh.

So King Arthur treasured Excalibur and the sword remained with him for all of his life, wherefore the name of Arthur and of Excalibur are one. So, I believe that that sword is the most famous of any that ever was seen or heard tell of in all the Courts of Chivalry.

As for the sheath of the blade, King Arthur lost that through the treachery of one who should, by rights, have been his dearest friend (as you shall hear of anon), and in the end the loss of that miraculous sheath brought it about that he suffered a very great deal of pain and sorrow.

All that also you shall read of, God willing, in due season.

So endeth the story of the winning of Excalibur, and may God give unto you in your life, that you may have His truth to aid you, like a shining sword, for to overcome your enemies; and may He give you Faith (for Faith containeth Truth as a scabbard containeth its sword), and may that Faith heal all your wounds of sorrow as the sheath of Excalibur healed all the wounds of him who wore that excellent weapon. For with Truth and Faith girded upon you, you shall be as well able to fight all your battles as did that noble hero of old, whom men called King Arthur.

PART III
THE WINNING OF A QUEEN

So, having told you how King Arthur obtained that very excellent sword, Excalibur, for a weapon of defence, I shall now presently recount sundry other noble and knightly adventures whereby he won for himself a most beautiful and gentle lady for his Queen.

For, though all the world is very well acquainted with the renown of that perfectly gracious dame, the Lady Guinevere, yet I do not think that the whole story of those adventures by the which King Arthur won her good favor hath ever yet been told.

So as the matter hereinafter to be related contains not only the narrative of that affair, but also the account of a certain enchanted disguise which King Arthur assumed for his purposes, as well as sundry adventures of very knightly daring which he undertook, I have great hope that he who reads what I have written shall find it both an agreeable and an entertaining history.

The Lady Guinevere.

CHAPTER FIRST

How King Arthur Went to Tintagalon With Four of His Court, and How He Disguised Himself for a Certain Purpose.

Now, upon a certain day King Arthur proclaimed a high feast, which was held at Carleon upon Usk. Many noble guests were bidden, and an exceedingly splendid Court gathered at the King's castle. For at that feast there sat seven kings and five queens in royal state, and there were high lords and beautiful ladies of degree, to the number of three score and seven; and there were a multitude of those famous knights of the King's Court who were reckoned the most renowned in arms in all of Christendom. And of all this great gathering of kings, lords, and knights, not one man looked askance at his neighbor, but all were united in good fellowship. Wherefore, when the young King looked about him and beheld such peace and amity among all these noble lords where, aforetime, had been discord and ill-regard: "Certes," quoth he to himself, "it is wonderful how this reign of mine hath knit men together in kindness and good fellowship!" And because of such thoughts as these, his spirit took wings like unto a bird and sang within him.

How King Arthur held a feast at Carleon upon Usk.

Now while the King sat thus at feast, lo! there came an herald-messenger from the west-country. And the herald came and stood before the King, and said: "Greeting to thee, King Arthur!"

Then the King said: "Speak, and tell me, what is thy message?"

To which the herald made reply: "I come from King Leodegrance of Cameliard, who is in sore trouble. For thus it is: His enemy and thine enemy, King Ryence of North Wales (he who at one time in contempt of thee commanded thee to send him thy beard for to trim his mantle), doth make sundry demands of my master, King Leodegrance, which demands King Leodegrance is altogether loath to fulfil. And King Ryence of North Wales threateneth to bring war into Cameliard because King Leodegrance doth not immediately fulfil those demands. Now King Leodegrance hath no such array of knights and armed men as he one time had gathered about him for to defend his kingdom against assault. For, since thou in thy majesty hath brought peace to this realm and hath reduced the power of all those kings under thee, those knights who once made the Court of King Leodegrance so famous have gone elsewhither for to seek better opportunities for their great valor and prowess at arms than his peaceful Court may afford. Wherefore my master, King Leodegrance, doth beseech aid of thee, who art his King and Overlord."

An herald-messenger comes from the west-country.

To these things that the herald-messenger said, King Arthur, and all that Court that feasted with him, listened in entire silence. And the King's countenance, which erstwhiles had been expanded with cheerfulness, became overcast and dark with anger. "Ha!" he cried, "this is, verily, no good news that thou hast brought hither to our feast. Now I will give what aid I am able to thy master, King Leodegrance, in this extremity, and that right speedily. But tell me, sir herald, what things are they that King Ryence demandeth of thy master?"

"That I will tell you, Lord," quoth the herald-messenger. "Firstly, King Ryence maketh demand upon my master of a great part of those lands of Cameliard that march upon the borders of North Wales. Secondly, he maketh demand that the Lady Guinevere, the King's daughter, be delivered in marriage unto Duke Mordaunt of North Umber, who is of kin unto King Ryence, and that Duke, though a mighty warrior, is so evil of appearance, and so violent of temper, that I believe that there is not his like for ugliness or for madness of humor in all of the world."

King Arthur is very angry at the message which the herald bringeth.

Now when King Arthur heard this that the messenger said he was immediately seized with an extraordinary passion of anger. For his eyes appeared, an it were, to shoot forth sparks of pure light, his face flamed like fire, and he ground his teeth together like the stones of a quern. Then he immediately rose from the chair where he sat and went forth from that place, and all those who beheld his anger shuddered thereat and turned their eyes away from his countenance.

Then King Arthur went into an inner room of the castle by himself, and there he walked up and down for a great while, and in that time no one of his household dared to come nigh to him. And the reason of the King's wrath was this: that ever since he had lain wounded and sick nigh unto death in the forest, he bare in mind how the Lady Guinevere had suddenly appeared before him like some tall, straight, shining angel who had descended unto him out of Paradise—all full of pity, and exceedingly beautiful. Wherefore, at thought of that wicked, mad Duke Mordaunt of North Umber making demand unto marriage with her, he was seized with a rage so violent that it shook his spirit like a mighty wind.

So, for a long while, he walked up and down in his wrath as aforesaid, and no one durst come nigh unto him, but all stood afar off, watching him from a distance.

Then, after a while, he gave command that Merlin, and Sir Ulfius, and Sir Kay should come to him at that place where he was. And when they had come thither he talked to them for a considerable time, bidding Merlin for to make ready to go upon a journey with him, and bidding Sir Ulfius and Sir Kay for to gather together a large army of chosen knights and armed men, and to bring that army straightway into those parts coadjacent to the royal castle of Tintagalon, which same standeth close to the borders of North Wales and of Cameliard.

So Sir Ulfius and Sir Kay went about to do as King Arthur commanded, and Merlin also went about to do as he commanded; and the next day King Arthur and Merlin, together with certain famous knights of the King's Court who were the most approved at arms of all those about him—to wit, Sir Gawaine and Sir Ewaine (who were nephews unto the King), and Sir Pellias and Sir Geraint, the son of Erbin—set forth for Tintagalon across the forest land of Usk.

So they travelled for all that day and a part of the next, and that without adventure or misadventure of any sort. So they came, at last, to that large and noble castle, hight Tintagalon, which guards the country bordering upon Cameliard and North Wales. Here King Arthur was received with great rejoicing; for whithersoever the King went the people loved him very dearly. Wherefore the folk of Tintagalon were very glad when he came unto them.

How King Arthur came to Tintagalon.

Now the morning after King Arthur had come into Tintagalon (the summer night having been very warm), he and Merlin were glad to arise betimes to go abroad for to enjoy the dewy freshness of the early daytime. So, in the cool of the day, they walked together in the garden (which was a very pleasant place), and beneath the shadow of a tall, straight tower. And all around about were many trees with a good shade, where the little birds sang sweetly in the cheerfulness of the summer weather.

And here King Arthur opened his mind very freely to Merlin, and he said: "Merlin, I do believe that the Lady Guinevere is the fairest lady in all of the world; wherefore my heart seems ever to be entirely filled with love for her, and that to such a degree that I think of her continually by day (whether I be eating, or drinking, or walking, or sitting still, or going about my business), and likewise I dream of her many times at night. And this has been the case with me, Merlin, ever since a month ago, when I lay sick in that hermit's cell in the forest, what time she came and stood beside me like a shining angel out of Paradise. So I am not willing that any other man than I should have her for his wife.

King Arthur openeth his heart to Merlin.

"Now I know very well that thou art wonderfully cunning in those arts of magic that may change a man in his appearance so that even those who know him best may not recognize him. Wherefore I very greatly desire it of thee that thou wilt so disguise me that I may go, unknown of any man, into Cameliard, and that I may dwell there in such a way that I may see the Lady Guinevere every day. For I tell thee very truly that I greatly desire to behold her in such a wise that she may not be in any way witting of my regard. Likewise I would fain see for myself how great may be the perils that encompass King Leodegrance—the King being my right good friend."

"My Lord King," said Merlin, "it shall be as thou desirest, and this morning I will cause thee to be so disguised that no one in all the world shall be able to know thee who thou art."

So that morning, a little before the prime, Merlin came unto the King where he was and gave him a little cap. And the cap was of such a sort that when the King set it upon his head he assumed, upon the instant, the appearance of a rude and rustic fellow from the country-side. Then the King commanded that a jerkin of rough frieze should be brought to him, and with this he covered his royal and knightly vestments, and with it he hid that golden collar and its jewel, pendent, which he continually wore about his neck. Then, setting the cap upon his head, he assumed at once the guise of that peasant hind.

King Arthur quits Tintagalon in disguise.

Whereupon, being thus entirely disguised, he quitted Tintagalon unknown of any man, and took his way a-foot unto the town of Cameliard.

Now toward the slanting of the day he drew nigh to that place, and lo! he beheld before him a large and considerable town of many comely houses with red walls and shining windows. And the houses of the town sat all upon a high, steep hill, the one overlooking the other, and the town itself was encompassed around about by a great wall, high and strong. And a great castle guarded the town, and the castle had very many towers and roofs. And all around about the tower were many fair gardens and lawns and meadows, and several orchards and groves of trees with thick and pleasing shade. Now at that time of the day the sky behind the tower was all, as it were, an entire flame of fire, so that the towers and the battlements of the castle and the roofs and the chimneys thereof stood altogether black against the brightness of the light. And, behold! great flocks of pigeons encircled the towers of the castle in a continual flight against that fiery sky. So, because King Arthur was a-weary with walking for all that day, it appeared to him that he had hardly ever beheld in all of his life so fair and pleasing a place as that excellent castle with its gardens and lawns and groves of trees.

King Arthur comes to Cameliard.

Thus came King Arthur unto the castle of Cameliard, in the guise of a poor peasant from the country-side, and no man in all of the world knew him who he was.

So, having reached the castle, he made inquiries for the head gardener thereof; and when he had speech with the gardener he besought him that he might be taken into service into that part of the garden that appertained to the dwelling-place of the Lady Guinevere. Then the gardener looked upon him and saw that he was tall and strong and well framed, wherefore he liked him very well and took him into service even as he desired.

And thus it was that King Arthur of Britain became a gardener's boy at Cameliard.

King Arthur dwelleth as gardener's boy at the castle.

Now the King was very glad to be in that garden; for in this pleasant summer season the Lady Guinevere came every day to walk with her damsels among the flowers, and King Arthur, all disguised as a peasant gardener boy, beheld her very many times when she came thither.

So King Arthur abode at that place for above a week, and he took no care that in all that time he enjoyed none of his kingly estate, but was only gardener's boy in the castle garden of Cameliard.

Now it happened upon a day when the weather was very warm, that one of the damsels who was in attendance upon the Lady Guinevere, arose all in the early morning whiles the air was still cool and refreshing. So, leaving the Lady Guinevere still sleeping, this damsel, whose name was Mellicene of the White Hand, went into the ante-room and, opening the casement thereof, looked forth into that garden of roses which adjoined the Lady Guinevere's bower.

Now there was at that place a carven marble figure of a youth, holding in his arms a marble ewer, and a fountain of water, as clear as crystal, flowed out from the ewer into a basin of marble. And the figure, and the fountain, and the marble basin into which the fountain flowed lay beneath the shadow of a linden-tree. And all around was a thick growth of roses, so that the place was entirely hidden, saving only from those windows the castle that were above.

So it befell that as the damsel looked down thitherward out of the window, she beheld a very wonderful sight. For, lo! a strange knight kneeled beside the fountain and bathed his face and his bosom in the crystal water thereof. And the damsel saw that the sunlight fell down through the leaves of the linden-tree and lay upon that strange knight. And she perceived that his hair and his beard were of the color of red gold—shining surpassingly in the brightness of the morning. And she beheld that his brow and his throat and his bosom were white like alabaster. And she beheld that around his neck and shoulders there hung a golden collar of marvellous beauty, so that when the sunlight shone upon it it flashed like pure lightning.

The damsel beholds a knight at the fountain.

So, beholding this strange appearance—as it were a vision—the damsel Mellicene stood for a long while, all entranced with wonder and with pleasure, and wist not whether that which she saw was a dream or no dream, nor whether he who sat there was a spirit, or whether he was a man of flesh and blood.

Then, by and by, recovering somewhat from her astonishment, she withdrew herself softly from the casement, and, turning about, ran fleetly down the turret stairs, and so came out thence into that fair and blooming garden at the foot of the tower. So she ran through the garden with all speed and silence, and thus came down an alley-way and to the marble fountain and the linden-trees and the rose-trees around about where she had anon beheld that strange knight bathing himself in the crystal waters.

But King Arthur had heard the coming of that damsel, and had speedily set the cap upon his head again. So that when the damsel Mellicene came thither, she found no one by the fountain but the gardener's boy. Of him she demanded: "Who art thou, fellow? And why sittest thou here by the fountain?"

The damsel findeth only the gardener's boy.

And unto her he replied: "I am the gardener's lad who came a short time ago to take service at this place."

"Then tell me, fellow," quoth she, "and tell me truly. Who was that young knight who was here beside the fountain but now, and whither hath he gone?" "Lady, whereunto," he said, "there has been no one at this fountain this day, but only I."

"Nay, fellow," she cried, "thou art deceiving me, for I do assure thee that with mine own eyes I beheld but now, where a strange young knight sat bathing himself in the waters of this fountain." And the gardener's boy said, "Lady, that which I have told you is the very truth, for indeed there hath no one been here this morn but only I. Wherefore, an thou deemest thou hast seen anyone else, thou art certainly mistaken."

At this the damsel set her look upon him, in great perplexity. Likewise, she marvelled very greatly, for she could not altogether disbelieve him. Nor yet could she entirely believe him either, because her eyes had beheld that which she had beheld, and she wotted that she had not been mistaken. Therefore she knew not what to think, and, because of her perplexity, she felt a very great displeasure at that gardener's boy. "Truly, wherefore," she said, "if thou art deceiving me, I shall certainly cause thee to suffer a great deal of pain, for I shall have thee whipped with cords." Thereupon she turned and went away from that place, much marvelling at that strange thing, and wondering what it all signified.

That morning she told unto the Lady Guinevere all that she had seen, but the Lady Guinevere only laughed at her and mocked her, telling her that she had been asleep and dreaming, when she beheld that vision. And, indeed, the damsel herself had begun to think this must be the case. Nevertheless, she thereafter looked out every morning from her casement window, albeit she beheld nothing for a great while, for King Arthur came not soon to that place again.

So, by and by, there befell another certain morning when she looked out of the casement and, lo! there sat that strange knight by the fountain once more as he had aforetime sat. And he bathed his face and his bosom in the water as he had aforetime done. And he appeared as comely and as noble as he had appeared before; and his hair and his young beard shone like gold as they had shone before in the sun. And this time she beheld that his collar of gold lay upon the brink of the fountain beside him, and it sparkled with great splendor in the sunlight the whiles he bathed his bosom. Then, after that damsel had regarded him for a considerable time, she ran with all speed to the chamber where the Lady Guinevere still lay, and she cried in a loud voice, "Lady! lady! arouse thee and come with me! For, lo! that same young knight whom I beheld before, is even now bathing himself at the fountain under the linden-tree."

Then the Lady Guinevere, greatly marvelling, aroused herself right quickly, and, dighting herself with all speed, went with the damsel unto that casement window which looked out into that part of the garden.

The Lady Guinevere beholds the knight at the fountain.

And there she herself beheld the young knight where he laved himself at the fountain. And she saw that his hair and his beard shone like gold in the sunlight; and she saw that his undervestment was of purple linen threaded with gold; and she saw that beside him lay that cunningly wrought collar of gold inset with many jewels of various colors, and the collar shone with great splendor where it lay upon the marble verge of the fountain.

Somewhiles she gazed, exceedingly astonished; then she commanded the damsel Mellicene for to come with her, and therewith she turned and descended the turret stairs, and went quickly out into the garden, as her damsel had done aforetime. Then, as that damsel had done, she straightway hastened with all speed down the alley-way toward the fountain.

But, behold! when she had come there, she found no young knight, but only the gardener boy, exactly as had happened with the damsel Mellicene aforetime. For King Arthur had heard her coming, and had immediately put that enchanted cap upon his head. Then the Lady Guinevere marvelled very greatly to find there only the gardener's boy, and she wist not what to think of so strange a thing. Wherefore she demanded of him, even as Mellicene had done, whither had gone the young knight whom she had beheld anon there at the fountain. And unto her the gardener lad made answer as aforetime: "Lady! there hath been no one at this place at any time this morning, but only I."

Now when King Arthur had donned his cap at the coming of the Lady, he had, in his great haste, forgotten his golden collar, and this Guinevere beheld where it lay shining very brightly, beside the margin of the fountain. "How now!" quoth she. "Wouldst thou dare to make a mock of me? Now tell me, thou fellow, do gardeners' boys in the land whence thou didst come wear golden collars about their necks like unto that collar that lieth yonder beside the fountain? Now, an I had thee well whipped, it would be thy rightful due. But take thou that bauble yonder and give it unto him to whom it doth rightfully belong, and tell him from me that it doth ill become a true belted knight for to hide himself away in the privy gardens of a lady." Then turned she with the damsel Mellicene, and left she that place and went back again into her bower.

Yet, indeed for all that day, as she sat over her 'broidery, she did never cease to marvel and to wonder how it was possible that that strange young knight should so suddenly have vanished away and left only the poor gardener's boy in his stead. Nor, for a long time, might she unriddle that strange thing.

Then, of a sudden, at that time when the heat of the day was sloping toward the cooler part of the afternoon, she aroused herself because of a thought that had come in an instant unto her. So she called the damsel Mellicene to come to her, and she bade her to go and tell the gardener's lad for to fetch her straightway a basket of fresh roses for to adorn her tower chamber.

So Mellicene went and did as she bade, and after considerable time the gardener's lad came bearing a great basket of roses. And, lo! he wore his cap upon his head. And all the damsels in waiting upon the Lady Guinevere, when they saw how he wore his cap in her presence, cried out upon him, and Mellicene of the White Hand demanded of him: "What! How now, Sir boor! Dost thou know so little of what is due unto a king's daughter that thou dost wear thy cap even in the presence of the Lady Guinevere? Now I bid thee straightway to take thy cap off thy head."

The gardener's boy weareth his cap before the Lady Guinevere.

And to her King Arthur made answer: "Lady, I cannot take off my cap."

Quoth the Lady Guinevere: "And why canst thou not take off thy cap, thou surly fellow?"

"Lady," said he, "I cannot take off my cap, because I have an ugly place upon my head."

"Then wear thy cap," quoth the Lady Guinevere. "Only fetch thou the roses unto me."

And so at her bidding, he brought the roses to her. But when he had come nigh unto the lady, she, of a sudden, snatched at the cap and plucked it off from his head. Then, lo! he was upon the instant transformed; for instead of the gardener's boy there stood before the Lady Guinevere and her damsel the appearance of a noble young knight with hair and beard like threads of gold. Then he let fall his basket of roses so that the flowers were scattered all over the floor, and he stood and looked at all who were there. And some of those damsels in attendance upon the Lady Guinevere shrieked, and others stood still from pure amazement and wist not how to believe what their eyes beheld. But not one of those ladies knew that he whom she beheld was King Arthur. Nevertheless the Lady Guinevere remembered that this was the knight whom she had found so sorely wounded, lying in the hermit's cell in the forest.

The Lady Guinevere discovers the knight of the fountain.

Then she laughed and flung him back his cap again. "Take thy cap," quoth she, "and go thy ways, thou gardener's boy who hath an ugly place upon his head." Thus she said because she was minded to mock him.

But King Arthur did not reply to her, but straightway, with great sobriety of aspect, set his cap upon his head again. So resuming his humble guise once more, he turned and quitted that place, leaving those roses scattered all over the floor even as they had fallen.

And after that time, whenever the Lady Guinevere would come upon the gardener's lad in the garden, she would say unto her damsel in such a voice that he might hear her speech: "Lo! yonder is the gardener's lad who hath an ugly place upon his head so that he must always wear his cap for to hide it."

Thus she spake openly, mocking at him; but privily she bade her damsels to say naught concerning these things, but to keep unto themselves all those things which had befallen.

JVSTISSIMVS·REX·

Two Knights do battle before Cameliard.

CHAPTER SECOND

How King Ryence Came to Cameliard and How King Arthur Fought With the Duke of North Umber.

NOW, UPON A CERTAIN DAY AT THIS TIME THERE CAME A MESSENGER TO the Court of King Leodegrance, with news that King Ryence of North Wales and Duke Mordaunt of North Umber were coming thither and that they brought with them a very noble and considerable Court of knights and lords. At this news King Leodegrance was much troubled in spirit, for he wist not what such a visit might betoken; and yet he greatly feared that it boded ill for him. So on that day when King Ryence and the Duke of North Umber appeared before the castle, King Leodegrance went forth to greet them and they three met together in the meadows that lie beneath the castle walls of Cameliard.

King Ryence and Duke Mordaunt come to Cameliard.

There King Leodegrance bade those others welcome in such manner as was fitting, desiring them that they should come into the castle with him so that he might entertain them according to their degree.

But to this courtesy upon the part of King Leodegrance, King Ryence deigned no pleasing reply. "Nay," quoth he, "we go not with thee into thy castle, King Leodegrance, until we learn whether thou art our friend or our enemy. For just now we are, certes, no such good friends with thee that we care to sit down at thy table and eat of thy salt. Nor may we be aught but enemies of thine until thou hast first satisfied our demands; to wit, that thou givest to me those lands which I demand of thee and that thou givest unto my cousin, Duke Mordaunt of North Umber, the Lady Guinevere to be his wife. In these matters thou hast it in thy power to make us either thy friends or thine enemies. Wherefore we shall abide here, outside of thy castle, for five days, in the which time thou mayst frame thine answer, and so we may know whether we shall be friends or enemies."

The King and the Duke send challenge to King Leodegrance.

"And in the meantime," quoth Duke Mordaunt of North Umber, "I do hold myself ready for to contest my right unto the hand of the Lady Guinevere with any knight of thy Court who hath a mind to deny my just title thereto; and if thou hast no knight in all thy Court who can successfully assay a bout of arms with me, thou thyself canst hardly hope to succeed in defending thyself against that great army of knights whom King Ryence hath gathered together to bring against thee in case thou denyest us that which we ask."

Then was King Leodegrance exceedingly cast down in his spirits, for he feared those proud lords and he wist not what to say in answer to them. Wherefore he turned and walked back into his castle again, beset with great anxiety and sorrow of spirit. And King Ryence, and Duke Mordaunt and their Court of lords and knights pitched their pavilions in those meadows over against the castle, so that the plain was entirely covered with those pavilions. And there they took up their inn with great rejoicing and with the sound of feasting and singing and merry-making, for it was an exceeding noble Court King Ryence had gathered about him.

And when the next morning had come Duke Mordaunt of North Umber went forth clad all in armor of proof. And he rode up and down the field before the castle and gave great challenge to those within; daring any knight to come forth for to meet him in knightly encounter. "Ho!" he cried, "how now, ye Knights of Cameliard! Is there no one to come forth to meet me? How then may ye hope to contend with the Knights of North Wales, an ye fear to meet with one single Knight from North Umber?" So he scoffed at them in his pride, and none dared to come forth from Camelaird against him. For the Duke of North Umber was one of the most famous knights of his day, and one of exceeding strength and success at arms, and there was now, in these times of peace, no one of King Leodegrance's Court who was at all able to face a warrior of his approved skill and valor. Wherefore, no one took up that challenge which the Duke of North Umber gave to the Court of Cameliard. Meantime many people gathered upon the walls of Cameliard and gazed down therefrom upon that proud and haughty duke, all bedight in his splendid armor, and all were grieved and ashamed that there was no one in that peaceful town to go out against him. And all the lords and knights of King Ryence's Court came and stood in front of the King's pavilion and laughed and clapped their hands together, and cheered Duke Mordaunt, as he so rode up and down before them. And the greater they were expanded with mirth, the more abashed were the people of Cameliard. "Ho! Ho!" cried that proud Duke. "How now! Will no one come forth to meet me? How then may ye of Cameliard

Duke Mordaunt rides before the castle.

hope to face the King of North Wales and all his knightly array of which I am but one man?" And the people of Cameliard, gathered upon the walls, listened to him with shame and sorrow.

Now all this while King Arthur digged in the garden; but, nevertheless, he was well aware of everything that passed and of how that the Duke of North Umber rode up and down so proudly before the castle walls. So, of a sudden, it came to him that he could not abide this any longer. Wherefore he laid aside his spade and went out secretly by a postern way, and so up into the town.

Now there was in Cameliard an exceedingly rich merchant, by name Ralph of Cardiff, and the renown of his possessions and his high estate had reached even unto King Arthur's ears at Carleon. Accordingly it was unto his house that King Arthur directed his steps.

And while he was in a narrow way, not far from the merchant's house, he took off his magic cap of disguise and assumed somewhat of his noble appearance once more, for he was now of a mind to show his knightliness unto those who looked upon him. Accordingly, when he stood before the rich merchant in his closet, and when the merchant looked up into his face, he wist not what to think to behold so noble a lord clad all in frieze. For though King Arthur was a stranger to the good man, so that he knew not his countenance, yet that merchant wist that he was no ordinary knight, but that he must assuredly be one of high degree and in authority, even though he was clad in frieze.

King Arthur seeks armor to do battle.

Then King Arthur opened the breast of his jerkin and showed the merchant the gold collar that hung around his neck. And also he showed beneath the rough coat of frieze how that there was an undergarment of fine purple silk embroidered with gold. And then he showed to the good man his own signet ring, and when the merchant saw it, he knew it to be the ring of the King of Britain. Wherefore, beholding these tokens of high and lordly authority, the merchant arose and stood before the King and doffed his cap.

"Sir Merchant," quoth the King, "know that I am a stranger knight in disguise in this place. Ne'theless, I may tell thee that I am a very good friend to King Leodegrance and wish him exceeding well. Thou art surely aware of how the Duke of North Umber rides continually up and down before the King's castle, and challenges anyone within to come forth for to fight against him in behalf of the Lady Guinevere. Now I am of a mind to assay that combat mine own self, and I hope a very great deal that I shall succeed in upholding the honor of Cameliard and of bringing shame upon its enemies.

"Sir Merchant, I know very well that thou hast several suits of noble armor in thy treasury, for the fame of them hath reached unto mine ears though I dwell a considerable distance from this place. Wherefore I desire that thou shalt provide me in the best manner that thou art able to do, so that I may straightway assay a bout of arms with that Duke of North Umber. Moreover, I do pledge thee my knightly word that thou shalt be fully recompensed for the best suit of armor that thou canst let me have, and that in a very little while."

"My Lord," said Master Ralph, "I perceive that thou art no ordinary errant knight, but rather someone of extraordinary estate; wherefore it is a very great pleasure to fulfil all thy behests. But even an thou wert other than thou art, I would be altogether willing to equip thee with armor, seeing that thou hast a mind to ride forth against yonder duke."

Upon this he rang a little silver bell that stood nigh to him, and in answer to its sound several attendants immediately appeared. Into their hands he intrusted the person of the King, bidding them to do him extraordinary honor. Accordingly, certain of those attendants prepared for the King a bath of tepid water perfumed with ambergris, very grateful to the person. And after he was bathed in this bath and was wiped with soft linen towels, other attendants conducted him to a hall all hung with tapestries and 'broideries, and at this place a noble feast had been spread ready for his refreshment. Here that lordly merchant himself ministered to the King's wants, serving him with various meats—very dainty, and of several sorts—and likewise with fine white bread. And he poured him wine of various countries—some as red as ruby, others as yellow as gold; and indeed the King had hardly ever enjoyed a better feast than that which the merchant, Ralph of Cardiff, had thus spread for him.

And after he had entirely refreshed himself with eating, there came six pages richly clad in sarsanet of azure, and these, taking the King to an apartment of great state, they there clad him in a suit of Spanish armor, very cunningly wrought and all inlaid with gold. And the like of that armor was hardly to be found in all of the land. The juppon and the several trappings of the armor were all of satin and as white as milk. And the shield was white, and altogether without emblazonment or device of any sort. Then these attendants conducted the King into the courtyard, and there stood a noble war-horse, as white as milk, and all the trappings of the horse were of milk-white cloth without emblazonment or adornment of any sort; and the bridle and the bridle rein were all studded over with bosses of silver.

King Arthur is armed by Ralph of Cardiff.

Then after the attendants had aided King Arthur to mount this steed, the lordly merchant came forward and gave him many words of good cheer, and so the king bade him adieu and rode away, all shining in white and glittering in fine armor, wherefore he resembled the full moon in harvest season.

And as he drave down the stony streets of the town, the people turned and gazed after him, for he made a very noble appearance as he passed along the narrow way between the houses of the town.

So King Arthur directed his way to the postern gate of the castle, and, having reached that place, he dismounted and tied his horse. Then he straightway entered the garden, and there, finding an attendant, he made demand that he should have present speech with the Lady Guinevere. So the attendant, all amazed at his lordly presence, went and delivered the message, and by and by the Lady Guinevere came, much wondering, and passed along a gallery with several of her damsels, until she had come over above where King Arthur was. And when King Arthur looked up and saw her above him, he loved her exceeding well. And he said to her: "Lady, I have great will to do thee such honor as I am able. For I go forth now to do combat with that Duke of North Umber who rides up and down before this castle. Moreover, I hope and verily believe that I shall encompass his downfall; accordingly, I do beseech of thee some token, such as a lady may give unto a knight for to wear when that knight rides forth to do her honor."

The Lady Guinevere accepts King Arthur for her champion.

Then the Lady Guinevere said: "Certes, Sir Knight, I would that I knew who thou art. Yet, though I know not, nevertheless I am altogether willing for to take thee for my champion as thou offerest. So, touching that to token thou speakest of, if thou wilt tell me what thing it is that thou desirest, I will gladly give it to thee."

"An that be so, Lady," said King Arthur, "I would fain have that necklace that thou wearest about thy throat. For, meseems that if I had that tied about my arm, I would find my valor greatly increased thereby."

"Pardee, Sir Knight," said the Lady, "what thou desirest of me thou shalt assuredly have." Thereupon speaking, she took from her long, smooth neck the necklace of pearls which she wore, and dropped the same down to King Arthur where he stood.

And King Arthur took the necklace and tied it about his arm, and he gave great thanks for it. Then he saluted the Lady Guinevere with very knightly grace, and she saluted him, and then, straightway, he went forth from that place, greatly expanded with joy that the Lady Guinevere had shown him such favor.

Now the report had gone about Cameliard that a knight was to go forth to fight the Duke of North Umber. Wherefore great crowds gathered upon the walls, and King Leodegrance and the Lady Guinevere and all the Court of the King came to that part of the castle walls overlooking the meadow where the Duke of North Umber defended. Wherefore, so great a concourse was presently assembled, that any knight might be encouraged to do his utmost before such a multitude as that which looked down upon the field.

Then of a sudden the portcullis of the castle was lifted, and the bridge let fall, and the White Champion rode forth to that encounter which he had undertaken. And, as he drave across that narrow bridge, the hoofs of his war-horse smote the boards with a noise like to thunder, and when he came out into the sunlight, lo! his armor flamed of a sudden like unto lightning, and when the people saw him they shouted aloud.

Then when the Duke of North Umber beheld a knight all clad in white, he rode straightway to him and spoke to him with words of knightly greeting. "Messire," he said, "I perceive that thou bearest no crest upon thy helm, nor hast thou a device of any sort upon thy shield, wherefore I know not who thou art. Ne'theless, I do believe that thou art a knight of good quality and of approved courage, or else thou wouldst not have thus come to this place."

"Certes, Sir Knight," said King Arthur, "I am of a quality equal to thine own. And as for my courage, I do believe that it hath been approved in as many encounters as even thine own hath been."

"Sir Knight," quoth the Duke of Umber, "thou speakest with a very large spirit. Ne'theless, thou mayst make such prayers as thou art able, for I shall now presently so cast thee down from thy seat, so that thou shalt never rise again; for so have I served better men than ever thou mayst hope to be."

To this King Arthur made answer with great calmness of demeanor: "That shall be according to the will of Heaven, Sir Knight, and not according to thy will."

So each knight saluted the other and rode to his assigned station, and there each dressed his spear and his shield, and made him ready for the encounter. Then a silence fell upon all so great that a man might hear his own heart beat in the stillness. So, for a small space, each knight sat like a statue made of iron. Then, of a sudden, each shouted to his war-horse, and drave spurs into his flank, and launched forth from his station. And so they met in the midst of the course with a noise like unto a violent thunder-clap. And lo! the spear of the Duke of North Umber burst into splinters unto the very truncheon thereof; but the spear of King Arthur broke not, but held, so that the Duke

King Arthur overthrows Duke Mordaunt.

was cast out of his saddle like a windmill—whirling in the air and smiting the earth so that the ground shuddered beneath him. And indeed he rolled full three times over and over ere he ceased to fall.

Then all the people upon the wall shouted with might and main, so that the noise thereof was altogether astonishing; for they had hardly hoped that their champion should have proved so extraordinarily strong and skilful.

Meanwhile, those of King Ryence's Court ran immediately to the Duke of Umber where he lay upon the earth, and they straightway unlaced his helm for to give him air. And first they thought that he was dead, and then they thought that he was like to die; for, behold! he lay without any life or motion. Nor did he recover from that swoon wherein he lay for the space of full two hours and more.

Now whilst the attendants were thus busied about Duke Mordaunt of North Umber, King Arthur sat his horse, very quietly, observing all that they did. Then, perceiving that his enemy was not dead, he turned him about and rode away from that place.

Nor did he return unto Cameliard at that time, for he deemed that he had not yet entirely done with these enemies to the peace of his realm, wherefore he was minded not yet to return the horse and the armor to the merchant, but to keep them for a while for another occasion.

So he bethought him of how, coming to Cameliard, he had passed through an arm of the forest where certain wood-choppers were at work felling the trees. Wherefore, remembering that place, he thought that he would betake him thither and leave his horse and armor in the care of those rude folk until he would need those things once more. So now he rode away into the country-side, leaving behind him the town and the castle and all the noise of shouting and rejoicing; nor did he once so much as turn his head to look back toward that place where he had so violently overthrown his enemy.

And now you shall presently hear of certain pleasant adventures of a very joyous sort that befell him ere he had accomplished all his purposes. For when a man is a king among men, as was King Arthur, then is he of such a calm and equal temper that neither victory nor defeat may cause him to become either unduly exalted in his own opinion or so troubled in spirit as to be altogether cast down into despair. So if you would become like to King Arthur, then you shall take all your triumphs as he took this victory, for you will not be turned aside from your final purposes by the great applause that many men may give you, but you will first finish your work that you have set yourself to perform, ere you give yourself ease to sit you down and to enjoy the fruits of your victory.

Yea, he who is a true king of men, will not say to himself, "Lo! I am worthy to be crowned with laurels"; but rather will he say to himself, "What more is there that I may do to make the world the better because of my endeavors?"

JVSTISSIMVS·REX·

he White Champion meets two Knights at the Mill.

CHAPTER THIRD

How King Arthur Encountered Four Knights and of What Befell Thereby.

Now, the day was extraordinarily sweet and pleasant unto one so lusty of frame and so lithe of heart as was good King Arthur. For the bright clouds swam smoothly across the blue sky in prodigious volumes of vapor, and the wind blew across the long grass of the meadow lands, and across the fields of growing wheat, so that a multitude of waves travelled over the hills and valleys like an it were across an entire sea of green. And now all the earth would be darkened with wide shadows from those clouds, and, anon, everything would burst out, of a sudden, into a wonderful radiance of sunlight once more. And the little birds they sang all gayly in the hedge-rows and the leafy thickets as though they would burst their tiny throats with singing, and the cock crowed, strong and lusty, from the farm croft, and all was so blithe and comely that the young King, with the visor of his helmet uplifted to the refreshment of the gentle breeze, would sometimes carol very joyously in his journeying. So travelled King Arthur in all that gay and tender summer season, when the earth was young and the time was of long-gone-by.

Now, you are to remember that when King Arthur had come from Carleon unto the castle of Tintagalon, he had brought with him four young knights for to bear him company. And those knights aforesaid were as follows: There was Sir Gawaine, the son of King Lot and of Queen Margaise, and there was Sir Ewaine, the son of King Uriens and of Queen Morgana la Fay (and these two were nephews, half in blood, unto the King), and there was Sir Pellias, and there was Sir Geraint, the son of Erbin. These were the four noble young knights who had come with King Arthur from Camelot unto Tintagalon.

Now it befell, as King Arthur rode all gayly in the summer time as aforesaid, that he came to a certain part of the road where he beheld before him a tall and comely tower that stood upon a green hillock immediately by the roadside. And lo! there stood upon the balcony of that tower three fair demoiselles, clad all in green taffeta.

King Arthur cometh upon a knight entertaining the ladies in green.

And on the high road in front of the castle there was a knight clad all in very fine armor. And the knight sat upon a noble war-horse, and in his hands he held a lute, and he played upon the lute and sang in a voice of extraordinary sweetness. Whiles he sang those three ladies in green taffeta listened to him with great cheerfulness of mien. And whenever that knight would stint his singing, then those three ladies would clap their hands together with great acclaim, and would bid him to sing to them again; and so he would do with great readiness of spirit.

All this King Arthur beheld, and it appeared to him to be a very pleasant sight, wherefore he rejoiced at it exceedingly.

And as he drew nigh, lo! he beheld that the knight who thus sat upon his horse and played upon the lute and sang unto the accompaniment thereof, was none other than Sir Geraint, the son of Erbin. For that knight wore upon his crest the figure of a gryphon, and the device upon his shield was two gryphons rampant facing one another upon a field azure, and King Arthur knew that this was the crest and the device of Sir Geraint. And when the King perceived who was the knight who sat there and sang, he laughed unto himself and straightway closed his visor and made him ready for such encounter as might, perchance, befall. So he drew nigh to where the knight sang and the ladies listened.

Now when Sir Geraint perceived King Arthur approach, he ceased singing and hung up his lute behind him across his shoulder. Then, casting upward his look to those three fair ladies above him, quoth he: "Mesdames, ye have been pleased to listen to that singing which I have assayed altogether in your honor. Now, likewise, in your honor, I will perform a deed of knightly prowess which I very much hope shall bring great glory to you. For, if ye will be pleased to lend me that encouragement which your very great beauty can so easily afford, ye shall behold me, I doubt not, overthrow yonder knight completely, and that to your great credit and renown."

"Sir Knight," said that lady who spoke for the others, "you are, truly, a lord of noble bearing and exceedingly pleasing of address, wherefore we do wish you great success in this undertaking; and we do believe that you will succeed in what which you assay to do."

Upon these Sir Geraint gave those three demoiselles great thanks for their words, and thereupon he closed the visor of his helmet. So, dressing his spear and shield, and saluting those three ladies with great humility of demeanor, he went forth to meet King Arthur where he now sat at a little distance, very quietly and soberly awaiting his pleasure.

Now Sir Geraint knew not King Arthur because he wore no crest upon his helm and no device upon his shield, wherefore as he saluted him he made speech to him in this wise: "Ha! Messire, I know not who thou art, seeing that thou bearest neither crest nor device. Ne'theless, I am minded to do thee such honor as I may in running a tilt with thee upon the behalf of those three demoiselles whom thou beholdest yonder upon that balcony. For I do affirm, and am ready to maintain the same with my knightly person, that those ladies are fairer than thy lady, whomsoever she may be."

"Sir Knight," quoth King Arthur, "I will gladly run a course with thee in honor of my lady; for, I may tell thee, she is a princess, and is held by many to be the most beautiful dame in all of the world. But I will only contend with thee upon one condition, and the condition is this—that he who is overthrown shall yield himself as servant unto the other for seven days, and in that time he shall do all that may be required of him."

"I will accept thy gage, Sir Unknown Knight," quoth Sir Geraint, "and when I have overthrown thee, I will yield thee unto those fair ladies yonder for to be their servant for seven days. And I do tell thee that there are a great many knights who would certainly regard that as being both a pleasant and an honorable task."

"And should I so chance as to overthrow thee," said King Arthur, "I will send thee for to serve my lady for that same period of time, and that will be even a pleasanter and a more honorable task than that which thou hast a mind for me to perform."

So each knight saluted the other, and thereupon each took such a stand as should cast the encounter immediately beneath where those three fair demoiselles looked down from the balcony. Then each knight dressed his spear and his shield, and, having made ready for the encounter, each sat for a small space entirely prepared. Then each shouted to his war-horse, and drave spur into its flank, and launched forth with wonderful speed to the assault. So they met in the very midst of the course with a force so vehement that the noise thereof was wonderfully appalling for to hear. And each knight smote the other in the very centre of his defences. And, lo! the spear of Sir Geraint burst into small pieces, even to the truncheon thereof; but the spear of King Arthur held, and Sir Geraint was cast so violently backward that both he and his horse were overthrown into the dust with a tumult like to a monstrous roaring of thunder.

King Arthur overthrows Sir Geraint.

And when Sir Geraint had recovered his footing, he was, for awhile, so astonished that he wist not where he stood, for never had he been so overthrown in all of his life before. Then, coming quickly unto himself again, he straightway drew forth his sword and called upon King Arthur with exceeding vehemence for to come down from out of his saddle, and to fight him afoot.

"Nay, not so, Sir Knight," said King Arthur, "I will not have to do with thee in that way. Moreover, thou art not to forget that thou hast promised to give thyself unto me as my servant for seven days, for, assuredly, I have entirely overcome thee in this encounter, and now thou art pledged unto me to be my servant."

Then Sir Geraint knew not what to say, being altogether abashed with shame and vexation at his overthrow. Ne'theless, he perceived that he must uphold his knightly word unto that which he had pledged himself to do; wherefore, he put up his sword again, though with exceeding discontent. "Sir Knight," said he, "I do acknowledge myself to have been overcome in this encounter, wherefore I yield myself now unto thy commands, according to my plighted word."

"Then I do place my commands upon thee in this wise," quoth King Arthur. "My command is, that thou goest straightway unto the Lady Guinevere at Cameliard, and that thou tellest her that thou hast been overthrown by that knight to whom she gave her necklace as a token. Moreover, I do desire that thou shalt obey her in everything that she may command thee to do, and that for the space of seven days to come."

King Arthur sendeth Sir Geraint to the Lady Guinevere.

"Sir Knight," quoth Sir Geraint, "that which thou biddest me to do, I will perform according to thy commands."

Thereupon he mounted his horse and went his way. And King Arthur went his way. And those three ladies who stood upon the balcony of the castle were exceedingly glad that they had beheld so noble an assay-at-arms as that which they had looked down upon.

Now, after King Arthur had travelled forward for the distance of two or three leagues or more, he came to a certain place of moorlands, where were many ditches of water, and where the heron and the marsh-hen sought harborage in the sedge. And here, at sundry points, were several windmills, with their sails all turning slowly in the sunlight before a wind which blew across the level plains of ooze. And at this place there was a long, straight causeway, with two long rows of pollard willows, one upon either hand. Now, when he had come nigh the middle of this causeway, King Arthur perceived two knights, who sat their horses in the shade of a great windmill that stood upon one side of the roadway. And a large shadow of the sails moved ever and anon across the roadway as the wheel of the mill turned slowly afore the wind. And all about the mill, and everywhere about, were great quantities of swallows that darted hither and thither like bees about a hive in midsummer. And King Arthur saw that those two knights, as they sat in the shadow of the mill, were eating of a great loaf of rye bread, fresh baked and of brittle crust; and they ate fair white cheese, which things the miller, all white with dust, served to them. But when these two knights perceived King Arthur, they immediately ceased eating that bread and cheese, and straightway closed their helmets. As for the miller, when he saw them thus prepare themselves, he went quickly back into the mill and shut the door thereof, and then went and looked out of a window which was over above where the knights were standing.

But King Arthur made very merry unto himself when he perceived that those two knights were Sir Gawaine and Sir Ewaine. For he knew that the one was Sir Gawaine because that the crest of his helmet was a leopard rampant, and because he bore upon his shield the device of a leopard rampant upon a field gules; and he knew that the other was Sir Ewaine, because he bore upon his crest an unicorn, and because the device upon his shield was that of a lady holding a naked sword in her hand, which same was upon a field or. Accordingly, whiles he was yet at some distance, King Arthur closed his helmet so that those two young knights might not know who he was.

King Arthur cometh upon two knights at the windmill.

So, when he had come anear to the two knights, Sir Gawaine rode forward for a little distance for to meet him. "Sir Knight," quoth he, "thou must know that this is soothly parlous ground whereon thou hast ventured; for there is no byway hence across the morass, and thou mayst not go forward without trying a tilt with me."

"Sir Knight," said King Arthur, "and I am very willing to run a tilt with thee. Ne'theless, I will only encounter thee upon one condition, and that is this: that he who is overthrown shall serve the other entirely for the space of seven full days."

"I do accept thy gage, Sir Knight," quoth Sir Gawaine. For he said unto himself, "Of a surety, so exceedingly strong and skilful a knight as I shall easily encompass the overthrow of this unknown knight."

So each knight immediately took his appointed station, and having dressed his spear and his shield, and having fully prepared himself in every manner, and having rested for a little space, each suddenly shouted to his horse, and drave spur into the flanks thereof, and so rushed to the encounter. And each knight smote the other in the midst of his defence, and lo! the spear of Sir Gawaine burst into fragments. But the spear of King Arthur held, so that Sir Gawaine was lifted entirely out of his saddle and over the crupper of his horse. And indeed he fell with wonderful violence into the dust.

King Arthur overthrows Sir Gawaine.

Nor could he immediately rise from that fall, but lay all bedazed for a little while. And when he did arise, he perceived that the white knight who had overthrown him sat nigh to him upon his horse.

Then King Arthur spake and said: "Sir Knight, I have altogether overthrown thee, and so thou must now serve me according to thy knightly word."

Then up spake Sir Ewaine, who sat nearby upon his horse. "Not so, Sir Knight," he said; "not so, nor until thou hast had to do with me. For I do make demand of thee that thou shalt straightway joust with me. And if I overthrow thee I will claim of thee that thou shalt release my cousin from that servitude unto which he hath pledged himself. But if thou overthrowst me, then will I serve thee even as he hath pledged himself to serve thee."

"Sir Knight," said King Arthur, "I do accept thy gage with all readiness of spirit!"

So each knight took his assigned place and dressed himself for the encounter. Then they shouted, and drave together, rushing the one upon the other like unto two rams upon the hillside. And the spear of Sir Ewaine was also shivered into pieces. But King Arthur's spear held, so that the girths of Sir Ewaine's saddle were burst apart, and both the saddle and the knight were swept off the horse's back with such violence that a tower falling could not have made a greater noise than did Sir Ewaine when he smote the dust of that causeway.

King Arthur overthrows Sir Ewaine.

Then Sir Ewaine arose to his feet and gazed upon him, all filled with entire amazement. To him came King Arthur, and bespake him thus: "Ha, Sir Knight, meseems that thou hast been fairly overcome this day. And so, according to your promises, both thou and yonder other knight must fulfil all my commands for the space of full seven days to come. Now this is the command that I set upon ye both: that ye shall straightway go unto the Lady Guinevere at Cameliard and shall take her greeting from her knight. And ye shall say to her that her knight unto whom she gave her necklace, hath sent ye, who are King's sons, for to do obedience unto her. And all that she shall command ye to do in the space of these seven days that are to come, that shall ye perform even unto the smallest grain."

King Arthur sendeth the two knights to the Lady Guinevere.

"Sir Knight," said Sir Gawaine, "so we will do according to thy commands, having pledged ourselves thereunto. But when these seven days are passed, I do make my vow that I shall seek thee out and shall carry this combat unto its entire extremity. For it may happen to any knight to be unhorsed as I have been, yet I do believe that I may have a better success with thee an I battle with thee to the extremity of my endeavor."

"Sir Knight," said King Arthur, "it shall be even as thou desirest. Yet I do verily believe that when these seven days are passed thou wilt not have such a great desire for to fight with me as thou now hast."

Having so spoken, King Arthur saluted those two knights and they saluted him. And then he turned his horse and went his way. And whenever he bethought him of how those two good knights had fallen before his assault, and when he thought of how astonished and abashed they had been at their overthrow, he laughed aloud for pure mirth, and vowed unto himself that he had never in all of his life engaged in so joyous an adventure as this.

So when Sir Ewaine had mended the girths of his saddle then he and Sir Gawaine mounted their horses and betook their way toward Cameliard much cast down in spirits.

Then the miller came forth from the mill once more, greatly rejoiced at having beheld such a wonderfully knightly encounter from so safe a place as that from which he had beheld it.

And so King Arthur rode onward with great content of mind until the slanting of the afternoon had come, and by that time he had come nigh to that arm of the forest-land which he had in mind as the proper place where he might leave his horse and his armor.

Now as he drew nigh to this part of the forest skirts, he perceived before him at the roadside a gnarled and stunted oak-tree. And he perceived that upon the oak-tree there hung a shield, and that underneath the shield were written these words in fair large letters:

"Whoso smiteth upon this shield
Doeth so at the peril of his body."

Then King Arthur was filled with a great spirit, and, uplifting his spear, he smote upon that shield so that it rang like thunder.

Then immediately King Arthur heard a voice issue out of the forest crying, "Who hath dared to assail my shield!" And straightway there came out thence a knight of large frame, riding upon a horse white, like that which King Arthur himself rode. And the trappings of the horse and of the knight were all white like unto the trappings of King Arthur and his horse. And the knight bore upon his helmet as his crest a swan with outspread wings, and upon his shield he bore the emblazonment of three swans upon a field argent. And because of the crest and

King Arthur smites the shield of the White Knight.

the emblazonment of the shield, King Arthur knew that this knight was Sir Pellias, who had come with him from Camelot to Tintagalon.

So when Sir Pellias had come nigh to where King Arthur waited for him, he drew rein and bespake him with great sternness of voice: "Ho! Ho! Sir Knight," quoted he. "Why didst thou dare to smite upon my shield! Verily, that blow shall bring thee great peril and dole. Now, prepare to defend thyself straightway because of what thou hast done."

"Stay! Stay! Sir Knight," said King Arthur, "it shall be as thou wouldst have it; and I will do combat with thee. Yet will I not assay this adventure until thou hast agreed that the knight who is overcome in the encounter shall serve the other in whatsoever manner that other may desire, for the space of one se'night from this time."

"Sir Knight," said Sir Pellias, "I do accept that risk, wherefore I bid thee now presently to prepare thyself for the encounter."

Thereupon each knight took his station and dressed his spear and shield. And when they had prepared themselves, they immediately launched together with a violence like to two stones cast from a catapult. So they met in the midst of the course, and again King Arthur was entirely successful in that assault which he made. For the spear of Sir Pellias burst to pieces, and the spear of King Arthur held; and Sir Pellias was cast with passing violence out of his saddle for the distance of more than half a spear's length behind the crupper of his horse. Nor did he altogether recover from that fall for a long time, so that King Arthur had to wait beside him for a considerable while ere he was able to lift himself up from the ground whereon he lay.

King Arthur overthrows Sir Pellias.

"Ha! Sir Knight," said King Arthur, "assuredly it hath not gone well with thee this day, for thou hast been entirely overthrown and now thou must straightway redeem thy pledge to serve me for seven days hereafter. Wherefore, I now set it upon thee as my command, that thou shalt go straightway unto Cameliard, and that thou shalt greet the Lady Guinevere from me, telling her that her knight unto whom she gave her necklace hath been successful in battle with thee. Likewise I set it upon thee that thou shalt obey her for the space of seven days in whatsoever she may command thee to do."

King Arthur sendeth Sir Pellias to the Lady Guinevere.

"Sir Knight," said Sir Pellias, "it shall even be as thou dost ordain. Yet I would that I knew who thou art, for I do declare that I have never yet in all my life been overthrown as thou hast overthrown me. And, indeed, I think that there are very few men in the world who could serve me as thou hast served me."

"Sir Knight," said King Arthur, "some time thou shalt know who I am. But, as yet, I am bound to entire secrecy."

Thereupon he saluted Sir Pellias and turned and entered the forest and was gone.

And Sir Pellias mounted his horse and betook him to Cameliard, much cast down and disturbed in spirit, yet much marvelling who that knight could be who had served him as he had been served.

So that day there came to Cameliard, first Sir Geraint and then Sir Gawaine and Sir Ewaine, and last of all there came Sir Pellias. And when these four beheld one another they were all abashed so that one scarce dared to look the other in the face. And when they came before the Lady Guinevere and made their condition known to her, and told her how that knight who wore her necklace had overthrown them all and had sent them thither to serve her for a se'night, and when she reckoned how great and famous were those four knights in deeds of chivalry, she was exceedingly exalted that her knight should have approved himself so great in those deeds of arms which he had undertaken to perform. But she greatly marvelled who that champion could be, and debated those things in her own mind. For it was a thing altogether unheard of that one knight, in one day, and with a single spear, should have overthrown five such well proved and famous knights as Duke Mordaunt of North Umber, Sir Geraint, Sir Gawaine, Sir Ewaine, and Sir Pellias. So she gave herself great joy that she had bestowed the gift of her necklace upon so worthy a knight, and she was exceeding uplifted with extraordinary pleasure at the thought of the credit he had endowed her withal.

The Lady Guinevere is pleased with her champion.

Now after King Arthur had entered the forest, he came by and by to where those wood-choppers, afore spoken of, plied their craft. And he abided with them for that night; and when the next morning had come, he intrusted them with his horse and armor, charging them to guard those things with all care, and that they should be wonderfully rewarded therefor. Then he took his departure from that place with intent to return unto Cameliard. And he was clad in that jerkin of frieze which he had worn ever since he had left Tintagalon.

King Arthur resumes his disguise.

And when he had reached the outskirts of the forest, he set his cap of disguise upon his head and so resumed his mean appearance once more. So, his knightliness being entirely hidden, he returned to Cameliard for to be gardener's boy as he had been before.

Four Knights serve the Gardener Lad.

CHAPTER FOURTH

How the Four Knights Served the Lady Guinevere.

Now, when King Arthur returned to Cameliard once more (which fell upon the afternoon of a second day), he found the gardener waiting for him, exceedingly filled with wrath. And the gardener had a long birchen rod which he had fetched thither for to punish his boy withal, when that he should have returned to the garden again. So when he saw King Arthur he said: "Thou knave! wherefore didst thou quit thy work to go a-gadding?" And King Arthur laughed and said: "Touch me not." At this, the gardener waxed so exceeding wroth, that he catched the King by the collar of his jerkin with intent to beat him, saying: "Dost thou laugh at me, knave, and make a mock at me? Now I will beat thee well for the offence thou hast committed."

The gardener chideth his boy.

Then, when King Arthur felt that man's hand laid upon him, and when he heard the words that the gardener spake in his wrath, his royal spirit waxed very big within him and he cried out: "Ha, wretch! wouldst thou dare to lay thy hands upon my sacred person?" So saying, he seized the gardener by the wrists, and took the rod straight away from him, and struck him with it across the shoulders. And when that poor knave felt himself thus in the powerful grasp of the angry King, and when he felt the rod upon his shoulders, he straightway lifted up a great outcry, albeit the blow hurt him not a whit. "Now get thee gone!" quoth King Arthur, "and trouble me no more; else will I serve thee in a way that will not at all belike thee." Herewith he loosed that poor man and let him go; and the gardener was so bemazed with terror, that both the earth and the sky swam before him. For King Arthur's eyes had flashed upon him like lightning, and those two hands had held his wrists with wonderful power. Wherefore, when the King let him go he gat him away as quickly as might be, all trembling and sweating with a great fear.

So he went straight to the Lady Guinevere and complained to her of the manner in which he had been treated. "Lady," quoth he, weeping with the memory of his terror,

The gardener complaineth to the Lady Guinevere.

"my boy goeth away for a day or more, I know not whither; and when I would whip him for quitting his work he taketh the rod straight away from me and beateth me with it. Wherefore, now, I prithee, deal with him as is fitting, and let several strong men drive him away from this place with rods."

Then the Lady Guinevere laughed. "Let be!" she said, "and meddle with him no more; for, indeed, he appeareth to be a very saucy fellow. As for thee! take thou no heed of his coming or his going, and haply I will deal with him in such a way as shall be fitting."

Whereupon the gardener went his way, greatly marveling that the Lady Guinevere should be so mild in dealing with that toward knave. And the Lady Guinevere went her way, very merry. For she began to bethink her that there was soothly some excellent reason why it should happen that when the White Champion, who did such wonderful deeds, should come thither, then that gardener's boy should go; and that when that same Champion should go, then the gardener's boy should come thitherward again. Wherefore she suspected many things, and was wonderfully merry and cheerful of spirit.

Now, that day, in the afternoon, the Lady Guinevere chanced to walk in the garden with her damsels, and with her walked those four noble knights who had been sent thither by her White Champion, to wit, Sir Gawaine, Sir Ewaine, Sir Geraint, and Sir Pellias. And the gardener's lad was digging in the gardens; and as they passed by where he was the Lady Guinevere laughed aloud and cried out: "Look! Look! Messires and Ladies! Yonder is a very saucy fellow for to be a gardener's lad, for he continually weareth his cap, even when he standeth in the presence of lords and ladies."

The Lady Guinevere mocketh the gardener's boy.

Then Sir Gawaine up and spake, saying: "Is it even so? Now will I straightway go to yonder knave, and will take his hat off for him, and that in a way so greatly to his misliking, that I do not believe that he will ever offend by wearing it in our presence again."

At this the Lady Guinevere laughed a very great deal. "Let be!" she said, "let be! Sir Gawaine! it would ill beseem one so gentle as thou art to have to do with yonder saucy fellow. Moreover, he doth assure us all that he hath an ugly place upon his head, wherefore let him wear his cap in God's mercy."

Thus the Lady Guinevere, though she suspected a very great deal, was yet pleased to make a mock of him whom she suspected.

Now that day Duke Mordaunt of North Umber had entirely recovered from those sore hurts that he had suffered from his overthrow at the hands of the White Champion. Wherefore, the next morning having come, he appeared again before the castle as he had appeared aforetime—clad all in complete armor. So this time there rode before him two heralds, and when the duke and the two heralds had come to that part of the meadows that lay immediately before the castle of Cameliard, the heralds blew their trumpets exceedingly loud. So at the sound of the trumpets many people came and gathered upon the walls; and King Leodegrance came, and took stand upon a lesser tower that looked down upon the plain where were the Duke of North Umber and the two heralds. Then the Duke of North Umber lifted up his eyes and beheld King Leodegrance where he stood over above him upon the top of that tower, and he cried out in a loud voice: "What ho! King Leodegrance! Thou shalt not think because I suffered a fall from my horse through the mischance of an assault at arms, that thou art therefore quit of me. Yet, ne'theless, I do now make this fair proffer unto thee. To-morrow day I shall appear before this castle with six knights-companion. Now if thou hast any seven knights who are able to stand against me and my companions in an assault at arms—whether with spears or swords, or ahorse or afoot—then shall I engage myself for to give over all pretence whatsoever unto the hand of the Lady Guinevere. But if thou canst not provide such champions to contend successfully against me and my knights-companion, then shall I not only lay claim to Lady Guinevere, but I shall likewise seize upon and shall hold for mine own, three certain castles of thine that stand upon the borders of North Umber. And, likewise, I shall seize upon and shall hold for mine own all the lands and glebes appertaining unto those same castles. Moreover, this challenge of mine shall hold only until to-morrow at set of sun; after the which time it shall be null and void. Wherefore, King Leodegrance, thou hadst best look to it straightway to provide thee with such champions as may defend thee from these demands aforesaid."

The Duke of North Umber issueth a second challenge.

Hereupon those two heralds blew their trumpets once more, and Duke Mordaunt of North Umber turned his horse about and went away from that place. Then King Leodegrance also went his way, very sorrowful and downcast in his spirits. For he said to himself: "Is it at all likely that another champion shall come unto me like that wonderful White Champion who came two days since, I know not whence, for to defend me against mine enemies? And, touching that same White Champion; if I know not whence he came, so also I know not whither he hath departed; how

King Leodegrance is downcast.

then shall I know where to seek him to beseech his further aid in this time of mine extremity?" Wherefore he went his way, very sorrowful, and wist not what he was to do for to defend himself. So being thus exceedingly troubled in his spirit, he went straight unto his own room, and there shut himself therein; nor would he see any man nor speak unto anyone, but gave himself over entirely unto sorrow and despair.

The Lady Guinevere beseecheth aid of the four knights.

Now in this extremity the Lady Guinevere bethought her of those four knights who had been pledged for to serve her for seven days. So she went unto them where they were and she bespoke them in this wise: "Messires, ye have been sent hither pledged for to serve me for seven days. Now I do ordain it of thee that you will take this challenge of Duke Mordaunt upon you at my behest, and I do much desire that you go forth to-morrow-day for to meet this Duke of North Umber and his knights-companion in battle. For ye are terribly powerful knights, and I do believe you may easily defend us against our enemies."

But Sir Gawaine said, "Not so, Lady; not so! For though we are pledged unto thy service, yet are we not pledged unto the service of King Leodegrance, thy father. Nor have we quarrel of any sort with this Duke of North Umber, nor with his six knights-companion. For we are knights of King Arthur, his Court, nor may we, except at his command, take any foreign quarrel upon us in the service of another king."

Then was the Lady Guinevere exceedingly angry, wherefore she said with great heat: "Either thou art a wonderfully faithful lord unto thy King, Sir Gawaine, or else thou fearest to meet this Duke of North Umber and his knights-companion."

And at this speech of the Lady Guinevere's, Sir Gawaine was also exceedingly wroth, wherefore he made reply: "An thou wert a knight and not a lady, Dame Guinevere, thou wouldst think three or four times ere thou wouldst find courage to speak those words unto me." Whereupon he arose and went out from that place with a countenance all inflamed with wrath. And the Lady Guinevere went away also from that place and to her bower, where she wept a very great deal, both from sorrow and from anger.

Now all this while King Arthur had been very well aware of everything that passed; wherefore he by and by arose and went out and found the gardener. And he took the gardener strongly by the collar of his coat and held him where he was. And he said to him: "Sirrah! I have a command to set upon thee, and thou shalt perform that command to the letter, else, an thou perform it not, a very great deal of pain may befall thee." Herewith speaking, he thrust his hand into the bosom of his jerkin and brought forth thence that necklace of pearls which the Lady Guinevere had given

King Arthur sendeth the gardener upon a mission.

him from about her neck. And he said further unto the gardener: "Thou shalt take this necklace to the Lady Guinevere and thou shalt say to her thus: that she is to send me forthwith bread and meat and wine and comfits from her own table. And thou shalt say unto her that I desire her to summon those four knights—to wit, Sir Gawaine, Sir Ewaine, Sir Geraint, and Sir Pellias—and that she is to bid those four for to come and serve me with those things for my refreshment. And thou art to say unto her that she is to lay her commands upon those knights that they are further to serve me according as I may command, and that they are henceforth to be my servants and not her servants. And these are the commands that I lay upon thee; that thou art to say these things unto the Lady Guinevere."

Now when the gardener heard those words he was so astonished that he wist not what to think, for he deemed that the gardener's lad had gone altogether mad. Wherefore he lifted up his voice and cried aloud, "How now! What is this thou sayest! Verily, should I do such a thing as this thou bidst me to do, either it will cost me my life or else it will cost thee thy life. For who would dare for to say such words unto the Lady Guinevere?"

But King Arthur said: "Ne'theless, thou shalt surely do as I command thee, sirrah. For if thou disobey in one single point, then I do assure thee it will go exceedingly ill with thee. For I have it in my power for to make thee suffer as thou hast never suffered before."

And upon this the gardener said, "I will go." For he said unto himself, "If I do as this fellow biddeth me, then will the Lady Guinevere have him punished in great measure, and so I shall be revenged upon him for what he did unto me yesterday. Moreover, it irks me exceedingly that I should have a lad for to work in the garden who behaves as this fellow does. Wherefore," he said, "I will go." So he took that necklace of pearls that King Arthur gave him, and he went forth and, after awhile, he found the Lady Guinevere where she was. And when he had found her, he bespoke her in this wise:

"Lady, my garden boy hath assuredly gone entirely mad. For, under the threat of certain great harm he would do unto me an I performed not his errand, he hath sent me to offer a very grievous affront unto thee. For he hath sent me with this string of large beads for to give to thee; and he bids me to tell thee that thou art to send to him bread and meat and sweetmeats and wine, such as thou usest at thine own table; and he bids me to tell thee that these things are to be served to him by the four noble knights who came hither the day before yesterday. And he saith that thou art to command those same knights that they are to obey him in whatsoever he may command, for that they are henceforth to be his servants and not thine. And, indeed, Lady, he would listen to naught that I might say to him contrariwise, but he hath threatened me with dire injury an I came not hither and delivered this message unto thee."

Now when the Lady Guinevere heard what the gardener said, and when she beheld the necklace which she had given unto that White Champion, and when she wist that the White Champion and the gardener's boy were indeed one, she was uplifted with an exceeding joy; wherefore she knew not whether to laugh or whether to weep for that pure joy. So she arose and took the necklace of pearls, and she bade the gardener for to come with her. Then she went forth until she found those four knights, and when she had found them she spake unto them thus:

"My Lords, awhile sin when I commanded you for to take my quarrel with Duke Mordaunt of North Umber upon you for my sake, ye would not do so. And thou, my lord Gawaine, didst speak such angry words as are not fitting that one who serveth should speak unto his mistress, far less that a knight should speak unto the daughter of a king. Accordingly I have it in my mind that ye shall perform a certain thing by way of a penance, which, an ye refuse to do, I will know very well that ye do not intend to fulfill that word which ye plighted to my knight when he overthrew you all four in fair combat. Now my command is this: that ye take certain food prepared for my table—meats and white bread and sweetmeats and wine—and that ye take that food unto my gardener's boy, whose cap, Sir Gawaine, thou didst threaten so valorously for to take away from him this very morning. And ye four are to serve the food unto him as though he were a royal knight. And when ye have so served him, ye are to obey him in whatsoever he may ordain. And this I put upon ye as a penalty because ye took not my quarrel upon ye as true knights should, for hereafter ye are to be servants unto that gardener's boy and not unto me. Wherefore ye are now to go unto the buttery of the castle, and ye are to bid the sewer for to give you meats such as are served upon mine own table. And the food ye are to serve upon silver plates, and the wine ye are to serve in silver cups and goblets. And ye are to minister unto that gardener's boy as though he were a great lord of exceeding fame and renown."

The Lady Guinevere commands the four knights to serve the gardener's boy.

Thus spake the Lady Guinevere, and when she had spoken, she turned and left those four knights, and she took with her the gardener, who was so astonished at that which he had heard, that he wist not whether he had gone mad or whether the Lady Guinevere had gone mad. And the Lady Guinevere bade the gardener to go to the gardener's boy and to tell him that all things should be fulfilled according to his commands. And so the gardener did as he was told.

Now turn we to those four knights whom the Lady Guinevere had left. For they were bemazed and abashed at the singular commands she had set upon them. And when they recovered from their amazement, they were inflamed with exceeding indignation that, for the time, they wist not whether that which they saw with their eyes was the light of day, or whether it was altogether darkness. Nor could one of them look at another in the face, so overcome were they with shame at the affront that had been put upon them. Then up and spake Sir Gawaine, and his voice so trembled with his exceeding anger that he could scarce contain it for to speak his words. "Messires," quoth he, "do ye not see how that this lady hath wantonly put a great affront upon us because we would not do that which she this morning bade us to do, and because we would not take up her quarrel against the Duke of North Umber? Now we will indeed serve this gardener's boy even as she hath ordained. For we will serve him with meat and drink as she hath commanded; and we will render our service unto him as she hath bidden us to do. But observe ye; we are no longer her servants, but we are his servants; wherefore we may serve him as we choose for to do. So, when we have fulfilled her commands and have served him with meat and drink, and when we have obeyed all the behests he layeth upon us; then do I make my vow that I, with mine own hand, shall slay that gardener's boy. And when I have slain him, I will put his head into a bag, and I will send that bag unto the Lady Guinevere by the meanest carrier whom I can find for that purpose. And so this proud lady shall receive an affront as great as that affront which she hath put upon us." And they all said that that which Sir Gawaine had planned should be exactly as he had said.

The four knights are angry.

So those four lords went unto the sewer of the castle, and they asked for the best of that food which was to be served unto the Lady Guinevere—meats and bread and sweetmeats and wine. Then they took them silver plates and platters and they placed the food upon them; and they took silver cups and silver goblets and they poured the wine into them; and they went forth with these things. And when they had come back of the castle nigh to the stables, they found the gardener's boy, and they bade him sit down and eat and to drink. And they waited upon him as though he had been some great lord. And not one of those four knights wist who he was, nor that he was the great King whose servant they, soothly, were. For he wore his cap of disguise upon his head, wherefore they deemed him to be only a poor peasant fellow.

The four knights serve the gardener's boy.

Now when Sir Ewaine beheld that he still wore his cap before them, he spake unto him with great indignation, saying: "Ha, villian! Wouldst thou wear thy cap even in the presence of great princes and lords such as we be?"

Unto this Sir Gawaine said, "Let be, it matters not." And then he said very bitterly unto the gardener's boy: "Eat thou well, sirrah! For thou shalt hardly eat another meal of food upon this earth."

To this the gardener's boy made reply: "Sir Knight, that, haply, shall lie unto another will than thine for to determine. For maybe, I shall eat many other meals than this. And, maybe, ye shall serve at them as ye are serving me now." And those four lords were astonished beyond measure that he should bespeak them thus so calmly and without any appearance of fear.

Then, after he had eaten, the gardener's boy said unto those knights, "Behold, Messires, I have had enough and am done; and now I have other commands for you to fulfil. And my next command is that ye shall make ready straightway to go abroad with me, and to that end ye shall clothe yourselves with complete armor. And thou, Sir Gawaine, shalt go to the head stable-keeper of this castle, and thou shalt demand of him that he shall make ready the Lady Guinevere's palfrey so that I may straightway ride forth upon it. And when ye are all encased in your armor, and when everything is duly appointed according to my command, ye shall bring that palfrey unto the postern gate of the castle, and there I shall meet ye for to ride forth with you."

And Sir Gawaine said: "It shall be done in every way according as thou dost command. But when we ride forth from this castle it shall be a sorry journey for thee."

And the gardener's boy said: "I think not so, Sir Gawaine."

Then those four went away and did according as the gardener's boy commanded. And when they had made themselves ready in full array of armor, and when they had obtained the Lady Guinevere's palfrey, they went unto the postern gate and there the gardener's boy met them. And when he saw that they sat their horses and that they moved not at his coming, he said: "Ha, Messires! would ye so entreat him whom ye have been ordained to serve? Now I do bid ye, Sir Gawaine and Sir Ewaine, for to come down and to hold my stirrup for me; and I bid ye, Sir Geraint and Sir Pellias, for to come down and to hold my palfrey for me whiles I mount."

Then those four noble knights did as they were commanded. And Sir Gawaine said: "Thou mayst command as thou dost list, and I do bid thee to make the most of it whiles thou mayst do so; for thou shalt have but a little while longer for to enjoy the great honor that hath fallen upon thee. For that honor which hath fallen upon thee—lo! it shall presently crush thee unto death."

And the gardener's boy said: "Not so; I believe I shall not die yet whiles." And again those four lords were greatly astonished at the calmness of his demeanor.

And so they rode forth from that place; and the gardener's boy would not permit that they should ride either before him or beside him, but he commanded them that they should ride behind him whiles they were still servants unto him.

So they rode as he assigned them for a considerable way. Then after they had gone forward a great distance, they drew nigh to a gloomy and dismal woodland that lay entirely beyond the country coadjacent to Cameliard. Then, when they had come nigh unto this woodland, Sir Gawaine rode a little forward, and he said: "Sir Gardener's Boy, seest thou yonder woodland? Now when we come into it thou shalt immediately die, and that by a sword that hath never yet been touched by any but noble or knightly blood."

King Arthur proclaimeth himself to the four knights.

And King Arthur turned him about in his saddle, and he said: "Ha! Sir Gawaine! Wouldst thou ride forward thus when I bid thee to ride behind me?"

And as he spake he took the cap from off his head, and, lo! they all beheld that it was King Arthur who rode with them.

Then a great silence of pure astonishment fell upon them all, and each man sat as though he were turned into an image of stone. And it was King Arthur who first spake. And he said: "Ha! how now, Sir Knights? Have ye no words of greeting for to pay to me? Certes, ye have served me with a very ill grace this day. Moreover, ye have threatened to slay me; and now, when I speak to you, ye say naught in reply."

Then those four knights immediately cried out aloud; and they leaped down from off their horses, and they kneeled down into the dust of the road. And when King Arthur beheld them kneeling there, he laughed with great joyfulness of spirit, and he bade them for to mount their horses again, for the time was passing by when there was much to do.

So they mounted their horses and rode away, and as they journeyed forward the King told them all that had befallen him, so that they were greatly amazed, and gave much acclaim unto the knightliness with which he had borne himself in those excellent adventures through which he had passed. And they rejoiced greatly that they had a king for to rule over them who was possessed of such a high and knightly spirit.

So they rode to that arm of the forest where King Arthur had left his horse and his armor.

The Gardener Lad takes off his Cap.

CHAPTER FIFTH

How King Arthur Overcame the Enemies of King Leodegrance, and How His Royalty Was Proclaimed.

Now, when the next day had come, the Duke of North Umber and six knights-companion appeared upon the field in front of the castle of Cameliard as he had duly declared that he and they would do. And those seven champions appeared in very great estate; for in front of them rode seven heralds with trumpets and tabards, and behind them there rode seven esquires, each esquire bearing the spear, the shield, the crest, and the banneret of the knight who was his lord and master. And the seven heralds blew their trumpets so exceedingly loud that the sound thereof penetrated unto the utmost parts of Cameliard, so that the people came running from everywhere. And while the heralds blew their trumpets the seven esquires shouted, and waved the spears and the bannerets. So those seven knights rode in such proud estate that those who looked upon them had hardly ever beheld such a splendid presentment of chivalry.

The Duke of North Umber and his six companions appear before the castle.

So they paraded up and down that field three times for its entire length, and, meantime, a great crowd of people, called thither by the blowing of the heralds' trumpets, stood upon the walls and gazed therefrom at that noble spectacle. And all the Court of King Ryence came, and stood upon the plain in front of the King's pavilion, and they shouted and cheered the Duke of North Umber and his six knights-companion.

Meanwhile, King Leodegrance of Cameliard was so cast down with trouble and shame that he did not choose to show his face, but hid himself away from all his Court. Nor would he permit anyone for to come into his presence at that time.

Nevertheless, the Lady Guinevere, with sundry of her damsels, went unto the King's closet where he was, and knocked upon the door thereof, and when the King denied her to come in to him, she spake to him through the door, giving him words

The Lady Guinevere cheereth her father.

of good cheer, saying: "My lord King and father, I prithee for to look up and to take good cheer unto thyself. For I do assure thee that there is one who hath our cause in his hands, and that one is, certes, a very glorious champion. And he shall assuredly come by and by ere this day is done, and when he cometh, he shall certainly overthrow our enemies."

But King Leodegrance opened not the door, but he said: "My daughter, that which thou sayest thou sayest for to comfort me. For there is no other help for me in this time of trouble only God, His good strong help and grace." And she said: "Nay, I say that which is the truth; and the help that God shall send unto thee he shall certainly send through a worthy champion who at this moment hath our cause in his hand."

So spake the Lady Guinevere, so that whilst King Leodegrance came not forth, yet he was greatly comforted at that which she said to him.

Thus passed all that morning and a part of the afternoon, and yet no one appeared for to take up that challenge which the seven knights had declared. But, whilst the sun was yet three or four hours high, there suddenly appeared at a great distance a cloud of dust. And in that cloud of dust there presently appeared five knights, riding at great speed, thitherward. And when these had come nigh unto the walls, lo! the people beheld that he who rode foremost of all was that same White Champion who had aforetime overthrown the Duke of North Umber. Moreover, they perceived that the four knights who rode with that White Champion were very famous knights and of great prowess and glory of arms. For the one was Sir Gawaine, and the other was Sir Ewaine, and the other was Sir Geraint, and the other was Sir Pellias. For the people of the castle and the town knew those four knights, because they had dwelt for two days at Cameliard, and they were of such exceeding renown that folk crowded from far and near for to look upon them whensoever they appeared for to walk abroad.

Five knights-defender appear at the field.

So when the people upon the walls beheld who those knights were, and when they perceived that White Champion who had aforetime brought them such exceeding honor, they shouted aloud for the second time with a voice mightier than that with which they had the first time shouted.

Now King Leodegrance heard the people shouting, whereupon hope awoke of a sudden within him. So he straightway came forth with all speed for to see what was ado, and there he beheld those five noble champions about to enter into the field below the castle walls.

And the Lady Guinevere also heard the shouting and she came forth likewise and, behold! there was that White Champion and those four other knights. So when she beheld that White Knight and his four companions-at-arms, her heart was like to break within her for pure joy and gladness, wherefore she wept for the passion thereof, and laughed the whiles she wept. And she waved her kerchief unto those five noble lords and kissed her hand unto them, and the five knights saluted her as they rode past her and into the field.

Now, when the Duke of North Umber was made aware that those five knights had come against him and his knights-companion for to take up his challenge, he straightway came forth from his pavilion and mounted his horse. And his knights-companion came forth and mounted their horses, and he and they went forth for to meet those who had come against them.

And when the Duke of North Umber had come nigh enough, he perceived that the chiefest of those five knights was the White Champion who had aforetime overthrown him. Wherefore he said unto that White Champion: "Sir Knight, I have once before condescended unto thee who art altogether unknown to me or to anybody else that is here. For without inquiring concerning thy quality, I ran a course with thee and, lo! by the chance of arms thou didst overthrow me. Now this quarrel is more serious than that, wherefore I and my companions-at-arms will not run a course with thee and thy companions; nor will we fight with thee until I first know what is the quality of him against whom I contend. Wherefore, I bid thee presently declare thyself, who thou art and what is thy condition."

The Duke of North Umber refuseth the combat.

Then Sir Gawaine opened the umbril of his helmet, and he said: "Sir Knight, behold my face, and know that I am Gawaine, the son of King Lot. Wherefore thou mayst perceive that my condition and estate are even better than thine own. Now I do declare unto thee that yonder White Knight is of such a quality that he condescends unto thee when he doeth combat with thee, and that thou dost not condescend unto him."

"Ho, Sir Gawaine!" quoth the Duke of Umber. "What thou sayest is a very strange thing, for, indeed, there are few in this world who are so exalted that they may condescend unto me. Ne'theless, since thou dost avouch for him, I may not gainsay that which thou sayest. Yet, there is still another reason why we may not fight with ye. For, behold! we are seven well-approved and famous knights, and ye are but five; so, consider how unequal are our forces, and that you stand in great peril in undertaking so dangerous an encounter."

Then Sir Gawaine smiled right grimly upon that Duke of North Umber. "Gramercy for thy compassion, and for the tenderness which thou showeth concerning our safety, Sir Duke," quoth he. "But ne'theless, thou mayst leave that matter unto us with entire content of spirit upon thy part. For I consider that the peril in which ye seven stand is fully equal to our peril. Moreover, wert thou other than a belted knight, a simple man might suppose that thou wert more careful of thine own safety in this matter, than thou art of ours."

Now at these words the countenance of the Duke of North Umber became altogether covered with red, for he wist that he had, indeed, no great desire for this battle, wherefore he was ashamed because of the words which Sir Gawaine spake to him. So, each knight closed his helmet, and all turned their horses, and the one party rode unto one end of the field, and the other party rode to the other end of the field, and there each took stand in the place assigned unto them.

And they arranged themselves thus: In the middle was King Arthur, and upon either hand were two knights; and in the middle was the Duke of North Umber, and upon either hand were three knights. So, when they had thus arrayed themselves they dressed their spears and their shields, and made them altogether ready for the onset. Then King Arthur and Duke Mordaunt each shouted aloud, and the one party hurled upon the other party with such violence that the ground shook and thundered beneath the hoofs of the horses, and the clouds of dust rose up against the heavens.

And so they met in the middle of the field with an uproar of such dreadful violence that one might have heard the crashing thereof for the distance of more than a mile away.

And when the one party had passed the other, and the dust of the encounter had arisen, lo! three of the seven had been overthrown, and not one of the five had lost his seat.

And one of those who had been overthrown was Duke Mordaunt of North Umber. And, behold! he never more arose again from the ground whereon he lay. For King Arthur had directed his spear into the very midst of his defences, and the spear had held, wherefore the point thereof had pierced the shield of the Duke of North Umber, and had pierced his body armor, and so violent was the stroke, that the Duke of North Umber had been lifted entirely out of his saddle, and had been cast a full spear's length behind the crupper of his horse. Thus died that wicked man, for as King Arthur drave past him, the evil soul of him quitted his body with a weak noise like to the squeaking of a bat, and the world was well rid of him.

King Arthur overturneth the Duke of North Umber.

Now when King Arthur turned him about at the end of the course and beheld that there were but four knights left upon their horses of all those seven against whom he and his companions had driven, he uplifted his spear, and drew rein upon his horse, and bespake his knights in this wise: "Messires, I am aweary of all this coil and quarrelling, and do not care to fight any more to-day, so go ye straightway and engage those knights in battle. As for me, I will abide here, and witness your adventure."

"Lord," said they, "we will do our endeavor as thou dost command."

So those four good knights did as he commanded, and they went forth straightway against those other four, much encouraged that their King looked upon their endeavor. And King Arthur sat with the butt of his spear resting upon his instep, and looked upon the field with great content of spirit, and a steadfast countenance.

As for those four knights-companion that remained of the Duke of North Umber's party, they came not forth to this second encounter with so much readiness of spirit as they had done aforetime. For they were now well aware of how great was the excellent prowess of those other knights, and they beheld that their enemies came forth to this second encounter very fiercely, and with great valor and readiness of spirit. Wherefore their hearts melted away within them with doubt and anxiety as to the outcome of this second encounter.

Nevertheless, they prepared themselves with such resolve as might be, and came forth as they were called upon to do.

Then Sir Gawaine drave straight up to the foremost knight, who was a very well-known champion, hight Sir Dinador of Montcalm. And when he had come sufficiently nigh to him, he lifted himself up in his stirrups and he smote Sir Dinador so fierce a blow that he cleft the shield of that knight asunder, and he cleft his helmet, and a part of the blade of his sword brake away and remained therein.

And when Sir Dinador felt that blow, his brains swam like water, and he was fain to catch the horn of his saddle for to save himself from falling therefrom. Then a great terror straightway fell upon him, so that he drew rein violently to one side. So he fled away from that place with the terror of death hanging above him like to a black cloud of smoke. And when his companions beheld that stroke that Sir Gawaine delivered, and when they beheld Sir Dinador flee away from before him, they also drew rein to one side and fled away with all speed, pursued with an entire terror of their enemies. And Sir Gawaine and Sir Ewaine and Sir Geraint and Sir Pellias pursued them as they fled. And they chased them straight through the Court of King Ryence,

The knights-challenger flee before the knights-defender.

so that the knights and nobles of that Court scattered hither and thither like chaff at their coming. And they chased those fleeing knights in among the pavilions of King Ryence's Court, and no man stayed them; and when they had chased those knights entirely away, they returned to that place where King Arthur still held his station, steadfastly awaiting them.

Now when the people of Cameliard beheld the overthrow of their enemies, and when they beheld how those enemies fled away from before the faces of their champions, they shouted with might and main, and made great acclaim. Nor did they stint their loud shouting when those four knights returned from pursuing their enemies and came back unto the White Champion again. And still more did they give acclaim when those five knights rode across the drawbridge and into the gateway of the town and into the town.

Thus ended the great bout-at-arms, which was one of the most famous in all the history of chivalry of King Arthur's Court.

King Arthur returneth his armor to the merchant.

Now when King Arthur had thus accomplished his purposes, and when he had come into the town again, he went unto that merchant of whom he had obtained the armor that he wore, and he delivered that armor back to him again. And he said, "To-morrow-day, Sir Merchant, I shall send thee two bags of gold for the rent of that armor which thou didst let me have."

To this the merchant said: "Lord, it is not needed that thou shouldst recompense me for that armor, for thou hast done great honor unto Cameliard by thy prowess."

But King Arthur said: "Have done, Sir Merchant, nor must thou forbid what I say. Wherefore take thou that which I shall send unto thee."

Thereupon he went his way, and, having set his cap of disguise upon his head, he came back into the Lady Guinevere's gardens again.

Now when the next morning had come the people of Cameliard looked forth and, lo! King Ryence had departed entirely away from before the castle. For that night he had struck his pavilions, and had withdrawn his Court, and had gone away from that place where he and his people had sat down for five days past. And with him he had taken the body of the Duke of North Umber, conveying it away in a litter surrounded by many lighted candles and uplifted by a peculiar pomp of ceremony. But when the people of Cameliard beheld that he was gone, they were exceedingly rejoiced, and made merry, and shouted and sang and laughed. For they wist not how deeply enraged King Ryence was against them; for his enmity aforetime toward King Leodegrance was but as a small flame when compared unto the anger that now possessed him.

Now that morning Lady Guinevere walked into her garden, and with her walked Sir Gawaine and Sir Ewaine, and lo! there she beheld the gardener's boy again.

Then she laughed aloud, and she said unto those two knights, "Messires behold! Yonder is the gardener's boy, who weareth his cap continually because he hath an ugly place upon his head."

Then those two knights, knowing who that gardener's boy was, were exceedingly abashed at her speech, and wist not what to say or whither to look. And Sir Gawaine spake, aside unto Sir Ewaine, and quoth he: "'Fore Heaven, that lady knoweth not what manner of man is yonder gardener's boy; for, an she did, she would be more sparing of her speech."

And the Lady Guinevere heard Sir Gawaine that he spoke, but she did not hear his words. So she turned unto Sir Gawaine, and she said: "Sir Gawaine, haply it doth affront thee that that gardener's boy should wear his cap before us, and maybe thou wilt go and take it off from his head as thou didst offer to do two or three days since."

And Sir Gawaine said: "Peace, Lady! Thou knowest not what thou sayest. Yonder gardener's boy could more easily take my head from off my shoulders than I could take his cap from off his head."

At this the Lady Guinevere made open laughter; but in her heart she secretly pondered that saying and greatly marvelled what Sir Gawaine meant thereby.

King Ryence threatened King Leodegrance.

Now about noon of that day there came an herald from King Ryence of North Wales, and he appeared boldly before King Leodegrance where the King sat in his hall with a number of his people about him. And the herald said: "My lord King: my master, King Ryence of North Wales, is greatly displeased with thee. For thou didst set certain knights upon Duke Mordaunt of North Umber, and those knights have slain that excellent nobleman, who was close kin unto King Ryence. Moreover, thou hast made no reply to those demands that my master, King Ryence, hath made touching the delivery unto him of certain lands and castles bordering upon North Wales. Wherefore my master is affronted with thee beyond measure. So my master, King Ryence, bids me to set forth to thee two conditions, and the conditions are these: Firstly, that thou dost immediately deliver into his hands that White Knight who slew the Duke of North Umber; secondly, that thou makest immediate promise that those lands in question shall be presently delivered unto King Ryence."

Then King Leodegrance arose from where he sat and spake to that herald with great dignity of demeanor. "Sir Herald," quoth he, "the demands that King Ryence maketh upon me pass all bounds for insolence. That death which the Duke of North Umber suffered, he suffered because of his own pride and folly. Nor would I deliver that White Knight into thy master's hands, even an I were able to do so. As for those lands that thy master demandeth of me, thou mayst tell King Ryence that I will not deliver unto him of those lands so much as a single blade of grass, or a single grain of corn that groweth thereon."

And the herald said: "If, so be, that is thine answer, King Leodegrance, then am I bidden for to tell thee that my master, King Ryence of North Wales, will presently come hither with an array of a great force of arms, and will take from thee by force those things which thou wilt not deliver unto him peacefully." Whereupon, so saying, he departed thence and went his way.

Now after the herald had departed, King Leodegrance went into his closet, and when he had come there he sent, privily, for the Lady Guinevere. So the Lady Guinevere came to him where he was. And King Leodegrance said to her: "My daughter, it hath happened that a knight clad all in white, and bearing no crest or device of any sort, hath twice come to our rescue and hath overthrown our enemies. Now it is said by everybody that that knight is thine own particular champion, and I hear say that he wore thy necklace as a favor when he first went out against the Duke of North Umber. Now I prithee, daughter, tell me who that White Champion is, and where he may be found."

King Leodegrance converses with the Lady Guinevere.

Then the Lady Guinevere was overwhelmed with a confusion, wherefore she looked away from her father's countenance; and she said: "Verily, my Lord, I know not who that knight may be."

Then King Leodegrance spake very seriously to the Lady Guinevere, and he took her by the hand and said: "My daughter, thou art now of an age when thou must consider being mated unto a man who may duly cherish thee and protect thee from thine enemies. For, lo! I grow apace in years, and may not hope to defend thee always from those perils that encompass one of our estate. Moreover, since King Arthur (who is a very great King indeed) hath brought peace unto this realm, all that noble court of chivalry which one time gathered about me has been scattered elsewhither where greater adventures may be found than in my peaceful realm. Wherefore (as all the world hath seen this week past) I have now not one single knight whom I may depend upon to defend us in such times of peril as these which now overshadow us.

Now, my daughter, it doth appear to me that thou couldst not hope to find anyone who could so well safeguard thee as this White Knight; for he doth indeed appear to be a champion of extraordinary prowess and strength. Wherefore it would be well if thou didst feel thyself to incline unto him as he appeareth to incline unto thee."

Then the Lady Guinevere became all rosy red as with a fire even unto her throat. And she laughed, albeit the tears overflowed her eyes and ran down upon her cheeks. So she wept, yet laughed in weeping. And she said unto King Leodegrance: "My Lord and father, an I give my liking unto any one in the manner thou speaketh of, I will give it only unto the poor gardener's boy who digs in my garden."

Then, at these words, the countenance of King Leodegrance became contracted with violent anger, and he cried out: "Ha, Lady! Wouldst thou make a mock and a jest of my words?"

Then the Lady Guinevere said: "Indeed, my Lord! I jest not and I mock not. Moreover, I tell thee for verity that that same gardener's boy knoweth more concerning the White Champion than anybody else in all of the world." Then King Leodegrance said: "What is this that thou tellest me?" And the Lady Guinevere said: "Send for that gardener's boy and thou shalt know." And King Leodegrance said: "Verily, there is more in this than I may at present understand."

So he called to him the chief of his pages, hight Dorisand, and he said to him: "Go, Dorisand, and bring hither the gardener's boy from the Lady Guinevere's garden."

So Dorisand, the page, went as King Leodegrance commanded, and in a little while he returned, bringing with him that gardener's boy. And with them came Sir Gawaine, and Sir Ewaine, and Sir Pellias and Sir Geraint. And those four lords stood over against the door, where they entered; but the gardener's boy came and stood beside the table where King Leodegrance sat. And the King lifted up his eyes and looked upon the gardener's boy, and he said: "Ha! Wouldst thou wear thy cap in our presence?"

Then the gardener's boy said: "I cannot take off my cap."

But the Lady Guinevere, who stood beside the chair of King Leodegrance, spake and said: "I do beseech thee, Messire, for to take off thy cap unto my father."

Whereupon the gardener's boy said: "At thy bidding I will take it off."

So he took the cap from off his head, and King Leodegrance beheld his face and knew him. And when he saw who it was who stood before him, he made a great outcry from pure amazement. And he said: "My Lord and my King! What is this!" Thereupon he arose from where he sat, and he went and kneeled down upon the ground before King Arthur. And he set the palms of his hands together

King Arthur discovereth himself to King Leodegrance.

and he put his hands within the hands of King Arthur, and King Arthur took the hands of King Leodegrance within his own. And King Leodegrance said: "My Lord! My Lord! Is it then thou who hast done all these wonderful things?"

Then King Arthur said: "Yea; such as those things were, I have done them." And he stooped and kissed King Leodegrance upon the cheek and lifted him up unto his feet and gave him words of good cheer.

Now the Lady Guinevere, when she beheld those things that passed, was astonished beyond measure. And lo! she understood of a sudden all these things with amazing clearness. Wherefore a great fear fell upon her so that she trembled exceedingly, and said unto herself: "What things have I said unto this great King, and how have I made a mock of him and a jest of him before all those who were about me!" And at the thought thereof, she set her hand upon her side for to still the extreme disturbance of her heart. So, whilst King Arthur and King Leodegrance gave to one another words of royal greeting and of compliment, she withdrew herself and went and stood over against the window nigh to the corner of the wall.

Then, by and by, King Arthur lifted up his eyes and beheld her where she stood afar off. So he went straightway unto her and he took her by the hand, and he said: "Lady, what cheer?"

King Arthur is betrothed to the Lady Guinevere.

And she said: "Lord, I am afeard of thy greatness." And he said: "Nay, Lady. Rather it is I who am afeard of thee. For thy kind regard is dearer unto me than anything else in all the world, else had I not served for these twelve days as gardener's boy in thy garden all for the sake of thy good will." And she said: "Thou hast my good will, Lord." And he said: "Have I thy good will in great measure?" And she said: "Yea, thou hast it in great measure."

Then he stooped his head and kissed her before all those who were there, and thus their troth was plighted.

Then King Leodegrance was filled with such an exceeding joy that he wist not how to contain himself therefore.

Now, after these things, there followed a war with King Ryence of North Wales. For Sir Kay and Sir Ulfius had gathered together a great army as King Arthur had bidden them to do, so that when King Ryence came against Cameliard he was altogether routed, and his army dispersed, and he himself chased, an outcast, into his mountains.

Then there was great rejoicing in Cameliard. For, after his victory, King Arthur remained there for awhile with an exceedingly splendid Court of noble lords and of beautiful ladies. And there was feasting and jousting and many famous bouts at arms, the like of which those parts had never before beheld. And King Arthur and the Lady Guinevere were altogether happy together.

Now, one day, whiles King Arthur sat at feast with King Leodegrance—they two being exceedingly expanded with cheerfulness—King Leodegrance said unto King Arthur: "My Lord, what shall I offer thee for a dowery with my daughter when thou takest her away from me for to be thy Queen?"

Then King Arthur turned to Merlin, who stood nigh to him, and he said: "Ha, Merlin! What shall I demand of my friend by way of that dowery?"

Unto him Merlin said: "My lord King, thy friend King Leodegrance hath one thing, the which, should he bestow it upon thee, will singularly increase the glory and renown of thy reign, so that the fame thereof shall never be forgotten."

And King Arthur said: "I bid thee, Merlin, tell me what is that thing."

So Merlin said: "My lord King, I will tell thee a story:

"In the days of thy father, Uther-Pendragon, I caused to be made for him a certain table in the shape of a ring, wherefore men called it the ROUND TABLE. Now, at this table were seats for fifty men, and these seats were designed for the fifty knights who were the most worthy knights in all the world. These seats were of such a sort, that whenever a worthy knight appeared, then his name appeared in letters of gold upon that seat that appertained unto him; and when that knight died, then would his name suddenly vanish from that seat which he had aforetime occupied.

Merlin telleth of the Round Table.

"Now, forty-and-nine of these seats, except one seat, were altogether alike (saving only one that was set aside for the King himself, which same was elevated above the other seats, and was cunningly carved and inlaid with ivory and with gold), and the one seat was different from all the others, and it was called the SEAT PERILOUS. For this seat was unlike the others both in its structure and its significance; for it was all cunningly inset with gold and silver of curious device, and it was covered with a canopy of satin embroidered with gold and silver; and it was altogether of a wonderful magnificence of appearance. And no name ever appeared upon this seat, for only one knight in all of the world could hope to sit therein with safety unto himself. For, if any other dared to sit therein, either he would die a sudden and violent death within three days' time, or else a great misfortune would befall him. Hence that seat was called the SEAT PERILOUS.

"Now, in the days of King Uther-Pendragon, there sat seven-and-thirty knights at the ROUND TABLE. And when King Uther-Pendragon died, he gave the ROUND TABLE unto his friend, King Leodegrance of Cameliard.

"And in the beginning of King Leodegrance's reign, there sat four-and-twenty knights at the ROUND TABLE.

"But times have changed since then, and the glory of King Leodegrance's reign hath paled before the glory of thy reign, so that his noble Court of knights have altogether quitted him. Wherefore there remaineth now not one name, saving only the name of King Leodegrance, upon all those fifty seats that surround the ROUND TABLE. So now that ROUND TABLE lieth beneath its pavilion altogether unused.

"Yet if King Leodegrance will give unto thee, my lord King, that ROUND TABLE for a dower with the Lady Guinevere, then will it lend unto thy reign its greatest glory. For in thy day every seat of that TABLE shall be filled, even unto the SEAT PERILOUS, and the fame of the knights who sit at it shall never be forgotten."

"Ha!" quoth King Arthur. "That would indeed be a dower worthy for any king to have with his queen."

King Leodegrance bestows the Round Table upon King Arthur.

"Then," King Leodegrance said, "that dower shalt thou have with my daughter; and if it bring thee great glory, then shall thy glory be my glory, and thy renown shall be my renown. For if my glory shall wane, and thy glory shall increase, behold! is not my child thy wife?"

And King Arthur said: "Thou sayest well and wisely."

Thus King Arthur became the master of that famous ROUND TABLE. And the ROUND TABLE was set up at Camelot (which some men now call Winchester). And by and by there gathered about it such an array of knights as the world had never beheld before that time, and which it shall never behold again.

Such was the history of the beginning of the ROUND TABLE in King Arthur's reign.

JVSTISSIMVS·REX·

King Arthur meets the Lady Guinevere.

CHAPTER SIXTH

How King Arthur Was Wedded in Royal State and How the Round Table Was Established.

AND NOW WAS COME THE EARLY FALL OF THE YEAR; THAT PLEASANT season when the meadow-land and the wold were still green with summer that had only just passed; when the sky likewise was as of summer-time—extraordinarily blue and full of large floating clouds; when a bird might sing here and another there, a short song in memory of spring-time, when all the air was tempered with warmth and yet the leaves were everywhere turning brown and red and gold, so that when the sun shone through them it was as though a cloth of gold, broidered with brown and crimson and green, hung above the head. At this season of the year it is exceedingly pleasant to be a-field among the nut-trees with hawk and hound, or to travel abroad in the yellow world, whether it be a-horse or a-foot.

Now this was the time of year in which had been set the marriage of King Arthur and the Lady Guinevere at Camelot, and at that place was extraordinary pomp and glory of circumstance. All the world was astir and in a great ferment of joy, for everybody was exceedingly glad that King Arthur was to have him a Queen.

In preparation for that great occasion the town of Camelot was bedight very magnificently, for the stony street along which the Lady Guinevere must come to the royal castle of the King was strewn thick with fresh-cut rushes smoothly laid. Moreover it was in many places spread with carpets of excellent pattern such as might be fit to lay upon the floor of some goodly hall. Likewise all the houses along the way were hung with fine hangings of woven texture interwoven with threads of azure and crimson, and everywhere were flags and banners afloat in the warm and gentle breeze against the blue sky, wherefore that all the world appeared to be alive with bright colors, so that when one looked adown that street, it was as though one beheld a crooked path of exceeding beauty and gayety stretched before him.

How Camelot town was adorned.

Thus came the wedding-day of the King—bright and clear and exceedingly radiant.

King Arthur sat in his hall surrounded by his Court awaiting news that the Lady Guinevere was coming thitherward. And it was about the middle of the morning when there came a messenger in haste riding upon a milk-white steed. And the raiment of that messenger and the trappings of his horse were all of cloth of gold embroidered with scarlet and white, and the tabard of the messenger was set with many jewels of various sorts so that he glistened from afar as he rode, with a singular splendor of appearance.

So this herald-messenger came straight into the castle where the King abided waiting, and he said: "Arise, my lord King, for the Lady Guinevere and her Court draweth nigh unto this place."

Upon this the King immediately arose with great joy, and straightway he went forth with his Court of Knights, riding in great state. And as he went down that marvellously adorned street, all the people shouted aloud as he passed by, wherefore he smiled and bent his head from side to side; for that day he was passing happy and loved his people with wonderful friendliness.

Thus he rode forward unto the town gate, and out therefrom, and so came thence into the country beyond where the broad and well-beaten highway ran winding down beside the shining river betwixt the willows and the osiers.

And, behold! King Arthur and those with him perceived the Court of the Princess where it appeared at a distance, wherefore they made great rejoicing and hastened forward with all speed. And as they came nigh, the sun falling upon the apparels of silk and cloth of gold, and upon golden chains and the jewels that hung therefrom, all of that noble company that surrounded the Lady Guinevere her litter flashed and sparkled with surpassing radiance.

Of the Court of the Lady Guinevere.

For seventeen of the noblest knights of the King's Court, clad in complete armor, and sent by him as an escort unto the lady, rode in great splendor, surrounding the litter wherein the Princess lay. And the framework of that litter was of richly gilded wood, and its curtains and its cushions were of crimson silk embroidered with threads of gold. And behind the litter there rode in gay and joyous array, all shining with many colors, the Court of the Princess—her damsels in waiting, gentlemen, ladies, pages, and attendants.

So those parties of the King and the Lady Guinevere drew nigh together until they met and mingled the one with the other.

Then straightway King Arthur dismounted from his noble horse and, all clothed with royalty, he went afoot unto the Lady Guinevere's litter, whiles Sir Gawaine and Sir Ewaine held the bridle of his horse. Thereupon one of her pages drew aside the silken curtains of the Lady Guinevere's litter, and King Leodegrance gave her his hand and she straightway descended therefrom, all embalmed, as it were, in exceeding beauty. So King Leodegrance led her to King Arthur, and King Arthur came to her and placed one hand beneath her chin and the other upon her head and inclined his countenance and kissed her upon her smooth cheek—all warm and fragrant like velvet for softness, and without any blemish whatsoever. And when he had thus kissed her upon the cheek, all those who were there lifted up their voices in great acclaim, giving loud voice of joy that those two noble souls had thus met together.

King Arthur greets the Lady Guinevere.

Thus did King Arthur give welcome unto the Lady Guinevere and unto King Leodegrance her father upon the highway beneath the walls of the town of Camelot, at the distance of half a league from that place. And no one who was there ever forgot that meeting, for it was full of extraordinary grace and noble courtliness.

Then King Arthur and his Court of Knights and nobles brought King Leodegrance and the Lady Guinevere with great ceremony unto Camelot and unto the royal castle, where apartments were assigned to all, so that the entire place was alive with joyousness and beauty.

King Arthur and the Lady Guinevere are wedded.

And when high noon had come, the entire Court went with great state and ceremony unto the cathedral, and there, surrounded with wonderful magnificence, those two noble souls were married by the Archbishop.

And all the bells rang right joyfully, and all the people who stood without the cathedral shouted with loud acclaim, and lo! the King and the Queen came forth all shining, like unto the sun for splendor and like unto the moon for beauty.

In the castle a great noontide feast was spread, and there sat thereat four hundred, eighty and six lordly and noble folk—kings, knights, and nobles—with queens and ladies in magnificent array. And near to the King and the Queen there sat King Leodegrance and Merlin, and Sir Ulfius, and Sir Ector the trustworthy, and Sir Gawaine, and Sir Ewaine, and Sir Kay, and King Ban, and King Pellinore and many other famous and exalted folk, so that no man had ever beheld such magnificent courtliness as he beheld at that famous wedding-feast of King Arthur and Queen Guinevere.

Of the feast at the King's castle.

✠ ✠ ✠

And that day was likewise very famous in the history of chivalry, for in the afternoon the famous Round Table was established, and that Round Table was at once the very flower and the chiefest glory of King Arthur's reign.

For about mid of the afternoon the King and Queen, preceded by Merlin and followed by all that splendid Court of kings, lords, nobles and knights in full array, made progression to that place where Merlin, partly by magic and partly by skill, had caused to be builded a very wonderful pavilion above the Round Table where it stood.

And when the King and the Queen and the Court had entered in thereat they were amazed at the beauty of that pavilion, for they perceived, an it were, a great space that appeared to be a marvellous land of Fay. For the walls were all richly gilded and were painted with very wonderful figures of saints and of angels, clad in ultramarine and crimson, and all those saints and angels were depicted playing upon various musical instruments that appeared to be made of gold. And overhead the roof of the pavilion was made to represent the sky, being all of cerulean blue sprinkled over with stars. And in the midst of that painted sky was an image, an it were, of the sun in his glory. And under foot was a pavement all of marble stone, set in squares of black and white, and blue and red, and sundry other colors.

Of the pavilion of the Round Table.

In the midst of the pavilion was a Round Table with seats thereat exactly sufficient for fifty persons, and at each of the fifty places was a chalice of gold filled with fragrant wine, and at each place was a paten of gold bearing a manchet of fair white bread. And when the King and his Court entered into the pavilion, lo! music began of a sudden for to play with a wonderful sweetness.

Then Merlin came and took King Arthur by the hand and led him away from Queen Guinevere. And he said unto the King, "Lo! this is the Round Table."

Then King Arthur said, "Merlin, that which I see is wonderful beyond the telling."

After that Merlin discovered unto the King the various marvels of the Round Table, for first he pointed to a high seat, very wonderfully wrought in precious woods and gilded so that it was exceedingly beautiful, and he said, "Behold, lord King, yonder seat is hight the 'Seat Royal,' and that seat is thine for to sit in." And as Merlin spake, lo! there suddenly appeared sundry letters of gold upon the back of that seat, and the letters of gold read the name,

King Arthur is seated at the Round Table.

ARTHUR, KING.

And Merlin said, "Lord, yonder seat may well be called the centre seat of the Round Table, for, in sooth, thou art indeed the very centre of all that is most worthy of true knightliness. Wherefore that seat shall be called the centre seat of all the other seats."

Then Merlin pointed to the seat that stood opposite to the Seat Royal, and that seat also was of a very wonderful appearance as afore told in this history. And Merlin said unto the King: "My lord King, that seat is called the Seat Perilous, for no man but one in all this world shall sit therein, and that man is not yet born upon the earth. And if any other man shall dare to sit therein that man shall either suffer death or a sudden and terrible misfortune for his temerity. Wherefore that seat is called the Seat Perilous."

"Merlin," quoth the King, "all that thou tellest me passeth the bound of understanding for marvellousness. Now I do beseech thee in all haste for to find forthwith a sufficient number of knights to fill this Round Table so that my glory shall be entirely complete."

Then Merlin smiled upon the King, though not with cheerfulness, and said, "Lord, why art thou in such haste? Know that when this Round Table shall be entirely filled in all its seats, then shall thy glory be entirely achieved and then forthwith shall thy day begin for to decline. For when any man hath reached the crowning of his glory, then his work is done and God breaketh him as a man might break a chalice from which such perfect ichor hath been drunk that no baser wine may be allowed to defile it. So when thy work is done and ended shall God shatter the chalice of thy life."

Then did the King look very steadfastly into Merlin's face, and said, "Old man, that which thou sayest is ever of great wonder, for thou speakest words of wisdom. Ne'theless, seeing that I am in God His hands, I do wish for my glory and for His good will to be accomplished even though He shall then entirely break me when I have served His purposes."

"Lord," said Merlin, "thou speakest like a worthy king and with a very large and noble heart. Ne'theless, I may not fill the Round Table for thee at this time. For, though thou hast gathered about thee the very noblest Court of Chivalry in all of Christendom, yet are there but two and thirty knights here present who may be considered worthy to sit at the Round Table."

Merlin chooseth the knights of the Round Table.

"Then, Merlin," quoth King Arthur, "I do desire of thee that thou shalt straightway choose me those two and thirty."

"So will I do, lord King," said Merlin.

Then Merlin cast his eyes around and lo! he saw where King Pellinore stood at a little distance. Unto him went Merlin and took him by the hand. "Behold, my lord King," quoth he. "Here is the knight in all the world next to thyself who at this time is most worthy for to sit at this Round Table. For he is both exceedingly gentle of demeanor unto the poor and needy and at the same time is so terribly strong and skilful that I know not whether thou or he is the more to be feared in an encounter of knight against knight."

Then Merlin led King Pellinore forward and behold! upon the high seat that stood upon the left hand of the Royal Seat there appeared of a sudden the name,

PELLINORE.

And the name was emblazoned in letters of gold that shone with extraordinary lustre. And when King Pellinore took his seat, great and loud acclaim long continued was given him by all those who stood round about.

Then after that Merlin had thus chosen King Arthur and King Pellinore he chose out of the Court of King Arthur the following knights, two and thirty in all, and these were the knights of great renown in chivalry who did first establish the Round Table. Wherefore they were surnamed "The Ancient and Honorable Companions of the Round Table."

To begin, there was Sir Gawaine and Sir Ewaine, who were nephews unto the King, and they sat nigh to him upon the right hand; there was Sir Ulfius (who held his seat but four years and eight months unto the time of his death, after which Sir Geheris—who was esquire unto his brother, Sir Gawaine—held that seat); and there was Sir Kay the Seneschal, who was foster brother unto the King; and there was Sir Baudwain of Britain (who held his seat but three years and two months until his death, after the which Sir Agravaine held that seat); and there was Sir Pellias and Sir Geraint and Sir Constantine, son of Sir Caderes the Seneschal of Cornwall (which same was king after King Arthur); and there was Sir Caradoc and Sir Sagramore, surnamed the Desirous, and Sir Dinadan and Sir Dodinas, surnamed the Savage, and Sir Bruin, surnamed the Black, and Sir Meliot of Logres, and Sir Aglaval and Sir Durnure, and Sir Lamorac (which three young knights were sons of King Pellinore), and there was Sir Griflet and Sir Ladinas and Sir Brandiles and Sir Persavant of Ironside, and Sir Dinas of Cornwall, and Sir Brian of Listinoise, and Sir Palomides and Sir Degraine and Sir Epinogres, the son of the King of North Umberland and brother unto the enchantress Vivien, and Sir Lamiel of Cardiff, and Sir Lucan the Bottler and Sir Bedevere his brother (which same bare King Arthur unto the ship of Fairies when he lay so sorely wounded nigh unto death after the last battle which he fought). These two and thirty knights were the Ancient Companions of the Round Table, and unto them were added others until there were nine and forty in all, and then was added Sir Galahad, and with him the Round Table was made entirely complete.

Now as each of these knights was chosen by Merlin, lo! as he took that knight by the hand, the name of that knight suddenly appeared in golden letters, very bright and shining, upon the seat that appertained to him.

But when all had been chosen, behold! King Arthur saw that the seat upon the right hand of the Seat Royal had not been filled, and that it bare no name upon it. And he said unto Merlin: "Merlin, how is this, that the seat upon my right hand hath not been filled, and beareth no name?"

And Merlin said: "Lord, there shall be a name thereon in a very little while, and he who shall sit therein shall be the greatest knight in all the world until that the knight cometh who shall occupy the Seat Perilous. For he who cometh shall exceed all other men in beauty and in strength and in knightly grace."

And King Arthur said: "I would that he were with us now." And Merlin said: "He cometh anon."

Thus was the Round Table established with great pomp and great ceremony of estate. For first the Archbishop of Canterbury blessed each and every seat, progressing from place to place surrounded by his Holy Court, the choir whereof singing most musically in accord, whiles others swung censers from which there ascended an exceedingly fragrant vapor of frankincense, filling that entire pavilion with an odor of Heavenly blessedness.

And when the Archbishop had thus blessed every one of those seats, the chosen knight took each his stall at the Round Table, and his esquire came and stood behind him, holding the banneret with his coat-of-arms upon the spear-point above the knight's head. And all those who stood about that place, both knights and ladies, lifted up their voices in loud acclaim.

Of the ceremony of installation of the Round Table.

Then all the knights arose, and each knight held up before him the cross of the hilt of his sword, and each knight spake word for word as King Arthur spake. And this was the covenant of their Knighthood of the Round Table: That they would be gentle unto the weak; that they would be courageous unto the strong; that they would be terrible unto the wicked and the evil-doer; that they would defend the helpless who should call upon them for aid; that all women should be held unto them sacred; that they would stand unto the defence of one another whensoever such defence should be required; that they would be merciful unto all men; that they would be gentle of deed, true in friendship, and faithful in love. This was their covenant, and unto it each knight sware upon the cross of his sword, and in witness thereof did kiss the hilt thereof. Thereupon all who stood thereabouts once more gave loud acclaim.

Then all the knights of the Round Table seated themselves, and each knight brake bread from the golden patten, and quaffed wine from the golden chalice that stood before him, giving thanks unto God for that which he ate and drank.

Thus was King Arthur wedded unto Queen Guinevere, and thus was the Round Table established.

Conclusion

So endeth this Book of King Arthur which hath been told by me with such joyousness of spirit that I find it to be a very great pleasure, in closing this first volume of my work, to look forward to writing a second volume, which now presently followeth.

In that volume there shall be told the history of several very noble worthies who were of the Court of the King, and it seems to me to be a good thing to have to do with the history of such noble and honorable knights and gentlemen. For, indeed, it might well please anyone to read such an history, and to hear those worthies speak, and to behold in what manner they behaved in times of trial and tribulation. For their example will doubtless help us all to behave in a like manner in a like case.

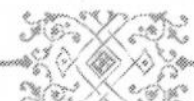

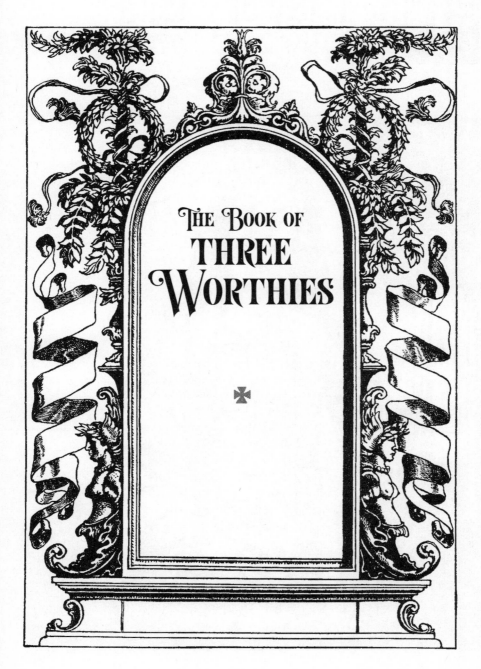

The Book of THREE WORTHIES

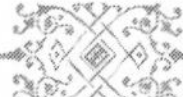

The Lady of ye Lake.

Foreword

Here beginneth the Second Book of the History of King Arthur, called The Book of Three Worthies, because it has to do with three very excellent, honorable Lords of the Court of King Arthur.

Of these three, the first is Merlin the Wise, the second is Sir Pellias, surnamed the Gentle Knight, and the third is Sir Gawaine, the son of King Lot of Orkney and the Isles.

So now presently follows the story of the passing of Merlin the Wise; in the which you shall see how the very wisdom that Merlin possessed in such great measure was the cause of his own undoing. Wherefore I do hope that you yourselves may take that story unto heart so that you shall see that those gifts of mind or person which God assigns unto you may not be so misused by you or others that they shall become the means of compassing your own downfall.

For it shall not excuse you in any wise that, as you journey forward in your life, you shall find many men who, like Merlin, have been endowed by the grace of God with very great gifts of talent which they might very easily use to the great benefit of mankind, but which they so misuse as to bring the greater ruin upon themselves and the greater harm unto other men. For, if you shall prove so weak or so wicked as to misuse your talents in that manner unto the harm of others and of yourself, it shall not make your fault the less that others shall have done greater evil than yourself.

Wherefore, let this story of Merlin be a warning unto you, I pray you all. For, though I do not believe that Merlin intended that his talents of magic should do harm unto others, yet, because of his folly, they did as great harm as though he himself had designed to do evil by means of them. Yea; it is hard to tell whether the wickedness or the follies of men do the greater harm in the world; therefore seek to guard yourself well, not only against sin, but against folly and weakness likewise.

JVSTISSIMVS·REX·

The Enchanter Merlin.

Prologue

UPON A CERTAIN DAY KING ARTHUR SAT IN THE ROYAL HALL OF CAMELOT with the Queen and all of his Court and all of her Court. And there was great joy and mirth at that place.

Whiles they sat there, there suddenly came an armed knight into the Hall, and his armor was all covered with blood and dust, and he had a great many wounds upon his body. Then all they who were at that place were astonished and affrighted at the aspect of that knight, for his appearance boded no good news to King Arthur. The knight-messenger came to where the King was, and he was nearly fainting with weakness and with the many wounds he had received, and he brought news unto those who were there present that five kings, enemies to King Arthur, had suddenly come into that land and that they were burning and harrying the country upon every side.

A messenger cometh to the King at Camelot.

And the knight-messenger said that these five kings were the King of Denmark, the King of Ireland, the King of Soleyse, the King of the Vale, and the King of Longtinaise. These had brought with them a great host and were laying waste the land all around about, so that all the realm was in sore travail and sorrow because of their devastations.

Upon this news, King Arthur smote his palms together with great vehemence and cried out, "Alas! who would be a king! Will the time never come when these wars and disturbances shall cease and we shall have entire peace in this land!" Therewith he arose in great agitation and went out from that place, and all who were there were in sore trouble.

So King Arthur immediately sent messengers to two friendly kings who were nearest to him—to wit, to King Pellinore and to King Uriens of Gore—and he bade them to come to his aid without any loss of time. Meantime he himself gathered together a large army with intent to go forth to meet his enemies forthwith.

King Arthur asketh aid of King Uriens and of King Pellinore.

So he went forth and upon the third day he came with his army unto the forest of Tintagalon and there he stayed with intent to rest for a little until King Pellinore and King Uriens should have joined him.

But the five kings, his enemies, had news that King Arthur was at that place, and thereupon they made a forced march through North Wales with intent to strike him ere those other two kings could come to his aid. So they came by night to where King Arthur was, and they fell upon him so unexpectedly that there was great danger of his army being put to rout before that assault.

But King Arthur drew his army together by his own courage and large-heartedness, and so they defended themselves with a great spirit until King Pellinore appeared with his army and joined in that battle.

King Arthur is victorious.

So in the end King Arthur won a great victory over his enemies; for they were put to rout and scattered in every direction. Likewise by means of that war, and because of the submissions of these five kings, King Arthur recovered all that realm that had once been his father's, and more besides.

Eight knights of the Round Table are slain in battle.

Now in that war eight of the knights of the Round Table lost their lives, and King Arthur mourned their loss with great dolor; for these were the first knights of the Round Table who had lost their lives in doing battle in his defence.

Whilst King Arthur was grieving very sorely for these eight knights, Merlin came unto him, and said, "Be not downcast, lord, for lo! thou hast many excellent knights still left about thee and thou canst certainly not have a very great deal of trouble in filling those eight places that have been thus made empty by death. Now if thou followest my counsel, thou must choose some very worthy adviser from the knights-companion of thy Round Table, and thou wilt consult with him in this matter (for the counsel of two is better than the counsel of one), and between ye ye may fill those places made vacant by war."

This counsel appeared very good to King Arthur, so he did as Merlin advised. For that morning he summoned King Pellinore to his privy closet and laid the matter before him and they two communed together thereupon. In that consultation King Pellinore advised King Arthur in this wise: That there should be four old and worthy knights chosen to fill four of those empty seats, and that there should be four young and ardent knights chosen to fill the other four seats, and in that manner all those eight seats should be filled.

King Arthur and King Pellinore choose eight old and worthy knights for the Round Table.

Now that advice appeared to King Arthur to be good, wherefore he said, "Let it be that way." So first they two chose the four old knights as follows: There was King Uriens of Gore, and King Lac, and Sir Hervise de Reuel, and Sir Galliar of Rouge. And from the younger knights of the Court they chose Sir Marvaise of Leisle, and Sir Lionel, the son of King Ban of Benwick, and Sir Cadar of Cornwall. So that there was one place yet to be filled.

Now it was a very hard thing to determine who should fill that place, for there were at that time two very honorable young knights at the Court. One of these was Sir Baudemagus, a young knight, brother of Sir Ewaine and son of King Uriens of Gore and Queen Morgana le Fay (which lady was half-sister unto King Arthur as hath been aforetold). And the other young knight was Sir Tor who, though late come to the Court, had performed several very famous adventures. And Sir Tor was a son of King Pellinore (though not of his Queen), and King Pellinore loved him a very great deal.

They choose three young knights for the Round Table.

Then King Pellinore said to King Arthur, "Lord, there are certainly but two knights in all thy Court to choose from for to fill this eighth seat at the Round Table: one of these is thy sister's son, Sir Baudemagus, and the other is my son, Sir Tor. Now I may not advise thee in this matter, wherefore do thou, Lord, choose the one or the other of these young knights to fill that place. But this I may say, that it will please me very greatly if thy favor should fall upon Sir Baudemagus, for then will all the world believe that I have been above reproach in my dealings in this affair, whereas should Sir Tor be chosen all men would say that I favored mine own son."

King Arthur chooseth Sir Tor for the Round Table.

Then King Arthur meditated upon this matter for a long while and by and by he spoke and said, "Sir, I have weighed this whole affair, and it is my belief that Sir Tor is the better knight of those twain. For he hath performed several very excellent adventures, whilst Sir Baudemagus, though a worthy knight, hath not yet made manifest any very great achievement in the fields of chivalry. So, in God's name, let Sir Tor be seated as companion of the Round Table."

Then King Pellinore said, "So be it," and thereupon they both arose and went forth from that place.

And, lo! that very moment the names of those eight worthies so chosen appeared each upon the back of the seat at the Round Table that appertained unto him, and so the decision of those two knights was confirmed in the sight of all the world in that manner.

Now when the word of all this reached the ears of Queen Morgana le Fay she was greatly affronted that Sir Baudemagus, her son, should have been passed by and that another should have been chosen in his stead. Wherefore she cried out against King Arthur in the hearing of several people, saying: "Ha! how is this! is blood and kinship of no account in the eyes of this King that he passes by so worthy a knight as his own nephew to choose one who is not of lawful birth in his stead? Now, my husband's house has suffered many grievous ills at the hands of King Arthur, for, lo! he hath taken away our royal power and hath made us all little better than captives in his own Court. This in itself is as great an affront as though we were his bitter enemies instead of his nigh of kin. But this that he hath now done to my son in thus passing him by is a greater affront than that other."

Queen Morgana le Fay is affronted with King Arthur.

And Queen Morgana le Fay spake in this wise not only to King Uriens, who was her husband, but to Sir Ewaine and to Sir Baudemagus, who were her sons. But King Uriens of Gore rebuked her for her speech, for he had grown to love King Arthur very much because of the high nobility of his nature, and likewise Sir Ewaine rebuked her saying that he would listen to no ill thing said of King Arthur, for that not only did he love King Arthur better than anyone else in all the world, but that the King was at once the looking-glass of all knighthood and likewise the very fountain-head of honor.

So spake these two; but Sir Baudemagus hearkened to what his mother, Queen Morgana said, for he was very angry with King Arthur because the King had passed him by. Wherefore he took his departure from the Court without asking leave of

King Arthur and went errant in quest of adventure, and at this King Arthur was very sorry.

Now, as aforesaid, Queen Morgana le Fay spake her indignation to several other people of the Court, so that word thereof came at last to the ears of King Arthur and grieved him a very great deal. So when Queen Morgana came to him one day and besought his leave for to quit the Court, he spake to her with great sadness of spirit, saying, "My sister, I am very sorry that you are not pleased with what I have done in this matter, for God knows that I have endeavored to do to the best of my power. And though I would rather a great deal that Sir Baudemagus were fellow of the Round Table, yet it was my very honest belief that, for several reasons, Sir Tor had the best right to a seat at that Table. Now if I chose otherwise than according to my right judgment, what virtue would the Round Table have, seeing that I should have shown favor unto a man because of his kinship to me?"

Then Queen Morgana le Fay said with great heat, "Sir, all that you say only adds to the affront that our house hath sustained at your hands. For now you not only deny my son that seat, but you belittle him by comparing him to his disadvantage with this low-born knight whom you have chosen. Now, the only pleasure that I can have in talking to you is to beseech you to let me go away from this place."

Then King Arthur, speaking with great dignity, said, "Lady, it shall be as you would have it, and you shall go whithersoever it pleases you. For God forbid that I should stay you in your wishes. Moreover, I shall see to it that you shall not depart from this place without such a Court for company as may very well befit one who is the wife of one king and the sister of another."

Queen Morgana le Fay leaveth the Court of King Arthur.

And so he did as he said he would do, for he sent Queen Morgana le Fay away from his Court with great honor and in high estate of circumstance. But the more patient King Arthur was with her and the more he showed her favor, the more angry Queen Morgana le Fay was with him and the more she hated him.

So she betook her way to an estuary of the sea and there she dismissed those whom the King had sent with her and embarked with her own Court in several ships, betaking her way to that enchanted isle, hight Avalon, which was her home.

This island of Avalon was a very strange, wonderful land, such as was not to be seen anywhere else in all the world. For it was like a Paradise for beauty, being covered all over with divers gardens of flowers, intermingled with plantations of fair trees, some bearing fruit and others all a-bloom with blossoms. And besides these were many terraces of lawns, and smooth slopes of grass lying all about the borders of the island, and overlooking the sea from tall white walls of pure marble. And in the midst of these gardens and orchards and plantations and lawns and terraces, were a multitude of castles and towers built up the one above the other—some as white as snow and others very gay with many colors.

And the greatest marvel of that wonderful island was this: that in the midst of all those castles and towers was a single tower built entirely of loadstone. And in that lay the great mystery of that place.

For the island floated upon the surface of the water, and that tower of loadstone possessed such a potency that Avalon would float from place to place according to the will of Queen Morgana le Fay, so that sometimes it would be here, and sometimes it would be there, as that royal lady willed it to be.

Nor was there a very many people who had seen that island, for somewhiles it would be all covered over with a mist of enchantment like to silver, so that no eyes could behold it unless they were fay. But sometimes it had been seen, as it were a vision of Paradise. What time he who beheld it would hear gay voices sounding from its lawns and plantations—very thin and clear because of the great distance (for no one ever came nigh to Avalon unless by authority of Queen Morgana le Fay), and he would hear music of so sweet a sort that it was likely that his soul would grow all faint because of the music. Then Avalon would suddenly disappear very marvellously, and he who had seen it would be aware that it was not likely that he would ever see it again.

Such was the island of Avalon, and if you would read of it more particularly you shall find much about it in a certain book written in French and called "Ogier le Danois."

Queen Morgana le Fay loved this island a very great deal, and it is said by many that King Arthur is yet alive in that place, lying there very peacefully and tranquilly whiles he awaits that certain time when he shall return unto the world to make right all that is wrong therein. So it is I have told you of it with these particulars at this place.

PART I
THE STORY OF MERLIN

Here followeth a particular account of the enchantment of Merlin by a certain damsel, hight Vivien, and of all the circumstances thereunto appertaining.

Likewise it is to be narrated how King Arthur was betrayed by his own sister, and of how he would certainly have been slain only for the help of that same enchantress Vivien who was the cause of Merlin's undoing.

Also it shall be told how the sheath of Excalibur was lost at that time.

The Enchantress Vivien.

CHAPTER FIRST

How Queen Morgana le Fay Meditated Evil Against King Arthur and How She Sent a Damsel to Beguile the Enchanter, Merlin.

NOW MORGANA LE FAY WAS A VERY CUNNING ENCHANTRESS, AND WAS so much mistress of magic that she could, by means of potent spells, work her will upon all things, whether quick or dead. For Merlin himself had been her master in times past, and had taught her his arts whilst she was still a young damsel at the Court of Uther-Pendragon. So it was that, next to Merlin, she was, at that time, the most potent enchanter in all the world. Nevertheless she lacked Merlin's foreknowledge of things to happen and his gift of prophecy thereupon, for these things he could not impart unto anyone, wherefore she had not learned them of him.

Queen Morgana contemplates evil against King Arthur.

Now, after Queen Morgana le Fay had come to the Island of Avalon as aforetold, she brooded a great deal over that affront which she deemed King Arthur had placed upon her house; and the more she brooded upon it the more big did it become in her mind. Wherefore, at last, it seemed to her that she could have no pleasure in life unless she could punish King Arthur for that which he had done. Yea; she would have been glad to see him dead at her feet because of the anger that she felt against him.

But Queen Morgana was very well aware that she could never do the King, her brother, an injury so long as Merlin was there to safeguard him, for Merlin would certainly foresee any danger that might threaten the King, and would counteract it, wherefore she was aware that if she would destroy the King, she must first destroy Merlin.

Now, there was at the Court of Queen Morgana le Fay, a certain damsel of such marvellous and bewitching beauty that her like was hardly to be seen in all of the world. This damsel was fifteen years old and of royal blood, being the daughter of the King of Northumberland; and her name was Vivien. This damsel, Vivien, was both wise and cunning beyond all measure for one so young. Moreover, she was without any heart, being cold and cruel to all who were contrary-minded to her wishes. So, because she was so cunning and wise, Queen Morgana liked her and taught her many things of magic and sorcery which she knew. But, notwithstanding all that Queen Morgana did for her, this maiden did not feel any love for her mistress, being altogether devoid of heart.

One day this damsel and Queen Morgana le Fay sat together in a garden of that magic island of Avalon, and the garden was upon a very high terrace and overlooked the sea. And the day was very fair and the sea so wonderfully blue that it appeared to be as though the blue sky had melted into water and the water into the sky. As Vivien and the Queen sat in this beautiful place, the Queen said to the damsel, "Vivien, what wouldst thou rather have than anything else in all the world?" To which Vivien replied, "Lady, I would rather have such wisdom as thou hast, than anything else."

Queen Morgana talketh with the Damsel Vivien.

Then Queen Morgana laughed and said, "It is possible for thee to be as wise as I am, and wiser too, if so be thou wilt do according to my ordination. For I know a way in which thou mayst obtain wisdom."

"How may I obtain that wisdom, Lady?" said Vivien.

Then Queen Morgana le Fay said, "Hearken and I will tell thee. Thou must know that Merlin, whom thou hast several times seen at the Court of King Arthur, is the master of all the wisdom that it is possible for anyone to possess in this world. All that I know of magic Merlin hath taught me, and he knoweth many things that he did not teach me, but which he withheld from me. For Merlin taught me, when I was a young damsel at the Court of my mother's husband, because I was beautiful in his eyes. For Merlin loveth beauty above all things else in the world, and so he taught me many things of magic and was very patient with me.

"But Merlin hath a gift which belongeth to him and which he cannot communicate to anyone else, for it is instinct with him. That gift is the gift of foreseeing into the future and the power of prophesying thereupon.

"Yet though he may foresee the fate of others, still he is blind to his own fate. For so he confessed to me several times: that he could not tell what was to happen in his own life when that happening concerned himself alone.

"Now thou, Vivien, art far more beautiful than I was at thine age. Wherefore I believe that thou wilt easily attract the regard of Merlin unto thee. And if I give thee, besides, a certain charm which I possess, I may cause it to be that Merlin may love thee so much that he will impart to thee a great deal more of his wisdom than ever he taught me when I was his disciple.

"But thou art to know, Vivien, that in winning this gift of knowledge from Merlin thou wilt put thyself in great peril. For, by and by, when the charm of thy beauty shall have waned with him, then he may easily regret what he hath done in imparting his wisdom to thee; in the which case there will be great danger that he may lay some spell upon thee to deprive thee of thy powers; for it would be impossible that both thou and he could live in the same world and each of ye know so much cunning of magic."

Now unto all this Vivien listened with a great deal of attention, and when Queen Morgana had ended the damsel said, "Dear Lady, all that thou tellest me is very wonderful, and I find myself possessed with a vehement desire to attain such knowledge in magic as that. Wherefore, if thou wilt help me in this matter so that I may beguile his wisdom from Merlin, thou wilt make of me a debtor unto thee for as long as I may live. And touching the matter of any danger that may fall to me in this affair, I am altogether willing to assume that; for I have a great hope that I may be able so to protect myself from Merlin that no harm shall befall me. For when I have drawn all the knowledge that I am able to obtain from him, then I will use that same knowledge to cast such a spell upon him that he shall never be able to harm me or anyone else again. In this I shall play my wit against his wisdom and my beauty against his cunning, and I believe that I shall win at that game."

Then Queen Morgana fell a-laughing beyond all measure, and when she had stinted her laughter, she cried, "Hey, Vivien! certes thou art cunning beyond anything that I ever heard tell of, and I believe that thou art as wicked as thou art cunning. For whoever heard of a child of fifteen years old who would speak such words as thou hast just now spoken; or whoever could suppose that so young a girl could conceive the thought of compassing the downfall of the wisest magician who hath ever lived."

Then Queen Morgana le Fay set to her lips a small whistle of ivory and gold and blew very shrilly upon it, and in reply there came running a young page of her Court. Queen Morgana commanded him to bring to her a certain casket of alabaster, cunningly carved and adorned with gold and set with several precious stones. And Queen Morgana opened the box and took from within it two rings of pure yellow gold, beautifully wrought and set, the one ring with a clear white stone of extraordinary brilliancy, and the other with a stone as red as blood. Then Queen Morgana said, "Vivien, behold these two rings! They possess each a spell of wonderful potency. For if thou wearest that ring with the white stone, whoever weareth the ring with the red stone shall love thee with such a passion of love that thou mayst do with him whatever thou hast a will to do. So take these rings and go to King Arthur's Court and use them as thy cunning may devise."

Queen Morgana giveth Vivien two enchanted rings.

So Vivien took the two rings and gave Queen Morgana le Fay thanks beyond all measure for them.

Now King Arthur took much pleasure in holding a great feast each Pentecost, at which time his Court was gathered about him with much mirth and rejoicing. At such times it delighted him to have some excellent entertainment for to amuse himself and his Court, wherefore it befell that nearly always something happened that gave much entertainment to the King. So came the Feast of Pentecost, and King Arthur sat at the table with a great many noble and lordly folk and several kings and queens. Now as they all sat at that feast, their spirits greatly expanded with mirth and good cheer, there suddenly came into the hall a very beautiful young damsel, and with her a dwarf, wonderfully misshapen and of a very hideous countenance. And the maiden was dressed all in flame-colored satin, very rich, and with beautiful embroidery of gold and embroidery of silver. And her hair, which was red like gold, was coiled into a net of gold. And her eyes were black as coals and extraordinarily bright and glistening. And she had about her throat a necklace of gold of three strands, so that with all that gold and those bright garments she shone with wonderful splendor as she entered the hall. Likewise, the dwarf who accompanied her was clad all in flame-colored raiment, and he bore in his hands a cushion of flame-colored silk with tassels of gold, and upon the cushion he bare a ring of exceeding beauty set with a red stone.

Vivien appears before King Arthur at the Feast of Pentecost.

So when King Arthur beheld this beautiful maiden he supposed nothing else, than that there was some excellent entertainment, and at that he rejoiced a very great deal.

But when he looked well at the damsel it appeared to him that he knew her face, wherefore he said to her, "Damsel, who art thou?" "Sir," she said, "I am the daughter of the King of Northumberland, and my name is Vivien," and thereat King Arthur was satisfied.

Then King Arthur said to her, "Lady, what is that thou hast upon yonder cushion, and why hast thou honored us by coming hitherward?" To the which Vivien made reply, "Lord, I have here a very good entertainment for to give you pleasure at this Feast of Pentecost. For here is a ring of such a sort that only he who is the most wise and the most worthy of all men here present may wear it." And King Arthur said, "Let us see the ring."

So Vivien took the ring from the cushion which the dwarf held and she came and brought it unto King Arthur, and the King took the ring into his own hand. And he perceived that the ring was extraordinary beautiful, wherefore he said, "Maiden, have I thy leave to try this ring upon my finger?" And Vivien said, "Yea, lord."

So King Arthur made attempt to place the ring upon his finger; but, lo! the ring shrank in size so that it would not pass beyond the first joint thereof. Wherefore King Arthur said, "It would appear that I am not worthy to wear this ring."

King Arthur trieth on the ring.

Then the damsel, Vivien, said, "Have I my lord's leave to offer this ring to others of his Court?" And King Arthur said, "Let the others try the ring." So Vivien took the ring to the various folk of the Court, both lords and ladies, but not one of these could wear the ring. Then last of all Vivien came to the place where Merlin sat, and she kneeled upon the ground before him and offered the ring to him; and Merlin, because this concerned himself, could not forecast into the future to know that harm was intended to him. Nevertheless he looked sourly upon the damsel and he said, "Child, what is this silly trick thou offerest me?" "Sir," quoth Vivien, "I beseech you for to try this ring upon your finger." Then Merlin regarded the damsel more closely, and he perceived that she was very beautiful, wherefore his heart softened toward her a great deal. So he spake more gently unto her and he said, "Wherefore should I take the ring?" To the which she made reply, "Because I believe that thou art the most wise and the most worthy of any man in all this place, wherefore the ring should belong to thee." Then Merlin smiled, and took the ring and placed it upon his finger, and, lo! it fitted the finger exactly. Thereupon Vivien cried out, "See! the ring hath fitted his finger and he is the most wise and the most worthy." And Merlin was greatly pleased that the ring which the beautiful damsel had given him had fitted his finger in that way.

Merlin secureth the ring.

Then, after a while, he would have withdrawn the ring but, behold! he could not, for the ring had grown to his finger as though it were a part of the flesh and the bone thereof. At this Merlin became much troubled in spirit and very anxious, for he did not understand what might be meant by the magic of the ring. So he said, "Lady, whence came this ring?" And Vivien said, "Sir, thou knowest all things, dost thou then not know that this ring was sent hitherward from Morgana le Fay?" Then again Merlin was greatly a-doubt, and he said, "I hope there may be no evil in this ring." And Vivien smiled upon him and said, "What evil could there be in it?"

Now by this time the great magic that was in the ring began to work upon Merlin's spirit, wherefore he regarded Vivien very steadily, and suddenly he took great pleasure in her beauty. Then the magic of the ring gat entire hold upon him and, lo! a wonderful passion immediately seized upon his heart and wrung it so that it was pierced as with a violent agony.

And Vivien beheld what passed in Merlin's mind, and she laughed and turned away. And several others who were there also observed the very strange manner in which Merlin regarded her, wherefore they said among themselves, "Of a surety Merlin is bewitched by the beauty of that young damoiselle."

So, after that time the enchantment of the ring of Morgana le Fay so wrought upon Merlin's spirit that he could in no wise disentangle himself from Vivien's witchery; for from that day forth, whithersoever she went, there he might be found not far away; and if she was in the garden, he would be there; and if she was in the Hall, he also would be there; and if she went a-hawking he would also be a-horseback. And all the Court observed these things and many made themselves merry and jested upon it. But, Vivien hated Merlin with all her might, for she saw that they all made merry at that folly of Merlin's, and he wearied her with his regard. But she dissembled this disregard before his face and behaved to him in all ways as though she had a great friendship for him.

The ring worketh its charm upon Merlin the Wise.

Now it happened upon a day that Vivien sat in the garden, and it was wonderfully pleasant summer weather, and Merlin came into the garden and beheld Vivien where she sat. But when Vivien perceived Merlin coming she suddenly felt so great a disregard for him that she could not bear for to be nigh him at that time, wherefore she arose in haste with intent to escape from him. But Merlin hurried and overtook her and he said to her, "Child, do you then hate me?" And Vivien said, "Sir, I do not hate you." But Merlin said, "In very truth I believe that you do hate me." And Vivien was silent.

Then in a little Merlin said, "I would that I knew what I might do for you so that you would cease to hate me, for I find that I have a wonderful love for you." Upon this Vivien looked at Merlin very strangely, and by and by she said, "Sir, if you would only impart your wisdom and your cunning unto me, then I believe that I could love you a very great deal. For, behold! I am but as a young child in knowledge and thou art so old and so wise that I am afraid of thee. If thou wouldst teach me thy wisdom so that I might be thine equal, then haply I might grow to have such a regard for thee as thou wouldst have me feel."

Upon this Merlin looked very steadily at Vivien and he said, "Damsel, thou art, certes, no such foolish child as thou dost proclaim thyself to be; for I see that thine eyes are very bright with a cunning beyond thy years. Now I misdoubt that if I should teach thee the wisdom which thou dost desire to possess, either it would be to thy undoing or else it would be to my undoing."

Then Vivien cried out with a very loud and piercing voice, "Merlin, if thou dost love me, teach me thy wisdom and the cunning of thy magic and then I will love thee beyond anyone else in all the world!"

But Merlin sighed very deeply, for his heart misgave him. Then by and by he said, "Vivien, thou shalt have thy will and I will teach thee all those things of wisdom and magic that thou desirest to know."

Upon this Vivien was filled with such vehement agony of joy that she did not dare to let Merlin look into her countenance lest he should read what was therein written. Wherefore she cast down her eyes and turned her face away from him. Then in a little while she said, "Master, when wilt thou teach me that wisdom?"

To this Merlin made reply, "I shall not teach thee to-day nor to-morrow nor at this place; for I can only teach thee those knowledges in such solitude that there shall be nothing to disturb thy studies. But to-morrow thou shalt tell King Arthur that thou must return unto thy father's kingdom. Then we will depart together accompanied by thy Court; and when we have come to some secluded place, there I will build a habitation by the means of my magic and we shall abide therein until I have instructed thee in wisdom."

Then Vivien made great joy, and she caught Merlin's hand in hers and she kissed his hand with great passion.

Merlin and Vivien depart from the Court of the King.

So the next day Vivien besought King Arthur that he would give her leave to return unto he father's Court, and upon the third day she and Merlin and a number of attendants who were in service upon the damsel, quitted the Court of King Arthur and departed as though to go upon their way to the Kingdom of Northumberland.

But after they had gone some little distance from the Court of the King, they turned to the eastward and took their way toward a certain valley of which Merlin was acquainted, and which was so fair and pleasant a place that it was sometimes called the Valley of Delight, and sometimes the Valley of Joyousness.

JVSTISSIMVS·REX·

Vivien bewitches Merlin.

CHAPTER SECOND

How Merlin Journeyed With Vivien Unto the Valley of Joyousness and How He Builded for Her a Castle at That Place. Also, How He Taught Her the Wisdom of Magic and of How She Compassed His Downfall Thereby.

So, Merlin and Vivien and those who were with them travelled for three days to the eastward, until, toward the end of the third day, they reached the confines of a very dark and dismal forest. And there they beheld before them trees so thickly interwoven together that the eyes could not see anything at all of the sky because of the thickness of the foliage. And they beheld the branches and the roots of the trees that they appeared like serpents all twisted together. Wherefore Vivien said, "Sir, this is a very dismal woodland."

Merlin and Vivien come to an enchanted forest.

"Yea," said Merlin, "so it appeareth to be. Ne'theless there lieth within this forest that place which is called by some the Valley of Joyousness, and by others the Valley of Delight, because of the great beauty of that place. And there are several pathways extending through this forest by the means of which that valley may be reached by a man, whether a-horse or afoot."

And after a while they found it was as Merlin said, for they came by and by upon one of those pathways and entered it and penetrated into the forest. And, lo! within that doleful woodland it was so dark that it appeared as though night-time had fallen, although it was bright daylight beyond the borders thereof, wherefore many of that party were very much afraid. But Merlin ever gave them good cheer and so they went forward upon their way. So, by and by, they came out at last from that place and into the open again, whereat they were greatly rejoiced and took much comfort.

Now, by this time, the evening had come, very peaceful and tranquil, and they beheld beneath them a valley spread out in that light and it was wonderfully beautiful. And in the centre of the valley was a small lake so smooth and clear, like to crystal, that it appeared like an oval shield of pure silver laid down upon the ground. And all

Merlin and Vivien come to the Valley of Joyousness.

about the margin of the lake were level meadows covered over with an incredible multitude of flowers of divers colors and kinds, very beautiful to behold.

When Vivien saw this place she cried unto Merlin, "Master, this is, indeed, a very joyous valley, for I do not believe that the blessed meadows of Paradise are more beautiful than this." And Merlin said, "Very well; let us go down into it." So they went down and, as they descended, the night fell apace and the round moon arose into the sky and it was hard to tell whether that valley was the more beautiful in the daytime or whether it was the more beautiful when the moon shone down upon it in that wise.

So they all came at last unto the borders of the lake and they perceived that there was neither house nor castle at that place.

Now upon this the followers of Merlin murmured amongst themselves, saying, "This enchanter hath brought us hitherward, but how will he now provide for us that we may find a resting-place that may shelter us from the inclement changes of the weather. For the beauty of this spot cannot alone shelter us from rain and storm." And Merlin overheard their murmurings and he said, "Peace! take ye no trouble upon that matter, for I will very soon provide ye a good resting-place." Then he said to them, "Stand ye a little distance aside till I show ye what I shall do." So they withdrew a little, as he commanded them, and he and Vivien remained where they were. And Vivien said, "Master, what wilt thou do?" And Merlin said, "Wait a little and thou shalt see."

Therewith he began a certain very powerful conjuration so that the earth began for to tremble and to shake and an appearance as of a great red dust arose into the air. And in this dust there began to appear sundry shapes and forms, and these shapes and forms arose very high into the air and by and by those who gazed thereon perceived that there was a great structure apparent in the midst of the cloud of red dust.

Merlin buildeth a castle by the means of his magic.

Then, after a while, all became quiet and the dust slowly disappeared from the air, and, behold! there was the appearance of a marvellous castle such as no one there had ever beheld before, even in a dream. For the walls thereof were of ultramarine and vermilion and they were embellished and adorned with figures of gold, wherefore that castle showed in the moonlight like as it were a pure vision of great glory.

Now Vivien beheld all that Merlin had accomplished and she went unto him and kneeled down upon the ground before him and took his hand and set it to her lips. And while she kneeled thus, she said, "Master, this is assuredly the most wonderful thing in the world. Wilt thou then teach me such magic that I may be able to build a castle like this castle out of the elements?" And Merlin said, "Yea; all this will I teach thee and more besides; for I will teach thee not only how thou mayst create such a structure as this out of invisible things, but will also teach thee how thou mayst, with a single touch of thy wand, dissipate that castle instantly into the air; even as a child, with a stroke of a straw, may dissipate a beautiful shining bubble, which, upon an instant is, and upon another instant is not. And I will teach thee more than that, for I will teach thee how to change and transform a thing into the semblance of a different thing; and I will teach thee spells and charms such as thou didst never hear tell of before."

Then Vivien cried out, "Master, thou art the most wonderful man in all of the world!" And Merlin looked upon Vivien and her face was very beautiful in the moonlight and he loved her a very great deal. Wherefore he smiled upon her and said, "Vivien, dost thou still hate me?" And she said, "Nay, master."

But she spake not the truth, for in her heart she was evil and the heart of Merlin was good, and that which is evil will always hate that which is good. Wherefore, though Vivien lusted for the knowledge of necromancy, and though she spake so lovingly with her lips, yet in her spirit she both feared and hated Merlin because of his wisdom. For she wist right well that, except for the enchantment of that ring which he wore, Merlin would not love her any longer in that wise. Wherefore she said in her heart, "If Merlin teaches me all of his wisdom, then the world cannot contain both him and me."

Now Merlin abided with Vivien in that place for a year and a little more, and in that time he taught her all of magic that he was able to impart. So at the end of that time he said unto her, "Vivien, I have now taught thee so much that I believe there is no one in all of the world who knoweth more than thou dost of these things of magic which thou hast studied in this time. For not only hast thou such power of sorcery that thou canst make the invisible elements take form at thy will, and not only canst thou transform at thy will one thing into the appearance of an altogether different thing, but thou hast such potent magic in thy possession that thou mayst entangle any living soul into the meshes thereof, unless that one hath some very good talisman to defend himself from thy wiles. Nor have I myself very much more power than this that I have given to thee."

Merlin teacheth magic to Vivien.

So said Merlin, and Vivien was filled with great joy. And she said in her heart, "Now, Merlin, if I have the good fortune to entangle thee in my spells, then shalt thou never behold the world again."

Now, when the next day had come, Vivien caused a very noble feast to be prepared for herself and Merlin. And by means of the knwledge which Merlin had imparted to her she produced a certain very potent sleeping-potion which was altogether without taste. This potion she herself infused into a certain noble wine, and the wine she poured into a golden chalice of extraordinary beauty.

Vivien setteth a feast for Merlin.

So when that feast was ended, and whiles she and Merlin sat together, Vivien said, "Master, I have a mind to do thee a great honor." And Merlin said, "What is it?" "Thou shalt see," said Vivien. Therewith she smote her hands together and there immediately came a young page unto where they were, and he bare that chalice of wine in his hand and gave it unto Vivien. Then Vivien took the chalice and she went to where Merlin sat and kneeled down before him and said, "Sir, I beseech thee to take this chalice and to drink the wine that is within it. For as that wine is both very noble and very precious, so is thy wisdom both very noble and very precious; and as the wine is contained within a chalice of priceless cost, so is thy wisdom contained within a life that hath been beyond all value to the world." Therewith she set her lips to the chalice and kissed the wine that was in it.

Then Merlin suspected no evil, but he took the chalice and quaffed of the wine with great cheerfulness.

After that, in a little, the fumes of that potent draught began to arise into the brains of Merlin and it was as though a cloud descended upon his sight, and when this came upon him he was presently aware that he was betrayed, wherefore he cried out thrice in a voice, very bitter and full of agony, "Woe! Woe! Woe!" And then he cried out, "I am betrayed!" And therewith he strove to arise from where he sat but he could not.

Merlin is overcome by the wine that Vivien giveth him.

That while Vivien sat with her chin upon her hands and regarded him very steadily, smiling strangely upon him. So presently Merlin ceased his struggles and sank into a sleep so deep that it was almost as though he had gone dead. And when that had happened Vivien arose and leaned over him and set a very powerful spell upon him. And she stretched out her forefinger and wove an enchantment all about him so that it was as though he was entirely encompassed with a silver web of enchantment. And when she had ended, Merlin could move neither hand nor foot nor even so much as a finger-tip, but was altogether like some great insect that a cunning and beautiful spider had enmeshed in a net-work of fine, strong web.

Now, when the next morning had come, Merlin awoke from his sleep and he beheld that Vivien sat over against him regarding him very narrowly. And they were in the same room in which he had fallen asleep. And when Vivien perceived that Merlin was awake, she laughed and said, "Merlin, how is it with thee?" And Merlin groaned with great passion, saying, "Vivien, thou hast betrayed me."

Vivien bewitches Merlin.

At this Vivien laughed again very shrilly and piercingly, and she said, "Behold! Merlin, thou art altogether in my power; for thou art utterly inwoven in those enchantments which thou, thyself, hast taught me. For lo! thou canst not move a single hair without my will. And when I leave thee, the world shall see thee no more and all thy wisdom shall be my wisdom and all thy power shall be my power, and there shall be no other in the whole world who shall possess the wisdom which I possess."

Then Merlin groaned with such fervor that it was as though his heart would burst asunder. And he said, "Vivien, thou hast brought me to such shame that even were I released from this spell I could not endure that any man should ever see my face again. For I grieve not for my undoings so much as I grieve at the folly that hath turned mine own wisdom against me to my destruction. So I forgive thee all things that thou hast done to me to betray me; yet there is one thing alone which I crave of thee."

And Vivien said, "Does it concern thee?" And Merlin said, "No, it concerns another." Thereupon Vivien said, "What is it?"

Then Merlin said, "It is this: Now I have received my gift of foresight again, and I perceive that King Arthur is presently in great peril of his life. So I beseech thee Vivien that thou wilt straightway go to where he is in danger, and that thou wilt use thy powers of sorcery for to save him. Thus, by fulfilling this one good deed, thou shalt haply lessen the sin of this that thou hast done to betray me."

Merlin maketh one request of Vivien.

Now at that time Vivien was not altogether bad as she afterward became, for she still felt some small pity for Merlin and some small reverence for King Arthur. Wherefore now she laughed and said, "Very well, I will do thy desire in this matter. Whither shall I go to save that King?"

Then Merlin replied, "Go into the West country and unto the castle of a certain knight hight Sir Domas de Noir, and when thou comest there then thou shalt immediately see how thou mayst be of aid to the good King." Upon this Vivien said, "I will do this thing for thee, for it is the last favor that anyone may ever render unto thee in this world."

Therewith Vivien smote her hands together and summoned many of her attendants. And when these had come in she presented Merlin before them, and she said, "Behold how I have bewitched him. Go! See for yourselves! Feel of his hands and his face and see if there be any life in him." And they went to Merlin and felt of him; his hands and arms and his face, and even they plucked at his beard, and Merlin could not move in any wise but only groan with great dolor. So they all laughed and made them merry at his woful state.

Then Vivien caused it by means of her magic that there should be in that place a great coffer of stone. And she commanded those who were there that they should lift Merlin up and lay him therein and they did as she commanded. Then she caused it that, by means of her magic, there should be placed a huge slab of stone upon that coffer such as ten men could hardly lift, and Merlin lay beneath that stone like one who was dead.

Vivien places Merlin beneath the stone.

Then Vivien caused it to be that the magic castle should instantly disappear and so it befell as she willed. Then she caused it that a mist should arise at that place, and the mist was of such a sort that no one could penetrate into it, or sever it asunder, nor could any human eye see what was within. Then, when she had done all this, she went her way with all of her Court from that valley, making great joy in that she had triumphed over Merlin.

Nevertheless she did not forget her promise, but went to the castle of Sir Domas de Noir, and after a while it shall all be told how it befell at that place.

Such was the passing of Merlin, and God grant it that you may not so misuse the wisdom He giveth you to have, that it may be turned against you to your undoing. For there can be no greater bitterness in the world than this: That a man shall be betrayed by one to whom he himself hath given the power of betraying him.

And now turn we unto King Arthur to learn how it fell with him after Merlin had thus been betrayed to his undoing.

JVSTISSIMVS·REX·

Queen Morgana le Fay.

CHAPTER THIRD

How Queen Morgana le Fay Returned to Camelot and to the Court With Intent to Do Ill to King Arthur. Also How King Arthur and Others Went a-Hunting and of What Befell Thereby.

Now, after Merlin had quitted the Court with Vivien in that manner aforetold, Queen Morgana le Fay returned again to Camelot. There she came unto King Arthur and kneeled before him, bowing her face, with an appearance of great humility. And she said, "Brother, I have meditated much upon these matters that have passed and I perceive that I have done very ill to talk against thee as I have done, and to be so rebellious against thy royalty. Wherefore I crave of thee to forgive me my evil words and thoughts against thee."

Queen Morgana le Fay and King Arthur are reconciled.

Then King Arthur was very much moved and he came to Queen Morgana and took her by the hand and lifted her up upon her feet and kissed her brow, and her eyes, saying, "My sister, I have no ill-will against thee, but nothing but love for thee in my heart." And so, Queen Morgana le Fay abode at the Court in the same manner as she had aforetime done, for King Arthur believed that they were reconciled.

Now one day, Queen Morgana and the King fell into a friendly talk concerning Excalibur, and Queen Morgana le Fay expressed a very great desire to see that noble weapon more closely than she had yet done, and King Arthur said he would sometime show it to her. So the next day he said, "Sister, come with me and I will show thee Excalibur." Therewith he took Queen Morgana by the hand and led her into another apartment where was a strong wooden coffer bound with bands of iron. Then the King opened the coffer and therein Queen Morgana le Fay beheld Excalibur where he lay in his sheath. Then King Arthur said to her, "Lady, take this sword and examine it as you please." Therewith Queen Morgana took Excalibur into her hands and lifted him out of the coffer. And she drew the sword

King Arthur showeth Excalibur to Queen Morgana.

out of the sheath and, lo! the blade flashed like lightning. Then she said, "Sir, this is a very beautiful sword and I would that I might take it hence and keep it for a little so that I might enjoy it in full measure."

Now King Arthur was of a mind to show the Queen great courtesy at this time of their reconciliation, wherefore he said to her, "Take it, and be thou its keeper for as long as thou wilt." So Queen Morgana took Excalibur and his sheath and bare them away with her to her inn, and she hid the sword in the bed in which she slept.

Then Queen Morgana sent for sundry goldsmiths, eight in number, and for certain armorsmiths, eight in number, and for certain cunning jewellers, eight in number, and she said unto them, "Make me a sword in every particular like this sword that I have here." And thereupon she showed then Excalibur in his sheath. So these goldsmiths and armorsmiths and lapidaries labored with great diligence, and in a fortnight they had made a sword so exactly like Excalibur that no eye could have told the difference betwixt the one and the other. And Queen Morgana le Fay kept both swords by her until her purposes should have been fulfilled.

It befell upon a certain day that King Arthur proclaimed a hunt, and he and all of his Court were party thereunto.

Now the day before this hunt took place Queen Morgana le Fay came to King Arthur and said, "Brother, I have here for thee a very beautiful and noble horse which I intend to give thee as a gift of love." Therewith she called aloud and there came two grooms bringing a horse as black as jet and all beset with trappings and harness of silver. And the horse was of such extraordinary beauty that neither King Arthur nor anybody who was with him had ever before seen its like for beauty. So a wonderful delight possessed the King at sight of the horse and he said, "Sister, this is the noblest gift I have had given to me for this long time." "Ha! brother," quoth Queen Morgana, "doth that horse then belike thee?" "Yea," said King Arthur, "it belikes me more than any horse that I ever beheld before." "Then," quoth Queen Morgana, "consider it as a gift of reconciliation betwixt thee and me. And in sign of that reconciliation I beg of thee that thou wilt ride that horse forth upon the hunt to-morrow day." And King Arthur said, "I will do so."

Queen Morgana le Fay giveth a horse to King Arthur.

So the next day he rode forth to the hunt upon that horse as he said that he would do.

Now it happened some time after noon that the hounds started a hart of extraordinary size, and the King and all of his Court followed the chase with great eagerness.

King Arthur rideth a-hunting.

But the horse of King Arthur soon outstripped all the other horses saving only that of a certain very honorable and worthy knight of the Court hight Sir Accalon of Gaul. So Sir Accalon and the King rode at a great pace through the forest, and they were so eager with the chase that they wist not whither they were riding. And at last they overtook the hart and found that it was embushed in a certain very thick and tangled part of the forest, and there King Arthur slew the stag, and so the chase was ended.

King Arthur and Sir Accalon of Gaul are lost in the forest.

Now after this had come to pass, the King and Sir Accalon would have retraced their way whither they had come, but in a little they perceived that they were lost in the mazes of the woodland and wist not where they were. For they had followed the chase so far that they were in an altogether strange country. So they wandered hither and thither at great length until eventide, at which time they were oppressed with hunger and weariness. Then King Arthur said to Sir Accalon, "Messire, meseems we shall have nowhere to rest ourselves to-night unless it be beneath a tree in this forest."

To this Sir Accalon made reply, "Lord, if thou wilt follow my counsel thou wilt let our horses seek their own way through this wilderness, so, haply, because of the instinct of such creatures, they shall bring us unto some place of habitation."

Now this advice appeared to be very good to King Arthur, wherefore he did as Sir Accalon advised and let loose his bridle-rein and allowed his horse to travel as it listed. So King Arthur's horse went along a certain path, and Sir Accalon followed after the King. And they went a great pass in this wise, and the night was descending upon them in the forest.

But, before it was entirely dark, they emerged out of that forest and into an open place where they beheld before them a very wide estuary, as it were an inlet of the sea. And before them was a beach of sand, very smooth, and white, and they two went down to that beach and stood upon the shore, and they wist not what to do, for there was no habitation in sight in any direction.

King Arthur and Sir Accalon see a wonderful ship.

Now, whiles they stood there a-doubt, they suddenly perceived a ship at a very great distance away. And this ship approached where they were, sailing very rapidly. As the ship drew nigh to that place they perceived that it was of a very strange and wonderful appearance, for it was painted in many divers colors, very gaudy and brilliant, and the sails were all of cloth of silk, woven in divers colors and embroidered with figures like to the figures of a tapestry; and King Arthur was very greatly amazed at the appearance of that ship.

Now, as they stood so watching the ship, they perceived that it drew nigher and nigher to that place where they were, and in a little it beached itself upon the shore of sand not very far away from them.

Then King Arthur said to Sir Accalon, "Sir, let us go forward to the shore where we may look into this ship, for never did I see its like before in all of my life, wherefore I have a thought that maybe it is fay."

So they two went to where the ship was and they stood upon the shore and looked down into it, and at first they thought that there was no one upon board of the ship, for it appeared to be altogether deserted. But as they stood there marvelling at the wonderfulness of that ship and at the manner in which it had come thither, they beheld, of a sudden, that certain curtains that hung before an apartment at the farther extremity of the ship were parted asunder and there came forth from that place twelve very beautiful damsels. Each of these was clad in a rich garment of scarlet satin very bright and shining, and each wore around her head a circlet of gold, and each had many bracelets of gold upon her arms. These damsels came forward unto where the two knights were and they said, "Welcome, King Arthur!" And they said, "Welcome, Sir Accalon!"

At this King Arthur was very much astonished that they should know him, and he said, "Fair ladies, how is this? Ye appear to know me very well, but I know ye not. Who are ye that know me and my companion and call us by name?"

Unto this the chiefest of those damsels made reply, "Sir, we are part fay and we know all about you; and we know how that ye have been following a very long chase; and we know that ye are aweary, anhungered, and athirst. Wherefore we beseech ye that ye come aboard of this ship and rest and refresh yourselves with food and drink."

Now, this appeared to King Arthur to be a very bel-adventure, wherefore he said to Sir Accalon, "Messire, I have a great mind for to go aboard this ship and to follow out this adventure." And Sir Accalon said, "Lord, if thou goest, I will go also."

So those ladies let fall a gangplank from the ship and King Arthur and Sir Accalon drave their horses up the gangplank and aboard the ship, and immediately they did so, the ship withdrew itself from the sands and sailed away as it had come—very swiftly—and it was now the early night-time with the moon very round and full in the sky like to a disk of pure shining silver.

Then those twelve damoiselles aided King Arthur and Sir Accalon to dismount; and some took their horses away and others led them into a fair chamber at the end of the ship. And in this chamber King Arthur beheld that a table had been placed as though for their entertainment, spread with a linen cloth and set with divers savory meats, and with manchets of white bread and with several different sorts of excellent wines. And at the sight King Arthur and Sir Accalon were very much rejoiced, for they were very greatly anhungered.

King Arthur and Sir Accalon enter the ship of damoiselles.

So they immediately sat themselves down at that table and they ate and drank with great heartiness, and whiles they did so some of those damsels served them with food, and others held them in pleasant discourse, and others made music upon lutes and citterns for their entertainment. So they feasted and made very merry.

But, after a while, a very great drowsiness of sleep began to descend upon King Arthur; albeit, he deemed that that drowsiness had come upon him because of the weariness of the chase. So presently he said, "Fair damsels, ye have refreshed us a very great deal and this hath been a very pleasant adventure. But I would now that ye had a place for us to sleep."

Unto this the chiefest of the damsels replied, "Lord, this boat hath been prepared for your refreshment, wherefore all things have been made ready for you with entire fulness."

Therewith some of those twelve damsels conducted King Arthur into a sleeping-chamber that had been prepared for him, and others led Sir Accalon into another chamber prepared for him. And King Arthur marvelled at the beauty of his chamber, for he thought that he had never beheld a more excellently bedight bed-chamber than that one into which he had now entered. So King Arthur laid himself down with much comfort to his body, and straightway he fell into a deep and gentle sleep, without dream or disturbance of any sort.

Now when King Arthur awoke from that sleep, he was astonished beyond all measure so that he wist not whether he was still asleep and dreaming, or whether he was awake. For, lo! he lay upon a pallet in a very dark and dismal chamber all of stone. And he perceived that this chamber was a dungeon, and all about him he heard the sound of many voices in woful complaint. Then King Arthur said to himself, "Where is that ship in which I was last night, and what hath become of those ladies with whom I spake?"

King Arthur findeth himself in a dreadful prison.

Upon this he looked about him and, behold! he saw that he was indeed in a dungeon and that there were many knights in very sad estate all about him. Wherefore he perceived that they also were captives and that it was they who had made that sound of woful lamentation which he had heard when awaking.

Then King Arthur aroused himself from where he lay and he saw that all those knights who were prisoners there were strangers unto him, and he knew not them and they knew not him. And of these knights there were two and twenty who were prisoners in that place.

Then King Arthur said, "Messires, who are you and where am I at these present?" To the which the chiefest of those knights who were prisoners made reply, "Sir, we are, like yourself, prisoners in a dungeon of this castle, and the castle belongs to a certain knight, hight Sir Domas, surnamed le Noir."

Then King Arthur made great marvel at what had befallen him, wherefore he said, "Messires, here is a very singular thing hath happened to me, for last night I was asleep in a very wonderful ship that I believe was fay, and with me was a knight-companion, and, lo! this morning I awake alone in this dungeon, and know not how I came hither."

"Sir," said the knight who spake for the others, "thou wert last night brought hither by two men clad in black, and thou wert laid down upon yonder pallet without awaking, wherefore it is very plain to me that thou art in the same case that we are in, and that thou art a prisoner unto this Sir Domas le Noir."

Then King Arthur said, "Tell me, who is this Sir Domas, for I declare that I never before heard of him." "I will tell you," said the captive knight, and therewith he did so as follows:

"I believe," said he, "that this Sir Domas is the falsest knight that liveth, for he is full of treason and leasing, and is altogether a coward in his heart. Yet he is a man of very great estate and very powerful in these parts.

"Now there are two brothers, and Sir Domas is one and the other is hight Sir Ontzlake, and Sir Domas is the elder and Sir Ontzlake is the younger. When the father of these two knights died, he left the one an equal patrimony with the other. But now it hath come about that Sir Domas hath nearly all of those estates and that Sir Ontzlake hath only one castle, which same he now holdeth by the force of arms and because of his own courage. For, though Sir Domas is altogether a coward in his heart, yet he hath cunning and guile beyond any man of whom I ever heard tell; wherefore it hath so come about that of his father's patrimony Sir Domas hath everything and Sir Ontzlake hath nothing saving only that one castle and the estate thereunto appertaining.

The knight-prisoner telleth King Arthur concerning Sir Domas.

"Now it would appear to be very strange that Sir Domas is not satisfied with all this, yet he is not satisfied, but he covets that one castle and that small estate that is his brother's, so that he can hardly have any pleasure in life because of his covetousness. Yet he knoweth not how to obtain that estate from his brother, for Sir Ontzlake is a very excellent knight, and the only way that Sir Domas can lay hands upon that estate is by having to do with his brother as man to man in a contest at arms, and this he is afraid to attempt.

"So, for a long time, Sir Domas hath been in search of a knight who may take up his case for him, and do battle against Sir Ontzlake in his behalf. Wherefore all the knights whom he can arrest he bringeth to this castle and giveth them their choice, either to take up his case against his brother, or else to remain in this place as his prisoner without ransom. So he hath arrested all of us, and hath made demand of each that he should do battle in his behalf. But not one of us will take up the case of such an evil-conditioned knight as Sir Domas, so we all remain his prisoners."

"Well," quoth King Arthur, "this is a very wonderful case. But methinks that if Sir Domas maketh his appeal to me, I will take up his case. For I would rather do that than remain a prisoner here for all my life. But if I should take upon me this battle and be successful therein, then I will afterward have to do with Sir Domas himself in such a manner as I do not believe would be very much to his liking."

A damsel cometh to King Arthur.

Now a little while after this the door of that prison-house was opened by the porter, and there entered a very fair young damsel. And this damsel came to King Arthur and she said to him, "What cheer?" "I cannot tell," quoth King Arthur, "but meseems I am in a very sorry pass in this place." "Sir," said the damsel, "I am grieved to see so noble-appearing a knight in so dolorous a case. But if you will undertake to defend the cause of the lord of this castle with your person against his enemy, then you shall have leave to go withersoever you please." To this King Arthur made reply, "Lady, this is a very hard case, that either I must fight a battle I care not for, or else remain a prisoner here without ransom for all of my days. But I would liever fight than live here all my life, and so I will undertake that adventure as thou wouldst have me do. But if I do battle for the lord of this castle, and if I should have Grace of Heaven to win that battle, then it must be that all these, my companions in imprisonment, shall also go forth with me into freedom."

King Arthur consents to do battle for Sir Domas.

To this the damsel said, "Very well, be it so, for that shall content the master of this castle."

Then King Arthur looked more closely at the maiden, and he said, "Damsel, meseems I should know thy face, for I think I have seen thee somewhere before this." "Nay, sir," said she, "that can hardly be, for I am the daughter of the lord of this castle."

But in this she was false, for she was one of the damsels of Morgana le Fay; and she was one of those who had beguiled King Arthur into the ship the night before; and it was she who had brought him to that castle and had delivered him into the hands of Sir Domas. And all these things she had done upon command of Queen Morgana le Fay.

Then King Arthur said, "But if I do this battle, thou must carry a message for me unto the Court of King Arthur, and that message must be delivered unto Queen Morgana le Fay into her own hands. Then, when that is done, I will do this battle for the cause of Sir Domas." And the damsel said, "It shall be done so."

Queen Morgana sendeth a false sword to King Arthur.

So King Arthur wrote a sealed letter to Queen Morgana le Fay that she should send to him his sword Excalibur; and he sent that message to her. And when Queen Morgana received that letter she laughed and said, "Very well, he shall have a sword that shall please his eye as well as Excalibur." And therewith she sent him that other sword that she had had made exactly like Excalibur.

So Sir Domas sent word unto his brother Sir Ontzlake, that he had now a champion for to do battle in his behalf to recover all that portion of their patrimony which Sir Ontzlake still withheld from him.

Now when Sir Ontzlake received this message he was thrown into great trouble of spirit, for a little while before he had been very sorely wounded in a tournament in the which a spear had been thrust through both his thighs, so that he was then abed with that wound and without power to arise therefrom. Wherefore he wist not what to do in this case, for he could not do battle upon his own behalf, and he had no one to do battle for him.

JUSTISSIMUS·REX·

ueen Morgana loses Excalibur his sheath.

CHAPTER FOURTH

What Befell Sir Accalon, and How King Arthur Fought an Affair-at-Arms With Swords, and How He Came Nigh to Losing His Life Thereby.

Here followeth the account of what happened unto Sir Accalon the morning after he went aboard that magic ship with King Arthur as aforetold.

Now when Sir Accalon awoke from that same sleep it was with him as it had been with King Arthur; for, at first, he wist not whether he was still asleep and dreaming or whether he was awake. For lo! he found himself to be lying beside a marble basin of clear water that gushed up very high from a silver tube. And he perceived that not far from this fountain was a large pavilion of parti-colored silk which stood upon the borders of a fair meadow of grass.

Sir Accalon findeth himself beside a fountain.

So Sir Accalon was altogether astonished to find himself in this place when he had fallen asleep on board that ship, wherefore he was afraid that all this was the fruit of some very evil spell. So he crossed himself and said, "God save King Arthur from any harm, for it seems to me that those damsels upon that ship have wrought some magic upon us for to separate us the one from the other." So saying, he arose from where he lay with intent to inquire further into that matter.

Now, as he made some noise in bestirring himself, there came forth from that pavilion aforementioned a very hideous dwarf, who saluted him with all civility and with high respect. Then Sir Accalon said to the dwarf, "Sirrah, who are you?" Unto which the dwarf made answer, "Messire, I belong unto the lady of yonder pavilion, and she hath sent me to bid you welcome to this place, and to invite you in for to partake of a repast with her." "Ha!" quoth Sir Accalon, "and how was it I came hither?" "Sir," said the dwarf, "I do not know, but when we looked forth this morning we saw you lying here by the fountain side."

Then Sir Accalon made great marvel at that which had happened to him, and by and by he said, "Who is thy lady?" To which the dwarf replied, "She is hight the Lady Gomyne of the Fair Hair, and she will be passingly glad of your company in her pavilion."

Sir Accalon enters the pavilion of the Lady Gomyne.

Upon this Sir Accalon arose, and, having laved himself at the fountain and so refreshed himself, he went with the dwarf unto the pavilion of that lady. And when he had come there he saw that in the centre of the pavilion was a table of silver spread with a fair white cloth and covered with very excellent food for a man to break his fast withal.

Now immediately Sir Accalon came into the pavilion, the curtains upon the further side thereof were parted and there entered from a further chamber a very beautiful lady and gave Sir Accalon welcome to that place. And Sir Accalon said to her, "Lady, methinks thou art very civil to invite me thus into thy pavilion." "Nay, sir," said the lady, "it took no great effort to be civil unto a knight so worthy as thou." Then she said to Sir Accalon, "Sir, wilt thou sit here at the table with me and break thy fast?"

At this Sir Accalon was very glad, for he was anhungered, and the beauty of the lady pleased him a very great deal, wherefore it afforded him great joy for to be in her company.

So they two sat at the table with a very cheerful and pleasant spirit and the dwarf waited upon them.

Now after Sir Accalon and the Lady of the Pavilion had broken their fasts she spake to him in this wise, "Sir knight, thou appearest to be a very strong and worthy lord and one very well used to feats of arms and to prowess in battle."

To this Sir Accalon made reply, "Lady, it does not beseem me to bespeak of my own worth, but this much I may freely say; I have engaged in several affrays at arms in such measure as a knight with belt and spurs may do, and I believe that both my friends and mine enemies have had reason to say that I have at all times done my devoirs to the best of my powers."

Then the damoiselle said, "I believe you are a very brave and worthy knight, and being such you might be of service to a good worthy knight who is in sad need of such service as one knight may render unto another."

To this Sir Accalon said, "What is that service?" And the damoiselle replied, "I will tell thee: There is, dwelling not far from this place, a certain knight hight Sir Ontzlake, who hath an elder brother hight Sir Domas. This Sir Domas hath served Sir Ontzlake very ill in many ways, and hath deprived him of well nigh all of his patrimony, so that only a little is left to Sir Ontzlake of all the great possessions that were one time his father's. But even such a small holding as that Sir Domas begrudges Sir Ontzlake, so that Sir Ontzlake must needs hold what he hath by such force of arms as he may himself maintain. Now Sir Domas hath found himself a champion who is a man of a great deal of strength and prowess, and through this champion Sir Domas challenges Sir Ontzlake's right to hold even that small part of those lands which were one time his father's; wherefore if Sir Ontzlake would retain what is his he must presently do battle therefore.

"Now this is a very sad case for Sir Ontzlake, for a short time since he was wounded by a spear at a tournament and was pierced through both of his thighs, wherefore he is not now able to sit upon his horse and to defend his rights against assault. Wherefore meseems that a knight could have no better cause to show his prowess than in the defence of so sad a case as this."

So spake that lady, and to all she said Sir Accalon listened with great attention, and when she had ended he said, "Lady, I would be indeed right willing to defend Sir Ontzlake's right, but, lo! I have no armor nor have I any arms to do battle withal."

Then that damoiselle smiled very kindly upon Sir Accalon and she said to him, "Sir, Sir Ontzlake may easily fit thee with armor that shall be altogether to thy liking. And as for arms, I have in this pavilion a sword that hath but one other fellow in all the world."

Upon this she arose and went back into that curtained recess from which she had come, and thence she presently returned, bringing a certain thing wrapped in a scarlet cloth. And she opened the cloth before Sir Accalon's eyes, and lo! that which she had there was King Arthur's sword Excalibur in his sheath. Then the damoiselle said, "This sword shall be thine if thou wilt assume this quarrel upon behalf of Sir Ontzlake."

Now when Sir Accalon beheld that sword he wist not what to think, and he said to himself, "Certes, either this is Excalibur or else it is his twin brother." Therewith he drew the blade from out of its shield and it shined with extraordinary splendor. Then Sir Accalon said, "I know not what to think for pure wonder, for this sword is indeed the very image of another sword I wot of." When he so spake that damoiselle smiled upon him again, and she said, "I have heard tell that there is in the world another sword like to this."

The Lady Gomyne showeth Excalibur to Sir Accalon.

Then Sir Accalon said, "Lady, to win this sword for myself I would be willing to fight in any battle whatsoever." And the damoiselle replied, "Then if thou wilt

Sir Accalon consents to do battle for Sir Ontzlake.

fight this battle for Sir Ontzlake thou art free to keep that sword for thine own," at the which Sir Accalon was rejoiced beyond all measure of gladness.

So it came about that, by the wiles of Queen Morgana le Fay, King Arthur was brought to fight a battle unknowingly with a knight very much beloved by him, and that that knight had Excalibur to use against his master. For all these things had come to pass through the cunning of Morgana le Fay.

Now a fair field was prepared for that battle in such a place as was convenient both to Sir Domas and to Sir Ontzlake, and thither they came upon the day assigned, each with his knight-champion and his attendants, Sir Ontzlake being brought thither in a litter because of the sore wound in his thighs. Also a great many other folk came to behold the combat, for the news thereof had gone forth to a great distance around about that place. So, all being in readiness, the two knights that were to do battle in that field were brought within the barriers of combat, each fully armed and each mounted upon a very good horse.

Now King Arthur was clad all in armor of Sir Domas, and Sir Accalon was clad in armor that belonged to Sir Ontzlake, and the head of each was covered by his helmet so that neither of those two knew the other.

Then the herald came forth and announced that the battle was toward, and each knight immediately put himself in readiness for the assault. Thereupon, the word for assault being given, the two rushed forth, each from his station, with such speed and fury that it was wonderful to behold. And so they met in the midst of the course with a roar as of thunder, and the spear of each knight was burst all into small pieces unto the truncheon which he held in his hand. Upon this each knight voided his horse with great skill and address, and allowed it to run at will in that field. And each threw aside the truncheon of his spear and drew his sword, and thereupon came, the one against the other, with the utmost fury of battle.

It was at this time that Vivien came to that place upon the behest of Merlin, and she brought with her such a Court and state of beauty that a great many people took notice of her with great pleasure. So Vivien and her Court took stand at the barriers whence they might behold all that was toward. And Vivien regarded those two knights and she could not tell which was King Arthur and which was his enemy, wherefore she said, "Well, I will do as Merlin desired me to do, but I must wait and

Vivien cometh to the field of battle.

see this battle for a while ere I shall be able to tell which is King Arthur, for it would be a pity to cast my spells upon the wrong knight."

So these two knights came together in battle afoot, and first they foined and then they both struck at the same time and, lo! the sword of King Arthur did not bite into the armor of Sir Accalon, but the sword of Sir Accalon bit very deeply into the armor of King Arthur and wounded him so sorely that the blood ran down in great quantities into his armor. And after that they struck very often and very powerfully, and as it was at first so it was afterward, for the sword of Sir Accalon ever bit into the armor of King Arthur, and the sword of King Arthur bit not at all into his enemy's armor. So in a little while it came that King Arthur's armor was stained all over red with the blood that flowed out from a great many wounds, and Sir Accalon bled not at all because of the sheath of Excalibur which he wore at his side. And the blood of King Arthur flowed down upon the ground so that all the grass around about was ensanguined with it. So when King Arthur beheld how all the ground was wet with his own blood, and how his enemy bled not at all, he began to fear that he would die in that battle; wherefore he said to himself, "How is this? Hath the virtue departed out of Excalibur and his sheath? Were it not otherwise I would think that that sword which cutteth me so sorely is Excalibur and that this sword is not Excalibur."

King Arthur is sorely wounded by Excalibur.

Upon this a great despair of death came upon him, and he ran at Sir Accalon and smote him so sore a blow upon the helm that Sir Accalon nigh fell down upon the ground.

But at that blow the sword of King Arthur broke short off at the cross of the handle and fell into the grass among the blood, and the pommel thereof and the cross thereof was all that King Arthur held in his hand.

Now at that blow Sir Accalon waxed very mad, so he ran at King Arthur with intent to strike him some dolorous blow. But when he saw that King Arthur was without weapon, he paused in his assault and he said, "Sir Knight, I see that thou art without weapon and that thou hast lost a great deal of blood. Wherefore I demand thee to yield thyself unto me as recreant."

Then King Arthur was again very much a-dread that his death was near to him; yet, because of his royalty, it was not possible for him to yield to any knight. So he said, "Nay, Sir Knight, I may not yield myself unto thee for I would liever die with honor than yield myself without honor. For though I lack a weapon, there are peculiar reasons why I may not lack worship. Wherefore thou mayst slay me as I am without weapon and that will be thy shame and not my shame."

"Well," said Sir Accalon, "as for the shame I will not spare thee unless thou dost yield to me." And King Arthur said, "I will not yield me." Thereupon Sir Accalon said, "Then stand thou away from me so that I may strike thee." And, when King Arthur had done as Sir Accalon bade him, Sir Accalon smote him such a woful blow that the King fell down upon his knees. Then Sir Accalon raised Excalibur with intent to strike King Arthur again, and with that all the people who were there cried out upon him to spare so worshipful a knight. But Sir Accalon would not spare him.

Then Vivien said unto herself, "Certes, that must be King Arthur who is so near to his death, and I do make my vow that it would be a great pity for him to die after he hath fought so fiercely." So when Sir Accalon raised his sword that second time with intent to strike his enemy, Vivien smote her hands with great force, and emitted at the same time a spell of such potency that it appeared to Sir Accalon upon the instant as though he had received some very powerful blow upon his arm. For with that spell his arm was benumbed all from the finger-tips unto the hollow of his armpit, and thereupon Excalibur fell out of Sir Accalon's hands and into the grass.

Vivien gets a spell upon Sir Accalon.

Then King Arthur beheld the sword and he perceived that it was Excalibur and therewith he knew that he had been betrayed. Wherefore he cried out thrice, in a very loud voice, "Treason! Treason! Treason!" and with that he set his knee upon the blade and before Sir Accalon could stay him he had seized it into his hands.

Then it appeared to King Arthur that a great virtue had come into him because of that sword. Wherefore he arose from his knees and ran at Sir Accalon and smote him so sorely that the blade penetrated his armor to the depth of half a palm's breadth. And he smote him again and again and Sir Accalon cried out in a loud voice, and fell down upon his hands and knees. Then King Arthur ran to him and catched the sheath of Excalibur and plucked it away from Sir Accalon and flung it away, and thereupon the wounds of Sir Accalon burst out bleeding in great measure. Then King Arthur catched the helmet of Sir Accalon and rushed it off his head with intent to slay him.

King Arthur overcometh Sir Accalon.

Now because King Arthur was blinded with his own blood he did not know Sir Accalon, wherefore he said, "Sir Knight, who art thou who hast betrayed me?" And Sir Accalon said, "I have not betrayed thee. I am Sir Accalon of Gaul and I am knight in good worship of King Arthur's Court."

But when King Arthur heard this he made great outcry and he said, "How is this? Know you who I am?" And Sir Accalon said, "Nay, I know you not." Then King

Arthur said, "I am King Arthur who am thy master." And upon this he took off his helmet and Sir Accalon knew him.

And when Sir Accalon beheld King Arthur he swooned away and lay like one dead upon the ground, and King Arthur said, "Take him hence."

Then when those who were there were aware who King Arthur was, they burst over the barriers and ran toward him with great outcry of pity. And King Arthur would have left this place but upon that he also swooned away because of the great issue of blood that had come from him, wherefore all those who were round about took great sorrow, thinking that he was dying, wherefore they bewailed themselves without stint.

Then came Vivien out into that field and she said, "Let me have him, for I believe that I shall be able to cure his hurts." So she commanded that two litters should be brought and she placed King Arthur in one of the litters and she placed Sir Accalon in the other, and she bore them both away to a priory of nuns that was at no great distance from that place.

So when Vivien had come there she searched the wounds of King Arthur and bathed them with a very precious balsam, so that they immediately began to heal. As for Sir Accalon, she would not have to do with his wounds, but let one of her attendants bathe him and dress his hurts.

Vivien healeth King Arthur.

Now when the next morning had come, King Arthur was so much recovered that he was able to arise, though very weak and sick nigh unto death. So he got up from his couch and he would not permit anyone to stay him, and he wrapped a cloak about him and went to the place where Sir Accalon lay. When he had come there he questioned Sir Accalon very narrowly and Sir Accalon told him all that had happened to him after he had left that ship, and how the strange damsel had given him a sword for to fight with. So when King Arthur heard all that Sir Accalon had to tell him, he said, "Messire, I think that thou art not to be blamed in this matter, but I much do fear me that there is treachery here to compass my ruin."

Then he went out from that place and he found Vivien and he said to her, "Damsel, I beseech thee to dress the wounds of that knight with the same balsam that thou didst use to dress my wounds." "Lord," said Vivien, "I cannot do so, for I have no more of that balsam." But what she said was false, for she did have more of that balsam, but she did not choose to use it upon Sir Accalon.

So that afternoon Sir Accalon died of his wounds which he had received in his battle with King Arthur.

Sir Accalon dieth of his wounds.

And that day King Arthur summoned Sir Domas and Sir Ontzlake into his presence and they came and stood before him, so filled with the terror of his majesty, that they had not the power to stand, but fell down upon their knees unto him.

Then King Arthur said, "I will pardon you, for ye knew not what ye did. But thou, Sir Domas, I believe, art a very false and treasonable knight, wherefore I shall deprive thee of all thy possessions but that one single castle which thy brother had and that I shall give unto thee, but all thy possessions I shall give unto Sir Ontzlake. And I shall further ordain that thou shalt never hereafter have the right to ride upon any horse but a palfrey, for thou art not worthy to ride upon a courser as a true knight hath a right to do. And I command it of thee that thou shall presently liberate all those knights who were my companions in captivity, and thou shalt recompense them for all the injury that thou hast done to them according as it shall be decided by a Court of Chivalry."

King Arthur dealeth with Sir Domas and Sir Ontzlake.

Therewith he dismissed those two knights, and they were very glad that he had dealt so mercifully with them.

Conclusion

Now shortly after that combat betwixt King Arthur and Sir Accalon the news thereof was brought to Queen Morgana le Fay, and the next day thereafter she heard that Sir Accalon was dead, and she wist not how it could be that her designs could have so miscarried. Then she was a-doubt as to how much King Arthur might know of her treachery, so she said to herself, "I will go and see my brother, the King, and if he is aware of my treason I will beseech him to pardon my transgression." So, having made diligent inquiry as to where it was that King Arthur lay, she gathered together her Court of knights and esquires and went thitherward.

Queen Morgana cometh to King Arthur.

So she came to that place upon the fifth day after the battle, and when she had come there she asked of those who were in attendance what cheer the King had. They answered her, "He is asleep and he must not be disturbed." To the which Queen Morgana le Fay replied, "No matter, I am not to be forbidden, for I must presently see him and speak with him." So they did not dare to stay her because she was the King's sister.

So Queen Morgana went into the chamber where the King lay and he did not waken at her coming. Then Queen Morgana was filled full of hatred and a great desire for revenge, wherefore she said to herself, "I will take Excalibur and his shield and will carry them away with me to Avalon, and my brother shall never see them again." So she went very softly to where King Arthur lay, and she looked upon him as he slept and perceived that he had Excalibur beside him and that he held the handle of the sword in his hand while he slept. Then Queen Morgana said, "Alas, for this, for if I try to take Excalibur away from him, haply he will awake and he will slay me for my treason." Then she looked and perceived where the sheath of Excalibur lay at the foot of the couch. So she took the sheath of Excalibur very softly and she wrapped it up in her mantle and she went out thence, and King Arthur did not awaken at her going.

Queen Morgana steals the sheath of Excalibur.

So Queen Morgana came out from the King's chamber and she said to those in attendance, "Do not waken the King, for he sleepeth very soundly." Therewith she mounted her horse and went her way from that place.

Now, after a considerable while, King Arthur awoke and he looked for the sheath of Excalibur, but he perceived that it was gone, wherefore he said immediately, "Who hath been here?" They in attendance made answer, "Queen Morgana le Fay had been here and she came in and saw you and went her way without waking you." Then King Arthur's heart misgave him, and he said, "I fear me that she hath dealt treacherously with me from the beginning to the end of these adventures."

Whereupon he arose and summoned all his knights and esquires and mounted his horse for pursuit of Queen Morgana, although he was still passing sick and faint from his sore wounds and loss of blood.

Now, as the King was about ready to depart, Vivien came to him where he was, and she said, "Lord, take me with thee, for if thou dost not do so thou wilt never recover Excalibur his sheath, nor wilt thou ever overtake Queen Morgana le Fay." And King Arthur said, "Come with me, damsel, in God's name." So Vivien went with him in pursuit of Queen Morgana.

Now, by and by, as she fled, Queen Morgana le Fay looked behind her and therewith she perceived that Vivien was with the party of King Arthur, wherefore her heart failed her and she said, "I fear me that I am now altogether ruined, for I have aided that damsel to acquire such knowledge of magic that I shall have no spells to save myself from her counter-spell. But at any rate it shall be that King Arthur shall never have the sheath of Excalibur again for to help him in his hour of need."

Queen Morgana throweth the sheath of Excalibur into the lake.

Now at that time they were passing beside the margin of a lake of considerable size. So Queen Morgana le Fay took the sheath of Excalibur in both her hands and swung it by its belt above her head and she threw it a great distance out into the water.

Then, lo! a very singular miracle occurred, for there suddenly appeared a woman's arm out of the water and it was clad in white. And it was adorned with many bracelets. And the hand of the arm catched the sheath of Excalibur and drew it underneath the water and no one ever beheld that sheath again.

So the sheath of Excalibur was lost, and that was a grievous thing for King Arthur in after time, as you may some time read.

Now after Queen Morgana le Fay had thus thrown the sheath of Excalibur into the lake, she went on a little farther to where was a very lonely place with a great many rocks and stones lying about upon the ground. And when she had come to that place she exercised very potent spells of magic that Merlin had taught her. So, by means of those spells, she transformed herself and all of her Court and all of their horses into large round stones of divers sizes.

Queen Morgana exercises her magic.

Then in a little while came King Arthur to that place with his knights and esquires, and he was exceedingly heavy of heart, for he had beheld from a great distance how Queen Morgana le Fay had thrown the sheath of Excalibur into that lake.

Now when the King and his Court had come to that spot the damsel Vivien called out upon him to stop and she said to him, "Lord, dost thou behold all those great round stones?" "Yea," said the King, "I do see them." Then Vivien said, "Lo! those stones are Queen Morgana le Fay and the Court who were with her. For this magic that she hath done to change herself and them into stones was a certain thing that Merlin had taught her. Now I myself know that magic, and I also know how to remove that magic at my will. Wherefore, if thou wilt promise to immediately punish that wicked woman for all her treason by depriving her of her life, then will I bring her back unto her true shape again so that thou mayst have her in thy power."

Then King Arthur looked upon Vivien with great displeasure, and he said, "Damsel, thou hast a cruel heart! Thou thyself hast suffered no injury at the hands of Queen Morgana; wherefore, then, wouldst thou have me slay her? Now, but for all thou hast done for me I would be very much affronted with thee. As for her, I forgive her all of this, and I shall forgive her again and again and yet again if she sin against me. For her mother was my mother, and the blood which flows in her veins and in my veins cometh from the same fountain-head, wherefore I will do no evil thing against her. Let us return again whence we came."

King Arthur chideth Vivien.

Then Vivien looked upon King Arthur very bitterly, and she laughed with great scorn, and said, "Thou art both a fool and a dotard," and therewith she vanished from the sight of all.

And after that, because King Arthur had rebuked her for her wickedness in the presence of others, she hated him even more than Morgana le Fay had hated him.

Some time after that, King Arthur heard how Merlin had been beguiled by Vivien, and he sorrowed with great bitterness that Merlin was lost unto the world in that wise.

So endeth the story of the passing of Merlin.

PART II
THE STORY OF SIR PELLIAS

Here followeth the story of Sir Pellias, surnamed by many the Gentle Knight. For Sir Pellias was of such a sort that it was said of him that all women loved him without disadvantage to themselves, and that all men loved him to their great good advantage.

Wherefore, when in the end he won for his beloved that beautiful Lady of the Lake, who was one of the chiefest damoiselles of Faëry, and when he went to dwell as lord paramount in that wonderful habitation which no other mortal than he and Sir Launcelot of the Lake had ever beheld, then were all men rejoiced at his great good fortune—albeit all the Court of King Arthur grieved that he had departed so far away from them never to return again.

So I believe that you will have pleasure in reading the history of the things concerning Sir Pellias hereinafter written for your edification.

Sir Pellias, the Gentle Knight.

CHAPTER FIRST

How Queen Guinevere Went a-Maying and of How Sir Pellias Took Upon Him a Quest in Her Behalf.

NOW IT BEFELL UPON A PLEASANT DAY IN THE SPRING-TIME, THAT Queen Guinevere went a-Maying with a goodly company of Knights and Ladies of her Court. And among those Knights were Sir Pellias, and Sir Geraint, and Sir Dinadan, and Sir Aglaval, and Sir Agravaine, and Sir Constantine of Cornwall, and sundry others, so that the like of that Court was hardly to be found in all of the world, either then or before or since.

Queen Guinevere goeth a-Maying.

The day was exceedingly pleasant with the sunlight all yellow, like to gold, and the breeze both soft and gentle. The small birds they sang with very great joy, and all about there bloomed so many flowers of divers sorts that the entire meadows were carpeted with their tender green. So it seemed to Queen Guinevere that it was very good to be abroad in the field and beneath the sky at such a season.

Now as the Queen and her Court walked in great joy among the blossoms, one of the damsels attendant upon the Lady Guinevere cried out of a sudden. "Look! Look! Who is that cometh yonder?" Thereupon Queen Guinevere lifted up her eyes, and she beheld that there came across the meadows a damsel riding upon a milk-white palfrey, accompanied by three pages clad in sky-blue raiment. That damsel was also clad entirely in azure, and she wore a finely wrought chain of gold about her neck and a fillet of gold about her brows, and her hair, which was as yellow as gold, was wrapped all about with bands of blue ribbon embroidered with gold. And one of the pages that followed the damsel bare a square frame of no very great size, and that the frame was enveloped and covered with a curtain of crimson satin.

There cometh a damsel to the May party.

Now when the Queen beheld that goodly company approaching, she bade one of the knights attendant upon her for to go forth to meet the damsel. And the knight who went forth in obedience to her command was Sir Pellias.

Sir Pellias talketh with the damsel.

So when Sir Pellias met the damsel and her three pages, he spake to her in this wise: "Fair damsel, I am commanded by yonder lady for to greet you and to crave of you the favor of your name and purpose."

"Sir Knight," said the damsel, "I do perceive from your countenance and address that you are some lord of very high estate and of great nobility, wherefore I will gladly tell to you that my name is Parcenet, and that I am a damsel belonging to the Court of a certain very high dame who dwelleth at a considerable distance from here, and who is called the Lady Ettard of Grantmesnle. Now I come hitherward desiring to be admitted into the presence of Queen Guinevere. Accordingly, if you can tell me whereabout I may find that noble lady, I shall assuredly be very greatly beholden unto you."

"Ha, Lady!" quoth Sir Pellias, "thou shalt not have very far to go to find Queen Guinevere; for, behold! yonder she walketh, surrounded by her Court of Lords and Ladies." Then the damsel said, "I prithee bring me unto her."

So Sir Pellias led Parcenet unto the Queen, and Queen Guinevere received her with great graciousness of demeanor, saying, "Damsel, what is it that ye seek of us?"

The damsel telleth Queen Guinevere of the Lady Ettard.

"Lady," quoth the damsel, "I will tell you that very readily. The Lady Ettard, my mistress, is considered by all in those parts where she dwelleth to be the most beautiful lady in the world. Now, of late, there hath come such a report of your exceeding beauty that the Lady Ettard hath seen fit for to send me hitherward to see with mine own eyes if that which is recorded of you is soothly true. And indeed, Lady, now that I stand before you, I may not say but that you are the fairest dame that ever mine eyes beheld unless it be the Lady Ettard aforesaid."

Then Queen Guinevere laughed with very great mirth. And she said, "It appears to me to be a very droll affair that thou shouldst have travelled so great a distance for so small a matter." Then she said, "Tell me, damsel, what is that thy page beareth so carefully wrapped up in that curtain of crimson satin?"

"Lady," quoth the damsel, "it is a true and perfect likeness of the Lady Ettard, who is my mistress."

Then Queen Guinevere said, "Show it to me."

Upon this the page who bore the picture dismounted from his palfrey and, coming to Queen Guinevere, he kneeled down upon one knee and uncovered the picture so that the Queen and her Court might look upon it. Thereupon they all beheld that that picture was painted very cunningly upon a panel of ivory framed with gold and inset with many jewels of divers colors. And they saw that it was the picture of a lady of such extraordinary beauty that all they who beheld it marvelled thereat. "Hey, damsel!" quoth Queen Guinevere, "thy lady is, indeed, graced with wonderful beauty. Now if she doth in sooth resemble that picture, then I believe that her like to loveliness is not to be found anywhere in the world."

The damsel showeth the Lady Ettard's picture to the Queen and her Court.

Upon this Sir Pellias spake out and said, "Not so, Lady; for I do protest, and am willing to maintain my words with the peril of my body, that thou thyself art much more beautiful than that picture."

"Hey day, Sir Knight!" quoth the damsel Parcenet, "it is well that thou dost maintain that saying so far away from Grantmesnle; for at that place is a certain knight, hight Sir Engamore of Malverat, who is a very strong knight indeed, and who maintaineth the contrary to thy saying in favor of the Lady Ettard against all comers who dare to encounter him."

Then Sir Pellias kneeled down before Queen Guinevere, and set his palms together. "Lady," he said, "I do pray thee of thy grace that thou wilt so far honor me as to accept me for thy true knight in this matter. For I would fain assay an adventure in thy behalf if I have thy permission for to do so. Wherefore, if thou grantest me leave, I will straightway go forth to meet this knight of whom the damsel speaketh, and I greatly hope that when I find him I shall cause his overthrow to the increasing of thy glory and honor."

Sir Pellias assumes the adventure in honor of the Queen.

Then Queen Guinevere laughed again with pure merriment. "Sir," quoth she, "it pleases me beyond measure that thou shouldst take so small quarrel as this upon thee in my behalf. For if, so be, thou dost assume so small a quarrel, then how much more wouldst thou take a serious quarrel of mine upon thee? Wherefore I do accept thee very joyfully for my champion in this affair. So go thou presently and arm thyself in such a way as may be fitting for this adventure."

"Lady," said Sir Pellias, "if I have thy leave, I will enter into this affair clad as I am. For I entertain hopes that I shall succeed in winning armor and accoutrements upon the way, in the which case this adventure will be still more to thy credit than it would otherwise be."

At this the Queen was very much pleased, that her knight should undertake so serious an adventure clad only in holiday attire; wherefore she said, "Let it be as thou wouldst have it." Thereupon she bade her page, Florian, for to go fetch the best horse that he might obtain for Sir Pellias; and Florian, running with all speed, presently returned with a noble steed, so black of hue that I believe there was not a single white hair upon him.

Then Sir Pellias gave adieu to Queen Guinevere, and her merry May-court, and they gave him adieu and great acclaim, and thereupon he mounted his horse and rode away with the damsel Parcenet and the three pages clad in blue.

Now when these had gone some distance the damsel Parcenet said, "Sir, I know not thy name or thy condition, or who thou art?"

Unto this Sir Pellias said, "Damsel, my name is Pellias and I am a knight of King Arthur's Round Table."

At that Parcenet was very much astonished, for Sir Pellias was held by many to be the best knight-at-arms alive, saving only King Arthur and King Pellinore.

Sir Pellias and Parcenet discourse together.

Wherefore she cried out, "Messire, it will assuredly be a very great honor for Sir Engamore to have to do with so famous a knight as thou." Unto this Sir Pellias said, "Damsel, I think there are several knights of King Arthur's Round Table who are better knights than I." But Parcenet said, "I cannot believe that to be the case."

Then after awhile Parcenet said to Sir Pellias, "Messire, how wilt thou get 'thyself armor for to fight Sir Engamore?" "Maiden," said Sir Pellias, "I do not know at these present where I shall provide me armor; but before the time cometh for me to have to do with Sir Engamore, I have faith that I shall find armor fit for my purpose. For thou must know that it is not always the defence that a man weareth upon his body that bringeth him success, but more often it is the spirit that uplifteth him unto his undertakings."

Then Parcenet said, "Sir Pellias, I do not believe that it is often the case that a lady hath so good a knight as thou for to do battle in her behalf." To which Sir Pellias said very cheerfully, "Damsel, when thy time cometh I wish that thou mayst have a very much better knight to serve thee than I." "Sir," quoth Parcenet, "such a thing as that is not likely to befall me." At the which Sir Pellias laughed with great lightness of heart. Then Parcenet said, "Heigh ho! I would that I had a good knight for to serve me."

To this Sir Pellias made very sober reply, "Maiden, the first one that I catch I will give unto thee for thy very own. Now wouldst thou have him fair or dark, or short or tall? For if thou wouldst rather have him short and fair I will let the tall, dark one go; but if thou wouldst have him tall and dark, I will let go the other sort."

Then Parcenet looked very steadily at Sir Pellias, and she said, "I would have him about as tall as thou art, and with the same color of hair and eyes, and with a straight nose like unto thine, and with a good wit such as thou hast."

"Alas!" said Sir Pellias, "I would that thou hadst told me this before we had come so far from Camelot; for I could easily have got thee such a knight at that place. For they have them there in such plenty that they keep them in wicker cages, and sell them two for a farthing." Whereat Parcenet laughed very cheerfully, and said, "Then Camelot must be a very wonderful place, Sir Pellias."

So, with very merry discourse they journeyed upon their way with great joy and good content, taking much pleasure in the spring-time and the pleasant meadows whereon they travelled, being without care of any sort, and heart-full of cheerfulness and good-will.

That night they abided at a very quaint, pleasant hostelry that stood at the outskirts of the Forest of Usk, and the next morning they departed betimes in the freshness of the early day, quitting that place and entering into the forest shadows.

Now, after they had travelled a considerable distance in that forest, the damsel Parcenet said to Sir Pellias, "Sir, do you know what part of the woods this is?" "Nay," said Sir Pellias. "Well," said Parcenet, "this part of the woodland is sometimes called Arroy, and is sometimes called the Forest of Adventure. For I must tell you it is a very wonderful place, full of magic of sundry sorts. For it is said that no knight may enter into this forest but some adventure shall befall him."

Sir Pellias and Parcenet come to the Forest of Adventure.

"Damsel," said Sir Pellias, "that which thou tellest me is very good news. For, maybe, if we should fall in with some adventure at this place I may then be able to obtain armor suitable for my purpose."

So they entered the Forest of Adventure forthwith, and then travelled therein for a long way, marvelling greatly at the aspect of that place into which they were come. For the Forest was very dark and silent and wonderfully strange and altogether different from any other place that they had ever seen. Wherefore it appeared to them that it would not be at all singular if some extraordinary adventure should befall them.

So after they had travelled in this wise for a considerable pass they came of a sudden out of those thicker parts of the woodland to where was an opening of considerable extent. And there they beheld before them a violent stream of water that flowed very turbulently and with great uproar of many noises. And they saw that by the side of the stream of water there was a thorn-tree, and that underneath the thorn-tree was a bank of green moss, and that upon the bank of moss there sat an aged woman of a very woful appearance. For that old woman was extraordinarily withered with age, and her eyes were all red as though with a continual weeping of rheum, and many bristles grew upon her cheeks and her chin, and her face was covered with such a multitude of wrinkles that there was not any place that was free from wrinkles.

They find an old woman beside the fountain.

Now when that old woman beheld Sir Pellias and Parcenet and the three pages approaching where she sat, she cried out in a loud voice, "Sir, wilt thou not bear me over this water upon thy horse? For, lo! I am very old and feeble and may not cross this river by myself."

Then Parcenet rebuked the old woman, saying, "Peace, be still! Who art thou to ask this noble knight for to do thee such a service as that?"

Then Sir Pellias was not pleased with Parcenet, wherefore he said, "Damsel, thou dost not speak properly in this matter, for that which beseemeth a true knight is to give succor unto anyone soever who needeth his aid. For King Arthur is the perfect looking-glass for knighthood, and he hath taught his knights to give succor unto all who ask succor of them, without regarding their condition." So saying Sir Pellias dismounted from his horse and lifted the old woman up upon the saddle thereof. Then he himself mounted once more and straightway rode into the ford of the river and so came across the torrent with the old woman in safety to the other side. And Parcenet followed him, marvelling very greatly at his knightliness, and the three pages followed her.

Sir Pellias carries the old woman across the water.

Now when they had reached the other side of the water, Sir Pellias dismounted with intent to aid the old woman to alight from the horse. But she waited not for his aid, but immediately leaped down very lightly from where she was. And, lo! Sir Pellias beheld that she whom he had thought to be only an aged and withered beldame was, in truth, a very strange, wonderful lady of extraordinary beauty. And, greatly marvelling, he beheld that she was clad in apparel of such a sort as neither he nor any who were there had ever beheld before. And because of her appearance he was aware that she was not like any ordinary mortal, but that she was doubtless of enchantment. For he perceived that her face was of a wonderful clearness, like to ivory for whiteness, and that her eyes were very black and extraordinarily bright, like unto two jewels set into ivory; and he perceived that she was clad all in green from head to foot and that her hair was long and perfectly black and like to fine silk for softness and for glossiness; and he perceived that she had about her neck a collar of opal stones and emeralds inset into gold, and that about her wrists were bracelets of finely wrought gold inset with opal stones and emeralds. Wherefore from all these circumstances he knew that she must be fay.

Of the wonderful Lady of the Lake.

(For thus was the Lady Nymue of the Lake; and so had she appeared unto King Arthur, and so did she appear unto Sir Pellias and those who were with him.)

So, beholding the wonderful magical quality of that lady, Sir Pellias kneeled down before her and set his hands together, palm to palm. But the Lady of the Lake said, "Sir, why dost thou kneel to me?" "Lady," quoth Sir Pellias, "because thou art so wonderfully strange and beautiful." "Messire," said the Lady of the Lake, "thou hast done a very good service to me and art, assuredly, a very excellent knight. Wherefore, arise and kneel no longer!" So Sir Pellias arose from his knees and stood before her, and he said, "Lady, who art thou?" To the which she made reply, "I am one who holdeth an exceedingly kind regard toward King Arthur and all his knights. My name is Nymue and I am the chiefest of those Ladies of the Lake of whom thou mayst have heard tell. I took upon me that form of a sorry old woman for to test thy knightliness, and, lo! I have not found thee amiss in worthy service." Then Sir Pellias said, "Lady, thou hast assuredly done me great favor in these." Upon that the Lady of the Lake smiled upon Sir Pellias very kindly, and she said, "Sir, I have a mind to do thee a greater favor than that."

Therewith, so saying, she immediately took from about her neck that collar of opal stones, of emeralds and gold, and hung it about the shoulders of Sir Pellias, so that it hung down upon his breast with a very wonderful glory of variegated colors.

The Lady of the Lake giveth Sir Pellias the collar of gold and jewels.

"Keep this," she said, "for it is of very potent magic."

Upon that she vanished instantly from the sight of those who were there, leaving them astonished and amazed beyond measure at what had befallen.

And Sir Pellias was like one who was in a dream, for he wist not whether that which he had beheld was a vision, or whether he had seen it with his waking eyes. Wherefore he mounted upon his horse in entire silence, as though he knew not what he did. And likewise in entire silence he led the way from that place. Nor did any of those others speak at that time; only after they had gone a considerable distance Parcenet said, speaking in a manner of fear, "Messire, that was a very wonderful thing that befell us." To which Sir Pellias said, "Yea, maiden."

Now that necklace which the Lady of the Lake had hung about the neck of Sir Pellias possessed such a virtue that whosoever wore it was beloved of all those who looked upon him. For the collar was enchanted with that peculiar virtue; but Sir Pellias was altogether unaware of that circumstance, wherefore he only took joy to himself because of the singular beauty of the jewel which the Lady of the Lake had given him.

JVSTISSIMVS·REX·

Sir Pellias encounters the Sorrowful Lady in Arroy.

CHAPTER SECOND

How Sir Pellias Overcame a Red Knight, Hight Sir Adresack, and of How He Liberated XXII Captives From That Knight's Castle.

NOW, AFTER THAT WONDERFUL HAPPENING, THEY JOURNEYED CONtinuously for a great while. Nor did they pause at any place until they came, about an hour after the prime of the day, to a certain part of the forest where charcoal-burners were plying their trade. Here Sir Pellias commanded that they should draw rein and rest for a while, and so they dismounted for to rest and to refresh themselves, as he had ordained that they should do.

Now as they sat there refreshing themselves with meat and drink, there came of a sudden from out of the forest a sound of great lamentation and of loud outcry, and almost immediately there appeared from the thickets, coming into that open place, a lady in woful array, riding upon a pied palfrey. And behind her rode a young esquire, clad in colors of green and white and seated upon a sorrel horse. And he also appeared to be possessed of great sorrow, being in much disarray and very downcast of countenance. And the lady's face was all beswollen and inflamed with weeping, and her hair hung down upon her shoulders with neither net nor band for to stay it in place, and her raiment was greatly torn by the brambles and much stained with forest travel. And the young esquire who rode behind her came with a drooping head and a like woful disarray of apparel, his cloak dragging behind him and made fast to his shoulder by only a single point.

There cometh a sorrowful lady and an esquire into the forest.

Now when Sir Pellias beheld the lady and the esquire in such sad estate, he immediately arose from where he sat and went straightway to the lady and took her horse by the bridle and stayed it where it was. And the lady looked at him, yet saw him not, being altogether blinded by her grief and distraction. Then Sir Pellias said to her, "Lady, what ails thee that thou sorrowest so greatly?" Whereunto she made reply, "Sir, it matters not, for thou canst not help me." "How know ye that?" said Sir Pellias. "I have a very good intention for to aid thee if it be possible for me to do so."

Then the lady looked more narrowly at Sir Pellias, and she perceived him as though through a mist of sorrow. And she beheld that he was not clad in armor, but only in a holiday attire of fine crimson cloth. Wherefore she began sorrowing afresh, and that in great measure, for she deemed that here was one who could give her no aid in her trouble. Wherefore she said, "Sir, thy intentions are kind, but how canst thou look to give me aid when thou hast neither arms nor defences for to help thee in taking upon thee such a quarrel?" But Sir Pellias said, "Lady, I know not how I may aid thee until that thou tellest me of thy sorrow. Yet I have good hope that I may serve thee when I shall know what it is that causes thee such disorder of mind." Thereupon, still holding the horse by the bridle, he brought the lady forward to that place where Parcenet still sat beside the napkin spread with food with which they had been refreshing themselves. And when he had come to that place, he, with all gentleness, constrained the lady for to dismount from her horse. Then, with equal gentleness, he compelled her to sit down upon the grass and to partake of the food. And when she had done so, and had drunk some of the wine, she found herself to be greatly refreshed and began to take to herself more heart of grace. Thereupon, beholding her so far recovered, Sir Pellias again demanded of her what was her trouble and besought her that she would open her heart unto him.

So, being encouraged by his cheerful words, she told to Sir Pellias the trouble that had brought her to that pass.

"Sir Knight," she said, "the place where I dwell is a considerable distance from this. Thence I came this morning with a very good knight, hight Sir Brandemere, who is my husband. We have been married but for a little over four weeks, so that our happiness until this morning was as yet altogether fresh with us. Now this morning Sir Brandemere would take me out a-hunting at the break of day, and so we went forth with a brachet of which my knight was wonderfully fond. So, coming to a certain place in the forest, there started up of a sudden from before us a doe, which same the brachet immediately pursued with great vehemence of outcry. Thereupon, I and my lord and this esquire followed thereafter with very great spirit and enjoyment of the chase. Now, when we had followed the doe and the hound for a great distance—the hound pursuing the doe with a great passion of eagerness—we came to a certain place where we beheld before us a violent stream of water which was crossed by a long and narrow bridge. And we beheld that upon the other side of the stream there stood a strong castle with seven towers, and that the castle was built up upon the rocks in such a way that the rocks and the castle appeared to be altogether like one rock.

The sorrowful lady telleth her story.

"Now, as we approached the bridge aforesaid, lo! the portcullis of the castle was lifted up and the drawbridge was let fall very suddenly and with a great noise, and there immediately issued forth from out of the castle a knight clad altogether in red. And all the trappings and the furniture of his horse were likewise of red; and the spear which he bore in his hand was of ash-wood painted red. And he came forth very terribly, and rode forward so that he presently stood at the other end of that narrow bridge. Thereupon he called out aloud to Sir Brandemere, my husband, saying: 'Whither wouldst thou go, Sir Knight?' And unto him Sir Brandemere made reply: 'Sir, I would cross this bridge, for my hound, which I love exceedingly, hath crossed here in pursuit of a doe.' Then that Red Knight cried out in a loud voice, 'Sir Knight, thou comest not upon this bridge but at thy peril; for this bridge belongeth unto me, and whosoever would cross it must first overthrow me or else he may not cross.'

"Now, my husband, Sir Brandemere, was clad at that time only in a light raiment such as one might wear for hunting or for hawking; only that he wore upon his head a light bascinet enwrapped with a scarf which I had given him. Ne'theless, he was so great of heart that he would not abide any challenge such as that Red Knight had given unto him; wherefore, bidding me and this esquire (whose name is Ponteferet) to remain upon the farther side of the bridge, he drew his sword and rode forward to the middle of the bridge with intent to force a way across if he was able so to do. Whereupon, seeing that to be his intent, that Red Knight, clad all in complete armor, cast aside his spear and drew his sword and rode forward to meet my knight. So they met in the middle of the bridge, and when they had thus met that Red Knight lifted himself in his stirrup and smote my husband, Sir Brandemere, upon the crown of his bascinet with his sword. And I beheld the blade of the Red Knight's sword that it cut through the bascinet of Sir Brandemere and deep into his brain-pan, so that the blood ran down upon the knight's face in great abundance. Then Sir Brandemere straightway fell down from his horse and lay as though he were gone dead.

"Having thus overthrown him, that Red Knight dismounted from his horse and lifted up Sir Brandemere upon the horse whence he had fallen so that he lay across the saddle. Then taking both horses by the bridles the Red Knight led them straight back across the bridge and so into his castle. And as soon as he had entered into the castle the portcullis thereof was immediately closed behind him and the drawbridge was raised. Nor did he pay any heed whatever either to me or to the esquire Ponteferet, but he departed leaving us without any word of cheer; nor do I now know whether my husband, Sir Brandemere, is living or dead, or what hath befallen him."

And as the lady spake these words, lo! the tears again fell down her face in great abundance.

Then Sir Pellias was very much moved with compassion, wherefore he said, "Lady, thy case is, indeed, one of exceeding sorrowfulness, and I am greatly grieved for thee. And, indeed, I would fain aid thee to all the extent that is in my power. So, if thou wilt lead me to where is this bridge and that grimly castle of which thou speakest, I make thee my vow that I will assay to the best of my endeavor to learn of the whereabouts of thy good knight, and as to what hath befallen him."

Sir Pellias assumes an adventure upon relief of the sorrowful lady.

"Sir," said the lady, "I am much beholden unto thee for thy good will. Yet thou mayst not hope for success shouldst thou venture to undertake so grave an adventure as that without either arms or armor for to defend thyself. For consider how grievously that Red Knight hath served my husband, Sir Brandemere, taking no consideration as to his lack of arms or defence. Wherefore, it is not likely that he will serve thee any more courteously." And to the lady's words Parcenet also lifted up a great voice, bidding Sir Pellias not to be so unwise as to do this thing that he was minded to do. And so did Ponteferet, the esquire, also call out upon Sir Pellias, that he should not do this thing, but that he should at least take arms to himself ere he entered upon this adventure.

But to all that they said Sir Pellias replied, "Stay me not in that which I would do, for I do tell you all that I have several times undertaken adventures even more perilous than this and yet I have 'scaped with no great harm to myself." Nor would he listen to anything that the lady and the damsel might say, but, arising from that place, he aided the lady and the damsel to mount their palfreys. Then mounting his own steed, and the esquire and the pages having mounted their steeds, the whole party immediately departed from that place.

So they journeyed for a great distance through the forest, the esquire, Ponteferet, directing them how to proceed in such a way as should bring them by and by to the castle of the Red Knight. So, at last they came to a more open place in that wilderness where was a steep and naked hill before them. And when they had reached to the top of that hill they perceived beneath them a river, very turbulent and violent. Likewise they saw that the river was spanned by a bridge, exceedingly straight and narrow, and that upon the farther side of the bridge and of the river there stood a very strong castle with seven tall towers. Moreover the castle and the towers were built up upon the rocks, very lofty and high, so that it was hard to tell where the rocks

They come to the castle of the Red Knight.

ceased and the walls began, wherefore the towers and the walls appeared to be altogether one rock of stone.

Then the esquire, Ponteferet, pointed with his finger, and said, "Sir Knight, yonder is the castle of the Red Knight, and into it he bare Sir Brandemere after he had been so grievously wounded." Then Sir Pellias said unto the lady, "Lady, I will presently inquire as to thy husband's welfare."

Therewith he set spurs to his horse and rode down the hill toward the bridge with great boldness. And when he had come nigher to the bridge, lo! the portcullis of the castle was lifted and the drawbridge was let fall with a great noise and tunult, and straightway there issued forth from out of the castle a knight clad all in armor and accoutrements of red, and this knight came forward with great speed toward the bridge's head. Then, when Sir Pellias saw him approaching so threateningly, he said unto those who had followed him down the hill: "Stand fast where ye are and I will go forth to bespeak this knight, and inquire into the matter of that injury which he hath done unto Sir Brandemere." Upon this the esquire, Ponteferet, said unto him, "Stay, Sir Knight, thou wilt be hurt." But Sir Pellias said, "Not so, I shall not be hurt."

So he went forth very boldly upon the bridge, and when the Red Knight saw him approach, he said, "Ha! who are thou who darest come thus upon my bridge?"

Unto him Sir Pellias made reply, "It matters not who I am, but thou art to know, thou discourteous knight, that I am come to inquire of thee where thou hast disposed of that good knight Sir Brandemere, and to ask of thee why thou didst entreat him so grievously a short time since."

At this the Red Knight fell very full of wrath. "Ha! ha!" he cried vehemently, "that thou shalt presently learn to thy great sorrow, for as I have served him, so shall I quickly serve thee, so that in a little while I shall bring thee unto him; then thou mayst ask him whatsoever thou dost list. But seeing that thou art unarmed and without defence, I would not do thee any bodily ill, wherefore I demand of thee that thou shalt presently surrender thyself unto me, otherwise it will be very greatly to thy pain and sorrow if thou compellest me to use force for to constrain thy surrender."

Then Sir Pellias said, "What! what! Wouldst thou thus assail a knight who is altogether without arms or defence as I am?" And the Red Knight said, "Assuredly shall I do so if thou dost not immediately yield thyself unto me."

"Then," quoth Pellias, "thou art not fit for to be dealt with as beseemeth a tried knight. Wherefore, should I encounter thee, thy overthrow must be of such a sort as may shame any belted knight who weareth golden spurs."

Thereupon he cast about his eyes for a weapon to fit his purpose, and he beheld how that a certain huge stone was loose upon the coping of the bridge. Now this stone was of such a size that five men of usual strength could hardly lift it. But Sir Pellias lifted it forth from its place with great ease, and, raising it with both hands, he ran quickly toward that Red Knight and flung the rock at him with much force. And the stone smote the Red Knight upon the middle of the shield and drave it back upon his breast, with great violence. And the force of the blow drave the knight backward from his saddle, so that he fell down to the earth from his horse with a terrible tumult and lay upon the bridgeway like one who was altogether dead.

Sir Pellias overthroweth the Red Knight with a great stone.

And when they within the castle who looked forth therefrom, saw that blow, and when they beheld the overthrow of the Red Knight, they lifted up their voices in great lamentation so that the outcry thereof was terrible to hear.

But Sir Pellias ran with all speed to the fallen knight and set his knee upon his breast. And he unlaced his helmet and lifted it. And he beheld that the face of the knight was strong and comely and that he was not altogether dead.

So when Sir Pellias saw that the Red Knight was not dead, and when he perceived that he was about to recover his breath from the blow that he had suffered, he drew that knight's misericordia from its sheath and set the point to his throat, so that when the Red Knight awoke from his swoon he beheld death, in the countenance of Sir Pellias and in the point of the dagger.

So when the Red Knight perceived how near death was to him he besought Sir Pellias for mercy, saying, "Spare my life unto me!" Whereunto Sir Pellias said, "Who art thou?" And the knight said, "I am hight Sir Adresack, surnamed of the Seven Towers." Then Sir Pellias said to him, "What hast thou done unto Sir Brandemere and how doth it fare with that good knight?" And the Red Knight replied, "He is not so seriously wounded as you suppose."

Now when Sir Brandemere's lady heard this speech she was greatly exalted with joy, so that she smote her hands together, making great cry of thanksgiving.

But Sir Pellias said, "Now tell me, Sir Adresack, hast thou other captives beside that knight, Sir Brandemere, at thy castle?" To which Sir Adresack replied, "Sir Knight, I will tell thee truly; there are in my castle one and twenty other captives besides him: to wit, eighteen knights and esquires of degree and three ladies. For I have defended this bridge for a long time and all who have undertaken to cross it, those have I taken captive and held for ransom. Wherefore I have taken great wealth and gained great estate thereby."

Then Sir Pellias said, "Thou art soothly a wicked and discourteous knight so to serve travellers that come thy way, and I would do well for to slay thee where thou liest. But since thou hast besought mercy of me I will grant it unto thee, though I will do so only with great shame unto thy knighthood. Moreover, if I spare to thee thy life there are several things which thou must perform. First thou must go unto Queen Guinevere at Camelot, and there must thou say unto her that the knight who left her unarmed hath taken thine armor from thee and hath armed himself therewith for to defend her honor. Secondly, thou must confess thy faults unto King Arthur as thou hast confessed them unto me and thou must beg his pardon for the same, craving that he, in his mercy, shall spare thy life unto thee. These are the things that thou must perform."

Sir Pellias layeth his injunctions upon the Red Knight.

To this Sir Adresack said, "Very well, these things do I promise to perform if thou wilt spare my life."

Then Sir Pellias permitted him to arise and he came and stood before Sir Pellias. And Sir Pellias summoned the esquire, Ponteferet, unto him, and he said, "Take thou this knight's armor from off of his body and put it upon my body as thou knowest how to do." And Ponteferet did as Sir Pellias bade him. For he unarmed Sir Adresack and he clothed Sir Pellias in Sir Adresack's armor, and Sir Adresack stood ashamed before them all. Then Sir Pellias said unto him, "Now take me into thy castle that I may there liberate those captives that thou so wickedly holdest as prisoners." And Sir Adresack said, "It shall be done as thou dost command."

Sir Pellias assumes the armor of Sir Adresack.

Thereupon they all went together unto the castle and into the castle, which was an exceedingly stately place. And there they beheld a great many servants and attendants, and these came at the command of Sir Adresack and bowed themselves down before Sir Pellias. Then Sir Pellias bade Sir Adresack for to summon the keeper of the dungeon, and Sir Adresack did so. And Sir Pellias commanded the keeper that he should conduct them unto the dungeon, and the keeper bowed down before him in obedience.

Now when they had come to that dungeon they beheld it to be a very lofty place and exceedingly strong. And there they found Sir Brandemere and those others of whom Sir Adresack had spoken.

But when that sorrowful lady perceived Sir Brandemere, she ran unto him with great voice of rejoicing and embraced him and wept over him. And he embraced her and wept and altogether forgot his hurt in the joy of beholding her again.

Sir Pellias liberates the captives.

And in the several apartments of that part of the castle, there were in all eighteen knights and esquires, and three ladies besides Sir Brandemere. Moreover, amongst those knights were two from King Arthur's Court: to wit, Sir Brandiles and Sir Mador de la Porte. Whereupon these beholding that it was Sir Pellias who had liberated them, came to him and embraced him with great joy and kissed him upon either cheek.

And all those who were liberated made great rejoicing and gave Sir Pellias such praise and acclaim that he was greatly contented therewith.

Then when Sir Pellias beheld all those captives who were in the dungeon he was very wroth with Sir Adresack, wherefore he turned unto him and said, "Begone, Sir Knight, for to do that penance which I imposed upon thee to perform, for I am very greatly displeased with thee, and fear me lest I should repent me of my mercy to thee."

Thereupon Sir Adresack turned him away and he immediately departed from that place. And he called to him his esquire and he took him and rode away to Camelot for to do that penance which he had promised Sir Pellias to do.

Then, after he was gone, Sir Pellias and those captives whom he had liberated, went through the divers parts of the castle. And there they found thirteen chests of gold and silver money and four caskets of jewels—very fine and of great brilliancy—all of which treasure had been paid in ransom by those captives who had aforetime been violently held prisoners at that place.

And Sir Pellias ordained that all those chests and caskets should be opened, and when those who were there looked therein, the hearts of all were wonderfully exalted with joy at the sight of that great treasure.

Then Sir Pellias commanded that all that treasure of gold and silver should be divided into nineteen equal parts, and when it had been so divided, he said, "Now let each of you who have been held captive in this place, take for his own one part of that treasure as a recompense for those sorrows which he hath endured." Moreover, to each of the ladies who had been held as captives in that place, he gave a casket of jewels, saying unto her, "Take thou this casket of jewels as a recompense for that sorrow which thou hast suffered. And unto Sir Brandemere's lady he gave a casket of the jewels for that which she had endured.

Sir Pellias divideth the treasures of Sir Adresack among the captives.

But then those who were there beheld that Sir Pellias reserved no part of that great treasure for himself, they all cried out upon him: "Sir Knight! Sir Knight! How is this? Behold, thou hast set aside no part of this treasure for thyself."

Then Sir Pellias made answer: "You are right, I have not so. For it needs not that I take any of this gold and silver, or any of these jewels, for myself. For, behold! ye have suffered much at the hands of Sir Adresack, wherefore ye should receive recompense therefore, but I have suffered naught at his hands, wherefore I need no such recompense."

Then were they all astonished at his generosity and gave him great praise for his largeness of heart. And all those knights vowed unto him fidelity unto death.

Then, when all these things were accomplished, Sir Brandemere implored all who were there that they could come with him unto his castle, so that they might refresh themselves with a season of mirth and good faring. And they all said that they would go with him, and they did go. And at the castle of Sir Brandemere there was great rejoicing with feasting and jousting for three days.

They abide at the castle of Sir Brandemere.

And all who were there loved Sir Pellias with an astonishing love because of that collar of emeralds and opals and of gold. Yet no one knew of the virtue of that collar, nor did Sir Pellias know of it.

So Sir Pellias abided at that place for three days. And when the fourth day was come he arose betimes in the morning and bade saddle his horse, and the palfrey of the damsel Parcenet, and the horses of their pages.

Then when all those who were there saw that he was minded to depart, they besought him not to go, but Sir Pellias said, "Stay me not, for I must go."

Then came to him those two knights of Arthur's Court, Sir Brandiles and Sir Mador de la Porte, and they besought him that he would let them go with him upon that adventure. And at first Sir Pellias forbade them, but they besought him the more, so that at last he was fain to say, "Ye shall go with me."

So he departed from that place with his company, and all those who remained gave great sorrow that he had gone away.

arcenet covers Sir Pellias with a cloak.

CHAPTER THIRD

How Sir Pellias Did Battle With Sir Engamore, Otherwise the Knight of the Green Sleeves, and of What Befell the Lady Ettard.

Now, Sir Pellias and his party and the damsel Parcenet and her party travelled onward until after awhile in the afternoon they came unto the utmost boundaries of the forest, where the woodlands ceased altogether and many fields and meadows, with farms and crofts and plantations of trees all a-bloom with tender leaves and fragrant blossoms, lay spread out beneath the sky.

And Sir Pellias said, "This is indeed a very beautiful land into which we have come." Whereat the damsel Parcenet was right well pleased, for she said, "Sir, I am very glad that that which thou seest belikes thee; for all this region belongeth unto the Lady Ettard, and it is my home. Moreover, from the top of yonder hill one mayst behold the castle of Grantmesnle which lieth in the valley beneath." Then Sir Pellias said, "Let us make haste! For I am wonderfully desirous of beholding that place."

So they set spurs to their horses and rode up that hill at a hand gallop. And when they had reached the top thereof, lo! beneath them lay the Castle of Grantmesnle in such a wise that it was as though upon the palm of a hand. And Sir Pellias beheld that it was an exceedingly fair castle, built altogether without of a red stone, and containing many buildings of red brick within the wall. And behind the walls there lay a little town, and from where they stood they could behold the streets thereof, and the people coming and going upon their businesses. So Sir Pellias, beholding the excellence of that castle, said, "Certes, maiden, yonder is a very fair estate."

They reach Grantmesnle.

"Yea," said Parcenet; "we who dwell there do hold it to be a very excellent estate."

Then Sir Pellias said to Parcenet: "Maiden, yonder glade of young trees nigh unto the castle appeareth to be a very cheerful spot. Wherefore at that place I and my companions in arms will take up our inn. There, likewise, we will cause to be set up three pavilions for to shelter us by day and by night. Meantime, I beseech of thee, that thou wilt go unto the lady, thy mistress, and say unto her that a knight hath come unto this place, who, albeit he knoweth her not, holdeth that the Lady Guinevere of Camelot is the fairest lady in all of the world. And I beseech thee to tell the lady that I am here to maintain that saying against all comers at the peril of my body. Wherefore, if the lady have any champion for to undertake battle in her behalf, him will I meet in yonder field to-morrow at mid-day a little before I eat my mid-day meal. For at that time I do propose for to enter into yonder field, and to make parade therein until my friends bid me for to come in to my dinner; and I shall take my stand in that place in honor of the Lady Guinevere of Camelot."

"Sir Pellias," said the damsel, "I will even do as thou desirest of me. And, though I may not wish that thou mayst be the victor in that encounter, yet am I soothly sorry to depart from thee. For thou art both a very valiant and a very gentle knight, and I find that I have a great friendship for thee."

Then Sir Pellias laughed, and he said, "Parcenet, thou art minded to give me praise that is far beyond my deserving." And Parcenet said, "Sir, not so, for thou dost deserve all that I may say to thy credit."

Thereupon they twain took leave of one another with very good will and much kindness of intention, and the maiden and the three pages went the one way, and Sir Pellias and his two companions and the several attendants they had brought with them went into the glade of young trees as Sir Pellias had ordained.

Sir Pellias and his knights-companion take up their inn in a glade of trees.

And there they set up three pavilions in the shade of the trees; the one pavilion of fair white cloth, the second of green cloth, and the third of scarlet cloth. And over each pavilion they had set a banner emblazoned with the device of that knight unto whom the pavilion appertained: above the white pavilion was the device of Sir Pellias: to wit, three swans displayed upon a field argent; above the red pavilion, which was the pavilion of Sir Brandiles, was a red banner emblazoned with his device: to-wit, a mailed hand holding in its grasp a hammer; above the green pavilion, which was that of Sir Mador de la Porte, was a green banner bearing his device, which was that of a carrion crow holding in one hand a white lily flower and in the other a sword.

So when the next day had come, and when mid-day was nigh at hand, Sir Pellias went forth into that field before the castle as he had promised to do, and he was clad all from head to foot in the red armor which he had taken from the body of Sir Adresack, so that in that armor he presented a very terrible appearance. So he rode up and down before the castle walls for a considerable while crying in a loud voice,

Sir Pellias issues challenge to Sir Engamore.

"What ho! What ho! Here stands a knight of King Arthur's Court and of his Round Table who doth affirm, and is ready to maintain the same with his body, that the Lady Guinevere, King Arthur's Queen of Camelot, is the most beautiful lady in all of the world, barring none whomsoever. Wherefore, if any knight maintaineth otherwise, let him straightway come forth for to defend his opinion with his body."

Now after Sir Pellias had thus appeared in that meadow there fell a great commotion within the castle, and many people came upon the walls thereof and gazed down upon Sir Pellias where he paraded that field. And after a time had passed, the drawbridge of the castle was let fall, and there issued forth a knight, very huge of frame and exceedingly haughty of demeanor. This knight was clad altogether from head to foot in green armor, and upon either arm he wore a green sleeve, whence he was sometimes entitled the Knight of the Green Sleeves.

So that Green Knight rode forward toward Sir Pellias, and Sir Pellias rode forward unto the Green Knight, and when they had come together they gave salute with a great deal of civility and knightly courtesy. Then the Green Knight said unto Sir Pellias, "Sir Knight, wilt thou allow unto me the great favor for to know thy name?"

Whereunto Sir Pellias made reply, "That will I so. I am Sir Pellias, a knight of King Arthur's Court and of his Round Table."

Then the Green Knight made reply, "Ha, Sir Pellias, it is a great honor for me to have to do with so famous a knight, for who is there in Courts of Chivalry who hath not heard of thee? Now, if I have the good fortune for to overthrow thee, then will all thy honor become my honor. Now, in return for thy courtesy for making proclamation of thy name, I give unto thee my name and title, which is Sir Engamore of Malverat, further known as the Knight of the Green Sleeves. And I may furthermore tell thee that I am the champion unto the Lady Ettard of Grantmesnle, and that I have defended her credit unto peerless beauty for eleven months, and that against all comers, wherefore if I do successfully defend it for one month longer, then do I become lord of her hand and of all this fair estate. So I am prepared to do the uttermost in my power in her honor."

Then Sir Pellias said, "Sir Knight, I give thee gramercy for thy words of greeting, and I too will do my uttermost in this encounter." Thereupon each knight saluted each other with his lance, and each rode to his appointed station.

Now a great concourse of people had come down to the lower walls of the castle and of the town for to behold the contest of arms that was toward, wherefore it would be hard to imagine a more worthy occasion where knights might meet in a glorious contest of friendly jousting, wherefore each knight prepared himself in all ways, and dressed him his spear and his lance with great care and circumspection. So when all had been prepared for that encounter, an herald, who had come forth from the castle into the field, gave the signal for assault. Thereupon in an instant, each knight drave spurs into his horse and rushed the one against the other, with such terrible speed that the ground shook and trembled beneath the beating of their horses' feet. So they met exactly in the centre of the field of battle, the one knight smiting the other in the midst of his defences with a violence that was very terrible to behold. And the spear of Sir Engamore burst into as many as thirty pieces, but the spear of Sir Pellias held so that the Green Knight was hurtled so violently from out of his saddle that he smote the earth above a spear's length behind the crupper of his horse.

Sir Pellias overthrows Sir Engamore.

Now when those who had stood upon the walls beheld how entirely the Green Knight was overthrown in the encounter, they lifted up their voices in great outcry; for there was no other such knight as Sir Engamore in all those parts. And more especially did the Lady Ettard make great outcry; for Sir Engamore was very much beloved by her; wherefore, seeing him so violently flung down upon the ground, she deemed that perhaps he had been slain.

Then three esquires ran to Sir Engamore and lifted him up and unlaced his helm for to give him air. And they beheld that he was not slain, but only in a deep swoon. So by and by he opened his eyes, and at that Sir Pellias was right glad, for it would have grieved him had he slain that knight. Now when Sir Engamore came back unto his senses once more, he demanded with great vehemence that he might continue that contest with Sir Pellias afoot and with swords. But Sir Pellias would not have it so. "Nay, Sir Engamore," quoth he, "I will not fight thee so serious a quarrel as that, for I have no such despite against thee." And at that denial Sir Engamore fell a-weeping from pure vexation and shame of his entire overthrow.

Then came Sir Brandiles and Sir Mador de la Porte and gave Sir Pellias great acclaim for the excellent manner in which he had borne himself in the encounter, and at the same time they offered consolation unto Sir Engamore and comforted him for the misfortune that had befallen him. But Sir Engamore would take but little comfort in their words.

Now whiles they thus stood all together, there issued out from the castle the Lady Ettard and an exceedingly gay and comely Court of esquires and ladies, and these came across the meadow toward where Sir Pellias and the others stood.

Then when Sir Pellias beheld that lady approach, he drew his misericordia and cut the thongs of his helmet, and took the helmet off of his head, and thus he went forward, bareheaded, for to meet her.

But when he had come nigh to her he beheld that she was many times more beautiful than that image of her painted upon the ivory panel which he had aforetime beheld, wherefore his heart went forth unto her with a very great strength of liking. So therewith he kneeled down upon the grass and set his hands together palm to palm, before her, and he said: "Lady, I do very greatly crave thy forgiveness that I should thus have done battle against thy credit. For, excepting that I did that endeavor for my Queen, I would rather, in another case, have been thy champion than that of any lady whom I have ever beheld."

Sir Pellias greets the Lady Ettard in courteous wise.

Now at that time Sir Pellias wore about his neck the collar of emeralds and opal stones and gold which the Lady of the Lake had given to him. Wherefore, when the Lady Ettard looked upon him, that necklace drew her heart unto him with very great enchantment. Wherefore she smiled upon Sir Pellias very cheerfully and gave him her hand and caused him to arise from that place where he kneeled. And she said to him, "Sir Knight, thou art a very famous warrior; for I suppose there is not anybody who knoweth aught of chivalry but hath heard of the fame of Sir Pellias, the Gentle Knight. Wherefore, though my champion Sir Engamore of Malverat hath heretofore overthrown all comers, yet he need not feel very much ashamed to have been overthrown by so terribly strong a knight."

Then Sir Pellias was very glad of the kind words which the Lady Ettard spake unto him, and therewith he made her known unto Sir Brandiles and Sir Mador de la Porte. Unto these knights also, the Lady Ettard spake very graciously, being moved thereto by the extraordinary regard she felt toward Sir Pellias. So she besought those knights that they would come into the castle and refresh themselves, with good cheer, and with that, the knights said that they would presently do so. Wherefore they returned each knight unto his pavilion, and there each bedight himself with fine raiment and with ornaments of gold and silver in such a fashion that he was noble company for any Court. Then those three knights betook themselves unto the castle of Grantmesnle, and when they had come thither everybody was astonished at the nobility of their aspect.

Sir Pellias and his knights-companion go to the castle of Grantmesnle.

But Sir Engamore, who had by now recovered from his fall, was greatly cast down, for he said unto himself, "Who am I in the presence of these noble lords?" So he stood aside and was very downcast of heart and oppressed in his spirits.

Then the Lady Ettard set a very fine feast and Sir Pellias and Sir Brandiles and Sir Mador de la Porte were exceedingly glad thereof. And upon her right hand she placed Sir Pellias, and upon her left hand she placed Sir Engamore. And Sir Engamore was still more cast down, for, until now, he had always sat upon the right hand of the Lady Ettard.

Now because Sir Pellias wore that wonderful collar which the Lady of the Lake had given unto him, the Lady Ettard could not keep her regard from him. So after they had refreshed themselves and had gone forth into the castle pleasaunce for to walk in the warm sunshine, the lady would have Sir Pellias continually beside her. And when it came time for those foreign knights to quit the castle, she besought Sir Pellias that he would stay a while longer. Now Sir Pellias was very glad to do that, for he was pleased beyond measure with the graciousness and the beauty of the Lady Ettard.

So by and by Sir Brandiles and Sir Mador de la Porte went back unto their pavilions, and Sir Pellias remained in the castle of Grantmesnle for a while longer.

Now that night the Lady Ettard let to be made a supper for herself and Sir Pellias, and at that supper she and Sir Pellias alone sat at the table, and the damsel Parcenet waited in attendance upon the lady. Whiles they ate, certain young pages and esquires played very sweetly upon harps, and certain maidens who were attendant upon the Court of the lady sang so sweetly that it expanded the heart of the listener to hear them. And Sir Pellias was so enchanted with the sweetness of the music, and with the beauty of the Lady Ettard, that he wist not whether he were indeed upon the earth or in Paradise, wherefore, because of his great pleasure, he said unto the Lady Ettard, "Lady, I would that I might do somewhat for thee to show unto thee how high is the regard and the honor in which I hold thee."

Sir Pellias and the Lady Ettard feast together.

Now as Sir Pellias sat beside her, the Lady Ettard had continually held in observation that wonderful collar of gold and of emerald and of opal stones which hung about his neck; and she coveted that collar exceedingly. Wherefore, she now said unto Sir Pellias, "Sir Knight, thou mayst indeed do me great favor if thou hast a mind for to do so." "What favor may I do thee, Lady?" said Sir Pellias. "Sir," said the Lady Ettard, "thou mayst give unto me that collar which hangeth about thy neck."

At this the countenance of Sir Pellias fell, and he said, "Lady, I may not do that; for that collar came unto me in such an extraordinary fashion that I may not part it from me."

Then the Lady Ettard said, "Why mayst thou not part it from thee, Sir Pellias?"

Thereupon Sir Pellias told her all of that extraordinary adventure with the Lady of the Lake, and of how that fairy lady had given the collar unto him.

At this the Lady Ettard was greatly astonished, and she said, "Sir Pellias, that is a very wonderful story. Ne'theless, though thou mayst not give that collar unto me, yet thou mayst let me wear it for a little while. For indeed I am charmed by the beauty of that collar beyond all manner of liking, wherefore I do beseech thee for to let me wear it for a little."

Sir Pellias lets the Lady Ettard wear the collar.

Then Sir Pellias could refuse her no longer, so he said, "Lady, thou shalt have it to wear for a while." Thereupon he took the collar from off of his neck, and he hung it about the neck of the Lady Ettard.

Then, after a little time the virtue of that jewel departed from Sir Pellias and entered into the Lady Ettard, and the Lady Ettard looked upon Sir Pellias with altogether different eyes than those with which she had before regarded him. Wherefore she said unto herself: "Hah! what ailed me that I should have been so enchanted with that knight to the discredit of my champion who hath served me so faithfully? Hath not this knight done me grievous discredit? Hath he not come hitherward for no other reason than for that purpose? Hath he not overthrown mine own true knight in scorn of me? What then hath ailed me that I should have given him such regard as I have bestowed upon him?" But though she thought all this, yet she made no sign thereof unto Sir Pellias, but appeared to laugh and talk very cheerfully. Nevertheless, she immediately began to cast about in her mind for some means whereby she might be revenged upon Sir Pellias; for she said unto herself, "Lo! is he not mine enemy and is not mine enemy now in my power? Wherefore should I not take full measure of revenge upon him for all that he hath done unto us of Grantmesnle?"

So by and by she made an excuse and arose and left Sir Pellias. And she took Parcenet aside, and she said unto the damsel Parcenet, "Go and fetch me hither presently a powerful sleeping-draught." Then Parcenet said, "Lady, what would you do?" And the Lady Ettard said, "No matter." And Parcenet said, "Would you give unto that noble knight a sleeping-draught?" And the lady said, "I would." Then Parcenet said, "Lady, that would surely be an ill thing to do unto one who sitteth in peace at your table and eateth of your salt." Whereunto the Lady Ettard said, "Take thou no care as to that, girl, but go thou straightway and do as I bid thee."

The Lady Ettard layeth plans against Sir Pellias.

Then Parcenet saw that it was not wise for her to disobey the lady. Wherefore she went straightway and did as she was bidden. So she brought the sleeping-draught to the lady in a chalice of pure wine, and the Lady Ettard took the chalice and said to Sir Pellias, "Take thou this chalice of wine, Sir Knight, and drink it unto me according to the measure of that good will thou hast unto me." Now Parcenet stood behind her lady's chair, and when Sir Pellias took the chalice she frowned and shook her head at him. But Sir Pellias saw it not, for he was intoxicated with the beauty of the Lady Ettard, and with the enchantment of the collar of emeralds and opal stones and gold which she now wore. Wherefore he said unto her, "Lady, if there were poison in that chalice, yet would I drink of the wine that is in it at thy command."

At that the Lady Ettard fell a-laughing beyond measure, and she said, "Sir Knight, there is no poison in that cup."

So Sir Pellias took the chalice and drank the wine, and he said, "Lady, how is this? The wine is bitter." To which the Lady Ettard made reply, "Sir, that cannot be."

Then in a little while Sir Pellias his head waxed exceedingly heavy as if it were of lead, wherefore he bowed his head upon the table where he sat. That while the Lady Ettard remained watching him very strangely, and by and by she said, "Sir Knight, dost thou sleep?" To the which Sir Pellias replied not, for the fumes of the sleeping-draught had ascended into his brains and he slept.

Sir Pellias sleepeth.

Then the Lady Ettard arose laughing, and she smote her hands together and summoned her attendants. And she said to them, "Take this knight away, and convey him into an inner apartment, and when ye have brought him thither, strip him of his gay clothes and of his ornaments so that only his undergarments shall remain upon him. And when ye have done that, lay him upon a pallet and convey him out of the castle and into that meadow beneath the walls where he overthrew Sir Engamore, so that when the morning shall arise he shall become a mock and a jest unto all who shall behold him. Thus shall we humiliate him in that same field wherein he overthrew Sir Engamore, and his humiliation shall be greater than the humiliation of Sir Engamore hath been."

Now when the damsel Parcenet heard this she was greatly afflicted, so that she withdrew herself apart and wept for Sir Pellias. But the others took Sir Pellias and did unto him as the Lady Ettard had commanded.

Now when the next morning had come, Sir Pellias awoke with the sun shining into his face. And he wist not at all where he was, for his brains were befogged by the sleeping-draught which he had taken. So he said unto himself, "Am I dreaming, or am I awake? for certes, the last that I remember was that I sat at supper with the Lady Ettard, yet here I am now in an open field with the sun shining upon me."

So he raised himself upon his elbow, and behold! he lay beneath the castle walls nigh to the postern gate. And above him, upon the top of the wall, was a great concourse of people, who, when they beheld that he was awake, laughed at him and mocked at him. And the Lady Ettard also gazed down at him from a window and he saw that she laughed at him and made herself merry. And lo! he beheld that he lay there clad only in his linen undervestment, and that he was in his bare feet as though he were prepared to sleep at night. So he sat upon the cot, saying unto himself, "Certainly this must be some shameful dream that oppresses me." Nor was he at all able to recover from his bewilderment.

The damsel Parcenet bringeth succor to Sir Pellias.

Now, as he sat thus, the postern gate was opened of a sudden, and the damsel Parcenet came out thence. And her face was all bewet with tears, and she bare in her hand a flame-colored mantle. Straightway she ran to Sir Pellias, and said, "Thou good and gentle knight, take thou this and wrap thyself in it."

Upon this Sir Pellias wist that this was no dream, but a truth of great shame; wherefore he was possessed with an extreme agony of shame, so that he fell to trembling, whilst his teeth chattered as though with an ague. Then he said to Parcenet, "Maiden, I thank thee." And he could find no more words to say. So he took the mantle and wrapped himself in it.

Now when the people upon the walls beheld what Parcenet had done, they hooted her and reviled her with many words of ill-regard. So the maiden ran back again into the castle, but Sir Pellias arose and went his way toward his pavilion wrapped in that mantle. And as he went he staggered and tottered like a drunken man, for a great burden of shame lay upon him almost more than he could carry.

Sir Pellias taketh great grief because of his shame.

So when Sir Pellias had reached his pavilion, he entered it and threw himself on his face upon his couch and lay there without saying anything. And by and by Sir Brandiles and Sir Mador de la Porte heard of that plight into which Sir Pellias had fallen, and thereupon they hastened to where he lay and made much sorrow over him. Likewise, they were exceedingly wroth at the shame that had been put upon him; wherefore they said, "We will get us aid from Camelot, and we will burst open yonder castle and we will fetch the Lady Ettard hither to crave thy pardon for this affront. This we will do even if we have to drag her hither by the hair of her head."

But Sir Pellias lifted not his head, only he groaned and he said, "Let be, Messires; for under no circumstance shall ye do that thing, she being a woman. As it is, I would defend her honor even though I died in that defence. For I know not whether I am bewitched or what it is that ails me, but I love her with a very great passion and I cannot tear my heart away from her."

At this Sir Brandiles and Sir Mador de la Porte were greatly astonished, wherefore they said the one to the other, "Certes, that lady hath laid some powerful spell upon him."

Then after a while Sir Pellias bade them go away and leave him, and they did so, though not with any very good will.

So Sir Pellias lay there for all that day until the afternoon had come. Then he aroused himself and bade his esquire for to bring him his armor. Now when Sir Brandiles and Sir Mador de la Porte heard news of this they went to where he was and said, "Sir, what have ye a mind to do?" To this Sir Pellias said, "I am going to try to win me unto the Lady Ettard's presence." Then they said, "What madness is this?" "I know not," said Sir Pellias, "but, meseems, that if I do not behold the Lady Ettard and talk with her I shall surely die of longing to see her." And they say, "Certes, this is madness." Whereunto he replied, "I know not whether it is madness or whether I am caught in some enchantment."

So the esquire fetched unto Sir Pellias his armor as he had commanded, and he clad Sir Pellias in it so that he was altogether armed from head to foot. Thereupon straightway Sir Pellias mounted his horse and rode out toward the castle of Grantmesnle.

Now when the Lady Ettard beheld Sir Pellias again parading the meadow below the castle, she called unto her six of her best knights, and she said unto them, "Behold, Messires, yonder is that knight who brought so much shame upon us yesterday. Now I bid ye for to go forth against him and to punish him as he deserveth."

So those six knights went and armed themselves, and when they had done so they straightway rode forth against Sir Pellias.

Sir Pellias overcometh six knights.

Now, when Sir Pellias beheld these approach, his heart overflowed with fury and he shouted in a great voice and drave forward against them. And for a while they withstood him, but he was not to be withstood, but fought with surpassing fury, wherefore they presently brake from before him and fled. So he pursued them with great fury about that field and smote four of them down from their horses. Then, when there were but two of those knights remaining, Sir Pellias of a sudden ceased to fight, and he cried out unto those two knights, "Messires, I surrender myself unto ye."

Now at that those two knights were greatly astonished, for they were entirely filled with the fear of his strength, and wist not why he should yield to them. Nevertheless they came and laid hands upon him and took him toward the castle. Upon this Sir Pellias said unto himself, "Now they will bring me unto the Lady Ettard, and I shall have speech with her." For it was for this that he had suffered himself to be taken by those two knights.

Sir Pellias yields himself prisoner.

But it was not to be as Sir Pellias willed it. For when they had brought him close under the castle, the Lady Ettard called unto them from a window in the wall. And she said, "What do you with that knight?" They said, "We bring him to you, Lady." Upon this she cried out very vehemently, "Bring him not to me, but take him and tie his hands behind his back and tie his feet beneath his horse's belly, and send him back unto his companions."

Then Sir Pellias lifted up his eyes unto that window and he cried out in a great passion of despair, "Lady, it was unto thee I surrendered, and not unto these unworthy knights."

But the Lady Ettard cried out all the more vehemently, "Drive him hence, for I do hate the sight of him."

So those two knights did as the Lady Ettard said; they took Sir Pellias and bound him hand and foot upon his horse. And when they had done so they allowed his horse for to bear him back again unto his companions in that wise.

The Lady Ettard puts shame upon Sir Pellias.

Now when Sir Brandiles and Sir Mador de la Porte beheld how Sir Pellias came unto them with his hands bound behind his back and his feet tied beneath his horse's belly, they were altogether filled with grief and despair. So they loosed those cords from about his hands and feet, and they cried out upon Sir Pellias, "Sir Knight, Sir Knight, art thou not ashamed to permit such infamy as this?" And Sir Pellias shook and trembled as though with an ague, and he cried out in great despair, "I care not what happens unto me!" They said, "Not unto thyself, Sir Knight; but what shame dost thou bring upon King Arthur and his Round Table!" Upon this Sir Pellias cried aloud, with a great and terrible voice, "I care not for them, either."

All of this befell because of the powerful enchantment of the collar of emeralds and opal stones and of gold which Sir Pellias had given unto the Lady Ettard, and which she continually wore. For it was beyond the power of any man to withstand the enchantment of that collar. So it was that Sir Pellias was bewitched and brought to that great pass of shame.

The Lady of the Lake sits by the Fountain in Arroy.

CHAPTER FOURTH

How Queen Guinevere Quarrelled With Sir Gawaine, and How Sir Gawaine Left the Court of King Arthur For a While.

NOW, IN THE SAME MEASURE THAT QUEEN GUINEVERE FELT HIGH regard for Sir Pellias, in that same degree she felt misliking for Sir Gawaine. For, though Sir Gawaine was said of many to have a silver tongue, and whiles he could upon occasion talk in such a manner as to beguile others unto his will, yet he was of a proud temper and very stern and haughty. Wherefore he would not always brook that the Lady Guinevere should command him unto her will as she did other knights of that Court. Moreover, she could not ever forget how Sir Gawaine did deny her that time at Cameliard when she besought him and his companions for aid, in her time of trouble, nor how discourteous his speech had been to her upon that occasion. So there was no great liking between these two proud souls, for Queen Guinevere held to her way and Sir Gawaine held to his way under all circumstances.

Now it happened upon an occasion that Sir Gawaine and Sir Griflet and Sir Constantine of Cornwall sat talking with five ladies of the Queen's Court in a pleached garden that lay beneath the tower of the Lady Guinevere, and they made very pleasant discourse together. For some whiles they would talk and make them merry with jests and contes, and other whiles one or another would take a lute that they had with them and would play upon it and would sing.

Sir Gawaine and others sit beneath the Queen's window.

Now while these lords and ladies sat thus enjoying pleasant discourse and singing in that manner, Queen Guinevere sat at a window that overlooked the garden, and which was not very high from the ground, wherefore she could overhear all that they said. But these lords and ladies were altogether unaware that the Queen could overhear them, so that they talked and laughed very freely, and the Queen greatly enjoyed their discourse and the music that they made.

That day was extraordinary balmy, and it being well toward the sloping of the afternoon, those lords and ladies were clad in very gay attire. And of all who were there

Sir Gawaine was the most gayly clad, for he was dressed in sky-blue silk embroidered with threads of silver. And Sir Gawaine was playing upon the lute and singing a ballad in an exceedingly pleasing voice so that Queen Guinevere, as she sat at the window beside the open casement, was very well content for to listen to him.

Sir Gawaine striketh the Queen's hound.

Now there was a certain greyhound of which Queen Guinevere was wonderfully fond; so much so that she had adorned its neck with a collar of gold inset with carbuncles. At that moment the hound came running into that garden and his feet were wet and soiled with earth. So, hearing Sir Gawaine singing and playing upon the lute, that hound ran unto him and leaped upon him. At this Sir Gawaine was very wroth, wherefore he clinched his hand and smote the hound upon the head with the knuckles thereof, so that the hound lifted up his voice with great outcry.

But when Queen Guinevere beheld that blow she was greatly offended, wherefore she called out from her window, "Why dost thou smite my dog, Messire?" And those lords and ladies who were below in the garden were very much surprised and were greatly abashed to find that the Queen was so nigh unto them as to overhear all that they had said and to behold all that they did.

But Sir Gawaine spake up very boldly, saying, "Thy dog affronted me, Lady, and whosoever affronteth me, him I strike."

Then Queen Guinevere grew very angry with Sir Gawaine, wherefore she said, "Thy speech is over-bold, Messire," and Sir Gawaine said, "Not over-bold, Lady; but only bold enough for to maintain my rights."

Of the quarrel of the Queen and Sir Gawaine.

At this speech the Lady Guinevere's face flamed like fire and her eyes shone very bright and she said, "I am sure that thou dost forget unto whom thou speakest, Sir Knight," at the which Sir Gawaine smiled very bitterly and said, "And thou, Lady, dost not remember that I am the son of a king so powerful that he needs no help from any other king for to maintain his rights."

At these words all those who were there fell as silent as though they were turned into stones, for that speech was exceedingly bold and haughty. Wherefore all looked upon the ground, for they durst not look either upon Queen Guinevere nor upon Sir Gawaine. And the Lady Guinevere, also, was silent for a long time, endeavoring to recover herself from that speech, and when she spake, it was as though she was half smothered by her anger. And she said, "Sir Knight, thou art proud and arrogant beyond measure, for I did never hear of anyone who dared to give reply unto his Queen as thou hast spoken unto me. But this is my Court, and I may command in it as I choose; wherefore I do now bid thee for to begone and to show thy face no more, either here nor in Hall nor any of the places where I hold my Court. For thou art an offence unto me, wherefore in none of these places shalt thou have leave to show thy face until thou dost ask my pardon for the affront which thou hast put upon me." Then Sir Gawaine arose and bowed very low to the Queen Guinevere and he said, "Lady, I go. Nor will I return thitherward until thou art willing for to tell me that thou art sorry for the discourteous way in which thou hast entreated me now and at other times before my peers."

So saying, Sir Gawaine took his leave from that place, nor did he turn his head to look behind him. And Queen Guinevere went into her chamber and wept in secret for anger and for shame. For indeed she was greatly grieved at what had befallen; yet was she so proud that she would in no wise have recalled the words that she had spoken, even had she been able for to have done so.

Now when the news of that quarrel had gone about the castle it came unto the ears of Sir Ewaine, wherefore Sir Ewaine went straightway unto Sir Gawaine, and asked him what was ado, and Sir Gawaine, who was like one distraught and in great despair, told him everything. Then Sir Ewaine said: "Thou wert certainly wrong for to speak unto the Queen as thou didst. Nevertheless, if thou art banished from this Court, I will go with thee, for thou art my cousin-german and my companion, and my heart cleaveth unto thee." So Sir Ewaine went unto King Arthur, and he said, "Lord, my cousin, Sir Gawaine, hath been banished from this Court by the Queen. And though I may not say that he hath not deserved that punishment, yet I would fain crave thy leave for to go along with him."

At this King Arthur was very grieved, but he maintained a steadfast countenance, and said, "Messire, I will not stay thee from going where it pleases thee. As for thy kinsman, I daresay he gave the Queen such great offence that she could not do otherwise than as she did."

So both Sir Ewaine and Sir Gawaine went unto their inns and commanded their esquires for to arm them. Then they, with their esquires, went forth from Camelot, betaking their way toward the forest lands.

Sir Gawaine and Sir Ewaine quit the Court.

There those two knights and their esquires travelled for all that day until the gray of the eventide, what time the birds were singing their last songs ere closing their eyes for the night. So, finding the evening drawing on apace, those knights were afraid that they would not be able to find kindly lodging ere the night should descend upon them, and they talked together a great deal concerning that thing. But as they came to the top of a certain hill, they beheld below them a valley, very fair and well tilled, with many cottages and farm-crofts. And in the midst of that valley was a goodly abbey very fair to look upon; wherefore Sir Gawaine said unto Sir Ewaine: "If yonder abbey is an abbey of monks, I believe we shall find excellent lodging there for to-night."

They come to an abbey of monks.

So they rode down into that valley and to the abbey, and they found a porter at the wicket of whom they learned that it was indeed an abbey of monks. Wherefore they were very glad and made great rejoicing.

But when the abbot of that abbey learned who they were and of what quality and high estate, he was exceedingly pleased for to welcome them, wherefore he brought them into that part of the abbey where he himself dwelt. There he bade them welcome and had set before them a good supper, whereat they were very much rejoiced. Now the abbot was merry of soul, and took great pleasure in discourse with strangers, so he diligently inquired of those two knights concerning the reason why they were errant. But they told him naught concerning that quarrel at Court, but only that they were in search of adventure. Upon this the abbot said, "Ha, Messires, if ye are in search of adventures, ye may find one not very far from this place."

So Sir Gawaine said, "What adventure is that?" And the abbot replied, "I will tell ye; if ye will travel to the eastward from this place, ye will come, after a while, to

The abbot telleth the knights of a good adventure.

a spot where ye shall find a very fair castle of gray stone. In front of that castle ye will find a good level meadow, and in the midst of the meadow a sycamore-tree, and upon the sycamore-tree a shield to which certain ladies offer affront in a very singular manner. If ye forbid those ladies to affront that shield you will discover a very good adventure."

Then Sir Gawaine said, "That is a very strange matter. Now, to-morrow morning we will go to that place and will endeavor to discover of what sort that adventure may be." And the abbot said, "Do so," and laughed in great measure.

So when the next morning had come, Sir Gawaine and Sir Ewaine gave adieu unto the abbot, and took their leave of that place, riding away unto the eastward, as the abbot had advised. And after they had ridden in that direction for two or three hours or more they beheld before them the borders of a forest all green and shady with foliage, and very cheerful in the warmth of the early summer day. And, lo! immediately at the edge of the woodland there stood a fair, strong castle of gray stone, with windows of glass shining very bright against the sky.

Then Sir Gawaine and Sir Ewaine beheld that everything was as the abbot had said; for in front of the castle was a smooth, level meadow with a sycamore-tree in the midst thereof. And as they drew near they perceived that a sable shield hung in the branches of the tree, and in a little they could see that it bore the device of three white goshawks displayed. But that which was very extraordinary was that in front of that shield there stood seven young damsels, exceedingly fair of face, and that these seven damsels continually offered a great deal of insult to that shield. For some of those damsels smote it ever and anon with peeled rods of osier, and others flung lumps of clay upon it, so that the shield was greatly defaced therewith. Now nigh to the shield was a very noble-appearing knight clad all in black armor, and seated upon a black war-horse, and it was very plain to be seen that the shield belonged unto that knight, for otherwise he had no shield. Yet, though that was very likely his shield, yet the knight offered no protest either by word or by act to stay those damoiselles from offering affront thereunto.

Sir Gawaine and Sir Ewaine behold the damsels assailing the shield.

Then Sir Ewaine said unto Sir Gawaine, "Yonder is a very strange thing that I behold; belike one of us is to encounter yonder knight." And Sir Gawaine said, "Maybe so." Then Sir Ewaine said, "If it be so then I will undertake the adventure." "Not so," said Sir Gawaine, "for I will undertake it myself, I being the elder of us twain, and the better seasoned in knighthood." So Sir Ewaine said, "Very well. Let it be that way, for thou art a very much more powerful knight than I, and it would be a pity for one of us to fail in this undertaking." Thereupon Sir Gawaine said, "Let be, then, and I will undertake it."

So he set spurs to his horse and he rode rapidly to where those damsels offered affront in that way to the sable shield. And he set his spear to rest and shouted in a loud voice, "Get ye away! Get ye away!" So when those damsels beheld the armed knight riding at them in that wise they fled away shrieking from before him.

Then the Sable Knight, who sat not a great distance away, rode forward in a very stately manner unto Sir Gawaine, and he said, "Sir Knight, why dost thou interfere with those ladies?" Whereunto Sir Gawaine replied, "Because they offered insult unto what appeared to me to be a noble and knightly shield." At this the Sable Knight spake very haughtily, saying, "Sir Knight, that shield belongeth unto me and I do assure thee that I am very well able for to take care of it without the interference of any other defender." To which Sir Gawaine said, "It would appear not, Sir Knight."

Then the Sable Knight said, "Messire, an thou thinkest that thou art better able to take care of that shield than I, I think that thou wouldst do very well to make thy words good with thy body." To this Sir Gawaine said, "I will do my endeavor to show thee that I am better able to guard that shield than thou art who ownest it."

Upon this the Sable Knight, without further ado, rode unto the sycamore-tree, and took down from thence the shield that hung there. And he dressed the shield upon his arm and took his spear in hand and made him ready for defence. And Sir Gawaine likewise made him ready for defence, and then each knight took such station upon the field as appeared unto him to be fitting.

Sir Gawaine and the Black Knight engage in battle.

Now, when the people of that castle perceived that a combat of arms was toward, they crowded in great numbers to the walls, so that there were as many as twoscore ladies and esquires and folk of different degrees looking down upon that field of battle from the walls.

So when those knights were altogether prepared, Sir Ewaine gave the signal for encounter and each knight shouted aloud and drave spurs into his charger and rushed forward to the assault with a noise like thunder for loudness.

Now, Sir Gawaine thought that he should easily overcome his adversary in this assault and that he would be able to cast him down from out of his saddle without much pains, for there was hardly any knight in that realm equal to Sir Gawaine for prowess. And, indeed, he had never yet been unhorsed in combat excepting by King Arthur. So when those two rode to the assault, the one against the other, Sir Gawaine thought of a surety that his adversary would fall before him. But it was not so, for in that attack Sir Gawaine's spear was broken into many pieces, but the spear of the Sable Knight held, so that Sir Gawaine was cast with great violence out of the saddle, smiting the dust with a terrible noise of falling. And so astonished was he at that fall that it appeared unto him not as though he fell from his saddle, but as though the earth rose up and smote him. Wherefore he lay for a while all stunned with the blow and with the astonishment thereof.

The Black Knight overthroweth Sir Gawaine.

But when he heard the shouts of the people upon the castle wall, he immediately aroused himself from where he lay in the dust, and he was so filled with rage and shame that he was like one altogether intoxicated. Wherefore he drew his sword and rushed with great fury upon his enemy with intent to hew him down by main strength. Then that other knight, seeing him come thus at him, immediately voided his own saddle and drew his sword and put himself in posture either for assault or for defence. So they lashed together, tracing this way and that, and smiting with such fury that the blows they gave were most terrible for to behold. But when Sir Ewaine beheld how fierce was that assault, he set spurs unto his horse and pushed him between the knights-contestant, crying out aloud, "Sir Knights! Sir Knights! what is this? Here is no cause for such desperate battle." But Sir Gawaine cried out very furiously, "Let be! let be! and stand aside! for this quarrel concerns thee not." And the Sable Knight said, "A-horse or afoot, I am ready to meet that knight at any time."

But Sir Ewaine said, "Not so; ye shall fight no more in this quarrel. For shame, Gawaine! For shame to seek such desperate quarrel with a knight that did but meet thee in a friendly fashion in a fair contest!"

Then Sir Gawaine was aware that Sir Ewaine was both just and right; wherefore he put up his sword in silence, albeit he was like to weep for vexation at the shame of his overthrow. And the Sable Knight put up his sword also, and so peace was made betwixt those two.

Then the Sable Knight said, "I am glad that this quarrel is ended, for I perceive, Messires, that ye are assuredly knights of great nobility and gentleness of breeding; wherefore I would that we might henceforth be friends and companions instead of enemies. Wherefore I do beseech ye for to come with me a little ways from here where I have taken up my inn, so that we may rest and refresh ourselves in my pavilion."

Unto this Sir Ewaine said, "I give thee gramercy for thy courtesy, Sir Knight; and we will go with thee with all the pleasure that it is possible to feel." And Sir Gawaine said, "I am content." So these three knights straightway left the field of battle.

And when they had come to the edge of the forest Sir Gawaine and Sir Ewaine perceived a very fine pavilion of green silk set up beneath the tree. And about that pavilion were many attendants of divers sorts all clad in colors of green and white. So Sir Gawaine perceived that the knight who had overthrown him was certainly someone of very high estate, wherefore he was very greatly comforted. Then the esquires of those three knights came and removed the helmet, each esquire from his knight, so that the knight might be made comfortable thereby. And when this was done Sir Gawaine and Sir Ewaine perceived that the Sable Knight was very comely of countenance, being ruddy of face and with hair like to copper for redness. Then Sir Ewaine said unto the knight, "Sir Unknown Knight, this knight, my companion, is Sir Gawaine, son of King Urien of Gore, and I am Ewaine, the son of King Lot of Orkney. Now, I crave of thee that wilt make thyself known unto us in like manner."

Sir Gawaine and Sir Ewaine come to the pavilion of the Black Knight.

"Ha," said the other; "I am glad that ye are such very famous and royal knights, for I am also of royal blood, being Sir Marhaus, the son of the King of Ireland."

Then Sir Gawaine was very glad to discover how exalted was the quality of that knight who overthrew him and he said unto Sir Marhaus, "Messire, I make my vow, that thou art one of the most terrible knights in the world. For thou hast done unto me this day what only one knight in all the world hath ever done, and that is King Arthur, who is my uncle and my lord. Now thou must certainly come unto the Court of King Arthur, for he will be wonderfully glad for to see thee, and maybe he will make thee a Knight of his Round Table—and there is no honor in all of the world that can be so great as that." Thus he spoke unthinkingly; and then he remembered. Wherefore he smote his fist against his forehead, crying out, "Aha! aha! who am I for to bid thee to come unto the Court of King Arthur, who only yesterday was disgraced and banished therefrom?"

Then Sir Marhaus was very sorry for Sir Gawaine, and he inquired concerning the trouble that lay upon him, and Sir Ewaine told Sir Marhaus all about that quarrel; at that Sir Marhaus was still more sorry for Sir Gawaine, wherefore he said, "Messires, I like ye both wonderfully well, and I would fain become your companion in the adventures ye are to undertake. For now I need remain here no longer. Ye must know that I was obliged to defend those ladies who assailed my shield until I had overthrown seven knights in their behalf. And I must tell ye that Sir Gawaine was the seventh knight I have overthrown. Wherefore, since I have now overthrown him, I am now released from my obligation and may go with ye."

Then Sir Gawaine and Sir Ewaine were very much astonished that any knight should lie beneath so strange an obligation as that—to defend those who assailed his shield—and they besought Sir Marhaus to tell them why he should have been obliged to fulfil such a pledge. So Sir Marhaus said, "I will tell ye. The case was this: Some whiles ago I was travelling in these parts with a hawk upon my wrist. At that time I was clad very lightly in holiday attire, to wit: I wore a tunic of green silk, and hosen one of green and one of white. And I had nothing upon me by way of defence but a light buckler and a short sword. Now, coming unto a certain stream of water, very deep and rapid, I perceived before me a bridge of stone crossing that stream, but so narrow that only one horseman might cross the bridge at a time. So I entered upon that bridge and was part way across it, when I perceived a knight in armor coming the other way. And behind the knight there sat upon a pillion a very fair lady with golden hair and very proud of demeanor. Now, when that knight perceived me upon the bridge, he cried aloud, 'Get back! get back! and suffer me to pass!' But this I would not do, but said, 'Not so, Sir Knight, for, having advanced so far upon this bridge, I have certes the right of way to complete my passage, and it is for you to wait and to permit me to cross.' But the knight would not do so, but immediately put himself in posture of offence and straightway came against me upon the bridge with intent either to slay me

Sir Marhaus telleth his story.

or to drive me back unto the other extremity of the bridge. But this he was not able to do, for I defended myself very well with my light weapons. And I so pushed my horse against his horse that I drave him backward from off the bridge and into the water, whereinto the horse and the knight and the lady all of them fell with a terrible uproar.

"At this the lady shrieked in great measure and both she and the knight were like to drown in the water, the knight being altogether clad in armor, so that he could not uplift himself above the flood. Wherefore, beholding their extremity, I leaped from off my horse and into the water, and with great ado and with much danger unto myself, I was able to bring them both unto the land.

"But that lady was very greatly offended with me, for her fair raiment was altogether wet and spoiled by the water, wherefore she upbraided me with great vehemence. So I kneeled down before her and besought her pardon with all humility, but she still continued to upbraid me. Then I offered unto her for to perform any penance that she might set upon me. At this the lady appeared to be greatly mollified, for she said, 'Very well, I will set thee a penance,' and when her knight had recovered she said, 'Come with us,' and so I mounted my horse and followed them. So after we had gone a considerable distance we came to this place and here she commanded me as follows: 'Sir Knight,' quoth she, 'this castle belongeth unto me and unto this knight who is my lord. Now, this shall be the penance for the affront thou hast given me: thou shalt take thy shield and hang it up in yonder sycamore-tree and every day I will send certain damsels of mine own out from the castle. And they shall offend against that shield and thou shalt not only suffer whatever offence they may offer, but thou shalt defend them against all comers until thou hast overcome seven knights.'

"So I have done until this morning, when thou, Sir Gawaine, camest hither. Thou art the seventh knight against whom I have contended, and as I have overcome thee, my penance is now ended and I am free."

Then Sir Gawaine and Sir Ewaine gave Sir Marhaus great joy that his penance was completed, and they were very well satisfied each party with the others. So Sir Gawaine and Sir Ewaine abided that night in the pavilion of Sir Marhaus and the next morning they arose and, having laved themselves in a forest stream, they departed from that place where they were.

So they entered the forest land once more and made their way by certain paths, they knew not whitherward; and they travelled all that morning and until the afternoon was come.

Now, as they travelled thus Sir Marhaus said of a sudden, "Messires, know ye where we are come to?" "Nay," they said, "we know not." Then Sir Marhaus said, "This part of the forest is called Arroy and it is further called 'The Forest of Adventure.' For it is very well known that when a knight, or a party of knights enter this forest, they will assuredly meet with an adventure of some sort, from which some come forth with credit while others fail therein." And Sir Ewaine said, "I am glad that we have come hither. Now let us go forward into this forest."

The three knights enter the Forest of Adventure.

So those three knights and their esquires continued onward in that woodland where was silence so deep that even the tread of their horses upon the earth was scarcely to be heard. And there was no note of bird and no sound of voice and hardly did any light penetrate into the gloom of that woodland. Wherefore those knights said unto one another, "This is soothly a very strange place and one, maybe, of enchantment."

Now when they had come into the very midst of these dark woodlands, they perceived of a sudden, in the pathway before them, a fawn as white as milk. And round the neck of the fawn was a collar of pure gold. And the fawn stood and looked at them, but when they had come nigh to it, it turned and ran along a very narrow path. Then Sir Gawaine said, "Let us follow that fawn and see where it goeth." And the others said, "We are content." So they followed that narrow path until of a sudden they came to where was a little open lawn very bright with sunlight. In the midst of the lawn was a fountain of water, and there was no fawn to be seen, but, lo! beside the fountain there sat a wonderfully beautiful lady, clad all in garments of green. And the lady combed her hair with a golden comb, and her hair was like to the wing of a raven for blackness. And upon her arms she wore very wonderful bracelets of emeralds and of opal stones inset into cunningly wrought gold. Moreover, the face of the lady was like ivory for whiteness and her eyes were bright like jewels set in ivory. Now, when this lady perceived the knights she arose and laid aside her golden comb and bound up the locks of her hair with ribbons of scarlet silk, and thereupon, she came to those knights and gave them greeting.

They behold a white fawn in the forest.

They behold a beautiful lady in the forest.

Then those three knights gat them down straightway from off their horses, and Sir Gawaine said, "Lady, I believe that thou art not of mortal sort, but that thou art of faërie." Unto this the lady said, "Sir Gawaine, thou art right," and Sir Gawaine marvelled that she should know his name so well. Then he said to her, "Lady, who art thou?" and she made answer, "My name is Nymue and I am the chiefest of those Ladies of the Lake of whom thou mayst have heard. For it was I who gave unto King

Arthur his sword Excalibur; for I am very friendly unto King Arthur and to all the noble Knights of his Court. So it is that I know ye all. And I know that thou, Sir Marhaus, shall become one of the most famous Knights of the Round Table." And all they three marvelled at the lady's words. Then she said, "I prithee tell me what it is that ye seek in these parts?" And they say, "We seek adventure." "Well," said she, "I will bring you unto adventure, but it is Sir Gawaine who must undertake it." And Sir Gawaine said, "That is very glad news." Then the lady said, "Take me behind you upon your saddle, Sir Gawaine, and I will show unto you that adventure." So Sir Gawaine took the lady up behind him upon the saddle, and lo! she brought with her a fragrance such as he had never known before; for that fragrance was so subtle that it seemed to Sir Gawaine that the forest gave forth that perfume which the Lady of the Lake brought with her.

So the Lady of the Lake brought them by many devious ways out from that part of the forest; and she brought them by sundry roads and paths until they came out into an open country, very fruitful and pleasant to behold; and she brought them up a very high hill, and from the top of the hill they looked down upon a fruitful and level plain as upon a table spread out before them. And they beheld that in the midst of the plain was a noble castle built all of red stone and of red bricks; and they beheld that there was a small town built also of red bricks.

Now as they sat their horses there on top of the hill they perceived of a sudden a knight clad all in red armor who came forth from a glade of trees. And they saw that the knight paraded the meadow that lay in front of the castle, and they saw that he gave challenge to those within the castle. Then they perceived that the drawbridge of the castle was let fall of a sudden and that there issued from thence ten knights clad in complete armor. And they beheld those ten knights assail the one knight in red armor, and they beheld the one knight assail the ten. And they beheld that for a while those ten withstood the one, but that he assailed them so terribly that he smote down four of them very quickly. Then they beheld that the rest brake and fled from before that one, and that the Red Knight pursued the others about the meadow with great fury. And they saw that he smote down one from out his saddle and another and another until but two of those knights were left.

The three knights behold a very singular assault-at-arms.

Then Sir Gawaine said, "That is certainly a very wonderful sight for to see." But the Lady of the Lake only smiled and said, "Wait a little."

So they waited and they saw that when the Red Knight had smitten down all of his enemies but those two, and that when he had put those two in great peril of their lives, he of a sudden sheathed his sword and surrendered himself unto them. And they saw that those two knights brought the Red Knight to the castle, and that when they had brought him there a lady upon the wall thereof bespake that Red Knight as with great violence of language. And they beheld that those two knights took the Red Knight and bound his hands behind his back, and that they bound his feet beneath his horse's belly, and that they drave him away from that place.

All this they beheld from the top of that hill, and the Lady of the Lake said unto Sir Gawaine, "There thou shalt find thy adventure, Sir Gawaine." And Sir Gawaine said, "I will go," and the Lady of the Lake said, "Do so."

Thereupon, lo! she vanished from their sight and they were greatly amazed.

JVSTISSIMVS·REX·

ir Gawaine sups with ye Lady Ettard.

CHAPTER FIFTH

How Sir Gawaine Met Sir Pellias and How He Promised to Aid Him With the Lady Ettard.

Now, after that wonderful lady had disappeared from their sight in that manner, those three knights stood for a little while altogether atonished, for they wist not how to believe what their eyes had beheld. Then, by and by, Sir Gawaine spake, saying, "Certes, that was a very wonderful thing that happened to us, for in all my life I never knew so strange a miracle to befall. Now, it is very plain that some excellent adventure lieth in what we have seen, wherefore let us descend into yonder valley, for there we shall doubtless discover what that signifies which we have just now beheld. For I make my vow that I have hardly ever seen so terribly powerful a knight as he who has just now fought yonder battle, wherefore I can in no wise understand why, when he should so nearly have obtained a victory over his enemies, he should have surrendered himself to them as he did."

And Sir Ewaine and Sir Marhaus agreed that it would be well to go down and inquire what was the meaning of that which they had beheld.

So they three and their attendants rode down into the valley.

And they rode forward until they had come to a certain glade of trees and there they beheld three goodly pavilions that stood there: the one pavilion of white cloth, the second pavilion of green cloth, and the third pavilion of scarlet cloth.

Now, as the three knights-companion drew nigh to the pavilions, there came forth two knights to meet them. And when Sir Gawaine and Sir Ewaine saw the shields of the two, they immediately knew that they were Sir Brandiles and Sir Mador de la Porte. And in the same manner Sir Brandiles and Sir Mador de la Porte knew Sir Gawaine and Sir Ewaine, and each party was very much astonished at thus meeting the other in so strange a place. So when they came together they gave one another very joyful greeting and clasped hands with strong love and good fellowship.

The three knights meet the two.

Then Sir Gawaine made Sir Marhaus acquainted with Sir Brandiles and Sir Mador de la Porte and thereupon the five knights all went together into those three pavilions, discoursing the while with great amity and pleasure. And when they had come into the pavilion of Sir Brandiles they found there spread a good refreshment of white bread and wine of excellent savor.

Then after a while Sir Gawaine said to Sir Brandiles and Sir Mador de la Porte, "Messires, we observed a little while ago a very singular thing; for, as we stood together at the top of yonder hill and looked down into this plain we beheld a single knight clad all in red amor who did battle with ten knights. And that one knight in red armor combated the ten with such fury that he drave them all from before him, though they were so many and he but one. And truly I make my vow that I have hardly ever seen a knight show such great prowess in arms as he. Yet, when he had overcome all but two of those knights, and was in fair way to win a clear victory, he suddenly yielded himself unto the two and suffered them to take him and bind him and drive him with great indignity from the field. Now, I pray ye, tell me what was the meaning of that which we beheld, and who was that knight who fought so great a battle and yet yielded himself so shamefully."

At this Sir Brandiles and Sir Mador de la Porte made no answer, but directed their looks another way, for they knew not what to say. But when Sir Gawaine beheld that they were abashed he began more than ever to wonder what that thing meant; wherefore he said, "What is this? Why do ye not answer me? I bid ye tell me what is the meaning of your looks, and who is that red knight!"

Then after a while Sir Mador de la Porte said, "I shall not tell you, but you may come and see."

Then Sir Gawaine began to think maybe there was something in this that it would be better not to publish, and that, haply, he had best examine further into the matter alone. So he said unto the other knights, "Bide ye here a little, Messires, and I will go with Sir Mador de la Porte."

So Sir Gawaine went with Sir Mador de la Porte, and Sir Mador led him into the white pavilion. And when they had come there Sir Mador drew aside the curtains of the pavilion, and he said, "Enter!" and Sir Gawaine entered.

Sir Mador de la Porte bringeth Sir Gawaine to Sir Pellias.

Now, when he had come into the pavilion he perceived that a man sat upon a couch of rushes covered with an azure cloth, and in a little he perceived that man was Sir Pellias. But Sir Pellias saw not him immediately, but sat with his head bowed, like one altogether overwhelmed by a great despair.

But when Sir Gawaine beheld who it was that sat upon the couch, he was greatly amazed and cried out, "Ha! is it thou, Sir Pellias? is it thou?"

But when Sir Pellias heard Sir Gawaine's voice, and when he perceived who it was that spake to him, he emitted an exceedingly bitter cry. And sprang to his feet and ran as far away as the walls of the pavilion would let him, and turned his face unto the walls thereof.

Then, after a while, Sir Gawaine spoke very sternly to Sir Pellias, saying, "Messire, I am astonished and very greatly ashamed that a Knight of King Arthur's Royal Court and of his Round Table should behave in so dishonorable a manner as I saw thee behave this day. For it is hardly to be believed that a knight of such repute and nobility as thou would suffer himself to be taken and bound by two obscure knights as thou didst suffer thyself this day. How couldst thou bring thyself to submit to such indignity and insult? Now, I do demand of thee that thou wilt explain this matter unto me."

Sir Gawaine rebukes Sir Pellias.

But Sir Pellias was silent and would not make any reply. Then Sir Gawaine cried out very fiercely, "Ha! wilt thou not answer me?" and Sir Pellias shook his head.

Then Sir Gawaine said, still speaking very fiercely, "Messire! thou shalt answer me one way or another! For either thou shalt tell me the meaning of thy shameful conduct, or else thou shalt do extreme battle with me. For I will not suffer it that thou shalt bring such shame upon King Arthur and his Round Table without myself defending the honor and the credit of him and of it. One while thou and I were dear friends, but unless thou dost immediately exculpate thyself I shall hold thee in contempt, and shall regard thee as an enemy."

Upon this Sir Pellias spake like unto one that was nigh distracted, and he said, "I will tell thee all." Then he confessed everything unto Sir Gawaine, telling all that had befallen since that time when he had left the May Court of Queen Guinevere to enter upon this adventure, and Sir Gawaine listened unto him with great amazement. And when Sir Pellias had made an end of telling all that had befallen him, Sir Gawaine said, "Certes, this is very wonderful. Indeed, I cannot understand how thou camest to be so entangled in the charms of this lady unless she hath bewitched thee with some great enchantment."

Unto this Sir Pellias said, "Yea, I believe that I have been bewitched, for I am altogether beside myself in this, and am entirely unable to contain my passion."

Then Sir Gawaine bethought him for a long while, considering that matter very seriously; and by and by he said, "I have a plan, and it is this: I will go unto the Lady

Ettard myself, and will inquire diligently into this affair. And if I find that anyone hath entangled thee in enchantments, it will go hard with me but I will punish that one with great dolor. For I shall not have it that another enchanter shall beguile thee as one hath already beguiled Merlin the Wise."

Then Sir Pellias said unto Sir Gawaine, "How wilt thou accomplish this matter so as to gain into the presence of the Lady Ettard?"

Sir Gawaine advises with Sir Pellias.

Thereupon Sir Gawaine replied, "That I will tell thee. We twain shall exchange armor, and I will go unto the castle in thy armor. When I have come there I shall say that I have overcome thee in an encounter, and have taken thine armor away from thee. Then they will haply admit me into the castle to hear my story, and I shall have speech with her."

Then Sir Pellias said, "Very well; it shall be as thou dost ordain."

So Sir Pellias summoned an esquire, and Sir Gawaine summoned his esquire, and those two removed the armor from Sir Pellias, and clad Sir Gawaine therein. After they had done that Sir Gawaine mounted upon the horse of Sir Pellias, and rode openly into that field wherein Sir Pellias had aforetime paraded.

Now, it happened that the Lady Ettard was at that time walking upon a platform within the castle walls, from which place she looked down into that meadow. So when she beheld a red knight parading in the meadow, she thought it was Sir Pellias come thither again, and at that she was vexed and affronted beyond all measure. Wherefore she said unto those nigh her, "That knight vexes me so wofully that I fear me I shall fall ill of vexation if he cometh here many more times. I would that I knew how to rid myself of him; for already, and only an hour ago, I sent ten good knights against him, and he overcame them all with great despatch and with much dishonor unto them and unto me."

So she beckoned to the Red Knight, and when he had come nigh to the walls of the castle, she said to him, "Sir Knight, why dost thou come hitherward to afflict me and to affront me thus? Canst thou not understand that the more often thou comest to tease me in this manner, the more do I hate thee?"

Then Sir Gawaine opened the umbril of his helmet and showed his face, and the Lady Ettard saw that the Red Knight was not Sir Pellias. And Sir Gawaine said, "Lady, I am not that one whom thou supposest me to be, but another. For, behold! I have thine enemy's armor upon my body, wherefore thou mayst see that I have overcome him. For thou mayst suppose that it is hardly to be thought that I could wear his armor unless I took it from him by force of arms. Wherefore thou needst trouble thyself no more about him."

Then the Lady Ettard could not think otherwise than this knight (whom she knew not) had indeed overthrown Sir Pellias in a bout of arms, and had taken his armor away from him. And indeed she was exceedingly astonished that such a thing could have happened; for it appeared to her that Sir Pellias was one of the greatest knights in the world; wherefore she marvelled who this knight could be who had overthrown him in battle. So she gave command to sundry of those in attendance upon her that they should go forth and bring that red knight into the castle and that they should pay him great honor; for that he must assuredly be one of the very greatest champions in the world.

Thus Sir Gawaine came into the castle and was brought before the Lady Ettard where she stood in a wonderfully large and noble hall. For that hall was illuminated by seven tall windows of colored glass, and it was hung around with tapestries and hangings, very rich and of a most excellent quality, wherefore Sir Gawaine was greatly astonished at the magnificence of all that he beheld in that place.

Sir Gawaine entereth Grantmesnle.

Now, Sir Gawaine had taken the helmet from off his head, and he bore it under his arm and against his hip, and his head was bare so that all who were there could see his face very plainly. Wherefore they all perceived that he was exceedingly comely, that his eyes were as blue as steel, his nose high and curved, and his hair and beard very dark and rich in color. Moreover, his bearing was exceedingly steadfast and haughty, so that those who beheld him were awed by the great knightliness of his aspect.

Then the Lady Ettard came to Sir Gawaine and gave him her hand, and he kneeled down and set it to his lips. And the lady bespoke him very graciously, saying, "Sir Knight, it would give me a great deal of pleasure if thou wouldst make us acquainted with thy name, and if thou wouldst proclaim thy degree of estate unto us."

Unto this Sir Gawaine made reply, "Lady, I cannot inform you of these things at these present, being just now vowed unto secrecy upon those points, wherefore I do crave your patience for a little."

Then the Lady Ettard said, "Sir Knight, it is a great pity that we may not know thy name and degree; ne'theless, though we are as yet in ignorance as to thy quality, I yet hope that thou wilt give us the pleasure of thy company awhile, and that thou wilt condescend to remain within this poor place for two days or three, whiles we offer thee such refreshment as we are able to do."

The magical necklace enchanteth Sir Gawaine.

Now here a very untoward thing befell. To wit, it was this: The Lady Ettard had come to love that necklace of emeralds and of opal stones and of gold that she had borrowed from Sir Pellias, and that to such a degree that she never let it depart from her whether by day or by night. Wherefore she wore it at that moment hanging about her neck and her throat. So, as she talked to Sir Gawaine, he looked upon that necklace, and the enchantment thereof began to take a very great hold upon him. For he presently began to feel as though his heart was drawn with exceeding ardency out of his bosom and unto the Lady Ettard; so much so that, in a little while, he could not at all keep his regard withdrawn from her. And the more that he looked upon the necklace and the lady the more did the enchantment of the jewel take hold upon his spirits. Accordingly, when the Lady Ettard spake so graciously unto him, he was very glad to accept of her kindness; wherefore he said, gazing very ardently at her the whiles, "Lady, thou art exceedingly gentle to extend so great a courtesy unto me; wherefore I shall be glad beyond measure for to stay with thee for a short while."

At these words the Lady Ettard was very greatly pleased, for she said to herself, "Certes, this knight (albeit I know not who he may be) must be a champion of extraordinary prowess and of exalted achievement. Now, if I can persuade him to remain in this castle as my champion, then shall I doubtless gain very great credit thereby; for I shall have one for to defend my rights who must assuredly be the greatest knight in all the world." Wherefore she set forth every charm and grace of demeanor to please Sir Gawaine, and Sir Gawaine was altogether delighted by the kindness of her manner.

Now, Sir Engamore was there present at that time, wherefore he was very greatly troubled in spirit. For in the same degree that Sir Gawaine received courtesy from the Lady Ettard, in that same degree Sir Engamore was cast down into great sorrow and distress—so much so that it was a pity for to see him. For Sir Engamore said to himself, "Aforetime, ere these foreign knights came hitherward, the Lady Ettard was very kind to me, and was willing to take me for her champion and lord. But first came Sir Pellias and overthrew me, and now cometh this strange knight and overthroweth him, wherefore, in the presence of such a great champion as this, I am come to be as nothing in her sight." So Sir Engamore withdrew himself from that place and went unto his closet, where he sat himself down alone in great sorrow.

Now the Lady Ettard had given command that a very noble and splendid feast should be prepared for Sir Gawaine and for herself, and whilst it was preparing she and Sir Gawaine walked together in the pleasaunce of the castle. For there was a very pleasant shade in the place, and flowers grew there in great abundance, and many birds sang very sweetly in among the blossoms of the trees. And as Sir Gawaine and the lady walked thus together, the attendants stood at a little distance and regarded them. And they said to one another, "Assuredly it would be a very good thing if the Lady Ettard would take this knight for her champion, and if he should stay here in Grantmesnle forever."

So Sir Gawaine and the lady walked together, talking very cheerfully, until sunset, and at that time the supper was prepared and they went in and sat down to it. And as they supped, a number of pages, very fair of face, played upon harps before them; and sundry damsels sang very sweetly in accord to that music, so that the bosom of Sir Gawaine was greatly expanded with joy. Wherefore he said to himself, "Why should I ever leave this place? Lo! I have been banished from King Arthur's Court; why then should I not establish here a Court of mine own that might, in time, prove to be like to his for glory?" And the Lady Ettard was so beautiful in his eyes that this seemed to him to be a wonderfully pleasant thought.

Sir Gawaine and the Lady Ettard feast together.

Now turn we unto Sir Pellias:

For after Sir Gawaine had left him, the heart of Sir Pellias began to misgive him that he had not been wise; and at last he said to himself, "Suppose that Sir Gawaine should forget his duty to me when he meeteth the Lady Ettard. For it seems that haply she possesses some potent charm that might well draw the heart of Sir Gawaine unto her. Wherefore if Sir Gawaine should come within the circle of such enchantment as that, he may forget his duty unto me and may transgress against the honor of his knighthood."

Sir Pellias is a-doubt.

And the more that Sir Pellias thought of this the more troubled he grew in his mind. So at last, when evening had fallen, he called an esquire unto him and he said, "Go, and fetch me hither the garb of a black friar, for I would fain go unto the castle of Grantmesnle in disguise." So the esquire went as he commanded and brought him such a garb, and Sir Pellias clad himself therein.

Now, by that time, the darkness had come entirely over the face of the earth so that it would not have been possible for anyone to know Sir Pellias, even if they had seen his face. So he went unto the castle, and they who were there, thinking that he was a black friar, as he appeared to be, admitted him into the castle by the postern gate.

So, as soon as Sir Pellias had come into the castle, he began to make diligent inquiry concerning where he might find that knight who had come thither in the afternoon, and those within the castle, still thinking him to be a friar of black orders, said

Sir Pellias cometh to the castle in disguise.

unto him, "What would ye with that knight?" To the which Sir Pellias said, "I have a message for him." They of the castle said, "Ye cannot come at that knight just now, for he is at supper with the Lady Ettard, and he holds her in pleasant discourse."

At this Sir Pellias began to wax very angry, for he greatly misliked the thought that Sir Gawaine should then make merry with the Lady Ettard. So he said, speaking very sternly, "I must presently have speech with that knight, wherefore I bid ye to bring me unto him without delay." Then they of the castle said, "Wait and we will see if that knight is willing to have you come to him."

So one of the attendants went unto that place where Sir Gawaine sat at supper with the Lady Ettard, and he said, "Sir Knight, there hath come hither a black friar who demandeth to have present speech with thee, and he will not be denied, but continually maketh that demand."

At this Sir Gawaine was greatly troubled in his conscience, for he knew that he was not dealing honorably by Sir Pellias, and he pondered whether or not this black friar might be a messenger from his friend. But yet he could not see how he might deny such a messenger speech with him. So, after a while of thought, he said, "Fetch the black friar hither and let him deliver his message to me."

So Sir Pellias, in the garb of a black friar, was brought by the attendants into the outer room of that place where Sir Gawaine sat at supper with the lady. But for a little time Sir Pellias did not enter the room, but stood behind the curtain of the ante-room and looked upon them, for he desired to make sure as to whether or no Sir Gawaine was true to him.

Now everything in that room where the knight and the lady sat was bedight with extraordinary splendor, and it was illuminated by a light of several score of waxen tapers that sent forth a most delightful perfume as they burned. And as Sir Pellias stood behind the curtains, he beheld Sir Gawaine and the Lady Ettard as they sat at the table together, and he saw that they were filled with pleasure in the company of one another. And he saw that Sir Gawaine and the lady quaffed wine out of the same chalice and that the cup was of gold. And as he saw those two making merry with one another, he was filled with great anger and indignation, for he now perceived that Sir Gawaine had betrayed him.

So, by and by, he could contain himself no longer, wherefore he took five steps into that room and stood before Sir Gawaine and the Lady Ettard. And, when they looked upon him in great surprise, he cast back the hood from his face and they knew him. Then the Lady Ettard shrieked with great vehemence, crying out, "I have been betrayed!" and Sir Gawaine sat altogether silent, for he had not a single word to say either to the lady or to Sir Pellias.

Then Sir Pellias came close to the Lady Ettard with such a fell countenance that she could not move for fear. And when he had come nigh to her he catched that necklace of emeralds and opal stones and gold with such violence that he brake the clasp thereof and so plucked it from her neck. Then he said, "This is mine and thou hast no right to it!" And therewith he thrust it into his bosom. Then he turned upon Sir Gawaine where he sat, and he said, "Thou art false both unto thy knighthood and unto thy friendship, for thou hast betrayed me utterly." Thereupon he raised his arm and smote Sir Gawaine upon the face with the back of his hand so violently that the mark of his fingers was left in red all across the cheek of Sir Gawaine.

Sir Pellias places affront upon Sir Gawaine.

Then Sir Gawaine fell as pale as ashes and he cried out, "Sir, I have in sooth betrayed thee, but thou hast offered such affront to me that our injury is equal." To the which Sir Pellias made reply, "Not so; for the injury I gave to thee is only upon thy cheek, but the injury thou gavest to me is upon my heart. Ne'theless, I will answer unto thee for the affront I have done thee. But thou also shalt answer unto me for the offence thou hast done unto me, in that thou hast betrayed me."

Then Sir Gawaine said, "I am willing to answer unto thee in full measure." And Sir Pellias said, "Thou shalt indeed do so." Thereupon he turned and left that place, nor did he so much as look again either at Sir Gawaine or at the Lady Ettard.

But, now that the Lady Ettard no longer had the magic collar about her neck, Sir Gawaine felt nothing of the great enchantment that had aforetime drawn him so vehemently unto her. Accordingly, he now suffered a misliking for her as great as that liking which had aforetime drawn him unto her. Wherefore he said to himself, "How was it possible that for this lady I could have so betrayed my knighthood and have done so much harm unto my friend!" So he pushed back his chair very violently and arose from that table with intent to leave her.

But when the Lady Ettard saw his intent she spake to him with very great anger, for she was very much affronted in that he had deceived her when he said that he had overcome Sir Pellias. Wherefore she said with great heat, "Thou mayst go, and I am very willing for to have thee do so, for thou didst say false when thou didst tell me that thou hadst overcome Sir Pellias. For now I perceive that he is both a stronger and a nobler knight than thou. For he smote thee as though thou wert his servant, and thou yet bearest the marks of his fingers upon thy cheek."

Sir Gawaine and the Lady Ettard speak bitterly together.

At this Sir Gawaine was exceedingly wroth and entirely filled with the shame of that which had befallen him, wherefore he said, "Lady, I think thou hast bewitched me to bring me to such a pass of dishonor. As for Sir Pellias, look forth into that meadow to-morrow and see if I do not put a deeper mark upon him than ever he hath put upon me." Thereupon he left that place and went down into the court-yard and called upon the attendants who were there for to fetch him his horse. So they did as he commanded and he straightway rode forth into the night.

And he was very glad of the darkness of the night, for it appeared to him that it was easier to bear his shame in the darkness, wherefore when he had come to the glade of trees he would not enter the pavilion where his friends were. And also, when Sir Ewaine and Sir Marhaus came out unto him and bade him to come in, he would not do so, but stayed without in the darkness; for he said unto himself, "If I go in where is a light, haply they will behold the mark of Sir Pellias his hand upon my face."

So he stayed without in the darkness and bade them to go away and leave him alone.

But when they had gone he called his esquire unto him and he said, "Take this red armor off me and carry it into the pavilion of Sir Pellias, for I hate it." So the esquire did as Sir Gawaine commanded, and Sir Gawaine walked up and down for the entire night, greatly troubled in spirit and in heart.

JVSTISSIMVS·REX·

The Lady of the Lake finds Sir Pellias wounded.

CHAPTER SIXTH

How the Lady of the Lake Took Back Her Necklace From Sir Pellias.

NOW, WHEN THE NEXT MORNING HAD COME, SIR GAWAINE SUMMONED his esquire unto him and said, "Fetch hither my armor and case me in it." And the esquire did so. Then Sir Gawaine said, "Help me unto my horse," and the esquire did so. And the morning was still very early, with the grass all lustrous and sparkling with dew, and the little birds singing with such vehemence that it might have caused anyone great joy to be alive. Wherefore, when Sir Gawaine was seated a-horseback and in armor, he began to take more courage unto himself, and the dark vapors that had whilom overshadowed him lifted themselves a little. So he bespoke his esquire with stronger voice, saying, "Take this glove of mine and bear it to Sir Pellias and tell him that Sir Gawaine parades in the meadow in front of the castle and that he there challenges Sir Pellias for to meet him a-horse or afoot, howsoever that knight may choose."

Sir Gawaine issues challenge to Sir Pellias.

At these that esquire was very much astonished, for Sir Gawaine and Sir Pellias had always been such close friends that there was hardly their like for friendship in all that land, wherefore their love for one another had become a byword with all men. But he held his peace concerning his thoughts and only said, "Wilt thou not eat food ere thou goest to battle?" And Sir Gawaine said, "Nay, I will not eat until I have fought. Wherefore do thou go and do as I have bid thee."

So Sir Gawaine's esquire went to Sir Pellias in his pavilion and he gave unto that knight the glove of Sir Gawaine, and he delivered Sir Gawaine's message to him. And Sir Pellias said, "Tell thy master that I will come forth to meet him as soon as I have broken my fast."

Now, when the news of that challenge had come to the ears of Sir Brandiles and Sir Mador de la Porte and Sir Ewaine and Sir Marhaus, those knights were greatly disturbed thereat, and Sir Ewaine said to the others, "Messires, let us go and make inquiries concerning this business." So the four knights went to the white pavilion where Sir Pellias was breaking his fast.

And when they had come into the presence of Sir Pellias, Sir Ewaine said to him, "What is this quarrel betwixt my kinsman and thee?" And Sir Pellias made reply, "I will not tell thee, so, let be and meddle not with it."

Then Sir Ewaine said, "Wouldst thou do serious battle with thy friend?" To which Sir Pellias said, "He is a friend to me no longer."

Then Sir Brandiles cried out, "It is a great pity that a quarrel should lie betwixt such friends as thou and Sir Gawaine. Wilt thou not let us make peace betwixt you?" But Sir Pellias replied, "Ye cannot make peace, for this quarrel cannot be stayed until it is ended."

Then those knights saw that their words could be of no avail and they went away and left Sir Pellias.

So when Sir Pellias had broken his fast he summoned an esquire named Montenoir, and he bade him case him in that red armor that he had worn for all this time, and Montenoir did so. Then, when Sir Pellias was clad in that armor, he rode forth into the meadow before the castle where Sir Gawaine paraded. And when he had come thither those four other knights came to him again and besought him that he would let peace be made betwixt him and Sir Gawaine, but Sir Pellias would not listen to them, and so they went away again and left him, and he rode forth into the field before the castle of Grantmesnle.

Now a great concourse of people had come down upon the castle walls for to behold that assault-at-arms, for news thereof had gone all about that place. And it had also come to be known that the knight that would do combat with Sir Pellias was that very famous royal knight hight Sir Gawaine, the son of King Lot of Orkney, and a nephew of King Arthur; wherefore all the people were very desirous to behold so famous a knight do battle.

Likewise the Lady Ettard came down to the walls and took her stand in a lesser tower that overlooked the field of battle. And when she had taken her stand at that place she beheld that Sir Pellias wore that necklace of emeralds and opal stones and gold above his body armor, and her heart went out to him because of it, wherefore she hoped that he might be the victor in that encounter.

Sir Pellias and Sir Gawaine do battle.

Then each knight took his station in such place as seemed to him to be fitting, and they dressed each his spear and his shield and made him ready for the assault. Then, when they were in all ways prepared, Sir Marhaus gave the signal for the assault. Thereupon each knight instantly quitted that station which he held, dashing against the other with the speed of lightning, and with such fury that the earth thundered and shook beneath their horses' hoofs. So they met fairly in the centre of the course, each knight striking the other in the very midst of his defences. And in that encounter the spear of Sir Gawaine burst even to the hand-guard, but the spear of Sir Pellias held, so that Sir Gawaine was cast out of his saddle with terrible violence, smiting the earth with such force that he rolled thrice over in the dust and then lay altogether motionless as though bereft of life.

Sir Pellias overthroweth Sir Gawaine.

At this, all those people upon the walls shouted with a great voice, for it was an exceedingly noble assault-at-arms.

Then the four knights who stood watching that encounter made all haste unto Sir Gawaine where he lay; and Sir Pellias also rode back and sat his horse nigh at hand. Then Sir Ewaine and Sir Gawaine's esquire unlaced the helmet of Sir Gawaine with all speed, and, behold! his face was the color of ashes and they could not see that he breathed.

Thereupon Sir Marhaus said, "I believe that thou hast slain this knight, Sir Pellias," and Sir Pellias said, "Dost thou think so?" "Yea," quoth Sir Marhaus, "and I deem it a great pity." Unto which Sir Pellias made reply, "He hath not suffered more than he deserved."

At these words Sir Ewaine was filled with great indignation, wherefore he cried out, "Sir Knight, I think that thou forgettest the quality of this knight. For not only is he a fellow-companion of the Round Table, to whom thou hast vowed entire brotherhood, but he is also the son of a king and the nephew of King Arthur himself."

But to this Sir Pellias maintained a very steadfast countenance and replied, "I would not repent me of this were that knight a king in his own right instead of the son of a king."

Then Sir Ewaine lifted up his voice with great indignation, crying out upon Sir Pellias, "Begone! or a great ill may befall thee." "Well," said Sir Pellias, "I will go."

Upon this he turned his horse and rode away from that place and entered the woodland and so was gone from their sight.

Then those others present lifted up Sir Gawaine and bare him away unto the pavilion late of Sir Pellias, and there they laid him upon the couch of Sir Pellias. But it was above an hour ere he recovered himself again; and for a great part of that while those nigh unto him believed him to have been dead.

Sir Pellias departs into the forest.

But not one of those knights wist what was the case; to wit, that Sir Pellias had been so sorely wounded in the side in that encounter that it was not to be hoped that he could live for more than that day. For, though the spear of Sir Gawaine had burst, and though Sir Pellias had overthrown him entirely, yet the head of Sir Gawaine's spear had pierced the armor of Sir Pellias, and had entered his side and had there broken off, so that of the iron of the spear, the length of the breadth of a palm had remained in the body of Sir Pellias a little above the midriff. Wherefore, while Sir Pellias sat there talking so steadfastly unto those four knights, he was yet whiles in a great passion of pain, and the blood ran down into his armor in abundance. So, what with the loss of the blood, and of the great agony which he suffered, the brain of Sir Pellias swam as light as a feather all the time that he held talk with those others. But he said not a word unto them concerning the grievous wound he had received, but rode away very proudly into the forest.

Sir Pellias is sore wounded.

But when he had come into the forest he could not forbear him any longer, but fell to groaning very sorely, crying out, "Alas! alas! I have certes got my death-wound in this battle!"

Now it chanced that morn that the damsel Parcenet had ridden forth to fly a young gerfalcon, and a dwarf belonging to the Lady Ettard had ridden with her for company. So, as the damsel and the dwarf rode through a certain part of the forest skirt, not a very great distance from Grantmesnle, where the thicker part of the woodland began and the thinner part thereof ceased, the damsel heard a voice in the woodlands, lamenting with very great dolor. So she stopped and harkened, and by and by she heard that voice again making a great moan. Then Parcenet said to the dwarf, "What is that I hear? Certes, it is the voice of someone in lamentation. Now let us go and see who it is that maketh such woful moan." And the dwarf said, "It shall be as thou sayest."

So the damsel and the dwarf went a little way farther and there they beheld a knight sitting upon a black horse beneath an oak-tree. And that knight was clad altogether in red armor, wherefore, Parcenet knew that it must be Sir Pellias. And she saw that Sir Pellias leaned with the butt of his spear upon the ground and so upheld himself upon his horse from which he would otherwise have fallen because of his great weakness, and all the while he made that great moan that Parcenet had heard. So, seeing him in this sorry condition, Parcenet was overcome with great pity, and she made haste to him crying out, "Alas! Sir Pellias, what ails thee?"

How Parcenet findeth Sir Pellias wounded in the forest.

Then Sir Pellias looked at her as though she were a great way removed from him, and, because of the faintness of his soul, he beheld her, as it were, through thin water. And he said, very faintly, "Maiden, I am sore hurt." Thereupon she said, "How art thou hurt, Sir Pellias?" And he replied, "I have a grievous wound in my side, for a spear's point standeth therein nigh a palm's breadth deep so that it reaches nearly to my heart, wherefore, meseems that I shall not live for very long."

Upon this the maiden cried out, "Alas! alas! what is this!" and she made great lament and smote her hands together with sorrow that that noble knight should have come to so grievous an extremity.

Then the dwarf that was with Parcenet, seeing how greatly she was distracted by sorrow, said, "Damsel, I know of a certain place in this forest (albeit it is a considerable distance from this) where there dwelleth a certain very holy hermit who is an extraordinarily skilful leech. Now, an we may bring this knight unto the chapel where that hermit dwelleth, I believe that he may be greatly holpen unto health and ease again."

Upon this Parcenet said, "Gansaret"—for Gansaret was the dwarf's name—"Gansaret, let us take this knight unto that place as quickly as we are able. For I tell thee sooth when I say that I have a very great deal of love for him." "Well," said the dwarf, "I will show thee where that chapel is."

So the dwarf took the horse of Sir Pellias by the bridle-rein and led the way through that forest, and Parcenet rode beside Sir Pellias and upheld him upon his saddle. For some whiles Sir Pellias fainted with sickness and with pain so that he would else have fallen had she not upheld him. Thus they went forward very sorrowfully and at so slow a pace that it was noontide ere they came to that certain very dense and lonely part of the forest where the hermit abided.

And when they had come unto that place the dwarf said, "Yonder, damsel, is the chapel whereof I spake."

Then Parcenet lifted up her eyes and she beheld where was a little woodland chapel built in among the leafy trees of the forest. And around this chapel was a little open lawn bedight with flowers, and nigh to the door of the hermitage was a fountain of water as clear as crystal. And this was a very secret and lonely place and withal very silent and peaceful, for in front of the chapel they beheld a wild doe and her fawn browsing upon the tender grass and herbs without any fear of harm. And when the dwarf and the maiden and the wounded knight drew nigh, the doe and the fawn looked up with great wide eyes and spread their large ears with wonder, yet fled not, fearing no harm, but by and by began their browsing again. Likewise all about the chapel in the branches of the trees were great quantities of birds, singing and chirping very cheerfully. And those birds were waiting for their mid-day meal that the hermit was used to cast unto them.

(Now this was that same forest sanctuary whereunto King Arthur had come that time when he had been so sorely wounded by Sir Pellinore as hath been aforetold in this history.)

As the maiden and the dwarf and the wounded knight drew nigh to this chapel, a little bell began ringing very sweetly so that the sound thereof echoed all through those quiet woodlands, for it was now the hour of noon. And Sir Pellias heard that bell as it were a great way off, and first he said, "Whither am I come?" and then he made shift to cross himself. And Parcenet crossed herself and the dwarf kneeled down and crossed himself. Then when the bell had ceased ringing, the dwarf cried out in a loud voice, "What ho! what ho! here is one needing help!"

Parcenet and the dwarf bring Sir Pellias to the hermit of the forest.

Then the door of the sanctuary was opened and there came forth from that place a very venerable man with a long white beard as it were of finely carded wool. And, lo! as he came forth, all those birds that waited there flew about him in great quantities, for they thought that he had come forth for to feed them; wherefore the hermit was compelled to brush those small fowls away with his hands as he came unto where the three were stationed.

And when he had come unto them he demanded of them who they were and why they had come thither with that wounded knight. So Parcenet told him how it was with them, and of how they had found Sir Pellias so sorely wounded in the forest that morning and had brought him hitherward.

Then, when the hermit had heard all of her story, he said, "It is well and I will take him in." So he took Sir Pellias into his cell, and when they had helped lay him upon the couch, Parcenet and the dwarf went their way homeward again.

After they had gone, the hermit examined the hurt of Sir Pellias, and Sir Pellias lay in a deep swoon. And the swoon was so deep that the hermit beheld that it was the death-swoon, and that the knight was nigh to his end. So he said, "This knight must assuredly die in a very little while, for I can do naught to save him." Wherefore he immediately quitted the side of Sir Pellias and set about in haste to prepare the last sacrament such as might be administered unto a noble knight who was dying.

Now whiles the hermit was about this business the door opened of a sudden and there came into that place a very strange lady clad all in green and bedight around the arms with armlets of emeralds and opal stones inset into gold. And her hair, which was very soft, was entirely black and was tied about with a cord of crimson ribbon. And the hermit beheld that her face was like to ivory for whiteness and that her eyes were bright, like unto jewels set into ivory, wherefore he knew that she was no ordinary mortal.

The Lady of the Lake cometh to Sir Pellias.

And this lady went straight to Sir Pellias and leaned over him so that her breath touched his forehead. And she said, "Alas! Sir Pellias, that thou shouldst lie so." "Lady," said the hermit, "thou mayst well say 'Alas,' for this knight hath only a few minutes to live." To this the lady said, "Not so, thou holy man, for I tell thee that this knight shall have a long while yet to live." And when she had said this she stooped and took from about his neck that necklace of emeralds and opal stones and gold that encircled it and she hung it about her own neck.

Now when the hermit beheld what she did, he said, "Lady, what is this that thou doest, and why dost thou take that ornament from a dying man?"

But the lady made reply very tranquilly, "I gave it unto him, wherefore I do but take back again what is mine own. But now I prithee let me be with this knight for a little while, for I have great hope that I may bring back life unto him again."

Then the hermit was a-doubt and he said, "Wilt thou endeavor to heal him by magic?" And the lady said, "If I do, it will not be by magic that is black."

So the hermit was satisfied and went away, and left the lady alone with Sir Pellias.

Now when the lady was thus alone with the wounded knight she immediately set about doing sundry very strange things. For first she brought forth a loadstone of great power and potency and this she set to the wound. And, lo! the iron of the spear-head came forth from the wound; and as it came Sir Pellias groaned with great passion. And when the spear-point came forth there burst out a great issue of blood like to a fountain of crimson. But the lady immediately pressed a fragrant napkin of fine cambric linen to the wound and stanched the blood, and it bled no more, for she held it within the veins by very potent spells of magic. So, the blood being stanched in this wise, the lady brought forth from her bosom a small crystal phial filled with an elixir of blue color and of a very singular fragrance. And she poured some of this elixir between the cold and leaden lips of the knight; and when the elixir touched his lips the life began to enter into his body once more; for, in a little while, he opened his eyes and gazed about him with a very strange look, and the first thing that he beheld was that lady clad in green who stood beside him, and she was so beautiful that he thought that haply he had died and was in Paradise, wherefore he said, "Am I then dead?"

The Lady of the Lake healeth Sir Pellias.

"Nay, thou art not dead," said the lady, "yet hast thou been parlously nigh to death." "Where then am I?" said Sir Pellias. And she replied, "Thou art in a deep part of the forest, and this is the cell of a saint-like hermit of the forest." At this Sir Pellias said, "Who is it that hath brought me back to life?" Upon this the lady smiled and said, "It was I."

Now for a little while Sir Pellias lay very silent, then by and by he spake and said, "Lady, I feel very strangely." "Yea," said the lady, "that is because thou hast now a different life." Then Sir Pellias said, "How is it with me?" And the lady said, "It is thus: that to bring thee back to life I gave thee to drink of a certain draught of an *elixir vitæ* so that thou art now only half as thou wert before; for if by the one half thou art mortal, by the other half thou art fay."

Then Sir Pellias looked up and beheld that the lady had about her neck the collar of emeralds and opal stones and gold which he had aforetime worn. And, lo! his heart went out to her with exceeding ardor, and he said, "Lady, thou sayest that I am half fay, and I do perceive that thou art altogether fay. Now, I pray thee to let it be that henceforth I may abide nigh unto where thou art." And the lady said, "It shall be as thou dost ask, for it was to that end I have suffered thee nearly to die, and then have brought thee back unto life again."

Sir Pellias loveth the Lady of the Lake.

Then Sir Pellias said, "When may I go with thee?" And she said, "In a little when thou hast had to drink." "How may that be?" said Sir Pellias, "seeing that I am but yet like unto a little child for weakness." To the which the lady made reply, "When thou hast drunk of water thy strength shall return unto thee, and thou shalt be altogether well and whole again."

So the Lady of the Lake went out, and presently returned, bearing in her hand an earthen crock filled with water from the fountain near at hand. And when Sir Pellias had drunk that water he felt, of a sudden, his strength come altogether back to him.

Yet he was not at all as he had been before, for now his body felt as light as air, and his soul was dilated with a pure joy such as he had never felt in his life before that time. Wherefore he immediately uprose from his couch of pain, and he said, "Thou hast given life unto me again, now do I give that life unto thee forever."

Then the lady looked upon him and smiled with great loving-kindness. And she said, "Sir Pellias, I have held thee in tender regard ever since I beheld thee one day in thy young knighthood drink a draught of milk at a cottager's hut in this forest. For the day was warm and thou hadst set aside thy helmet, and a young milkmaid, brown of face and with bare feet, came and brought thee a bowl of milk, which same thou didst drink of with great appetite. That was the first time that I beheld thee—although thou didst not see me. Since that time I have had great friendship for all thy fellowship of King Arthur's Court and for King Arthur himself, all for thy sake."

Then Sir Pellias said, "Lady, wilt thou accept me for thy knight?" and she said, "Aye." Then Sir Pellias said, "May I salute thee?" And she said, "Yea, if it pleasures thee." So Sir Pellias kissed her upon the lips, and so their troth was plighted.

Now return we unto Parcenet and the dwarf:

After those two had left that hermitage in the woodland, they betook their way again toward Grantmesnle, and when they had come nigh out of the forest at a place not far from the glade of trees wherein those knights-companion had taken up their inn, they met one of those knights clad in half-armor, and that knight was Sir Mador de la Porte. Then Parcenet called upon him by name, saying, "Alas! Sir Mador, I have but this short time quitted a hermit's cell in the forest where I left Sir Pellias sorely wounded to death, so I fear me he hath only a little while to live."

Parcenet bringeth news of Sir Pellias to Sir Mador de la Porte.

Then Sir Mador de la Porte cried out, "Ha! maiden, what is this thou tellest me? That is a very hard thing to believe; for when Sir Pellias quitted us this morn he gave no sign of wound or disease of any sort."

But Parcenet replied, "Ne'theless, I myself beheld him lying in great pain and dole, and, ere he swooned his death-swoon, he himself told me that he had the iron of a spear in his side."

Then Sir Mador de la Porte said, "Alas! alas! that is sorry news! Now, damsel, by thy leave and grace, I will leave thee and hasten to my companions to tell them this news." And Parcenet said, "I prithee do so."

So Sir Mador de la Porte made haste to the pavilion where were his companions, and he told them the news that he had heard.

Now at this time Sir Gawaine was altogether recovered from the violent overthrow he had suffered that morning, wherefore when he heard the news that Sir Mador de la Porte brought to him, he smote his hands together and cried out aloud, "Woe is me! what have I done! For first I betrayed my friend, and now I have slain him. Now I will go forth straightway to find him and to crave his forgiveness ere he die."

But Sir Ewaine said, "What is this that thou wouldst do? Thou art not yet fit to undertake any journey."

Sir Gawaine said, "I care not, for I am determined to go and find my friend." Nor would he suffer any of his companions to accompany him; but when he had summoned

Sir Gawaine departeth to find Sir Pellias.

his esquire to bring him his horse, he mounted thereon and rode away into the forest alone, betaking his way to the westward, and lamenting with great sorrow as he journeyed forward.

Now when the afternoon had fallen very late, so that the sun was sloping to its setting, and the light fell as red as fire through the forest leaves, Sir Gawaine came to that hermit's cell where it stood in the silent and solitary part of the forest woodland. And he beheld that the hermit was outside of his cell digging in a little garden of lentils. So when the hermit saw the armed knight come into that lawn all in the red light of the setting sun, he stopped digging and leaned upon his trowel. Then Sir Gawaine drew nigh, and, as he sat upon his horse, he told the holy man of the business whereon he had come.

To this the hermit said, "There came a lady hither several hours ago, and she was clad all in green, and was of a very singular appearance, so that it was easy to see that she was fay. And by means of certain charms of magic that lady cured thy friend, and after she had healed him, the two rode away into the forest together."

Then Sir Gawaine was very much amazed, and he said, "This is a very strange thing that thou tellest me, that a knight who is dying should be brought back to life again in so short a time, and should so suddenly ride forth from a bed of pain. Now, I prithee tell me whither they went." The hermit said, "They went to the westward." Whereupon, when Sir Gawaine heard this, he said, "I will follow them."

So he rode away and left the hermit gazing after him. And as he rode forward upon his way, the twilight began to fall apace, so that the woodlands after a while grew very dark and strange all around him. But as the darkness descended a very singular miracle happened, for, lo! there appeared before Sir Gawaine, a light of a pale blue color, and it went before him and showed him the way, and he followed it, much marvelling.

Sir Gawaine follows a singular light.

Now after he had followed the light for a very long time he came at last, of a sudden, to where the woodland ceased, and where there was a wide, open plain of very great extent. And this plain was all illuminated by a singular radiance which was like that of a clear full moonlight, albeit no moon was shining at that time. And in that pale and silver light Sir Gawaine could see everything with wonderful distinctness; wherefore he beheld that he was in a plain covered all over with flowers of divers sorts, the odors whereof so filled the night that it appeared to press upon the bosom with a great pleasure. And he beheld that in front of him lay a great lake, very wide and still. And all those things appeared so strange in that light that Sir Gawaine wotted that he had come into a land of faëry. So he rode among tall flowers toward that lake in a sort of fear, for he wist not what was to befall him.

Now as he drew near the lake he perceived a knight and a lady approaching him; and when they had come nigh he beheld that the knight was Sir Pellias, and that his countenance was exceedingly strange. And he beheld that the lady was she whom he had aforetime seen all clad in green apparel when he had travelled in the Forest of Adventure with Sir Ewaine and Sir Marhaus.

Now when Sir Gawaine first beheld Sir Pellias he was filled with a great fear, for he thought it was a spirit that he saw. But when he perceived that Sir Pellias was alive, there came into his bosom a joy as great as that fear had been; wherefore he made haste toward Sir Pellias. And when he had come near to Sir Pellias, he leaped from off his horse, crying out, "Forgive! Forgive!" with great vehemence of passion. Then he would have taken Sir Pellias into his arms, but Sir Pellias withdrew himself from the contact of Sir Gawaine, though not with any violence of anger. And Sir Pellias spake in a voice very thin and of a silvery clearness as though it came from a considerable distance, and he said, "Touch me not, for I am not as I was aforetime, being not all human, but part fay. But concerning my forgiveness: I do forgive thee whatsoever injury I may have suffered at thy hands. And more than this I give unto thee my love, and I greatly hope for thy joy and happiness. But now I go away to leave thee, dear friend, and haply I shall not behold thee again, wherefore I do leave this with thee as my last behest; to wit, that thou dost go back to King Arthur's Court and make thy peace with the Queen. So thou mayst bring them news of all that hath happened unto me."

Sir Gawaine findeth Sir Pellias.

Then Sir Gawaine cried out in great sorrow, "Whither wouldst thou go?"

And Sir Pellias said, "I shall go to yonder wonderful city of gold and azure which lieth in yonder valley of flowers."

Then Sir Gawaine said, "I see no city but only a lake of water."

Whereupon Sir Pellias replied, "Ne'theless, there is a city yonder and thither I go, wherefore I do now bid thee farewell."

Then Sir Gawaine looked into the face of Sir Pellias and beheld again that strange light that it was of a very singular appearance, for, lo! it was white like to ivory and his eyes shone like jewels set in ivory, and a smile lay upon his lips and grew neither more nor less, but always remained the same. (For those who were of that sort had always that singular appearance and smiled in that manner—to wit, the Lady of the Lake, and Sir Pellias, and Sir Launcelot of the Lake.)

Then Sir Pellias and the Lady of the Lake turned and left Sir Gawaine where he stood, and they went toward the lake, and they entered the lake, and when the feet of the horse of Sir Pellias had touched the water of the lake, lo! Sir Pellias was gone and Sir Gawaine beheld him no more, although he stood there for a long time weeping with great passion.

Sir Pellias disappeareth into the lake.

So endeth the story of Sir Pellias.

But Sir Gawaine returned unto the Court of King Arthur as he had promised Sir Pellias to do, and he made his peace with Queen Guinevere and, thereafter, though the Queen loved him not, yet there was a peace betwixt them. And Sir Gawaine published these things to the Court of King Arthur and all men marvelled at what he told.

And only twice thereafter was Sir Pellias ever seen of any of his aforetime companions.

And Sir Marhaus was made a Companion of the Round Table and became one of the foremost knights thereof.

And the Lady Ettard took Sir Engamore into favor again, and that summer they were wedded and Sir Engamore became lord of Grantmesnle.

So endeth this story.

PART III
THE STORY OF SIR GAWAINE

Here followeth the story of Sir Gawaine and of how he discovered such wonderful faithfulness unto King Arthur, who was his lord, that I do not believe that the like of such faithfulness was ever seen before.

For indeed, though Sir Gawaine was at times very rough and harsh in his manner, and though he was always so plain-spoken that his words hid the gentle nature that lay within him, yet, under this pride of manner, was much courtesy; and at times he was so urbane of manner and so soft of speech that he was called by many the Knight of the Silver Tongue.

So here ye shall read how his faithfulness unto King Arthur brought him such high reward that almost anyone in all the world might envy him his great good fortune.

Sir Gawaine the Son of Lot, King of Orkney.

CHAPTER FIRST

How a White Hart Appeared Before King Arthur, and How Sir Gawaine and Gaheris, His Brother, Went in Pursuit Thereof, and of What Befell Them in That Quest.

Upon a certain time King Arthur, together with Queen Guinevere and all of his Court, were making progression through that part of his kingdom which was not very near to Camelot. At this time the King journeyed in very great state, and Queen Guinevere had her Court about her, so there were many esquires and pages; wherefore, what with knights, lords, and ladies in attendance, more than six score of people were with the King and Queen.

Now it chanced that at this time the season of the year was very warm, so that when the middle of the day had come the King commanded that a number of pavilions should be spread for their accommodation, wherein that they might rest there until the heat of the day had passed. So the attendants spread three pavilions in a pleasant glade upon the outskirts of the forest.

When this had been done, the King gave command that the tables, whereat they were to eat their mid-day meal, should be spread beneath the shadow of that glade of trees; for there was a gentle wind blowing and there were many birds singing, so that it was very pleasant to sit in the open air.

Accordingly the attendants of the Court did as the King commanded, and the tables were set upon the grass beneath the shade, and the King and Queen and all the lords and ladies of their Courts sat down to that cheerful repast.

A white hart and a white hound appear before King Arthur at feast.

Now whiles they sat there feasting with great content of spirit, and with much mirth and goodly talk among themselves, there came of a sudden a great outcry from the woodland that was near by, and therewith there burst forth from the cover of that leafy wilderness a very beautiful white hart pursued by a white brachet of equal beauty. And there was not a hair upon either of these animals that was not as white as milk, and each wore about its neck a collar of gold very beautiful to behold.

The hound pursued the white hart with a very great outcry and bellowing, and the hart fled in the utmost terror. In this wise they ran thrice around the table where King Arthur and his Court sat at meat, and twice in that chase the hound caught the hart and pinched it on its haunch, and therewith the hart leaped away, and all they who sat there observed that there was blood at two places upon its haunch where the hound had pinched it. But each time the hart escaped from the hound, and the hound followed after it with much outcry of yelling so that King Arthur and Queen Guinevere and all their Court were annoyed at the noise and tumult that those two creatures made. Then the hart fled away into the forest again by another path, and the hound pursued it and both were gone, and the baying of the hound sounded more and more distant as it ran away into the woodland.

Now, ere the King and Queen and their Court had recovered from their astonishment at these things, there suddenly appeared at that part of the forest whence the hart and the hound had emerged, a knight and a lady, and the knight was of very lordly presence and the lady was exceedingly beautiful. The knight was clad in half-armor, and the lady was clad in green as though for the chase; and the knight rode upon a charger of dapple gray, and the lady upon a piebald palfrey. With them were two esquires, also clad for the chase.

These, seeing the considerable company gathered there, paused as though in surprise, and whilst they stood so, there suddenly appeared another knight upon a black horse, clad in complete armor, and he seemed to be very angry. For he ran upon the half-armed knight and smote him so sorry a blow with his sword, that the first knight fell down from his horse and lay upon the ground as though dead; whereat the lady who was with him shrieked with great dolor.

Then the full-armed knight upon the black horse ran to the lady and catched her, and he lifted her from her palfrey and laid her across the horn of his saddle, and thereupon he rode back into the forest again. The lady screamed with such vehemence of violent outcry, that it was a great pity to hear her, but the knight paid no attention to her shrieking, but bore her away by main force into the forest.

King Arthur and his Court behold a knight carry off a lady prisoner.

Then, after he and the lady had gone, the two esquires came and lifted up the wounded knight upon his horse, and then they also went away into the forest and were gone.

All this King Arthur and his Court beheld from a distance, and they were so far away that they could not stay that knight upon the black horse from doing what he did to carry away the lady into the forest; nor could they bring succor to that other knight in half-armor whom they had beheld struck down in that wise. So they were very greatly grieved at what they had beheld and knew not what to think of it. Then King Arthur said to his Court, "Messires, is there not some one of you who will follow up this adventure and discover what is the significance of that which we have seen, and compel that knight to tell why he behaved as he did?"

Upon this Sir Gawaine said, "Lord, I shall be very glad indeed to take upon me this adventure if I have thy leave to do so." And King Arthur said, "Thou hast my leave." Then Sir Gawaine said, "Lord, I would that thou would also let me take my younger brother, Gaheris, with me as mine esquire in this undertaking, for he groweth apace unto manhood, and yet he hath never beheld any considerable adventure at arms." So King Arthur said, "Thou hast my leave to take thy brother with thee."

Sir Gawaine and Gaheris undertake the adventure of these things.

At this Gaheris was very glad, for he was of an adventurous spirit, wherefore the thought of going with his brother upon this quest gave him great pleasure.

So they two went to the pavilion of Sir Gawaine, and there Gaheris aided Sir Gawaine as his esquire to don his armor. Then they rode forth upon that quest which Sir Gawaine had undertaken.

Now they journeyed onward for a very considerable distance, following that direction which they had seen the hart take when it had sped away from before the hound, and when, from time to time, they would meet some of the forest folk, they would inquire of them whither had fled that white brachet and the white hart, and whither had fled the knight and the lady, and so they followed that adventure apace.

By and by, after a long pass—it being far advanced in the afternoon—they were suddenly aware of a great uproar of conflict, as of a fierce battle in progress. So they followed this sound, and after a while they came to an open meadow-land with very fair and level sward. Here they beheld two knights fighting with great vehemence of passion, and with a very deadly purpose. Then Sir Gawaine said, "What is this? Let us go see." So he and Gaheris rode forward to where those two knights were engaged, and as they approached, the two knights paused in their encounter, and rested upon their weapons. Then Sir Gawaine said, "Ha! Messires, what is to do and why do ye fight with such passion, the one against the other, in that wise?" Then one of the knights said to Sir Gawaine, "Sir, this does not concern you"; and the other said, "Meddle not with us, for this battle is of our own choosing."

They behold two knights fighting.

"Messires," said Sir Gawaine, "I would be very sorry to interfere in your quarrel, but I am in pursuit of a white hart and a white brachet that came this way, and also of a knight who hath carried off a lady upon the same pass. Now I would be greatly beholden to ye if you would tell me if ye have seen aught of one or the other."

Then that knight who had first spoken said, "Sir, this is a very strange matter, for it was upon account of that very white hart and that brachet, and of the knight and the lady that we two were just now engaged in that battle as thou didst behold. For the case is this: We two are two brothers, and we were riding together in great amity when that hart and that hound came hitherward. Then my brother said he very greatly hoped that the white hart would escape from the hound, and I said that I hoped that the hound would overtake the hart and bring it to earth. Then came that knight with that lady, his captive, and I said that I would follow that knight and rescue the lady, and my brother said that he would undertake that adventure.

One of the knights tells their story.

"Upon these points we fell into dispute; for it appeared to me that I felt great affection for that hound, and my brother felt as extraordinary regard for the white hart, and that as I had first spoken I should have the right to follow that adventure; but my brother felt affection for the hart, and he considered that as he was the elder of us twain, he had the best right to the adventure. So we quarrelled, and by and by we fell to upon that fight in which thou did see us engaged."

At this Sir Gawaine was very greatly astonished, and he said, "Messires, I cannot understand how so great a quarrel should have arisen from so small a dispute; and, certes, it is a great pity for two brothers to quarrel as ye have done, and to give one another such sore cuts and wounds as I perceive you have both received."

"Messires," said the second knight, "I think thou art right, and I now find myself to be very much ashamed of that quarrel." And the other said, "I too am sorry for what I have done."

Then Sir Gawaine said, "Sirs, I would be very glad indeed if you would tell me your names." And the one knight said, "I am called Sir Sorloise of the Forest." And the other said, "I am called Sir Brian of the Forest."

Then Sir Sorloise said, "Sir Knight, I would deem it a very great courtesy if thou wouldst tell me who thou art."

"I would be very glad to do that," said Sir Gawaine, and therewith he told them his name and condition. Now, when they heard who Sir Gawaine was, those two knights were very greatly astonished and pleased; for no one in all the courts of chivalry was more famous than Sir Gawaine, the son of King Lot of Orkney. Wherefore those two brothers said, "It is certainly a great joy to us to meet so famous a knight as thou art, Sir Gawaine."

Then Sir Gawaine said, "Sir Knights, that hart and that hound came only a short while ago to where King Arthur and Queen Guinevere and their Courts of lords and ladies were at feast, and there, likewise, all we beheld that knight seize upon the lady and make her captive. Wherefore, I and my brother have come forth upon command of King Arthur for to discover what is the meaning of that which we beheld. Now I shall deem it a very great courtesy upon your part if you will cease from this adventure and will go in amity unto the Court of the King, and will tell him of what ye beheld and of how you quarrelled and of how we met. For otherwise I myself will have to engage ye both, and that would be a great pity; for ye are weary with battle and I am fresh."

Then these two knights said, "Sir, we will do as you desire, for we have no wish to have to do with so powerful a knight as you."

Thereupon those two knights departed and went to the Court of King Arthur as Sir Gawaine ordained, and Sir Gawaine and his brother rode forward upon their adventure.

Now, by and by they came nigh to a great river, and there they beheld before them a single knight in full armor, who carried a spear in his hand and a shield hanging to his saddle-bow. Thereupon Sir Gawaine made haste forward and he called aloud to the knight, and the knight paused and waited until Sir Gawaine had overtaken him. And when Sir Gawaine came up to that knight he said, "Sir Knight, hast thou seen a white hart and a white hound pass by this way? And hast thou seen a knight bearing off a captive lady?"

Sir Gawaine and Gaheris meet a knight beside the river.

Unto this the knight said, "Yea, I beheld them both, and I am even now following after them with intent to discover whither they are bound." Then Sir Gawaine said, "Sir Knight, I bid thee not to follow this adventure farther, for I myself am set upon it. Wherefore I desire thee for to give it over so that I may undertake it in thy stead." "Sir," said the other knight, speaking with a very great deal of heat, "I know not who thou art, nor do I care a very great deal. But touching the pursuance of this adventure, I do tell thee that I myself intend to follow it to the end and so will I do, let who will undertake to stay me."

Thereupon Sir Gawaine said, "Messire, thou shalt not go forward upon this adventure unless thou hast first to do with me." And the knight said, "Sir, I am very willing for that."

So each knight took such stand upon that field as appeared to him to be best, and each put himself into a posture of defence and dressed his shield and his spear. Then, when they were thus prepared in all ways, they immediately launched forth, the one against the other, rushing together with great speed and with such an uproar that the ground trembled and shook beneath them. So they met together in the midst of the course and the spear of the strange knight burst all into small pieces, but the spear of Sir Gawaine held; wherefore he hurled that knight out of his saddle with such violence that he smote the ground with a blow like an earthquake.

Sir Gawaine overthroweth the knight.

Then Sir Gawaine rode back to where his enemy was (for that knight was unable to arise), and he removed the helmet from the head of the fallen knight and beheld that he was very young and comely.

Now, when the fresh air smote upon the knight's face, he presently awoke from his swoon and came back unto his senses again, whereupon Sir Gawaine said, "Dost thou yield unto me?" And the knight said, "I do so." Then Sir Gawaine said, "Who art thou?" And the knight said, "I am called Sir Alardin of the Isles." "Very well," said Sir Gawaine; "then I lay my command upon thee in this wise: that thou shalt go to the Court of King Arthur and deliver thyself to him as a captive of my prowess. And thou art to tell him all that thou knowest of the hart and the hound and the knight and the lady. And thou shalt tell him all that hath befallen thee in this assault."

So the knight said that he would do that, and thereupon they parted, the one party going the one way and the other party going the other way.

After that Sir Gawaine and his brother, Gaheris, rode a considerable distance until they came, by and by, through a woodland into an open plain, and it was now about the time of sunset. And they beheld in the midst of the plain a very stately and noble castle with five towers and of very great strength.

And right here they saw a sight that filled them with great sorrow, for they beheld the dead body of that white brachet lying beside the road like any carrion. And they saw that the hound was pierced through with three arrows, wherefore they wist that it had been slain very violently.

Sir Gawaine and Gaheris behold the dead brachet.

Now when Sir Gawaine beheld that beautiful hound lying dead in that wise, he was filled with great sorrow. "What a pity it is," he cried, "that this noble hound should be slain in this wise; for I think that it was the most beautiful hound that ever I saw in all my life. Here hath assuredly been great treachery against it; for it hath been foully dealt with because of that white hart which it pursued. Now, I make my vow that if I can find that hart I will slay it with mine own hands, because it was in that chase that this hound met its death."

After that they rode forward toward that castle, and as they drew nigh, lo! they beheld that white hart with the golden collar browsing upon the meadows before the castle.

Now, as soon as the white hart beheld those two strangers, it fled with great speed toward the castle, and it ran into the court-yard of the castle. And when Sir Gawaine beheld the stag, he gave chase in pursuit of it with great speed, and Gaheris followed after his brother.

Sir Gawaine slayeth the white hart.

So Sir Gawaine pursued the white hart into the courtyard of the castle and from thence it could not escape. Then Sir Gawaine leaped him down from his horse and drew his sword and slew the hart with a single blow of his weapon.

This he did in great haste, but when he had done that and it was too late to mend it, he repented him of what he had done very sorely.

Now with all this tumult, there came out the lord and the lady of that castle; and the lord was one of very haughty and noble aspect, and the lady was extraordinarily graceful and very beautiful of appearance. And Sir Gawaine looked upon the lady and he thought he had hardly ever seen so beautiful a dame, wherefore he was more sorry than ever that, in his haste, he had slain that white hart.

But when the lady of the castle beheld the white hart, that it lay dead upon the stone pavement of the court-yard, she smote her hands together and shrieked with such shrillness and strength, that it pierced the ears to hear her. And she cried out, "Oh, my white hart, art thou then dead?" And therewith she fell to weeping with great passion. Then Sir Gawaine said, "Lady, I am very sorry for what I have done, and I would that I could undo it." Then the lord of that castle said to Sir Gawaine, "Sir, didst thou slay that stag?" "Yea," said Sir Gawaine. "Sir," said the lord of the castle, "thou hast done very ill in this matter, and if thou wilt wait a little I will take full vengeance upon thee." Unto which Sir Gawaine said, "I will wait for thee as long as it shall please thee."

Then the lord of the castle went into his chamber and clad himself in his armor, and in a little while he came out very fiercely. "Sir," said Sir Gawaine, "what is thy quarrel with me?" And the lord of the castle said, "Because thou hast slain the white hart that was so dear to my lady." To the which Sir Gawaine said, "I would not have slain the white hart only that because of it the white brachet was so treacherously slain." Upon this the lord of the castle was more wroth than ever, and he ran at Sir Gawaine and smote him unawares, so that he clave through the epaulier of his armor and cut through the flesh and unto the bone of the shoulder, so that Sir Gawaine was put to a great agony of pain at the stroke. Then Sir Gawaine was filled with rage at the pain of the wound, wherefore he smote the knight so woful a blow that he cut through his helmet and into the bone beneath, and thereupon the knight fell down upon his knees because of the fierceness of the blow, and he could not rise up again. Then Sir Gawaine catched his helmet and rushed it off from his head.

The knight of the castle assaileth Sir Gawaine.

Upon this the knight said in a weak voice, "Sir Knight, I crave mercy of you, and yield myself to you."

But Sir Gawaine was very furious with anger because of that unexpected blow which he had received and because of the great agony of the wound, wherefore he would not have mercy, but lifted up his sword with intent to slay that knight.

Sir Gawaine maketh to slay the knight of the castle.

Then the lady of the castle beheld what Sir Gawaine was intent to do, and she brake away from her damsels and ran and flung herself upon the knight so as to shield him with her own body. And in that moment Sir Gawaine was striking and could not stay his blow; nevertheless, he was able to turn his sword in his hand so that the edge thereof did not smite the lady. But the flat of the sword struck her upon the neck a very grievous blow, and the blade cut her a little, so that the blood ran down her smooth white neck and over her kerchief; and with the violence of the blow the lady fell down and lay upon the ground as though she were dead.

Sir Gawaine striketh the lady of the castle without intent.

Now when Sir Gawaine beheld that, he thought that he had slain that lady in his haste, and he was all a-dread at what he had done, wherefore he cried, "Woe is me! what have I done?"

"Alas!" said Gaheris, "that was a very shameful blow that thou didst strike; and the shame of it is mine also because thou art my brother. Now I wish I had not come with thee to this place."

Then Sir Gawaine said to the lord of that castle, "Sir, I will spare thy life, for I am very sorry for what I have done in my haste."

But the knight of the castle was filled with great bitterness, because he thought that his lady was dead, wherefore he cried out as in despair, "I will not now have thy mercy, for thou art a knight without mercy and without pity. And since thou hast slain my lady, who is dearer to me than my life, thou mayst slay me also. For that is the only service which thou canst now render me."

But by now the damsels of the lady had come to her where she lay, and the chiefest of these cried out to the lord of the castle, "Ha, sir, thy lady is not dead, but only in a swoon from which she will presently recover."

Then when the lord of the castle heard that, he fell to weeping in great measure from pure joy; for now that he knew his lady was alive he could not contain himself for joy. Therewith Sir Gawaine came to him and lifted him up from the ground where he was, and kissed him upon the cheek. Then certain others came and bare the lady away into her chamber, and there in a little while she recovered from that swoon and was but little the worse for the blow she had received.

That night Sir Gawaine, and his brother, Gaheris, abided with the knight and the lady, and when the knight learned who Sir Gawaine was, he felt it great honor to have so famous a knight in that place. So they feasted together that evening in great amity.

Now, after they had refreshed themselves, Sir Gawaine said, "I beseech you, sir, to tell me what was the meaning of the white hart and the white brachet which led me into this adventure."

To this the lord of the castle (whose name was Sir Ablamor of the Marise) said, "I will do so." And therewith he spake as follows:

"You must know, sir, that I have a brother who hath always been very dear to me, and when I took this, my lady, unto wife, he took her sister as his wife.

The lord of the castle telleth the story of the white hart and the white hound.

"Now, my brother dwelt in a castle nigh to this, and we held commerce together in great amity. But it befell a day that my lady and my brother's lady were riding through this forest together discoursing very pleasantly. What time there appeared a lady unto them, exceedingly beautiful, and of very strange appearance, for I do not think that either my lady or her sister ever beheld her like before.

"This strange lady brought unto those two ladies a white hart and a white brachet, and the hart and the hound she held each by a silver chain attached to a golden collar that encircled its neck. And the white hart she gave unto my lady and the white brachet she gave unto my lady's sister. And then she went away leaving them very glad.

"But their gladness did not last for very long, for ever since that time there hath been nothing else but discord between my brother and myself, and between my lady and her sister, for the white hound hath ever sought the white hart for to destroy it, wherefore I and my lady have entertained very great offence against my brother and his lady because they did not keep the white brachet at home. So it has come to pass that a number of times we have sought to destroy the hound, so that my brother and his lady have held equal offence against us.

"Now this day it chanced I was toward the outskirts of the forest to the east of us, when I heard a great outcry in the woodland, and by and by the white hart that belonged to my lady came fleeing through the woodland, and the white brachet that belonged to my brother's lady was in pursuit of it; and my brother and his lady and two esquires followed rapidly after the hart and the brachet.

"Then I was very greatly angered, for it seemed to me that they were chasing that white hart out of despite of my lady and myself, wherefore I followed after them with all speed.

"So I came upon them at the outskirts of the woodland, nigh to where there were a number of pavilions pitched in the shade of a glade of trees in the midst of the meadow, and there, in mine anger, I struck my brother a great blow so that I smote him down from his horse. And I catched his lady and I threw her across the horn of my saddle and I bore her here away to this castle, and here I have held her out of revenge because they pursued the white hart which belonged to my lady. For my lady loved that hart as she loved nothing else in the world, excepting myself."

"Sir," said Sir Gawaine, "this is a very strange matter. Now I beseech thee to tell me of what appearance was that lady who gave the white hart and the white hound unto those two ladies?" "Messire," said the knight, "she was clad all in crimson, and about her throat and arms were a great many ornaments of gold beset with stones of divers colors, and her hair was red like gold and was enmeshed in a net of gold, and her eyes were very black and shone with exceeding brightness, and her lips were like coral, so that she possessed a very strange appearance."

Sir Gawaine heareth of Vivien.

"Ha!" said Sir Gawaine, "from this description methinks that lady could have been none other than the sorceress Vivien. For now she spendeth all of her time in doing such mischief as this by means of her enchantment, out of pure despite. And, indeed, I think it would be a very good thing if she were put out of this world so that she could do no more such mischief. But tell me, Messire, where now is that lady, thy wife's sister?" "Sir," said the knight, "she is in this castle and is a prisoner of honor." "Well," quoth Sir

Gawaine, "since now both the hart and the hound are dead, ye can assuredly bear no more enmity toward her and your brother, wherefore I do beseech you that you will let her go free, and will enter again into a condition of amity and good-will the one with the other, in such a manner as hath afore obtained between you." And the lord of the castle said, "Sir, it shall be so."

And so he set the lady free at that time, and thereafter there was amity between them as Sir Gawaine had ordained.

And the next day Sir Gawaine and his brother, Gaheris, returned unto this Court of the King and he told King Arthur and his Court all that had befallen, hiding nothing from them.

Now, Queen Guinevere was very much displeased when she heard how Sir Gawaine would show no mercy to that knight and how he had struck the lady with his sword. Wherefore she said aside to one of those who stood nigh to her, "It seems to me to be a very strange thing for a belted knight to do, to refuse to give mercy unto a fallen enemy and to strike a lady with his sword; for I should think that any sword that had drawn blood from a lady in such wise would be dishonored for aye; and I cannot think that anyone who would strike a lady in that wise would hold himself guiltless unto his vow of knighthood."

Queen Guinevere is displeased with Sir Gawaine.

This Sir Gawaine overheard and he was exceedingly wroth thereat. But he concealed his anger at that time. Only after he had gone away he said to Gaheris, his brother, "I believe that lady hateth me with all her heart; but some time I will show to her that I have in me more courtesy and am more gentle than she believes me to be. As for my sword, since she deemeth it to be dishonored by that blow, I will not use it any more." So he took the sword out of its sheath and brake it across his knee and flung it away.

Sir Gawaine breaketh his sword.

Now all this hath been told to set forth that which follows; for there ye shall learn what great things of nobility Sir Gawaine could do when it behooved him to do them. For, haply, ye who have read this story may feel as Queen Guinevere did, that Sir Gawaine was not rightwise courteous as a belted knight should have been in that adventure aforetold.

ing Arthur findeth ye old woman in ye hut.

CHAPTER SECOND

How King Arthur Became Lost in the Forest, and How He Fell Into a Very Singular Adventure in a Castle Unto Which He Came.

NOW, IT BEFELL UPON A TIME SOME WHILE AFTER THIS, THAT KING Arthur was at Tintagalon upon certain affairs of state. And Queen Guinevere and her Court and the King's Court made progression from Camelot unto Carleon, and there they abided until the King should be through his business at Tintagalon and should join them at Carleon.

Now that time was the spring of the year, and all things were very jolly and gay, wherefore King Arthur became possessed with a great desire for adventure. So he called unto him a certain favorite esquire, hight Boisenard, and he said to him, "Boisenard, this day is so pleasant that I hardly know how I may contain myself because of the joy I take in it, for it seems to be that my heart is nigh ready to burst with a great pleasure of desiring. So I am of a mind to go a-gadding with only thee for companion."

To this Boisenard said, "Lord, I know of nothing that would give to me a greater pleasure than that."

So King Arthur said, "Very well, let us then go away from this place in such a manner that no one will be aware of our departure. And so we will go to Carleon and surprise the Queen by coming unexpectedly to that place."

So Boisenard brought armor, without device, and he clad the King in that armor; and then they two rode forth together, and no one wist that they had left the castle.

King Arthur sets forth with his esquire.

And when they came forth into the fields, King Arthur whistled and sang and jested and laughed and made himself merry; for he was as a war-horse turned forth upon the grass that taketh glory in the sunshine and the warm air and becometh like unto a colt again.

So by and by they came into the forest and rode that way with great content of spirit; and they took this path and they took that path for no reason but because the day was so gay and jolly. So, by and by, they lost their way in the mazes of the woodland and knew not where they were.

Now when they found themselves to be lost in that wise they journeyed with more circumspection, going first by this way and then by that, but in no manner could they find their way out from their entanglement. And so fell night-time and they knew not where they were; but all became very dark and obscure, with the woodland full of strange and unusual sounds around about them.

They are lost in the forest.

Then King Arthur said, "Boisenard, this is a very perplexing pass and I do not know how we shall find lodging for this night."

To this Boisenard said, "Lord, if I have thy permission to do so, I will climb one of these trees and see if I can discover any sign of habitation in this wilderness." And King Arthur said, "Do so, I pray thee."

Boisenard beholdeth a light.

So Boisenard climbed a very tall tree and from the top of the tree he beheld a light a great distance away, and he said, "Lord, I see a light in that direction." And therewith he came down from the tree again.

So King Arthur and Boisenard went in the direction that Boisenard had beheld the light, and by and by they came out of the forest and into an open place where they beheld a very great castle with several tall towers, very grim and forbidding of appearance. And it was from this castle that the light had appeared that Boisenard had seen. So they two rode up to the castle and Boisenard called aloud and smote upon the gate of the castle. Then immediately there came a porter and demanded of them what they would have. Unto him Boisenard said, "Sirrah, we would come in to lodge for to-night, for we are a-weary." So the porter said, "Who are you?"—speaking very roughly and rudely to them, for he could not see of what condition they were because of the darkness. Then Boisenard said, "This is a knight of very good quality and I am his esquire, and we have lost our way in the forest and now we come hither seeking shelter."

"Sir," said the porter, "if ye know what is good for you, ye will sleep in the forest rather than come into this place, for this is no very good retreat for errant knights to shelter themselves."

Upon this King Arthur bespake the porter, for that which the porter said aroused great curiosity within him. So he said, "Nay, we will not go away from here and we demand to lodge here for this night."

Then the porter said, "Very well; ye may come in." And thereupon he opened the gate and they rode into the court-yard of that castle.

Now at the noise of their coming, there appeared a great many lights within the castle, and there came running forth divers attendants. Some of these aided King Arthur and Boisenard to dismount, and others took the horses, and others again brought basins of water for them to wash withal. And after they had washed their faces and hands, other attendants brought them into the castle.

King Arthur and his esquire enter the castle.

Now as they came into the castle, they were aware of a great noise of very many people talking and laughing together, with the sound of singing and of harping. And so they came into the hall of the castle and beheld that it was lighted with a great number of candles and tapers and torches. Here they found a multitude of people gathered at a table spread for a feast, and at the head of the table there sat a knight, well advanced in years and with hair and beard white as milk. Yet he was exceedingly strong and sturdy of frame, having shoulders of wonderful broadness and a great girth of chest. This knight was of a very stern and forbidding appearance, and was clad altogether in black, and he wore around his neck a chain of gold, with a locket of gold hanging pendant from it.

Now when this knight beheld King Arthur and Boisenard come into the hall, he called aloud to them in a very great voice bidding them to come and sit with him at the head of the table; and they did so, and those at the head of the table made place for them, and thus they sat there beside the knight.

Now King Arthur and Boisenard were exceedingly hungry, wherefore they ate with great appetite and made joy of the entertainment which they received, and meantime the knight held them in very pleasant discourse, talking to them of such things as would give them the most entertainment. So after a while the feast was ended and they ceased from eating.

Then, of a sudden, the knight said to King Arthur, "Messire, thou art young and lusty of spirit and I doubt not but thou hath a great heart within thee. What say you now to a little sport betwixt us two?" Upon this King Arthur regarded that knight very steadily and he believed that his face was not so old as it looked; for his eyes were exceedingly bright and shone like sparks of light; wherefore he was a-doubt and he said, "Sir, what sport would you have?" Upon this the knight fell a-laughing in great measure and he said, "This is a very strange sport that I have in mind, for it is this: That thou and I shall prove the one unto the other what courage each of us may have." And King Arthur said, "How shall we prove that?" Whereunto the knight made reply, "This is what we shall do: Thou and I shall stand forth in the

The knight of the castle challenges King Arthur to an adventure.

middle of this hall, and thou shalt have leave to try to strike off my head; and if I can receive that blow without dying therefrom, then I shall have leave to strike thy head off in a like manner."

Upon his speech King Arthur was greatly a-dread and he said, "That is very strange sport for two men to engage upon."

Now when King Arthur said this, all those who were in the hall burst out laughing beyond all measure and as though they would never stint from their mirth. Then, when they had become in a measure quiet again, the knight of that castle said, "Sir, art thou afraid of that sport?" Upon which King Arthur fell very angry and he said, "Nay, I am not afeared, for no man hath ever yet had reason to say that I showed myself afeared of anyone." "Very well," said the knight of the castle; "then let us try that sport of which I spake." And King Arthur said, "I am willing."

Then Boisenard came to King Arthur where he was, and he said, "Lord, do not thou enter into this thing, but rather let me undertake this venture in thy stead, for I am assured that some great treachery is meditated against thee." But King Arthur said, "Nay; no man shall take my danger upon himself, but I will assume mine own danger without calling upon any man to take it." So he said to the knight of the castle, "Sir, I am ready for that sport of which thou didst speak, but who is to strike that first blow and how shall we draw lots therefor?" "Messire," said the knight of the castle, "there shall be no lots drawn. For, as thou art the guest of this place, so shall thou have first assay at that sport."

King Arthur cuts off the head of the knight of the castle.

Therewith that knight arose and laid aside his black robe, and he was clad beneath in a shirt of fine linen very cunningly worked. And he wore hosen of crimson. Then he opened that linen undergarment at the throat and he turned down the collar thereof so as to lay his neck bare to the blow. Thereupon he said, "Now, Sir Knight, thou shalt have to strike well if thou wouldst win at this sport."

But King Arthur showed no dread of that undertaking, for he arose and drew Excalibur so that the blade of the sword flashed with exceeding brightness. Then he measured his distance, and lifted the sword, and he smote the knight of the castle with all his might upon the neck. And, lo! the blade cut through the neck of the knight of the castle with wonderful ease, so that the head flew from the body to a great distance away.

But the trunk of the body of that knight did not fall, but instead of that it stood, and it walked to where the head lay, and the hands of the trunk picked up the head and they set the head back upon the body, and, lo! that knight was as sound and whole as ever he had been in all his life.

Upon this all those of the castle shouted and made great mirth, and they called upon King Arthur that it was now his turn to try that sport. So the King prepared himself, laying aside his surcoat and opening his undergarment at the throat, as the knight of the castle had done. And at that Boisenard made great lamentation. Then the knight of the castle said, "Sir, art thou afeared?" And King Arthur said, "No, I am not afeared, for every man must come to his death some time, and it appears that my time hath now come, and that I am to lay down my life in this foolish fashion for no fault of mine own."

Then the knight of the castle said, "Well, stand thou away a little distance so that I may not strike thee too close, and so lose the virtue of my blow."

The knight torments King Arthur.

So King Arthur stood forth in the midst of the hall, and the knight of the castle swung his sword several times, but did not strike. Likewise, he several times laid the blade of the sword upon King Arthur's neck, and it was very cold. Then King Arthur cried out in great passion, "Sir, it is thy right to strike, but I beseech thee not to torment me in this manner." "Nay," said the knight of the castle, "it is my right to strike when it pleases me, and I will not strike any before that time. For if it please me I will torment thee for a great while ere I slay thee." So he laid his sword several times more upon King Arthur's neck, and King Arthur said no more, but bore that torment with a very steadfast spirit.

Then the knight of the castle said, "Thou appearest to be a very courageous and honorable knight, and I have a mind to make a covenant with thee." And King Arthur said, "What is that covenant?" "It is this," said the knight of the castle, "I will spare thee thy life for a year and a day if thou wilt pledge me thy knightly word to return hither at the end of that time."

Then King Arthur said, "Very well; it shall be so." And therewith he pledged his knightly word to return at the end of that time, swearing to that pledge upon the cross of the hilt of Excalibur.

The knight of the castle sets King Arthur a riddle.

Then the knight of the castle said, "I will make another covenant with thee." "What is it?" said King Arthur. "My second covenant is this," quoth the knight of the castle, "I will give to thee a riddle, and if thou wilt answer that riddle when thou returnest hither, and if thou makest no mistake in that answer, then will I spare thy life and set thee free." And King Arthur said, "What is that riddle?" To which the knight made reply, "The riddle is this: What is it that a woman desires most of all in the world?"

"Sir," said King Arthur, "I will seek to find the answer to that riddle, and I give thee gramercy for sparing my life for so long a time as thou hast done, and for giving me the chance to escape my death." Upon this the knight of the castle smiled very sourly, and he said, "I do not offer this to thee because of mercy to thee, but because I find pleasure in tormenting thee. For what delight canst thou have in living thy life when thou knowest that thou must, for a surety, die at the end of one short year? And what pleasure canst thou have in living even that year when thou shalt be tormented with anxiety to discover the answer to my riddle?"

Then King Arthur said, "I think thou art very cruel." And the knight said, "I am not denying that."

So that night King Arthur and Boisenard lay at the castle, and the next day they took their way thence. And King Arthur was very heavy and troubled in spirit; ne'theless he charged Boisenard that he should say nothing concerning that which had befallen, but that he should keep it in secret. And Boisenard did as the King commanded, and said nothing concerning that adventure.

Now in that year which followed, King Arthur settled his affairs. Also he sought everywhere to find the answer to that riddle. Many there were who gave him answers in plenty, for one said that a woman most desired wealth, and another said she most desired beauty, and one said she desired power to please, and another said that she most desired fine raiment; and one said this, and another said that; but no answer appeared to King Arthur to be good and fitting for his purpose.

So the year passed by, until only a fortnight remained; and then King Arthur could not abide to stay where he was any longer, for it seemed to him his time was very near to hand, and he was filled with a very bitter anxiety of soul, wherefore he was very restless to be away.

So he called Boisenard to him, and he said, "Boisenard, help me to arm, for I am going away."

Then Boisenard fell a-weeping in very great measure, and he said, "Lord, do not go."

At this King Arthur looked very sternly at his esquire, and said, "Boisenard, how is this? Wouldst thou tempt me to violate mine honor? It is not very hard to die, but it would be very bitter to live my life in dishonor; wherefore tempt me no more, but do my bidding and hold thy peace. And if I do not return in a month from this time, then mayst thou tell all that hath befallen. And thou mayst tell Sir Constantine of Cornwall that he is to search the papers in my cabinet, and that there he will find all that is to be done should death overtake me."

So Boisenard put a plain suit of armor upon King Arthur, though he could hardly see what he was about for the tears that flowed down out of his eyes in great abundance. And he laced upon the armor of the King a surcoat without device, and he gave the King a shield without device. Thereupon King Arthur rode away without considering whither his way took him. And of everyone whom he met he inquired what that thing was that a woman most desired, and no one could give him an answer that appeared to him to be what it should be, wherefore he was in great doubt and torment of spirit.

King Arthur set forth to return to the castle of the evil knight.

Now the day before King Arthur was to keep his covenant at that castle, he was wandering through the adjacent forest in great travail of soul, for he wist not what he should do to save his life. As he wandered so, he came of a sudden upon a small hut built up under an overhanging oak-tree so that it was very hard to tell where the oak-tree ended and the hut began. And there were a great many large rocks all about covered with moss, so that the King might very easily have passed by the hut only that he beheld a smoke to arise therefrom as from a fire that burned within. So he went to the hut and opened the door and entered. At first he thought there was no one there, but when he looked again he beheld an old woman sitting bent over a small fire that burned upon the hearth. And King Arthur had never beheld such an ugly beldame as that one who sat there bending over that fire, for her ears were very huge and flapped, and her hair hung down over her head like to snakes, and her face was covered all over with wrinkles so that there were not any places at all where there was not a wrinkle; and her eyes were bleared and covered over with a film, and the eyelids were red as with the continual weeping of her eyes and she had but one tooth in her mouth, and her hands, which she spread out to the fire, were like claws of bone.

King Arthur cometh to the hut of an old woman.

Then King Arthur gave her greeting and she gave the King greeting, and she said to him, "My lord King, whence come ye? and why do ye come to this place?"

Then King Arthur was greatly astonished that that old woman should know him, who he was, and he said, "Who are you that appeareth to know me?" "No matter," said she, "I am one who meaneth you well; so tell me what is the trouble that brings you here at this time." So the King confessed all his trouble to that old woman, and he asked her if she knew the answer to that riddle, "What is it that a woman most desires?" "Yea," said the old woman, "I know the answer to that riddle very well, but I will not tell it to thee unless thou wilt promise me something in return."

At this King Arthur was filled with very great joy that the old woman should know the answer to that riddle, and he was filled with doubt of what she would demand of him, wherefore he said, "What is it thou must have in return for that answer?"

Then the old woman said, "If I aid thee to guess thy riddle aright, thou must promise that I shall become wife unto one of the knights of thy Court, whom I may choose when thou returnest homeward again."

"Ha!" said King Arthur, "how may I promise that upon the behalf of anyone?" Upon this the old woman said, "Are not the knights of thy Court of such nobility that they will do that to save thee from death?" "I believe they are," said King Arthur. And with that he meditated a long while, saying unto himself, "What will my kingdom do if I die at this time? I have no right to die." So he said to the old woman, "Very well, I will make that promise."

Then she said unto the King, "This is the answer to that riddle: That which a woman most desires is to have her will." And the answer seemed to King Arthur to be altogether right.

The old woman telleth King Arthur to answer the riddle.

Then the old woman said, "My lord King, thou hast been played upon by that knight who hath led thee into this trouble, for he is a great conjurer and a magician of a very evil sort. He carrieth his life not within his body, but in a crystal globe which he weareth in a locket hanging about his neck; wherefore it was that when thou didst cut the head from off his body, his life remained in that locket and he did not die. But if thou hadst destroyed that locket, then he would immediately have died."

"I will mind me of that," said King Arthur.

So King Arthur abided with that old woman for that night, and she refreshed him with meat and drink and served him very well. And the next morning he set forth unto that castle where he had made his covenant, and his heart was more cheerful than it had been for a whole year.

JVSTISSIMVS·REX·

Sir Gawaine finds the beautiful Lady.

CHAPTER THIRD

How King Arthur Overcame the Knight-Enchanter, and How Sir Gawaine Manifested the Nigh Nobility of His Knighthood.

NOW, WHEN KING ARTHUR CAME TO THE CASTLE, THE GATEWAY THEREOF was immediately opened to him and he entered. And when he had entered, sundry attendants came and conducted him into the hall where he had aforetime been. There he beheld the knight of that castle and a great many people who had come to witness the conclusion of the adventure. And when the knight beheld King Arthur he said to him, "Sir, hast thou come to redeem thy pledge?" "Yea," said King Arthur, "for so I made my vow to thee." Then the knight of the castle said, "Sir, hast thou guessed that riddle?" And King Arthur said, "I believe that I have." The knight of the castle said, "Then let me hear thy answer thereto. But if thou makest any mistake, or if thou dost not guess aright, then is thy life forfeit." "Very well," said King Arthur, "let it be that way. Now this is the answer to thy riddle: That which a woman most desires is to have her will."

King Arthur returneth to the castle of the evil knight.

Now when the lord of the castle heard King Arthur guess aright he wist not what to say or where to look, and those who were there also perceived that the King had guessed aright.

Then King Arthur came very close to that knight with great sternness of demeanor, and he said, "Now, thou traitor knight! thou didst ask me to enter into thy sport with thee a year ago, so at these present it is my turn to ask thee to have sport with me. And this is the sport I will have, that thou shalt give me that chain and locket that hang about thy neck, and that I shall give thee the collar which hangeth about my neck."

At this, the face of that knight fell all pale, like to ashes, and he emitted a sound similar to the sound made by a hare when the hound lays hold upon it. Then King Arthur catched him very violently by the arm, and he catched the locket and brake it away from about the knight's neck, and upon that the knight shrieked very loud,

King Arthur slayeth the knight of the castle.

and fell down upon his knees and besought mercy of the King, and there was great uproar in that place. Then King Arthur opened the locket and lo! there was a ball as of crystal, very clear and shining. And King Arthur said, "I will have no mercy," and therewith he flung the ball violently down upon the stone of the pavement so that it brake with a loud noise. Then, upon that instant, the knight-conjurer gave a piercing bitter cry, and fell down upon the ground; and when they ran to raise him up, behold! he was entirely dead.

Now when the people of that castle beheld their knight thus suddenly dead, and when they beheld King Arthur how he stood in the fury of his kingly majesty, they were greatly afeared so that they shrunk away from the King where he stood. Then the King turned and went out from that castle and no one stayed him, and he mounted his horse and rode away, and no one gave him let or hindrance in his going.

Now when the King had left the castle in that wise, he went straight to the hut where was the old beldame and he said to her, "Thou hast holpen me a very great deal in mine hour of need, so now will I fulfil that pledge which I made unto thee, for I will take thee unto my Court and thou shalt choose one of my knights for thy husband. For I think there is not one knight in all my Court but would be very glad to do anything that lieth in his power to reward one who hath saved me as thou hast done this day."

Therewith he took that old woman and he lifted her up upon the crupper of his horse; then he himself mounted upon his horse, and so they rode away from that place. And the King comported himself to that aged beldame in all ways with the utmost consideration as though she had been a beautiful dame of the highest degree in the land. Likewise he showed her such respect that had she been a lady of royal blood, he could not have shown greater respect to her.

King Arthur taketh the old woman away with him.

So in due time they reached the Court, which was then at Carleon. And they came there nigh about mid-day.

Now about that time it chanced that the Queen and a number of the lords of the Court, and a number of the ladies of the Court, were out in the fields enjoying the pleasantness of the Maytime; for no one in all the world, excepting the esquire, Boisenard, knew anything of the danger that beset King Arthur; hence all were very glad of the pleasantness of the season. Now as King Arthur drew nigh to that place, these lifted up their eyes and beheld him come, and they were astonished beyond all measure to see King Arthur come to them across that field with that old beldame behind him upon the saddle, wherefore they stood still to wait until King Arthur reached them.

But when King Arthur had come to them, he did not dismount from his horse, but sat thereon and regarded them all very steadfastly; and Queen Guinevere said, "Sir, what is this? Hast thou a mind to play some merry jest this day that thou hast brought hither that old woman?"

"Lady," said King Arthur, "excepting for this old woman it were like to have been a very sorry jest for thee and for me; for had she not aided me I would now have been a dead man and in a few days you would doubtless all have been in great passion of sorrow."

Then all they who were there marvelled very greatly at the King's words. And the Queen said, "Sir, what is it that hath befallen thee?"

Thereupon King Arthur told them all that had happened to him from the very beginning when he and Boisenard had left the castle of Tintagalon. And when he had ended his story, they were greatly amazed.

Now there were seventeen lords of the Court there present. So when King Arthur had ended his story, he said unto these, "Messires, I have given my pledge unto this aged woman that any one of you whom she may choose, shall take her unto him as his wife, and shall treat her with all the regard that it is possible for him to do; for this was the condition that she laid upon me. Now tell me, did I do right in making unto her my pledge that I would fulfill that which she desired?" And all of those who were present said, "Yea, lord, thou didst right, for we would do all in the world for to save thee from such peril as that from which thou hast escaped."

Then King Arthur said to that old woman, "Lady, is there any of these knights here whom you would choose for to be your husband?" Upon this, the old woman pointed with her very long, bony finger unto Sir Gawaine, saying, "Yea, I would marry that lord, for I see by the chain that is around his neck and by the golden circlet upon his hair and by the haughty nobility of his aspect, that he must be the son of a king."

The old woman chooseth Sir Gawaine.

Then King Arthur said unto Sir Gawaine, "Sir, art thou willing to fulfil my pledge unto this old woman?" And Sir Gawaine said, "Yea, lord, whatsoever thou requirest of me, that will I do." So Sir Gawaine came to the old woman and took her hand into his and set it to his lips; and not one of all those present so much as smiled. Then they all turned their faces and returned unto the King's castle; and they were very silent and downcast, for this was sore trouble that had come upon that Court.

Sir Gawaine taketh the old woman to wife.

Now after they had returned unto the Court, they assigned certain apartments therein to that old woman, and they clad her in rich raiment such as a queen might wear, and they assigned unto her a Court such as was fit for a queen; and it seemed to all the Court that, in the rich robes which she wore, she was ten times more ugly than she was before. So when eleven days had passed, Sir Gawaine was wedded to that old woman in the chapel of the King's Court with great ceremony and pomp of circumstance, and all of those who were there were as sad and as sorrowful as though Sir Gawaine had been called upon to suffer his death.

Afterward that they were married, Sir Gawaine and the old woman went to Sir Gawaine's house and there Sir Gawaine shut himself off from all the world and suffered no one to come nigh him; for he was proud beyond all measure, and in this great humiliation he suffered in such a wise that words cannot tell how great was that humiliation. Wherefore he shut himself away from the world that no one might behold his grief and his shame.

And all the rest of that day he walked continually up and down his chamber, for he was altogether in such despair that it came unto his mind that it would be well if he took his own life; for it seemed to him impossible for to suffer such shame as that which had come upon him. So after a while it fell the dark of the early night and therewith a certain strength came to Sir Gawaine and he said, "This is a shame for me for to behave in this way; for since I have married that lady she is my true wedded wife and I do not treat her with that regard unto which she hath the right." So he went out of that place and sought the apartment of that old woman who was his wife, and by that time it was altogether dark. But when Sir Gawaine had come into that place where she was, that old woman upbraided him, crying out upon him, "So, Sir! You have treated me but ill upon this our wedding-day, for you have stayed all the afternoon away from me and now only come to me when it is dark night." And Sir Gawaine said, "Lady, I could not help it, for I was very sore oppressed with many cares. But if I have disregarded thee this day, I do beseech thy forgiveness therefore, and I will hold myself willing to do all that is in my power to recompense thee for any neglect that I have placed upon thee." Then the lady said, "Sir, it is very dark in this place; let us then have a light." "It shall be as thou dost desire," said Sir Gawaine, "and I, myself, will go and fetch a light for thee."

Sir Gawaine is in great sorrow.

So Sir Gawaine went forth from that place and he brought two waxen tapers, one in either hand, and he bore them in candlesticks of gold; for he was minded to show all respect unto that old woman. And when he came into the room he perceived that she was at the farther end of the apartment and he went toward her, and she arose and stood before him as he approached.

Of the beautiful lady who appeareth to Sir Gawaine.

But when the circle of light fell upon that old woman, and when Sir Gawaine beheld her who stood before him, he cried out aloud in a very great voice because of the great marvel and wonder of that which he saw. For, instead of that old woman whom he had left, he beheld a lady of extraordinary beauty and in the very flower of her youth. And he beheld that her hair was long and glossy and very black, and that her eyes were likewise black like to black jewels, and that her lips were like coral, and her teeth were like pearls. So, for a while, Sir Gawaine could not speak, and then he cried out, "Lady! lady! who art thou?"

Then that lady smiled upon Sir Gawaine with such loving-kindness that he wist not what to think, other than that this was an angel who had descended to that place out of paradise. Wherefore he stood before her for a long time and could find no more words to say, and she continued to smile upon him very kindly in that wise. Then by and by Sir Gawaine said to her, "Lady, where is that dame who is my wife?" And the lady said, "Sir Gawaine, I am she." "It is not possible," cried out Sir Gawaine, "for she was old and extraordinarily ugly, but I believe that thou art beautiful beyond any lady whom I have beheld." And the lady said, "Nevertheless, I am she and because thou hast taken me for thy wife with thine own free will and with great courtesy, so is a part of that enchantment that lay upon me removed from me. For I will now be able to appear before thee in mine own true shape. For whiles I was a little while ago so ugly and foul as thou didst behold me to be, now am I to be as thou seest me, for one-half the day—and the other half thereof I must be ugly as I was before."

Then Sir Gawaine was filled beyond all words with great joy. And with that joy there came an extreme passion of loving regard for that lady. So he cried out aloud several times, "This is surely the most wonderful thing that ever befell any man in all the world." Therewith he fell down upon his knees and took that lady's hands into his own hands, and kissed her hands with great fervor, and all the while she smiled upon him as she had done at first.

Then again the lady said, "Come, sit thee down beside me and let us consider what part of the day I shall be in the one guise, and what part of the day I shall be in the other guise; for all day I may have the one appearance, and all night I may have the other appearance."

Then Sir Gawaine said, "I would have thee in this guise during the night time, for then we are together at our own inn; and since thou art of this sort that I now see thee, I do not at all reckon how the world may regard thee."

Upon this the lady spake with great animation, saying, "No, sir, I would not have it that wise, for every woman loveth the regard of the world, and I would fain enjoy such beauty as is mine before the world, and not endure the scorn and contempt of men and women."

To this Sir Gawaine said, "Lady, I would have it the other way."

And she said, "Nay, I would have it my way."

Sir Gawaine giveth the lady her will.

Then Sir Gawaine said, "So be it. For since I have taken thee for my wife, so must I show thee respect in all matters; wherefore thou shalt have thy will in this and in all other things."

Then that lady fell a-laughing beyond all measure and she said, "Sir, I did but put this as a last trial upon thee, for as I am now, so shall I always be."

Upon this Sir Gawaine was so filled with joy that he knew not how to contain himself.

So they sat together for a long time, hand in hand. Then after a while Sir Gawaine said, "Lady, who art thou?" Unto which she made reply, "I am one of the Ladies of the Lake; but for thy sake I have become mortal like to other women and have quit that very beautiful home where I one time dwelt. I have kept thee in my heart for a considerable while, for I was not very far distant at that time when thou didst bid adieu to Sir Pellias beside the lake. There I beheld how thou didst weep and bewail thyself when Sir Pellias left thee, wherefore my heart went out to thee with great pity. So, after a while, I quitted that lake and became mortal for thy sake. Now, when I found the trouble into which King Arthur had fallen I took that occasion to have him fetch me unto thee so that I might test the entire nobility of thy knighthood; and, lo! I have found it all that I deemed it possible to be. For though I appeared to thee so aged, so ugly, and so foul, yet hast thou treated me with such kind regard that I do not believe that thou couldst have behaved with more courtesy to me had I been the daughter of a king. Wherefore it doth now afford me such pleasure for to possess thee for my knight and my true lord, that I cannot very well tell thee how great is my joy therein."

Then Sir Gawaine said, "Lady, I do not think it can be so great as my joy in possessing thee." And thereupon he came to her and laid his hand upon her shoulder and kissed her upon the lips.

Then, after that, he went forth and called with a great voice all through that house, and the people of the house came running from everywhere. And he commanded that the people should bring lights and refreshments, and they brought the lights, and when they had brought them and beheld that beautiful lady instead of the aged dame, they were filled with great wonder and joy; wherefore they cried out aloud and clapped their hands together and made such sound of rejoicing. And they set a great feast for Sir Gawaine and his lady, and in place of the sorrow and darkness that had been, there was joy and light, and music and singing; wherefore those of the King's Court, beholding this from a distance, said, "It is very strange that Sir Gawaine should have taken so much joy of having wedded that old beldame."

Sir Gawaine lets make great rejoicing.

But when the next morning had come, that lady clad herself in raiment of yellow silk, and she hung about her many strands of precious stones of several colors, and she set a golden crown upon her head. And Sir Gawaine let call his horse, and he let call a snow-white palfrey for the lady, and thereupon they rode out from that place and entered the Court of the King. But when the King and the Queen and their several Courts beheld that lady, they were filled with such great astonishment that they wist not what to say for pure wonder. And when they heard all that had happened, they gave great joy and loud acclaim so that all their mourning was changed into rejoicing. And, indeed, there was not one knight there of all that Court who would not have given half his life to have been so fortunate in that matter as was Sir Gawaine, the son of King Lot of Orkney.

Such is the story of Sir Gawaine, and from it I draw this significance: as that poor ugly beldame appeared unto the eyes of Sir Gawaine, so doth a man's duty sometimes appear to him to be ugly and exceedingly ill-favored unto his desires. But when he shall have wedded himself unto that duty so that he hath made it one with him as a bridegroom maketh himself one with his bride, then doth that duty become of a sudden very beautiful unto him and unto others.

So may it be with ye that you shall take duty unto yourselves no matter how much it may mislike ye to do so. For indeed a man shall hardly have any real pleasure in his life unless his inclination becometh wedded unto his duty and cleaveth unto it as a husband cleaveth unto his wife. For when inclination is thus wedded unto duty, then doth the soul take great joy unto itself as though a wedding had taken place betwixt a bridegroom and a bride within its tabernacle.

Likewise, when you shall have become entirely wedded unto your duty, then shall you become equally worthy with that good knight and gentleman Sir Gawaine; for it needs not that a man shall wear armor for to be a true knight, but only that he shall do his best endeavor with all patience and humility as it hath been ordained for him to do. Wherefore, when your time cometh unto you to display your knightness by assuming your duty, I do pray that you also may approve yourself as worthy as Sir Gawaine approved himself in this story which I have told you of as above written.

Conclusion

So endeth this volume wherein hath been told, with every circumstance of narration, the history of those Three Worthies who were of the Court of King Arthur.

And now, if God will give me the grace to do so, I will some time, at no very great time from this, write the further history of sundry other knights and worthies of whom I have not yet spoken.

And among the first of these shall be Sir Launcelot, whom all the world knoweth to have been the greatest knight in prowess of arms of any who has lived, excepting Sir Galahad, who was his son. And I shall tell you the story of Sir Ewaine and Sir Geraint, and of Sir Percival and of sundry others.

But of this another time. For now, with great regret I bid you adieu and bring this history unto a close.

So may God grant us to come together at another time with such happiness and prosperity that you may have a free and untroubled heart to enjoy the narrated history of those excellent men which I shall then set before you. Amen.

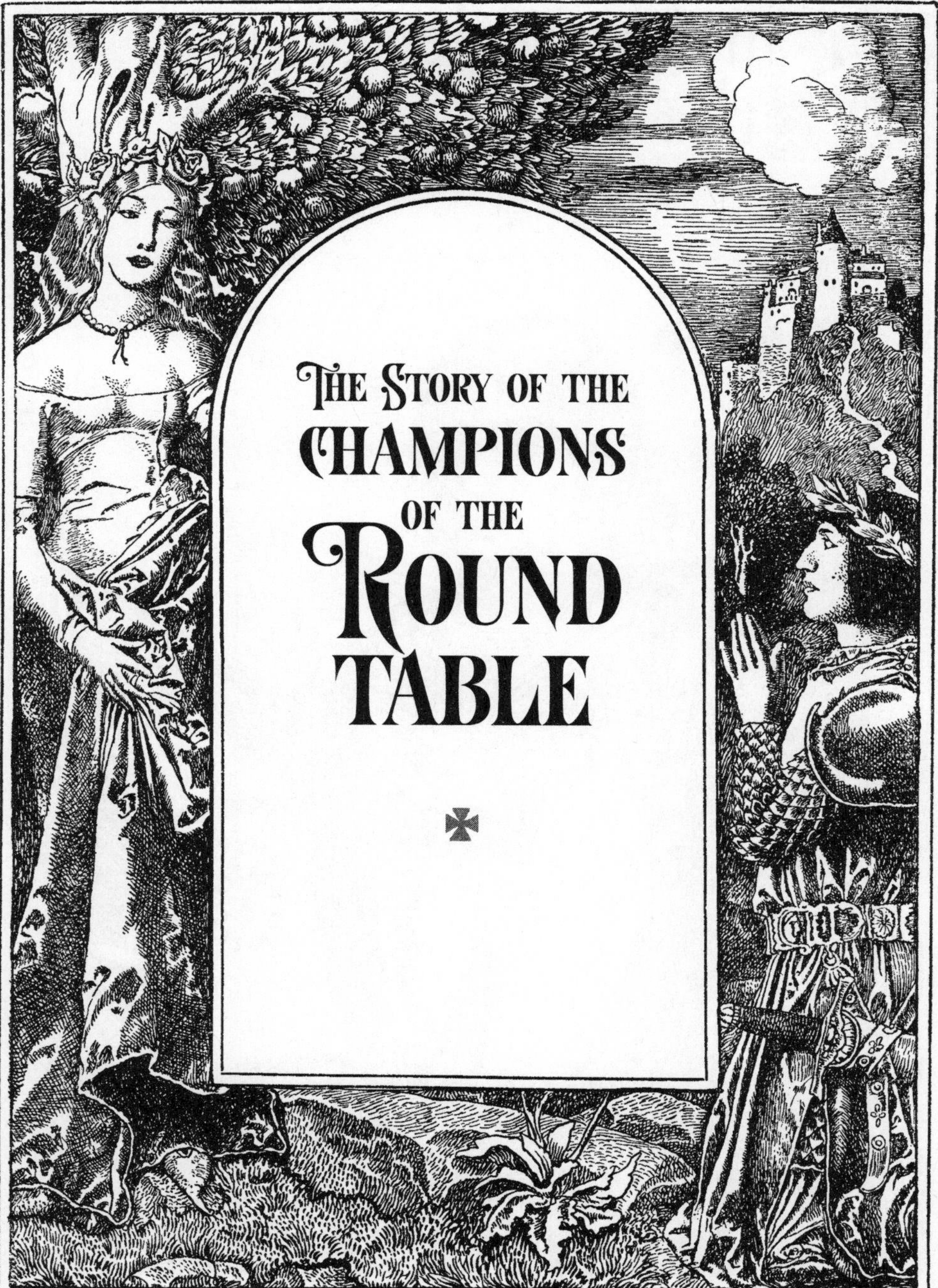
THE STORY OF THE
CHAMPIONS
OF THE
ROUND
TABLE

Sir Launcelot of the Lake.

Foreword

In a book which was written by me aforetime, and which was set forth in print, I therein told much of the history of King Arthur; of how he manifested his royalty in the achievement of that wonderful magic sword which he drew forth out of the anvil; of how he established his royalty; of how he found a splendid sword yclept Excalibur in a miraculously wonderful manner; of how he won the most beautiful lady in the world for his queen; and of how he established the famous Round Table of noble worthy knights, the like of whose prowess the world hath never seen, and will not be likely ever to behold again.

Also I told in that book the adventures of certain worthy knights and likewise how the magician Merlin was betrayed to his undoing by a sorceress hight Vivien.

Now, if you took any joy in reading that book, I have great hope that that which follows may be every whit as pleasing to you; for I shall hereinafter have to do with the adventures of certain other worthies with whom you may have already become acquainted through my book and otherwise; and likewise of the adventures of certain other worthies, of whom you have not yet been told by me.

More especially, I believe, you will find entertainment in what I shall have to tell you of the adventures of that great knight who was altogether the most noble of spirit, and the most beautiful, and the bravest of heart, of any knight who ever lived—excepting only his own son, Galahad, who was the crowning glory of his house and of his name and of the reign of King Arthur.

However, if Sir Launcelot of the Lake failed now and then in his behavior, who is there in the world shall say, "I never fell into error"? And if he more than once offended, who is there shall have hardihood to say, "I never committed offence"?

Yea, that which maketh Launcelot so singularly dear to all the world, is that he was not different from other men, but like other men, both in his virtues and his shortcomings; only that he was more strong and more brave and more untiring than those of us who are his brethren, both in our endeavors and in our failures.

Contents

✠ ✠ ✠

The Story of Launcelot

The Book of Sir Tristram

PART I

The Book of Sir Percival

✠ List of Illustrations ✠

The Lady Nymue beareth away Launcelot into the Lake.

Prologue

IT HATH ALREADY BEEN SET FORTH IN PRINT IN A VOLUME WRITTEN BY ME concerning the adventures of King Arthur when he first became king, how there were certain lesser kings who favored him and were friendly allies with him, and how there were certain others of the same sort who were his enemies.

Among those who were his friends was King Ban of Benwick, who was an exceedingly noble lord of high estate and great honor, and who was of a lineage so exalted that it is not likely that there was anyone in the world who was of a higher strain.

Of King Ban and his misfortunes.

Now, upon a certain time, King Ban of Benwick fell into great trouble; for there came against him a very powerful enemy, to wit, King Claudas of Scotland. King Claudas brought unto Benwick a huge army of knights and lords, and these sat down before the Castle of Trible with intent to take that strong fortress and destroy it.

This noble Castle of Trible was the chiefest and the strongest place of defence in all King Ban's dominions, wherefore he had intrenched himself there with all of his knights and with his Queen, hight Helen, and his youngest son, hight Launcelot.

Now this child, Launcelot, was dearer to Queen Helen than all the world besides, for he was not only large of limb but so extraordinarily beautiful of face that I do not believe an angel from Paradise could have been more beautiful than he. He had been born with a singular birth-mark upon his shoulder, which birth-mark had the appearance as of a golden star enstamped upon the skin; wherefore, because of this, the Queen would say: "Launcelot, by reason of that star upon thy shoulder I believe that thou shalt be the star of our house and that thou shalt shine with such remarkable glory that all the world shall behold thy lustre and shall marvel thereat for all time to come." So the Queen took extraordinary delight in Launcelot and loved him to the very core of her heart—albeit she knew not, at the time she spake, how that prophecy of hers concerning the star was to fall so perfectly true.

Now, though King Ban thought himself very well defended at his Castle of Trible, yet King Claudas brought so terribly big an army against that place that it covered the entire plain. A great many battles were fought under the walls of the castle, but ever King Claudas waxed greater and stronger, and King Ban's party grew weaker and more fearful.

So by and by things came to such a pass that King Ban bethought him of King Arthur, and he said to himself: "I will go to my lord the King and beseech help and aid from him, for he will certainly give it me. Nor will I trust any messenger in this affair other than myself; for I myself will go to King Arthur and will speak to him with my own lips."

King Ban bethinks him of King Arthur.

Having thus bethought him, he sent for Queen Helen to come into his privy closet and he said to her: "My dear love, nothing remaineth for me but to go unto the court of King Arthur and beseech him to lend his powerful aid in this extremity of our misfortunes; nor will I trust any messenger in this affair but myself. Now, this castle is no place for thee, when I am away, therefore, when I go upon this business, I will take thee and Launcelot with me, and I will leave you both in safety at King Arthur's court with our other son, Sir Ector, until this war be ended and done." And to these Queen Helen lent her assent.

So King Ban summoned to him the seneschal of the castle, who was named Sir Malydor le Brun, and said to him: "Messire, I go hence to-night by a secret pass, with intent to betake me unto King Arthur, and to beseech his aid in this extremity. Moreover, I shall take with me my lady and the young child Launcelot, to place them within the care of King Arthur during these dolorous wars. But besides these, I will take no other one with me but only my favorite esquire, Foliot. Now I charge thee, sir, to hold this castle in my behalf with all thy might and main, and yield it not to our enemies upon any extremity; for I believe I shall in a little while return with sufficient aid from King Arthur to compass the relief of this place."

So when night had fallen very dark and still, King Ban, and Queen Helen, and the young child Launcelot, and the esquire Foliot left the town privily by means of a postern gate. Thence they went by a secret path, known only to a very few, that led down a steep declivity of rocks, with walls of rock upon either side that were very high indeed, and so they came out in safety beyond the army of King Claudas and into the forest of the valley below. And the forest lay very still and solemn and dark in the silence of the nighttime.

King Ban with Queen Helen and Launcelot escape from Trible.

Having thus come out in safety into the forest, that small party journeyed on with all celerity that they were able to achieve until, some little time before dawn, they came to where was a lake of water in an open meadow of the forest. Here they rested for a little while, for Queen Helen had fallen very weary with the rough and hasty journey which they had travelled.

Now whilst they sat there resting, Foliot spake of a sudden, saying unto King Ban: "Lord, what is that light that maketh the sky so bright yonder-ways?" Then King Ban looked a little and presently said: "Methinks it must be the dawn that is breaking." "Lord," quoth Foliot, "that cannot very well be; for that light in the sky lieth in the south, whence we have come, and not in the east, where the sun should arise."

Foliot seeth a light.

Then King Ban's heart misgave him, and his soul was shaken with a great trouble. "Foliot," he said, "I believe that you speak sooth and that that light bodes very ill for us all." Then he said: "Stay here for a little and I will go and discover what that light may be." Therewith he mounted his horse and rode away in the darkness.

Now there was a very high hill near-by where they were, and upon the top of the hill was an open platform of rock whence a man could see a great way off in every direction. So King Ban went to this place, and, when he had come there, he cast his eyes in the direction of the light and he straightway beheld with a manner of terror that the light came from Trible; and then, with that terror still growing greater at his heart, he beheld that the town and the castle were all in one great flame of fire.

King Ban beholdeth the burning of Trible.

When King Ban saw this he sat for a while upon his horse like one turned into a stone. Then, after a while, he cried out in a great voice: "Woe! Woe! Woe is me!" And then he cried out still in a very loud voice, "Certes, God hath deserted me entirely."

Therewith a great passion of grief took hold upon him and shook him like to a leaf, and immediately after that he felt that something brake within him with a very sharp and bitter pain, and he wist that it was his heart that had broken. So being all alone there upon the hilltop, and in the perfect stillness of the night, he cried out, "My heart! My heart!" And therewith, the shadows of death coming upon him, he could not sit any longer upon his horse, but fell down upon the ground. And he knew very well that death was nigh him, so, having no cross to pray upon, he took two blades of grass and twisted them into that holy sign, and he kissed it and prayed unto it that God would forgive him his sins. So he died all alone upon that hilltop.

The death of King Ban.

Meanwhile, Queen Helen and Foliot sat together waiting for him to return and presently they heard the sound of his horse's hoofs coming down that rocky path. Then Queen Helen said: "Foliot, methinks my lord cometh." So in a little came the horse with the empty saddle. When Foliot beheld that he said: "Lady, here meseems is great trouble come to us, for methinks something hath befallen my lord, and that he is in sore travail, for here is his horse without him."

Then it seemed to Queen Helen as though the spirit of life suddenly went away from her, for she foresaw what had befallen. So she arose like one in a dream, and, speaking very quietly, she said: "Foliot, take me whither my lord went awhile since!" To this Foliot said: "Lady, wait until the morning, which is near at hand, for it is too dark for you to go thitherward at this present." Whereunto the Lady Helen replied: "Foliot, I cannot wait, for if I stay here and wait I believe I shall go mad." Upon this, Foliot did not try to persuade her any more but made ready to take her whither she would go.

Now the young child Launcelot was then asleep upon the Queen's knees, wherefore she took her cloak and wrapped the child in it and laid him very gently upon the ground, so that he did not wake. Then she mounted upon her palfrey and Foliot led the palfrey up the hill whither King Ban had gone a short time since.

When they came to that place of open rocks above told of, they found King Ban lying very quiet and still upon the ground and with a countenance of great peace. For I believe of a surety that God had forgiven him all his sins, and he would now suffer no more because of the cares and the troubles of this life. Thus Queen Helen found him, and finding him she made no moan or outcry of any kind, only she looked for a long while into his dead face, which she could see very plainly now, because that the dawn had already broken. And by and by she said: "Dear Lord, thou art at this time in a happier case than I." And by and by she said to Foliot: "Go and bring his horse to this place,

The Lady Helen findeth the King.

that we may bear him hence." "Lady," said Foliot, "it is not good for you to be left here alone." "Foliot," said the Queen, "thou dost not know how much alone I am; thy leaving me here cannot make me more alone." Therewith she fell to weeping with great passion.

Then Foliot wept also in great measure and, still weeping like rain, he went away and left her. When he came again with King Ban's horse the sun had risen and all the birds were singing with great jubilation and everything was so blithe and gay that no one could have believed that care and trouble could dwell in a world that was so beautiful.

So Queen Helen and Foliot lifted the dead king to his horse and then the Queen said: "Come thou, Foliot, at thine own gait, and I will go ahead and seek my child, for I have yet Launcelot to be my joy. Haply he will be needing me at this moment." So the Queen made haste down the steep hill ahead of Foliot and by and by she came to the margin of that little lake where they had rested awhile since.

The Lady Helen bringeth her dead down from the Mountain.

By now the sun had risen very strong and warm so that all the lake, and the meadows circumadjacent, and the forest that stood around about that meadow were illumined with the glory of his effulgence.

Now as Queen Helen entered that meadow she beheld that a very wonderful lady was there, and this lady bare the child Launcelot in her arms. And the lady sang to Launcelot, and the young child looked up into her face and laughed and set his hand against her cheek. All this Queen Helen beheld; and she likewise beheld that the lady was of a very extraordinary appearance, being clad altogether in green that glistered and shone with a wonderful brightness. And she beheld that around the neck of the lady was a necklace of gold, inset with opal stones and emeralds; and she perceived that the lady's face was like ivory—very white and clear—and that her eyes, which were very bright, shone like jewels set into ivory. And she saw that the lady was very wonderfully beautiful, so that the beholder, looking upon her, felt a manner of fear—for that lady was Fay.

(And that lady was the Lady of the Lake, spoken of aforetime in the Book of King Arthur, wherein it is told how she aided King Arthur to obtain that wonderful, famous sword yclept Excalibur, and how she aided Sir Pellias, the Gentle Knight, in the time of his extremity, and took him into the lake with her. Also divers other things concerning her are told of therein.)

Then the Queen came near to where the lady was, and she said to her, "Lady, I pray you give me my child again!" Upon this the Lady of the Lake smiled very strangely and said: "Thou shalt have thy child again, lady, but not now; after a little thou shalt have him again." Then Queen Helen cried out with great agony of passion: "Lady, would you take my child from me? Give him to me again, for he is all I have left in the world. Lo, I have lost house and lands and husband, and all the other joys that life has me to give, wherefore, I beseech you, take not my child from me." To this the Lady of the Lake said: "Thou must endure thy sorrow a while longer; for it is so ordained that I must take thy child; for I take him only that I may give him to thee again, reared in such a wise that he shall make the glory of thy house to be the glory of the world. For he shall become the greatest knight in the world, and from his loins shall spring a greater still than he, so that the glory of the House of King Ban shall be spoken of as long as mankind shall last." But Queen Helen cried out all the more in a great despair: "What care I for all this? I care only that I shall have my little child again! Give him to me!"

The Lady of the Lake taketh Launcelot into the Lake.

Therewith she would have laid hold of the garments of the Lady of the Lake in supplication, but the Lady of the Lake drew herself away from Queen Helen's hand and said: "Touch me not, for I am not mortal, but Fay." And thereupon she and Launcelot vanished from before Queen Helen's eyes as the breath vanishes from the face of a mirror.

For when you breathe upon a mirror the breath will obscure that which lieth behind; but presently the breath will disappear and vanish, and then you shall behold all things entirely clear and bright to the sight again. So the Lady of the Lake vanished away, and everything behind her where she had stood was clear and bright, and she was gone.

Then Queen Helen fell down in a swoon, and lay beside the lake of the meadow like one that is dead; and when Foliot came he found her so and wist not what to do for her. There was his lord who was dead and his lady who was so like to death that he knew not whether she was dead or no. So he knew not what to do but sat down and made great lamentation for a long while.

The Lady Helen taketh to a Nunnery.

What time he sat thus there came that way three nuns who dwelt in an abbey of nuns which was not a great distance away from that place. These made great pity over that sorrowful sight, and they took away from there the dead King and the woful Queen, and the King they buried in holy ground, and the Queen they let live with them and she was thereafter known as the "Sister of Sorrows."

Now Launcelot dwelt for nigh seventeen years with the Lady Nymue of the Lake in that wonderful, beautiful valley covered over with the appearance of such a magical lake as hath been aforetime described in the Book of King Arthur.

How Launcelot dwelt in the lake.

And that land of the lake was of this sort that shall here be described:—

Unto anyone who could enter into the magic water of that lake (and there were very few of those who were mortal who were allowed to come to those meadows of Faery that were there concealed beneath those enchanted waters) he would behold before him a wide and radiant field of extraordinary beauty. And he would behold that that field was covered all over with such a multitude of exquisite and beautiful flowers that the heart of the beholder would be elated with pure joy to find himself in the midst of that waving sea of multitudinous and fragrant blossoms. And he would behold many fair and shady groves of trees that here and there grew up from that valley, each glade overshadowing a fountain of water as clear as crystal. And he would perhaps behold, at such pleasant places beneath the shade of those trees, some party of the fair and gentle folk of that country; and he would see them playing in sport, or he would hear them chanting to the music of shining golden harps. And he would behold in the midst of that beautiful plain a wonderful castle with towers and roofs uplifted high into the sky, and all shining in the peculiar radiance of that land, like to castles and battlements of pure gold.

Such was the land unto which Launcelot was brought, and from what I have told you you may see what a wonderful, beautiful place it was.

And the mystery of that place entered into the soul of Launcelot, so that thereafter, when he came out thence, he was never like other folk, but always appeared to be in a manner remote and distant from other of his fellow-mortals with whom he dwelt.

For though he smiled a great deal, it was not often that he laughed; and if he did laugh, it was never in scorn, but always in loving-kindness.

It was here in this land that Sir Pellias had now dwelt for several years, with great peace and content. (For it hath been told in the Book of King Arthur how, when he was upon the edge of death, the Lady Nymue of the Lake brought him back to life again, and how, after that time, he was half fay and half mortal.)

And the reason why Launcelot was brought to that place was that Sir Pellias might teach him and train him in all the arts of chivalry. For no one in all the world was more skilful in arms than Sir Pellias, and no one could so well teach Launcelot the duties of chivalry as he.

So Sir Pellias taught Launcelot all that was best of knighthood, both as to conduct of manner, and as to the worthiness and skill at arms, wherefore it was that when Launcelot was completely taught, there was no knight in all the world who was his peer in strength of arms or in courtesy of behavior, until his own son, Sir Galahad, appeared in the courts of chivalry as shall by and by be told of.

So when Launcelot came forth into the world again he became the greatest knight in all the history of chivalry, wherefore that prophecy of his mother was fulfilled as to his being like to a bright star of exceeding lustre.

Accordingly, I have herein told you with great particularity all these circumstances of his early history so that you may know exactly how it was that he was taken away into the lake, and why it was that he was afterward known as Sir Launcelot, surnamed of the Lake.

As to how he came into the world to achieve that greatness unto which he had been preordained, and as to how King Arthur made him knight, and as to many very excellent adventures that befell him, you shall immediately read in what followeth.

PART I
THE STORY OF LAUNCELOT

Here beginneth the story of Sir Launcelot, surnamed of the Lake, who was held by all men to be the most excellent, noble, perfect knight-champion who was ever seen in the world from the very beginning of chivalry unto the time when his son, Sir Galahad, appeared like a bright star of extraordinary splendor shining in the sky of chivalry.

In this Book it shall be told how he was taken into a magic lake, how he came out thence to be made knight by King Arthur, and of how he undertook several of those adventures that made him at once the wonder and the admiration of all men, and the chiefest glory of the Round Table of Arthur-Pendragon.

Sir Launcelot greets Queen Guinevere.

CHAPTER FIRST

How Sir Launcelot Came Forth From the Enchanted Castle of the Lake and Entered Into the World Again, and How King Arthur Made Him Knight.

I KNOW NOT ANY TIME OF THE YEAR THAT IS MORE FULL OF JOYFULNESS than the early summer season; for that time the sun is wonderfully lusty and strong, yet not so very hot; that time the trees and shrubs are very full of life and very abundant of shade and yet have not grown dry with the heats and droughts of later days; that time the grass is young and lush and green, so that when you walk athwart the meadow-lands it is as though you walked through a fair billowy lake of magical verdure, sprinkled over with a great multitude of little flowers; that time the roses are everywhere a-bloom, both the white rose and the red, and the eglantine is abundant; that time the nests are brimful of well-fledged nestlings, and the little hearts of the small parent fowls are so exalted with gladness that they sing with all their mights and mains, so that the early daytime is filled full of the sweet jargon and the jubilant medley of their voices. Yea; that is a goodly season of the year, for though, haply, the spirit may not be so hilarious as in the young and golden springtime, yet doth the soul take to itself

Of the springtime of long ago.

so great a content in the fulness of the beauty of the world, that the heart is elated with a great and abundant joy that it is not apt to feel at another season.

Now it chanced upon the day before Saint John's day in the fulness of a summer-time such as this, that King Arthur looked forth from his chamber very early in the morning and beheld how exceedingly fair and very lusty was the world out-of-doors—all in the freshness of the young daylight. For the sun had not yet risen, though he was about to rise, and the sky was like to pure gold for brightness; all the grass and leaves and flowers were drenched with sweet and fragrant dew, and the birds were singing so vehemently that the heart of any man could not but rejoice in the fulness of life that lay all around about him.

There were two knights with King Arthur at that time, one was Sir Ewain, the son of Morgana le Fay (and he was King Arthur's nephew), and the other was Sir Ector de Maris, the son of King Ban of Benwick and of Queen Helen—this latter a very noble, youthful knight, and the youngest of all the Knights of the Round Table who were at that time elected. These stood by King Arthur and looked forth out of the window with him and they also took joy with him in the sweetness of the summer season. Unto them, after a while, King Arthur spake, saying: "Messires, meseems this is too fair a day to stay within doors. For, certes, it is a shame that I who am a king should be prisoner within mine own castle, whilst any ploughman may be free of the wold and the green woods and the bright sun and the blue sky and the wind that blows over hill and dale. Now, I too would fain go forth out of doors and enjoy these things; wherefore I ordain that we shall go a-hunting this day and that ye and I shall start before any others of the lords and the ladies that dwell herein are awake. So let us take our horses and our hounds and let us take certain foresters and huntsmen, and let us go forth a-hunting into the green forest; for this day shall be holiday for me and for you and we shall leave care behind us, and for a while we shall disport ourselves in pleasant places."

King Arthur and two knights ride a-hunting.

So they all did as King Arthur bade; they made them each man ready with his own hands, and they bade the huntsmen and the foresters to attend thereupon as the King had ordained. Then they rode forth from the castle and out into the wide world that lay beyond, and it was yet so early in the morning that none of the castle folk were astir to know of their departure.

All that day they hunted in the forest with much joy and with great sport, nor did they turn their faces toward home again until the day was so far spent that the sun had sunk behind the tops of the tall leafy trees. Then, at that time, King Arthur gave command that they should bend their ways toward Camelot once more.

Now this time, being the Eve of Saint John, fairies and those folk who are fay come forth, as is very well known, into the world from which they dwell apart at other times. So when King Arthur and those two knights and their several foresters and huntsmen came to a certain outlying part of the forest, they were suddenly aware of a damsel and a dwarf waiting where the road upon which they were travelling crossed another road, and they perceived, from her very remarkable appearance, that the damsel was very likely Fay. For both she and her dwarf sat each upon a milk-white horse, very strangely still, close to where was a shrine by a hedge of hawthorne; and the damsel was so wonderfully fair of face that it was a marvel to behold her. Moreover, she was clad all in white samite from top to toe and her garments were embroidered with silver; and the trappings and garniture of her horse were of white samite studded with bright silver bosses, wherefore, because of this silver, she glistered with a sudden lustre whensoever she moved a little. When King Arthur and the two knights who were with him drew nigh this damsel, much marvelling at her appearance, she hailed him in a voice that was both high and clear, crying: "Welcome, King Arthur! Welcome, King Arthur! Welcome, King Arthur!" saying three words three times; and "Welcome, Sir Ewain!" "Welcome, Sir Ector de Maris!" addressing each of those lords by his name.

King Arthur and his companions find a strange damsel and a dwarf.

"Damsel," quoth King Arthur, "it is very singular that you should know who we are and that we should not know you. Now, will you not tell us your name and whence you come and whither you go? For of a surety I believe you are Fay."

"Lord," said the damsel, "it matters not who I am, saving that I am of the court of a wonderful lady who is your very good friend. She hath sent me here to meet you and to beseech you to come with me whither I shall lead you, and I shall lead you unto her."

"Damsel," said King Arthur, "I shall be right glad to go with you as you desire me to do. So, if you will lead me to your lady, I and my knights will gladly follow you thitherway to pay our court unto her."

Upon this the damsel waved her hand, and drawing her bridle-rein she led the way, accompanied by the dwarf, and King Arthur and the two knights followed her, and all their party of foresters and huntsmen and hounds and beagles followed them.

King Arthur and his knights follow the damsel.

By this time the sun had set and the moon had risen very fair and round and as yellow as gold, making a great light above the silent tree-tops. Everything now was embalmed in the twilight, and all the world was enshrouded in the mystery of the midsummer eve. Yet though the sun had gone the light was wonderfully bright, wherefore all that the eye could see stood sharp-cut and very clear to the vision.

So the damsel and the dwarf led the way for somewhat of a distance, though not for so very far, until they came of a sudden to where was an open meadow in the forest, hedged all around with the trees of the woodland. And here the King and his knights were aware of a great bustle of many people, some working very busily in setting up several pavilions of white samite, and others preparing a table as for a feast, and others upon this business and others upon that; and there were various sumpter-mules and pack-horses and palfreys all about, as though belonging to a party of considerable estate.

Then King Arthur and those who were with him beheld that, at some distance away upon the other side of the meadow, there were three people sitting under a crab-apple tree upon a couch especially prepared for them, and they were aware that these people were the chief of all that company.

The first party of the three was a knight of very haughty and noble appearance, clad all in armor as white as silver; and his jupon was white embroidered with silver, and the scabbard of the sword and the sword-belt were white, and his shield hung in the crab-tree above him and that, too, was all white as of silver. This knight still wore his helmet, so that his countenance was not to be seen. The second party of the three was a lady clad all in white raiment. Her face was covered by her wimple so that her countenance also was not to be seen very clearly, but her garments were of wonderful sort, being of white sarcenet embroidered over with silver in the pattern of lily flowers. Also she wore around her breast and throat a chain of shining silver studded with bright and sparkling gems of divers sorts. The third party of the three was a youth of eighteen years, so beautiful of face that it seemed to King Arthur that he had never beheld so noble a being. For his countenance was white and shining, and his hair was as soft as silk and as black as it was possible to be, and curled down upon his shoulders; and his eyes were large and bright and extraordinarily black, and his eyebrows arched so smoothly that if they had been painted they could not have been marked upon his forehead more evenly than they were; and his lips, which pouted a little, though not very much, were as red as coral, and his upper lip was shaded with a soft down of black. Moreover, this youth was clad altogether in white cloth of satin with no ornaments whatsoever saving only a fine chain of shining silver set with opal-stones and emeralds that hung about his neck.

King Arthur and his companions are brought to speak with strange folk.

Then when King Arthur approached near enough he perceived by certain signs that the lady was the chiefest of those three, wherefore he paid his court to her especially, saying to her: "Lady, it seems that I have been brought hitherward unto you and that you were aware of my name and estate when you sent for me. Now I should be exceedingly glad if you would enlighten me in the same manner as to yourself."

"Sir," she said, "that I shall be glad to do; for if I have known you aforetime, you have also seen me afore time and have known me as your friend." Therewith the lady lowered the wimple from her face and King Arthur perceived that it was the Lady of the Lake.

Upon this he kneeled down upon one knee and took her hand and set it to his lips. "Lady," quoth he, "I have indeed cause to know you very well, for you have, as you affirm, been a friend to me and to my friends upon many several occasions." Then King Arthur turned to that knight who was with that Lady of the Lake, and he said unto him: "Messire, if I mistake not, I should know you also; and I doubt not, if you will lift the umbril of your helmet, we shall all three know your face." Upon this the knight without more ado lifted his umbril as King Arthur had desired him to do and the three beheld that it was Sir Pellias, the Gentle Knight.

King Arthur findeth Sir Pellias again.

Now it hath already been very fully told about Sir Pellias in the Book of King Arthur, and those of you who read of him therein will remember, no doubt, how sorely he was wounded in a combat with Sir Gawaine, who was his best friend, and of how the Lady of the Lake took him to dwell with her in that wonderful city that was hidden by the appearance as of an enchanted lake, and of how it was Sir Gawaine who last beheld him upon that occasion. But if Sir Gawaine was the dearest friend that Sir Pellias had at that time, then Sir Ewain was only less dear to him. Therefore, when Sir Ewain beheld that the strange knight was Sir Pellias, he wist not what to think for pure wonder; for no mortal eyes had ever beheld Sir Pellias since he had gone into the lake with the Lady of the Lake that time as foretold, and it was not thought that anyone would ever see him again.

So when Sir Ewain beheld that the knight was Sir Pellias he emitted a great cry of joy and ran to him and catched him in his arms, and Sir Pellias forbade him not. For though at most times those who are of Faëry do not suffer themselves to be touched by mortal hands, yet, upon the Eve of Saint John's Day, fairies and mortals may commune as though they were of the same flesh and blood. Wherefore Sir Pellias did not forbid Sir Ewain, and they embraced, as one-time brethren-in-arms should embrace. And each kissed the other upon the face, and each made great joy the one over the other. Yea, so great was their joy that all those who stood about were moved with pure happiness at beholding them.

Then Sir Pellias came to King Arthur and kneeled down before him and kissed his hand, as is the bounden duty of every knight unto his lord. "Ha, Messire," quoth King Arthur, "methought when I beheld this lady, that you would not be very far distant from her." Then he said unto the Lady of the Lake: "Lady, I prithee tell me, who is this fair youth who is with you. For methinks I never beheld before so noble and so beautiful a countenance as his. Maybe you will make us acquainted with him also."

"Lord," said the Lady Nymue, "who he is, and of what quality, shall, I hope, be made manifest in due time; just now I would not wish that he should be known even unto you. But touching him, I may say that it was for his sake that I sent my damsel to meet you at the cross-roads awhile ago. But of that, more anon; for see! the feast is now spread which we have prepared for your entertainment. So let us first eat and drink and make merry together, and then we shall speak further of this matter."

So they all six went and sat down to the table that had been spread for them in the open meadow-land. For the night was very pleasant and warm and a wonderful full moon shone down upon them with a marvellous lustre, and there was a pleasant air, soft and warm, from the forest, and, what with the scores of bright waxen tapers that stood in silver candlesticks upon the table (each taper sparkling as bright as any star), the night was made all illuminate like to some singular mid-day. There was set before them a plenty of divers savory meats and of several excellent wines, some as yellow as gold, and some as red as carbuncle, and they ate and they drank and they made merry in the soft moonlight with talk and laughter. Somewhiles they told Sir Pellias and the lady of all that was toward at court at Camelot; otherwhiles Sir Pellias and the lady told them such marvellous things concerning the land in which they two dwelt that it would be hard to believe that the courts of Heaven could be fairer than the courts of Fairyland whence they had come.

The Lady of the Lake prepareth a feast for King Arthur.

Then, after the feast was ended, the Lady of the Lake said to King Arthur: "Sir, an I have won your favor in any way, there is a certain thing I would ask of you." To the which King Arthur made reply: "Ask it, Lady, and it shall be granted thee, no matter what it may be." "Sir," said the Lady of the Lake, "this is what I would ask of you. I would ask you to look upon this youth who sits beside me. He is so dear to me that I cannot very well make you know how dear he is. I have brought him hither from our dwelling-place for one certain reason; to wit, that you should make him knight. That is the great favor I would ask of you. To this intent I have brought armor and all the appurtenances of knighthood; for he is of such noble lineage that no armor in the world could be too good for him."

"Lady," quoth King Arthur, "I will do what you ask with much pleasure and gladness. But, touching that armor of which you speak, it is my custom to provide anyone whom I make a knight with armor of mine own choosing."

To this the Lady of the Lake smiled very kindly, saying, "Lord, I pray you, let be in this case, for I daresay that the armor which hath been provided for this youth shall be so altogether worthy of your nobility and of his future credit that you will be entirely contented with it." And with that, King Arthur was altogether satisfied.

And, touching that armor, the ancient history that speaketh of these matters saith that it was of such a sort as this that followeth, and that it was brought from that enchanted court of the lake in this wise; to wit, in the front came two youths, leading two white mules, and the mules bore two chests studded with silver bosses. In one chest was the hauberk of that armor and in the other were the iron boots. These were bright like to silver and were inlaid with cunningly devised figures, all of pure gold. Next to them came two esquires, clad in white robes and mounted upon white horses, bearing the one a silver shield and the other a shining helmet, as of silver—it likewise being very wonderfully inlaid with figures of pure gold. After these came two other esquires, the one bearing a sword in a white sheath embossed with studs of silver (the belt whereof was of silver with facets of gold) and the other leading a white charger, whose coat was as soft and as shining as silk. And all the gear and furniture of this horse was of silver and of white samite embellished with silver. So from this you can see how nobly that young acolyte was provided with all that beseemed his future greatness. For, as you may have guessed, this youth was Launcelot, King Ban's son of Benwick, who shortly became the greatest knight in the world.

Of the armor, etc., of Sir Launcelot.

Now there was in that part of the forest border a small abbey of monks, and in the chapel of that abbey Launcelot watched his armor for that night and Sir Ewain was with him for all that time. Meantime King Arthur and Sir Ector de Maris slept each in a silken pavilion provided for them by the Lady of the Lake.

Launcelot guards his armor at night.

In the morning Sir Ewain took Launcelot to the bath and bathed him, for such was the custom of those who were being prepared for knighthood.

Now, whilst Sir Ewain was bathing the youth, he beheld that on his shoulder was a mark in the likeness of a golden star and he marvelled very much thereat; but he made no mention of it at that time, but held his peace concerning what he saw; only he marvelled very greatly thereat.

Then, after Sir Ewain had bathed Launcelot, he clothed him in raiment fitted for that ceremony unto which he was ordained, and when the youth was so clothed, Sir Ewain brought him to King Arthur, and King Arthur knighted Launcelot with great ceremony, and buckled the belt around him with his own hands. After he had done this Sir Ewain and Sir Ector de Maris set the golden spurs to his heels, and Sir Ector wist not that he was performing such office for his own brother.

King Arthur creates Sir Launcelot a Knight-Royal.

So Sir Launcelot was made knight with great estate and ceremony, whereof I have told you all, unto every particular. For it is fitting that all things should be so told concerning that most great and famous knight.

After King Arthur had so dubbed Sir Launcelot knight, it was time that those two parties should part company—to wit, the party of the Lady of the Lake and the party of King Arthur. But when they were about to leave one another the Lady of the Lake took Sir Launcelot aside, and she spake to him after this manner:

"Launcelot, forget not that you are a king's son, and that your lineage is as noble as that of anyone upon earth—for so I have often told you aforetime. Wherefore, see to it that your worthiness shall be as great as your beauty, and that your courtesy and gentleness shall be as great as your prowess. To-day you shall go unto Camelot with King Arthur to make yourself known unto that famous Court of Chivalry. But do not tarry there, but, ere the night cometh, depart and go forth into the world to prove your knighthood as worthily as God shall give you grace to do. For I would not have you declare yourself to the world until you have proved your worthiness by your deeds. Wherefore, do not yourself proclaim your name, but wait until the world proclaimeth it; for it is better for the world to proclaim the worthiness of a man than that the man should proclaim his own worthiness. So hold yourself ready to undertake any adventure whatsoever that God sendeth to you to do, but never let any other man complete a task unto which you yourself have set your hand." Then, after the Lady of the Lake had so advised Sir Launcelot, she kissed him upon the face, and therewith gave him a ring curiously wrought and set with a wonderful purple stone, which ring had such power that it would dissolve every enchantment. Then she said: "Launcelot, wear this ring and never let it be from off your finger." And

The Lady of the Lake gives Sir Launcelot good advice.

Launcelot said: "I will do so." So Sir Launcelot set the ring upon his finger and it was so that it never left his finger whilst he drew the breath of life.

Then King Arthur and Sir Ewain and Sir Ector de Maris and the young Sir Launcelot laid their ways toward Camelot. And, as they journeyed so together, Sir Ewain communicated privily to Sir Ector de Maris how that the youth had a mark as of a golden star upon the skin of his shoulder, and upon this news Sir Ector fell very silent. For Sir Ector knew that that sign was upon his own brother's shoulder, and he did not know how it could be upon the shoulder of any other man. Wherefore, he wist not what to think that it should be upon the shoulder of this youth. But he said naught of these thoughts to Sir Ewain, but held his peace.

Sir Launcelot cometh to Camelot.

So they reached Camelot whilst it was still quite early in the morning and all they who were there made great joy at the coming of so wonderfully fair and noble a young knight as Sir Launcelot appeared to be. Wherefore, there was great sound of rejoicing at his coming.

Then, after a while, King Arthur said: "Let us go and see if, haply, this youth's name is marked upon any of the seats of the Round Table, for I think it should be there." So all they of the court went to that pavilion afore described, where the Round Table was established, and they looked; and lo! upon the seat that King Pellinore had one time occupied was this name:

THE KNIGHT OF THE LAKE.

So the name stood at first, nor did it change until the name of Sir Launcelot of the Lake became so famous in all the world. Then it became changed to this:

SIR LAUNCELOT OF THE LAKE.

Sir Launcelot becometh knight of the Round Table.

So Sir Launcelot remained at Camelot for that entire day and was made acquainted with a great many of the lords and ladies and knights and dames of King Arthur's court. And all that while he was like one that walked in a dream, for he had never before beheld anything of the world of mankind since he had been carried away into the lake, wherefore he wist not very well whether what he saw was real or whether he beheld it in a vision of enchantment. For it was all very new and wonderful to him and he took great delight in it because that he was a man and because this world was the world of mankind. Wherefore, though that Castle of the Lake was so beautiful, yet he felt his heart go forth to this other and less beautiful land as it did not go forth to that, because he was human and this was human.

Nevertheless, though that was so joyful a day for him, yet Sir Launcelot did not forget what the Lady of the Lake had said concerning the time he was to abide there! Wherefore, when it drew toward evening he besought leave of King Arthur to depart from that place in search of adventures, and King Arthur gave him leave to do as he desired.

So Sir Launcelot prepared to depart, and whilst he was in his chamber making ready there came in unto him Sir Ector de Maris. And Sir Ector said unto him: "Sir, I prithee tell me—is it true that you bear upon your right shoulder a mark like unto a golden star?" And Sir Launcelot made reply: "Yea, that is true." Then Sir Ector said: "I beseech you to tell me if your name is Launcelot." And Sir Launcelot said: "Yea, that is my name."

Upon this Sir Ector broke out into great weeping and he catched Sir Launcelot in his arms and he cried out: "Launcelot, thou art mine own brother! For thy father was my father, and my mother was thy mother! For we are both sons unto King Ban of Benwick, and Queen Helen was our mother." Therewith he kissed Sir Launcelot with great passion upon the face. And Sir Launcelot upon his part kissed Sir Ector with a great passion of joy that he had found a brother in this strange world into which he had so newly come. But Sir Launcelot charged Sir Ector that he should say nothing of this to any man; and Sir Ector pledged his knightly word to that effect. (Nor did he ever tell anyone who Sir Launcelot was until Sir Launcelot had performed such deeds that all the world spake his name.)

Of the brotherhood of Sir Ector and Sir Launcelot.

For when Sir Launcelot went out into the world in that wise he undertook several very weighty achievements and brought them all to a successful issue, so that his name very quickly became known in every court of chivalry.

First he removed an enchantment that overhung a castle, hight Dolorous Gard; and he freed that castle and liberated all the sad, sorry captives that lay therein. (And this castle he held for his own and changed the name from Dolorous Gard to Joyous Gard and the castle became very famous afterward as his best-loved possession. For this was the first of all his possessions that he won by the prowess of his arms and he loved it best of all and considered it always his home.) After that Sir Launcelot, at the bidding of Queen Guinevere, took the part of the Lady of Nohan against the King of

Northumberland, and he overcame the King of Northumberland and made him subject unto King Arthur. Then he overcame Sir Gallehaut, King of the Marches, and sent him captive to the court of King Arthur (and afterward Sir Gallehaut and Sir Launcelot became great friends for aye). So in a little while all the world spoke of Sir Launcelot, for it was said of him, and truly, that he had never been overcome by any other knight, whether upon horseback or upon foot, and that he always succeeded in every adventure which he undertook, whether that adventure were great or whether it were small. So it was as the Lady of the Lake desired it to be, for Sir Launcelot's name became famous, not because he was his father's son, but because of the deeds which he performed upon his own account.

Of sundry adventures of Sir Launcelot.

So Sir Launcelot performed all these famous adventures, and after that he returned again to the court of King Arthur crowned with the glory of his successful knighthood, and there he was received with joy and acclaim and was duly installed in that seat of the Round Table that was his. And in that court he was held in the greatest honor and esteem of all the knights who were there. For King Arthur spake many times concerning him to this effect: that he knew not any honor or glory that could belong to a king greater than having such a knight for to serve him as was Sir Launcelot of the Lake. For a knight like Sir Launcelot came hardly ever into the world, and when he did come his glory must needs illuminate with its effulgence the entire reign of that king whose servant he was.

So it was that Sir Launcelot was greatly honored by everybody at the court of King Arthur, and he thereafter abided at that court for the most part of his life.

And now I must needs make mention of that friendship that existed betwixt Sir Launcelot and Queen Guinevere, for after he thus returned to the court of the king, they two became such friends that no two people could be greater friends than they were.

Now I am aware that there have been many scandalous things said concerning that friendship, but I do not choose to believe any such evil sayings. For there are always those who love to think and say evil things of others. Yet though it is not to be denied that Sir Launcelot never had for his lady any other dame than the Lady Guinevere, still no one hath ever said with truth that she regarded Sir Launcelot otherwise than as her very dear friend. For Sir Launcelot always avouched with his knightly

Of Sir Launcelot and Queen Guinevere.

word, unto the last day of his life, that the Lady Guinevere was noble and worthy in all ways, wherefore I choose to believe his knightly word and to hold that what he said was true. For did not he become an hermit, and did not she become a nun in their latter days, and were they not both broken of heart when King Arthur departed from this life in so singular a manner as he did? Wherefore I choose to believe good of such noble souls as they, and not evil of them.

How Sir Launcelot dwelt at Camelot.

Yet, though Sir Launcelot thus abided at the court of the King, he ever loved the open world and a life of adventure above all things else. For he had lived so long in the Lake that these things of the sturdy life of out-of-doors never lost their charm for him. So, though he found, for a while, great joy in being at the court of the King (for there were many jousts held in his honor, and, whithersoever he rode forth, men would say to one another: "Yonder goeth that great knight, Sir Launcelot, who is the greatest knight in the world"), yet he longed ever to be abroad in the wide world again. So one day he besought King Arthur for leave to depart thence and to go forth for a while in search of adventures; and King Arthur gave him leave to do as he desired.

So now shall be told of several excellent adventures that Sir Launcelot undertook, and which he carried through with entire success, and to the great glory and renown of the Round Table, of which he was the foremost knight.

JVSTISSIMVS·REX·

ir Lionel of Britain.

CHAPTER SECOND

How Sir Launcelot and Sir Lionel Rode Forth Errant Together and How Sir Lionel Met Sir Turquine to His Great Dole. Also How Sir Ector Grieved for the Departure of His Brother Launcelot and So, Following Him, Fell Into a Very Sorry Adventure.

Now after King Arthur had thus given Sir Launcelot leave to go errant and whilst Sir Launcelot was making himself ready to depart there came to him Sir Lionel, who was his cousin germain, and Sir Lionel besought leave to go with him as his knight-companion, and Sir Launcelot gave him that leave.

Sir Launcelot and Sir Lionel depart in search of adventure.

So when King Arthur confirmed Sir Launcelot's permission Sir Lionel also made himself ready very joyfully, and early of the morning of the next day they two took their leave of the court and rode away together; the day being very fair and gracious and all the air full of the joy of that season—which was in the flower of the spring-time.

So, about noon-tide, they came to a certain place where a great apple-tree stood by a hedge, and by that time they had grown an-hungered. So they tied their horses near-by in a cool and shady place and straightway sat them down under the apple-tree in the soft tall grass, which was yet fresh with the coolness of the morning.

Sir Launcelot sleepeth beneath an apple-tree.

Then when they had ended their meal Sir Launcelot said: "Brother, I have a great lust to sleep for a little space, for I find myself so drowsy that mine eyelids are like scales of lead." Unto which Sir Lionel made reply: "Very well; sleep thou for a while, and I will keep watch, and after that thou shalt watch, and I will sleep for a little space." So Sir Launcelot put his helmet beneath his head and turned upon his side, and in a little had fallen into a sleep which had neither dream nor thought of any kind, but which was deep and pure like to a clear well of water in the forest.

And, whilst he slept thus, Sir Lionel kept watch, walking up and down in the shade of a hedge near-by.

Where they were was upon the side of a hill, and beneath them was a little valley; and a road ran through the valley, very white and shining in the sunlight, like a silken ribbon, and the road lay between growing fields of corn and pasture-land. Now as Sir Lionel walked beside the hedge he beheld three knights come riding into that valley and along that road with very great speed and in several clouds of dust; and behind them came a fourth knight, who was very huge of frame and who was clad altogether in black armor. Moreover, this knight rode upon a black horse and his shield was black and his spear was black and the furniture of his horse was black, so that everything appertaining to that knight was as black as any raven.

Sir Lionel perceives how one knight pursues three knights.

And Sir Lionel beheld that this one knight pursued those other three knights and that his horse went with greater speed than theirs, so that by and by he overtook the hindermost knight. And Sir Lionel beheld that the sable knight smote the fleeing knight a great buffet with his sword, so that that knight fell headlong from his horse and rolled over two or three times upon the ground and then lay as though he were dead. Then the black knight catched the second of the three, and served him as he had served his fellow. Then the third of the three, finding that there was no escape for him, turned as if to defend himself; but the black knight drave at him, and smote him so terrible a blow that I believe had a thunderbolt smitten him he would not have fallen from his horse more suddenly than he did. For, though that combat was full three furlongs away, yet Sir Lionel heard the sound of that blow as clearly as though it had been close by.

Then after the black knight had thus struck down those three knights he went to each in turn and tied his hands behind his back. Then, lifting each man with extraordinary ease, he laid him across the saddle of that horse from which he had fallen, as though he were a sack of grain. And all this Sir Lionel beheld with very great wonder, marvelling much at the strength and prowess of that black knight. "Ha," quoth he to himself, "I will go and inquire into this business, for it may haply be that yonder black knight shall not find it to be so easy to deal with a knight of the Round Table as with those other three knights."

So, with this, Sir Lionel loosed his horse very quietly and went his way so softly that Sir Launcelot was not awakened. And after he had gone some way, he mounted his steed and rode off at a fast gallop down into that valley.

Sir Lionel addresses the sable knight.

When Sir Lionel had come to that place where the knight was, he found that he had just bound the last of the three knights upon the saddle of his horse as aforetold. So Sir Lionel spoke to the sable knight in this wise: "Sir, I pray you tell me your name and degree and why you treat those knights in so shameful a fashion as I behold you to do."

"Messire," said the black knight very fiercely, "this matter concerns you not at all; yet I may tell you that those knights whom I have overthrown are knights of King Arthur's court, and so I serve all such as come into this place. So will I serve you, too, if you be a knight of King Arthur's."

"Well," said Sir Lionel, "that is a very ungracious thing for you to say. And as for that, I too am a knight of King Arthur's court, but I do not believe that you will serve me as you have served those three. Instead of that, I have great hope that I shall serve you in such a fashion that I shall be able to set these knights free from your hands."

Thereupon, without more ado, he made him ready with spear and shield, and the black knight, perceiving his design, also made him ready. Then they rode a little distance apart so as to have a fair course for a tilt upon the roadway. Then each set spur to his horse and the two drave together with such violence that the earth shook beneath them. So they met fair in the middle of the course, but lo! in that encounter the spear of Sir Lionel broke into as many as thirty or forty pieces, but the spear of the black knight held, so that Sir Lionel was lifted clean out from his saddle and over the crupper of his horse with such violence that when he smote the ground he rolled three times over ere he ceased to fall. And because of that fierce, terrible blow he swooned away entirely, and all was black before his eyes, and he knew nothing.

The sable knight overcomes Sir Lionel.

Therewith the black knight dismounted and tied Sir Lionel's arms behind his back and he laid him across the saddle of his horse as he had laid those others across the saddles of their horses; and he tied him there very securely with strong cords so that Sir Lionel could not move.

And all this while Sir Launcelot slept beneath the apple-tree upon the hillside, for he was greatly soothed by the melodious humming of the bees in the blossoms above where he lay.

Now you are to know that he who had thus taken Sir Lionel and those three knights prisoner was one Sir Turquine, a very cruel, haughty knight, who had a great and strong castle out beyond the mouth of that valley in which these knights took combat as aforetold. Moreover, it was the custom of Sir Turquine to make prisoner

Of Sir Turquine the sable knight.

all the knights and ladies who came that way; and all the knights and ladies who were not of King Arthur's court he set free when they had paid a sufficient ransom unto him; but the knights who were of King Arthur's court, and especially those who were of the Round Table, he held prisoner for aye within his castle. The dungeon of that castle was a very cold, dismal, and unlovely place, and it was to this prison that he proposed to take those four knights whom he had overcome, with intent to hold them prisoner as aforetold.

And now turn we to King Arthur's court and consider what befell there after Sir Launcelot and Sir Lionel had left it in search of adventures.

When Sir Ector found that Sir Launcelot and Sir Lionel had gone away in that fashion he was very much grieved in spirit; wherefore he said to himself, "Meseems my brother might have taken me with him as well as our cousin." So he went to King Arthur and besought his leave to quit the court and to ride after those other two and to join in their adventures, and King Arthur very cheerfully gave him that leave. So Sir Ector made him ready with all despatch, and rode away at a great gait after Sir Launcelot and Sir Lionel. And ever as Sir Ector rode he made diligent inquiry and he found that those two knights had ridden before him, so he said to himself: "By and by I shall overtake them—if not to-day, at least by night, or by to-morrow day."

Sir Ector follows Sir Launcelot and Sir Lionel.

But after a while he came to a cross-roads, and there he took a way that Sir Launcelot and Sir Lionel had not taken; so that, after he had gone a distance, he found that he had missed them by taking that road. Nevertheless, he went on until about the prime of the day, what time he met a forester, to whom he said: "Sirrah, saw you two knights ride this way—one knight clad in white armor with a white shield upon which was depicted the figure of a lady, and the other knight clad in red armor with the figure of a red gryphon upon his shield?" "Nay," said the forester, "I saw not such folk." Then said Sir Ector, "Is there any adventure to be found hereabouts?" Upon this the forester fell to laughing in great measure. "Yea," he said, "there is an adventure to be found hard by and it is one that many have undertaken and not one yet hath ever fulfilled." Then Sir Ector said, "Tell me what that adventure is and I will undertake it."

Sir Ector seeks adventure.

"Sir," said the forester, "if you will follow along yonder road for a distance you will find a very large, strong castle surrounded by a broad moat. In front of that castle is a stream of water with a fair, shallow ford, where the roadway crosses the water. Upon this side of that ford there groweth a thorn-tree, very large and sturdy, and upon it hangs a basin of brass. Strike upon that basin with the butt of your spear, and you shall presently meet with that adventure concerning which I have just now spoken." "Fellow," said Sir Ector, "gramercy for your news." And, therewith, straightway he rode off in search of that adventure.

He rode a great distance at a very fast gait and by and by he came to the top of a hill and therewith he saw before him the mouth of a fair valley. Across from where he stood was another hill not very large or high, but exceedingly steep and rocky. Upon this farther hill was builded a tall, noble castle of gray stone with many towers and spires and tall chimneys and with several score of windows, all shining bright in the clear weather. A fair river ran down into the mouth of that valley and it was as bright and as smooth as silver, and on each side of it were smooth level meadow-lands—very green—and here and there shady groves of trees and plantations of fruit-trees. And Sir Ector perceived that the road upon which he travelled crossed the aforesaid river by a shallow ford, and he wist that this must be the ford whereof the forester had spoken. So he rode down unto that ford, and when he had come nigh he perceived the thorn-tree of which the forester had told him, and he saw that a great basin of brass hung to the thorn-tree, just as the forester had said.

Sir Ector smites upon the brazen basin.

Then Sir Ector rode to that thorn-tree and he smote upon that basin of brass with the butt of his spear, so that the basin rang with a noise like thunder; and he smote it again and again, several times over. But though he was aware of a great commotion within that fair castle, yet no adventure befell him, although he smote the brazen basin several times.

Now, his horse being athirst, Sir Ector drove him into the ford that he might drink, and whilst he was there he was suddenly aware where, on the other side of the stream, was a singular party coming along the roadway. For first of all there rode a knight entirely clad in black, riding upon a black horse, and all the harness and furniture of that horse entirely of black. Behind him, that knight led four horses as though they were pack-horses, and across each one of those four horses was a knight in full armor, bound fast to the saddle like to a sack of grain, whereat Sir Ector was very greatly astonished.

As soon as that sable knight approached the castle, several came running forth and relieved him of those horses he led and took them into the castle, and as soon as he had been thus relieved the sable knight rode very violently up to where Sir Ector was. As soon as he had come to the water's edge he cried out: "Sir Knight, come forth from out of that water and do me battle."

"Very well," said Sir Ector, "I will do so, though it will, I think, be to thy very great discomfort."

Sir Ector essays battle with the sable knight.

With that he came quickly out from the ford, the water whereof was all broken and churned into foam at his passing, and straightway he cast aside his spear and drew his sword and, driving against that sable knight, he smote him such a buffet that his horse turned twice about.

"Ha," said the black knight, "that is the best blow that ever I had struck me in all of my life." Therewith he rushed upon Sir Ector, and without using a weapon of any sort he catched him about the body, underneath the arms, and dragged him clean out of his saddle, and flung him across the horn of his own saddle. Thereupon, having accomplished this marvellous feat, and with Sir Ector still across his saddle-bow, he rode up unto his castle, nor stopped until he had reached the court-yard of the keep. There he set Sir Ector down upon the stone pavement. Then he said: "Messire, thou hast done to me this day what no other knight hath ever done to me before, wherefore, if thou wilt promise to be my man from henceforth, I will let thee go free and give thee great rewards for thy services as well."

But Sir Ector was filled very full of shame, wherefore he cried out fiercely, "Rather would I lie within a prison all my life than serve so catiff a knight as thou, who darest to treat other knights as thou hast just now treated me."

"Well," said the black knight very grimly, "thou shalt have thy choice." Therewith he gave certain orders, whereupon a great many fierce fellows set upon Sir Ector and stripped him of all his armor, and immediately haled him off, half-naked, to that dungeon aforementioned.

There he found many knights of King Arthur's court, and several of the Round Table, all of whom he knew, and when they beheld Sir Ector flung in unto them in that fashion they lifted up their voices in great lamentation that he should have been added to their number, instead of freeing them from their dolorous and pitiable case. "Alas," said they, "there is no knight alive may free us from this dungeon, unless it be Sir Launcelot. For this Sir Turquine is, certes, the greatest knight in all the world, unless it be Sir Launcelot."

The sable knight makes prisoner of Sir Ector.

JVSTISSIMVS·REX·

Queen Morgana appears unto Sir Launcelot.

CHAPTER THIRD

How Sir Launcelot Was Found in a Sleep by Queen Morgana le Fay and Three Other Queens Who Were With Her, and How He Was Taken to a Castle of Queen Morgana's and of What Befell Him There.

So Sir Launcelot lay in deep slumber under that apple-tree, and knew neither that Sir Lionel had left him nor what ill-fortune had befallen that good knight. Whilst he lay there sleeping in that wise there came by, along the road, and at a little distance from him, a very fair procession of lordly people, making a noble parade upon the highway. The chiefest of this company were four ladies, who were four queens. With them rode four knights, and, because the day was warm, the four knights bore a canopy of green silk by the four corners upon the points of their lances in such wise as to shelter those queens from the strong heat of the sun. And those four knights rode all armed cap-a-pie on four noble war-horses, and the four queens, bedight in great estate, rode on four white mules richly caparisoned with furniture of divers colors embroidered with gold. After these lordly folk there followed a very excellent court of esquires and demoiselles to the number of a score or more; some riding upon horses and some upon mules that ambled very easily.

Four Queens and their courts pass by where Sir Launcelot lies sleeping.

Now all these folk of greater or lesser degree were entirely unaware that Sir Launcelot lay sleeping so nigh to them as they rode by chattering very gayly together in the spring-time weather, taking great pleasure in the warm air, and in growing things, and the green fields, and the bright sky; and they would have had no knowledge that the knight was there, had not Sir Launcelot's horse neighed very lustily. Thereupon, they were aware of the horse, and then they were aware of Sir Launcelot where he lay asleep under the apple-tree, with his head lying upon his helmet.

Now foremost of all those queens was Queen Morgana le Fay (who was King Arthur's sister, and a potent, wicked enchantress, of whom much hath been told in the

Book of King Arthur), and besides Queen Morgana there was the Queen of North Wales, and the Queen of Eastland, and the Queen of the Outer Isles.

Now when this party of queens, knights, esquires, and ladies heard the war-horse neigh, and when they beheld Sir Launcelot where he lay, they drew rein and marvelled very greatly to see a knight sleeping so soundly at that place, maugre all the noise and tumult of their passing. So Queen Morgana called to her one of the esquires who followed after them, and she said to him: "Go softly and see if thou knowest who is yonder knight; but do not wake him."

So the esquire did as she commanded; he went unto that apple-tree and he looked into Sir Launcelot's face, and by hap he knew who it was because he had been to Camelot erstwhiles and he had seen Sir Launcelot at that place. So he hastened back to Queen Morgana and he said to her: "Lady, I believe that yonder knight is none other than the great Sir Launcelot of the Lake, concerning whom there is now such report; for he is reputed to be the most powerful of all the knights of King Arthur's Round Table, and the greatest knight in the world, so that King Arthur loves him and favors him above all other knights."

An esquire knoweth Sir Launcelot.

Now when Queen Morgana le Fay was aware that the knight who was asleep there was Sir Launcelot, it immediately entered her mind for to lay some powerful, malignant enchantment upon him to despite King Arthur. For she too knew how dear Sir Launcelot was to King Arthur, and so she had a mind to do him mischief for King Arthur's sake. So she went softly to where Sir Launcelot lay with intent to work some such spell upon him. But when she had come to Sir Launcelot she was aware that this purpose of mischief was not possible whilst he wore that ring upon his finger which the Lady of the Lake had given him; wherefore she had to put by her evil design for a while.

But though she was unable to work any malign spell upon him, she was able to cause it by her magic that that sleep in which he lay should remain unbroken for three or four hours. So she made certain movements of her hands above his face and by that means she wove the threads of his slumber so closely together that he could not break through them to awake.

Queen Morgana le Fay sets a mild enchantment upon Sir Launcelot.

After she had done this she called to her several of the esquires who were of her party, and these at her command fetched the shield of Sir Launcelot and laid him upon it. Then they lifted him and bore him away, carrying him in that manner to a certain castle in the forest that was no great distance away. And the name of that castle was Chateaubras and it was one of Queen Morgana's castles.

And all that while Sir Launcelot wist nothing, but lay in a profound sleep, so that when he awoke and looked about him he was so greatly astonished that he knew not whether he was in a vision or whether he was awake. For whilst he had gone asleep beneath that apple-tree, here he now lay in a fair chamber upon a couch spread with a coverlet of flame-colored linen.

Sir Launcelot awakens in a fair chamber.

Then he perceived that it was a very fair room in which he lay, for it was hung all about with tapestry hangings representing fair ladies at court and knights at battle. And there were woven carpets upon the floor, and the couch whereon he lay was of carved wood, richly gilt. There were two windows to that chamber, and when he looked forth he perceived that the chamber where he was was very high from the ground, being built so loftily upon the rugged rocks at its foot that the forest lay far away beneath him like a sea of green. And he perceived that there was but one door to this chamber and that the door was bound with iron and studded with great bosses of wrought iron, and when he tried that door he found that it was locked.

So Sir Launcelot was aware from these things that he was a prisoner—though not a prisoner in a hard case—and he wist not how he had come thither nor what had happened to him.

Now when the twilight of the evening had fallen, a porter, huge of frame and very forbidding of aspect, came and opened the door of the chamber where Sir Launcelot lay, and when he had done so there entered a fair damsel, bearing a very good supper upon a silver tray. Moreover, she bore upon the tray three tapers of perfumed wax set in three silver candlesticks, and these gave a fair light to the entire room. But, when Sir Launcelot saw the maiden coming thus with intent to serve him, he arose and took the tray from her and set it himself upon the table; and for this civility the damsel made acknowledgement to him. Then she said to him: "Sir Knight, what cheer do you have?" "Ha, damsel," said Sir Launcelot, "I do not know how to answer you that, for I wist not what cheer to have until I know whether I be with friends or with enemies. For though this chamber wherein I lie is very fair and well-bedight, yet meseems I must have been brought here by some enchantment, and that I am a prisoner in this place; wherefore I know not what cheer to take."

A fair damsel beareth light and food unto Sir Launcelot.

Then the damsel looked upon Sir Launcelot, and she was very sorry for him. "Sir," quoth she, "I take great pity to see you in this pass, for I hear tell you are the best knight in the world and, of a surety, you are of a very noble appearance. I must tell you that

The damsel has pity for Sir Launcelot.

this castle wherein you lie is a castle of enchantment, and they who dwell here mean you no good; wherefore I would advise you to be upon your guard against them."

"Maiden," said Sir Launcelot, "I give you gramercy for your kind words, and I will be upon my guard as you advise me."

Then the damsel would have said more, but she durst not for fear that she should be overheard and that evil should befall her, for the porter was still without the door. So in a little she went away and Sir Launcelot was left alone.

But though the damsel bade Sir Launcelot have good cheer, yet he had no very good cheer for that night, as anyone may well suppose, for he wist not what was to befall him upon the morrow.

Now when the morning had come Sir Launcelot was aware of someone at his chamber door, and when that one entered it was Queen Morgana le Fay.

How Queen Morgana cometh to Sir Launcelot.

She was clad in all the glory at her command, and her appearance was so shining and radiant that when she came into that room Sir Launcelot knew not whether it was a vision his eyes beheld or whether she was a creature of flesh and blood. For she came with her golden crown upon her head, and her hair, which was as red as gold, was bound around with ribbons of gold; and she was clad all in cloth of gold; and she wore golden rings with jewels upon her fingers and golden bracelets upon her arms and a golden collar around her shoulders; wherefore, when she came into the room she shone with an extraordinary splendor, as if she were a marvellous statue made all of pure gold—only that her face was very soft and beautiful, and her eyes shone exceedingly bright, and her lips, which were as red as coral, smiled, and her countenance moved and changed with all the wiles of fascination that she could cause it to assume.

When Sir Launcelot beheld her come thus gloriously into his room he rose and greeted her with a very profound salutation, for he was astonished beyond measure at beholding that shining vision. Then Queen Morgana gave him her hand, and he kneeled, and took her jewelled fingers in his and set her hand to his lips. "Welcome, Sir Launcelot!" quoth she; "welcome to this place! For it is indeed a great honor to have here so noble and famous a knight as you!"

"Ha, Lady," said Sir Launcelot, "you are gracious to me beyond measure! But I pray you tell me how I came to this place and by what means? For when I fell asleep yesterday at noon I lay beneath an apple-tree upon a hillside; and when I awoke—lo! I found myself in this fair chamber."

To this Queen Morgana le Fay made smiling reply as follows: "Sir, I am Queen Morgana le Fay, of whom you may have heard tell, for I am the sister of King Arthur, whose particular knight you are. Yesterday, at noon, riding with certain other queens and a small court of knights, esquires, and demoiselles, we went by where you lay sleeping. Finding you lying so, alone and without any companion, I was able, by certain arts which I possess, to lay a gentle enchantment upon you so that the sleep wherein you lay should remain unbroken for three or four hours. So we brought you to this place in hopes that you would stay with us for two or three days or more, and give us the pleasure of your company. For your fame, which is very great, hath reached even as far as this place, wherefore we have made a gentle prisoner of you for this time being."

Queen Morgana seeks to beguile Sir Launcelot.

"Lady," said Sir Launcelot, "such constraint as that would be very pleasing to me at another time. But when I fell asleep I was with my cousin, Sir Lionel, and I know not what hath become of him, and haply he will not know what hath become of me should he seek me. Now I pray you let me go forth and find my cousin, and when I have done so I will return to you again at this place with an easy spirit."

"Well, Messire," said Queen Morgana, "it shall be as you desire, only I require of you some pledge of your return." (Herewith she drew from her finger a golden ring set very richly with several jewels.) "Now take this ring," she said, "and give me that ring which I see upon your finger, and when you shall return hither each shall have his ring again from the other."

"Lady," said Sir Launcelot, "that may not be. For this ring was placed upon my finger with such a pledge that it may never leave where it is whilst my soul abideth in my body. Ask of me any other pledge and you shall have it; but I cannot give this ring to you."

Upon this Queen Morgana's cheeks grew very red, and her eyes shone like sparks of fire. "Ha, Sir Knight," she said, "I do not think you are very courteous to refuse a lady and a queen so small a pledge as that. I am much affronted with you that you should have done so. Wherefore, I now demand of you, as the sister of King Arthur whom you serve, that you give me that ring."

Queen Morgana hath anger for Sir Launcelot.

"Lady," said Sir Launcelot, "I may not do that, though it grieveth me much to refuse you."

Then Queen Morgana looked at Sir Launcelot awhile with a very angry countenance, but she perceived that she was not to have her will with him, wherefore she presently turned very quickly and went out of the room, leaving Sir Launcelot much perturbed in spirit. For he knew how great were the arts of Queen Morgana le Fay, and he could not tell what harm she might seek to work upon him by those arts. But he ever bore in mind how that the ring which he wore was sovereign against such malignant arts as she practised, wherefore he took what comfort he could from that circumstance.

Nevertheless, he abode in that chamber in great uncertainty for all that day, and when night came he was afraid to let himself slumber, lest they of the castle should come whilst he slept and work him some secret ill; wherefore he remained awake whilst all the rest of the castle slept. Now at the middle of the night, and about the time of the first cock-crow, he was aware of a sound without and a light that fell through the crack of the door. Then, in a little, the door was opened and there entered that young damsel who had served him with his supper the night before, and she bare a lighted taper in her hand.

When Sir Launcelot perceived that damsel he said: "Maiden, do you come hither with good intent or with evil intent?" "Sir," she said, "I come with good intent, for I take great pity to see you in such a sorry case as this. I am a King's daughter in attendance upon Queen Morgana le Fay, but she is so powerful an enchantress that, in good sooth, I am in great fear lest she some time do me an ill-hap. So to-morrow I leave her service and return unto my father's castle. Meantime, I am of a mind to help you in your adversity. For Queen Morgana trusts me, and I have knowledge of this castle and I have all the keys thereof, wherefore I can set you free. And I will set you free if you will, upon your part, serve me in a way that you can very easily do."

The damsel cometh again to Sir Launcelot.

"Well," said Sir Launcelot, "provided I may serve you in a way fitting my knightly honor, I shall be glad to do so under any condition. Now I pray you tell me what it is you would have of me."

"Sir," said the damsel, "my father hath made a tournament betwixt him and the King of North Wales upon Tuesday next, and that is just a fortnight from this day. Now, already my father hath lost one such a tournament, for he hath no very great array of knights upon his side, and the King of North Wales hath three knights of King Arthur's Round Table to aid his party. Because of the great help of these knights of the Round Table, the King of North Wales won the last tournament and my father lost it, and now he feareth to lose the tournament that is to be. Now if you will enter upon my father's side upon the day of the tournament, I doubt not that he shall win that tournament; for all men say that you

The damsel speaketh to Sir Launcelot of her father, King Bagdemagus.

are the greatest knight in the world at this time. So if you will promise to help my father and will seal that promise with your knightly word, then will I set you free of this castle of enchantment."

"Fair maiden," said Sir Launcelot, "tell me your name and your father's name, for I cannot give you my promise until I know who ye be."

Sir Launcelot promises to aid King Bagdemagus.

"Sir," said the demoiselle, "I am called Elouise the Fair, and my father is King Bagdemagus." "Ha!" quoth Sir Launcelot, "I know your father, and I know that he is a good king and a very worthy knight besides. If you did me no service whatsoever, I would, at your simple asking, were I free of this place, lend him such aid as it is in my power to give."

At this the damsel took great joy and gave Sir Launcelot thanks beyond measure. So they spoke together as to how that matter might be brought about so that Sir Launcelot should be brought to talk to King Bagdemagus. And the damsel Elouise said: "Let it be this way, Sir Launcelot. Imprimis—thou art to know that somewhat of a long distance to the westward of that place where thou didst fall asleep yesterday, there standeth a very large, fair abbey known as the Abbey of Saint James the Lesser. This abbey is surrounded by an exceedingly noble estate that lieth all around about it so that no man that haps in that part of the country can miss it if he make inquiry for it. Now I will go and take lodging at that abbey a little while after I leave this place. So when it suits thee to do so, come thou thither and thou wilt find me there and I will bring thee to my father."

"Very well," said Sir Launcelot, "let it be that way. I will come to that place in good time for the tournament. Meantime, I prithee, rest in the assurance that I shall never forget thy kindness to me this day, nor thy gracious behavior and speech unto me. Wherefore I shall deem it not a duty but a pleasure to serve thee."

So, having arranged all these matters, the damsel Elouise opened the door of that room and led Sir Launcelot out thence; and she led him through various passages and down several long flights of steps, and so brought him at last unto a certain chamber, where was his armor. Then the damsel helped Sir Launcelot to encase him in his armor, so that in a little while he was altogether armed as he had been when he fell asleep under that apple-tree. Thereafter the damsel brought him out past the court-yard and unto the stable where was Sir Launcelot's horse, and the horse knew him when he came. So he saddled the horse by the light of a half-moon which sailed like a boat high up in the sky through the silver, floating clouds, and

The damsel bringeth Sir Launcelot to freedom.

therewith he was ready to depart. Then the damsel opened the gate and he rode out into the night, which was now drawing near the dawning of the day.

Thus Elouise the Fair aided Sir Launcelot to escape from that castle of enchantment, where else great ill might have befallen him.

And now it shall be told how Sir Launcelot did battle with Sir Turquine and of what happened thereat.

JVSTISSIMVS·REX·

Sir Launcelot doeth battle with Sir Turquine.

CHAPTER FOURTH

How Sir Launcelot Sought Sir Lionel and How a Young Damsel Brought Him to the Greatest Battle That Ever He Had in All His Life.

So Sir Launcelot rode through the forest, and whilst he rode the day began to break. About sunrise he came out into an open clearing where certain charcoal-burners were plying their trade.

To these rude fellows he appeared out of the dark forest like some bright and shining vision; and they made him welcome and offered him to eat of their food, and he dismounted and sat down with them and brake his fast with them. And when he had satisfied his hunger, he gave them gramercy for their entertainment, and took horse and rode away.

Sir Launcelot breaks his fast in the forest.

He made forward until about the middle of the morning, what time he came suddenly upon that place where, two days before, he had fallen asleep beneath the blooming apple-tree. Here he drew rein and looked about him for a considerable while; for he thought that haply he might find some trace of Sir Lionel thereabouts. But there was no trace of him, and Sir Launcelot wist not what had become of him.

Sir Launcelot cometh again to the place of the apple-tree.

Now whilst Sir Launcelot was still there, not knowing what to do to find Sir Lionel, there passed that way a damsel riding upon a white palfrey. Unto her Sir Launcelot made salutation, and she made salutation to him and asked him what cheer. "Maiden," said Sir Launcelot, "the cheer that I have is not very good, seeing that I have lost my companion-at-arms and know not where he is." Then he said: "Did you haply meet anywhere with a knight with the figure of a red gryphon upon his shield?" whereunto the damsel answered: "Nay, I saw none such." Then Sir Launcelot said: "Tell me, fair damsel, dost thou know of any adventure hereabouts that I may undertake? For, as thou seest, I am errant and in search of such."

Sir Launcelot perceives a damsel upon a palfrey.

Upon this the damsel fell a-laughing: "Yea, Sir Knight," said she, "I know of an adventure not far away, but it is an adventure that no knight yet that ever I heard tell of hath accomplished. I can take thee to that adventure if thou hast a desire to pursue it."

"Why should I not pursue it," said Sir Launcelot, "seeing that I am here for that very cause—to pursue adventure?"

"Well," said the damsel, "then come with me, Sir Knight, I will take thee to an adventure that shall satisfy thee."

So Sir Launcelot and that damsel rode away from that place together; he upon his great war-horse and she upon her ambling palfrey beside him. And the sun shone down upon them, very pleasant and warm, and all who passed them turned to look after them; for the maiden was very fair and slender, and Sir Launcelot was of so noble and stately a mien that few could behold him even from a distance without looking twice or three times upon him. And as they travelled in that way together they fell into converse, and the damsel said to Sir Launcelot: "Sir, thou appearest to be a very good knight, and of such a sort as may well undertake any adventure with great hope of success. Now I prithee to tell me thy name and what knight thou art."

The damsel leads Sir Launcelot to an adventure.

"Fair maiden," said Sir Launcelot, "as for telling you my name, that I will gladly do. I am called Sir Launcelot of the Lake, and I am a knight of King Arthur's court and of his Round Table."

At this the damsel was very greatly astonished and filled with admiration. "Hah!" quoth she, "it is a great pleasure to me to fall in with you, Sir Launcelot, for all the world now bespeaketh your fame. Little did I ever think to behold your person, much less speak with you, and ride in this way with you. Now I will tell you what this adventure is on which we are set; it is this—there is, some small distance from this, a castle of a knight hight Sir Turquine, who hath in his prison a great many knights of King Arthur's court, and several knights of his Round Table. These knights he keepeth there in great dole and misery, for it is said that their groans may be heard by the passers along the high-road below the castle. This Sir Turquine is held to be the greatest knight in the world (unless it be thou) for he hath never yet been overcome in battle, whether a-horseback or a-foot. But, indeed, I think it to be altogether likely that thou wilt overcome him."

Sir Launcelot and the maiden discourse together.

"Fair damsel," quoth Sir Launcelot, "I too have hope that I shall hold mine own with him, when I meet him, and to that I shall do my best endeavor. Yet this and all other matters are entirely in the hands of God."

Then the damsel said, "If you should overcome this Sir Turquine, I know of still another adventure which, if you do not undertake it, I know of no one else who may undertake to bring it to a successful issue."

Quoth Sir Launcelot, "I am glad to hear of that or of any other adventure, for I take great joy in such adventuring. Now, tell me, what is this other adventure?"

"Sir," said the damsel, "a long distance to the west of this there is a knight who hath a castle in the woods and he is the evilest disposed knight that ever I heard tell of. For he lurks continually in the outskirts of the woods, whence he rushes forth at times upon those who pass by. Especially he is an enemy to all ladies of that country, for he hath taken many of them prisoners to his castle and hath held them in the dungeon thereof for ransom; and sometimes he hath held them for a long while. Now I am fain that thou undertake that adventure for my sake."

The maiden tells Sir Launcelot of the savage forest knight.

"Well," said Sir Launcelot, "I believe it would be a good thing for any knight to do to rid the world of such an evil-disposed knight as that, so if I have the good fortune to overcome this Sir Turquine, I give my knightly word that I will undertake this adventure for thy sake, if so be thou wilt go with me for to show me the way to his castle."

"That I will do with all gladness," said the damsel, "for it is great pride for any lady to ride with you upon such an adventure."

Thus they talked, and all was arranged betwixt them. And thus they rode very pleasantly through that valley for the distance of two leagues or a little more, until they came to that place where the road crossed the smooth stream of water afore told of; and there was the castle of Sir Turquine as afore told of; and there was the thorn-bush and the basin hanging upon the thorn-bush as afore told of. Then the maiden said: "Sir Launcelot, beat upon that basin and so thou shalt summon Sir Turquine to battle with thee."

So Sir Launcelot rode to that basin where it hung and he smote upon it very violently with the butt of his spear. And he smote upon that basin again and again until he smote the bottom from out it; but at that time immediately no one came.

Sir Launcelot smites upon the basin.

Then, after a while, he was ware of one who came riding toward him, and he beheld that he who came riding was a knight very huge of frame, and long and strong of limb. And he beheld that the knight was clad entirely in black, and that the horse upon which he rode and all the furniture of the horse was black. And he beheld that this knight drave before him another horse, and that across the saddle of that other horse there lay an armed knight, bound hand and foot; and Sir Launcelot wist that the sable knight who came riding was that Sir Turquine whom he sought.

So Sir Turquine came very rapidly along the highway toward where Sir Launcelot sat, driving that other horse and the captive knight before him all the while. And as they came nearer and nearer Sir Launcelot thought that he should know who the wounded knight was; and when they came right close, so that he could see the markings of the shield of that captive knight, he wist that it was Sir Gaheris, the brother of Sir Gawaine, and the nephew of King Arthur, whom Sir Turquine brought thither in that wise.

The sable knight bringeth Sir Gaheris captive.

At this Sir Launcelot was very wroth; for he could not abide seeing a fellow-knight of the Round Table treated with such disregard as that which Sir Gaheris suffered at the hands of Sir Turquine; wherefore Sir Launcelot rode to meet Sir Turquine, and he cried out: "Sir Knight! put that wounded man down from his horse, and let him rest for a while, and we two will prove our strength, the one against the other! For it is a shame for thee to treat a noble knight of the Round Table with such despite as thou art treating that knight."

"Sir," said Sir Turquine, "as I treat that knight, so treat I all knights of the Round Table—and so will I treat thee if thou be of the Round Table."

"Well," said Sir Launcelot, "as for that, I am indeed of the Round Table, and I have come hither for no other reason than for to do battle with thee."

"Sir Knight," said Sir Turquine, "thou speakest very boldly; now I pray thee to tell me what knight thou art and what is thy name."

"Messire," said Sir Launcelot, "I have no fear to do that. I am called Sir Launcelot of the Lake, and I am a knight of King Arthur's, who made me knight with his own hand."

"Ha!" said Sir Turquine, "that is very good news to me, for of all knights in the world thou art the one I most desire to meet, for I have looked for thee for a long while with intent to do battle with thee. For it was thou who didst slay my brother Sir Caradus at Dolorous Gard, who was held to be the best knight in all the world. Wherefore, because of this, I have the greatest despite against thee of any man in the world, and it was because of that despite that I waged particular battle against all the knights of King Arthur's court. And in despite of thee I now hold five score and eight knights, who are thy fellows, in the dismallest dungeon of my castle. Also I have to tell thee that among those knights is thine own brother, Sir Ector, and thy kinsman, Sir Lionel. For I overthrew Sir Ector and Sir Lionel only a day or two ago, and now they lie almost naked in the lower parts of that castle yonder. I will put down this knight as thou biddst me, and when I have done battle with thee I hope to tie thee on his saddle-horn in his place."

So Sir Turquine loosed the cords that bound Sir Gaheris and set him from off the horse's back, and Sir Gaheris, who was sorely wounded and very weak, sat him down upon a slab of stone near-by.

Sir Launcelot and Sir Turquine do battle together.

Then Sir Launcelot and Sir Turquine made themselves ready at all points, and each took such stand as seemed to him to be best; and when each was ready for the assault, each set spurs to his horse and rushed the one against the other with such terrible violence that they smote together like a clap of thunder.

So fierce was that onset that each horse fell back upon the ground and only by great skill and address did the knight who rode him void his saddle, so as to save himself from a fall. And in that meeting the horse of Sir Turquine was killed outright and the back of Sir Launcelot's horse was broken and he could not rise, but lay like dead upon the ground.

Then each knight drew his sword and set his shield before him and they came together with such wrath that it appeared as though their fierce eyes shot sparks of fire through the occulariums of their helmets. So they met and struck; and they struck many scores of times, and their blows were so violent that neither shield nor armor could withstand the strokes they gave. For their shields were cleft and many pieces of armor were hewn from their limbs, so that the ground was littered with them. And each knight gave the other so many grim wounds that the ground presently was all sprinkled with red where they stood.

Now that time the day had waxed very hot, for it was come high noontide, so presently Sir Turquine cried out: "Stay thee, Sir Launcelot, for I have a boon to ask!" At this Sir Launcelot stayed his hand and said: "What is it thou hast to ask, Sir Knight?" Sir Turquine said: "Messire, I am athirst—let me drink." And Sir Launcelot said: "Go and drink."

So Sir Turquine went to that river and entered into that water, which was presently stained with red all about him. And he stooped where he stood and drank his fill, and presently came forth again altogether refreshed.

Therewith he took up his sword once more and rushed at Sir Launcelot and smote with double strength, so that Sir Launcelot bent before him and had much ado to defend himself from these blows.

Then by and by Sir Launcelot waxed faint upon his part and was athirst, and he cried out: "I crave of thee a boon, Sir Knight!" "What wouldst thou have?" said Sir

Turquine. "Sir Knight," said Sir Launcelot, "bide while I drink, for I am athirst." "Nay," said Sir Turquine, "thou shalt not drink until thou quenchest thy thirst in Paradise." "Ha!" cried Sir Launcelot, "thou art a foul churl and no true knight. For when thou wert athirst, I let thee drink; and now that I am athirst, thou deniest me to quench my thirst."

Therewith he was filled with such anger that he was like one gone wode; wherefore he flung aside his shield and took his sword in both hands and rushed upon Sir Turquine and smote him again and again; and the blows he gave were so fierce that Sir Turquine waxed somewhat bewildered and bore aback, and held his shield low for faintness.

Sir Launcelot overcometh Sir Turquine.

Then when Sir Launcelot beheld that Sir Turquine was faint in that wise, he rushed upon him and catched him by the beaver of his helmet and pulled him down upon his knees. And Sir Launcelot rushed Sir Turquine's helmet from off his head. And he lifted his sword and smote Sir Turquine's head from off his shoulders, so that it rolled down upon the ground.

Then for a while Sir Launcelot stood there panting for to catch his breath after that sore battle, for he was nearly stifled with the heat and fury thereof. Then he went down into the water, and he staggered like a drunken man as he went, and the water ran all red at his coming. And Sir Launcelot stooped and slaked his thirst, which was very furious and hot.

Thereafter he came up out of the water again, all dripping, and he went to where the damsel was and he said to her; "Damsel, lo, I have overcome Sir Turquine; now I am ready to go with thee upon that other adventure, as I promised thee I would."

At this the damsel was astonished beyond measure, wherefore she cried: "Sir, thou art sorely hurt, and in need of rest for two or three days, and maybe a long time more, until thy wounds are healed."

"Nay," said Sir Launcelot, "no need to wait; I will go with thee now."

Then Sir Launcelot went to Sir Gaheris—for Sir Gaheris had been sitting for all that while upon that slab of stone. Sir Launcelot said to Sir Gaheris: "Fair Lord, be not angry if I take your horse, for I must presently go with this damsel, and you see mine own horse hath broke his back."

"Sir Knight," said Sir Gaheris, "this day you have saved both me and my horse, wherefore it is altogether fitting that my horse or anything that is mine should be yours to do with as you please. So I pray you take my horse, only tell me your name and what knight you are; for I swear by my sword that I never saw any knight in all the world do battle so wonderfully as you have done to-day."

"Sir," said Sir Launcelot, "I am called Sir Launcelot of the Lake, and I am a knight of King Arthur's. So it is altogether fitting that I should do such service unto you as this, seeing that you are the brother of that dear knight, Sir Gawaine. For if I should not do this battle that I have done for your sake, I should yet do it for the sake of my lord, King Arthur, who is your uncle and Sir Gawaine's uncle."

Sir Launcelot makes himself known to Sir Gaheris.

Now when Sir Gaheris heard who Sir Launcelot was, he made great exclamation of amazement. "Ha, Sir Launcelot!" he cried, "and is it thou! Often have I heard of thee and of thy prowess at arms! I have desired to meet thee more than any knight in the world; but never did I think to meet thee in such a case as this." Therewith Sir Gaheris arose, and went to Sir Launcelot, and Sir Launcelot came to him and they met and embraced and kissed one another upon the face; and from that time forth they were as brethren together.

Then Sir Launcelot said to Sir Gaheris: "I pray you, Lord, for to go up unto yonder castle, and bring succor to those unfortunates who lie therein. For I think you will find there many fellow-knights of the Round Table. And I believe that you will find therein my brother, Sir Ector, and my cousin, Sir Lionel. And if you find any other of my kindred I pray you to set them free and to do what you can for to comfort them and to put them at their ease. And if there is any treasure in that castle, I bid you give it unto those knights who are prisoners there, for to compensate them for the pains they have endured. Moreover, I pray you tell Sir Ector and Sir Lionel not to follow after me, but to return to court and wait for me there, for I have two adventures to undertake and I must essay them alone."

Sir Launcelot bids Sir Gaheris to free the castle captives.

Then Sir Gaheris was very much astonished, and he cried out upon Sir Launcelot: "Sir! Sir! Surely you will not go forth upon another adventure at this time, seeing that you are so sorely wounded."

But Sir Launcelot said: "Yea, I shall go now; for I do not think that my wounds are so deep that I shall not be able to do my devoirs when my time cometh to do them."

At this Sir Gaheris was amazed beyond measure, for Sir Launcelot was very sorely wounded, and his armor was much broken in that battle, wherefore Sir Gaheris had never beheld a person who was so steadfast of purpose as to do battle in such a case.

So Sir Launcelot mounted Sir Gaheris' horse and rode away with that young damsel, and Sir Gaheris went to the castle as Sir Launcelot had bidden him to do.

Sir Launcelot departs with the damsel.

In that castle he found five score and eight prisoners in dreadful case, for some who were there had been there for a long time, so that the hair of them had grown down upon their shoulders, and their beards had grown down upon their breasts. And some had been there but a short time, as was the case of Sir Lionel and Sir Ector. But all were in a miserable sorry plight; and all of those sad prisoners but two were knights of King Arthur's court, and eight of them were knights of the Round Table. All these crowded around Sir Gaheris, for they saw that he was wounded and they deemed that it was he had set them free, wherefore they gave him thanks beyond measure.

Sir Gaheris frees the castle captives.

"Not so," said Sir Gaheris, "it was not I who set you free; it was Sir Launcelot of the Lake. He overcame Sir Turquine in such a battle as I never before beheld. For I saw that battle with mine own eyes, being at a little distance seated upon a stone slab and wounded as you see. And I make my oath that I never beheld so fierce and manful a combat in all of my life. But now your troubles are over and done, and Sir Launcelot greets you all with words of good cheer and bids me tell you to take all ease and comfort that you can in being free, and in especial he bids me greet you, Sir Ector, and you, Sir Lionel, and to tell you that you are to follow him no farther, but to return to court and bide there until he cometh; for he goeth upon an adventure which he must undertake by himself."

Sir Lionel and Sir Ector and Sir Kay follow after Sir Launcelot.

"Not so," said Sir Lionel, "I will follow after him, and find him." And so said Sir Ector likewise, that he would go and find Sir Launcelot. Then Sir Kay the Seneschal said that he would ride with those two; so the three took horse and rode away together to find Sir Launcelot.

As for those others, they ransacked throughout the castle of Sir Turquine, and they found twelve treasure-chests full of treasure, both of silver and of gold, together with many precious jewels; and they found many bales of cloth of silk and of cloth of gold. So, as Sir Launcelot had bid them do so, they divided the treasure among themselves, setting aside a part for Sir Ector and a part for Sir Lionel and a part for Sir Kay. Then, whereas before they had been mournful, now they were joyful at having been made so rich with those precious things.

Thus happily ended that great battle with Sir Turquine which was very likely the fiercest and most dolorous fight that ever Sir Launcelot had in all of his life. For, unless it was Sir Tristram, he never found any other knight so big as Sir Turquine except Sir Galahad, who was his own son.

And now it shall be told how Sir Launcelot fared upon that adventure which he had promised the young damsel to undertake.

Sir Launcelot sits with Sir Hilaire and Croisette.

CHAPTER FIFTH

How Sir Launcelot Went Upon an Adventure With the Damsel Croisette as Companion, and How He Overcame Sir Peris of the Forest Sauvage.

Now after Sir Launcelot had finished that battle with Sir Turquine as aforetold, and when he had borrowed the horse of Sir Gaheris, he rode away from that place of combat with the young damsel, with intent to carry out the other adventure which he had promised her to undertake.

But though he rode with her, yet, for a while, he said very little to her, for his wounds ached him sorely and he was in a great deal of pain. So, because of this, he had small mind to talk, but only to endure what he had to endure with as much patience as he might command. And the damsel upon her part was somewhat aware of what Sir Launcelot was suffering and she was right sorry for him, wherefore she did not trouble him with idle discourse at that moment, but waited for a while before she spake.

How Sir Launcelot's wounds pain him.

Then by and by she said to him: "Messire, I would that thou wouldst rest for some days, and take thine ease, and have thy wounds searched and dressed, and have thy armor looked to and redded. Now there is a castle at some distance from this, and it is my brother's castle, and thither we may go in a little pass. There thou mayst rest for this night and take thine ease. For I know that my brother will be wonderfully glad to see thee because thou art so famous."

Then Sir Launcelot turned his eyes upon the damsel: "Fair maiden," quoth he, "I make confession that I do in sooth ache a very great deal, and that I am somewhat aweary with the battle I have endured this day. Wherefore I am very well content to follow thy commands in this matter. But I prithee, damsel, tell me what is thy name, for I know not yet how thou art called."

"Sir," she said, "I am called Croisette of the Dale, and my brother is called Sir Hilaire of the Dale, and it is to his castle that I am about to take thee to rest for this time."

Then Sir Launcelot said: "I go with thee, damsel, wherever it is thy will to take me."

So they two rode through that valley at a slow pace and very easily. And toward the waning of the afternoon they left the valley by a narrow side way, and so in a little while came into a shallow dale, very fertile and smiling, but of no great size. For the more part that dale was all spread over with fields and meadow-lands, with here and there a plantation of trees in full blossom and here and there a farm croft. A winding river flowed down through the midst of this valley, very quiet and smooth, and brimming its grassy banks, where were alder and sedge and long rows of pollard willows overreaching the water.

Of how Sir Launcelot and the damsel ride together.

At the farther end of the valley was a castle of very comely of appearance, being built part of stone and part of bright red bricks; and the castle had many windows of glass and tall chimneys, some a-smoke. About the castle and nigh to it was a little village of thatched cottages, with many trees in blossom and some without blossom shading the gables of the small houses that took shelter beneath them.

Sir Launcelot and Croisette come to a fair valley.

Now when Sir Launcelot and Croisette came into that little valley it was at the declining of the day and the sky was all alight with the slanting sun, and the swallows were flying above the smooth shining surface of the river in such multitudes that it was wonderful to behold them. And the lowing herds were winding slowly along by the river in their homeward way, and all was so peaceful and quiet that Sir Launcelot drew rein for pure pleasure, and sat for some while looking down upon that fair, happy dale. Then by and by he said: "Croisette, meseems I have never beheld so sweet and fair a country as this, nor one in which it would be so pleasant to live."

Upon this Croisette was very much pleased, and she smiled upon Sir Launcelot. "Think you so, Sir Launcelot?" quoth she. "Well, in sooth, I am very glad that this valley pleasures you; for I love it beyond any other place in all the world. For here was I born and here was I raised in that castle yonder. For that is my brother's castle and it was my father's castle before his time; wherefore meseems that no place in all the world can ever be so dear to my heart as this dale."

Thereupon they went forward up that little valley, and along by the smoothly flowing river, and the farther they went the more Sir Launcelot took pleasure in all that he beheld. Thus they came through the pretty village where the folk stood and watched with great admiration how that noble knight rode that way; and so they came to the castle and rode into the court-yard thereof. Then presently there came the lord of that castle, who was Sir Hilaire of the Dale. And Sir Hilaire

Croisette bringeth Sir Launcelot to her brother's house.

greeted Sir Launcelot, saying: "Welcome, Sir Knight. This is great honor you do me to come into this quiet dale with my sister, for we do not often have with us travellers of such quality as you."

"Brother," said Croisette, "you may well say that it is an honor to have this knight with us, for this is none other knight than the great Sir Launcelot of the Lake. This day I beheld him overcome Sir Turquine in fair and honorable battle. So he doth indeed do great honor for to visit us in this wise."

Then Sir Hilaire looked at Sir Launcelot very steadily, and he said: "Sir Launcelot, your fame is so great that it hath reached even unto this peaceful outland place; wherefore it shall not soon be forgotten here how you came hither. Now, I pray you, come in and refresh yourself, for I see that you are wounded and I doubt not you are weary."

Upon this several attendants came, and they took Sir Launcelot and led him to a pleasant chamber. There they unarmed him and gave him a bath in tepid water, and there came a leech and searched his wounds and dressed them. Then those in attendance upon him gave him a soft robe of cloth of velvet, and when Sir Launcelot had put it on he felt much at ease, and in great comfort of body.

Sir Launcelot is made at ease.

By and by, when evening had fallen, a very good, excellent feast was spread in the hall of the castle, and there sat down thereto Sir Launcelot and Sir Hilaire and the damsel Croisette. As they ate they discoursed of various things, and Sir Launcelot told many things concerning his adventures, so that all who were there were very quiet, listening to what he said. For it was as though he were a visitor come to them from some other world, very strange and distant, of which they had no knowledge, wherefore they all listened so as not to lose a single word of what he told them. So that evening passed very pleasantly, and Sir Launcelot went to his bed with great content of spirit.

So Sir Launcelot abided for several days in that place until his wounds were healed. Then one morning, after they had all broken their fast, he made request that he and the damsel might be allowed to depart upon that adventure which he had promised her to undertake, and unto this Sir Hilaire gave his consent.

How Sir Launcelot abides at the castle of Sir Hilaire.

Now, during this while, Sir Launcelot's armor had been so pieced and mended by the armor-smiths of that castle that when he donned it it was, in a measure, as sound as it had ever been, and of that Sir Launcelot was very glad. So having made ready in all ways he and Croisette took leave of that place, and all they who were there bade them adieu and gave Sir Launcelot God-speed upon that adventure.

Now some while after they left that dale they rode through a very ancient forest, where the sod was exceedingly soft underfoot and silent to the tread of the horses, and where it was very full of bursting foliage overhead. And as they rode at an easy pace through that woodland place they talked of many things in a very pleasant and merry discourse.

Quoth the damsel unto Sir Launcelot: "Messire, I take very great wonder that thou hast not some special lady for to serve in all ways as a knight should serve a lady."

"Ha, damsel," said Sir Launcelot, "I do serve a lady in that manner and she is peerless above all other ladies; for that lady is the Lady Guinevere, who is King Arthur's queen. Yet though I am her servant I serve her from a very great distance. For in serving her I am like one who standeth upon the earth, yet looketh upward ever toward the bright and morning star. For though such an one may delight in that star from a distance, yet may he never hope to reach an altitude whereon that star standeth."

Sir Launcelot and Croisette discourse together.

"Heyday!" quoth Croisette, "for that matter, there are other ways of serving a lady than that wise. Were I a knight meseems I would rather serve a lady nearer at hand than at so great distance as that of which thou speakest. For in most cases a knight would rather serve a lady who may smile upon him nigh at hand, and not stand so far off from him as a star in the sky." But to this Sir Launcelot made no reply but only smiled. Then in a little Croisette said: "Dost thou never think of a lady in that wise, Sir Launcelot?"

"Nay," said Sir Launcelot, "and neither do I desire so to serve any lady. For it is thus with me, Croisette—for all that while of my life until I was eighteen years of age I lived in a very wonderful land beneath a magical lake, of which I may not tell thee. Then I came out of that lake and into this world and King Arthur made me a knight. Now because I was so long absent from this world of mankind and never saw aught of it until I was grown into a man, meseems I love that world so greatly that I cannot tell thee how beautiful and wonderful it seems to me. For it is so wonderful and so beautiful that methinks my soul can never drink its fill of the pleasures thereof. Yea; methinks I love every blade of grass upon the fields, and every leaf upon every tree: and that I love everything that creepeth or that flyeth, so that when I am abroad

Sir Launcelot speaketh of the Lady Guinevere.

under the sky and behold those things about me I am whiles like to weep for very joy of them. Wherefore it is, Croisette, that I would rather be a knight-errant in this world which I love so greatly than to be a king seated upon a throne with a golden crown upon my head and all men kneeling unto me. Yea; meseems that because of my joy in these things I have no room in my heart for such a love of lady as thou speakest of, but only for the love of knight-errantry, and a great wish for to make this world in which I now live the better and the happier for my dwelling in it. Thus it is, Croisette, that I have no lady for to serve in the manner thou speakest of. Nor will I ever have such, saving only the Lady Guinevere, the thought of whom standeth above me like that bright star afore spoken of."

"Ha," quoth Croisette, "then am I sad for the sake of some lady, I know not who. For if thou wert of another mind thou mightest make some lady very glad to have so great a knight as thou art to serve her." Upon this Sir Launcelot laughed with a very cheerful spirit, for he and the damsel were grown to be exceedingly good friends, as you may suppose from such discourse as this.

So they wended their way in this fashion until somewhat after the prime of day, and by that time they had come out of that forest and into a very rugged country. For this place into which they were now come was a sort of rocky valley, rough and bare and in no wise beautiful. When they had entered into it they perceived, a great way off, a castle built up upon the rocks. And that castle was built very high, so that the roofs and the chimneys thereof stood wonderfully sharp and clear against the sky; yet the castle was so distant that it looked like a toy which you might easily take into your hand and hold betwixt your fingers.

Sir Launcelot perceives the Castle of Sir Peris.

Then Croisette said to Sir Launcelot: "Yonder is the castle of that evil-minded knight of whom I spake to thee yesterday, and his name is Sir Peris of the Forest Sauvage. Below that castle, where the road leads into that woodland, there doth he lurk to seize upon wayfarers who come thitherward. And indeed he is a very catiff knight, for, though he is strong and powerful, he doth not often attack other knights, but only ladies and demoiselles who come hither. For these he may take captive without danger to himself. For I believe that though he is so big of frame yet is he a coward in his heart."

Then Sir Launcelot sat for a while and regarded that castle, and fell into thought; and he said, "Damsel, if so be this knight is such a coward as thou sayest, meseems that if I travel with thee I shall have some ado to come upon him; because, if he sees me with thee, he may keep himself hidden in the thicket of the forest from my

Sir Launcelot advises Croisette what to do.

sight. Now I will have it this way; do thou ride along the highway in plain sight of the castle, and I will keep within the woodland skirts, where I may have thee in sight and still be hidden from the sight of others. Then if this knight assail thee, as I think it likely he may do, I will come out and do battle with him ere he escapes."

So it was arranged as Sir Launcelot said and they rode in that wise: Croisette rode along the highway, and Sir Launcelot rode under the trees in the outskirts of the forest, where he was hidden from the eyes of anyone who might be looking that way. So they went on for a long pass until they came pretty nigh to where the castle was.

Then, as they came to a certain part of the road that dipped down toward a small valley, they were suddenly aware of a great noise, and immediately there issued out from the forest a knight, large and strong of frame, and followed close behind by a squire dressed altogether in scarlet from head to foot. This knight bore down with great speed upon where Croisette was, and the esquire followed close behind him. When these two had come near to Croisette, the esquire leaped from off his horse and caught her palfrey by the bridle, and the knight came close to her and catched her as though to drag her off from her horse.

Sir Peris attacks Croisette.

With that Croisette shrieked very loud, and immediately Sir Launcelot broke out from the woods and rode down upon where all this was toward with a noise like to thunder. As he came he cried aloud in a great and terrible voice: "Sir Knight, let go that lady, and turn thou to me and defend thyself!"

Then Sir Peris of the Forest Sauvage looked this way and that with intent to escape, but he was aware that he could not escape from Sir Launcelot, wherefore he took his shield in hand and drew his sword and put himself into a position of defence; for, whereas he could not escape, he was, perforce, minded to do battle. Then Sir Launcelot threw aside his spear, and he set his shield before him and he took his sword in his hand, and he drave his horse against Sir Peris. And when he had come nigh to Sir Peris he raised himself in his stirrups and struck him such a buffet that I believe nothing in the world could withstand its force. For though Sir Peris raised his shield against that blow, yet the sword of Sir Launcelot smote through the shield and it smote down the arm that held the shield, and it smote with such a terrible force upon the helm of Sir Peris that Sir Peris fell down from his horse and lay in a swoon without any motion at all.

Sir Launcelot overthrows Sir Peris.

Then Sir Launcelot leaped down from his horse and rushed off the helm of Sir Peris, and lifted his sword with intent to strike off his head.

Upon that the senses of Sir Peris came somewhat back to him, and he set his palms together and he cried out, though in a very weak voice: "Spare me, Sir Knight! I yield myself to thee!"

"Why should I spare thee?" said Sir Launcelot.

"Sir," said Sir Peris, "I beseech thee, by thy knighthood, to spare me."

"Well," said Sir Launcelot, "since thou hast besought me upon my knighthood I cannot do else than spare thee. But if I do spare thee, thou shalt have to endure such shame that any true knight in thy stead would rather die than be spared in such a manner."

"Sir Knight," said Sir Peris, "I am content with anything thou mayst do, so be that thou wilt spare my life."

Upon this Sir Launcelot bade Sir Peris rise. And he took the halter of Sir Peris's horse, and he bound Sir Peris's arms behind his back, and when he had done this he drove him up to his castle at the point of his lance. And when they came to the castle he bade Sir Peris have open the castle; and Sir Peris did so; and thereupon Sir Launcelot and Sir Peris entered the castle and the damsel and the squire followed after them.

In that castle were fourteen ladies of high degree held captive for ransom; and some of these had been there for a considerable time, to their great discomfort. All these were filled with joy when they were aware that Sir Launcelot had set them free. So they came to Sir Launcelot and paid their court to him and gave him great thanks beyond measure.

Sir Launcelot liberates the captive ladies.

Sir Launcelot and Croisette abode in that castle all that night, and when the next morning had come Sir Launcelot made search all over that castle, and he found a considerable treasure of silver and gold, which had been gathered there by the ransom of the ladies and the damsels of degree whom Sir Peris had made prisoner aforetime. All this treasure Sir Launcelot divided among those ladies who were prisoners, and a share of the treasure he gave to the damsel Croisette, because that they two were such good friends and because Croisette had brought him thither to that adventure, and thereof Croisette was very glad. But Sir Launcelot kept none of that treasure for himself.

Sir Launcelot gives the castle treasure to the captive ladies.

Then Croisette said: "How is this, Sir Launcelot? You have not kept any of this treasure for yourself, yet you won it by your own force of arms, wherefore it is altogether yours to keep if you will to do so."

"Croisette," said Sir Launcelot, "I do not care for such things as this treasure; for when I lived within that lake of which I have spoken to thee, such things as this treasure were there as cheap as pebbles which you may gather up at any river-bed, wherefore it has come to pass that such things have no value to me."

Now, after all this had been settled, Sir Launcelot had Sir Peris of the Forest Sauvage haled before him, and Sir Launcelot said: "Catiff Knight, now is it time for thy shame to come upon thee." Therewith he had Sir Peris stripped of all armor and raiment, even to his jerkin and his hose, and he had his arms tied behind his back, and he had a halter set about his neck; and Sir Launcelot tied the halter that was about the neck of Sir Peris to the horn of the saddle of his own horse, so that when he rode away with Croisette Sir Peris must needs follow behind him at whatever gait the horse of Sir Launcelot might take.

Sir Launcelot makes Sir Peris a dishonored captive.

So Sir Launcelot and Croisette rode back to the manor of Sir Hilaire of the Dale with Sir Peris running behind them, and when they had come there Sir Launcelot delivered Sir Peris unto Sir Hilaire, and Sir Hilaire had Sir Peris bound upon a horse's back with his feet underneath the belly of the horse; and sent him to Camelot for King Arthur to deal with him as might seem to the King to be fit.

Sir Hilaire sendeth Sir Peris to King Arthur.

But Sir Launcelot remained with Sir Hilaire of the Dale all the next day and he was very well content to be in that pleasant place. And upon the day after that, which was Sunday, he set forth at about the prime of the day to go to that abbey of monks where he had appointed to meet the damsel Elouise the Fair, as aforetold.

And now you shall hear how Sir Launcelot behaved at the tournament of King Bagdemagus, if it please you to read that which herewith immediately followeth.

JVSTISSIMVS·REX·

Sir Launcelot and Elouise the Fair.

CHAPTER SIXTH

How Sir Launcelot Took Part in the Tournament Between King Bagdemagus and the King of North Wales, and How He Won That Battle for King Bagdemagus.

Sir Launcelot rode by many highways and many byways at a very slow pace, stopping now and then when it pleased him to do so, for he took great joy in being free in the open air again. For the day was warm and that time the clouds were very thick, drifting in great abundance across the sky. And anon there would fall a sudden shower of rain, and anon the sun would shine forth again, very warm and strong, so that all the world sparkled as with incredible myriads of jewels. Then the cock crowed lustily because the shower was past, and another cock answered him far away, and all the world suddenly smiled, and the water trickled everywhere, and the little hills clapped their hands for joy. So Sir Launcelot took great pleasure in the day and he went his way at so easy a pace that it was night-time ere he reached that abbey of monks where he was to meet Elouise the Fair.

How Sir Launcelot rode to find Elouise the Fair.

Now that evening Elouise was sitting in a certain apartment of the abbey overlooking the court-yard, and a maiden was reading to her by the light of several waxen tapers from a book of painted pictures. And the maiden read in a voice that was both high and clear; meanwhile, Elouise sat very still and listened to what she read. Now while Elouise the Fair sat so, there was of a sudden the sound of a great horse coming on the stone pavement of the court below. Therewith Elouise arose hastily and ran to the window and looked down into that court-yard. Then she saw who he was that came, and that it was Sir Launcelot of the Lake. For the light was not yet altogether gone from the sky, which was all shining with gray, so that she could see who it was who came there.

Then Elouise gave great exclamation of joy, and clapped her hands. And she ran down to the court where Sir Launcelot was, and several of her maidens went with her.

Elouise the Fair gives welcome to Sir Launcelot.

When she had come to the court she gave great welcome to Sir Launcelot, and she summoned many attendants and she bade them look to Sir Launcelot. So some of them aided Sir Launcelot to dismount and some took his horse, and some brought him up to a chamber that had been set apart for him, and there unarmed and served him, and set him at his ease.

Then Elouise sent to him a soft robe of purple cloth of velvet, lined with fur, and Sir Launcelot put it upon him and took great comfort in it.

After that Sir Launcelot descended to where Elouise was, and he found that a fair supper had been set for his refreshment. So he sat and ate, and Elouise the Fair herself served him.

Elouise sends for King Bagdemagus.

Meanwhile she had sent for her father, King Bagdemagus, who was at that time no great distance away, and a little after Sir Launcelot had finished his supper King Bagdemagus came to that place, much wondering why Elouise had sent for him.

When King Bagdemagus came, Elouise took him by the hand and led him to Sir Launcelot, and she said: "Sire, here is a knight who, for my sake, is come to help you in this tournament upon Tuesday."

Now King Bagdemagus had never before seen Sir Launcelot, so he knew not who that knight was. Wherefore he said to him: "Messire, I am much beholden to you for coming to my aid in this battle. Now I pray you that you tell me your name and what knight you are."

"Lord," said Sir Launcelot, "I am hight Launcelot, and am surnamed 'He of the Lake.'"

Now when King Bagdemagus heard this he was astonished beyond measure, wherefore he cried out, "This is wonderful, that you who are the very flower of knighthood should be here, and that you should come to aid me in my battle!"

"Sire," said Sir Launcelot, "I know not how much aid I may be to thee until that matter is proven. But of a surety I owe it to this damsel to do what I am able at her request, in return for all that she hath done for me to aid me in my time of great peril. So it is a very small repayment for me to aid thee, her father, in thy time of difficulties. Wherefore if, by good hap, I may be of use to thee in this battle which is nigh at hand, then I shall be glad beyond measure that I have paid some part of that debt which I owe to this lady."

Sir Launcelot talks with King Bagdemagus.

"Messire," said King Bagdemagus, "I give thee gramercy for thy good will in this matter. I am sure that, with thy aid, I shall be successful in this battle, and that it will always be most renowned in the history of chivalry because thou hast taken part in it."

So spake they with great courtesy to one another. Then, by and by, Sir Launcelot said: "Sir, I pray you tell me who are those knights of King Arthur's court who are upon the part of the King of North Wales? For I would fain know against whom I am to do battle." To which King Bagdemagus said: "Messire, those three knights of the Round Table are as follows—there is Sir Mordred, nephew unto King Arthur, and there is Sir Galahantine, and there is Sir Mador de la Porte."

"Ha," quoth Sir Launcelot, "these are three very good knights indeed, and I am not at all astonished that the King of North Wales should have had such good fortune aforetime in that other tournament with you, seeing that he had three such knights as they to do battle upon his side."

After this they fell into discourse as to the manner in which they should do battle upon the morrow, and Sir Launcelot advised in this wise: "Lord, let me take three knights of yours, such as you trust, and such as you hold to be the strongest knights of your party. Let these three knights paint their shields altogether white and I will paint mine white, and then no man will know who we are. For I would have it so that I should not be known to be in this battle until I shall have approved myself in it. Now, when you have chosen those three knights, we four will take hiding in some wood or glade nigh to the place of combat, and when you are most busily engaged, and when you begin to be hard-pressed, then we will come forth and fall upon the flank of the party of the King of North Wales with intent to throw them into confusion. Then you will push your assault very hard, and I doubt not by the grace of God that we shall betwixt us be able to bear back their array in confusion."

Sir Launcelot arranges the order of battle with King Bagdemagus.

This advice seemed very good to King Bagdemagus, and so he did as Sir Launcelot said. He chose him three very strong, worthy, honorable knights, and these made their shields white as Sir Launcelot directed.

Thus, all things being arranged as Sir Launcelot willed, it came to be the eve before the battle. So a little after sunset Sir Launcelot and those three knights whom King Bagdemagus had chosen rode over toward the place of tourney (which was some twelve miles from the abbey where the damsel Elouise was lodged). There they found a little woodland of tall, leafy trees fit for Sir Launcelot's purpose, and that wood stood to one side of the meadow of battle and at about the distance of three furlongs from it. In this little wood Sir Launcelot and the three knights-companion whom King Bagdemagus had chosen laid themselves down upon the ground and wrapped, each man, his cloak about him. So they slept there until the morrow, when the battle was ordained to be.

Now there had been very great preparation made for this tournament for on three sides of the meadow of battle scaffolds had been built and rows of seats had been placed. These were covered over with tapestries and hangings of divers colors—some of figured and some of plain weaving—so that the green and level meadow-land was hung all about with these gay and gaudy colors.

Now when the morning had come, the folk who came to witness that tournament began to assemble from all directions—lords and ladies of high degree, esquires and damsels of lesser rank, burghers and craftsmen with their wives, townspeople from the town, yeomen from the woodlands, and freeholders from the farm crofts. With these came many knights of the two parties in contest, and with the knights came their esquires in attendance. Now these knights were all in full armor, shining very bright, and the esquires were clad in raiment of many textures and various colors, so that they were very gay and debonair. So, with all this throng moving along the highway toward the meadow of battle, it seemed as though the entire world was alive with gay and moving figures.

Sir Launcelot and his companions lie near the place of tournament.

Now the place where Sir Launcelot and those three knights who were with him lay hidden was not far from the highway, so, whence they lay, they could see all that goodly procession of folk taking their way toward the lists, and they could look down upon the meadow of battle, which, as hath been said, was not more than three furlongs distant, and they could see the crowds of people of high and low degree taking their places upon those seats according to their rank and station. And they could see how the knights-contestant arrayed themselves upon this side of the field and upon that, and how the esquires and attendants hurried hither and thither, busying themselves in making their lords ready for the encounter that was soon to befall. Yea, all this could they see as plainly as though it lay upon the palm of a hand.

So they saw that about noontide all those who had come thither had taken their places, and that the field was clean, and that the two parties of combat were arrayed in order for battle.

Then Sir Launcelot perceived that the party of the King of North Wales was very much greater than the party of King Bagdemagus; for while the party of the King of North Wales had nigh eight score of helms, the party of King Bagdemagus had hardly four score of helms. So Sir Launcelot perceived that that party of King Bagdemagus would have much labor to do if it was to win in the battle.

Now, all being prepared, the marshal stood forth and blew upon his trumpet, and therewith those two parties of knights rushed the one against the other, each in so great a cloud of dust that one could hardly see the knights in their passage. Therewith they met in the midst of the meadow of battle, with such a crash and uproar of splintered lances as was terrible to hear.

How the battle began.

And for a while no man could see what was toward, so great was the dust and the tumult. But by and by the dust raised itself a little and then Sir Launcelot perceived that the party of King Bagdemagus had been pushed back by that other party, as might have been supposed in such a case.

So Sir Launcelot looked upon the battle for some while and he saw that the party of King Bagdemagus was pushed farther and farther back. Then by and by Sir Launcelot said to his knights-companion: "Messires, methinks now is our time to enter this engagement."

Therewith he and they rode forth out of that woods, and they rode down the hill and across the fields and so came into that meadow-of-battle.

At that time the party of the King of North Wales was so busily engaged in its assault upon the party of King Bagdemagus that very few of those knights engaged were aware of those four knights coming, and those who were aware of them thought but very little of the coming of so small a number. So no one interfered with their coming, wherefore they were able to bear down with great speed upon the flank of the party of the King of North Wales. Therewith they struck that flank with such force that both horses and horsemen were overturned by their assault.

Sir Launcelot and his companions enter the battle.

In that encounter Sir Launcelot carried a spear that was wonderfully strong and tough. With it he ran with great fierceness into the very thickest of the press, and before he was checked he struck down five knights with that one spear. And likewise those three knights that were with him did such good service that all that flank of the party of the King of North Wales was thrown into great confusion and wist not what to do for to guard themselves against that fierce, furious onset.

Then Sir Launcelot and his three companions bore back a little, and when they got their distance they ran again into the press, and this time Sir Launcelot overthrew the King of North Wales himself, and that with such violence that the bone of his thigh was broken, and he had to be carried away out of that field by his attendants. And in this second assault Sir Launcelot and the three knights who were with him overthrew eleven knights besides the King of North Wales, wherefore all that part of the press began to break away from them and to seek some place where they could defend themselves from such another assault.

Now when the party of King Bagdemagus saw into what confusion the other party were thrown by these four knights-champion, they began a very fierce and furious attack, and with such vehemence that in a little the party of the King of North Wales began to bear back before them. So, what with those who withdrew before Sir Launcelot's assault, and what with those who withdrew from the assault of King Bagdemagus, there was a great deal of confusion in the ranks of the party of the King of North Wales.

Now those three knights who were of King Arthur's court perceived how Sir Launcelot and his knights-companion were throwing the ranks of the party of the King of North Wales into confusion, and they knew that unless the onset of Sir Launcelot was checked, the day would of a surety be lost unto them. Wherefore said Sir Mador de la Porte: "Yonder is a very strong and fierce-fighting knight; if we do not check his onset we will very likely be brought to shame in this battle." "Yea," said Sir Mordred, "that is so. Now I will take it upon me to joust with that knight and to overthrow him." Upon that those other two knights bade him go and do as he said. So Sir Mordred made way to where Sir Launcelot was, coming forward very fiercely and with great violence, and Sir Launcelot was aware of Sir Mordred's coming and made him ready for that assault. So the two came together with terrible violence and Sir Launcelot struck Sir Mordred such a buffet that the breast-band of Sir Mordred's saddle brake, and both the saddle and Sir Mordred flew over his horse's tail. Therewith Sir Mordred fell upon his head and struck with such violence upon the ground that his neck was nigh broken, and he lay altogether in a dead swoon and had to be carried out of the lists by his attendants.

Sir Launcelot overthrows Sir Mordred.

This saw Sir Mador de la Porte, and he cried out: "Ha! see what hath befallen Sir Mordred!" And therewith he also bare down upon Sir Launcelot with all his might and main with intent to overthrow him. And Sir Launcelot ran against him, and they struck together so fiercely that it was terrible to behold. But the spear of Sir Mador de la Porte burst into pieces, whilst the spear of Sir Launcelot held, so that both Sir Mador and his horse were overthown, the horse rolling upon the man. And in that encounter Sir Mador's shoulder went out of place, and he also had to be borne away by his attendants.

Sir Launcelot overthrows Sir Mador.

Then Sir Galahantine took a great spear from his esquire, who was nigh him, and he also ran against Sir Launcelot with all his might; and Sir Launcelot met him in full course and that onset was more terrible than either of the other two. For the spear of each knight was burst into splinters, even to the butt thereof. Then each threw away the butt of his spear and drew out his sword, and Sir Galahantine struck Sir Launcelot such a blow that the legs of Sir Launcelot's horse trembled under him because of the weight of that stroke. At this Sir Launcelot waxed wroth beyond measure and he rose in his stirrups and he smote Sir Galahantine such a buffet that the blood burst out from his nose and his ears, and all his senses so went away from him that he might hardly behold the light of day because of the swimming of his sight.

Sir Launcelot strikes Sir Galahantine a sad blow.

Therewith Sir Galahantine's head hung down upon his breast and he had no power to guide his horse, wherefore his horse made way out of the press and galloped off, bearing Sir Galahantine away, whether he would or no. And after the horse had galloped a little distance Sir Galahantine could not any longer sit upon his saddle, but he fell off of his horse and rolled over upon the ground and had not strength to rise therefrom.

Then Sir Launcelot catched another spear, great and strong, from the esquire who followed him, and before ever that spear broke he overthrew sixteen knights therewith. Wherefore all who beheld him were amazed and terrified at what he did.

By now the party of the King of North Wales began to bear more and more aback and in a little they broke, and then the party of King Bagdemagus pursued them hither and thither, and those who did not surrender were overthrown so that it was not possible for them to make any new order of battle. Then that party surrendered itself as conquered, one and all, and so King Bagdemagus won that tournament with the greatest glory that it was possible for him to have. For it had never been heard of before that a party of four-score knights should overcome in that way a party of eight-score knights, with three knights of the Round Table to champion them. Nor would such a victory have been possible only for what Sir Launcelot did in that battle.

Sir Launcelot wins the battle for King Bagdemagus.

So Sir Launcelot won that tournament for King Bagdemagus, and after the battle was over and done King Bagdemagus came to Sir Launcelot and said to him: "Messire, thou hast brought to me the greatest glory this day that ever fell to my lot in all of my life. Now I prithee come with me and refresh thyself with me, so that I may give thee fitting thanks for all thou hast done, and so that I may reward thee in such a way as is fit for a king to reward a knight-champion such as thou art."

Unto this Sir Launcelot made reply: "Lord, I give you thanks for your courtesy, but I need no reward; for it is meet that I should have done what I could for the sake of

Sir Launcelot departs without reward.

the demoiselle Elouise the Fair, seeing that she rescued me from the mischiefs that Queen Morgana had intent to do me."

Then King Bagdemagus besought Sir Launcelot that he would tarry awhile and rest, but Sir Launcelot would not do so, but would be going upon his way without any tarrying. But he said to King Bagdemagus: "I prithee greet your daughter for me, and say to her that if ever she hath need of my services again let her send to me, and I will come to her even if it be to the end of the earth. For I have not yet repaid her for what she hath done for me."

Therewith Sir Launcelot went his way from that meadow of battle, and, coming to the skirts of the forest he entered therein, and those who were there at the meadow of battle did not see him any more.

So endeth the history of that famous tournament betwixt King Bagdemagus and the King of North Wales.

JVSTISSIMVS·REX·

Sir Launcelot climbs to catch the lady's falcon.

CHAPTER SEVENTH

How Sir Launcelot Fell Into the Greatest Peril That Ever He Encountered in All His Life. Also How He Freed a Misfortunate Castle and Town From the Giants Who Held Them, and How He Released the Lord Thereof From a Dungeon.

NOW SIR LAUNCELOT WANDERED ERRANT FOR MANY DAYS, MEETING NO adventure of any moment, but taking great joy in all that he beheld of the wide world about him, and in that time he found lodging wheresoever he chanced to be (if not in house, then beneath the skies), and he endured all sorts of weather, both wet and dry.

Upon a certain day, in the prime of the morning, he came across a hilltop, and beheld beneath him a valley, very fertile and well-tilled, with fields and meadow-lands spread all over it like to a fair green carpet woven in divers patterns. And in the midst of the valley was a very large and noble castle, with many towers, and tall, steep roofs, and clustering chimneys. So Sir Launcelot descended into that valley, and the road which he took ended in front of the castle and under the shade of the tall gray walls thereof. But he did not stop at that castle but went on by it.

Sir Launcelot cometh to a fair valley with a castle.

Now after Sir Launcelot had passed by that castle it seemed to him that he heard very delicate silver bells ringing sweetly in the air above him, and when he looked up he beheld that a falcon was flying over his head toward a high elm tree that stood at a little distance, and he wist that it was the bells upon the cap of the falcon that rang so sweetly. And Sir Launcelot beheld that long lunes hung from the feet of the falcon as she flew, wherefore he was aware that the falcon had slipped her lunes and had flown from her owner.

So Sir Launcelot watched the falcon, and he beheld that she lit in a tall elm tree, where she took her perch and rested, balancing with her wings part spread. Then by and by she would have taken her flight again, but the lunes about her feet had

Sir Launcelot beholdeth a falcon entangled.

become entangled around the bough on which she sat, so that when she would have flown she could not do so. Now Sir Launcelot was very sorry to see the falcon beating herself in that wise, straining to escape from where she was prisoner, but he knew not what to do to aid her, for the tree was very high, and he was no good climber of trees.

While he stood there watching that falcon he heard the portcullis of the castle lifted, with a great noise, and the drawbridge let fall, and therewith there came a lady riding out of the castle very rapidly upon a white mule, and she rode toward where Sir Launcelot watched the falcon upon the tree. When that lady had come nigh to Sir Launcelot, she cried out to him: "Sir Knight, didst thou see a falcon fly this way?" Sir Launcelot said: "Yea, Lady, and there she hangs, caught by her lunes in yonder elm-tree."

Then when that lady beheld how that her falcon hung there she smote her hands together, crying out: "Alas, alas! what shall I do? That falcon is my lord's favorite hawk! While I was playing with her a while since, she slipped from me and took flight, and has sped as thou dost see. Now when my lord findeth that I have lost his hawk in that wise he will be very angry with me, and will haply do me some grievous hurt."

Quoth Sir Launcelot: "Lady, I am very sorry for you." "Sir," she said, "it boots nothing for you to be sorry for me unless you can aid me." "How may I aid you in this?" said Sir Launcelot. "Messire," quoth she, "how otherwise could you aid me than by climbing up into this tree for my hawk? For if you aid me not in such a fashion, I know not what I shall do, for my lord hath a very hot and violent temper, and he is not likely to brook having his favorite hawk lost to him, as it is like to be."

The Lady beseeches Sir Launcelot to get her the falcon again.

Upon this Sir Launcelot was put to a great pass and knew not what to do, for he had no good mind to climb that tree. "Lady," quoth he, "I prithee tell me what is thy lord's name." "Messire," she replied, "he is hight Sir Phelot, and is a knight of the court of the King of North Wales."

"Well, Lady," said Sir Launcelot, "thou dost put upon me a very sore task in this, for God knoweth I am no climber of trees. Yea, I would rather do battle with twenty knights than to climb one such tree as this. Ne'ertheless, I cannot find it in me to refuse the asking of any lady, if so be it lieth at all in my power to perform her will. Now if you will aid me to unarm myself, I will endeavor to climb this tree and get your hawk."

So the lady dismounted from her mule, and Sir Launcelot dismounted from his horse, and the lady aided Sir Launcelot to unarm himself. And when he had unarmed himself he took off all his clothes saving only his hosen and his doublet. Then he climbed that tree, though with great labor and pain to himself, and with much dread lest he should fall. So he, at last, reached the falcon where it was, and he loosened the lunes from where they were entangled about the branch, and he freed the bird. Then he brake off a great piece of rotten bough of the tree and he tied the lunes of the falcon to it and he tossed the falcon down to where the lady was; and the lady ran with great joy and caught the falcon and loosed it from the piece of branch and tied the lunes to her wrist, so that it could not escape again.

Sir Launcelot climbs the tree.

Then Sir Launcelot began to descend the tree with as great labor and pain as he had climbed into it.

But he had not come very far down when he perceived a knight who came riding very rapidly toward that tree, and he saw that the knight was in full armor. When this knight came to the tree he drew rein and bespoke the lady who was there, though Sir Launcelot could not hear what he said. So, after he had spoken for a little, the knight dismounted from his horse and went to Sir Launcelot's shield and looked upon the face of it very carefully. Then presently he looked upward toward Sir Launcelot, and he said: "Art thou Sir Launcelot of the Lake?" And Sir Launcelot said: "Yea." "Very well," said the knight, "I am pleased beyond measure at that. For I am Sir Phelot, the lord of this castle, and the brother of that Sir Peris of the Forest Sauvage, whom thou didst treat so shamefully after thou hadst overcome him in battle."

Sir Phelot threatens Sir Launcelot's life.

"Sir," said Sir Launcelot, "I treated him nowise differently from what he deserved." "No matter for that," said Sir Phelot, "he was my brother, and thou didst put great despite and shame upon him. So now I will be revenged upon thee, for now I have thee where I would have thee, and I will slay thee as shamefully as thou didst put shame upon him. So say thy prayers where thou art, for thou shalt never go away from this place alive."

"Sir Knight," said Sir Launcelot, "I do not believe that thou wouldst really assault a naked and harmless man, for it would certainly be a great shame to thee to do me a harm in that wise. For lo! thou art armed in full, and I am a naked man, and to slay me as I am would be both murder and treason."

"No matter for that," said Sir Phelot; "as for the shame of it, I take no thought of it. I tell thee thou shalt have no grace nor mercy from me. Wherefore make thy peace with Heaven, for thine hour is come."

"Sir Knight," said Sir Launcelot, "I ask only one boon of thee; if thou art of a mind to take so much shame upon thee, as appears to be the case, let me not, at least, die like a felon without any weapon. Let me have my sword in my hand, even if I have no other defence. For if a knight must die, it is a shame for him to die without weapons. So hang my sword upon yonder bough, where I may reach it, and then thou mayst slay me."

"Nay," said Sir Phelot, "I will not do that, for I know very well how wonderful is thy prowess. Wherefore I believe that even if thou wert otherwise unarmed thou mightst overcome me if thou hadst thy sword. So I will give thee no such chance, but will have my will of thee as thou art."

Then Sir Launcelot was put to a great pass of anxiety, for he wist not what to do to escape from that danger in which he lay. Wherefore he looked all about him and above him and below him, and at last he beheld a great branch of the elm tree just above his head, very straight and tough. So he catched this branch and broke it off from the tree and shaped it to a club of some sort. Then he came lower, and the knight waited to strike him with his sword, when he was low enough; but Sir Launcelot did not come low enough for that.

Sir Launcelot is put to a sad pass to escape.

Then Sir Launcelot perceived that his horse stood below him and a little to one side, so of a sudden he ran out along the branch whereon he stood and he leaped quickly down to the earth upon the farther side of his horse from where the knight stood.

At this Sir Phelot ran at him and lashed at him with his sword, thinking to slay him before he had recovered from his leap. But Sir Launcelot was quicker than he, for he recovered his feet and put away the blow of Sir Phelot with his club which he held. Then he ran in upon Sir Phelot under his sword arm, and before he could use his sword he struck Sir Phelot with all his might upon the side of his head. And he struck him very quickly again, and he struck him the third time, all in the space whilst one might count two. And those blows he struck were so direful that Sir Phelot fell down upon his knees, all stunned and bedazed, and the strength went out of his thews because of faintness. Then Sir Launcelot took the sword out of the hand of Sir Phelot and Sir Phelot did not have strength to deny him. And Sir Launcelot plucked off Sir Phelot's helm and catched him by the hair and dragged his neck forward so as to have ease to strike his head from off his body.

Sir Launcelot overcomes Sir Phelot with a strange weapon.

Now all this while the lady had been weeping and watching what befell. But when she saw the great danger Sir Phelot was in, she ran and clasped her arms about him, and cried out in a very loud and piercing voice upon Sir Launcelot to spare Sir

Phelot and to slay him not. But Sir Launcelot, still holding him by the hair of the head, said: "Lady, I cannot spare him, for he has treated me more treacherously than any other knight with whom I ever had dealings." But the lady cried out all the more vehemently, "Sir Launcelot, thou good knight, I beseech thee, of thy knighthood, to spare him."

"Well," said Sir Launcelot, "it hath yet to be said of me that I have denied anything that I was able to grant unto any lady that hath asked it of me upon my knighthood. And yet I know not how to trust either of ye. For thou didst not say one word in my behalf when I was in danger of being slain so treacherously just now. As for this knight, I perceive that he is every whit as great a traitor and a coward as was his brother Sir Peris of the Sauvage Forest. So I will spare him, but I will not trust him, lest he turn against me ere I arm myself again. Wherefore give me hither the halter rein of your mule." So the lady gave Sir Launcelot the halter rein, weeping amain as she did so. And Sir Launcelot took the halter rein and he tied the arms of Sir Phelot behind him. Then he bade the lady of Sir Phelot to help him arm himself from head to foot, and she did so, trembling a very great deal. Then, when she had done so, quoth Sir Launcelot: "Now I fear the treachery of no man." Therewith he mounted his horse and rode away from that place. And he looked not behind him at all, but rode away as though he held too much scorn of that knight and of that lady to give any more thought to them.

Sir Launcelot spares Sir Phelot's life.

So after that Sir Launcelot travelled for a while through the green fields of that valley, till by and by he passed out of that valley, and came into a forest through which he travelled for a very long time.

For it was about the slanting of the afternoon ere he came forth out of that forest and under the open sky again. And when he came out of the forest he beheld before him a country of perfectly level marish, very lush and green, with many ponds of water and sluggish streams bordered by rushes and sedge, and with pollard willows standing in rows beside the waters. In the midst of this level plain of green (which was like to the surface of a table for flatness) there stood a noble castle, part built of brick and part of stone, and a town of no great size and a wall about the town. And this castle and town stood upon an island surrounded by a lake of water, and a long bridge, built upon stone buttresses, reached from the mainland to the island. And this castle and town were a very long distance away, though they appeared very clear and

Sir Launcelot cometh to a marish country.

distinct to the sight across the level marish, like, as it were, to a fine bit of very small and cunning carving.

Now the way that Sir Launcelot travelled, led somewhat toward that town, wherefore he went along that way with intent to view the place more near by. So he conveyed by that road for some time without meeting any soul upon the way. But at last he came of a sudden upon an archer hiding behind an osier tree with intent to shoot the water-fowl that came to a pond that was there—for he had several such fowl hanging at his girdle. To him Sir Launcelot said: "Good fellow, what town is that yonderway?" "Sir," said the yeoman, "that is called the Town of the Marish because it stands in these Fenlands. And that castle is called the Castle of the Fenlands for the same reason."

Quoth Sir Launcelot: "What manner of place is that? Is it a good place, or is it otherwise?" "Sir," said the archer, "that place was one while a very good, happy place; for in times gone by there was a lord who dwelt there who was both just and noble, and kind to all folk, wherefore he was loved by all the people. But one night there came two very grim and horrible giants thither from the Welsh Mountains and these entered into the castle by treachery and made prisoner of the lord of the castle. Him they cast into the dungeon of the castle, where they held him prisoner as an hostage. For they threaten that if friends of that lord's should send force against them to dispossess them, they will slay him. As for any other rescue, there is no knight who dareth to go against them because of their terrible size, and their strength, and their dreadful, horrible countenances."

Sir Launcelot talks with a yeoman.

"Well," said Sir Launcelot, "that is a pity and I am sorry for that noble lordling. Now, since there is no other single knight who dareth to undertake this adventure, I myself will go and encounter these giants."

"Nay, Sir Knight," said the yeoman, "do not do so, for they are not like mortal men, but rather like monsters that are neither beast nor man. Wherefore anyone who beholdeth them, feareth them."

"Gramercy for thy thought of me, good fellow," quoth Sir Launcelot, "but if I shall refuse an adventure because I find it perilous, then I am not like to undertake any adventure at all."

Therewith he bade good den to that yeoman and rode upon his way, directing his course toward that town at an easy pass.

So he came at last to the long bridge that reached from the land to the island, and he saw that at the farther end of the bridge was the gateway of the town and through the arch thereof he could perceive a street of the town, and the houses upon either side of the street, and the people thereof coming and going.

So he rode forth upon the bridge and at the noise of his coming (for the hoofs of his horse sounded like thunder upon the floor of the bridge) the people of the town came running to see who it was that dared to come so boldly into their town.

Sir Launcelot crosses the bridge to the town.

These, when Sir Launcelot came nigh, began to call to him on high, crying: "Turn back, Sir Knight! Turn back! Else you will meet your death at this place."

But Sir Launcelot would not turn back, but advanced very steadfastly upon his way.

Now somewhat nigh the farther end of that bridge there stood a little lodge of stone, built to shelter the warden of the bridge from stress of weather. When Sir Launcelot came nigh to this lodge there started suddenly out from it a great churl, above seven feet high, who bore in his hand a huge club, shod with iron and with great spikes of iron at the top. This churl ran to Sir Launcelot and catched his horse by the bridle-rein and thrust it back upon its haunches, crying out in a great hoarse voice: "Whither goest thou, Sir Knight, for to cross this bridge?" Sir Launcelot said: "Let go my horse's rein, Sir Churl." Whereunto the churl made answer: "I will not let go thy horse's rein, and thou shalt not cross this bridge."

At this Sir Launcelot waxed very angry, and he drew his sword and struck the churl a blow with the flat thereof upon the shoulder, so that he dropped the rein very quickly. Therewith that churl drew back and took his great iron-shod club in both hands and struck at Sir Launcelot a blow that would have split a millstone. But Sir Launcelot put by the blow with his sword so that it did him no harm. But therewith he waxed so wroth that he ground his teeth together with anger, and, rising in his stirrups, he lashed that churl so woful a blow that he cleft through his iron cap and his head and his breast even to the paps.

Sir Launcelot slays the huge churl.

Now when the people of the town beheld that terrible blow they lifted up their voices in a great outcry, crying out: "Turn back, Sir Knight! Turn back! For this is a very woful thing for thee that thou hast done!" and some cried out: "Thou hast killed the giants' warder of the bridge!" And others cried: "Thou art a dead man unless thou make haste away from this." But to all this Sir Launcelot paid no heed, but wiped his sword and thrust it back into its sheath. Then he went forward upon his way across the bridge as though nothing had befallen, and so came to the farther side. Then, without paying any heed

The folk warn Sir Launcelot.

to all the people who were there, he rode straight to the castle and into the gate of the castle and into the court-yard thereof.

Now by this time all the castle was astir, and in great tumult, and many people came running to the windows and looked down upon Sir Launcelot. And Sir Launcelot sat his horse and looked all about him. So he perceived that beyond the court-yard was a fair space of grass, very smooth and green, well fitted for battle, wherefore he dismounted from his horse and tied it to a ring in the wall, and then he went to that green field and made him ready for whatever might befall.

Meantime all those people who were at the windows of the castle cried out to him, as the people of the town had done: "Go away, Sir Knight! Go away whilst there is still time for you to escape, or else you are a dead man!"

But Sir Launcelot replied not, but stood there and waited very steadfastly. Then the great door of the castle hall opened, and there came forth therefrom those two giants of whom he had heard tell.

And in truth Sir Launcelot had never beheld such horrible beings as they; for they were above ten feet high, and very huge of body and long of limb. And they were clad in armor of bull-hide with iron rings upon it, and each was armed with a great club, huge and thick, and shod with iron, and studded with spikes. These came toward Sir Launcelot swinging their clubs and laughing very hideously and gnashing their long white teeth, for they thought to make easy work of him.

Two giants attack Sir Launcelot.

Then Sir Launcelot, seeing them coming thus, set his shield before him, and made ready for that assault with great calmness of demeanor. Then the giants rushed suddenly upon him and struck at him, the both of them together; for they deemed that by so doing the enemy could not escape both blows, but if one failed the other would slay him. But Sir Launcelot put aside the blow of one giant with his sword and of the other with his shield, with marvellous dexterity. Thereupon, ere they could recover themselves, he turned upon that giant who was upon his left hand and he struck him so terrible a blow upon the shoulder that he cut through the armor and through the shoulder and half-way through the body, so that the head and one arm of the giant leaned toward one way, and the other arm and the shoulder leaned toward the other way. Therewith the giant fell down upon the ground bellowing, so that it was most terrible to hear; and in a little he had died where he had fallen.

How Sir Launcelot slays the first giant.

Now when the fellow of that giant beheld that dreadful, horrible stroke, he was so possessed with terror that he stood for a while trembling and like one in a maze. But when he saw Sir Launcelot turn upon him with intent to make at him also, he let fall his club and ran away with great and fearful outcry. Therewith he ran toward the castle and would have entered therein, but those within the castle had closed the doors and the gates against him, so that he could not escape in that way. So the giant ran around and around the court with great outcry, seeking for some escape from his pursuer, and Sir Launcelot ran after him. And Sir Launcelot struck him several times with his sword, so that at last, what with terror and pain and weariness, that giant stumbled and fell upon the ground. Therewith Sir Launcelot ran at him, and, ere he could rise, he took his sword in both hands and smote off his head so that it rolled down upon the ground like a ball. Then Sir Launcelot stood there panting for breath, for he had raced very hard after the giant, and could hardly catch his breath again. As he stood so, many of those of the castle and many of those who were of the town came to him from all sides; and they crowded around him and gave him great acclaim for ridding that place of those giants.

How Sir Launcelot slays the second giant.

Then Sir Launcelot said to them: "Where is your lord?" Whereunto they made reply: "Sir, he lieth in the dungeon of the castle under the ground chained to the walls thereof, and there he hath been for three years or more, and no one hath dared to bring him succor until you came hither." "Go find him," said Sir Launcelot, "and set him free, and lose no time in doing so. And put him at all ease that you can."

They say: "Will you not stay and see him, Messire, and receive his acknowledgements for what you have done?" But Sir Launcelot replied: "Nay, not so." Then they say: "Will you not have some refreshment after this battle?" Whereunto Sir Launcelot said: "I do not need such refreshment." Then they say: "But will you not rest a little?" "Nay," said Sir Launcelot: "I may not tarry, for I have far to go and several things to do, so that I do not care to stay." So he loosed his horse from the ring in the wall, and mounted upon it and rode away from that castle and from that town and across the bridge whence he had come. And all the people followed after him, giving him great acclaim.

Sir Launcelot departs without refreshment.

So Sir Launcelot left the castle, not because he needed no rest, but because he could not endure to receive the thanks of those whom he benefited. For though he loved to bring aid to the needy, yet he did not love to receive their thanks and their praise. Wherefore, having freed the lord of that castle from that brood of giants, he was content therewith and went his way without resting or waiting for thanks.

For so it was with those noble gallant knights of those days; that whilst they would perform signal service for mankind, yet they were not pleased to receive thanks or reward for the same, but took the utmost satisfaction, not in what they gained by their acts, but in the doing of knightly deeds, for they found all their reward in their deeds, because that thereby they made the world in which they lived better; and because they made the glory of the King, whose servants they were, the more glorious.

And I hold that such behavior upon the part of anyone makes him the peer of Sir Launcelot or Sir Tristram or Sir Lamorack or Sir Percival; yea, of Sir Galahad himself. For it does not need either the accolade or the bath to cause a man to be a true knight of God's making; nor does it need that a mortal King should lay sword upon shoulder to constitute a man the fellow of such knightly company as that whose history I am herewith writing; it needs only that he should prove himself at all times worthy in the performance of his duty, and that he shall not consider the hope of reward, or of praise of others in the performance of that duty.

So look to it that in all your services you take example of the noble Sir Launcelot of the Lake, and that you do your uttermost with might and main, and that you therewith rest content with having done your best, maugre any praise. So you shall become a worthy fellow of Sir Launcelot and of his fellows.

JVSTISSIMVS·REX·

Sir Launcelot takes the armor of Sir Kay.

CHAPTER EIGHTH

How Sir Launcelot Rescued Sir Kay From a Perilous Pass. Also How He Changed Armor With Sir Kay and What Befell.

One day Sir Launcelot came at early nightfall to a goodly manor-house and there he besought lodging for the night, and lodging was granted to him very willingly.

Now there was no lord of that manor, but only an old gentlewoman of very good breeding and address. She made Sir Launcelot right welcome and gave such cheer as she could, setting before him a very good supper, hot and savory, and a great beaker of humming mead wherewith to wash it down. Whilst Sir Launcelot ate, the gentlewoman inquired of him his name and he told her it was Sir Launcelot of the Lake. "Ha!" quoth she, "I never heard that name before, but it is a very good name."

The old gentlewoman makes Sir Launcelot welcome.

At this Sir Launcelot laughed: "I am glad," said he, "that my name belikes thee. As for thy not having heard of it—well, I am a young knight as yet, having had but three years of service. Yet I have hopes that by and by it may be better known than it is at this present."

"Thou sayest well," quoth she, "for thou art very young yet, wherefore thou mayst not know what thou canst do till thou hast tried." And therewith Sir Launcelot laughed again, and said: "Yea, that is very true."

Now after Sir Launcelot had supped, his hostess showed him to the lodging she had provided for him wherein to sleep, and the lodging was in a fair garret over the gateway of the court. So Sir Launcelot went to his bed and, being weary with journeying, he presently fell into a deep and gentle sleep.

Now about the middle of the night there fell of a sudden the noise of someone beating upon the gate and calling in a loud voice and demanding immediate admittance thereat. This noise awoke Sir Launcelot, and he arose from his couch and went

Sir Launcelot is aroused from sleep.

to the window and looked out to see who it was that shouted so loudly and made such uproar.

The moon was shining at that time, very bright and still, and by the light thereof Sir Launcelot beheld that there was a knight in full armor seated upon horseback without the gate, and that the knight beat upon the gate with the pommel of his sword, and shouted that they should let him in.

But ere anyone could run to answer his call there came a great noise of horses upon the highroad, and immediately after there appeared three knights riding very fiercely that way, and these three knights were plainly pursuing that one knight. For, when they perceived him, they rode very violently to where he was, and fell upon him fiercely, all three at one time; wherefore, though that one knight defended himself as well as he could, yet was he in a very sorry way, and altogether likely to be overborne. For those three surrounded him so close to the gate that he could do little to shift himself away from their assaults.

Now when Sir Launcelot beheld how those three knights attacked that one knight, he said to himself: "Of a surety, yonder knight is in a very sorry way. I will do what I can to help him; for it is a shame to behold three knights attack one knight in that way. And if he be slain in this assault, meseems I shall be a party to his death."

Sir Launcelot goeth to the rescue of the knight assaulted.

Therewith he ran and put his armor upon him, and made ready for battle. Then he drew the sheet from his bed, and he tied the sheet to the bar of the window and by it he let himself quickly down to the ground not far from where those knights were doing battle. So being safely arrived in that way he cried out in a very loud voice: "Messires, leave that knight whom ye assail, and turn to me, for I have a mind to do battle with you myself."

Then one of those knights, speaking very fiercely, said: "Who are you, and what business have you here?"

"It matters not who I am," said Sir Launcelot, "but I will not have it that you three shall attack that one without first having had to do with me."

"Very well," said that knight who had spoken, "you shall presently have your will of that."

Therewith he and his fellows immediately descended from their horses, and drew their swords and came at Sir Launcelot upon three sides at once. Then Sir Launcelot set his back against the gate and prepared to defend himself.

Therewith that knight whom he would defend immediately got down from his horse with intent to come to the aid of Sir Launcelot, but Sir Launcelot forbade him very fiercely, saying: "Let be, Sir Knight, this is my quarrel, and you shall not meddle in it."

Upon this, those three knights rushed upon him very furiously, and they struck at him all at once, smiting at him wherever they could and with all their might and main. So Sir Launcelot had much ado to defend himself from their assault. But he made shift that they should not all rush in upon him at once, and by and by he found his chance with one of them. Whereupon he turned suddenly upon that one, and suddenly he lashed so terrible a buffet at him that the knight fell down and lay as though he had been struck dead with the force thereof.

Sir Launcelot does battle with three knights.

Then, ere those other two had recovered themselves, he ran at a second and struck him so fierce a blow that his wits left him, and he staggered like a drunken man and ran around and around in a circle, not knowing whither he went. Then he rushed upon the third and thrust him back with great violence, and as he went back Sir Launcelot struck him, too, as he had struck his companions and therewith that knight dropped his sword and fell down upon his knees and had not power to raise himself up.

Then Sir Launcelot ran to him and snatched off his helmet, and catched him by the hair with intent to cut off his head. But at that the fallen knight embraced Sir Launcelot about the knees, crying out: "Spare my life!"

"Why should I spare you?" said Sir Launcelot. "Sir," cried the knight, "I beseech you of your knighthood to spare me."

"What claim have you upon knighthood," said Sir Launcelot, "who would attack a single knight, three men against one man?"

Then the other of those knights who had been staggered by Sir Launcelot's blow, but who had by now somewhat recovered himself, came and kneeled to Sir Launcelot, and said: "Sir, spare his life, for we all yield ourselves unto you, for certes, you are the greatest champion in all the world."

Then Sir Launcelot was appeased, but he said: "Nay, I will not take your yielding unto me. For as you three assaulted this single knight, so shall you all three yield to him."

"Messire," said the knight who kneeled: "I am very loth to yield us to that knight, for we chased him hither, and he fled from us, and we would have overcome him had you not come to his aid."

"Well," said Sir Launcelot, "I care nothing for all that, but only that you do as I will. And if ye do not do it, then I must perforce slay your companions and you two. Wherefore you may take your choice."

The three knights must yield to the one knight.

Then said that knight who kneeled: "Messire, I see no other thing to do than to yield us as you would have, wherefore we submit ourselves unto this knight whom you have rescued from us."

Then Sir Launcelot turned to that knight to whom he had brought aid in that matter, and he said: "Sir Knight, these knights yield themselves unto you to do as you command them. Now I pray you of your courtesy to tell me your name and who you are."

"Sir," said that knight, "I am Sir Kay the Seneschal, and am King Arthur's foster-brother, and a knight of the Round Table. I have been errant now for some time in search of Sir Launcelot of the Lake. Now, I deem either that you are Sir Launcelot, or else that you are the peer of Sir Launcelot."

"Thou art right, Sir Kay," said Sir Launcelot, "and I am Sir Launcelot of the Lake." So thereat they two made great joy over one another, and embraced one another as brothers-in-arms should do.

Then Sir Kay told Sir Launcelot how it was with those three knights who had assailed him; that they were three brethren, and that he had overthrown the fourth brother in an adventure at arms and had hurt him very sorely thereby. So those three had been pursuing him for three days with intent to do him a harm.

Sir Kay taketh submission of the three knights.

Now Sir Kay was very loath to take submission of those three knights, but Sir Launcelot would have it so and no other way. So Sir Kay consented to let it be as Sir Launcelot willed. Thereupon those three knights came and submitted themselves to Sir Kay, and Sir Kay ordained that they should go to Camelot and lay their case before King Arthur, and that King Arthur should adjudge their case according to what he considered to be right and fitting.

Then those three knights mounted upon their horses and rode away, and when they had done so the gates of the manor were opened, and Sir Launcelot and Sir Kay entered in. But when the old lady who was his hostess beheld Sir Launcelot come in, she was very greatly astonished, for she wist he was still asleep in his bed-chamber. Wherefore she said: "Sir, methought you were in bed and asleep." "So indeed I was," said Sir Launcelot, "but when I saw this knight in peril of his life against three knights, I leaped out of my window and went to his aid." "Well," said his hostess, "meseems that you will sometime be a very good knight, if you have so much courage whilst you are so young." And at that both Sir Launcelot and Sir Kay laughed a great deal.

Then the chatelaine set bread and wine before Sir Kay, and he ate and refreshed himself, and thereafter he and Sir Launcelot went to that garret above the gate, and there fell asleep with great ease of body.

Now before the sun arose Sir Launcelot awoke but Sir Kay still slept very soundly. Then Sir Launcelot beheld how Sir Kay slept, and he had a mind for a jest. So he clad himself in Sir Kay's armor altogether from head to foot, and he took Sir Kay's shield and spear, and he left his armor and shield and spear for Sir Kay to use. Then he went very softly from that room, and left Sir Kay still sleeping. And he took Sir Kay's horse and mounted upon it and rode away; and all that while Sir Kay knew not what had befallen, but slept very deeply.

Sir Launcelot takes Sir Kay's armor.

Now after a while Sir Kay awoke, and he found that Sir Launcelot was gone, and when he looked he found that his own armor was gone and that Sir Launcelot's armor was left. Then he wist what Sir Launcelot had done, and he said: "Ha! what a noble, courteous knight is the gentleman. For he hath left me his armor for my protection, and whilst I wear it and carry his shield and ride his horse, it is not likely that anyone will assail me upon my way. As for those who assail him, I do not believe that they will be likely to find great pleasure in their battle."

Therewith he arose and clad himself in Sir Launcelot's armor, and after he had broken his fast he thanked his hostess for what she had given him, and rode upon his way with great content of spirit.

(And it was as Sir Kay had said, for when he met other knights upon the road, and when they beheld the figure upon his shield, they all said: "It is not well to meddle with that knight, for that is Sir Launcelot." And so he came to Camelot without having to do battle with any man.)

As for Sir Launcelot, he rode upon his way with great cheerfulness of spirit, taking no heed at all of any trouble in the world, but chanting to himself as he rode in the pleasant weather. But ever he made his way toward Camelot, for he said: "I will return to Camelot for a little, and see how it fares with my friends at the court of the King."

How Sir Launcelot travels toward Camelot.

So by and by he entered into the country around about Camelot, which is a very smooth and fertile country, full of fair rivers and meadows with many cots and hamlets, and with fair hedge-bordered highways, wonderfully pleasant to journey in. So travelling he came to a very large meadow where were several groves of trees standing here and there along by a river. And as he went through this meadow he saw before him a long bridge, and at the farther side of the bridge were three pavilions of silk of divers colors, which pavilions had been cast in the shade of a grove of beech-trees. In front of each pavilion stood a great spear thrust in the earth, and from the spear hung the shield of the knight to whom the pavilion belonged. These shields Sir Launcelot read very easily, and so knew the knights who were there. To wit: that they were Sir Gunther, Sir Gylmere, and Sir Raynold, who were three brothers of the Court of King Arthur. As Sir Launcelot passed their pavilions, he saw that the three knights sat at feast in the midmost pavilion of the three, and that a number of esquires and pages waited upon them and served them, for those knights were of very high estate, and so they were established as high lords should be.

Sir Launcelot perceives three knights at feast.

Now when those knights perceived Sir Launcelot they thought it was Sir Kay because of the armor he wore, and Sir Gunther, who was the eldest of the three brothers, cried out: "Come hither, Sir Kay, and eat with us!" But to this Sir Launcelot made no reply, but rode on his way. Then said Sir Gunther: "Meseems Sir Kay hath grown very proud this morning. Now I will go and bring him back with me, or else I will bring down his pride to earth." So he made haste and donned his helmet and ran and took his shield and his spear, and mounted his horse and rode after Sir Launcelot at a hard gallop. As he drew nigh to Sir Launcelot he cried out: "Stay, Sir Knight! Turn again, and go with me!" "Why should I go with you?" said Sir Launcelot. Quoth Sir Gunther: "Because you must either return with me or do battle with me." "Well," said Sir Launcelot, "I would rather do battle than return against my will." And at that Sir Gunther was astonished, for Sir Kay was not wont to be so ready for a battle. So Sir Launcelot set his shield and spear and took his stand, and Sir Gunther took his stand. Then, when they were in all ways prepared, each set spur to his horse and rushed together with terrible speed. So each knight struck the other in the midst of his shield, but the onset of Sir Launcelot was so terrible that it was not to be withstood, wherefore both Sir Gunther and his horse were overthrown in such a cloud of dust that nothing at all was to be seen of them until that cloud lifted.

The three knights bid Sir Launcelot come to feast with them.

Sir Launcelot overthrows Sir Gunther.

At this both Sir Raynold and Sir Gylmere were astonished beyond measure, for Sir Gunther was reckoned to be a much better knight than Sir Kay, wherefore they wist not how it was that Sir Kay should have overthrown him in that fashion.

So straightway Sir Gylmere, who was the second of those brothers, called out to Sir Launcelot to tarry and do battle. "Very well," said Sir Launcelot, "if I cannot escape thee I must needs do battle. Only make haste, for I would fain be going upon my way."

So Sir Gylmere donned his helm in haste and ran and took his shield and spear and mounted upon his horse. So when he had made himself ready in all ways he rushed upon Sir Launcelot with all his might and Sir Launcelot rushed against him.

In that encounter each knight struck the other in the midst of his shield, and the spear of Sir Gylmere burst into pieces, but Sir Launcelot's spear held, so the breast-strap of Sir Gylmere's saddle bursting, both saddle and knight were swept entirely off the horse and to the earth, where Sir Gylmere lay altogether stunned.

Sir Launcelot overthrows Sir Gylmere.

Then Sir Raynold came against Sir Launcelot in like manner as the others had done, and in that encounter Sir Launcelot overthrew both horse and man so that, had not Sir Raynold voided his horse, he would likely have been very sadly hurt.

Sir Launcelot wins from Sir Raynold.

Then Sir Raynold drew his sword and cried out in a loud voice: "Come, Sir Knight, and do me battle afoot!" But Sir Launcelot said: "Why will you have it so, Sir Knight? I have no such quarrel with you as to do battle with swords." "Ha!" said Sir Raynold, "you shall fight with me. For though you wear Sir Kay's armor, I wot very well that you are not Sir Kay, but a great deal bigger man than ever Sir Kay is like to be."

"Nay," said Sir Launcelot, "I will not do any more battle with you." And therewith he drew rein and rode away, leaving Sir Raynold standing very angry in the middle of the highway.

After that Sir Launcelot rode very easily at a quiet gait, with no great thought whither he rode, until after a while he came to a place where a road went across a level field with two rows of tall poplar trees, one upon either side of the highway. Then Sir Launcelot perceived where, beneath the shade of these poplar trees, were four knights standing each by his horse. And these four knights were conversing very pleasantly together. Now as Sir Launcelot drew nigh he perceived that those were four very famous noble knights of the Round Table; to wit: one of those knights was his own brother, Sir Ector de Maris, another was Sir Gawain, another was Sir Ewain, and the fourth was Sir Sagramore le Desirous.

Sir Launcelot meets four noble knights.

Now as Sir Launcelot drew nigh Sir Gawain said: "Look, yonder cometh Sir Kay the Seneschal." Unto this Sir Sagramore le Desirous said: "Yea, this is he; now bide you here for a little while, and I will go and take a fall of him."

So straightway he mounted upon his horse, and he rode toward Sir Launcelot, and he cried out: "Stay, Sir Knight, you cannot go farther until you have had to do with me." "What would you have of me?" quoth Sir Launcelot. "Sir," said Sir Sagramore, "I will have a fall of you." "Well," said Sir Launcelot, "I suppose I must pleasure you, since it cannot be otherwise."

Therewith he dressed his shield and his spear and Sir Sagramore dressed his shield and his spear, and when they were in all ways prepared they ran together at full tilt. In that encounter Sir Sagramore's spear broke, but Sir Launcelot struck so powerful a blow that he overthrew both horse and man into a ditch of water that was near-by.

Sir Launcelot overthrows Sir Sagramore.

Then Sir Ector de Maris said: "Ha, surely some very ill chance has befallen Sir Sagramore for to be overthrown by Sir Kay. Now I will go and have ado with him, for if the matter rests here there will be no living at court with the jests which will be made upon us."

So he took horse and rode to where Sir Launcelot was, and he went at a very fast gallop. When he had come near to Sir Launcelot he cried out: "Have at thee, Sir Kay, for it is my turn next!" "Why should I have at thee?" said Sir Launcelot, "I have done thee no harm." "No matter," said Sir Ector, "you can go no farther until you have had to do with me." "Well," said Sir Launcelot, "if that is so, the sooner I have to do with thee, the sooner shall I be able to go upon my way."

Sir Launcelot overthrows Sir Ector.

Therewith each knight made himself ready and when they were in all ways prepared they came together with such force that Sir Launcelot's spear went through Sir Ector's shield and smote him upon the shoulder, and Sir Ector was thrown down upon the ground with such violence that he lay where he had fallen, without power to move.

Then said Sir Ewain to Sir Gawain where they stood together: "That is the most wonderful thing that ever I beheld, for never did I think to behold Sir Kay bear himself in battle in such a fashion as that. Now bide thee here and let me have a try at him." Therewith Sir Ewain mounted his horse and rode at Sir Launcelot, and there were no words spoken this time, but each knight immediately took his stand to do battle. Then they ran their horses together, and Sir Launcelot gave Sir Ewain such a buffet that he was astonished, and for a little he knew not where he was, for his spear fell down out of his hand, and he bore his shield so low that Sir Launcelot might have slain him where he stood if he had been minded to do so.

Sir Ewain yields to Sir Launcelot.

Then Sir Launcelot said: "Sir Knight, I bid thee yield to me." And Sir Ewain said: "I yield me. For I do not believe that thou art Sir Kay but a bigger man than he shall ever be. Wherefore I yield me." "Then that is well," said Sir Launcelot. "Now stand thou a little aside where thou mayst bring succor unto these other two knights, for I see that Sir Gawain has a mind to tilt with me."

And it was as Sir Launcelot said, for Sir Gawain also had mounted his horse and had made himself ready for that encounter. So Sir Gawain and Sir Launcelot took stand at such place as suited them. Then each knight set spurs to his horse and rushed together like thunder, and each knight smote the other knight in the midst of his shield; and in that encounter the spear of Sir Gawain brake in twain but the spear of Sir Launcelot held, and therewith he gave Sir Gawain such a buffet that Sir Gawain's horse reared up into the air, and it was with much ado that he was able to void his saddle ere his horse fell over backward. For if he had not leaped to earth the horse would have fallen upon him.

Sir Gawain fails with Sir Launcelot.

Then Sir Gawain drew his sword and cried very fiercely: "Come down and fight me, Sir Knight! For thou art not Sir Kay!"

"Nay, I will not fight thee that way," said Sir Launcelot, and therewith he passed on his way without tarrying further.

But he laughed to himself behind his helmet as he rode, and he said: "God give Sir Kay joy of such a spear as this, for I believe there came never so good a spear as this into my hand. For with it I have overthrown seven famous knights in this hour."

As for those four knights of the Round Table, they comforted one another as best they could, for they knew not what to think of that which had befallen them. Only Sir Ector said: "That was never Sir Kay who served us in this wise, but such a man as is better than ten Sir Kays, or twice ten Sir Kays, for the matter of that."

Now Sir Launcelot came to Camelot about eventide, what time King Arthur and his court were assembled at their supper. Then there was great joy when news was brought of his coming and they brought him in to the court and set him beside the King and the Lady Guinevere all armed as he was. Then King Arthur said: "Sir Launcelot, how is it with thee?" and Sir Launcelot said: "It is well." Then King Arthur said: "Tell us what hath befallen thee." And Sir Launcelot told all that had happened

How Sir Launcelot returned to Camelot.

in that month since he had left court. And all they who were there listened, and were much astonished.

But when Sir Launcelot told how he had encountered those seven knights, in the armor of Sir Kay, all laughed beyond measure excepting those of the seven who were there, for they took no very good grace to be laughed at in that wise.

So now I hope I have made you acquainted with Sir Launcelot of the Lake, who was the greatest knight in the world. For not only have I told you how he was created a knight at the hands of King Arthur, but I have also led you errant along with him, so that you might see for yourself how he adventured his life for other folk and what a noble and generous gentleman he was; and how pitiful to the weak and suffering, and how terrible to the evil-doer. But now I shall have to leave him for a while (but after a while in another book that shall follow this, I shall return to him to tell you a great many things concerning other adventures of his), for meantime it is necessary that I should recount the history of another knight, who was held by many to be nearly as excellent a knight as Sir Launcelot was himself.

Conclusion

Here endeth the story of Sir Launcelot. That which followeth is the story of Sir Tristram of Lyonesse, who was knit with Sir Launcelot into such close ties of friendship that if they had been brothers of the same blood, with the same father and mother, they could not have loved one another more than they did.

For indeed it would not be possible to tell any history of Sir Launcelot of the Lake without telling that of Sir Tristram of Lyonesse as well, for as the web of a fair fabric is woven in with the woof thereof, so were the lives of Sir Launcelot and Sir Tristram woven closely together.

Wherefore you shall now hear tell of the goodly adventures of Sir Tristram of Lyonesse; and God grant that you may have the same joy in reading thereof that I shall have in telling of them to you.

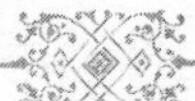

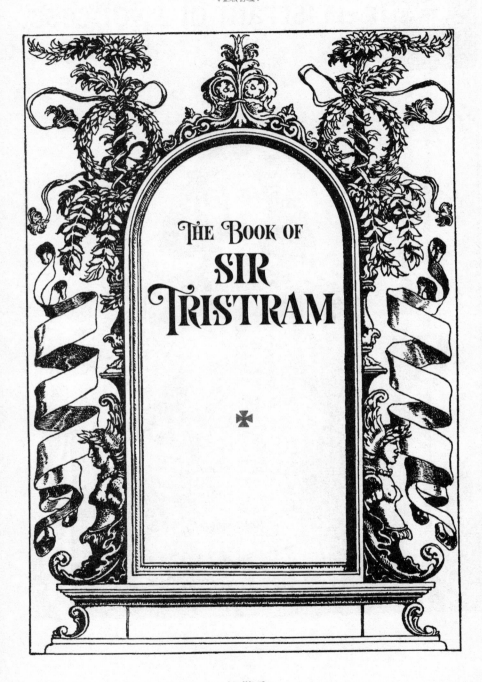

THE BOOK OF SIR TRISTRAM

ir Tristram of Lyonesse.

Prologue

THERE WAS A CERTAIN KINGDOM CALLED LYONESSE, AND THE KING OF that country was hight Meliadus, and the Queen thereof who was hight the Lady Elizabeth, was sister to King Mark of Cornwall.

In the country of Lyonesse, there was a very beautiful lady, who was a cunning and wicked sorceress. This lady took great love for King Meliadus, who was of an exceedingly noble appearance, and she meditated continually how she might bring him to her castle so as to have him near her.

Now King Meliadus was a very famous huntsman, and he loved the chase above all things in the world, excepting the joy he took in the love of his Queen, the Lady Elizabeth. So, upon a certain day, in the late autumn season he was minded to go forth a-hunting, although the day was very cold and bleak.

King Meliadus rides a-hunting.

About the prime of the day the hounds started, of a sudden, a very wonderful stag. For it was white and its horns were gilded very bright, shining like pure gold, so that the creature itself appeared like a living miracle in the forest. When this stag broke cover, the hounds immediately set chase to it with a great outcry of yelling, as though they were suddenly gone frantic, and when the King beheld the creature, he also was immediately seized as with a great fury for chasing it. For, beholding it, he shouted aloud and drove spurs into his horse, and rushed away at such a pass that his court was, in a little while, left altogether behind him, and he and the chase were entirely alone in the forest.

The stag, with the hounds close behind it, ran at a great rate through the passes of the woodlands, and King Meliadus pursued it with might and main until the chase burst out of the forest into an open plain beyond the woodland. Then King Meliadus beheld that in the midst of the plain was a considerable lake of water; and that in the midst of the water was an island; and that upon the island was a very tall and stately castle. Toward this castle the stag ran with great speed, and so, coming to the lake, it leaped into the water and swam across to the island—and there was a thin sheet of clear ice upon the water close to either bank.

King Meliadus chases the stag.

But when the hounds that pursued the stag came to that frozen water, they stinted their pursuit and stood whimpering upon the brink, for the ice and the water repelled them. But King Meliadus made no such pause, but immediately leaped off from his horse, and plunged into the water and swam across in pursuit of the stag. And when he reached the other side, he chased the stag afoot with great speed, and therewith the stag ran to the castle and into the court-yard thereof, and King Meliadus ran after it. Then, immediately he had entered in, the gates of the castle were shut and King Meliadus was a prisoner.

(Now you are to know that that castle was the abode of the beautiful enchantress afore spoken of, and you are to know that she had sent that enchanted stag to beguile King Meliadus to her court, and so she made King Meliadus her captive. Further, it is to be told that when she had him there within her castle, she wove a web of enchantment all about him so that he forgot the Lady Elizabeth and his court and his kingdom and thought of nothing but that beautiful sorceress who had thus beguiled him into her power.)

King Meliadus is made prisoner at an enchanted castle.

Now, when those who were with the King returned to the castle of Lyonesse without him, and when the King did not return that day nor the next day nor at any time, the Lady Elizabeth grew more and more distracted in her anxiety because of him. And when a fortnight had gone by and still there was no news of the King, her grief and apprehension became so great that she turned distracted and they had to set watch and ward upon her lest she do herself a harm in her madness.

The Lady Elizabeth grieves to distraction.

So for a long time they kept her within the castle; but upon a certain day she broke away from her keepers and ran out from the castle and into the forest ere those in attendance upon her knew she had gone. Only one gentlewoman saw her, and she called upon a young page to follow her, and thereupon ran after the Queen whither she went, with intent to bring her back again.

But the Lady Elizabeth ran very deep into the forest, and the gentlewoman and the page ran after her; and the Queen thought that she was going to find her lord in the forest. So she ran very rapidly for a great distance, until by and by she waxed faint with weariness from running and sank down upon the ground; and there they that followed her found her lying. And they found that the Queen was in a great passion of pain and sick to death. For the day was very wintry, with a fine powder of snow all over the ground, so that the cold of the weather pierced through the garments of the Lady Elizabeth and entered into her body and chilled her to the heart.

The Lady Elizabeth escapes into the forest.

Now the gentlewoman, seeing how it was with the Queen, called the page to her and said: "Make haste! Go back to the castle of Lyonesse, and bring some of the knights of the castle with all speed, else the Queen will die at this place." And upon that the page ran off with great speed to do her bidding and the Queen was left alone with her gentlewoman.

Then the gentlewoman said, "Lady, what cheer?" And the Queen said, "Alas, I am sick to death." The gentlewoman said, "Lady, cannot you bear up a little until help cometh?" Thereupon the Lady Elizabeth fell to weeping very piteously, and said, "Nay, I cannot bear up any longer, for the cold hath entered into my heart." (Yea, even at that time death was upon her because of the cold at her heart.)

Then by and by in the midst of her tears and in very sore travail a man-child was born to the Queen, and when that came to pass a great peace fell suddenly upon her.

Then she said, speaking to the nurse like one in great weariness, "What child is it that I have given unto the world?" The nurse said, "It is a man-child." The Queen said to her, "Hold him up until I see him." Thereupon the nurse held the child up and the Queen looked at him, though she could hardly see him because it was as though a mist lay upon her eyes which she could not clear away from her sight; for at that time she was drawing deep draughts of death. Then, when she had seen the child and had beheld that he was very strong and lusty and exceedingly comely, she said: "Behold, this is my child, born in the midst of sore travail and great sorrow; wherefore his name shall be called Tristram because he hath caused so many tears to be shed."

How Tristram is born in the forest.

Then in a little while the Lady died, and the gentlewoman stood weeping beside her, making great outcry in that cold and lonely forest.

Anon there came those knights who were sent from the castle to find the Queen; and when they came to that place, they beheld that she lay upon the ground all cold and white like to a statue of marble stone. So they lifted her up and bare her away upon a litter, and the gentlewoman followed weeping and wailing in great measure, and bearing the child wrapped in a mantle.

So Tristram was born in that wise, and so his name was given to him because of the tears that were shed at his birth.

And now it is to be told how King Meliadus returned from that castle of enchantment where he was held prisoner.

At this time Merlin was still living in the world, for Vivien had not yet bewitched him, as hath been told in the Book of King Arthur. So by and by it came to pass that he discovered where King Meliadus was imprisoned and how it fared with him in the castle of that enchantress. So he made greater spells than those that enmeshed King Meliadus, and he brought King Meliadus back into his memory of the Queen and his kingdom. Then straightway the King broke out from the castle of the enchantress and returned to his kingdom. But when he came there it was to find everything in great sorrow and dole; for the Lady Elizabeth was no longer upon this earth to bring joy to the heart of the King. So for a long while after his return King Meliadus lay altogether stricken down with the grief of that bereavement.

King Meliadus is released from durance.

Here followeth the story of Tristram, how he passed his youth, and how he became a knight of Cornwall of King Mark's making.

PART I

THE STORY OF SIR TRISTRAM AND THE LADY BELLE ISOULT

Here followeth the story of Sir Tristram of Lyonesse, who, with Sir Launcelot of the Lake, was deemed to be one of the two most worthy and perfect knights champion of his day.

Likewise herein shall be told the story of the Lady Belle Isoult, who next to Queen Guinevere, was reckoned to be the most fair, gentle lady in all of the world.

Tristram succors the Lady Moeya.

CHAPTER FIRST

How the New Queen of Lyonesse Sought Tristram's Life; How He Went to France, and How He Returned Again to Lyonesse and Was Received With Love at That Place.

So King Meliadus grieved very bitterly for the Lady Elizabeth for the space of seven years, and in that time he took but little pleasure in life, and still less pleasure in that son who had been born to him in that wise. Then one day a certain counsellor who was in great favor with the King came to him and said: "Lord, it is not fitting that you should live in this wise and without a mate; for you should have a queen, and you should have other children besides Tristram, else all the fate of this kingdom shall depend upon the life of that one small child."

And King Meliadus took this counsel to heart, and after a while he said: "What you tell me is true, and so I shall take another Queen, even though it is not in me to love any other woman in all of the world but that dear one who is dead and gone." So a while after that he took to wife the Lady Moeya, who was the daughter of King Howell of Britain.

King Meliadus taketh the Lady Moeya to second wife.

Now Queen Moeya had been married to an Earl of Britain, and by him she had a son who was about the age of Tristram. So she brought this son to Lyonesse with her, and he and Tristram were very good companions.

But the Lady Moeya took great hatred of Tristram, for she said in her heart: "Except for this Tristram, mayhap my son might be King and overlord of this land." And these thoughts brooded with her, so that after a while she began to meditate how she might make away with Tristram so that her own son might come into his inheritance.

Now at that time Tristram was about thirteen years of age and very large and robust of form and of extraordinary strength of body and beauty of countenance. But the son of Queen Moeya was not of such a sort, so the more beautiful and noble Tristram was the more the Queen hated him. So one day she called to her a very cunning chemist and she said to him: "Give me a drink of such and such a sort, so that he who drinks thereof shall certainly die, maugre help of any kind." And the chemist gave her what she desired, and it was in a phial and was of a golden color.

Now Tristram and the son of the Lady Moeya were wont to play ball in a certain court of the castle, and when they would play there they would wax all of a heat with their sport. This the Lady Moeya was well aware of; so one day she took that phial of poison and she poured a part of it into a chalice and she filled the chalice with clear water and she set the chalice upon a bench where those two would play at ball. For she said to herself: "When they grow warm with their play, Tristram will certainly drink of this water to quench his thirst, and then my son will maybe enter into his inheritance."

The Lady Moeya devises mischief against Tristram.

So the two youths played very fiercely at their game, and they waxed exceedingly hot and presently were both very violently athirst. Then Tristram said, "I would I had somewhat to drink," and his stepbrother said, "Look, yonder is a chalice of water; drink! and when thou hast quenched thy thirst, then I will drink also." But Tristram said: "Nay, brother, drink thou first, for thou art more athirst than I." Then at first the son of the Lady Moeya would not have it so, but would have Tristram drink; but afterward he did as Tristram bade him, and, taking the chalice in both hands, he drank freely of that poison which his own mother had prepared. Then when he had drunk his fill, Tristram took the chalice and would have drunk too; but the other said, "Stay, Tristram, there is great bitterness in that chalice"; and then he said, "Methinks I feel a very bitter pang within my vitals," and then he cried out, "Woe is me! I am in great pain!" Therewith he fell down upon the ground and lay there in a great passion of agony. Then Tristram cried aloud for help in a piercing voice; but when help came thither it was too late, for the son of the Lady Moeya was dead.

The son of the Queen drinks of the poison.

Then the Lady Moeya was in great torment of soul, and beat her breast and tore her hair and King Meliadus had much ado for to comfort her. And after this she hated Tristram worse than ever before, for she would say to herself: "Except for this Tristram, my own son would yet be alive!"

So she brooded upon these things until she could not rest, whether by day or night. Then one day she took the rest of the poison that was in the phial and poured it into a goblet of yellow wine. This goblet she gave to one of her pages, saying: "Take this to Tristram, and offer it to him when I shall tell you to do so!"

Therewith she went down to the hall where Tristram was, and she said, "Tristram, let there be peace betwixt us." And Tristram said: "Lady, that meets my wishes, for I have never had in my heart aught but loving-kindness toward you, and so I would have it in your heart toward me." With this the page came in the hall with that goblet of yellow wine. Then the Lady Moeya took the goblet and said: "Take this cup, and drink of the wine that is in it, and so there shall be peace betwixt us forever." And as she said that she looked very strangely upon Tristram, but Tristram was altogether innocent of any evil against him. So he reached out his hand to take the cup which the page brought to him.

The Lady Moeya seeks Tristram's life a second time.

Now at that moment King Meliadus came into the hall fresh from the chase, and he was much heated and greatly athirst, wherefore, when he saw that cup of wine he said: "Stay, Tristram, let me drink, for I am greatly athirst. After I have quenched my thirst, then thou shalt drink."

Therewith he took the goblet of wine and made to lift it to his lips. But at that the Lady Moeya cried out, in a very loud and piercing voice, "Do not drink of that wine!" The King said, "Why should I not drink of it?" "No matter," said the Lady Moeya, "thou shalt not drink of it, for there is death in it."

Therewith she ran to the King and catched him by the hand, and she plucked away the goblet so that the wine was spilled out of it upon the ground.

Then King Meliadus gazed at the Lady Moeya, and he thought of many things in very little time. Thereupon he seized her by the hair and dragged her forward, so that she fell down upon her hands and knees to the pavement of the hall. And King Meliadus drew his great sword so that it flashed like lightning, and he cried: "Tell me what thou hast done, and tell me quickly, or thou shalt not be able to tell me at all!" Then the Lady Moeya clutched King Meliadus about the thighs, and she cried out: "Do not slay me with thine own hand, or else my blood will stain thee with dishonor! I will tell

King Meliadus threatens to slay the Queen.

thee all, and then thou mayst deal with me according to the law, for indeed I am not fit to live." So therewithal the Lady Moeya confessed everything to the King.

Then King Meliadus shouted aloud and called the attendants and said: "Take this woman and cast her into prison, and see that no harm befall her there; for the lords of this country shall adjudge her, and not I." And therewith he turned away and left her.

And thereafter, in due season, the Lady Moeya was brought to trial and was condemned to be burned at the stake.

Now when the day came that she was to be burnt, Tristram was very sorry for her. So when he beheld her tied fast to the stake he came to where King Meliadus was and he kneeled before him, and he said, "Father, I crave a boon of thee." Thereupon King Meliadus looked upon Tristram, and he loved him very tenderly and he said: "My son, ask what thou wilt, and it shall be thine." Then Tristram said: "Father, I pray thee, spare the life of this lady, for methinks she hath repented her of her evil, and surely God hath punished her very sorely for the wickedness she hath tried to do."

Tristram begs mercy for the Queen.

Then King Meliadus was very wroth that Tristram should interfere with the law; but yet he had granted that boon to his son and could not withdraw. So after a while of thought he said: "Well, I have promised, and so I will perform my promise. Her life is thine; go to the stake and take her. But when thou hast done so I bid thee go forth from this place and show thy face here no more. For thou hast interfered with the law, and hast done ill that thou, the son of the King, should save this murderess. So thou shalt leave this place, for I mistrust that between you two some murder will befall in this country."

So Tristram went weeping to where the Queen was bound to the stake; and he cut her bonds with his dagger and set her free. And he said: "Lady, thou art free; now go thy way, and may God forgive thee as I do." Then the Queen wept also, and said, "Tristram, thou art very good to me." And because she was barefoot and in her shift, Tristram took his cloak and wrapped it about her.

After that, Tristram straightway left Lyonesse, and King Meliadus appointed that a noble and honorable lord of the court, hight Gouvernail, should go with him. They two went to France, and there they were made very welcome at the court of the King. So Tristram dwelt in France till he was eighteen years old, and everyone at the court of the King of France loved him and honored him so that he dwelt there as though he were of the blood of France.

Tristram departs from Lyonesse.

During the time that he was in France he became the greatest hunter in the world, and he wrote many books on venery that were read and studied long after he had ceased to live. Also he became so skilful with the harp that no minstrel in the world was his equal. And ever he waxed more sturdy of frame and more beautiful of countenance, and more well-taught in all the worship of knighthood. For during that time he became so wonderfully excellent in arms that there was no one in France who was his equal.

Thus Tristram dwelt at peace in that land for five years, but even he longed for his own home with all the might and main of his heart. So one day he said to Gouvernail: "Gouvernail, I cannot deny myself any longer from seeing my father and my own country, for I feel that I must see them or else my heart will certainly break because of its great longing." Nor would he listen to anything that Gouvernail might say contrary to this. So they two took their departure from France, and Tristram travelled as a harper and Gouvernail as his attendant. Thus they came to Lyonesse in that wise.

How Tristram returns to Lyonesse.

One day whilst King Meliadus sat at meat, they two came into the hall, and Gouvernail wore a long white beard which altogether disguised him so that no one knew him. But Tristram shone with such a great radiance of beauty and of youth that all who looked upon him marvelled at him. And the heart of King Meliadus went out to Tristram very strongly, and he said before all of his court, "Who art thou, fair youth? And whence comest thou?" To which Tristram made reply: "Lord, I am a harper, and this is my man, and we have come from France." Then King Meliadus said to Tristram: "Sir, have you seen a youth in France whom men call Tristram?" And Tristram replied, "Yea, I have seen him several times." King Meliadus said, "Doth he do well?" "Yea," said Tristram, "he doeth very well, though at times he is sore oppressed with a great desire for his own country." At this King Meliadus turned away his face, for his heart went very strongly out at the thought of his son. Then by and by he said to Tristram, "Wilt thou play upon thy harp?" And Tristram said, "Yea, if it will please thee to hear me." Therewith he took his harp and he set it before him, and he struck the strings and played upon it, and he sang in such a wise that no one who was there had ever heard the like thereof.

Then King Meliadus' heart was melted at Tristram's minstrelsy, and he said: "That is wonderful harping. Now ask what thou wilt of me, and it shall be thine, whatever it may be."

To this Tristram said, "Lord, that is a great thing that thou sayest." "Nevertheless," said King Meliadus, "it shall be as I say." Then Tristram left his harp and he came to where King Meliadus sat, and he kneeled down before him and he said: "Lord, if so be that is the case, then that which I ask of thee is this: that thou wilt forgive me and bring me back into thy favor again."

At that King Meliadus was filled with a great wonder, and he said: "Fair youth, who art thou, and what have I to forgive thee?" "Lord," said Tristram, "I am thy son, and ask thee to forgive me that I should have saved the life of that lady who is thy Queen."

King Meliadus is reconciled to Tristram.

At this King Meliadus cried out with joy, and he came down from where he sat and he took Tristram into his arms and kissed him upon the face, and Tristram wept and kissed his father upon the face.

So they were reconciled.

After that, Tristram abode in peace in Lyonesse for some while, and during that time he made peace betwixt King Meliadus and Queen Moeya, and the Queen loved him because he was so good to her.

Now after the return of Tristram as aforesaid, King Meliadus would have made him a knight, but Tristram would not suffer the honor of knighthood to be bestowed upon him at that time, but always said: "Lord, think not ill of me if I do not accept knighthood at this time. For I would fain wait until the chance for some large adventure cometh; then I would be made a knight for to meet that adventure, so that I might immediately win renown. For what credit could there be to our house if I should be made knight, only that I might sit in hall and feast and drink and make merry?"

Tristram refuses knighthood.

So spoke Sir Tristram, and his words sounded well to King Meliadus, wherefore from thenceforth King Meliadus refrained from urging knighthood upon him.

Now the way that Sir Tristram achieved knighthood shall be told in that which followeth, and also it shall then be told how he fought his first battle, which was one of the most famous that ever he fought in all of his life.

JVSTISSIMVS·REX·

ing Mark of Cornwall.

CHAPTER SECOND

How Sir Tristram Was Made Knight by the King of Cornwall, and How He Fought a Battle With a Famous Champion.

NOW FIRST OF ALL IT IS TO BE HERE SAID THAT AT THAT TIME THERE was great trouble come to King Mark of Cornwall (who, as aforesaid, was uncle to Sir Tristram) and the trouble was this:

The King of Cornwall and the King of Ireland had great debate concerning an island that lay in the sea betwixt Cornwall and Ireland. For though that island was held by Cornwall, yet the King of Ireland laid claim to it and demanded that the King of Cornwall should pay him truage for the same. This King Mark refused to do, and there was great contention betwixt Cornwall and Ireland, so that each country made ready for war.

The King of Ireland claims truage of Cornwall.

But the King of Ireland said: "Let there not be war betwixt Ireland and Cornwall concerning this disagreement, but let us settle this affair in some other way. Let us each choose a champion and let those two champions decide the rights of this case by a combat at arms. For so the truth shall be made manifest."

Now you are to know that at that time the knights of Cornwall were held in great disregard by all courts of chivalry; for there was not in those days any knight of repute in all the court of Cornwall. Wherefore King Mark knew not where he should find him a champion to meet that challenge from the King of Ireland. Yet he must needs meet it, for he was ashamed to refuse such a challenge as that, and so to acknowledge that Cornwall had no knight-champion to defend it. So he said it should be as the King of Ireland would have it, and that if the King of Ireland would choose a champion, he also would do the same.

Thereupon the King of Ireland chose for his champion Sir Marhaus of Ireland, who was one of the greatest knights in the world. For in the Book of King Arthur (which I wrote aforetime) you may there read in the story of Sir Pellias how great and

The King of Ireland chooses Sir Marhaus for his champion.

puissant a champion Sir Marhaus was, and how he overthrew Sir Gawaine and others with the greatest ease. Wherefore at that time he was believed by many to be the greatest knight in the world (it being before the days of Sir Launcelot of the Lake), and even in the days of Sir Launcelot it was doubted whether he or Sir Launcelot were the greater champion.

So King Mark could not find any knight in Cornwall to stand against Sir Marhaus. Nor could he easily find any knight outside of Cornwall to do battle with him. For Sir Marhaus, being a knight of the Round Table, no other knight of the Round Table would fight against him—and there were no other knights so great as that famous brotherhood of the Table Round.

Accordingly, King Mark knew not where to turn to find him a champion to do battle in his behalf.

In this strait, King Mark sent a letter by a messenger to Lyonesse, asking if there was any knight at Lyonesse who would stand his champion against Sir Marhaus, and he offered great reward if such a champion would undertake his cause against Ireland.

Now when young Tristram heard this letter of his uncle King Mark, he straightway went to his father and said: "Sire, some whiles ago you desired that I should become a knight. Now I would that you would let me go to Cornwall upon this occasion. For when I come there I will beseech my uncle King Mark to make me a knight, and then I will go out against Sir Marhaus. For I have a great mind to undertake this adventure in behalf of King Mark, and to stand his champion against Sir Marhaus. For though Sir Marhaus is so great a knight and so famous a hero, yet if I should have the good fortune to overcome him in battle, there would, certes, be great glory to our house through my knighthood."

Tristram asks leave to go to Cornwall.

Then King Meliadus looked upon Tristram and loved him very dearly, and he said: "Tristram, thou hast assuredly a very great heart to undertake this adventure, which no one else will essay. So I bid thee go, in God's name, if so be thy heart bids thee to go. For maybe God will lend the strength necessary to carry this adventure through to a successful issue."

So that very day Tristram departed from Lyonesse for Cornwall, taking with him only Gouvernail as his companion. So, by ship, he reached Cornwall, and the castle of Tintagel, where King Mark was then holding court.

And it was at the sloping of the afternoon when he so came, and at that time King Mark was sitting in hall with many of his knights and lords about him. And the King was brooding in great trouble of spirit. Unto him came an attendant, saying: "Lord, there are two strangers who stand without, and crave to be admitted to your presence. One of them hath great dignity and sobriety of demeanor, and the other, who is a youth, is of so noble and stately an appearance that I do not believe his like is to be found in the entire world."

To this the King said, "Show them in."

So those two were immediately admitted into the hall and came and stood before King Mark; and the one of them was Gouvernail and the other was young Tristram. So Tristram stood forth before Gouvernail and Gouvernail bore the harp of Tristram, and the harp was of gold and shone most brightly and beautifully. Then King Mark looked upon Tristram, and marvelled at his size and beauty; for Tristram stood above any man in that place, so that he looked like a hero amongst them. His brow was as white as milk and his lips were red like to coral and his hair was as red as gold and as plentiful as the mane of a young lion, and his neck was thick and sturdy and straight like to a round pillar of white-stone, and he was clad in garments of blue silk embroidered very cunningly with threads of gold and set with a countless multitude of gems of divers colors. So because of all this he glistened with a singular radiance of richness and beauty.

Tristram and Gouvernail come to Cornwall.

So King Mark marvelled at the haughtiness of Tristram's appearance, and he felt his heart drawn toward Tristram with love and admiration. Then, after a little, he spoke, saying: "Fair youth, who are you, and whence come you, and what is it you would have of me?"

"Lord," said Tristram, "my name is Tristram, and I come from the country of Lyonesse, where your own sister was one time Queen. Touching the purpose of my coming hither, it is this: having heard that you are in need of a champion to contend for your rights against the champion of Ireland, I come hither to say that if you will make me a knight with your own hand, I will take it upon me to stand your champion and to meet Sir Marhaus of Ireland upon your behalf."

Tristram offers himself as champion for Cornwall.

Then King Mark was filled with wonder at the courage of Tristram, and he said: "Fair youth, are you not aware that Sir Marhaus of Ireland is a knight well set in years and of such great and accredited deeds of arms that it is supposed that, excepting Sir Launcelot of the Lake, there is not his peer in any court of chivalry in all of the world? How then can you, who are altogether new to the use of arms, hope to stand against so renowned a champion as he?"

"Lord," quoth Tristram, "I am well aware of what sort of knight Sir Marhaus is, and I am very well aware of the great danger of this undertaking. Yet if one who covets knighthood shall fear to face a danger, what virtue would there then be in the chivalry of knighthood? So, Messire, I put my trust in God, His mercies, and I have great hope that He will lend me both courage and strength in my time of need."

Then King Mark began to take great joy, for he said to himself: "Maybe this youth shall indeed bring me forth in safety out of these dangers that menace my honor." So he said: "Tristram, I do believe that you will stand a very excellent chance of success in this undertaking, wherefore it shall be as you desire; I will make you a knight, and besides that I will fit you with armor and accoutrements in all ways becoming to the estate of a knight-royal. Likewise I will provide you a Flemish horse of the best strain, so that you shall be both furnished and horsed as well as any knight in the world hath ever been."

So that night Tristram watched his armor in the chapel of the castle, and the next day he was made knight with all the circumstances appertaining to a ceremony of such solemnity as that. And upon the afternoon of the day upon which he was thus made knight, King Mark purveyed a ship in all ways befitting the occasion, and in the ship Tristram and Gouvernail set sail for that island where Sir Marhaus was known to be abiding at that time.

Tristram is made knight-royal.

Now upon the second day of their voyaging and about the middle of the day they came to a land which they knew must be the place which they were seeking, and there the sailors made a safe harbor. As soon as they were at anchor a gangway was set from the ship to the shore and Sir Tristram and Gouvernail drave their horses across the gangway and so to the dry land.

Thereafter they rode forward for a considerable distance, until about the first slanting of the afternoon they perceived in the distance three very fair ships drawn up close to the shore. And then they were aware of a knight, clad in full armor and seated upon a noble horse under the shadow of those ships, and they wist that that must be he whom Sir Tristram sought.

Then Gouvernail spake to Sir Tristram, saying: "Sir, that knight resting yonder beneath the shelter of the ships must be Sir Marhaus."

"Yea," said Sir Tristram, "that is assuredly he." So he gazed very steadily at the knight for a long while, and by and by he said: "Gouvernail, yonder seems to me to be a very great and haughty knight for a knight so young as I am to have to do with in his first battle; yet if God will lend me His strong aid in this affair, I shall assuredly win me great credit at his hands." Then after another short while he said: "Now go,

Sir Tristram goes forth to meet Sir Marhaus.

Gouvernail, and leave me alone in this affair, for I do not choose for anyone to be by when I have to do with yonder knight. For either I shall overcome him in this combat or else I will lay down my life at this place. For the case is thus, Gouvernail; if Sir Marhaus should overcome me and if I should yield me to him as vanquished, then mine uncle must pay truage to the King of Ireland for the land of Cornwall; but if I died without yielding me to mine enemy, then he must yet do battle with another champion at another time, if my uncle the King can find such an one to do battle in his behalf. So I am determined either to win this battle or to die therein."

Now when Gouvernail heard this, he fell a-weeping in great measure; and he cried out: "Sir, let not this battle be of that sort!" To him Sir Tristram said very steadfastly: "Say no more, Gouvernail, but go as I bid thee." Whereupon Gouvernail turned and went away, as he was bidden to do, weeping very bitterly as he went.

Now by this Sir Marhaus had caught sight of Sir Tristram where he stood in that field, and so presently he came riding thitherward to meet Sir Tristram. When he had come nigh, Sir Marhaus said: "Who art thou, Sir Knight?" Unto these Sir Tristram made reply: "Sir, I am Sir Tristram of Lyonesse, son of King Meliadus of that land, and nephew of King Mark of Cornwall. I am come to do battle upon behalf of the King of Cornwall, to release him from the demands of truage made by the King of Ireland." Quoth Sir Marhaus: "Messire, are you a knight of approval and of battles?" "Nay," said Sir Tristram, "I have only been created knight these three days."

Sir Tristram proclaims his degree.

"Alas!" said Sir Marhaus, "I am very sorry for thee and for thy noble courage that hath brought thee hither to this place. Thou art not fit to have to do with me, for I am one who hath fought in more than twice twenty battles, each one of which was, I believe, greater than this is like to be. Also I have matched me with the very best knights in the world, and have never yet been overcome. So I advise thee, because of thy extreme youth, to return to King Mark and bid him send me another champion in thy stead, who shall be better seasoned than thou art."

"Sir," said Sir Tristram, "I give thee gramercy for thy advice. But I may tell thee that I was made knight for no other purpose than to do battle with thee; so I may not return without having fulfilled mine adventure. Moreover, because of thy great renown and thy courage and prowess, I feel all the more desirous to have to do with thee; for if I should die at thy hand, then there will be no shame to me, but if I should win this battle from thee, then I shall have very great renown in the courts of chivalry."

"Well," said Sir Marhaus, "it is not likely that thou shalt die at my hand. For because of thy youth I will not have it that this battle shall be so desperate as that."

"Say not so," said Sir Tristram, "for either I shall die at thy hand, or else I shall overcome thee in this battle, for I make my vow to God that I will not yield myself to thee so long as there is life within my body."

"Alas!" said Sir Marhaus, "that is certes a great pity. But as thou hast fore-ordained it, so it must needs be." Therewith he saluted Sir Tristram and drew rein and rode aside to a little distance where he straightway made ready for that battle. Nor was Sir Tristram behind him in making preparation, albeit he was filled with doubts as to the outcome of that undertaking.

Then when they were in all ways prepared, each gave shout and drave spurs into his horse and rushed toward the other with such fury that it was terrible to behold.

Sir Tristram is wounded.

And each smote the other with his spear in the centre of his shield, and in that encounter Sir Marhaus smote through Sir Tristram's shield and gave Sir Tristram a great wound in his side. Then Sir Tristram felt the blood gush out of that wound in such abundance that it filled his iron boots, so that they were sodden therewith, and he thought he had got his death-wound. But in spite of that grievous bitter stroke, he held his seat and was not overthrown. Then so soon as he had recovered himself he voided his horse and drew his sword and set his shield before him; and when Sir Marhaus saw his preparations, he likewise voided his horse and made ready for battle upon foot. So straightway they came together with terrible fury, lashing at each other with such fearful strength and evil will that it was dreadful to behold. And each gave the other many grievous strokes, so that whole pieces of armor were hewn off from their bodies; and each gave the other many deep wounds, so that that part of the armor that still hung to them became red as though it were painted with red. Likewise the ground was all besprinkled red where they stood, yet neither gave any thought to quitting that battle in which they were engaged.

Now for a while Sir Tristram feared because of the wound which he had at first received that he would die in that battle, but by and by he perceived that he was stouter than Sir Marhaus and better winded; wherefore great hope came to him and uplifted him with redoubled strength. Then presently Sir Marhaus fell back a little and when Sir Tristram perceived that he ran in upon him and smote him several times, such direful strokes that Sir Marhaus could not hold up his shield against that assault. Then Sir Tristram perceived that Sir Marhaus was no longer able to hold up his shield, and therewith he smote him a great blow with his sword upon the helmet. So direful was that blow that the sword of Sir Tristram pierced very deep through the helm of Sir Marhaus and into the brain-pan. And Sir Tristram's sword stuck fast in the helm and the brain-pan of Sir Marhaus so that Sir Tristram could not pull it out again. Then Sir Marhaus, half a-swoon, fell down upon his knees, and therewith a part of the edge of the blade brake off from Sir Tristram's sword, and remained in the wound that he had given to Sir Marhaus.

Sir Tristram gives Sir Marhaus a death-wound.

Then Sir Marhaus was aware that he had got his death-wound, wherefore a certain strength came to him so that he rose to his feet staggering like a drunken man. And at first he began going about in a circle and crying most dolorously. Then as he wist all that had happed he threw away his sword and his shield, and made away from that place, staggering and stumbling like one who had gone blind; for he was all bewildered with that mortal wound, and wist not very well what he was doing or whither he was going. Then Sir Tristram would have made after him to stop him, but he could not do so because he himself was so sorely wounded and so weak from the loss of blood. Yet he called after Sir Marhaus: "Stay, stay, Sir Knight! Let us finish this battle now we are about it!" But to this Sir Marhaus made no answer, but went on down to his ships, staggering and stumbling like a blind man as aforesaid, for the sore wound which he had received still lent him a false strength of body so that he was able to go his way. Then those who were aboard the ships, beholding him thus coming staggering toward them, came down and met him and lifted him up and bore him away to his own ship. Thereafter, as soon as might be they hoisted sail and lifted anchor and took their way from that place.

Sir Marhaus leaves the field.

Then by and by came Gouvernail and several others of Sir Tristram's party to where Sir Tristram was; and there they found him leaning upon his sword and groaning very sorely because of the great wound in his side. So presently they perceived that he could not walk, wherefore they lifted him up upon his own shield and bore him thence to that ship that had brought him thither.

And when they had come to the ship they laid him down upon a couch and stripped him of his armor to search his wounds. Then they beheld what a great wound it was that Sir Marhaus had given him in the side, and they lifted up their voices in sorrow, for they all believed that he would die.

So they set sail, and in two days brought him back to King Mark, where he sat at Tintagel in Cornwall. And when King Mark saw how pale and wan and weak Sir Tristram was, he wept and grieved very sorely for sorrow of that sight, for he too thought that Sir Tristram was certainly about to die.

Sir Tristram returns to Cornwall.

But Sir Tristram smiled upon King Mark, and he said: "Lord, have I done well for thy sake?" And King Mark said, "Yea," and fell to weeping again.

"Then," quoth Tristram, "it is time for me to tell thee who I am who have saved thy kingdom from the shame of having to pay truage to Ireland, and that I am thine own sister's son. For my father is King Meliadus of Lyonesse, and my mother was the Lady Elizabeth, who was thine own sister till God took her soul to Paradise to dwell there with His angels."

Sir Tristram proclaims himself to King Mark.

But when King Mark heard this he went forth from that place and into his own chamber. And when he had come there he fell down upon his knees and cried out aloud: "Alas, alas, that this should be! Rather, God, would I lose my entire kingdom than that my sister's son should come to his death in this wise!"

Now it remaineth to say of Sir Marhaus that those who were with him brought him back to Ireland and that there in a little while he died of the wound that Sir Tristram had given him upon the head. But ere he died, and whilst they were dressing that hurt, the Queen of Ireland, who was sister to Sir Marhaus, discovered the broken piece of the blade still in that grim wound. This she drew forth and set aside, and hid very carefully, saying to herself: "If ever I meet that knight to whose sword this piece of blade fitteth, then it will be an evil day for him."

Thus I have told you all the circumstances of that great battle betwixt Sir Tristram of Lyonesse and Sir Marhaus of Ireland. And now you shall hear how it befell Sir Tristram thereafter; so harken to what followeth.

JVSTISSIMVS·REX·

The Lady Belle Isoult.

CHAPTER THIRD

How Sir Tristram Went to Ireland to Be Healed of His Wound by the King's Daughter of Ireland, and of How He Came to Love the Lady Belle Isoult. Also Concerning Sir Palamydes and the Lady Belle Isoult.

Now that grievous hurt which Sir Tristram had received at the hands of Sir Marhaus did not heal, but instead grew even more rankled and sore, so that there were many who thought that there had been treachery practised and that the spearhead had been poisoned to cause such a malignant disease as that with which the wounded man suffered. So by and by Sir Tristram grew so grievously sick of his hurt that all those who were near him thought that he must certainly die.

Then King Mark sent everywhere and into all parts for the most wise and learned leeches and chirurgeons to come to Cornwall and search the wounds of Sir Tristram, but of all these no one could bring him any ease.

Now one day there came to the court of King Mark a very wise lady, who had travelled much in the world and had great knowledge of wounds of all sorts. At the bidding of the King, she went to where Sir Tristram lay, and searched the wound as so many had already done. And when she had done that she came out of Sir Tristram's chamber and unto King Mark, where he was waiting for her. Then King Mark said to her: "Well, how will it be with yonder knight?" "Lord," quoth she, "it is thus; I can do nothing to save his life, nor do I know of any one who may save it unless it be the King's daughter of Ireland, who is known as the Belle Isoult because of her wonderful beauty. She is the most skilful leech in all of the world, and she alone may hope to bring Sir Tristram back to life and health again, for I believe that if she fail no one else can save him."

How Sir Tristram lieth sick in Cornwall.

Then after the aforesaid lady had gone, King Mark went to where Sir Tristram lay, and he told him all that she had said concerning his condition; and King Mark said: "Tristram, wilt thou go to the King's daughter of Ireland and let her search thy wound?"

Then Sir Tristram groaned at the thought of the weariness and pain of moving, and he said: "Lord, this is a great undertaking for one who is so sick. Moreover, it is a great risk for me, for, if I go to Ireland, and if it be found that I am he who slew Sir Marhaus, then it is hardly likely that I shall ever escape from that country again with my life. Ne'theless, I am so sorely sick of this wound that I would rather die than live as I am living; wherefore I will go to Ireland for the sake of being healed, if such a thing is possible."

Accordingly, a little while after that, King Mark provided a ship to carry Sir Tristram to Ireland. This ship he furnished with sails of silk of divers colors, and he had it hung within with fine embroidered cloth, and fabrics woven with threads of silver and gold, so that in its appearance it was a worthy vessel even for a great king to sail in. Then, when all was ready, King Mark had a number of attendants carry Sir Tristram down to the ship in a litter, and he had them lay Sir Tristram upon a soft couch of crimson satin, which was set upon the deck beneath a canopy of crimson silk, embroidered with threads of silver and garnished with fringe of silver, and Sir Tristram lay there at ease where the breezes of the ocean came pleasantly to him, and breathed upon his face and his temples and his hair and his hands with coolness; and Gouvernail was with Sir Tristram all the while in attendance upon him.

Sir Tristram sails to Ireland to have his wound searched.

So they set sail for Ireland, the weather being very fair and pleasant, and on the third day, at about the time of sunset, they came to a part of the coast of Ireland where there was a castle built upon the rocks that rose out of the sea.

Now there were several fishermen fishing in boats near that castle, and of these the pilot of Sir Tristram's boat made inquiry what castle that was. To him the fisherman replied: "That castle is the castle of King Angus of Ireland." And the fisherman said: "It so happens that the King and Queen and their daughter, hight the Lady Belle Isoult, and all of their court are there at this very while."

This Sir Tristram heard and said: "This is good news, for indeed I am very sick and am right glad that my voyaging is ended." So he gave orders that the pilot should bring the ship close under the walls of that castle, and that he should there let go anchor; and the pilot did as Sir Tristram had commanded him.

Now, as aforesaid, that ship was of a very wonderful appearance, like to the ship of a king or a high prince, wherefore many people came down to the walls of the castle and stood there and gazed at the vessel as it sailed into the harbor. And by that time the sun had set and all the air was illuminated with a marvellous golden light; and in this sky of gold the moon

How Sir Tristram came to Ireland.

hung like a shield of silver, very bright and steady above the roofs and towers of the castle. And there came from the land a pleasing perfume of blossoms; for it was then in the fulness of the spring-time, and all the fruit-bearing trees were luxuriant with bloom so that the soft air of evening was full of fragrance thereby.

Then there came a great content into the heart of Sir Tristram, wherefore he said to Gouvernail: "Gouvernail, either I shall soon be healed of this wound, or else I shall presently die and enter into Paradise free of pain, for I am become very full of content and of peace toward all men." And then he said: "Bring me hither my harp, that I may play upon it a little, for I have a desire to chant in this pleasant evening-time."

So Gouvernail brought to Sir Tristram his shining harp, and when Sir Tristram had taken it into his hands he tuned it, and when he had tuned it he struck it and sang; and, because of the stillness of the evening, his voice sounded marvellously clear and sweet across the level water, so that those who stood upon the castle walls and heard it thought that maybe an angel was singing on board of that ship.

Sir Tristram sings.

That time the Lady Belle Isoult sat at the window of her bower enjoying the pleasantness of the evening. She also heard Sir Tristram singing, and she said to those damsels who were with her, "Ha, what is that I hear?" Therewith she listened for a little while, and then she said: "Meseems that must be the voice of some angel that is singing." They say: "Nay, Lady, it is a wounded knight singing, and he came to this harbor in a wonderful ship some while ago." Then the Lady Belle Isoult said to a page who was in attendance: "Bid the King and Queen come hither, that they may hear this singing also, for never did I think to hear such singing beyond the walls of Paradise."

So the page ran with all speed, and in a little the King and Queen came to the bower of the Lady Belle Isoult; and she and they leaned upon the window-ledge and listened to Sir Tristram whilst he sang in the soft twilight. Then by and by King Angus said: "Now I will have yonder minstrel brought hither to this castle to do us pleasure, for I believe that he must be the greatest minstrel in all the world to sing in that wise." And the Lady Belle Isoult said: "I pray you, sir, do so, for it would be great joy to everybody to have such singing as that in this place."

So King Angus sent a barge to that ship, and besought that he who sang should be brought to the castle. At that Sir Tristram was very glad, for he said: "Now I shall be brought to the Lady the Belle Isoult and maybe she will heal me." So he had them bare him to the barge of the King of Ireland, and so they brought him to the castle of King Angus, where they laid him upon a bed in a fair room of the castle.

Then King Angus came to Sir Tristram where he lay, and he said: "Messire what can I do for you to put you more at your ease than you are?" "Lord," said Sir Tristram, "I pray you to permit the Lady Belle Isoult to search a great wound in my side that I received in battle. For I hear that she is the most skilful leech in all the world, and so I have come hither from a great distance, being in such pain and dole from my grievous hurt that I shall die in a little while unless it be healed."

King Angus cometh to Tristram.

"Messire," said King Angus, "I perceive that you are no ordinary knight, but somebody of high nobility and estate, so it shall be as you desire." And then King Angus said: "I pray you, tell me your name and whence you come."

Upon this, Sir Tristram communed within his own mind, saying: "An I say my name is Tristram, haply there may be someone here will know me and that I was the cause why the brother of the Queen of this place hath died." So he said: "Lord, my name is Sir Tramtris, and I am come from a country called Lyonesse, which is a great distance from this."

Quoth King Angus, "Well, Sir Tramtris, I am glad that you have come to this place. Now it shall be done to you as you desire, for to-morrow the Lady Belle Isoult shall search your wound to heal it if possible."

And so it was as King Angus said, for the next day the Lady Belle Isoult came with her attendants to where Sir Tristram lay, and one of the attendants bare a silver basin and another bare a silver ewer, and others bare napkins of fine linen. So the Lady Belle Isoult came close to Sir Tristram and kneeled beside the couch whereon he lay and said, "Let me see the wound." Therewith Sir Tristram laid bare his bosom and his side and she beheld it. Then she felt great pity for Sir Tristram because of that dolorous wound, and she said: "Alas, that so young and so fair and so noble a knight should suffer so sore a wound as this!" Therewith still kneeling beside Sir Tristram she searched the wound with very gentle, tender touch (for her fingers were like to rose leaves for softness) and lo! she found a part of the blade of a spear-head embedded very deep in the wound of Sir Tristram.

My Lady Belle Isoult searches the wound.

This she drew forth very deftly (albeit Sir Tristram groaned with a great passion of pain) and therewithafter came forth an issue of blood like a crimson fountain, whereupon Sir Tristram swooned away like one who had gone dead. But he did not die, for they quickly staunched the flow, set aromatic spices to his nostrils, so that in a little he revived in spirit to find himself at great ease and peace in his body (albeit it was for a while like to the peace of death).

Thus it was that the Lady Belle Isoult saved the life of Sir Tristram, for in a little while he was able to be about again, and presently waxed almost entirely hale and strong in limb and body.

Sir Tristram is healed.

And now it is to be told how Sir Tristram loved the Lady Belle Isoult and how she loved Sir Tristram. Also how a famous knight, hight Sir Palamydes the Saracen, loved Belle Isoult and of how she loved not him.

For, as was said, it came about that in a little while Sir Tristram was healed of that grievous wound aforetold of so that he was able to come and go whithersoever he chose. But always he would be with the Lady Belle Isoult, for Sir Tristram loved her with a wonderfully passionate regard. And so likewise the lady loved Sir Tristram. For if he loved her because she had saved his life, then she also loved him for the same reason. For she did not ever forget how she had drawn out the head of that spear from the wound at his side, and of how he had groaned when she brought it forth, and of how the blood had gushed out of that wound. Wherefore she loved him very aboundingly for the agony of pain she had one time caused him to suffer.

Sir Tristram loves the Lady Belle Isoult.

So they two fair and noble creatures were always together in bower or in hall, and no one in all that while wist that Sir Tramtris was Sir Tristram, and that it was his hand that had slain Sir Marhaus of Ireland.

So Sir Tristram was there in Ireland for a year, and in that time he grew to be altogether well and sturdy again.

Now it was in those days that there came Sir Palamydes the Saracen knight to that place, who was held to be one of the very foremost knights in the world. So great rejoicing was made over him because he had come thither, and great honor was shown to him by everyone.

Sir Palamydes cometh to Ireland.

But when Sir Palamydes beheld the Lady Belle Isoult and when he saw how fair she was, he came in a short while to love her with almost as passionate a regard as that with which Sir Tristram loved her, so that he also sought ever to be with her whenever the chance offered.

But Belle Isoult felt no regard for Sir Palamydes, but only fear of him, for all of her love was given to Sir Tristram. Nevertheless, because Sir Palamydes was so fierce and powerful a knight, she did not dare to offend him; wherefore she smiled upon him and treated him with all courtesy and kindness although she loved him not, dissembling her regard for him.

All this Sir Tristram beheld from aside and it displeased him a very great deal to see how Sir Palamydes was always beside the lady. But Belle Isoult beheld how

Sir Tristram is displeased.

Sir Tristram was displeased, wherefore she took occasion to say to him: "Tramtris, be not displeased, for what am I to do? You know very well that I do not love this knight, but I am afraid of him because he is so fierce and so strong."

To this Sir Tristram said: "Lady, it would be a great shame to me if I, being by, should suffer any knight to come betwixt you and me and win your regard through fear of him."

She said: "Tramtris, what would you do? Would you give challenge to this knight? Lo, you are not yet entirely healed of your hurt, and Sir Palamydes is in perfect strength of body. For indeed it is for you I am most of all afraid lest you and Sir Palamydes should come to battle and lest he should do you a harm before you are entirely healed."

"Lady," quoth Sir Tristram, "I thank God that I am not at all afraid of this knight, or of any other knight, and I have to thank you that I am now entirely recovered and am as strong as ever I was. Wherefore I have now a mind to deal with this knight in your behalf. So if you will provide me with armor I will deal with him so that maybe he will not trouble you again. Now I will devise it in this way:—tell your father, King Angus, to proclaim a great jousting. In that jousting I will seek out Sir Palamydes and will encounter him, and I hope with God's aid that I shall overcome him, so that you shall be free from him."

Sir Tristram desires to do battle.

Belle Isoult said, "Tramtris, are you able for this?" He said, "Yea, I am as ready as ever I shall be in all of my life." Whereat Belle Isoult said, "It shall be as you will have it."

Then Sir Tristram charged Belle Isoult that she should keep secret all this that had been said betwixt them. And more especially she was to keep it secret that he was to take part in such a tournament as that which they had devised. And he said to her: "Lady, I lie here under a great peril to my life, though I cannot tell you what that peril is. But I may tell you that if my enemies should discover me at this place, it would go hard with me to preserve my life from them. Wherefore, if I take part in any such affair as this, it must be altogether a secret betwixt us."

So therewith they parted and Lady Belle Isoult went to her father and besought him to proclaim a great day of jousting in honor of Sir Palamydes, and the King said that he would do so. So the King sent forth proclamation to all the courts of that nation that a great tournament was to be held and that great rewards and great honors were to be given to the best knight thereat. And that tournament was talked about in all the courts of chivalry where there were knights who desired to win glory in such affairs at arms.

And now it shall be told concerning that tournament and how it befell with Sir Tristram thereat, and with Sir Palamydes thereat.

The Queen of Ireland seeks to slay Sir Tristram.

CHAPTER FOURTH

How Sir Tristram Encountered Sir Palamydes at the Tournament and of What Befell. Also How Sir Tristram Was Forced to Leave the Kingdom of Ireland.

So came the time for the tournament that King Angus of Ireland had ordained; and that was a very famous affair at arms indeed. For it hath very rarely happened that so noble a gathering of knights hath ever come together as that company which there presented itself for that occasion at the court of the King of Ireland.

For you may know how excellent was the court of chivalry that fore gathered thereat when you shall hear that there came to that tournament, the King of an Hundred Knights and the King of the Scots, and that there came several knights of the Round Table, to wit: Sir Gawaine, Sir Gaheris and Sir Agravaine; and Sir Bagdemagus and Sir Kay and Sir Dodinas, and Sir Sagramore le Desirous, and Sir Gumret the Less, and Sir Griflet; and that there came besides these many other knights of great renown.

Of the court of chivalry at Ireland.

These and many others gathered at the court of King Angus of Ireland, so that all those meadows and fields coadjacent to the place of battle were gay as beds of flowers with the multitude of tents and pavilions of divers colors that were there emplanted.

And on the day of the tournament there came great crowds of people into the lists, so that all that place was alive with movement. For it was as though a sea of people had arisen to overflow the seats and stalls thereof.

Now that tournament was to last for three days, and upon the third day there was to be a grand mêlée in which all these knights contestant were to take stand upon this side or upon that.

But upon the first two of those three days Sir Tristram sat in the stall of the King and looked down upon the jousting, for, because of the illness from which he had recovered, he was minded to save his body until the right time should come, what time he should be called upon to do his uttermost.

And in those two days, Sir Tristram beheld that Sir Palamydes did more wonderfully in battle than he would have believed it possible for any knight to do. For Sir Palamydes was aware that the eyes of the Lady Belle Isoult were gazing upon him, wherefore he felt himself uplifted to battle as with the strength of ten. Wherefore he raged about that field like a lion of battle, seeking whom he might overthrow and destroy. And upon the first day he challenged Sir Gawaine to joust with him, and then he challenged Sir Gaheris, and the King of an Hundred Knights, and Sir Griflet, and Sir Sagramore le Desirous and fourteen other knights, and all of these he met and many he overcame, and that without any mishap to himself. And upon the second day he met with great success Sir Agravaine and Sir Griflet and Sir Kay and Sir Dodinas and twelve other knights. Wherefore those who beheld how he did gave great shouts and outcries of applause and acclaim, saying: "Certes, there was never knight in all of the world so great as this knight. Yea; even Sir Launcelot himself could not do more than that knight doeth."

Sir Palamydes performeth wonders.

Then Belle Isoult was troubled in her mind, and she said: "Tramtris, yonder in very truth is a most fierce and terrible knight. Now somewhiles I have fear that you may not be able to overcome him."

Thereat Sir Tristram smiled very grimly, and said: "Lady, already I have overcome in battle a bigger knight than ever Sir Palamydes has been or is like to be." But the Lady Belle Isoult wist not that that knight of whom Sir Tristram spake was Sir Marhaus of Ireland.

Now upon the evening of the second day of that tournament, Sir Palamydes came to where the Lady Belle Isoult was, and he said: "Lady, all these things I have done for your sake. For had it not been for my love for you, I would not have been able to do a third part of that which I did. Now I think you should have pity and regard for one who loves you so strongly as that; wherefore I beseech you to bestow some part of your good-will upon me."

Sir Palamydes bespeaks the Lady Belle Isoult.

"Sir," said the Lady Belle Isoult, "you are not to forget that there is still another day of this battle, and in it you may not happen to have the same fortune that favored you to-day; so I will wait until you have won that battle also before I answer you."

"Well," said Sir Palamydes, "you shall see that I shall do even more worthily to-morrow for your sake than I have done to-day."

But the Lady Belle Isoult was not very well pleased with that saying, for she began again to fear that maybe the will of Sir Palamydes was so strong that Sir Tristram would not have any success against him.

So came the third day of that very famous contest at arms, and when this morning was come there began to gather together in the two parties those who were to contest the one against the other. Of one of these parties, Sir Palamydes was the chiefest knight, and upon that side was also Sir Gawaine and several of the knights who were with him. For these said, "There shall certes be greater credit to be had with Sir Palamydes than against him," and so they joined them with his party. Of the other party the chiefest knights were the King of an Hundred Knights and the King of Scots, and both of these were very famous and well-approved champions, of high courage and remarkable achievements.

Now when the time was nigh ready for that tournament, Sir Tristram went to put on the armor that the Lady Belle Isoult had provided him, and when he was armed he mounted very lightly upon the horse which she had given him. And the armor of Sir Tristram was white, shining like to silver, and the horse was altogether white, and the furniture and trappings thereof were all white, so that Sir Tristram glistened with extraordinary splendor.

Belle Isoult arms Sir Tristram.

Now when he was armed and prepared in all ways, the Lady Belle Isoult came to where he was and she said, "Tramtris, are you ready?" And he answered "Yea." Therewith she took the horse of Sir Tristram by the bridle and she led him to the postern gate of the castle, and put him out that way into a fair field that lay beyond; and Sir Tristram abided in the fields for some while until the tournament should have begun.

But the Lady Belle Isoult went to the tournament with her father, the King, and her mother, the Queen, and took her station at that place assigned to her whence she might overlook the field.

So in a little while that friendly battle began. And again Sir Palamydes was filled with the vehement fury of contest, wherefore he raged about the field, spreading terror whithersoever he came. For first he made at the King of an Hundred Knights, and he struck that knight so direful a blow that both horse and man fell to the ground with the force thereof. Then in the same manner he struck the King of Scots with his sword, and smote him straightway out of the saddle also. Then he struck down one after another, seven other knights, all of well-proved strength and prowess, so that all those who looked thereon cried out, "Is he a man or is he a demon?" So, because of the terror of Sir Palamydes, all those in that contest bore away from him as they might do from a lion in anger.

How Sir Palamydes fought in the tournament.

At this time came Sir Tristram, riding at a free pace, shining like to a figure of silver. Then many saw him and observed him and said to one another: "Who is this knight, and what party will he join with to do battle?" These had not long to wait to know what side he would join, for immediately Sir Tristram took stand with that party which was the party of the King of an Hundred Knights and the King of Scots, and at that the one party was very glad, and the other party was sorry; for they deemed that Sir Tristram was certes some great champion.

Then straightway there came against Sir Tristram four knights of the other party, and one of these was Sir Gaheris, and another was Sir Griflet and another was Sir Bagdemagus and another was Sir Kay. But Sir Tristram was possessed with a great joy of battle, so that in a very short time he had struck down or overthrown all those knights, beginning with Sir Gaheris, and ending with Sir Kay the seneschal.

Sir Tristram enters the tournament.

This Sir Gawaine beheld, and said to Sir Sagramore: "Yonder is certes a knight of terrible strength; now let us go and see of what mettle he be."

Therewith Sir Gawaine pushed against Sir Tristram from the one side, and Sir Sagramore came against him on the other side, and so they met him both at once. Then first Sir Gawaine struck Sir Tristram such a buffet that the horse of Sir Tristram turned twice about with the force of that stroke; and therewith Sir Sagramore smote him a buffet upon the other side so that Sir Tristram wist not upon which side to defend himself.

Then, at those blows Sir Tristram waxed so exceedingly fierce that it was as though a fire of rage flamed up into his brains and set them into a blaze of rage. So with that he rose up in his stirrups and launched so dreadful a blow upon Sir Gawaine that I believe nothing could have withstood the force of that blow. For it clave through the shield of Sir Gawaine and it descended upon the crown of his helmet and it clave away a part of his helmet and a part of the épaulière of his shoulder; and with the force of that dreadful, terrible blow, Sir Gawaine fell down upon the ground and lay there as though he were dead.

Then Sir Tristram wheeled upon Sir Sagramore (who sat wonder-struck at that blow he had beheld) and thereafter he smote him too, so that he fell down and lay upon the ground in a swoon from which he did not recover for more than two hours.

Now Sir Palamydes also had beheld those two strokes that Sir Tristram had given, wherefore he said: "Hah! Yonder is a very wonderful knight. Now if I do not presently meet him, and that to my credit, he will have more honor in this battle than I."

So therewith Sir Palamydes pushed straight against Sir Tristram, and when Sir Tristram beheld that he was very glad, for he said: "Now it will either be Sir

Palamydes his day, or else it will be mine." So he upon his part pushed against Sir Palamydes with good intent to engage him in battle, and then they two met in the midst of the field.

Sir Palamydes rides against Sir Tristram.

Then immediately Sir Palamydes smote Sir Tristram such a buffet that Sir Tristram thought a bolt of lightning had burst upon him, and for a little while he was altogether bemazed and wist not where he was. But when he came to himself he was so filled with fury that his heart was like to break therewith.

Thereupon he rushed upon Sir Palamydes and smote him again and again and again with such fury and strength that Sir Palamydes was altogether stunned at the blows he received and bare back before them. Then Sir Tristram perceived how that Sir Palamydes bare his shield low because of the fierceness of that assault, and thereupon he rose up in his stirrups and struck Sir Palamydes upon the crown of the helmet so dreadful a buffet that the brains of Sir Palamydes swam like water, and he must needs catch the pommel of his saddle to save himself from falling. Then Sir Tristram smote him another buffet, and therewith darkness came upon the sight of Sir Palamydes and he rolled off from his horse into the dust beneath its feet.

Sir Tristram smites Sir Palamydes.

Then all who beheld the encounter shouted very loud and with great vehemence, for it was the very best and most notable assault at arms that had been performed in all that battle. But most of those who beheld that assault cried out "The Silver Knight!" For at that time no one but the Lady Belle Isoult wist who that silver knight was. But she wist very well who he was, and was so filled with the glory of his prowess that she wept for joy thereof.

Then the King of Ireland said: "Who is yonder knight who hath so wonderfully overthrown Sir Palamydes? I had not thought there was any knight in the world so great as he; but this must be some great champion whom none of us know." Upon that the Lady Belle Isoult, still weeping for joy, could contain herself no longer, but cried out: "Sir, that is Tramtris, who came to us so nigh to death and who hath now done us so great honor being of our household! For I knew very well that he was no common knight but some mighty champion when I first beheld him."

Belle Isoult declares Sir Tristram.

At that the King of Ireland was very much astonished and overjoyed, and he said: "If that is indeed so, then it is a very great honor for us all."

Now after that assault Sir Tristram took no more part in that battle but withdrew to one side. But he perceived where the esquires attendant upon Sir Palamydes came to him and lifted him up and took him away. Then by and by he perceived that Sir

Palamydes had mounted his horse again with intent to leave that meadow of battle, and in a little he saw Sir Palamydes ride away with his head bowed down like to one whose heart was broken.

All this Sir Tristram beheld and did not try to stay Sir Palamydes in his departure. But some while after Sir Palamydes had quitted that place, Sir Tristram also took his departure, going in that same direction that Sir Palamydes had gone. Then after he had come well away from the meadow of battle, Sir Tristram set spurs to his horse and rode at a hard gallop along that way that Sir Palamydes had taken.

So he rode at such a gait for a considerable pass until, by and by, he perceived Sir Palamydes upon the road before him; and Sir Palamydes was at that time come to the edge of a woods where there were several stone windmills with great sails swinging very slowly around before a strong wind that was blowing.

Now this was a lonely place, and one very fit to do battle in, wherefore Sir Tristram cried out to Sir Palamydes in a loud voice: "Sir Palamydes! Sir Palamydes! Turn you about! For here is the chance for you to recover the honor that you have lost to me." Thereupon Sir Palamydes, hearing that loud voice, turned him about. But when he beheld that the knight who called was he who had just now wrought such shame upon him, he ground his teeth together with rage, and therewith drave his horse at Sir Tristram, drawing his sword so that it flashed like lightning in the bright sunlight. And when he came nigh to Sir Tristram, he stood up in his stirrups and lashed a blow at him with all his might and main; for he said to himself: "Maybe I shall now recover mine honor with one blow which I lost to this knight a while since." But Sir Tristram put aside that blow of Sir Palamydes with his shield with very great skill and dexterity, and thereupon, recovering himself, he lashed at Sir Palamydes upon his part. And at that first stroke Sir Tristram smote down the shield of Sir Palamydes, and gave him such a blow upon the head that Sir Palamydes fell down off his horse upon the earth. Then Sir Tristram voided his own horse very quickly, and running to Sir Palamydes where he lay he plucked off his helmet with great violence. Therewith he cried out very fiercely: "Sir Knight, yield thee to me, or I will slay thee." And therewithal he lifted up his sword as though to strike off the head of Sir Palamydes.

Sir Tristram overthrows Palamydes again.

Then when Sir Palamydes saw Sir Tristram standing above him in that wise, he dreaded his buffets so that he said: "Sir Knight, I yield me to thee to do thy commands, if so be thou wilt spare my life."

Thereupon Sir Tristram said, "Arise," and at that Sir Palamydes got him up to his knees with some ado, and so remained kneeling before Sir Tristram.

"Well," said Sir Tristram, "I believe you have saved your life by thus yielding yourself to me. Now this shall be my commandment upon you. First of all, my commandment is that you forsake the Lady Belle Isoult, and that you do not come near her for the space of an entire year. And this is my second commandment; that from this day you do not assume the arms of knighthood for an entire year and a day."

"Alas!" said Sir Palamydes, "why do you not slay me instead of bringing me to such shame as this! Would that I had died instead of yielding myself to you as I did." And therewith he wept for shame and despite.

"Well," said Sir Tristram, "let that pass which was not done. For now you have yielded yourself to me and these are my commands." So with that Sir Tristram set his sword back again into its sheath, and he mounted his horse and rode away, leaving Sir Palamydes where he was.

But after Sir Tristram had gone, Sir Palamydes arose, weeping aloud. And he said: "This is such shame to me that I think there can be no greater shame." Thereupon he drew his misericordia, and he cut the thongs of his harness and he tore the pieces of armor from off his body and flung them away very furiously, upon the right hand and upon the left. And when he had thus stripped himself of all of his armor, he mounted his horse and rode away into the forest, weeping like one altogether brokenhearted.

Sir Palamydes disarms himself.

So Sir Tristram drave Sir Palamydes away from the Lady Belle Isoult as he had promised to do.

Now when Tristram came back to the castle of the King of Ireland once more, he thought to enter privily in by the postern-gate as he had gone out. But lo! instead of that he found a great party waiting for him before the castle and these gave him loud acclaim, crying, "Welcome, Sir Tramtris! Welcome, Sir Tramtris!" And King Angus came forward and took the hand of Sir Tristram, and he also said: "Welcome, Sir Tramtris, for you have brought us great honor this day!"

But Sir Tristram looked at the Lady the Belle Isoult with great reproach and by and by when they were together he said: "Lady, why did you betray me who I was when you had promised me not to do so?" "Sir," she said, "I meant not to betray you, but in the joy of your victory I know not very well what I said." "Well," said Sir Tristram, "God grant that no harm come of it." She said, "What harm can come of it, Messire?" Sir Tristram said: "I may not tell you, Lady, but I fear that harm will come of it."

Sir Tristram chides Belle Isoult.

Anon the Queen of Ireland came and said: "Tramtris, one so nigh to death as you have been should not so soon have done battle as you have done. Now I will have a bain prepared and you shall bathe therein, for you are not yet hale and strong."

"Lady," said Tristram, "I do not need any bain, for I believe I am now strong and well in all wise."

"Nay," said the Queen, "you must have that bain so that no ill may come to you hereafter from this battle which you have fought."

So she had that bain prepared of tepid water, and it was very strong and potent with spices and powerful herbs of divers sorts. And when that bain was prepared, Sir Tristram undressed and entered the bath, and the Queen and the Lady Belle Isoult were in the adjoining chamber which was his bed-chamber.

The Queen of Ireland beholds Sir Tristram's sword.

Now whilst Sir Tristram was in that bath, the Queen and Belle Isoult looked all about his chamber. And they beheld the sword of Sir Tristram where it lay, for he had laid it upon the bed when he had unlatched the belt to make himself ready for that bath. Then the Queen said to the Lady Belle Isoult, "See what a great huge sword this is," and thereupon she lifted it and drew the blade out of its sheath, and she beheld what a fair, bright, glistering sword it was. Then in a little she saw where, within about a foot and a half from the point, there was a great piece in the shape of a half-moon broken out of the edge of the sword; and she looked at that place for a long while. Then of a sudden she felt a great terror, for she remembered how even such a piece of sword as that which had been broken off from that blade, she had found in the wound of Sir Marhaus of which he had died. So she stood for a while holding that sword of Sir Tristram in her hand and looking as she had been turned into stone. At this the Lady Belle Isoult was filled with a sort of fear, wherefore she said, "Lady, what ails you?" The Queen said, "Nothing that matters," and therewith she laid aside the sword of Sir Tristram and went very quickly to her own chamber. There she opened her cabinet and took thence the piece of sword-blade which she had drawn from the wound of Sir Marhaus, and which she had kept ever since. With this she hurried back to the chamber of Sir Tristram, and fitted that piece of the blade to the blade; and lo! it fitted exactly, and without flaw.

The Queen assails Sir Tristram.

Upon that the Queen was seized as with a sudden madness; for she shrieked out in a very loud voice, "Traitor! Traitor! Traitor!" saying that word three times. Therewith she snatched up the sword of Sir Tristram and she ran with great fury into the room where he lay in his bath. And she beheld him where he was there all naked in his bath, and therewith she rushed at him and lashed at him with his sword. But Sir Tristram threw himself to one side and so that blow failed of its purpose. Then the Queen would have lashed at him again or have thrust him through with the weapon; but at that Gouvernail and Sir Helles ran to her and catched her and held her back, struggling and screaming very violently. So they took the sword away from her out of her hands, and all the while she shrieked like one gone entirely distracted.

Then as soon as Gouvernail and Sir Helles loosed her, she ran very violently out of that room with great outcry of screaming, and so to King Angus and flung herself upon her knees before him, crying out: "Justice! Justice! I have found that man who slew my brother! I beseech of you that you will deal justice upon him."

Then King Angus rose from where he sat, and he said: "Where is that man? Bring me to him." And the Queen said: "It is Tramtris, who hath come hither unknown unto this place."

King Angus said: "Lady, what is this you tell me? I cannot believe that what you say is true." Upon this the Queen cried out: "Go yourself, Lord, and inquire, and find out how true it is."

Then King Angus rose, and went forth from that place, and he went to the chamber of Sir Tristram. And there he found that Sir Tristram had very hastily dressed himself and had armed himself in such wise as he was able. Then King Angus came to Tristram, and he said: "How is this, that I find thee armed? Art thou an enemy to my house?" And Tristram wept, and said: "Nay, Lord, I am not your enemy, but your friend, for I have great love for you and for all that is yours, so that I would be very willing to do battle for you even unto death if so be I were called upon to do so."

Then King Angus said: "If that is so, how is it that I find thee here armed as if for battle, with thy sword in thy hand?" "Lord," said Sir Tristram, "although I be friends with you and yours, yet I know not whether you be friends or enemies unto me; wherefore I have prepared myself so that I may see what is your will with me, for I will not have you slay me without defence upon my part." Then King Angus said: "Thou speakest in a very foolish way, for how could a single knight hope to defend himself against my whole household? Now I bid thee tell me who thou art, and what is thy name, and why thou camest hither knowing that thou hadst slain my brother?"

Then Sir Tristram said, "Lord, I will tell thee all the truth." And therewith he confessed everything to King Angus, to wit: who was his father and his mother, and how he was born and reared; how he fought Sir Marhaus, and for what reason; and of how he came hither to be healed of his wound, from which else he must die in very

Sir Tristram confesses to King Angus.

grievous pain. And he said: "All this is truth, Lord, and it is truth that I had no ill-will against Sir Marhaus; for I only stood to do battle with him for the sake of mine uncle, King Mark of Cornwall, and to enhance mine own honor; and I took my fortune with him as he took his with me. Moreover, I fought with Sir Marhaus upon the same day that I was made knight, and that was the first battle which I fought, and in that battle I was wounded so sorely that I was like to die as you very well know. As for him, he was a knight well-tried and seasoned with many battles, and he suffered by no treachery but only with the fortune of war."

So King Angus listened to all that Sir Tristram said, and when he had ended, quoth he: "As God sees me, Tristram, I cannot deny that you did with Sir Marhaus as a true knight should. For it was certes your part to take the cause of your uncle upon you if you had the heart to do so, and it was truly a real knightly thing for you who were so young to seek honor at the hands of so famous a knight as Sir Marhaus. For I do not believe that until you came his way there was any knight in the world who was greater than he, unless it were Sir Launcelot of the Lake. Wherefore, from that, and from what I saw you do at the tournament, some time ago, I believe that you are one of the strongest knights in the world, and the peer of Sir Launcelot, or of anybody else.

"But though all this is true, nevertheless it will not be possible for me to maintain you in this country, for if I keep you here I shall greatly displease not only the Queen and her kin, but many of those lords and knights who were kin to Sir Marhaus or who were united to him in pledges of friendship. So you must even save yourself as you can and leave here straightway, for I may not help or aid you in any way."

Then Sir Tristram said: "Lord, I thank you for your great kindness unto me, and I know not how I shall repay the great goodness that my Lady Belle Isoult hath showed to me. For I swear to you upon the pommel of my sword which I now hold up before me that I would lay down my life for her sake. Yea, and my honor too! for she hath the entire love of my heart, so that I would willingly die for her, or give up for her all that I have in the world. Now as for my knighthood, I do believe that I shall in time become a knight of no small worship, for I feel within my heart that this shall be so. So if my life be spared, it may be that you will gain more having me for your friend and your true servant than you will by taking my life in this outland place. For whithersoever I go I give you my knightly word that I shall be your daughter's servant, and that I shall ever be her true knight in right or in wrong, and that I shall never fail her if I shall be called upon to do her service."

Then King Angus meditated upon this for a while, and he said: "Tristram, what thou sayest is very well said, but how shall I get you away from this place in safety?"

Sir Tristram said: "Lord, there is but one way to get me away with credit unto yourself. Now I beseech you of your grace that I may take leave of my lady your daughter, and that I may then take leave of all your knights and kinsmen as a right knight should. And if there be any among them who chooses to stop me or to challenge my going, then I must face that one at my peril, however great it may be."

"Well," said King Angus, "that is a very knightly way to behave, and so it shall be as you will have it."

So Sir Tristram went down stairs to a certain chamber where Belle Isoult was. And he went straight to her and took her by the hand; and he said: "Lady, I am to go away from this place, if I may do so with credit to my honor; but before I go I must tell you that I shall ever be your own true knight in all ways that a knight may serve a lady. For no other lady shall have my heart but you, so I shall ever be your true knight. Even though I shall haply never see your face again, yet I shall ever carry your face with me in my heart, and the thought of you shall always abide with me withersoever I go."

At this the Lady Belle Isoult fell to weeping in great measure, and thereat the countenance of Sir Tristram also was all writhed with passion, and he said, "Lady, do not weep so!" She said, "Alas I cannot help it!" Then he said: "Lady, you gave me my life when I thought I was to lose it, and you brought me back from pain unto ease, and from sorrow unto joy. Would God I were suffering all those pangs as aforetime, so that there might be no more tears upon your face."

Then, King Angus being by, he took her face into his hands and kissed her upon the forehead, and the eyes, and the lips. Therewith he turned and went away, all bedazed with his sorrow, and feeling for the latch of the door ere he was able to find it and go out from that place.

Sir Tristram parts from Belle Isoult.

After that Sir Tristram went straight unto the hall of the castle, and there he found a great many of the lords of the castle and knights attendant upon the King. For the news of these things had flown fast, and many of them were angry and some were doubtful. But Tristram came in very boldly, clad all in full armor, and when he stood in the midst of them he spoke loud and with great courage, saying: "If there be any man here whom I have offended in any way, let him speak, and I will give him entire satisfaction whoever he may be. But let such speech be now or never, for here is my body to make good my knighthood against the body of any man, whomsoever he may be."

At this all those knights who were there stood still and held their peace, and no man said anything against Sir Tristram (although there were several knights and lords who were kin to the Queen), for the boldness of Tristram overawed them, and no one had the heart to answer him.

So after a little while Sir Tristram left that place, without turning his head to see if any man followed him.

Sir Tristram departs from Ireland.

So he left that castle and Gouvernail went with him, and no one stopped him in his going. After that, he and Gouvernail came to the shore and took a boat and they came to the ship of Sir Tristram, and so they sailed away from Ireland. But the heart of Sir Tristram was so full of sorrow that he wished a great many times that he was dead.

So Sir Tristram, though as to his body he was very whole and sound, was, as to his spirit, very ill at ease; for though he was so well and suffered no pain, yet it appeared to him that all the joy of his life had been left behind him, so that he could nevermore have any more pleasure in this world which lieth outside of the walls of Paradise.

JVSTISSIMVS·REX·

Sir Tristram harpeth before King Mark.

CHAPTER FIFTH

How Sir Tristram Was Sent by Command of King Mark to Go to Ireland to Bring the Lady the Belle Isoult from Ireland to Cornwall and How It Fared With Him.

So Sir Tristram came back again to Cornwall, and King Mark and all the knights and lords of the court of the King gave him great welcome and made much joy over him because he had returned safely.

But Sir Tristram took no joy in their joy because he was filled with such heavy melancholy that it was as though even the blue sky had turned to sackcloth to his eyes, so that he beheld nothing bright in all the world.

But though he had no great pleasure in life, yet Sir Tristram made many very good songs about Belle Isoult; about her beauty and her graciousness; about how he was her sad, loving knight; about how he was pledged unto her to be true to her all of his life even though he might never hope to see her again.

Sir Tristram tells of the Lady Belle Isoult.

These like words he would sing to the music of his shining, golden harp, and King Mark loved to listen to him. And sometimes King Mark would sigh very deeply and maybe say: "Messire, that lady of thine must in sooth be a very wonderful, beautiful, gracious lady." And Sir Tristram would say, "Yea, she is all that."

So it was at that time that King Mark had great love for Sir Tristram; in a little while all that was very different, and his love was turned to bitter hate, as you shall presently hear tell.

Now in those days the knights of Cornwall were considered to be the least worthy of all knights in that part of the world, for they had so little skill and prowess at arms that they were a jest and a laughing-stock to many courts of chivalry. It was said of them that a knight-champion of Cornwall was maybe a knight, but certes was no champion at all; and this was great shame to all those of Cornwall, more especially as that saying was in a great measure true.

One day there came to the court of Cornwall a very noble, haughty knight, hight Sir Bleoberis de Ganys, who was brother to Sir Blamor de Ganys and right cousin to Sir Launcelot of the Lake. This knight was a fellow of King Arthur's Round Table, and so he was received with great honor at Cornwall, and much joy was taken of his being there; for it was not often that knights of such repute as he came to those parts. At that time Sir Tristram was not present at the court, having gone hunting into the forest, but a messenger was sent to him with news that Sir Bleoberis was present at the court of the King and that King Mark wished him to be at court also.

Sir Bleoberis comes to Cornwall.

Now whilst Sir Tristram was upon his way to return to the court in obedience to these commands, there was held a feast at the castle of the King in honor of Sir Bleoberis. There was much strong wine drunk at that feast, so that the brains of Sir Bleoberis and of others grew very much heated therewith. Then, what with the heat of the wine and the noise and tumult of the feast, Sir Bleoberis waxed very hot-headed, and boastful. So, being in that condition and not knowing very well how he spake, he made great boast of the prowess of the knights of King Arthur's court above those of Cornwall. And in this boastful humor he said: "It is perfectly true that one single knight of the Round Table is the peer of twenty knights of Cornwall, for so it is said and so I maintain it to be."

Upon that there fell a silence over all that part of the feast, for all the knights and lords who were there heard what Sir Bleoberis said, and yet no one knew how to reply to him. As for King Mark, he looked upon Sir Bleoberis, smiling very sourly, and as though with great distaste of his words, and he said: "Messire, inasmuch as thou art our guest, and sitting here at feast with us, it is not fit that we should take thy words seriously; else what thou sayst might be very easily disproved."

Upon this the blood rushed with great violence into the face and head of Sir Bleoberis, and he laughed very loud. Then he said: "Well, Lord, it need not be that I should be a guest here very long. And as for what I say, you may easily put the truth thereof to the proof."

Therewith Sir Bleoberis arose and looked about him, and he perceived that there was near by where he stood a goblet of gold very beautifully chased and cunningly carved. This Sir Bleoberis took into his hand, and it was half full of red wine. So he stood up before them all, and he cried in a very loud voice: "Messires, and all you knights of Cornwall, here I drink to your more excellent courage and prowess, and wish that you may have better fortune in arms than you have heretofore

Sir Bleoberis challenges the knights of Cornwall.

proved yourselves to have?" And therewith he drank all the wine that was in the goblet. Then he said: "Now I go away from here and take this goblet with me; and if any knight of Cornwall may take it away from me and bring it back again to the King, then I am very willing to own that there are better knights in this country than I supposed there to be." Therewith he turned and went out from that place very haughtily and scornfully, taking that goblet with him, and not one of all those knights who were there made any move to stay him, or to reprove him for his discourteous speech.

Now after he had come out of the hall and into the cool of the air, the heat of the wine soon left him, and he began to repent him of what he had done; and he said: "Alas! meseems I was not very courteous to King Mark, who was mine host." So for a while he was minded to take that goblet back again and make amends for what he had said; but afterward he could not do this because of his pride. So he went to the chamber that had been allotted to him and clad himself in his armor, and after that he rode away from the court of King Mark carrying the goblet with him.

Now some while after he had gone, Sir Tristram came into the hall where the others were, and there he found them all sitting with ill countenances, and no man daring, for shame, to look at his fellow. So Sir Tristram came to King Mark and said: "Where is Sir Bleoberis?" And King Mark said, "He is gone away." Sir Tristram said, "Why did he go?" Thereupon King Mark told Sir Tristram of what had befallen, and how Sir Bleoberis had taken away that goblet to the great shame and scorn of all those who were there. Upon this the blood flew very violently into Sir Tristram's face, and he said: "Was there no knight here with spirit enough to call reproof upon Sir Bleoberis, or to stay him in his going?" Therewith he looked all about that hall, and he was like a lion standing among them, and no man dared to look him in the face or to reply to him. Then he said: "Well, if there is no knight in Cornwall who hath the will to defend his King, then is there a knight of Lyonesse who will do so because he received knighthood at the hands of the King of Cornwall." And therewith he turned and went away, and left them very haughtily, and they were all still more abashed than they had been before.

Sir Tristram is angry.

Then Sir Tristram went to his chamber and had himself armed in all wise; and he took his horse and mounted and rode away in the direction that Sir Bleoberis had gone, and Gouvernail went with him.

So Sir Tristram and Gouvernail rode at a good pace for a long time, making inquiry of whomsoever they met if Sir Bleoberis had passed that way. At last they entered the forest and rode therein a

Sir Tristram follows Sir Bleoberis.

great way, meeting no one till toward the latter part of the afternoon. By and by they saw before them two knights, very large and strong of frame and clad all in bright and shining armor, and each riding a great war-horse of Flemish strain.

"Gouvernail," said Sir Tristram, "ride forward apace and see for me who are yonder knights." So Gouvernail rode forward at a gallop, and so, in a little, came near enough to the two knights to see the devices upon their shields. Upon that he returned to Sir Tristram, and said: "Messire, those are two very famous worthy knights of King Arthur's Court, and of the two you are acquainted with one, but the other is a stranger to you. For the one is Sir Sagramore le Desirous, who was at that tournament in Ireland, and the other is Sir Dodinas le Sauvage."

Sir Tristram comes to two knights.

"Well," said Sir Tristram, "those are indeed two very good, worthy knights. Now if you will sit here for a while, I will go forward and have speech with them." "Messire," said Gouvernail, "I would counsel you not to have to do with those knights, for there are hardly any knights more famous at arms than they, so it is not likely that you can have success of them if you should assay them."

But to this Sir Tristram said: "Peace, Gouvernail! Hold thy peace, and bide here while I go forward!"

Now those knights when they became aware that Sir Tristram and Gouvernail were there, had halted at a clear part of the woodland to await what should befall. Unto them Sir Tristram came, riding with great dignity and haughtiness, and when he had come nigh enough he drew rein and spoke with great pride of bearing, saying: "Messires, I require of you to tell me whence you come, and whither you go, and what you do in these marches?"

Unto him Sir Sagramore made reply, speaking very scornfully: "Fair knight, are you a knight of Cornwall?" and Sir Tristram said: "Why do you ask me that?" "Messire," said Sir Sagramore, "I ask you that because it hath seldom been heard tell that a Cornish knight hath courage to call upon two knights to answer such questions as you have asked of us."

"Well," said Sir Tristram, "for the matter of that, I am at this present a knight of Cornwall, and I hereby let you know that you shall not go away from here unless you either answer my question or give me satisfaction at arms."

Then Sir Dodinas spoke very fiercely, saying: "Sir Cornish knight, you shall presently have all the satisfaction at arms that you desire and a great deal more than you desire." Therewith he took a very stout spear in his hand and rode to a little distance, and Sir Tristram, beholding his intent to do battle, also rode to a little distance, and took stand in such a place as seemed to him to be best. Then, when they were in all wise prepared, they rushed together with such astonishing vehemence that the earth shook and trembled beneath them.

Therewith they met in the middle of their course with a great uproar of iron and wood. But in that onset the spear of Sir Dodinas broke into a great many small pieces, but the spear of Sir Tristram held, so that in the encounter he lifted Sir Dodinas entirely out of his saddle, and out behind the crupper of his horse. And he flung Sir Dodinas down so violently that his neck was nearly broken, and he lay for a while in a deep swoon like one who has been struck dead.

Sir Tristram does battle with Sir Dodinas.

Then Sir Sagramore said: "Well, Sir Knight, that was certes a very great buffet that you gave my fellow, but now it is my turn to have ado with you."

So therewith he took also his spear in hand and chose his station for an assault as Sir Dodinas had done, and Sir Tristram also took station as he had done before. Then immediately they two ran together with the same terrible force that Sir Tristram and Sir Dodinas had coursed, and in that encounter Sir Tristram struck Sir Sagramore so direful a buffet with his spear that he overthrew both horse and man, and the horse, falling upon Sir Sagramore, so bruised his leg that he could not for a while arise from where he lay.

Sir Tristram does battle with Sir Sagramore.

Therewith Sir Tristram, having run his course, came back to where those two knights lay upon the ground, and he said, "Fair Knights, will you have any more fighting?" They said, "No, we have had fighting enough." Then Sir Tristram said: "I pray you, tell me, are there any bigger knights at the court of King Arthur than you? If it is not so, then I should think you would take great shame to yourselves that you have been overthrown the one after the other by a single knight. For this day a knight of Cornwall hath assuredly matched you both to your great despite."

Then Sir Sagramore said: "Sir, I pray you upon your true knighthood to tell us who you are, for you are assuredly one of the greatest knights in the world." Upon this Sir Tristram laughed, "Nay," quoth he, "I am as yet a young knight, who has had but little proof in battle. As for my name, since you ask it of me, upon my knighthood I am not ashamed to tell you that I am hight Sir Tristram, and that I am King Meliadus' son of Lyonesse."

Sir Tristram acknowledges his degree.

"Ha!" said Sir Sagramore, "if that be so, then there is little shame in being overthrown by you. For not only do I well remember how at the court of the King of

Ireland you overthrew six knights of the Round Table, and how easily you overthrew Sir Palamydes the Saracen, but it is also very well known how you did battle with Sir Marhaus, and of how you overcame him. Now Sir Marhaus and Sir Palamydes were two of the best knights in the world, so it is not astonishing that you should have done as you did with us. But, since you have overthrown us, what is it you would have us do?"

"Messires," said Sir Tristram, "I have only to demand two things of you. One of them is that you give me your word that you will go to Cornwall and confess to King Mark that you have been overthrown by a Cornish knight; and the second thing is that you tell me if you saw Sir Bleoberis de Ganys pass this way?"

They say: "Messire, touching that demand you make upon us to go to King Mark and to confess our fall, that we will do as you desire; and as for Sir Bleoberis, we met him only a short while ago, and he cannot even now be very far from this place."

"Well," said Sir Tristram, "I give you good den, and thank you for your information. I have some words to say to Sir Bleoberis before he leave these marches."

So thereafter he called Gouvernail, and they two rode into the forest and on their way as fast as they were able. As for Sir Dodinas and Sir Sagramore, they betook their course to the court of King Mark, as they had promised to do.

Sir Tristram comes to Sir Bleoberis.

Now, by and by, after Sir Tristram and Gouvernail had gone some considerable distance farther upon that road, they beheld Sir Bleoberis before them in a forest path, riding very proudly and at an easy pass upon his way. At that time the sun was setting very low toward the earth, so that all the tops of the forest trees were aflame with a very ruddy light, though all below in the forest was both cool and gray. Now when Sir Tristram and Gouvernail with him had come pretty nigh to Sir Bleoberis, Sir Tristram called to him in a very loud voice, and bade him turn and stand. Therewith Sir Bleoberis turned about and waited for Sir Tristram to come up with him. And when Sir Tristram was come near by, he said to Sir Bleoberis: "Messire, I hear tell that you have with you a very noble goblet which you have taken in a shameful way from the table of King Mark of Cornwall. Now I demand of you that you give me that goblet to take back unto the King again." "Well," said Sir Bleoberis, "you shall freely have that goblet if you can take it from me, and if you will look, you will see where it hangs here from my saddle-horn. But I may tell you that I do not believe that there is any Cornish knight who may take away that goblet against my will."

"As for that," said Sir Tristram, "we shall see in a little while how it may be."

Therewith each knight took his spear in hand and rode a little distance away, and made himself in all wise ready for the assault. Then when they were in all ways prepared, each launched himself against the other, coming together with such violence that sparks of fire flew out from the points of their spears. And in that assault the horse of each knight was overthrown, but each knight voided his saddle and leaped very lightly to earth, without either having had a fall. Then each drew his sword and set his shield before him, and therewith came together, foining and lashing with all the power of their might. Each gave the other many sore strokes, so that the armor of each was indented in several places and in other places was stained with red. Then at last Sir Tristram waxed very wode with anger and he rushed at Sir Bleoberis, smiting him so fiercely that Sir Bleoberis bare back and held his shield low before him. This Sir Tristram perceived, and therewith, rushing in upon Sir Bleoberis, he smote that knight such a great buffet upon the head that Sir Bleoberis fell down upon his knees, without having strength to keep his feet. Then Sir Tristram rushed off the helmet of Sir Bleoberis, and he said, "Sir Knight, yield to me or I shall slay you."

Sir Tristram overcometh Sir Bleoberis.

"Messire," said Sir Bleoberis, "I yield myself to you, and indeed you are as right a knight as ever I met in all of my life." Then Sir Tristram took Sir Bleoberis by the hand and he lifted him up upon his feet, and he said: "Sir, I am very sorry for to have had to do with you in this fashion, for almost would I rather that you should have overcome me than that I should have overcome you. For I do not at any time forget that you are cousin unto Sir Launcelot of the Lake, and I honor Sir Launcelot above all men else in the world, and would rather have his friendship than that of any man living. So I have had no despite against you in this battle, but have only fought with you because it behooved me to do so for the sake of the King of Cornwall, who is my uncle."

Then Sir Bleoberis said, "Messire, I pray you tell me who you are?" "Lord," said Sir Tristram, "I am a very young knight hight Tristram, and I am the son of King Meliadus of Lyonesse and the Lady Elizabeth, sister unto King Mark of Cornwall."

"Ha," said Sir Bleoberis, "I have heard great report of you, Sir Tristram, and now I know at mine own cost that you are one of the best knights in the world. Yea; I have no doubt that at some time you will be the peer of Sir Launcelot of the Lake himself, or of Sir Lamorak of Gales, and they two are, certes, the best knights in the world. Now I believe that I would have given you this goblet, even without your having to fight for it, had I known who you were; and as it is I herewith give it to you very freely."

Sir Bleoberis gives the goblet to Sir Tristram.

So Sir Bleoberis untied the goblet from where it hung at his saddle-bow, and Sir Tristram took the goblet and gave him gramercy for it; and therewith having recovered their horses, each knight mounted, and betook his way whither he was going.

So a little after nightfall Sir Tristram came to the King of Cornwall and his court, and he said to King Mark: "Here is your goblet which I have brought back to you; and I would God that some of your knights who are so much older than I had the courage to do for you what I have had to do." And therewith he went away and left them all sitting ashamed.

Now it chanced some little while after these things happened as aforesaid, that King Mark lay down upon his couch after his midday meal for to sleep a little space during the heat of the day; and it likewise happened that the window near by where he lay was open so that the air might come into the room. Now at that time three knights of the court sat in the garden beneath where the window was. These knights talked to one another concerning Sir Tristram, and of how he had brought back that goblet from Sir Bleoberis de Ganys, and of what honor it was to have such a champion in Cornwall for to stand for the honor of that court. In their talk they said to one another that if only the King of Cornwall were such a knight as Sir Tristram, then there would be plenty of knights of good worth who would come to that court, and Cornwall would no longer have to be ashamed of its chivalry as it was nowadays. So they said: "Would God our King were such a knight as Sir Tristram!"

All this King Mark overheard, and the words that they said were like a very bitter poison in his heart. For their words entered into his soul and abided there, and thereupon at that same hour all his love for Tristram was turned into hate. Thus it befell that, after that day, King Mark ever pondered and pondered upon that which he had heard, and the longer he pondered it, the more bitter did his life become to him, and the more he hated Sir Tristram. So it came to pass that whenever he was with Sir Tristram and looked upon him, he would say in his heart: "So they say that you are a better knight than I? Would God you were dead or away from this place, for I believe that some day you will be my undoing!" Yea; there were times when he would look upon Sir Tristram in that wise and whisper to himself: "Would God would send a blight upon thee, so that thou wouldst wither away!"

King Mark takes hatred to Sir Tristram.

But always the King dissembled this hatred for Sir Tristram, so that no one suspected him thereof; least of all did Sir Tristram suspect how changed was the heart of the King toward him.

Now one day Sir Tristram was playing upon his harp and singing before King Mark, and the King sat brooding upon these things as he gazed at Tristram. And Sir Tristram, as he ofttimes did nowadays, sang of the Lady Belle Isoult, and of how her face was like to a rose for fairness, and of how her soul was like to a nightingale in that it uplifted the spirit of whosoever was near her even though the darkness of sorrow as of night might envelop him. And whilst Sir Tristram sang thus, King Mark listened to him, and as he listened a thought entered his heart and therewith he smiled. So when Sir Tristram had ended his song of the Belle Isoult, King Mark said: "Fair nephew, I would that you would undertake a quest for me." Sir Tristram said, "What quest is that, Lord?" "Nay," said King Mark, "I will not tell you what quest it is unless you will promise me upon your knighthood to undertake it upon my behalf." Then Sir Tristram suspected no evil, wherefore he smiled and said: "Dear Lord, if the quest is a thing that it is in my power to undertake, I will undertake it upon your asking, and unto that I pledge my knighthood." King Mark said, "It is a quest that you may undertake." Sir Tristram said, "Then I will undertake it, if you will tell me what it is."

King Mark said: "I have listened to your singing for this long while concerning the Lady Belle Isoult. So the quest I would have you undertake is this: that you go to Ireland, and bring thence the Lady Belle Isoult to be my Queen. For because of your songs and ballads I have come to love her so greatly that I believe that I shall have no happiness in life until I have her for my Queen. So now, since you have pledged me your word upon your knighthood to do my bidding in this case, such is the quest that I would send you upon." And therewith he smiled upon Sir Tristram very strangely.

King Mark betrays Sir Tristram to a promise.

Then Sir Tristram perceived how he had been betrayed and he put aside his harp and rose from where he sat. And he gazed for a long while at King Mark, and his countenance was wonderfully white like that of a dead man. Then by and by he said: "Sir, I know not why you have put this upon me, nor do I know why you have betrayed me. For I have ever served you truly as a worthy knight and a kinsman should. Wherefore I know not why you have done this unto me, nor why you seek to compass my death. For you know very well that if I return to Ireland I shall very likely be slain either by the Queen or by some of her kindred, because that for your sake I slew in battle Sir Marhaus, the Queen's brother of Ireland. Yet, so far as that is concerned, I would rather lose my life than succeed in this quest, for if so be I do not lose my

How Sir Tristram fell into despair.

life, then I must do that which I would liever die than do. Yea; I believe that there was never any knight loved a lady as I love the Lady Belle Isoult. For I love her not only because of her beauty and graciousness, but because she healed mine infirmities and lent ease unto my great sufferings and brought me back from death unto life. Wherefore that which you bid me fulfil is more bitter to me than death."

"Well," said King Mark, "I know nothing of all this—only I know that you have given me your knightly word to fulfil this quest."

"Very well," said Sir Tristram, "if God will give me His good help in this matter, then I will do that which I have pledged my knighthood to undertake." Therewith he turned and went out from that place in such great despair that it was as though his heart had been turned into ashes. But King Mark was filled with joy that he should have caused Sir Tristram all that pain, and he said to his heart: "This is some satisfaction for the hate which I feel for this knight; by and by I shall maybe have greater satisfaction than that."

After that Sir Tristram did not come any more where King Mark was, but he went straight away from the King's court and into a small castle that King Mark had given him some while since for his own. There he abided for several days in great despair of soul, for it seemed to him as though God had deserted him entirely. There for a while Gouvernail alone was with him and no one else, but after a while several knights came to him and gave him great condolence and offered to join with him as his knights-companion. And there were eighteen of these knights, and Sir Tristram was very glad of their comradeship.

These said to him: "Sir, you should not lend yourself to such great travail of soul, but should bend yourself as a true knight should to assume that burden that God hath assigned you to bear."

So they spoke, and by and by Sir Tristram aroused himself from his despair and said to himself: "Well, what these gentlemen say is true, and God hath assuredly laid this very heavy burden upon me; as that is so, I must needs assume it for His sake."

Sir Tristram departs from Cornwall.

So Sir Tristram and the knights who were with him abode in that place for a day or two or three, and then one morning Sir Tristram armed himself and they armed themselves, and all took their departure from that castle and went down to the sea. Then they took ship with intent to depart to Ireland upon that quest Sir Tristram had promised King Mark he would undertake, and in a little they hoisted sail and departed from Cornwall for Ireland.

But they were not to make their quest upon that pass so speedily as they thought, for, upon the second day of their voyaging, there arose a great storm of wind of such a sort that the sailors of that ship had never seen the like thereof in all of their lives. For the waves rose up like mountains, and anon the waters sank away into deep valleys with hills of water upon either side all crested over with foam as white as snow. And anon that ship would be uplifted as though the huge sea would toss it into the clouds; and anon it would fall down into a gulf so deep that it appeared as though the green waters would swallow it up entirely. The air roared as though it were full of demons and evil spirits out of hell, and the wind was wet and very bitter with brine. So the ship fled away before that tempest, and the hearts of all aboard were melted with fear because of the great storm of wind and the high angry waves.

Then toward evening those who were watching from the lookout beheld a land and a haven, and they saw upon the land overlooking the haven was a noble castle and a fair large town, surrounded by high walls of stone. So they told the others of what they saw, and all gave great rejoicing for that they were so nigh the land. Therewith they sailed the ship toward the haven, and having entered therein in safety, they cast anchor under the walls of the castle and the town, taking great joy that God had brought them safe and sound through that dreadful peril of the tempest.

Then Sir Tristram said to Gouvernail: "Knowest thou, Gouvernail, what place is this to which we have come?" "Messire," said Gouvernail, "I think it is Camelot." And then those knights of Cornwall who stood by said, "Yea, that is true, and it is Camelot." And one of them said: "Messire, it is likely that King Arthur is at that place at this very time, for so it was reported that he was, and so I believe it to be."

Sir Tristram comes to Camelot.

"Ha," quoth Tristram, "that is very good news to me, for I believe that it would be the greatest joy to me that the world can now give to behold King Arthur and those noble knights of his court ere I die. More especially do I desire above all things to behold that great, noble champion, Sir Launcelot of the Lake. So let us now go ashore, and mayhap it shall come to pass that I shall see the great King and Sir Launcelot and mayhap shall come to speak with the one or the other." And that saying of Sir Tristram's seemed good to those knights who were with him, for they were weary of the sea, and desired to rest for a while upon the dry land.

So they presently all went ashore and bade their attendants set up their pavilions in a fair level meadow that was somewhat near a league distant away from the castle and the town. In the midst of the other pavilions upon that plain was set the pavilion of Sir Tristram. It

Sir Tristram sets up his pavilion.

was of fine crimson cloth striped with silver and there was the figure of a gryphon carved upon the summit of the centre pole of the pavilion. The spear of Sir Tristram was emplanted by the point of the truncheon in the ground outside the pavilion, and thereunto his shield was hung so that those who passed that way might clearly behold what was the device thereon.

And now shall be told how Sir Tristram became united in friendship with the brotherhood of good knights at King Arthur's court.

JVSTISSIMVS·REX·

Sir Tristram sits with Sir Launcelot.

CHAPTER SIXTH

How Sir Tristram Had to Do in Battle With Three Knights of the Round Table. Also How He Had Speech With King Arthur.

SO CAME THE NEXT MORNING, AND UPROSE THE SUN IN ALL THE SPLENDOR of his glory, shedding his beams to every quarter with a rare dazzling effulgence. For by night the clouds of storm had passed away and gone, and now all the air was clear and blue, and the level beams of light fell athwart the meadowlands so that countless drops of water sparkled on leaf and blade of grass, like an incredible multitude of shining jewels scattered all over the earth. Then they who slept were awakened by the multitudinous voicing of the birds; for at that hour the small fowl sang so joyous a roundelay that all the early morning was full of the sweet jargon of their chanting.

At this time, so early in the day, there came two knights riding by where Sir Tristram and his companions had set up their pavilions. These were two very famous knights of King Arthur's court and of the Round Table; for one was Sir Ector de Maris and the other was Sir Morganor of Lisle.

How two knights came to the pavilion of Sir Tristram.

When these two knights perceived the pavilions of Sir Tristram and his knights-companion, they made halt, and Sir Ector de Maris said, "What knights are these who have come hither?" Then Sir Morganor looked and presently he said: "Sir, I perceive by their shields that these are Cornish knights, and he who occupies this central pavilion must be the champion of this party." "Well," quoth Sir Ector, "as for that I take no great thought of any Cornish knight, so do thou strike the shield of that knight and call him forth, and let us see of what mettle he is made."

"I will do so," said Sir Morganor; and therewith he rode forward to where the shield of Sir Tristram hung from the spear, and he smote the shield with the point of his lance, so that it rang with a very loud noise.

Upon this, Sir Tristram immediately came to the door of his pavilion, and said, "Messires, why did you strike upon my shield?" "Because," said Sir Ector, "we are of a mind to try your mettle what sort of a knight you be." Quoth Sir Tristram: "God forbid that you should not be satisfied. So if you will stay till I put on my armor you shall immediately have your will in this matter."

Thereupon he went back into his tent and armed himself and mounted his horse and took a good stout spear of ash-wood into his hand.

Then all the knights of Cornwall who were with Sir Tristram came forth to behold what their champion would do, and all their esquires, pages, and attendants came forth for the same purpose, and it was a very pleasant time of day for jousting.

Sir Tristram overthrows Sir Morganor.

Then first of all Sir Morganor essayed Sir Tristram, and in that encounter Sir Tristram smote him so dreadful, terrible a blow that he cast him a full spear's length over the crupper of his horse, and that so violently that the blood gushed out of the nose and mouth and ears of Sir Morganor, and he groaned very dolorously and could not arise from where he lay.

"Hah," quoth Sir Ector, "that was a very wonderful buffet you struck my fellow. But now it is my turn to have ado with you, and I hope God will send me a better fortune."

Sir Tristram overthrows Sir Ector.

So he took stand for battle as did Sir Tristram likewise, and when they were in all wise prepared they rushed very violently to the assault. In that encounter Ector suffered hardly less ill fortune than Sir Morganor had done. For he brake his spear against Sir Tristram into as many as an hundred pieces, whilst Sir Tristram's spear held so that he overthrew both the horse and the knight-rider against whom he drove.

Then all the knights of Cornwall gave loud acclaim that their knight had borne himself so well in those encounters. But Sir Tristram rode back to where those two knights still lay upon the ground, and he said: "Well, Messires, this is no very good hap that you have had with me."

Upon that speech Sir Ector de Maris gathered himself up from the dust and said: "Sir Knight, I pray you of your knighthood to tell us who you be and what is your degree, for I declare to you, I believe you are one of the greatest knights-champion of the world."

"Sir," said Sir Tristram, "I am very willing to tell you my name and my station; I am Sir Tristram, the son of King Meliadus of Lyonesse."

"Ha," quoth Sir Ector, "I would God I had known that before I had ado with you, for your fame hath already reached to these parts, and there hath been such report of your prowess and several songs have been made about you by minstrels and poets. I who speak to you am Sir Ector, surnamed de Maris, and this, my companion, is Sir Morganor of Lisle."

"Alas!" cried out Sir Tristram, "I would that I had known who you were ere I did battle with you. For I have greater love for the knights of the Round Table than all others in the world, and most of all, Sir Ector, do I have reverence for your noble brother Sir Launcelot of the Lake. So I take great shame to myself that any mishap should have befallen you this day through me."

Upon this Sir Ector laughed. "Well," quoth he, "let not that trouble lie with you, for it was we who gave you challenge without inquiry who you were, and you did but defend yourself. We were upon our way to Camelot yonder, when we fell into this mishap, for King Arthur is at this time holding court at that place. So now, if we have your leave to go upon our way, we will betake ourselves to the King and tell him that you are here, for we know that he will be very glad of that news."

Upon this Sir Tristram gave them leave to depart, and they did so with many friendly words of good cheer. And after they had gone Sir Tristram went back into his pavilion again and partook of refreshment that was brought to him.

Now, some while after Sir Ector and Sir Morganor had left that place, and whilst Sir Tristram was still resting in his pavilion, there came a single knight riding that way, and this knight was clad altogether in white armor and his shield was covered over with a covering of white leather, so that one could not see what device he bare thereon.

There comes a knight in white armor.

When this white knight came to the place where Sir Tristram and his companions had pitched their pavilions, he also stopped as Sir Ector and Sir Morganor had done, for he desired to know what knights these were. At that time Gouvernail was standing alone in front of Sir Tristram's pavilion, and unto him the white knight said: "Sir, I pray you, tell me who is the knight to whom this pavilion belongs."

Now Gouvernail thought to himself: "Here is another knight who would have ado with my master. Perhaps Sir Tristram may have glory by him also." So he answered the white knight: "Sir, I may not tell you the name of this knight, for he is my master, and if he pleases to tell you his name he must tell it himself."

"Very well," said the white knight, "then I will straightway ask him."

Therewith he rode to where the shield of Sir Tristram hung, and he struck upon the shield so violent a blow that it rang very loud and clear.

Then straightway came forth Sir Tristram and several of his knights-companion from out of the pavilion, and Sir Tristram said, "Sir Knight, wherefore did you strike upon my shield?"

"Messire," quoth the white knight, "I struck upon your shield so that I might summon you hither for to tell me your name, for I have asked it of your esquire and he will not tell me."

"Fair Knight," quoth Sir Tristram, "neither will I tell you my name until I have wiped out that affront which you have set upon my shield by that stroke you gave it. For no man may touch my shield without my having to do with him because of the affront he gives me thereby."

"Well," said the white knight, "I am satisfied to have it as you please."

So therewith Sir Tristram went back into his pavilion and several went with him. These put his helmet upon his head and they armed him for battle in all ways. After that Sir Tristram came forth and mounted his horse and took his spear in hand and made himself in all ways ready for battle, and all that while the white knight awaited his coming very calmly and steadfastly. Then Sir Tristram took ground for battle, and the white knight did so likewise. So being in all ways prepared, each launched forth against the other with such amazing and terrible violence that those who beheld that encounter stood as though terrified with the thunder of the onset.

Sir Tristram does battle with the white knight.

Therewith the two knights met in the midst of the course, and each knight smote the other directly in the centre of the shield. In that encounter the spear of each knight broke all to small pieces, even to the truncheon which he held in his fist. And so terrible was the blow that each struck the other that the horse of each fell back upon his haunches, and it was only because of the great address of the knight-rider that the steed was able to recover his footing. As for Sir Tristram, that was the most terrible buffet he ever had struck him in all his life before that time.

Then straightway Sir Tristram voided his saddle and drew his sword and dressed his shield. And he cried out: "Ha, Sir Knight! I demand of you that you descend from your horse and do me battle afoot."

"Very well," said the white knight, "thou shalt have thy will." And thereupon he likewise voided his horse and drew his sword and dressed his shield and made himself in all ways ready for battle as Sir Tristram had done.

Therewith they two came together and presently fell to fighting with such ardor that sparks of fire flew from every stroke. And if Sir Tristram struck hard and often, the white knight struck as hard and as often as he, so that all the knights of Cornwall who stood about marvelled at the strength and fierceness of the knights-combatant. Each knight gave the other many sore buffets so that the armor was here and there dinted and here and there was broken through by the edge of the sword so that the red blood flowed out therefrom and down over the armor, turning its brightness in places into an ensanguined red. Thus they fought for above an hour and in all that time neither knight gave ground or gained any vantage over the other.

Then after a while Sir Tristram grew more weary of fighting than ever he had been in all of his life before, and he was aware that this was the greatest knight whom he had ever met. But still he would not give ground, but fought from this side and from that side with great skill and address until of a sudden, he slipped upon some of that blood that he himself had shed, and because of his great weariness, fell down upon his knees, and could not for the instant rise again.

Sir Tristram falls in the battle.

Then that white knight might easily have struck him down if he had been minded to do so. But, instead, he withheld the blow and gave Sir Tristram his hand and said: "Sir Knight, rise up and stand upon thy feet and let us go at this battle again if it is thy pleasure to do so; for I do not choose to take advantage of thy fall."

Then Sir Tristram was as greatly astonished at the extraordinary courtesy of his enemy as he had been at his prowess. And because of that courtesy he would not fight again, but stood leaning upon his sword panting. Then he said: "Sir Knight, I pray thee of thy knighthood to tell me what is thy name and who thou art."

"Messire," said the white knight, "since you ask me that upon my knighthood, I cannot refuse to tell you my name. And so I will do, provided you, upon your part, will do me a like courtesy and will first tell me your name and degree."

Quoth Sir Tristram: "I will tell you that. My name is Sir Tristram of Lyonesse, and I am the son of King Meliadus of that land whereby I have my surname."

"Ha, Sir Tristram," said the white knight, "often have I heard of thee and of thy skill at arms, and well have I proved thy fame this day and that all that is said of thee is true. I must tell thee that I have never yet met my match until I met thee this day. For I know not how this battle might have ended hadst thou not slipped and fallen by chance as thou didst. My name is Sir Launcelot, surnamed of the Lake, and I am King Ban's son of Benwick."

Sir Launcelot confesses himself.

At this Sir Tristram cried out in a loud voice: "Sir Launcelot! Sir Launcelot! Is it thou against whom I have been doing battle! Rather I would that anything should have happened to me than that, for of all men in the world I most desire thy love and friendship."

Then, having so spoken, Sir Tristram immediately kneeled down upon his knees and said: "Messire, I yield myself unto thee, being overcome not more by thy prowess

Sir Tristram yields to Sir Launcelot.

than by thy courtesy. For I freely confess that thou art the greatest knight in the world, against whom no other knight can hope to stand; for I could fight no more and thou mightest easily have slain me when I fell down a while since."

"Nay, Sir Tristram," said Sir Launcelot, "arise, and kneel not to me, for I am not willing to accept thy submission, for indeed it is yet to be proved which of us is the better knight, thou or I. Wherefore let neither of us yield to the other, but let us henceforth be as dear as brothers-in-arms the one toward the other."

Then Sir Tristram rose up to his feet again. "Well, Sir Launcelot," he said, "whatsoever thou shalt ordain shall be as thou wouldst have it. But there is one thing I must do because of this battle."

Then he looked upon his sword which he held naked and ensanguined in his hand and he said: "Good sword; thou hast stood my friend and hast served me well

Sir Tristram breaks his sword.

in several battles, but this day thou hast served me for the last time." Therewith he suddenly took the blade of the sword in both hands—the one at the point and the other nigh the haft—and he brake the blade across his knee and flung the pieces away.

Upon this Sir Launcelot cried out in a loud voice: "Ha, Messire! why didst thou do such a thing as that? To break thine own fair sword?"

"Sir," quoth Sir Tristram, "this sword hath this day received the greatest honor that is possible for any blade to receive; for it hath been baptized in thy blood. So, because aught else that might happen to it would diminish that honor, I have broken it so that its honor might never be made less than it is at this present time."

Upon this Sir Launcelot ran to Sir Tristram and catched him in his arms, and he cried out: "Tristram, I believe that thou art the noblest knight whom ever I beheld!" And Sir Tristram replied: "And thou, Launcelot, I love better than father or kindred." Therewith each kissed the other upon the face, and all they who stood by were so moved at that sight that several of them wept for pure joy.

Thereafter they two went into Sir Tristram's pavilion and disarmed themselves. Then there came sundry attendants who were excellent leeches and these searched

Sir Tristram and Sir Launcelot feast together.

their hurts and bathed them and dressed them. And several other attendants came and fetched soft robes and clothed the knights therein so that they were very comfortable in their bodies. Then still other attendants brought them good strong wine and manchets of bread and they sat together at table and ate very cheerfully and were greatly refreshed.

So I have told you of that famous affair-at-arms betwixt Sir Launcelot and Sir Tristram, and I pray God that you may have the same pleasure in reading of it that I had in writing of it.

Now, as Sir Launcelot and Sir Tristram sat in the pavilion of Sir Tristram making pleasant converse together, there suddenly entered an esquire to where they were sitting. This esquire proclaimed: "Messires, hither cometh King Arthur, and he is very near at hand." Thereupon, even as that esquire spoke, there came from without the pavilion a great noise of trampling horses and the pleasant sound of ringing armor, and then immediately a loud noise of many voices uplifted in acclamation.

King Arthur comes to Sir Tristram's pavilion.

Therewith Sir Launcelot and Sir Tristram arose from where they sat, and as they did so the curtains at the doorway of the pavilion were parted and there entered King Arthur himself enveloped, as it were, with all the glory of his royal estate.

Unto him Sir Tristram ran, and would have fallen upon his knees, but King Arthur stayed him from so doing. For the great king held him by the hand and lifted him up, and he said, "Sir, are you Sir Tristram of Lyonesse?" "Yea," said Sir Tristram, "I am he." "Ha," said King Arthur, "I am gladder to see you than almost any man I know of in the world," and therewith he kissed Sir Tristram upon the face, and he said: "Welcome, Messire, to these parts! Welcome! And thrice welcome!"

Then Sir Tristram besought King Arthur that he would refresh himself, and the King said he would do so. So Sir Tristram brought him to the chiefest place, and there King Arthur sat him down. And Sir Tristram would have served him with wine and with manchets of bread with his own hand, but King Arthur would not have it so, but bade Sir Tristram to sit beside him on his right hand, and Sir Tristram did so. After that, King Arthur spake to Sir Tristram about many things, and chiefly about King Meliadus, the father of Sir Tristram, and about the court of Lyonesse.

Then, after a while King Arthur said: "Messire, I hear tell that you are a wonderful harper." And Sir Tristram said, "Lord, so men say of me." King Arthur said, "I would fain hear your minstrelsy." To which Sir Tristram made reply: "Lord, I will gladly do anything at all that will give you pleasure."

So therewith Sir Tristram gave orders to Gouvernail, and Gouvernail brought him his shining golden harp, and the harp glistered with great splendor in the dim light of the pavilion.

Sir Tristram took the harp in his hands and tuned it and struck upon it. And he played upon the harp, and he sang to the music thereof so wonderfully that they

Sir Tristram sings before King Arthur.

who sat there listened in silence as though they were without breath. For not one of them had ever heard such singing as that music which Sir Tristram sang; for it was as though some angel were singing to those who sat there harkening to his chanting.

So after Sir Tristram had ended, all who were there gave loud acclaim and much praise to his singing. "Ha, Messire!" quoth King Arthur, "many times in my life have I heard excellent singing, but never before in my life have I heard such singing as that. Now I wish that we might always have you at this court and that you would never leave us." And Sir Tristram said: "Lord, I too would wish that I might always be with you and with these noble knights of your court, for I have never met any whom I love as I love them."

So they sat there in great joy and friendliness of spirit, and, for the while, Sir Tristram forgot the mission he was upon and was happy in heart and glad of that terrible storm that had driven him thitherward.

And now I shall tell you the conclusion of all these adventures, and of how it fared with Sir Tristram.

JVSTISSIMVS·REX·

elle Isoult and Sir Tristram drink the love draught.

CHAPTER SEVENTH

How Sir Tristram Had Speech With King Angus of Ireland; How He Undertook to Champion the Cause of King Angus and of What Happened Thereafter.

Now, as Sir Tristram and King Arthur and Sir Launcelot sat together in the pavilion of Sir Tristram in pleasant, friendly discourse, as aforetold, there came Gouvernail of a sudden into that place. He, coming to Sir Tristram, leaned over his shoulder and he whispered into his ear: "Sir, I have just been told that King Angus of Ireland is at this very time at Camelot at the court of the King."

Upon this Sir Tristram turned to King Arthur and said: "Lord, my esquire telleth me that King Angus of Ireland is here at Camelot; now I pray you tell me, is that saying true?" "Yea," said King Arthur, "that is true; but what of it?" "Well," said Sir Tristram, "I had set forth to seek King Angus in Ireland, when I and my companions were driven hither by a great storm of wind. Yet when I find him, I know not whether King Angus may look upon me as a friend or as an unfriend."

Sir Tristram hears news of King Angus.

"Ha," said King Arthur, "you need not take trouble concerning the regard in which King Angus shall hold you. For he is at this time in such anxiety of spirit that he needs to have every man his friend who will be his friend, and no man his enemy whom he can reconcile to him. He is not just now in very good grace, either with me or with my court, for the case with him is thus: Some while ago, after you left the court of Ireland, there came to that place Sir Blamor de Ganys (who is right cousin to Sir Launcelot of the Lake) and with Sir Blamor a knight-companion hight Sir Bertrand de la Riviere Rouge. These two knights went to Ireland with intent to win themselves honor at the court of Ireland. Whilst they were in that kingdom there were held many jousts and tourneys, and in all of them Sir Blamor and Sir Bertrand were victorious, and all the knights of Ireland who came against them were put to shame at their hands. Many of the Irish knights were exceedingly angry at this, and so likewise was

How Sir Bertrand was killed in Ireland.

the King of Ireland. Now it happened one day that Sir Bertrand was found dead and murdered at a certain pass in the King's forest, and when the news thereof was brought to Sir Blamor, he was very wroth that his knight-companion should have been thus treacherously slain. So he immediately quitted Ireland and returned hither straightway, and when he had come before me he accused King Angus of treason because of that murder. Now at this time King Angus is here upon my summons for to answer that charge and to defend himself therefrom; for Sir Blamor offers his body to defend the truth of his accusation, and as for the King of Ireland, he can find no knight to take his part in that contention. For not only is Sir Blamor, as you very well know, one of the best knights in the world, but also nearly everybody here hath doubt of the innocence of King Angus in this affair. Now from this you may see that King Angus is very much more in need of a friend at this time than he is of an enemy."

"Lord," said Sir Tristram, "what you tell me is very excellent good news, for now I know that I may have talk with King Angus with safety to myself, and that he will no doubt receive me as a friend."

So after King Arthur and his court had taken their departure—it being then in the early sloping of the afternoon—Sir Tristram called Gouvernail to him and bade him make ready their horses, and when Gouvernail had done so, they two mounted and rode away by themselves toward that place where King Angus had taken up his lodging. When they had come there, Sir Tristram made demand to have speech with the King, and therewith they in attendance ushered him in to where the King Angus was.

King Angus welcomes Sir Tristram.

But when King Angus saw Sir Tristram who he was, and when he beheld a face that was both familiar and kind, he gave a great cry of joy, and ran to Sir Tristram and flung his arms about him, and kissed him upon the cheek; for he was rejoiced beyond measure to find a friend in that unfriendly place.

Then Sir Tristram said, "Lord, what cheer have you?" Unto that King Angus replied: "Tristram, I have very poor cheer; for I am alone amongst enemies with no one to befriend me, and unless I find some knight who will stand my champion to-morrow or the next day I am like to lose my life for the murder of Sir Bertrand de la Riviere Rouge. And where am I to find any one to act as my champion in defence of my innocence in this place, where I behold an enemy in every man whom I meet? Alas, Tristram! There is no one in all the world who will aid me unless it be you, for you alone of all the knights in the world beyond the circle of the knights of the Round Table may hope to stand against so excellent and so strong a hero!"

"Lord," quoth Sir Tristram, "I know very well what great trouble overclouds you at this time, and it is because of that that I am come hither for to visit you. For I have not at any time forgotten how that I told you when you spared my life in Ireland that mayhap the time might come when I might serve as your friend in your day of need. So if you will satisfy me upon two points, then I myself will stand for your champion upon this occasion."

"Ah, Tristram," quoth King Angus, "what you say is very good news to me indeed. For I believe there is no other knight in all the world (unless it be Sir Launcelot of the Lake) who is so strong and worthy a knight as you. So tell me what are those two matters concerning which you would seek satisfaction, and, if it is possible for me to do so, I will give you such an answer as may please you."

"Lord," said Sir Tristram, "the first matter is this: that you shall satisfy me that you are altogether innocent of the death of Sir Bertrand. And the second matter is this: that you shall grant me whatsoever favor it is that I shall have to ask of you."

Then King Angus arose and drew his sword and he said: "Tristram, behold; here is my sword—and the guard thereof and the blade thereof and the handle thereof make that holy sign of the cross unto which all Christian men bow down to worship. Look! See! Here I kiss that holy sign and herewith I swear an oath upon that sacred symbol, and I furthermore swear upon the honor of my knighthood, that I am altogether guiltless of the death of that noble, honorable knight aforesaid. Nor do I at all know how it was he met his death, for I am innocent of all evil knowledge thereof. Now, Messire, art thou satisfied upon that point?" And Sir Tristram said, "I am satisfied."

King Angus swears innocence to Sir Tristram.

Then King Angus said: "As to the matter of granting you a favor, that I would do in any case for the love I bear you. So let me hear what it is that you have to ask of me."

"Lord," cried out Sir Tristram, "the favor is one I had liever die than ask. It is this: that you give me your daughter, the Lady Belle Isoult, for wife unto mine uncle, King Mark of Cornwall."

Sir Tristram asks his boon.

Upon these words, King Angus sat in silence for a long while, gazing very strangely upon Sir Tristram. Then by and by he said: "Messire, this is a very singular thing you ask of me; for from what you said to me aforetime and from what you said to my daughter I had thought that you desired the Lady Belle Isoult for yourself. Now I can in no wise understand why you do not ask for her in your name instead of asking for her in the name of King Mark."

Then Sir Tristram cried out as in great despair: "Messire, I love that dear lady a great deal more than I love my life; but in this affair I am fulfilling a pledge made upon the honor of my knighthood and unto the King of Cornwall, who himself made me knight. For I pledged him unaware, and now I am paying for my hastiness. Yet I would God that you might take the sword which you hold in your hand and thrust it through my heart; for I had liefer die than fulfil this obligation to which I am pledged."

"Well," said King Angus, "you know very well that I will not slay you, but that I will fulfil your boon as I have promised. As for what you do in this affair, you must answer for it to God and to the honor of your own knighthood whether it is better to keep that promise which you made to the King of Cornwall or to break it."

Then Sir Tristram cried out again in great travail of soul: "Lord, you know not what you say, nor what torments I am at this present moment enduring." And therewith he arose and went forth from that place, for he was ashamed that anyone should behold the passion that moved him.

And now is to be told of that famous battle betwixt Sir Tristram and Sir Blamor de Ganys of which so much hath been written in all the several histories of chivalry that deal with these matters.

Now when the next morning had come—clear and fair and with the sun shining wonderfully bright—a great concourse of people began to betake themselves to that place where the lists had been set up in preparation for that ordeal of battle. That place was on a level meadow of grass very fair bedight with flowers and not far from the walls of the town nor from the high road that led to the gate of the same.

And, indeed, that was a very beautiful place for battle, for upon the one hand was the open countryside, all gay with spring blossoms and flowers; and upon the other hand were the walls of the town. Over above the top of those walls was to be seen a great many tall towers—some built of stone and some of brick—that rose high up into the clear, shining sky all full of slow-drifting clouds, that floated, as it were, like full-breasted swans in a sea of blue. And beyond the walls of the town you might behold a great many fair houses with bright windows of glass all shining against the sky. So you may see how fair was all that place, where that fierce battle was presently to be fought.

Of the meadow of battle.

Meanwhile, great multitudes of people had gathered all about the meadow of battle, and others stood like flies upon the walls of the town and looked down into that fair, pleasant meadow-land, spread with its carpet of flowers. All along one side of the ground of battle was a scaffolding of seats fair bedraped with fabrics of various colors and textures. In the midst of all the other seats were two seats hung with cloth of scarlet, and these seats were the one for King Arthur and the other for King Angus of Ireland.

In the centre of the meadow-land Sir Blamor rode up and down very proudly. He was clad in red armor, and the trappings and the furniture of his horse were all of red, so that he paraded the field like a crimson flame of fire.

"Sir." quoth King Arthur to King Angus, "yon is a very strong, powerful, noble knight; now where mayst thou find one who can hope to stand against him in this coming battle?"

"Lord," said King Angus, "I do believe that God hath raised up a defender for me in this extremity. For Sir Tristram of Lyonesse came to me yesterday, and offered for to take this quarrel of mine upon him. Now I do not believe that there is any better knight in all of Christendom than he, wherefore I am to-day uplifted with great hopes that mine innocence shall be proved against mine accuser."

King Angus presents Sir Tristram for his champion.

"Ha!" quoth King Arthur, "if Sir Tristram is to stand thy champion in this affair, then I do believe that thou hast indeed found for thyself a very excellent, worthy defender."

So anon there came Sir Tristram riding to that place, attended only by Gouvernail. And he was clad all in bright, polished armor so that he shone like a star of great splendor as he entered the field of battle. He came straight to where King Arthur sat and saluted before him. King Arthur said, "Sir, what knight art thou?" "Lord," answered he, "I am Sir Tristram of Lyonesse, and I am come to champion King Angus who sits beside you. For I believe him to be innocent of that matter of which he is accused, and I will emperil my body in that belief for to prove the truth of the same."

"Well," quoth King Arthur, "this King accused hath, certes, a very noble champion in thee. So go and do thy devoirs, and may God defend the right."

Thereupon each knight took a good stout spear into his hand and chose his place for the encounter, and each set his shield before him and feutered his lance in rest. Then, when each was ready, the marshal blew a great blast upon his trumpet, and thereupon, in an instant, each knight launched against the other like a bolt of thunder. So they met in the very middle of the course with such violence that the spear of each knight was shattered all into pieces unto the very truncheon thereof. Each horse fell back upon his haunches, and each would no doubt, have fallen entirely, had not the knight-rider recovered his steed with the greatest skill and address.

Sir Tristram does battle with Sir Blamor.

Then each knight voided his saddle and each drew his sword and set his shield before him. Therewith they came to battle on foot like two wild boars—so fiercely and felly that it was terrible to behold. For they traced this way and that and foined and struck at one another so that whole pieces of armor were hewn from the bodies of each.

But in all this battle Sir Tristram had so much the better that, by and by after they had fought for above an hour, Sir Blamor de Ganys began to bare back before him, and to give ground, holding his shield low for weariness. This Sir Tristram perceived, and, running in suddenly upon Sir Blamor, he struck him so terrible a blow upon the right shoulder that Sir Blamor's arm was altogether benumbed thereby, and he could no longer hold his sword in his hand.

Sir Tristram overcomes Sir Blamor.

So the sword of Sir Blamor fell down into the grass, and Sir Tristram, perceiving this, ran and set his foot upon it. Then Sir Blamor could not stand any longer, but fell down upon his knees because of a great weariness and faintness that lay upon him like the weariness and faintness of approaching death.

Then Sir Tristram said: "Sir Knight, thou canst fight no longer. Now I bid thee for to yield thyself to me as overcome in this battle."

Thereunto Sir Blamor made reply, speaking very deep and hollow from out of his helmet: "Sir Knight, thou hast overcome me by thy strength and prowess, but I will not yield myself to thee now nor at any time. For that would be so great shame that I would rather die than endure it. I am a knight of the Round Table, and have never yet been overcome in this wise by any man. So thou mayst slay me, but I will not yield myself to thee."

Then Sir Tristram cried out: "Sir Knight, I beseech thee to yield thyself, for thou art not fit to fight any more this day."

Sir Blamor said, "I will not yield, so strike and have done with it."

So Sir Tristram wist not what to do, but stood there in doubt looking down upon Sir Blamor. Then Sir Blamor said, again: "Strike, Sir Knight, and have done with it."

Upon this Sir Tristram said: "I may not strike thee, Sir Blamor de Ganys, to slay thee, for thou art very nigh of blood to Sir Launcelot of the Lake, and unto him I have sworn brotherhood in arms; wherefore I pray thee now to yield thyself to me."

Sir Blamor said, "Nay, I will not yield me to thee."

"Well," said Sir Tristram, "then I must fain act this day in a manner like as I acted yesterday."

Therewith speaking, he took his sword into both his hands and he swung it several times around his head and when he had done that he flung it to a great distance away, so that he was now entirely unarmed saving only for his misericordia. After that he gave Sir Blamor his hand and lifted him up upon his feet. And he stooped and picked up Sir Blamor's sword out of the grass and gave it back to Sir Blamor into his hands, and he said: "Sir Knight, now thou art armed and I am entirely unarmed, and so thou hast me at thy mercy. Now thou shalt either yield thyself to me or slay me as I stand here without any weapon; for I cannot now strike thee, and though I have overcome thee fairly yet thou hast it now in thy power to slay me. So now do thy will with me in this matter."

Sir Tristram gives Sir Blamor back his sword.

Then Sir Blamor was greatly astonished at the magnanimity of Sir Tristram, and he said, "Sir Knight, what is thy name?" Sir Tristram said, "It is Tristram, surnamed of Lyonesse."

Upon this Sir Blamor came to Sir Tristram and put his arms about his shoulders, and he said: "Tristram, I yield myself to thee, but in love and not in hate. For I yield myself not because of thy strength of arms (and yet I believe there is no knight in the world, unless it be my cousin Sir Launcelot of the Lake, who is thy peer), but I yield me because of thy exceeding nobility. Yet I would that I might only be satisfied that this King of Ireland is no traitor."

"Messire," said Sir Tristram, "of that I have assured myself very strongly ere I entered into this contest, wherefore I may now freely avouch upon mine own knightly word that he is innocent."

"Then," said Sir Blamor, "I also am satisfied, and I herewith withdraw all my impeachment against him."

Then those two noble, excellent knights took one another by the hand and went forward together to where King Arthur sat in high estate, and all those who looked on and beheld that reconciliation gave loud acclaim. And when King Arthur beheld them coming thus, he arose from where he sat and met them and embraced them both, and he said: "I do not believe that any king can have greater glory in his life than this, to have such knights about him as ye be."

Sir Tristram and Sir Blamor are reconciled.

So ended this famous battle with great glory to Sir Tristram and yet with no disregard to that famous knight against whom he did battle.

After that, they and King Arthur and King Angus of Ireland and all the court went up unto the castle of Camelot, and there the two knights-combatant were bathed in tepid water and their wounds were searched and dressed and they were put at their ease in all ways that it was possible.

Now that very day, as they all sat at feast in the castle of Camelot, there came one with news that the name of Sir Tristram had suddenly appeared upon one of the seats of the Round Table. So after they had ended their feast they all immediately went to see how that might be. When they came to the pavilion of the Round Table, there, behold! was his name indeed upon that seat that had once been the seat of King Pellinore. For this was the name that now was upon that seat:

SIR TRISTRAM
OF
LYONESSE

So the next day Sir Tristram was duly installed as a knight-companion of the Round Table with a great pomp and estate of circumstance, and a day or two after that he set sail for Ireland with King Angus, taking with him Gouvernail and those Cornish knights who were his companions.

Sir Tristram becomes knight of the Round Table.

So they all reached Ireland in safety, and, because Sir Tristram had aided the King of Ireland in the day of his extremity, the Queen forgave him all the despite she held against him, so that he was received at the court of the King and Queen with great friendship and high honor.

For a while Sir Tristram dwelt in Ireland and said nothing concerning that purpose for which he had come. Then one day he said to King Angus: "Lord, thou art not to forget to fulfil that promise which thou madst to me concerning the Lady Belle Isoult."

How Sir Tristram dwelt in Ireland.

To this King Angus made reply: "I had hoped that now we were come to Ireland you had changed your purpose in that matter. Are you yet of the same mind as when you first spake to me?"

"Yea," said Sir Tristram, "for it cannot be otherwise."

"Well, then," said King Angus, "I shall go to prepare my daughter for this ill-hap that is to befall her, though indeed it doth go against my heart to do such a thing. After I have first spoken to her, you are to take the matter into your own hands, for, to tell you the truth, I have not the heart to contrive it further."

So King Angus went away from where Sir Tristram was, and he was gone a long while. When he returned he said: "Sir, go you that way and the Lady Belle Isoult will see you."

So Sir Tristram went in the direction King Angus had said, and a page showed him the way. So by and by he came to where the Lady Belle Isoult was, and it was a great chamber in a certain tower of the castle and high up Under the eaves of the roof.

The Lady Belle Isoult stood upon the farther side of this chamber so that the light from the windows shone full upon her face, and Sir Tristram perceived that she was extraordinarily beautiful, and rather like to a shining spirit than to a lady of flesh and blood. For she was clad altogether in white and her face was like to wax for whiteness and clearness, and she wore ornaments of gold set with shining stones of divers colors about her neck and about her arms so that they glistered with a wonderful lustre. Her eyes shone very bright and clear like one with a fever, and Sir Tristram beheld that there were channels of tears upon her face and several tears stood upon her white cheeks like to shining jewels hanging suspended there.

How Lady Belle Isoult appeared to Sir Tristram.

So, for a while, Sir Tristram stood still without speaking and regarded her from afar. Then after a while she spake and said, "Sir, what is this you have done?" "Lady," he said, "I have done what God set me to do, though I would rather die than do it."

She said, "Tristram, you have betrayed me." Upon the which he cried out in a very loud and piercing voice, "Lady, say not so!"

She said: "Tristram, tell me, is it better to fulfil this pledge you have made, knowing that in so doing you sacrifice both my happiness and your happiness to satisfy your pride of honor; or is it better that you sacrifice your pride and break this promise so that we may both be happy? Tristram, I beseech you to break this promise you have made and let us be happy together."

At this Sir Tristram cried out in a very loud voice: "Lady, did you put your hand into my bosom and tear my naked heart, you could not cause me so much pain as that which I this moment endure. It cannot be as you would have it, for it is thus with me: were it but myself whom I might consider, I would freely sacrifice both my life and my honor for your sake. But it may not be so, lady; for I am held to be one of the chiefest of that order of knighthood to which I belong, wherefore I may not consider myself, but must ever consider that order. For if I should violate a pledge given upon my knighthood, then would I dishonor not myself, but that entire order to which I belong. For, did I so, all the world would say, what virtue is there in the order of knighthood when one of the chiefest of that order may violate his pledge when it pleases him to do so? So, lady, having assumed that great honor of knighthood I must perform its obligations even to the uttermost; yea, though in fulfilling my pledge I sacrifice both thee and myself."

Then Belle Isoult looked upon Sir Tristram for some little while, and by and by she smiled very pitifully and said: "Ah, Tristram, I believe I am more sorry for thee than I am for myself."

"Lady," said Tristram, "I would God that I lay here dead before you. But I am not able to die, but am altogether strong and hale—only very sorrowful at heart." And therewith he turned and left that place. Only when he had come to a place where he was entirely by himself with no one but God to see him, he hid his face in his hands and wept as though his heart were altogether broken. So it was that Sir Tristram fulfilled his pledge.

After that, King Angus furnished a very noble and beautiful ship with sails of satin embroidered with figures of divers sorts, and he fitted the ship in all ways such as became the daughter of a king and the wife of a king to embark upon. And that ship was intended for the Lady Belle Isoult and Sir Tristram in which to sail to the court of Cornwall.

Belle Isoult and Sir Tristram depart for Cornwall.

And it was ordained that a certain very excellent lady of the court of the Queen, who had been attendant upon the Lady Belle Isoult when she was a little child and who had been with her in attendance ever since that time, should accompany her to the Court of Cornwall. And the name of this lady was the Lady Bragwaine.

Now the day before the Lady Belle Isoult was to take her departure from Ireland, the Queen of Ireland came to the Lady Bragwaine and she bare with her a flagon of gold very curiously wrought. And the Queen said: "Bragwaine, here is a flask of a very singular and precious sort of an elixir; for that liquor it is of such a sort that when a man and a woman drink of it together, they two shall thereafter never cease to love one another as long as they shall have life. Take this flask, and when you have come to Cornwall, and when the Lady Belle Isoult and King Mark have been wedded, then give them both to drink of this elixir; for after they have drunk they shall forget all else in the world and cleave only to one another. This I give you to the intent that the Lady Isoult may forget Sir Tristram, and may become happy in the love of King Mark whom she shall marry."

The Queen of Ireland provides a love potion for King Mark and Belle Isoult.

Soon thereafter the Lady Belle Isoult took leave of the King and the Queen and entered into that ship that had been prepared for her. Thus, with Sir Tristram and with Dame Bragwaine and with their attendants, she set sail for Cornwall.

Now it happened that, whilst they were upon that voyage, the Lady Bragwaine came of a sudden into the cabin of that ship and there she beheld the Lady Belle Isoult lying upon a couch weeping. Dame Bragwaine said, "Lady, why do you weep?"

Whereunto the Lady Belle Isoult made reply: "Alas, Bragwaine, how can I help but weep seeing that I am to be parted from the man I love and am to be married unto another whom I do not love?"

Dame Bragwaine laughed and said: "Do you then weep for that? See! Here is a wonderful flask as it were of precious wine. When you are married to the King of Cornwall, then you are to quaff of it and he is to quaff of it and after that you will forget all others in the world and cleave only to one another. For it is a wonderful love potion and it hath been given to me to use in that very way. Wherefore dry your eyes, for happiness may still lay before you."

When the Lady Belle Isoult heard these words she wept no more but smiled very strangely. Then by and by she arose and went away to where Sir Tristram was.

When she came to him she said, "Tristram, will you drink of a draught with me?" He said, "Yea, lady, though it were death in the draught." She said, "There is not death in it, but something very different," and thereupon she went away into the cabin where that chalice aforesaid was hidden. And at that time Dame Bragwaine was not there.

Then the Lady Belle Isoult took the flagon from where it was hidden, and poured the elixir out into a chalice of gold and crystal and she brought it to where Sir Tristram was. When she had come there, she said, "Tristram, I drink to thee," and therewith she drank the half of the elixir there was in the chalice. Then she said, "Now drink thou the rest to me."

Upon that Sir Tristram took the chalice and lifted it to his lips, and drank all the rest of that liquor that was therein.

Now immediately Sir Tristram had drunk that elixir he felt it run like fire through every vein in his body. Thereupon he cried out, "Lady, what is this you have given me to drink?" She said: "Tristram, that was a powerful love potion intended for King Mark and me. But now thou and I have drunk of it and never henceforth can either of us love anybody in all of the world but the other."

Sir Tristram and Belle Isoult drink the love potion.

Then Sir Tristram catched her into his arms and he cried out: "Isoult! Isoult! what hast thou done to us both? Was it not enough that I should have been unhappy but that thou shouldst have chosen to be unhappy also?"

Thereat the Lady Belle Isoult both wept and smiled, looking up into Sir Tristram's face, and she said: "Nay, Tristram; I would rather be sorry with thee than happy with another." He said, "Isoult, there is much woe in this for us both." She said, "I care not, so I may share it with thee."

Thereupon Sir Tristram kissed her thrice upon the face, and then immediately put her away from him and he left her and went away by himself in much agony of spirit.

Thereafter they reached the kingdom of Cornwall in safety, and the Lady Belle Isoult and King Mark were wedded with much pomp and ceremony and after that there was much feasting and every appearance of rejoicing.

PART II

THE STORY OF SIR TRISTRAM AND SIR LAMORACK

And now shall be told the story of Sir Tristram and Sir Lamorack of Gales, how they became brothers-in-arms; how Sir Lamorack took offence at Sir Tristram, and how they became reconciled again.

But first of all you must know that Sir Lamorack of Gales was deemed to be one of the greatest knights alive. For it was said that there were three knights that were the greatest in all of the world, and those three were Sir Launcelot of the Lake, Sir Tristram of Lyonesse, and Sir Lamorack of Gales.

Sir Lamorack was the son of King Pellinore, of whom it hath already been told in the Book of King Arthur that he was the greatest knight during that time; and he was the brother of Sir Percival, of whom it is to be told hereinafter that he was the peer even of Sir Launcelot of the Lake. So because that house produced three such great and famous knights, the house of King Pellinore hath always been singularly renowned in all histories of chivalry. For indeed there was not any house so famous as it saving only the house of King Ban of Benwick, which brought forth those two peerless knights beyond all compare:—to wit, Sir Launcelot of the Lake and Sir Galahad, who achieved the quest of the San Grail.

So I hope that you may find pleasure in the story of how Sir Tristram and Sir Lamorack became acquainted, and of how they became brothers-in-arms.

Sir Lamorack of Gales.

CHAPTER FIRST

How Sir Lamorack of Gales Came to Tintagel and How He and Sir Tristram Sware Friendship Together in the Forest.

After these happenings, Sir Tristram abode for awhile at the Court of Cornwall, for so King Mark commanded him to do. And he sought in every way to distract his mind from his sorrows by deeds of prowess. So during this time he performed several adventures of which there is not now space to tell you. But these adventures won such credit to his knighthood that all the world talked of his greatness.

And ever as he grew more and more famous, King Mark hated him more and more. For he could not bear to see Sir Tristram so noble and so sorrowful with love of the Lady Belle Isoult.

Also Sir Tristram spent a great deal of time at chase with hawk and hound; for he hoped by means also of such sports to drive away, in some measure, his grief for the loss of Belle Isoult.

Now the season whereof this chapter speaketh was in the autumn of the year, what time all the earth is glorious with the brown and gold of the woodlands. For anon, when the wind would blow, then the leaves would fall down from the trees like showers of gold so that everywhere they lay heaped like flakes of gold upon the russet sward, rustling dry and warm beneath the feet, and carpeting all the world with splendor. And the deep blue sky overhead was heaped full of white, slow-moving clouds, and everywhere the warm air was fragrant with the perfume of the forest, and at every strong breeze the nuts would fall pattering down upon the ground like hailstones.

Sir Tristram rides ahunting.

And because the world was so beautiful and so lusty, Sir Tristram took great pleasure in life in spite of that trouble that lay upon him. So he and his court rode very joyfully amid the trees and thickets, making the woodlands merry with the music of winding horns and loud-calling voices and with the baying of hounds sounding like sweet tolling bells in the remoter aisles of the forest spaces.

Thus Sir Tristram made sport all one morning, in such an autumn season, and when noon had come he found himself to be anhungered. So he gave orders to those who were in attendance upon him that food should be spread at a certain open space in the forest; and therewith, in accordance with those orders, they in attendance immediately opened sundry hampers of wicker, and therefrom brought forth a noble pasty of venison, and manchets of bread and nuts and apples and several flasks and flagons of noble wine of France and the Rhine countries. This abundance of good things they set upon a cloth as white as snow which they had laid out upon the ground.

Now just as Sir Tristram was about to seat himself at this goodly feast he beheld amid the thin yellow foliage that there rode through a forest path not far away a very noble-seeming knight clad all in shining armor and with vestments and trappings of scarlet so that he shone like a flame of fire in the woodlands.

Then Sir Tristram said to those who stood near him, "Know ye who is yonder knight who rides alone?" They say, "No, Lord, we know him not." Sir Tristram said, "Go and bid that knight of his courtesy that he come hither and eat with me."

So three or four esquires ran to where that knight was riding, and in a little they came attending him to where Sir Tristram was, and Sir Tristram went to meet him.

Then Sir Tristram said: "Sir Knight, I pray you for to tell me your name and degree, for it seems to me that you are someone very high in order of knighthood."

Sir Lamorack meets Sir Tristram.

"Messire," quoth the other, "I shall be very glad to tell you my name if so be you will do the like courtesy unto me. I am Sir Lamorack of Gales, and I am son of the late King Pellinore, who was in his days held to be the foremost knight in this realm. I come to these parts seeking Sir Tristram of Lyonesse, of whose fame I hear told in every court of chivalry whither I go. For I have never beheld Sir Tristram, and I have a great desire to do so."

"Well," quoth Sir Tristram, "meseems I should be greatly honored that you should take so much trouble for nothing else than that; for lo! I am that very Sir Tristram of Lyonesse whom you seek."

Then Sir Lamorack immediately leaped down from his war-horse and putting up the umbril of his helmet, he came to Sir Tristram and took him by the hand and kissed him upon the cheek. And Sir Tristram kissed Sir Lamorack again, and each made great joy of the other.

After that, Sir Lamorack, with the aid of these esquires attendant upon Sir Tristram, put aside his armor, and bathed his face and neck and hands in a cold forest brook, as clear as crystal, that came brawling down out of the woodlands. Therewith, being greatly refreshed he and Sir Tristram sat down to that bountiful feast together, and ate and drank with great joy and content of spirit. And whiles they ate each made inquiry of the other what he did, and each told the other many things concerning the goodly adventures that had befallen him.

And after they were through eating and drinking, Sir Tristram took his harp in hand and sang several excellent ballads and rondels which he had made in honor of Belle Isoult, and Sir Lamorack listened and made great applause at each song that Sir Tristram sang. And so each knight loved the other more and more the longer they sat together.

Sir Tristram sings to Sir Lamorack.

Then, after a while, Sir Tristram said: "Dear friend, let us swear brotherhood to one another, for I find that my heart goeth out to thee with a wonderful strength."

"Ha, Tristram," said Sir Lamorack, "I would rather live in brotherhood with thee than with any man whom I know, for I find that the longer I am with thee, the greater and the stronger my love groweth for thee."

Then Sir Tristram drew from his finger a very splendid ring (for the ring held an emerald carved into the likeness of the head of a beautiful woman, and that emerald was set into the gold of the ring) and Sir Tristram said: "Give me that ring upon thy finger, O Lamorack! and take thou this ring in its stead; so we shall have confirmed our brotherhood to one another."

Then Sir Lamorack did very joyfully as Sir Tristram bade him, and he took the ring that Sir Tristram gave him and kissed it and put it upon his finger; and Sir Tristram kissed the ring that Sir Lamorack gave him and put it upon his finger.

Thus they confirmed brotherhood with one another that day as they sat together in the forest at feast, with the golden leaves falling about them. And so they sat together all that afternoon and until the sun began to hang low in the west; after that, they arose and took horse, and rode away together toward Tintagel in great pleasure of companionship.

Now all the court at Tintagel was greatly rejoiced at the presence of so famous a knight as Sir Lamorack of Gales; so there was great celebration upon that account, and everybody did the most that he was able to give pleasure to Sir Lamorack. And during the time that Sir Lamorack was at Tintagel there were several joustings held in his honor, and in all these assays at arms Sir Lamorack himself took part and overthrew everyone who came against him, so that he approved himself to be so wonderful a champion that all men who beheld his performance exclaimed with astonishment at his prowess.

Sir Lamorack is honored at Tintagel.

But from all these affairs at arms Sir Tristram held himself aloof, and would not take part in them. For he took such pleasure in Sir Lamorack's glory that he would not do anything that might imperil the credit that his friend thus gained by his prowess. For though Sir Tristram dearly loved such affairs, he would ever say to himself: "Perhaps if I should enter the lists against my friend it might be my mishap to overthrow him and then his glory would be forfeited unto me."

Now upon a certain time there was held a great day of jousting in honor of Sir Lamorack, and in that affair at arms twenty of the best knights, both of Cornwall and the countries circumadjacent, took the field to hold it against all comers. Of these knights, several were well-known champions, so that they maintained the field for a long while, to the great credit both of themselves and of Cornwall. But some while after the prime of day, there came Sir Lamorack into that field, and, the day being cool and fresh, he was filled with a wonderful strength and spirit of battle. So he challenged first one of those Cornish champions and then another, and in all such challenges he was successful, so that he overthrew of those knights, the one after the other, fifteen men, some of whom were sorely hurt in the encounter. Upon this, the other five of those champions, beholding the prowess and strength and skill of Sir Lamorack said to one another: "Why should we venture against this man? Of a verity, this knight is no mere man, but a demon of strength and skill. Wherefore no man may hope to stand against him in an assault of arms; for lo! if he doth but touch a man with his lance that man straightway falleth from his saddle." So they withdrew themselves from that encounter and would not have to do with Sir Lamorack.

Sir Lamorack does famous battle.

Now at that time Sir Tristram was sitting with the court of the King, and not far from the Lady Belle Isoult, overlooking the meadow of battle.

To him King Mark said: "Messire, why do you take no part against this knight? Is it that you fear him?"

To this Sir Tristram replied with great calmness: "Nay, I fear not him nor any man alive, and that you know, Lord, better than anyone in all of the world."

"I am glad to hear of your courage and fearlessness," quoth King Mark, "for meseems it is a great shame to all of us that this gentleman, who is a stranger amongst us, should win so much credit to the disadvantage of all the knights of Cornwall. Now, as you say you have no fear of him, I pray you go down into the field and do battle with him in our behalf." So said King Mark, for he thought to himself: "Perhaps Sir Lamorack may overthrow Sir Tristram, and so bring him into disrepute with those who praise him so greatly."

But Sir Tristram said: "No; I will not go down to battle against Sir Lamorack this day whatever I may do another day. For I have sworn brotherhood to that noble and gentle champion, and it would ill beseem me to assault him now, when he is weary and short of breath from this great battle which he hath done to-day against such odds. For if I should overthrow him now, it would bring great shame upon him. Some other day and in some other place I may assay him in friendliness, with honor and credit both to myself and him."

"Well," said King Mark, "as for that, I do not choose to wait. Nor am I pleased that you should sit by and suffer this knight to carry away all the credit of arms from Cornwall in despite of the knights of Cornwall. For not only would this be a great shame to the knights of Cornwall (of whom you are the acknowledged champion), but it would be equally a shame unto this lady whom you have fetched hither from Ireland to be Queen of Cornwall. So I lay this command upon you—not only because I am your King, but because I am he who made you knight—that you straightway go down into yonder meadow and do battle with this knight who beareth himself so proudly in our midst."

King Mark commands Sir Tristram to do battle.

Then Sir Tristram looked upon King Mark with great anger and bitterness, and he said: "This is great shame and despite which you seek to put upon me by giving such commands unto me. Verily, it would seem that in all ways you seek to put shame and sorrow upon me. And yet I have ever been your true knight, and have saved your kingdom from truage to Ireland and have served you very faithfully in all ways. Would to God I had been made knight by any man in the world rather than by you."

At this King Mark smiled very bitterly upon Tristram. "Sirrah," quoth he, "meseems you speak very outrageously to me who am your King. Now I herewith command you to go straightway down into that field without any further words and to do my bidding against yonder knight."

Then Sir Tristram groaned in spirit, and then he said, "I go."

So Sir Tristram arose and went away from that place very full of bitterness and anger against the King and his court. For whiles there were some of that court who were sorry for the affront that King Mark had put upon him in public before the eyes of the entire court, yet there were others who smiled and were glad of his humiliation. For even so true and noble a gentleman as Sir Tristram, when he groweth great and famous, is like to have as many enemies as friends. For there are ever those who envy truth and nobility in a man, as well as others who hate meanness and falsity, and so Sir Tristram ever had many enemies whithersoever he went. And that also was the case with Sir Launcelot and Sir Lamorack, and with other noble knights at that time.

But though Sir Tristram was so filled with indignation he said nothing to any man, but went to his lodging and summoned Gouvernail, and bade Gouvernail to help him to his armor and his horse.

Sir Tristram arms himself.

Gouvernail said: "Lord, what would you do for to arm and horse yourself at this hour?" Sir Tristram made reply: "The King hath commanded me to do battle with Sir Lamorack, and yet Sir Lamorack is my very dear friend and sworn brother-in-arms. He is already weary with battle, and of a surety I shall be very likely to overthrow him in an assault at arms at this time." Gouvernail said, "Lord, that would be great shame to you as well as to him." And Sir Tristram said, "Yea, it is great shame." Then Gouvernail beheld Sir Tristram's face, how it was all filled with a passion of shame and indignation, and so he guessed what had passed, and held his peace.

So when Sir Tristram was armed and mounted, he rode down into the meadow of battle, where was Sir Lamorack parading with great glory before the applause of all who looked down upon that field.

But when Sir Lamorack beheld that it was Sir Tristram who came against him, he was greatly astonished, and cried out: "Ha, Tristram, how is this? Is it you who come against me? Have you then forgot that I am your brother-in-arms and a fellow of the Round Table?"

Sir Lamorack speaks to Sir Tristram.

To this Sir Tristram said: "Messire, I come not of my own free will, but only because I must needs come, being so commanded by the King of Cornwall."

"Very well," said Sir Lamorack, "so be it as you will, though I am very much surprised that you should do battle against me, after all that hath passed betwixt us. More especially at this season when, as you very well know, I am weary and winded with battle."

Thereupon and without further parley, each knight took stand for the encounter at the position assigned to him. Then when they were in all ways prepared, the marshal of the field blew upon his trumpet a call for the assault.

So rushed those two together like two stones, flung each out of a catapult; and therewith they two smote together in the midst of their course like to a clap of thunder.

Sir Tristram overthrows Sir Lamorack.

In that encounter the spear of Sir Lamorack brake into as many as twenty or thirty pieces; but the spear of Sir Tristram held, so that the horse of Sir Lamorack, which was weary with the several charges he had made, was overthrown into a great cloud of dust.

But Sir Lamorack did not fall with his steed; for he voided his saddle with a very wonderful agility and dexterity, so that he himself kept his feet, although his horse fell as aforesaid. Then he was filled with great rage and shame that he had been so overthrown before all those who looked upon him; wherefore he immediately drew his sword and cried out aloud: "Come down, Sir Knight, and do battle with me afoot, for though my horse hath failed me because of his weariness, yet you shall find that my body shall not so fail me."

But that while Sir Tristram sat very sorrowful, and he said: "Nay, I will not have to do with thee again this day, for it was against my will that I came hither to do battle with thee, and it is to my shame that I did so. Wherefore I will not now do further battle with thee. But wait until to-morrow and until thou art fresh, and then I will give thee the chance of battle again."

To this Sir Lamorack made answer very bitterly: "Sir, I think you talk to amuse me; for first you put shame upon me in this encounter, and then you bid me wait until to-morrow ere I purge me of that shame. Now I demand of you to do battle with me upon this moment and not to-morrow."

Sir Tristram said: "I will not do battle with thee, Lamorack, for I have done wrong already, and I will not do more wrong."

Sir Lamorack reproves Sir Tristram.

Upon this, Sir Lamorack was so filled with anger that he scarce knew what to say or to do. Wherefore he turned him to several who had come down into the meadow of battle, and he said: "Hear ye all, and listen to my words: This knight came against me in this field after I had had to do with fifteen other knights. In that encounter he overthrew me, because of the weariness of my horse. Having done that unknightly deed, he now refuseth me any further test of battle, but allows me to lie beneath that shame which he put upon me. Now I bid you who stand here to take this word to

Sir Launcelot of the Lake; I bid ye tell Sir Launcelot that Sir Tristram of Lyonesse, having sworn brotherhood-in-arms to me, and being a fellow-knight of the Round Table, hath come against me when I was weary with battle and he was fresh. Tell Sir Launcelot that so Sir Tristram overthrew me with shame to himself and with discredit to me, and that he then refused me all satisfaction such as one true knight should afford another."

Then Sir Tristram cried out in a loud voice, "I pray you, hear me speak, Messire!" But Sir Lamorack replied, "I will not hear thee!" and therewith turned and went away, leaving Sir Tristram where he was. And Sir Tristram sat there without movement, like to a statue of stone.

After that Sir Lamorack did not tarry longer at Tintagel, but immediately left the King's court without making speech with anyone. And thereafter he went down to the seashore and embarked in a boat with intent to sail to Camelot where King Arthur was then holding court. For his heart was still so bitter against Sir Tristram that he intended to lay complaint against him before the court of chivalry at Camelot.

Sir Lamorack leaves Tintagel.

But Sir Lamorack did not reach Camelot upon that voyage; for, whilst he was in passage, there suddenly arose a great tempest of wind, and in spite of all that the mariners could do, that small ship wherein he sailed was driven upon a cruel headland of rocks and cliffs where it was dashed to pieces.

But Sir Lamorack had foreseen that that small boat was to be wrecked, wherefore, before the end came, he stripped himself entirely naked and leaped into the waters and swam for his life.

So he swam for a long time until he was wellnigh exhausted and upon the point of drowning in the waters. But at that moment he came by good hap to where was a little bay of quiet water, whereinto he swam and so made shift to come safe to land—but faint and weak, and so sick that he feared that he was nigh to death. Then Sir Lamorack perceived that there was heather at that place growing upon the rocks of the hillside, so he crawled into the heather and lay him down therein in a dry spot and immediately fell into such a deep sleep of weariness that it was more like to the swoon of death than to slumber.

Sir Lamorack is shipwrecked upon a strange land.

Now the lord of that country whereunto Sir Lamorack had come was a very wicked knight, huge of frame and very cruel and hard of heart. The name of this knight was Sir Nabon, surnamed le Noir; for he was very swarth of hue, and he always wore armor entirely of black. This knight had several years before slain the lord of that land, and had seized upon all of the island as his own possession, and no one dared to come against him for to recover these possessions, for his prowess was so remarkable and his body so huge that all the world was afraid of him. So he dwelt there unmolested in a strong castle of stone built up upon a rock near to the seashore, whence he might behold all the ships that passed him by. Then, whenever he would see such a ship pass by, he would issue forth in his own ships and seize upon that other vessel, and either levy toll upon it or sink it with all upon board. And if he found any folk of high quality aboard such a ship, that one he would seize and hold for ransom. So Sir Nabon made himself the terror of all that part of the world, and all men avoided the coasts of so inhospitable a country. Such was the land upon which Sir Lamorack had been cast by the tempest.

Of Sir Nabon le Noir.

Now whilst Sir Lamorack lay sleeping in the heather in that wise as aforetold, there came by that way several fisher-folk; these, when they saw him lying there, thought at first that he was dead. But as they stood talking concerning him, Sir Lamorack was aware of their voices and woke and sat up and beheld them.

The fisher-folk disarm Sir Lamorack.

Then the chiefest of those fisher-folk spake and said, "Who are you, and how came you here?" Him Sir Lamorack answered: "Alas! friend! I am a poor soul who was cast ashore from a shipwreck, naked as you see me. Now I pray you, give me some clothes to cover my nakedness, and give me some food to eat, and lend me such succor as man may give to man in distress."

Then the chief fisherman perceived the ring upon Sir Lamorack's finger that Sir Tristram had given him, and he said, "How got you that ring upon your finger?" Sir Lamorack said, "He who was my friend gave it to me." "Well," quoth the fisherman, "I will give you clothes to wear and food to eat, but if I do so you must give me that ring that I see upon your hand. As for lending you aid, I must tell you that the lord of this island hath ordained upon peril of our lives that all who come hither must straightway be brought before him to be dealt with as he may deem fitting. Wherefore, after I have fed you and clothed you I must immediately take you to him."

"Alas!" quoth Sir Lamorack, "this is certes an inhospitable land into which I have come! Ne'ertheless, as I am naked and starving, I see that I have no choice other than that which ye put upon me." So therewith he gave the chief of the fisher-folk the ring that Sir Tristram had given him, and in return the fishermen gave him such garments as they could spare to cover his nakedness; and they gave him black bread and

The fisher-folk give Sir Lamorack clothes and food.

cheese to eat, and bitter ale to drink from a skin that they carried with them. After that they tied Sir Lamorack's hands behind his back, and so, having made him prisoner, they brought him to the castle of Sir Nabon, and before Sir Nabon who was there at that time.

Now it chanced that the swineherd of Sir Nabon's castle had been slain in a quarrel with one of his fellows, so that when Sir Nabon beheld Sir Lamorack, that he was big and sturdy of frame, he said: "I will spare this fellow his life, but I will make him my swineherd. So take ye him away and let him herd my swine."

So they led Sir Lamorack away, and he became swineherd to Sir Nabon surnamed le Noir, and presently in a little while he grew so rough and shaggy that his own mother would hardly have known him had she beheld him.

Sir Lamorack turns swineherd.

So endeth this adventure of Sir Lamorack. And now it shall be told how it befel with Sir Tristram after Sir Lamorack had left Tintagel as aforetold.

JVSTISSIMVS·REX·

Sir Tristram cometh to ye castle of Sir Nabon.

CHAPTER SECOND

How Sir Tristram Started to Go to Camelot, and How He Stayed by the Way to Do Battle With Sir Nabon le Noir.

Now after Sir Lamorack had quit the court of King Mark of Cornwall as aforetold, Sir Tristram was very sad at heart for a long while. Nevertheless, he tried to comfort himself by saying: "Well, it was not by my will that I did battle with my friend and brother-in-arms, for I had no choice as to that which I was compelled to do." So he spake to himself, and took what comfort he was able from such considerations, and that comfort was not very great.

Then one day there came from Sir Launcelot of the Lake a letter in which Sir Launcelot said that he had heard that Sir Tristram had assailed Sir Lamorack when that knight was weary and spent with battle. And in that letter Sir Launcelot further said: "It is very strange to me, Messire, that such things should be said of you, and that by several mouths. Now, I pray you, set this matter at right, for I do not choose to have such a thing said of you; that you would wait until a knight was weary with fighting before you would do battle with him. Moreover, Sir Lamorack is your sworn brother-at-arms, and a fellow-knight of the Round Table, and is, besides, one of the noblest and gentlest knights in Christendom. Wherefore I beseech you to set this matter right, so that those who accuse you of unknightliness may be brought to confusion."

Sir Launcelot sends a letter to Sir Tristram.

So wrote Sir Launcelot, and at those words Sir Tristram was cast into a great deal of pain and trouble of spirit; for he wist not how to answer that letter of Sir Launcelot's so as to make the matter clear to that knight. Wherefore he said: "I will straightway go to Camelot and to Sir Launcelot and will speak to him by word of mouth, and so will make him understand why I did that which I had to do."

So when the next day had come Sir Tristram arose and took horse and rode away from Tintagel with intent to betake himself to Camelot where King Arthur was then holding court, and where

Sir Tristram rides to Camelot.

he might hope to find Sir Launcelot abiding. And Sir Tristram took no companion with him, not even Gouvernail.

And now I shall tell you how Sir Tristram rode: the way that he took led him down by the seashore, and by and by to a deep forest, which was then nearly altogether devoid of leaves, so that the branches above him were in some places like to the meshes of a net spread against the sky. Here that young knight rode upon a deep carpet of leaves, so that the steps of his war-horse were silenced save only for the loud and continued rustling of his footfalls in the dry and yellow foliage. And as Sir Tristram rode he sang several songs in praise of the Lady Belle Isoult, chanting in a voice that was both clear and loud and very sweet, and that sounded to a great distance through the deep, silent aisles of the forest.

Thus he travelled, anon singing as aforetold of, and anon sank in meditation, so travelling until the day declined and the early gray of the evening began to fall. Then he began to bethink him how he should spend the night, and he thought he would have to sleep abroad in the forest. But just as the gray of the evening was fading away into darkness he came to a certain place of open land, where, before him, he perceived a tall castle, partly of stone and partly of red bricks, built up upon a steep hill of rocks. And upon one side of this castle was the forest, and upon the other side was the wide and open stretch of sea.

And Sir Tristram perceived that there were lights shining from several windows of that castle, and that all within was aglow with red as of a great fire in the hall of the castle; and at these signs of good cheer, his heart was greatly expanded with joy that he should not after all have to spend that night in the darkness and in the chill of the autumn wilds.

So Sir Tristram set spurs to his good horse and rode up to the castle and made request for rest and refreshment for the night. Then, after a little parley, the drawbridge was lowered, and the portcullis was raised, and he rode with a great noise into the stone-paved courtyard of the castle.

Sir Tristram comes to a friendly castle.

Thereupon there came several attendants of the castle, and took his horse and aided him to descend from the saddle; and then other attendants came and led him away into the castle and so to an apartment where there was a warm bath of tepid water, and where were soft towels and napkins of linen for to dry himself upon after he was bathed. And when he had bathed and refreshed himself, there came still other attendants bearing soft warm robes for him in which to clothe himself after his journey; and Sir Tristram clothed himself and felt greatly at his ease, and was glad that he had come to that place.

For thus it was that worthy knights like Sir Tristram travelled the world in those days so long ago; and so they were received in castle and hall with great pleasure and hospitality. For all folk knew the worth of these noble gentlemen and were glad to make them welcome whithersoever they went. And so I have told to you how Sir Tristram travelled, that you might, perchance, find pleasure in the thought thereof.

Now after Sir Tristram had refreshed himself and clothed himself as aforesaid, there came the steward of the castle and besought him that he would come to where the lady of the castle was awaiting him for to welcome him. And Sir Tristram went with the steward, and the steward brought him where the lady sat at a table prepared for supper. And Sir Tristram perceived that the lady was very beautiful, but that she was clad in the deep weeds of a widow.

Sir Tristram meets the lady of the castle.

When the lady perceived Sir Tristram, she arose and went to meet him, and gave him welcome, speaking in a voice both soft and very sweet. "Messire," quoth she, "I am grieved that there is no man here to welcome you in such a manner as is fitting. But, alas! as you may see by the weeds in which I am clad, I am alone in the world and without any lord of the castle to do the courtesies thereof as is fitting. Yet such as I am, I give you welcome with my entire heart."

"Lady," quoth Sir Tristram, "I give you gramercy for your courtesy. And indeed I am grieved to see you in such sorrow as your dress foretells. Now if there is any service I may render to you, I beseech you to call upon me for whatever aid I may give you."

"Nay," quoth she, "there is nothing you can do to help me." And therewith the lady, who was hight Loise, took Sir Tristram by the hand and led him to the table and sat him down beside her. Then straightway there came sundry attendants, and set a noble feast before them, with good excellent wines, both white and red; and they two ate and drank together with great appetite and enjoyment.

Sir Tristram feasts with the chatelaine.

Now after that feast was over and done, Sir Tristram said: "Lady, will you not of your courtesy tell me why you wear the weeds of sorrow in which you are clad? This I ask, not from idle humor, but because, as I said before, I may haply be able to aid you in whatever trouble it is under which you lie."

"Alas, Sir Knight!" quoth she, "my trouble lieth beyond your power to aid or to amend. For can you conquer death, or can you bring the dead back to life again? Nevertheless, I will tell you what my sorrow is, and how it came unto me. You must know

The Lady telleth Sir Tristram of Sir Nabon le Noir.

that some distance away across the sea, which you may behold from yonder window, there lieth an island. The present lord of that island is a very wicked and cruel knight, huge of frame and big of limb, hight Sir Nabon surnamed le Noir. One time the noble and gentle knight who was my husband was the lord of that island and the castle thereon, and of several other castles and manors and estates upon this mainland as well. But one evil day when I and my lord were together upon that island, this Sir Nabon came thither by night, and with certain evil-disposed folk of the island he overcame my lord and slew him very treacherously. Me also he would have slain, or else have taken into shameful captivity, but, hearing the noise of that assault in which my lord was slain, I happily escaped, and so, when night had come, I got away from that island with several attendants who were faithful to me, and thus came to this castle where we are. Since that time Sir Nabon has held that castle as his own, ruling it in a very evil fashion. For you are to know that the castle sits very high upon the crags overlooking the sea, and whenever a vessel passeth by that way, Sir Nabon goeth forth to meet it; and upon some of these crafts he levies toll, and other ships he sinks after slaying the mariners and sailor-folk who may by evil hap be aboard thereof. And if anyone is by chance cast ashore upon that island, that one he either slays or holds for ransom, or makes thereof a slave for to serve him. Because of this, very few ships now go by that way, for all people shun the coasts of so evil a country as that. So Sir Nabon took that land away from me; nor have I any kin who will take up this quarrel for me, and so I must endure my losses as best I may."

"Ha!" quoth Sir Tristram, "and is there then no good knight-champion in this country who will rid the world of such an evil being as that Sir Nabon of whom you speak?"

"Nay," said the lady, "there is no one who cares to offer challenge to that knight, for he is as strong and as doughty as he is huge of frame, and he is as fierce and cruel as he is strong and masterful, wherefore all men hold him in terror and avoid him."

"Well," said Sir Tristram, "meseems it is the business of any knight to rid the world of such a monster as that, whatever may be the danger to himself. Now as there is no knight hereabouts who hath heart to undertake such an adventure, I myself shall undertake it so soon as to-morrow shall have come."

"Sir," said the lady, "I beseech you to think twice before you enter into such an affair as that. Or rather be ruled by me and do not undertake this quest at all; for I misdoubt that anyone could conquer this huge and powerful champion, even if that knight were such as Sir Launcelot of the Lake or Sir Tristram of Lyonesse."

At this Sir Tristram laughed with great good-will, and he said, "Lady, do you not then know who I am?" "Nay," said she, "I know you not." "Well," said Sir Tristram, "then I may tell you that I am that Sir Tristram of Lyonesse of whom you spoke just now. And I also tell you that I shall undertake this adventure to-morrow morning."

Sir Tristram confesses his degree to the chatelaine.

Now when the lady found that the stranger she had taken in was Sir Tristram of Lyonesse, she made great exclamation of surprise and pleasure at having him at that place, for at that time all the world was talking of Sir Tristram's performances. So she took great pleasure and pride that her castle should have given him shelter. She made many inquiries concerning his adventures, and Sir Tristram told her all she asked of him.

Then the lady said: "Messire, I hear tell that you sing very sweetly, and that you are a wonderful harper upon the harp. Now will you not chaunt for me a song or two or three?" And Sir Tristram said: "Lady, I will do whatsoever you ask me that may give you pleasure."

So the lady bade them bring a harp and they did so. And Sir Tristram took the harp and set it before him and tuned it and played upon it, and sang so sweetly that they of the castle said: "Certes, this is no knight-errant who sings, but an angel from Paradise who hath come among us. For surely no one save an angel from Paradise could sing so enchantingly."

Sir Tristram sings to the lady.

So passed that evening very pleasantly until the hours waxed late. Then Sir Tristram retired to a very noble apartment where a soft couch spread with flame-colored linen had been prepared for him, and where he slept a soft sleep without disturbance of any kind.

Now when the next morning had come, Sir Tristram armed himself and mounted upon his war-horse, and rode him to a certain place on the shore. There he found some mariners in haven with a large boat, and to these he paid ten pieces of silver money to bear him across the sea to that island where Sir Nabon le Noir abided. At first these mariners said they would not sail to such a coast of danger and death; but afterward they said they would, and they did do so. But still they would not bring Sir Tristram to land nigh to the castle, but only at a place that was a great way off, and where they deemed themselves to be more safe from the cruel lord of that land.

Sir Tristram departs for the island of Sir Nabon.

As for Sir Tristram he made merry with their fear, saying: "It is well that we who are knights-errant have more courage than you who are sailor-men, else it would not be possible that monsters such as this Sir Nabon should ever be made an end of."

Upon this the captain of these sailors replied: "Well, Messire, for the matter of that, it is true that mariners such as we have not much courage, for we are the first of our order who have dared to come hither. But it is also true that you are the first errant-knight who hath ever had courage to come hither. So what say you for the courage of your own order?" And at that Sir Tristram laughed with great good will and rode his way.

Thereafter he rode forward along the coast of that land for several leagues, with the noise of the sea ever beating in his ears, and the shrill clamor of the sea-fowl ever sounding in the air about him. By and by he came to a place of certain high fells, and therefrom perceived before him in the distance a tall and forbidding castle standing upon a high headland of the coast. And the castle was built of stone, that was like the rocks upon which it stood, so that at first one could not tell whether what one beheld was a part of the cliffs or whether it was the habitation of man. But when Sir Tristram had come somewhat nearer, he perceived the windows of the castle shining against the sky, and he saw the gateway thereof, and the roofs and the chimneys thereof, so that he knew that it was a castle of great size and strength and no wall of rock as he had at first supposed it to be; and he wist that this must be the castle of that wicked and malignant knight, Sir Nabon, whom he sought.

Sir Tristram arrives at the castle of Sir Nabon.

Now as Sir Tristram wended his way toward that castle by a crooked path meditating how he should come at Sir Nabon for to challenge him to battle, he was by and by aware of a fellow clad in pied black and white, who walked along the way in the direction that he himself was taking. At the first that fellow was not aware of Sir Tristram; then presently he was aware of him and turned him about, and beheld that a strange knight was riding rapidly down toward him upon a horse.

Then at first that fellow stood like one struck with amazement; but in a moment he cried out aloud as with a great fear, and instantly turned again and ran away, yelling like one who had gone mad.

But Sir Tristram thundered after him at speed, and, in a little, came up with him, and catched him by the collar of his jerkin and held him fast. And Sir Tristram said: "Fellow, who are you?"

"Lord," quoth the fellow, "I am an attendant upon the knight of yonder castle, which same is hight Sir Nabon surnamed le Noir."

Then Sir Tristram said: "Sirrah, why did you run from me when you first beheld me?" And the fellow replied: "Messire, you are the first stranger who hath dared to come hither to this country; wherefore, seeing you, and seeing that you rode upon horseback, and not knowing how you came to this land, I wist not whether you were a man of flesh and blood, or whether you were a spirit come hither for to punish us for our sins; so I ran away from you."

Sir Tristram talks with a knave of the earth.

"Well," said Sir Tristram, "as you see, I am no spirit, but a man of flesh and blood. Yet I have great hope that I have indeed been sent hither for to punish those who have done evil, for I come hither seeking the knight of yonder castle for to do battle with him in behalf of that lady whose lord he slew so treacherously as I have heard tell. And I hope to take away from him this island and return it to the Lady Loise, to whom it belongeth."

"Alas, Messire," quoth the fellow, "this is for you a very sorry quest upon which you have come. For this Sir Nabon whom you seek is accounted to be the most potent knight in all of the world. Yea; he is held to be a bigger knight than even Sir Launcelot of the Lake or Sir Tristram of Lyonesse or Sir Lamorack of Gales. Wherefore I beseech you to turn about and go away whither you have come whilst there is still the chance for you to escape."

"Gramercy for your pity, good fellow," quoth Sir Tristram, "and may God grant that it may not be deserved. Nevertheless, in spite of the danger in this quest, I am still of the same mind as I was when I came hither. So do you presently go to your lord and tell him from me that a knight hath come to do battle with him upon the behalf of the lady to whom this island by rights belongeth."

Sir Tristram sends challenge to Sir Nabon.

Therewith Sir Tristram let the fellow go, and he ran off with great speed and so away to the postern of the castle and entered in and shut the door behind him.

Now at that time Sir Nabon le Noir was walking along the wall of the castle, and his son, who was a lad of seventeen years, was with him. There the messenger from Sir Tristram found him and delivered his message. Thereupon Sir Nabon looked over the battlements and down below and he beheld that there was indeed a tall and noble knight seated upon horseback in a level meadow that reached away, descending inland from the foot of the crags whereon the castle stood.

But when Sir Nabon perceived that a stranger knight had dared to come thus into his country, he was filled with amazement at the boldness of that knight that he wist not what to think. Then, presently a great rage got hold upon him, and he ground his teeth together, and the cords on his neck stood out like knots on the trunk of a tree. For a while he stood as though bereft of speech; then anon he roared out in a voice like that of a bull, crying to those who were near him: "Go! Haste ye! Fetch me straightway my horse and armor and I will go immediately forth and so deal with yonder champion of ladies that he shall never take trouble upon their account again."

Then those who were in attendance upon Sir Nabon were terrified at his words and ran with all speed to do his bidding, and presently fetched his armor and clad him in it; and they fetched his horse into the courtyard of the castle and helped him to mount upon it. And lo! the armor of Sir Nabon was as black as ink; and the great horse upon which he sat was black; and all the trappings and furniture of the armor and of the horse were black, so that from top to toe he was altogether as black and as forbidding as Death himself.

So when Sir Nabon was thus in all wise prepared for battle, the portcullis of the castle was lifted up, and he rode forth to meet Sir Tristram; and his young son rode with him as his esquire. Then all the people of the castle gathered together upon the walls to see that battle that was to be, and not one of those several score of folk thought otherwise than that Sir Tristram would certainly be overcome in that encounter.

Sir Nabon rides forth to meet Sir Tristram.

Sir Nabon rode straight up to Sir Tristram and he said very fiercely, "Sirrah, what is it brings you hither to this land?"

"As to that," said Sir Tristram, "the messenger whom I have sent to you hath, I believe, told you what I come for, and that it is to redeem this island from your possession, and to restore it to the Lady Loise, to whom it belongeth. Likewise that I come to punish you for all the evil you have done."

"And what business is all this of yours?" quoth Sir Nabon, speaking with great fury of voice.

"Messire," quoth Sir Tristram, "know ye not that it is the business of every true knight to rid the world of all such evil monsters as you be?"

"Ha!" quoth Sir Nabon, "that was very well said, for whatever mercy I should have been willing before this to show you hath now been forfeited unto you. For now I shall have no mercy upon you but shall slay you."

"Well," quoth Sir Tristram, "as for that, meseems it will be time enough to offer me mercy after you have overcome me in battle."

So thereupon each knight took his place for assault, and when they were in all ways prepared, each set spurs to his horse and dashed the one against the other, with a dreadful, terrible fury of onset. Each smote the other in the very midst of his shield, and at that blow the lance of each was altogether shivered into pieces to the very truncheon thereof. But each knight recovered his horse from the fall and each leaped

Sir Tristram does battle with Sir Nabon.

to earth and drew his sword, and each rushed against the other with such fury that it was as though sparks of pure fire flew out from the oculariums of the helmets. Therewith they met together, and each lashed and smote at the other such fell strokes that the noise thereof might easily have been heard several furlongs away. Now in the beginning of that battle Sir Tristram was at first sore bestead and wist that he had met the biggest knight that ever he had encountered in all of his life, unless it was Sir Launcelot of the Lake, whom he had encountered as aforetold of in this history. So at first he bore back somewhat from the might of the blows of Sir Nabon. For Sir Nabon was so huge of frame and the blows he struck were so heavy that they drove Sir Tristram back as it were in spite of himself.

Then Sir Tristram began to say to himself: "Tristram, if you indeed lose this battle, then there will be no one to defend your honor before Sir Launcelot who hath impeached it." Therewith it was as though new strength and life came back to him, and of a sudden he rushed that battle, and struck with threefold fury, and gave stroke upon stroke with such fierceness of strength that Sir Nabon was astonished and fell back before his assault. Then Sir Tristram perceived how Sir Nabon held his shield passing low, and therewith he rushed in upon him and smote him again and again and yet again. And so he smote Sir Nabon down upon his knees. Then he rushed in upon him and catched his helmet and plucked it off from his head. And he catched Sir Nabon by the hair of his head and drew his head forward. And Sir Tristram lifted his sword on high and he smote Sir Nabon's head from off his body so that it rolled down into the dust upon the ground.

Sir Tristram slays Sir Nabon.

Now when the son of Sir Nabon perceived how that his father was slain, he shrieked like a woman. And he fell down upon his knees and crawled upon his knees to Sir Tristram and catched him about the thighs, crying out to him, "Spare me, and slay me not!"

But Sir Tristram thrust him away and said, "Who art thou?"

"Messire," said the youth, "I am the son of him whom thou hast just slain."

Then Sir Tristram looked closely into his face, and he perceived that it was wicked and treacherous and malevolent like to the face of Sir Nabon. Thereupon Sir Tristram said: "If a man shall slay the wolf and spare the whelp of the wolf, what shall the world be the better therefor?" Therewith he catched the son of Sir Nabon by the hair and dragged him down and smote off his head likewise as he had smitten off the head of his father, so that it fell upon the ground beside the head of Sir Nabon.

Sir Tristram slays the son of Sir Nabon.

And now it shall be told how Sir Tristram discovered Sir Lamorack upon the island and how he made amends to him, so that they became friends and brethren-in-arms once more as they had been before.

JVSTISSIMVS·REX

ir Lamorack herds the swine of Sir Nabon.

CHAPTER THIRD

How Sir Tristram Did Justice in the Island, and Thereby Released Sir Lamorack From Captivity. Also How Sir Tristram and Sir Lamorack Renewed Their Great Tenderness Toward One Another.

Now after Sir Tristram had overcome Sir Nabon le Noir, and had slain the son of Sir Nabon as has been just told, he went straightway to the castle that had been Sir Nabon's, and commanded that they should bring forth the seneschal and the officers thereof unto him. Meantime, being a little wounded in that battle, he sat himself down upon a bench of wood that stood in the hall of the castle, and there he held his court.

So, in a little while, there came the seneschal and several of the officers of the household to where Sir Tristram was, and when the seneschal came before Sir Tristram, he fell down upon his knees and besought pardon and mercy.

Sir Tristram talks with the castle help.

Then Sir Tristram said: "I will consider thy case anon, and if I may assure myself that thou and these others are truly repentant, and if I may have assurity that ye will henceforth be faithful in your duty toward that lady who is now again the mistress of this castle and land, then I shall have mercy. But if ye show yourselves recreant and treacherous, according to the manners of this Sir Nabon who is dead, then I shall of a surety return hither and shall punish you even as ye beheld me punish that wicked knight and his young son."

Then Sir Tristram said, "Who is the porter of this castle?" And the porter lifted his hand and said, "Lord, I am he." Sir Tristram said, "What captives have ye in this place?" The porter said: "Lord, there be four knights and three ladies who are held captive here for ransom." Then Sir Tristram said, "Bring them forth hither to me."

So the porter and several other of the castle folk departed with all speed and presently returned bringing with them those miserable captives whom they had liberated from the dungeons of the castle. These they led to where Sir Tristram still sat in justice upon the bench of wood. And Sir Tristram looked upon them with pity

Sir Tristram comforts the captives.

and beheld that they were in a very sad and forlorn condition and so sorrowful from their captivity that some of them wept from pure weakness of heart. Then Sir Tristram said: "Comfort ye, and take no more sorrow to yourselves, for now your troubles are past and gone, and happiness lieth before you. Sir Nabon is dead, and so is his son, and there is no one now to torment you. Moreover, I dare say that there is much treasure gathered at this place by Sir Nabon, and all that treasure shall be divided amongst you, for to comfort ye, wherefore when ye leave this place, ye shall go away a great deal richer than ye were when ye came."

So spake Sir Tristram, promising them much for to comfort them a little.

As to that treasure he spake of, ye shall immediately be told how it was. For when Sir Tristram had summoned the treasurer of that place, he brought Sir Tristram down into the vaults of the castle and there he beheld seven strong chests bolted and locked. Then Sir Tristram summoned the locksmith of that castle; and the smith came and burst open the chests; and lo! the eyes of all were astonished and bedazzled with the treasure which they therewith beheld; for in those chests was heaped an incalculable treasure of gold and silver and precious gems of many divers sorts.

And besides this treasure, you are to know that they found in that vault many bales of cloths—some of silk and velvet, and some of tissues of cloth of gold and silver; and they found many precious ornaments, and many fine suits of armor, and many other valuable things. For in several years Sir Nabon had gathered all that treasure in toll from those ships that had sailed past that land.

All this treasure Sir Tristram had them bring forth into the light of day, and he divided it into seven equal parcels. Then he said to those sad, sorrowful captives: "Look! See! all this shall be yours for to comfort ye! Take each of you one parcel and depart hence in joy!" Then all they were greatly astonished at Sir Tristram's generosity, and they said: "Lord, how is this? Do you not then take any of this treasure for yourself?"

Sir Tristram divides the treasure amongst the captives.

To them Sir Tristram made reply: "Nay, why should I take it? I am not sad, nor sick, nor troubled at heart as you poor captives are. All this I have taken for to comfort you, and not for to satisfy my own covetousness. So let each take his share of it and see that ye all use it in comfort and peace and for the advantage of other men and women who are in trouble as ye have been. For, as hitherto this treasure hath been used for evil purpose, so shall it be henceforth that it shall be used to good purpose."

So there was great rejoicing amongst all those poor people who had been so sad and sorrowful before.

Now, after all this had been settled, Sir Tristram cast about how he might put that land under good government upon behalf of the Lady Loise. To this intent he chose from amongst those captives whom he had liberated a certain very worthy honorable knight of Cornwall hight Sir Segwarides. Him Sir Tristram appointed to be governor of that island, giving him liberty to rule it as he chose saving only that he should do homage to the Lady Loise as lady paramount. And Sir Tristram ordained that Sir Segwarides should pay tribute to that lady every year such an amount as should be justly determined upon betwixt them. For Sir Tristram wist that some strong worthy knight should rule that island, or else, from its position, it might again some time fall from the Lady Loise's possession into the hands of such an evil and malignant overlord as Sir Nabon had been.

Sir Tristram appoints Sir Segwarides governor of the castle.

So it was done as Sir Tristram had ordained. And it may here be said that Sir Segwarides ruled that land very justly and that he and the Lady Loise became dear friends, so that at the end of three years from that time he and she were made husband and wife.

Now Sir Tristram remained in that island several days, with intent to see to it that the power of Sir Segwarides should be established. And he made all the people of that land come before Sir Segwarides for to pledge obedience to him.

Amongst these came Sir Lamorack in the guise of a swineherd, and Sir Tristram knew him not, because that he was clad in rags and in the skins of animals and because that his beard and his hair were uncut and unkempt, and hung down very shaggy upon his breast. But Sir Lamorack knew Sir Tristram yet would not acknowledge him, being ashamed that Sir Tristram should discover him in such a guise and so ragged and forlorn as he then was. So he kept his eyes from Sir Tristram, and Sir Tristram passed him by and knew him not.

But amongst other of the people of the castle that passed before Sir Tristram, there came a woman, very fair to look upon, and she had been a house-slave to Sir Nabon. As this woman passed before Sir Tristram, he beheld that she wore upon her thumb a very fair and shining ring, that bare a green stone set in wrought gold. And when he looked again he saw it was that ring of carven emerald that he had given to Sir Lamorack as aforetold.

Sir Tristram beholds Sir Lamorack's ring.

At this Sir Tristram was astonished beyond measure, and he ordered that woman to come before him, and she came and stood before him trembling. Then Sir Tristram said: "Fear not, but tell me where got ye that ring that I behold upon your hand?" And the woman said: "Lord, I will tell you the very truth. My husband is the chief fisherman of this place, and one day, some while ago, he gave me this ring when I had favor in his sight."

Sir Tristram said, "Where is your husband?" The slave-woman said, "Yonder he stands." Then Sir Tristram said: "Come hither, Sirrah!" And therewith the fisherman came and stood before Sir Tristram as his wife had done, and he also trembled with fear as she had done.

To him Sir Tristram said, "Why do you tremble so?" And the fisher-man said, "Lord, I am afeard!" Sir Tristram said: "Have no fear, unless you have done wrong, but tell me the truth. Where got ye that ring that yonder woman weareth?" "Lord," said the fisherman, "I will tell you the perfect truth. One day I and several of my fellows found a man lying naked in a bed of heather near the seaside. At first we thought he was dead, but he awoke and arose when he heard our voices. He was naked and hungry, and he besought us for clothes to cover his nakedness and for food to eat. So we gave him what we could, demanding that ring in payment. So he gave the ring to me, who am the chief of the fishermen, and I gave it to that woman who is my wife; and that, lord, is the very truth."

Sir Tristram questions the fisherman.

Then Sir Tristram was very much disturbed in mind, for he feared that it might have gone ill with Sir Lamorack. And he said, "Where now is that man of whom ye speak?" The fisherman replied: "Lord, he was set to keep the swine, and he is the swine-herd of the castle to this day."

At this Sir Tristram was very glad that no more ill had befallen Sir Lamorack, and that he was yet alive.

Then, after the fisherman had departed from that place, Sir Tristram sat for a while sunk into deep thought. And he said to himself: "Alas, that so noble a knight should be brought to such a pass as that! How greatly must my friend be abased when he would not acknowledge himself to me nor claim my assistance because of the shame of his appearance! Meseems it is not fitting for me to send for him to come to me in the guise which he now wears, for it would be discourteous a thing for me to do, to make him so declare himself. So first I shall see to it that he is clothed in such a manner as shall be fitting to his high estate, and then haply he will be willing to make himself manifest to me. After that, perhaps his love will return to me again, and remain with me as it was at first."

So Sir Tristram called to him several of the people of that castle, and he bade them do certain things according to his command, and straightway they departed to do as he ordained.

Now turn we to Sir Lamorack: whilst he sat keeping watch over his swine there came to him four men from the castle. These say to him, "You must come straightway with us." Sir Lamorack said, "Whither would you take me?" They say: "That we are not permitted to tell you, only that you are to go with us as we bid you."

So Sir Lamorack arose and went with those four, much wondering what it was that was to befall him, and whether that which was to happen was good or evil.

The four men brought him to the castle and they entered in thereat, and they escorted Sir Lamorack, still greatly wondering, up the stairway of the castle, and so into a noble and stately apartment, hung with tapestries and embroidered hangings. And there Sir Lamorack beheld a great bath of tepid water, hung within and without with linen. There were at this place several attendants; these took Sir Lamorack and unclothed him and brought him to the bath, and bathed him and dried him with soft linen and with fine towels. Then there came the barber and he shaved Sir Lamorack and clipped his hair, and when he was thus bathed and trimmed, his nobility shone forth again as the sun shines forth from a thick cloud that hides its effulgence for a while, only to withdraw so that the glorious day-star may shine forth again with redoubled splendor.

Sir Lamorack is brought to the castle.

Then there came divers other attendants and clothed Sir Lamorack in rich and handsome garments such as were altogether fitting for a knight-royal to wear. And after that there came several esquires and brought a very splendid suit of armor; and they clad Sir Lamorack in that armor; and the armor gleamed as bright as daylight, being polished to a wonderful clearness, and inlaid with figures of arabesqued silver.

Sir Lamorack is armed in armor.

Then Sir Lamorack said, "What means all this that ye do to me?" And they said, "Wait, Messire, and you shall see."

So after all these things were done, five other esquires appeared to conduct Sir Lamorack away from that place. These led him through several passages and hallways until at last they came to a great space of hall wherein stood a single man; and that man was Sir Tristram.

And Sir Tristram gazed upon Sir Lamorack and his heart yearned over him with great loving-kindness. But he would not betray his love to those who had come with Sir Lamorack, so he contained himself for a little, and he said to those in attendance, "Get ye gone," and straightway they departed.

Then Sir Lamorack lifted up his eyes and he came to where Sir Tristram was standing and he said: "Is it thou, Tristram, who hath bestowed all these benefits upon me?" And he said: "From thy nobility of soul such things may be expected."

Then Sir Tristram wept for joy, and he said: "Lamorack, it is little that I have done to pleasure thee, and much that I have done to affront thee." Then Sir Lamorack

Sir Tristram and Sir Lamorack are reconciled.

said: "Nay; it is much that thou hast done to comfort me, and little to cause me discomfort. For lo! thou hast uplifted me from misery into happiness, and thou hast brought me from nakedness and want into prosperity and ease, and what more may one man do for another man than that?"

"Lamorack," said Sir Tristram, "there is much more than one man may do for another man than that. For if one man hath given offence to another man, he may be reconciled to that one so offended, and so the soul of that other shall be clothed with peace and joy, even as thy body hath been clothed with garments of silk and fine linen." Then Sir Tristram took Sir Lamorack by the hand, and he said, "Dear friend, art thou now strong and fresh of body?" And Sir Lamorack, greatly wondering, said, "Ay."

"Then," said Sir Tristram, "I may now offer thee reparation for that offence which I one time unwillingly committed against thee. For lo! I have had thee clad in the best armor that it is possible to provide, and now that thou art fresh and hale and strong, I am ready to do battle with thee at any time thou mayst assign. For if, before, thou wert overcome because thou wert weary with battle, now thou mayst prove thy prowess upon me being both strong and sound in wind and limb."

But upon this Sir Lamorack ran to Sir Tristram and catched him in his arms and kissed him upon the cheek. And he said: "Tristram, thou art indeed a very noble soul. I will do no battle with thee, but instead I will take thee into my heart and cherish thee there forever."

Sir Tristram said, "Art thou altogether satisfied?" And Sir Lamorack said, "Yea." And therewith Sir Tristram wept for pure joy.

Then Sir Tristram said: "Let us go to Sir Launcelot of the Lake, so that I may make my peace with him also. For he hath writ me a letter chiding me for having done battle with thee when thou wert weary and winded with fighting. And I was upon my way to see Sir Launcelot and to plead my cause with him when I came hither by good hap, and was able to uplift thee out of thy distress." To this Sir Lamorack said: "I will go with thee to Sir Launcelot whenever it shall please thee; and I will bear full testimony to thy knightliness and to thy courtesy."

Sir Tristram and Sir Lamorack depart from the island.

So when the next morning had come they took boat and sailed away from that island. And the night of that day they abided at the castle of the Lady Loise, who gave thanks without measure to Sir Tristram for ridding the world of so wicked and malign a being as Sir Nabon, and for restoring her inheritance of that land unto her again. And upon the morning of the next day those two good knights betook their way to Camelot, where they found Sir Launcelot. There Sir Lamorack exculpated Sir Tristram, and Sir Launcelot immediately withdrew his rebuke for that battle which Sir Tristram had aforetime done against Sir Lamorack.

After that Sir Tristram and Sir Lamorack abode at the court of King Arthur for nigh a year, and during that time they went upon many quests and adventures of various sorts—sometimes alone, sometimes together. All these have been set down in ancient histories that tell of the adventures of Sir Tristram and Sir Lamorack. Some of them I would like right well to tell you of, but should I undertake to do so, the story of those happenings would fill several volumes such as this. Nevertheless, I may tell you that they did together many knightly deeds, the fame whereof hath been handed down to us in several histories of chivalry. Therein you may read of those things if you should care to do so.

All this I leave to tell you how Sir Tristram returned into Cornwall, and likewise to tell you of one more famous adventure that he did at this time.

Sir Tristram had been at the court of King Arthur for about a year when one day there came a messenger unto the court at Camelot with news that Sir Palamydes, the Saracen knight aforetold of in this history, had through a cunning trick seized the Lady Belle Isoult and had carried her away to a lonely tower in the forest of Cornwall. The messenger bore a letter from King Mark beseeching Sir Tristram to return as immediately as possible unto Cornwall and to rescue that lady from her captivity. And the letter further said that two knights of Cornwall had already essayed to rescue the Lady Belle Isoult, but that they had failed, having been overcome and sorely wounded in battle by Sir Palamydes. And the letter said that it was acknowledged by all men that Sir Tristram was the only knight of Cornwall who could achieve the rescue of Belle Isoult from so wonderful and puissant a knight as Sir Palamydes.

Sir Tristram hears from Cornwall of Sir Palamydes.

So in answer to that letter, Sir Tristram immediately left the court of King Arthur and returned in all haste to Cornwall, and there he found them all in great perturbation that the Lady Belle Isoult had thus been stolen away.

But Sir Tristram did not remain at court very long for, after he had obtained such information as he desired, he immediately left Tintagel and plunged into the forest with Gouvernail as his companion in quest of that lonely tower where Belle Isoult was said to be held prisoner.

After several adventures of no great note he came at last very, very deep into the forest and into an open space thereof; and in the midst of that open space he beheld a lonely tower surrounded by a moat. And he wist that that must be the place where the Lady Belle Isoult was held prisoner.

But when Sir Tristram drew nigh to this tower he perceived a single knight sitting at the base of the tower with head hanging down upon his breast as though he were broken-hearted with sorrow. And when he came still more nigh, Sir Tristram was astonished to perceive that that mournful knight was Sir Palamydes the Saracen, and he wondered why Sir Palamydes should be so broken-hearted.

Sir Tristram finds Sir Palamydes in the forest.

And now it must be told why it was that Sir Palamydes came to be in such a sorry case as that; for the truth was that he was locked and shut outside of the tower, whilst the Lady Belle Isoult was shut and locked inside thereof.

Now it hath already been told how the letter of King Mark had said to Sir Tristram that two knights of Cornwall went both against Sir Palamydes for to challenge him and to rescue the Lady Belle Isoult.

The second of these knights was Sir Adthorp, and he had followed Sir Palamydes so closely through the forest that he had come to the forest tower not more than an hour after Sir Palamydes had brought the Lady Belle Isoult thither.

Therewith Sir Adthorp gave loud challenge to Sir Palamydes to come forth and do him battle, and therewith Sir Palamydes came immediately out against him, full of anger that Sir Adthorp should have meddled in that affair.

But immediately Sir Palamydes had thus issued forth to do battle with Sir Adthorp, the Lady Belle Isoult ran down the tower stairs and immediately shut the door through which he had passed, and she locked it and set a great bar of oak across the door.

So when Sir Palamydes had overthrown the Cornish knight, and when he would have returned to the tower, he could not, for lo! it was fastened against him. So now for three days he had set there at the foot of the tower and beside the moat, sunk in sorrow like to one who had gone out of his mind.

How Sir Palamydes came without the tower.

So Sir Tristram found him, and perceiving that it was Sir Palamydes who was sitting there, he said to Gouvernail: "Go thou and bid that knight to come and do battle with me."

So Gouvernail went to Sir Palamydes and he said: "Sir, arise, for here is a knight would speak with you!" But Sir Palamydes would not move. Then Gouvernail touched him with his lance, and said: "Sir Palamydes, arise and bestir yourself, for here is Sir Tristram come to do battle with you." With that, Sir Palamydes awoke from his stupor and arose very slowly and stiffly. And he gathered up his helmet which was lying beside him and put it upon his head. Then he took down his shield from where it hung against the wall and he mounted upon his horse, doing all as though he were moving in a dream.

But as soon as he was upon horseback he suddenly aroused himself, for his fierce spirit had come back to him once more. Then he gnashed his teeth, crying out in a loud voice, "Tristram, this time either thou or I shall perish."

Therewith he rushed upon Sir Tristram and smote him so violently that Sir Tristram had much ado to defend himself. And Sir Palamydes smote him again and again; and with that Sir Tristram smote in return. And if the blows of Sir Palamydes were terrible, the blows of Sir Tristram were terrible likewise. Then by and by Sir Tristram smote Sir Palamydes so sore a buffet that the Saracen knight fell down from his horse and was unable immediately to arise. Then Sir Tristram ran to him and rushed off his helmet and catched him by the hair with intent to cut his head from off his body.

Sir Tristram overcomes Sir Palamydes.

But with that the Lady Belle Isoult came running from out the tower and cried out: "Tristram, is it thou? Spare that mistaken knight and have mercy upon him as thou hopest for mercy."

"Lady," said Sir Tristram, "for thy sake and at thy bidding I will spare him." Then he said to Sir Palamydes, "Arise." And Sir Palamydes arose very painfully, and Sir Tristram said: "Get thee hence, and go to the court of King Arthur and make thy confession to the King and ask him to forgive thee, and if he forgive thee, then also I will forgive thee."

Therewith Sir Palamydes mounted upon his horse and rode away without speaking another word, his head bowed with sorrow upon his breast for shame and despair.

Then Sir Tristram took the Lady Belle Isoult up behind him on his horse, and he and she and Gouvernail departed from that place.

So Sir Tristram brought the Lady Isoult back to Cornwall, and there he was received with loud praise and great rejoicing, for everybody was glad that Belle Isoult had been brought safely back again.

Sir Tristram brings Belle Isoult back to Cornwall.

And now it shall be told what reward Sir Tristram received for this deed of arms.

For, though at first King Mark was greatly beholden to Sir Tristram, that he had thus rescued the Lady Belle Isoult, yet, by little and little, he grew to hate that noble knight more bitterly than ever. For he heard men say to one another: "Lo, Sir Tristram is, certes, the very champion of Cornwall, for who is there in this country is his equal?" So King Mark, hearing these things said to himself: "The more noble Tristram is, the more ignoble will men deem me to be who am under obligations to such an enemy." So he would say in his heart, "Yea, Tristram; I hate thee more than death."

PART III

THE MADNESS OF SIR TRISTRAM

Here followeth the story of how Sir Tristram was driven out of Cornwall and of how he went mad because of his troubles. Likewise it shall be told how he performed several very wonderful adventures whilst he was in that state, and of how he was brought back into his senses again.

ir Tristram assaults King Mark.

CHAPTER FIRST

How Sir Tristram Was Discovered With the Lady Belle Isoult; How He Assaulted King Mark, and How He Escaped from Tintagel Into the Forest.

After Sir Tristram had thus rescued the Lady Belle Isoult from the hand of Sir Palamydes, he dwelt very peacefully at the court of Cornwall for all of that winter and until the spring that followed, and during that time he was given every meed of praise and honor. But although King Mark and his court gave praise to Sir Tristram with the lips, yet he and many of his people hated Sir Tristram at heart, and there were many mischief-makers about the court who were ever ready to blow the embers of the King's wrath into a flame.

Now the chiefest of all these mischief-makers was Sir Andred, who was nephew unto King Mark, and cousin-germaine unto Sir Tristram. Sir Andred was a fierce strong knight, and one very dextrous at arms; but he was as mean and as treacherous as Sir Tristram was generous and noble, wherefore he hated Sir Tristram with great bitterness (though he dissembled that hatred) and sought for every opportunity to do Sir Tristram a harm by bringing him and the King into conflict.

So Sir Andred set spies upon Sir Tristram, and he himself spied upon his cousin, yet neither he nor they were able to find anything with which to accuse Sir Tristram. Then one day Sir Andred came to Sir Tristram and said: "Sir, the Lady Belle Isoult wishes to see you to talk with you." Sir Tristram said, "Where is she?"

Sir Andred of Cornwall sets spies upon Sir Tristram.

And Sir Andred said, "She is in her bower." Then Sir Tristram said, "Very well, I will go to her."

So Sir Tristram arose and departed from where he was with intent to find the lady; and therewith Sir Andred hurried to where King Mark was, and said: "Lord, arise, for Sir Tristram and the Lady Isoult are holding converse together."

King Mark said, "Where are they?" And Sir Andred said, "They are in the bower of the Queen." At that King Mark's rage and jealousy blazed up into a flame, so that he was like one seized with a sudden frensy. So, in that madness of rage, he looked about for some weapon with which to destroy Sir Tristram, and he perceived a great sword where it hung against the wall. Thereupon he ran to the sword and took it down from where it was, and ran with all speed to that place where Sir Tristram and the Lady Isoult were, and Sir Andred guided him thither.

King Mark assaults Sir Tristram.

And when King Mark reached the bower of the Lady Isoult he flung open the door and found Sir Tristram and the Lady Isoult sitting together in the seat of a deep window. And he perceived that the Lady Isoult wept and that Sir Tristram's face was very sorrowful because of her sorrow. Then King Mark twisted him about and bent double as with a great pain, and then he cried out thrice in a voice very hoarse and loud: "Traitor! Traitor! Traitor!" Saying those words three times. Therewith he ran at Sir Tristram and struck furiously at him with that sword he held, with intent to slay him.

Now Sir Tristram was at that time altogether without armor and was clad in clothes of scarlet silk. Accordingly, he was able to be very quick and alert in his movements. So perceiving King Mark rushing upon him with intent to slay him he leaped aside and so avoided the blow. Then immediately he rushed in upon King Mark and catched him by the wrist and wrenched the sword out of his hand.

Then Sir Tristram was blinded with his rage and might have slain his uncle, but the Lady Isoult, beholding the fury in his face, shrieked in a very piercing voice, "Forbear! Forbear!" And therewith he remembered him how that King Mark was his mother's brother and that it was his hand that had made him a knight.

Sir Tristram beats King Mark.

So he turned the sword in his hand and he smote King Mark with the flat thereof again and again, and at those blows King Mark was filled with terror so that he howled like a wild beast. And King Mark fled away from that place, striving to escape, but Sir Tristram ever pursued him, grinding his teeth like a wild boar in rage, and smiting the King as he ran, over and over again, with the flat of the sword so that the whole castle was filled with the tumult and uproar of that assault.

Then many of the knights of Cornwall came running with intent to defend the King, and with them came Sir Andred. But when Sir Tristram saw them, his rage suddenly left the King and went out toward them; so therewith, naked of armor as he was, he rushed at them, and he struck at them so fiercely that they were filled with the terror of his fury, and fled away from before his face. And Sir Tristram chased them through the courts of the castle, striking right and left until he was weary with striking, and many he struck down with the fierceness of his blows, and amongst them was Sir Andred who was sorely wounded. So after a while Sir Tristram grew weary of that battle, and he cried out, "Certes, these are not knights, but swine!" And therewith he ceased striking, and allowed those who could do so to escape.

Thereafter he went to his chamber and armed himself without summoning Gouvernail, and after that he took horse and rode away altogether from that place. And not even Gouvernail went with him, but only his favorite hound, hight Houdaine, which same followed him into the forest as he rode thitherward. And in his going Sir Tristram looked neither to the right nor to the left but straight before him very proudly and haughtily, and no one dared to stay him in his going.

Sir Tristram departs from Tintagel.

Yet, though he appeared so steadfast, he was like one who was brokenhearted, for he wist that in going away from that place he was leaving behind him all that he held dear in the world, wherefore he was like one who rode forth from a pleasant garden into an empty wilderness of sorrow and repining.

Then, some little while after Sir Tristram had gone, Gouvernail also took horse and rode into the forest, and he searched for a long while in the forest without finding his master. But after a while he came upon Sir Tristram seated under a tree with his head hanging down upon his breast. And Houdaine lay beside Sir Tristram and licked his hand, but Sir Tristram paid no heed to him, being so deeply sunk in his sorrow that he was unaware that Houdaine licked his hand in that wise.

Gouvernail finds Sir Tristram in the forest.

Then Gouvernail dismounted from his horse and came to where Sir Tristram was, and Gouvernail wept at beholding the sorrow of Sir Tristram. And Gouvernail said: "Messire, look up and take cheer, for there must yet be joy for thee in the world."

Then Sir Tristram raised his eyes very slowly (for they were heavy and dull like lead) and he looked at Gouvernail for some while as though not seeing him. Then by and by he said: "Gouvernail, what evil have I done that I should have so heavy a curse laid upon me?" Gouvernail said, still weeping: "Lord, thou hast done no ill, but art in all wise a very noble, honorable gentleman." "Alas!" quoth Sir Tristram, "I must unwittingly have done some great evil in God's sight, for certes the hand of God lieth grievously heavy upon me." Gouvernail said: "Lord, take heart, and tell me whither shall we go now?" And Sir Tristram said, "I know not."

Then Gouvernail said: "Lord, let us go hence, I care not where, for I reckon nothing of storm or rain or snow or hail if it so be that I am with you."

Then Sir Tristram looked upon Gouvernail and smiled, and he said: "Gouvernail, it is great joy to me that you should love me so greatly as you do. But this time you may not go with me whither I go, for the Lady Belle Isoult hath few friends at the court of Cornwall, and many enemies, wherefore I would have you return unto her for my sake, so that you may befriend her and cherish her when that I am no longer by her for to stand her friend in her hour of need. And take this dog Houdaine with you and bid the Lady Belle Isoult for to keep him by her to remind her of my faithfulness unto her. For even as this creature is faithful unto me under all circumstances, so am I faithful unto her whether she be glad or sorry, or in good or evil case. So return to Tintagel as I bid thee, and see that thou pay thy duty unto that lady even as thou payst it unto me. For she is so singularly dear unto me that, even as a man's heart is the life of his body, so is her happiness the life of my life."

Sir Tristram bids Gouvernail return to Tintagel.

Then Gouvernail wept again in very great measure, and he said, "Lord, I obey." Therewith he mounted his horse, still weeping with a great passion of sorrow, and rode away from that place, and Houdaine followed after him and Sir Tristram was left sitting alone in the deep forest.

After that Sir Tristram wandered for several days in the forest, he knew not whither for he was bewildered with that which had happened; so that he ate no food and took no rest of any sort for all that time. Wherefore, because of the hardship he then endured, he by and by became distraught in his mind. So, after a while, he forgot who he himself was, and what was his condition, or whence he came or whither he wended. And because his armor weighed heavily upon him, he took it off and cast it away from him, and thereafter roamed half naked through the woodlands.

Sir Tristram wanders in the forest mad.

Now upon the sixth day of this wandering he came to the outskirts of the forest and nigh to the coast of the sea at a spot that was not very far away was the castle of the Lady Loise, where he had once stayed at the time that he undertook the adventure against Sir Nabon as aforetold. There, being exhausted with hunger and weariness, he laid himself down in the sunlight out beyond the borders of the forest and presently fell into a deep sleep that was like to a swoon.

Now it chanced at that time that there came that way a certain damsel attendant upon the Lady Loise. She perceiving that a man lay there on the grass at the edge of the forest was at first of a mind to quit that place. Then, seeing that the man lay very strangely still as though he were dead, she went forward very softly and looked into his face.

Now that damsel had beheld Sir Tristram a great many times when he was at the castle of the Lady Loise; wherefore now, in spite of his being so starved and shrunken, and so unkempt and unshaved, she remembered his face and she knew that this was Sir Tristram.

Therewith the damsel hurried away to the Lady Loise (and the lady was not a very great distance away) and she said: "Lady, yonder way there lieth a man by the forest side and I believe that it is Sir Tristram of Lyonesse. Yet he is but half-clad and in great distress of body so that I know not of a surety whether it is really Sir Tristram or not. Now I pray you come with me and look upon his face and see if you may know him."

So the Lady Loise went with the damsel to where Sir Tristram lay and looked into his face, and she knew Sir Tristram in spite of his ill condition.

Then the Lady Loise touched Sir Tristram upon the shoulder and shook him, and thereupon Sir Tristram awoke and sat up. Then the Lady Loise said, "Sir Tristram, is it thou who liest here?" And Sir Tristram said, "I know not who I am." The Lady Loise said, "Messire, how came you here in this sad case?" And Sir Tristram said: "I know not whence I came, nor how I came hither, nor who I am, nor what it is that ails me, for I cannot hold my mind with enough steadiness to remember those things." Then the lady sighed for sorrow of Sir Tristram, and she said: "Alas, Sir Tristram, that I should find you thus! Now I pray you, lord, for to come with me to my castle which is hard by. There we may care for you and may perhaps bring you back to health again."

The Lady Loise finds Sir Tristram.

To this Sir Tristram said: "Lady, I may not go with you. For though I cannot remember whence I came, nor who I am, this much I know—I know that I am mad, and that the forest is the only fit place for such as I am come to be."

The lady said: "Alas, Sir Tristram, thou wilt die if thou art left alone here in the forest." And Sir Tristram said: "Lady, I know not what you mean when you say I am to die. What is it to die?" So at these words the Lady Loise saw how it was with Sir Tristram; that his brains were altogether turned; and she wist that some sore trouble must have befallen to bring him to such a pass. Then she bethought her of how dearly he loved the music of the harp, and she said to herself: "Mayhap by means of music

I may bring him back into his senses again." So she said to that damsel who had brought her thither: "Go thou and bring hither my little harp of gold, and let us see if music may charm him to remembrance."

So the damsel ran to the castle and brought the harp thence, and the Lady Loise took the harp and tuned it and struck it and played upon it. And the lady sang very sweetly a ballad that she knew Sir Tristram loved.

The Lady Loise harps to Sir Tristram.

Then when Sir Tristram heard the sound of the music and singing he aroused himself. For first he listened with great pleasure, and then he said, "Give it to me! Give it to me!" and he reached out his hands and would have taken the harp from the lady.

Sir Tristram comes to the Lady's castle.

But the Lady Loise laughed and shook her head, and she walked away from Sir Tristram and toward the castle, still playing upon the little harp and singing; and Sir Tristram followed close after, saying ever, "Give it to me! Give it to me!" and reaching out his hands for the harp. So the Lady Loise led him away from that place across the meadows; and she led him to the castle and into the castle; and ever Sir Tristram followed after her, beseeching her for to give the harp unto him. And the lady led Sir Tristram that way until she had brought him to a fair room, and there she gave him the harp, and Sir Tristram took it very eagerly into his hands and struck upon it and played and sang most sweetly and with great joy and pleasure.

Afterward, being so much comforted, he ate and drank with appetite, and then fell into a fair sound sleep.

Yet, though he so slept, still Sir Tristram's wits in no wise recovered themselves; for when he awoke from that slumber he still could not remember who he was or whence he came, neither could he remember the faces of any of those who were around about him. But, though he was thus mad, he was still gentle and kind in his madness and courteous and civil to all those who came nigh him.

So Sir Tristram remained a gentle captive in the castle of the Lady Loise for nigh upon a month, and somewhiles she would sing and harp to him, and otherwhiles he himself would harp and sing. But ever and anon, when he found the chance for to do so, he would escape from the captivity of the castle and seek the forest; for he was aware of his madness and he ever sought to hide that madness in the deep and shady woodland where only the wild creatures of the forest might see him.

Yet always when he so escaped the Lady Loise would take her little golden harp and go forth to the skirts of the forest and play upon it, and when the music thereof would reach Sir Tristram's ears he would return to the castle, being led thither by the music.

But one day he wandered so far astray that the music of the harp could not reach his ears, and then he wandered on farther and farther until he was altogether lost. At that Lady Loise took much sorrow for she had much love for Sir Tristram. So she sent many of her people to search the forest for him, but none of these were able to find him and thereafter he came no more to the castle.

Sir Tristram quits the Lady's castle.

Thus Sir Tristram escaped from that castle and after that he wandered in the forest as he had done at the first. And in that time he took no food and but little rest. And the brambles tore his clothes, so that in a short time he was wellnigh altogether naked.

And somewhiles during this time of wandering he would be seized as with a fury of battle, and in such case he would shout aloud as though in challenge to an enemy. And then he would rend and tear great branches from the trees in the fury of his imaginings. But otherwhiles he would wander through the leafy aisles of the forest in gentler mood, singing so sweetly that had you heard him you would have thought that it was some fairy spirit of the forest chanting in those solitudes.

So he wandered until he failed with faintness, and sank down into the leaves; and I believe that he would then have died, had it not been that there chanced to come that way certain swineherds of the forest who fed their swine upon acorns that were to be therein found. These found Sir Tristram lying there as though dead, and they gave him to eat and to drink so that he revived once more. After that they took him with them, and he dwelt with them in those woodlands. There these forest folk played with him and made merry with him, and he made them great sport. For he was ever gentle and mild like a little child for innocence so that he did no harm to anyone, but only talked in such a way that the swineherds found great sport in him.

Sir Tristram dwells with the swineherds.

Now Sir Andred of Cornwall very greatly coveted the possessions of Sir Tristram, so that when several months had passed by and Sir Tristram did not return to Tintagel, he said to himself: "Of a surety, Tristram must now be dead in the forest, and, as there is no one nigher of kin to him than I, it is altogether fitting that I should inherit his possessions."

But as Sir Andred could not inherit without proof of the death of Sir Tristram, he suborned a certain very beautiful but wicked lady who dwelt in the forest, persuading her that she should give false evidence of Sir Tristram's death. Accordingly, he one day brought that lady before King Mark, and she gave it as her evidence that Sir Tristram had died in the forest and that she had been with him when he died. And she showed them a new-made grave in the forest, and she said: "That is the grave of Sir Tristram, for I saw him die and I saw him buried there with mine own eyes."

So everybody believed this evidence, and thought that Sir Tristram was really dead, and so Sir Andred seized upon all the possessions of Sir Tristram. And there were many who were very sorry that Sir Tristram was dead and there were others who were glad thereof in the same measure. But when the news was brought to Belle Isoult that Sir Tristram was dead, she shrieked aloud and swooned away. And she lay in that swoon so long that they thought for a while she would never recover from it. But by and by she awoke therefrom, crying, "Would to God that I were dead with Tristram and had never awakened!"

Sir Andred seizes Sir Tristram's possessions.

And thereafter she mourned continually for Sir Tristram and would not be comforted; for she was like to a woman who hath been widowed from a lover of her youth.

And now it shall be told of how it fared with Sir Tristram in the forest where he dwelt with the swineherds, and of how he achieved a very notable adventure therein.

JVSTISSIMVS·REX·

Sir Kay and the Forest Madman.

CHAPTER SECOND

How Sir Tristram Got Him a Sword From Sir Kay and How He Slew Therewith a Huge Knight in the Forest and Rescued a Lady in Very Great Distress. Also How Sir Launcelot Found Sir Tristram in the Forest and Brought Him Thence to Tintagel Again.

NOW IT CHANCED ONE DAY THAT SIR KAY THE SENESCHAL CAME RIDING through those parts of the forest where Sir Tristram abided with the swineherds, and with Sir Kay there came a considerable court of esquires. And with him besides there travelled Sir Dagonet, King Arthur's Fool.

Now, you are to know that though Sir Dagonet was the King's jester, and though he was slack of wit, yet he was also a knight of no mean prowess. For he had performed several deeds of good repute and was well held in all courts of chivalry. So Sir Dagonet always went armed; though he bore upon his shield the device of a cockerel's head as a symbol of his calling.

Sir Kay and Sir Dagonet come to the forest.

The time that Sir Kay and his court travelled as aforesaid was in the summer season and the day was very warm, so that Sir Kay was minded to take rest during the midday and until the coolness of the afternoon should come. So they all dismounted from their horses and sat them down under the shade of the trees where it was cool and pleasant and where the breezes reached them to breathe upon their faces.

But whilst Sir Kay and his court thus rested themselves, Sir Dagonet must needs be gadding, for he was of a very restless, meddlesome disposition. So, being at that time clad only in half armor, he wandered hither and thither through the forest as his fancy led him. For somewhiles he would whistle and somewhiles he would gape, and otherwhiles he would cut a caper or two. So, as chance would have it, he came by and by to that open glade of the forest where the swineherds were gathered; and at that time they were eating their midday meal of black bread and cheese, and were drinking beer; some talking and laughing and others silent as they

Sir Dagonet wanders in the woodland.

ate their food. Unto these Sir Dagonet appeared, coming out of the forest in very gay attire, and shining in the half armor he wore, so that he appeared like a bright bird of the woodland.

Then Sir Dagonet, seeing where those rude boors were eating their meal of food, came to them and stood amongst them. And he said, "Who are ye fellows?" Whereunto they replied, "We are swineherds, Messire; who be ye?"

Quoth Sir Dagonet: "I am King Arthur's Fool. And whilst there are haply many in the world with no more wits than I possess, yet there are few so honest as I to confess that they are fools."

At these words those swineherds laughed very loudly. "Well," quoth one, "if King Arthur hath his fool, so have we, and yonder he is," and therewith he pointed to where Sir Tristram lay in the shade of the trees some distance away and beside a deep well of the forest.

Upon that Sir Dagonet must needs go to where Sir Tristram lay, nearly naked, upon the ground. And when he had come there he said, "Arise, fool." Whereunto Sir Tristram replied: "Why should I arise? Lo! I am weary."

Then Sir Dagonet said: "It is not fitting that thou, who art the fool of swineherds shouldst lie upon the grass, whilst I who am the fool of a king stand upright upon my shanks. So, fool, I bid thee bestir thyself and arise."

But Sir Tristram said, "I will not arise." And therewith Sir Dagonet took his sword and pricked the thigh of Sir Tristram with the point thereof with intent to make him bestir himself.

Sir Tristram souses Sir Dagonet in the well.

Now when Sir Tristram felt the prick of Sir Dagonet's sword, a certain part of his memory of knighthood came back to him and he was seized with a sudden fury against Sir Dagonet. So he arose and ran at Sir Dagonet and catched him in his arms, and lifted Sir Dagonet off his feet and he soused him in the well four or five times so that he was like to have drowned him.

As for those swineherds, when they saw what their fool did to that other fool, they roared with laughter so that some of them rolled down upon the ground and lay grovelling there for pure mirth. But others of them called out to Sir Tristram, "Let be, or thou wilt drown that man"; and therewith Sir Tristram let Sir Dagonet go, and Sir Dagonet ran away.

Nor did Sir Dagonet cease to run until he came to his party under the shade of the trees. But when Sir Kay perceived what a sorry plight it was in which Sir Dagonet appeared, he said, "What hath befallen thee?"

To this Sir Dagonet replied as follows: "Messire, I, who am a fool, went into the forest and met another fool. I fool would have a jest with he fool, but he fool catched I fool and soused I fool in a well of cold water. So it came about that while I fool had the jest, he fool had the sport of the jest."

Then Sir Kay understood in some manner what had befallen, and he was very angry that Sir Dagonet should have been so served. Wherefore he said, "Where did this befall thee?" And Sir Dagonet said, "Over yonder ways." Then Sir Kay said: "I will avenge thee for the affront that hath been put upon thee. For no boor shall serve a knight of King Arthur's court in such a fashion!" So therewith Sir Kay arose and put on his armor and mounted his horse and rode away; and after a while he came to that place where the swineherds were.

Sir Kay seeks to avenge Sir Dagonet.

Then Sir Kay said very sternly: "Which of ye is that boor who put so grievous an affront upon a gentleman of my party?" The swineherds say: "Yonder he is lying by the well; but he is slack of wit, wherefore we beseech you to do him no harm."

Then Sir Kay rode to where Sir Tristram was, and he said: "Sirrah, why did you souse Sir Dagonet into the water?" To this Sir Tristram did not reply, but only looked at Sir Kay and laughed, for it pleased him wonderfully to behold that knight all in shining armor. But when Sir Kay beheld Sir Tristram laugh in that wise, he waxed exceedingly wroth. Wherefore he drew his sword straightway, and rode at Sir Tristram with intent to strike him with the blade thereof. But when Sir Tristram saw the sword of Sir Kay shining like lightning in the sunlight, somewhat of his knightly spirit arose within him and took wing like to a bird springing up out of the marish grass into the clear air. For beholding that bright flashing sword he cried out aloud and arose and came very steadily toward Sir Kay, and Sir Kay rode toward Sir Tristram. Then when Sir Kay had come near enough to strike, he arose in his stirrups and lifted the blade on high with intent to strike Sir Tristram with it. But therewith Sir Tristram ran very quickly in beneath the blow, so that the stroke of Sir Kay failed of its mark. Then Sir Tristram leaped up and catched Sir Kay around the body and dragged him down from off his horse very violently upon the ground, and with that the sword of Sir Kay fell down out of his hands and lay in the grass. Then Sir Tristram lifted up Sir Kay very easily and ran with him to the well of water and soused him therein several times until Sir Kay cried out, "Fellow, spare me or I strangle!" Upon that Sir Tristram let go Sir Kay, and Sir Kay ran to his horse and mounted thereon and rode away from that place with might and main, all streaming with water like to a fountain.

Sir Tristram souses Sir Kay in the water.

And all that while those swineherds roared with great laughter, ten times louder than they had laughed when Sir Tristram had soused Sir Dagonet into the well.

Then Sir Tristram beheld the sword of Sir Kay where it lay in the grass and forthwith he ran to it and picked it up. And when he held it in his hands he loved it with a great passion of love, wherefore he hugged it to his bosom and kissed the pommel thereof.

But when the swineherds beheld the sword in Sir Tristram's hands, they said, "That is no fit plaything for a madman to have," and they would have taken it from him, but Sir Tristram would not permit them, for he would not give them the sword, and no one dared to try to take it from him.

Sir Tristram keeps the sword of Sir Kay.

So thereafter he kept that sword ever by him both by night and by day, and ever he loved it and kissed it and fondled it; for, as aforesaid, it aroused his knightly spirit to life within him, wherefore it was he loved it.

So it hath been told how Sir Tristram got him a sword, and now it shall be told how well he used it.

Now there was at that time in the woodlands of that part of Cornwall a gigantic knight hight Sir Tauleas, and he was the terror of all that district. For not only was he a head and shoulders taller than the tallest of Cornish men, but his strength and fierceness were great in the same degree that he was big of frame. Many knights had undertaken to rid the world of this Sir Tauleas, but no knight had ever yet encountered him without meeting some mishap at his hands.

(Yet it is to be said that heretofore no such knight as Sir Launcelot or Sir Lamorack had come against Sir Tauleas, but only the knights of Cornwall and Wales, whose borders marched upon that district where Sir Tauleas ranged afield.)

Now one day there came riding through the forest a very noble, gallant young knight, hight Sir Daynant, and with him rode his lady, a beautiful dame to whom he had lately been wedded with a great deal of love. These wayfarers in their travelling came to that part of the forest where the swineherds abode, and where were the open glade of grass and the fair well of water aforespoken of.

Sir Daynant and his lady come to the forest.

Hereunto coming, and the day being very warm, these two travellers dismounted and besought refreshment of the swineherds who were there, and those rude good fellows gladly gave them to eat and to drink of the best they had.

Whilst they ate, Sir Tristram came and sat nigh to Sir Daynant and his lady and smiled upon them, for he loved them very greatly because of their nobility and

Sir Daynant regards Sir Tristram.

beauty. Then Sir Daynant looked upon Sir Tristram and beheld how strong and beautiful of body and how noble of countenance he was, and he saw that beautiful shining sword that Sir Tristram carried ever with him. And Sir Daynant said, "Fair friend, who are you, and where gat ye that sword?"

"I know not who I am," said Sir Tristram, "nor know I whence I came nor whither I go. As for this sword, I had it from a gentleman who came hither to us no great while ago."

Then the chiefest of the swineherds said: "Lord, this is a poor madman whom we found naked and starving in the forest. As for that sword, I may tell you that he took it away from a knight who came hither to threaten his life, and he soused that knight into the well so that he was wellnigh drowned."

Sir Daynant said: "That is a very strange story, that a naked madman should take the sword out of the hands of an armed knight and treat that knight as ye tell me. Now maybe this is some famous hero or knight who hath lost his wits through sorrow or because of some other reason, and who hath so come to this sorry pass."

(So said Sir Daynant, and it may here be said that from that time those rude swineherds began to look upon Sir Tristram with different eyes than before, saying amongst themselves: "Maybe what that knight said is true, and this is indeed no common madman.")

Now whilst Sir Daynant sat there with his lady, holding converse with the swineherds concerning Sir Tristram in that wise, there came a great noise in the forest, and out therefrom there came riding with great speed that huge savage knight Sir Tauleas aforetold of. Then Sir Daynant cried out, "Alas, here is misfortune!" And therewith he made all haste to put his helmet upon his head.

Sir Tauleas strikes down Sir Daynant.

But ere he could arm himself in any sufficient wise, Sir Tauleas drave down very fiercely upon him. And Sir Tauleas rose up in his stirrups and lashed so terrible a blow at Sir Daynant that it struck through Sir Daynant's helmet and into his brain-pan, wherefore Sir Daynant immediately fell down to the ground as though he had been struck dead.

Sir Tauleas bears away the lady.

Then Sir Tauleas rode straightway to where the lady of Sir Daynant was, and he said: "Lady, thou art a prize that it is very well worth while fighting for! And lo! I have won thee." Therewith he catched her and lifted her up, shrieking and screaming and struggling, and sat her upon the saddle before him and held her there maugre all her struggles. Then straightway he rode away into the forest, carrying her with him; and all that while Sir Tristram stood as though in a maze, gazing with a sort of terror upon what befell and not rightly knowing what it all meant. For there lay Sir Daynant as though dead upon the ground, and he could yet hear the shrieks of the lady sounding out from the forest whither Sir Tauleas had carried her.

Then the chief of the swineherds came to Sir Tristram, and said: "Fellow, as thou hast a sword, let us see if thou canst use it. If thou art a hero as that knight said of thee a while since, and not a pure madman, then follow after that knight and bring that lady back hither again."

Then Sir Tristram awoke from that maze and said, "I will do so." And therewith he ran away very rapidly into the forest, pursuing the direction that Sir Tauleas had taken. And he ran for a great distance, and by and by, after a while, he beheld Sir Tauleas before him where he rode. And by that time the lady was in a deep swoon and lay as though dead across the saddle of Sir Tauleas. Then Sir Tristram cried out in a great voice: "Stay, Sir Knight, and turn this way, for I come to take that lady away from thee and to bring her back unto her friend again!"

Sir Tristram follows Sir Tauleas.

Then Sir Tauleas turned him and beheld a naked man running after him with a sword in his hand, whereupon he was seized with a great rage of anger, so that he put that lady he carried down to the ground. And he drew his sword and rushed at Sir Tristram very violently with intent to slay him. And when he came nigh to Sir Tristram he arose up on his stirrups and lashed so terrible a blow at him that, had it met its mark, it would have cloven Sir Tristram in twain. But Sir Tristram leaped aside and turned the blow very skilfully; and therewith a memory of his knightly prowess came upon him and he, upon his part, lashed a blow at Sir Tauleas that Sir Tauleas received very unexpectedly. And that blow struck Sir Tauleas so terrible a buffet upon the head that the brain of Sir Tauleas swam, and he swayed about and then fell down from off his horse. Therewith Sir Tristram ran to him and rushed his helmet from off his head. And when he beheld the naked head of Sir Tauleas he catched it by the hair and drew the neck of Sir Tauleas forward. Then Sir Tauleas cried out, "Spare me, fellow!" But Sir Tristram said, "I will not spare thee for thou art a wicked man!" And therewith he lifted his sword on high and smote off the head of Sir Tauleas so that it rolled down upon the ground.

Sir Tristram slays Sir Tauleas.

After that, Sir Tristram went to the Lady and he chafed her hands and her face so that she revived from her swoon. And when she was revived, he said: "Lady, take cheer; for look yonder and thou wilt see thy enemy is dead, and so now I may take thee back again unto thy friend." And therewith the lady smiled upon Sir Tristram and catched his hand in hers and kissed it.

Then Sir Tristram lifted the lady upon the horse of Sir Tauleas, and after that he went back again to where he had left Sir Daynant and the swineherds; and he led the horse of Sir Tauleas by the bridle with the lady upon the back thereof and he bore the head of Sir Tauleas in his hand by the hair.

But when those swineherds saw Sir Tristram come forth thus out of the forest bringing that lady and bearing the head of Sir Tauleas, they were amazed beyond measure, and they said to one another: "Of a certainty what this young knight hath just said is sooth and this madman is indeed some great champion in distress. But who he is no one may know, since he himself doth not know."

And when Sir Daynant had recovered from that blow that Sir Tauleas had given him, he also gave Sir Tristram great praise for what he had done. And Sir Tristram was abashed at all the praise that was bestowed upon him.

Then Sir Daynant and his lady besought Sir Tristram that he would go with them to their castle so that they might care for him, but Sir Tristram would not, for he said: "I wist very well that I am mad, and so this forest is a fit place for me to dwell and these kind rude fellows are fit companions for me at this time whilst my wits are wandering."

Thus it was with this adventure. And now you shall hear how Sir Launcelot found Sir Tristram in the forest and how he brought him out thence and likewise what befell thereafter.

For only the next day after all these things had happened, Sir Launcelot came riding through the forest that way, seeking for Sir Tauleas with intent to do battle with him because of his many evil deeds. For Sir Launcelot purposed either to slay him or else to bring him captive to King Arthur.

Sir Launcelot enters the forest.

So it came to pass that Sir Launcelot came to that place where Sir Tristram and the swineherds abode.

There Sir Launcelot made pause for to rest and to refresh himself, and whilst he sat with his helmet lying beside him so that the breezes might cool his face, all those rude swineherds gathered about and stared at him. And Sir Launcelot smiled upon them, and he said: "Good fellows, I pray you tell me; do you know where, hereabouts, I shall find a knight whom men call Sir Tauleas?"

Unto this the chief swineherd made reply, saying: "Lord, if you come hither seeking Sir Tauleas, you shall seek him in vain. For yesterday he was slain, and if you look yonder way you may see his head hanging from a branch of a tree at the edge of the glade."

Upon this Sir Launcelot cried out in great amazement, "How hath that come to pass?" and therewith he immediately arose from where he sat and went to that tree where the head hung. And he looked into the face of the head, and therewith he saw that it was indeed the head of Sir Tauleas that hung there. Then Sir Launcelot said: "This is very wonderful. Now I pray you, tell me what knight was it who slew this wicked wretch, and how his head came to be left hanging here?"

To this the chief of the swineherds made reply: "Messire, he who slew Sir Tauleas was no knight, but a poor madman whom we found in the forest and who has dwelt with us now for a year past. Yonder you may see him, lying half naked, sleeping beside that well of water."

Sir Launcelot said, "Was it he who did indeed slay Sir Tauleas?" And the swineherd said, "Yea, lord, it was he."

Sir Launcelot said, "Do ye not then know who he is?" The swineherd replied: "No, lord, we only know that one day we found him lying in the forest naked and nigh to death from hunger and that we fed him and clothed him, and that since then he hath dwelt ever with us, showing great love for us all."

Sir Launcelot regards Sir Tristram.

Then Sir Launcelot went to where Sir Tristram lay, and he looked upon him as he slept and he knew him not; for the beard and the hair of Sir Tristram had grown down all over his breast and shoulders and he was very ragged and beaten by the weather. But though Sir Launcelot knew him not, yet he beheld that the body of Sir Tristram was very beautiful and strong, for he saw how all the muscles and thews thereof were cut very smooth and clean as you might cut them out of wax, wherefore Sir Launcelot gazed for a long while and felt great admiration for his appearance.

Then Sir Launcelot beheld how the sleeping man held a naked sword in his arms very caressingly, as though he loved it, and thereat he was very much surprised to find such a sword as that in the hands of this forest madman. Wherefore he said to those swineherds, "Where got this man that sword?"

"Messire," said the swineherd who had afore spoken, "some while since there came a knight hitherward who ill-treated him. Thereupon this poor man ran at the knight and overthrew him and took the sword away from him and soused him several times in the well. After that he hath ever held fast to this sword and would not give it up to any of us."

"Ha!" said Sir Launcelot, "that is a very wonderful story, that a naked man should overthrow an armed knight and take his sword away from him. Now I deem that this is no mere madman, but some noble knight in misfortune."

Therewith he reached forward and touched Sir Tristram very gently on the shoulder, and at that Sir Tristram awoke and opened his eyes and sat up. And Sir Tristram looked upon Sir Launcelot, but knew him not, albeit some small memory moved very deeply within him. Nevertheless, though he knew not Sir Launcelot, yet he felt great tenderness for that noble knight in arms, and he smiled very lovingly upon him. And Sir Launcelot felt in return a very great deal of regard for Sir Tristram, but wist not why that was; yet it seemed to Sir Launcelot that he should know the face of Sir Tristram, and that it was not altogether strange to him.

Sir Launcelot awakens Sir Tristram.

Then Sir Launcelot said, "Fair friend, was it thou who slew Sir Tauleas?" And Sir Tristram said, "Ay." Sir Launcelot said, "Who art thou?" Whereunto Sir Tristram made reply: "I know not who I am, nor whence I come, nor how I came hither."

Then Sir Launcelot felt great pity and tenderness for Sir Tristram, and he said: "Friend, wilt thou go with me away from this place and into the habitations of men? There I believe thy mind maybe made whole again, and that it may be with thee as it was beforetime. And verily, I believe that when that shall come to pass, the world shall find in thee some great knight it hath lost."

Sir Tristram said: "Sir Knight, though I know not who I am, yet I know that I am not sound in my mind; wherefore I am ashamed to go out in the world and amongst mankind, but would fain hide myself away in this forest. Yet I love thee so much that, if thou wert to bid me go with thee to the ends of the world, I believe I would go with thee."

Then Sir Launcelot smiled upon Sir Tristram very kindly and said, "I do bid thee come with me away from here," and Sir Tristram said, "I will go."

So Sir Launcelot bade the swineherds clothe Sir Tristram in such a wise that his nakedness might be covered, and he bade them give Sir Tristram hosen and shoon, and when Sir Tristram was thus decently clad, Sir Launcelot made ready to take his departure from that place.

Sir Tristram quits the forest with Sir Launcelot.

But ere the two left, all those good fellows crowded around Sir Tristram, and embraced him and kissed him upon the cheek; for they had come to love him a very great deal.

Then the two went away through the forest, Sir Launcelot proudly riding upon his great horse and Sir Tristram running very lightly beside him.

But Sir Launcelot had other business at that time than to seek out Sir Tauleas as aforetold. For at that time there were three knights of very ill-repute who harried the west coast of that land that overlooked the sea toward the Kingdom of Ireland, and Sir Launcelot was minded to seek them out after he had finished with Sir Tauleas. So ere he returned to the court of King Arthur he had first of all to go thitherward.

Now you are to know that the castle of Tintagel lay upon the way that he was to take upon that adventure, and so it was that he brought Sir Tristram to the castle of Tintagel, where King Mark of Cornwall was then holding court. For Sir Launcelot was minded to leave Sir Tristram there whilst he went upon that adventure aforetold of.

And Sir Launcelot was received in Tintagel with very great honor and acclaim, for it was the first time he had ever been there. And King Mark besought Sir Launcelot for to abide a while in Tintagel; but Sir Launcelot refused this hospitality, saying: "I have an adventure to do for the sake of my master, King Arthur, and I may not abide here at this present. But I pray you to grant me a favor, and it is this: that you cherish this poor madman whom I found in the forest, and that you keep him here, treating him kindly until I shall return from the quest I am upon. For I have great love for this poor fellow and I would not have any harm befall him whilst I am away."

Sir Tristram comes to Tintagel.

Then King Mark said: "I am sorry you will not remain with us, but as to this thing it shall be done as you desire, for we will cherish and care for this man while you are away." So said King Mark, speaking with great cheerfulness and courtesy; for neither he nor any of his court at that time wist who Sir Tristram was.

So Sir Launcelot went upon his way, and King Mark gave orders that Sir Tristram should be well-clothed and fed, and it was done as he commanded.

Thus it was that Sir Tristram was brought back to the castle of Tintagel again. And now it shall be told how it befell with him thereat.

JVSTISSIMVS·REX·

Sir Tristram leaps into ye sea.

CHAPTER THIRD

How Sir Tristram Was Discovered at Tintagel and of What Befell Thereby.

Now during the time that Sir Tristram abode thus unknown at the court of Tintagel, he was allowed to wander thereabouts whithersoever he chose, and no one hindered him either in going or in coming. For none in all that place suspected who he was, but everyone thought that he was only a poor gentle madman of the forest; so he was allowed to wander at will as his fancy led him.

And Sir Tristram's memory never awoke; but though it awoke not, yet it stirred within him. For though he could not remember what this place was whereunto he had come, yet it was very strangely familiar to him, so that whithersoever he went, he felt that those places were not altogether strange to him. And in some of those places he felt great pleasure and in other places somewhat of pain, yet he knew not why he should have the one feeling or the other.

How Sir Tristram dwelt at Tintagel.

Now of all those places whereunto he wandered, Sir Tristram found most pleasure in the pleasance of the castle where was a fair garden and fruit trees; for it was there that he and the Lady Belle Isoult had walked together aforetime ere his affliction had befallen him, and he remembered this place better than any other, and took more pleasure in it. Now one day Sir Tristram came wandering thus into that pleasance and, the day being warm, he sat under the shade of an appletree beside a marble fountain of water; and the appletree above his head was all full of red and golden fruit. So Sir Tristram sat there, striving to remember how it was that he had once aforetime beheld that fountain and that garden and that appletree beneath which he sat.

So whilst he sat there pondering in that wise, there came the Lady Belle Isoult into the garden of that pleasance and her lady, the dame Bragwaine, was with her, and the hound, hight Houdaine, which Sir Tristram had sent to her by Gouvernail, walked beside her on the other side. Then Belle Isoult perceived that there was a man sitting under the appletree, and she said to dame Bragwaine: "Who is yonder man who hath dared to come hither into our privy garden?" Unto this, dame Bragwaine replied: "That, lady, is the gentle madman of the forest whom Sir Launcelot brought hither two days ago."

Then the Lady Belle Isoult said, "Let us go nearer and see what manner of man he is"; and so they went forward toward where Sir Tristram sat, and the dog Houdaine went with them.

Then Sir Tristram was aware that someone was nigh; and therewith he turned his face and beheld the Lady Isoult for the first time since he had gone mad in the forest; and the lady was looking at him, but knew him not.

Then of a sudden, because of his great love for Belle Isoult, the memory of Sir Tristram came all back to him in the instant, and upon that instant he knew who he was and all that had befallen him, and how he had been brought there as a madman out of the forest. But though he knew her in that wise, yet, as has been said, she knew not him.

Then Sir Tristram was all overwhelmed with shame that he should be thus found by that dear lady; wherefore he turned away his face and bowed his head so that she might not remember him, for he perceived that as yet she did not know him who he was.

Now at that moment the dog, Houdaine, was aware of the savor of Sir Tristram; wherefore he leaped away from the Lady Belle Isoult and ran to Sir Tristram and smelt very eagerly of him. And with that he knew his master.

Houdaine knoweth Sir Tristram.

Then the two ladies who looked beheld Houdaine fall down at the feet of Sir Tristram and grovel there with joy. And they beheld that he licked Sir Tristram's feet and his hands, and that he leaped upon Sir Tristram and licked his neck and face, and at that they were greatly astonished.

Then of a sudden a thought came to dame Bragwaine, and she catched the Lady Isoult by the arm and she said: "Lady, know you not who yonder madman is?" But the Lady Belle Isoult said: "Nay, I know not who he is. Who is he, Bragwaine?" And Bragwaine said: "Certes, that is Sir Tristram, and no one else in all the world."

Belle Isoult knows Sir Tristram.

Therewith, at those words, the scales suddenly fell from Lady Belle Isoult's eyes and she knew him. Then, for a little space, she stood as though turned into stone; then she emitted a great loud cry of joy and ran to Sir Tristram where he sat, and flung herself down upon the ground at the feet of Sir Tristram and embraced him about the knees. And she cried out in a voice of great passion: "Tristram! Tristram! Is it thou? They told me thou wert dead, and lo! thou art come to life again!" And with that she fell to weeping with such fury of passion that it was as though the soul of her were struggling to escape from her body.

Then Sir Tristram got to his feet in great haste and agitation and he said: "Lady! Lady! This must not be—arise, and stay your passion or else it will be our ruin. For behold, I am alone and unarmed in this castle, and there are several herein who seek my life. So if it be discovered who I am, both thou and I are lost."

Then, perceiving how that Belle Isoult was in a way distracted and out of her mind with joy and grief and love, he turned him unto Bragwaine and said to her: "Take thy lady hence and by and by I will find means whereby I may come to speech with her in private. Meanwhile it is death both for her and for me if she remain here to betray me unto the others of this castle."

So Bragwaine and Sir Tristram lifted up the Lady Belle Isoult, and Bragwaine led her thence out of that place; for I believe that Belle Isoult knew not whither she went but walked like one walking half in a swoon.

Now it chanced at that time that Sir Andred was in a balcony overlooking that pleasance, and, hearing the sound of voices and the sound of a disturbance that was suppressed, he looked out and beheld all that passed. Then he also wist who was that madman whom Sir Launcelot had fetched to that place out of the forest, and that he was Sir Tristram.

Sir Andred knoweth Sir Tristram.

Therewith he was filled with a great rage and fury and was likewise overwhelmed with great fear lest, if Sir Tristram should escape from that castle with his life, he would reclaim those possessions that he, Sir Andred, had seized upon.

So therewith he withdrew himself from that balcony very softly, into the apartment behind. And he sat down in that apartment for a little while as though not knowing rightly what to do. But after a little while he arose and went to King Mark; and King Mark looked up and beheld him and said, "What news do you bring, Messire?" Thereunto Sir Andred made reply: "Lord, know you who that madman is whom Sir Launcelot hath fetched hither?" King Mark said, "Nay, I know not who he is." But with that he fell to trembling throughout his entire body, for he began to bethink him who that madman was. "Lord," said Sir Andred, "it is Sir Tristram, and meseems Sir Launcelot was aware who it was, and that he was plotting treason when he fetched him hither."

Sir Andres betrays Sir Tristram to King Mark.

At that King Mark smote his hands together and he cried in a terrible voice, "I know it! I know it!" And then he said: "Blind! Blind! How was it that I knew him not?" Then after a little he fell to laughing and he said to Sir Andred: "Lo! God hath assuredly delivered that traitor, Sir Tristram, into mine hands so that I may punish him for his treasons. For, behold! he is here in our midst and he is altogether unarmed. Go, Messire, with all haste, gather together such force as may be needful, and seize upon him and bind him so that he may do no further harm to any man. Then let justice be executed upon him so soon as it is possible to do so." And Sir Andred said: "Lord, it shall be done according to your demands and upon the instant."

Therewith Sir Andred went forth from where the King was, and he armed himself in complete armor, and he gathered together a number of knights and esquires and he led them to that place where he knew Sir Tristram would be; and there he found Sir Tristram sitting sunk in thought. And when Sir Tristram beheld those armed men come in thus upon him, he arose to defend himself. But then Sir Andred cried out in a loud voice: "Seize him ere he can strike and bind him fast, for he is unarmed and may do you no harm!"

With that a dozen or more of those who were with Sir Andred flung themselves upon Sir Tristram, shouting and roaring like wild beasts. And they bore him to the earth by numbers, and after a while, by dint of great effort, they held him and bound his hands together by the wrists. Then they lifted up Sir Tristram and stood him upon his feet, and lo! his bosom heaved with his struggles, and his eyes were all shot with blood and his lips afroth with the fury of his fighting; and his clothes were torn in that struggle so that his body was half naked. And they held him there, a knight in armor with a naked sword standing upon his right hand and another armed knight with a naked sword standing upon his left hand.

The castle folk seize Sir Tristram.

Then Sir Andred came and stood in front of Sir Tristram and taunted him, saying: "Ha, Tristram, how is it with thee now?" Lo! thou camest like a spy into this place, and now thou art taken with all thy treason upon thee. So thou shalt die no knightly death, but, in a little while, thou shalt be hanged like a thief."

Then he came close to Sir Tristram, and he laughed and said: "Tristram where is now the glory of thy strength that one time overcame all thine enemies? Lo! thou art helpless to strike a single blow in defence of thine honor." And therewith Sir Andred lifted his hand and smote Sir Tristram upon the face with the palm thereof.

At that blow the rage of Sir Tristram so flamed up in him that his eyes burned as with pure green fire. And in an instant, so quickly that no man wist what he did, he turned with amazing suddenness upon that knight who stood at his left hand, and he lifted up both hands that were bound, and he smote that knight such a blow upon the face that the knight

Sir Tristram slays Sir Andred.

fell down upon the ground and his sword fell out of his hand. Then Sir Tristram snatched the sword and, turning with astonishing quickness, he smote the knight upon his right hand such a buffet that he instantly fell down upon his knees and then rolled over upon the ground in a swoon. Then Sir Tristram turned upon Sir Andred, and lifting high the sword with both hands tied, he smote him so terrible a blow that the blade cut through his epulier and half through his body as far as the paps. At that great terrible blow the breath fled out of Sir Andred with a deep groan, and he fell down upon the ground and immediately died.

Now all this had happened so suddenly that they who beheld it were altogether amazed and stood staring as though bewitched by some spell. But when they beheld Sir Tristram turn upon them and make at them with that streaming sword lifted on high, the terror of his fury so seized upon them that they everywhere broke from before him and fled, yelling, and with the fear of death clutching them in the vitals. And Sir Tristram chased them out of that place and into the courtyard of the castle, and some he smote down and others escaped; but all who could do so scattered away before him like chaff before the wind.

Then, when they were gone, Sir Tristram stood panting and glaring about him like a lion at bay. Then he set the point of his sword upon the pavement of the court and the pommel thereof he set against his breast, and he drew the bonds that held his wrists across the edge of the sword so that they were cut and he was free.

But Sir Tristram wist that in a little the whole castle would be aroused against him, and that he would certainly be overwhelmed by dint of numbers, wherefore he looked about him for some place of refuge; and he beheld that the door of the chapel which opened upon the courtyard stood ajar. So he ran into the chapel and shut to that door and another door and locked and bolted them both, and set a heavy bar of wood across both of them so that for a while he was safe.

Sir Tristram defends the chapel.

But yet he was only safe for a little while, for about the time of early nightfall, which came not long thereafter, a great party of several score of King Mark's people came against the chapel where he was. And when they found that the doors were locked and barred, they brought rams for to batter in the chief door of the chapel.

Then Sir Tristram beheld how parlous was his case, and that he must in a little while die if he did not immediately do something to save himself. So with that he ran to a window of the chapel and opened it and looked out thence. And lo! below him and far beneath was the sea, and the rocks of the shore upon which the castle was built; and the sea and the rocks lay twelve fathoms beneath him.

Sir Tristram leaps into the sea.

But Sir Tristram said, "Better death there than here"; and therewith finding that the door was now falling in beneath the rams, he leaped out from the window-ledge, and thence he dived down into the sea; and no one saw that terrible leap that he made.

So he sank down deep into the sea, but met no rocks, so that he presently came up again safe and sound. Then, looking about him, he perceived in the twilight a cave in the rocks, and thither he swam with the intent to find shelter for a little.

Now when they who had come against him had broken into the chapel they all ran in in one great crowd, for they expected to find Sir Tristram and to do battle with him. But lo! Sir Tristram was not there, but only the empty walls. Then at first they were greatly astonished, and knew not what to think. And some who came cried out: "Is that man then a spirit that he can melt away into thin air?" But after a little, one of them perceived where the window of the chapel stood open, and therewith several of them ran thereunto and looked out, and they wist that Sir Tristram had leaped out thence into the sea.

Then they said to one another: "Either that knight is now dead, or else he will perish when the tide rises and covers the rocks; so to-night we will do no more with this business; but to-morrow we will go and find his body where it lies among the rocks of the shore." So thereupon they shut the window and went their ways.

Now Gouvernail was not at that time at Tintagel, nor did he return thereunto until all this affair was over and done. But when he came there, there were many voices to tell him what had befallen, and to all of them Gouvernail listened without saying anything.

But afterward Gouvernail went and sought out a certain knight hight Sir Santraille de Lushon, who, next to himself, was the most faithful friend to Sir Tristram at that place. To him Gouvernail said: "Messire, I do not think that Sir Tristram is dead, for he hath always been a most wonderful swimmer and diver. But if he be alive, and we do not save him, he will assuredly perish when the tide comes up and covers over those rocks amongst which he may now be hidden."

So Gouvernail and Sir Santraille went to that chapel unknown to anyone, and they went to that window whence Sir Tristram had leaped, and they opened the window, and leaned out and called upon Sir Tristram in low voices: "Sir Tristram, if thou art alive, arise and answer us, for we are friends!"

Then after a while Sir Tristram recognized Gouvernail's voice and answered them: "I am alive; but save me, or I perish in a little while." Then Gouvernail said: "Lord, are you hurt, or are you whole?" Sir Tristram replied, "I am strong and well in body, but the tide rises fast." Gouvernail said, "Messire, can you wait a little?" Sir Tristram said, "Ay; for a little, but not for too long."

Then Gouvernail and Sir Santraille withdrew from where they were and they made all haste, and they got together a great number of sheets and napkins, and tied these together and made a rope, and lowered the rope down to the rocks where Sir Tristram was. Then Sir Tristram climbed up the rope of linen and so reached the chapel in safety. And at that time it was nigh to midnight and very dark.

Gouvernail and Sir Santraille rescue Sir Tristram.

But when Sir Tristram stood with them in the chapel, he gave them hardly any greeting, but said at once: "Messires, how doth it fare with the Lady Belle Isoult?" For he thought of her the first of all and above all things else.

To this Sir Santraille made reply: "Sir, the lady hath been shut into a tower, and the door thereof hath been locked upon her, and she is a close prisoner."

Then Sir Tristram said: "How many knights are there in the place who are my friends, and who will stand with me to break out hence?" To this Gouvernail said: "Lord, there are twelve besides ourselves, and that makes fourteen in all who are with thee in this quarrel unto life or death."

Sir Tristram said: "Provide me presently with arms and armor and bring those twelve hither armed at all points. But first let them saddle horses for themselves and for us, and for the Lady Belle Isoult and for her waiting-woman, Dame Bragwaine. When this is done, we will depart from this place unto some other place of refuge, and I do not think there will be any in the castle will dare stop or stay us after we are armed."

So it was done as Sir Tristram commanded, and when all those were gathered together, and their horses ready, Sir Tristram and several of the knights of his party went openly to that tower where the Lady Belle Isoult was prisoner. And they burst open the doors and went in with torches, and found Belle Isoult and her attendant in the upper part of the castle.

Sir Tristram arms himself.

But when Belle Isoult beheld the face of Sir Tristram, she said: "Is it thou, my love; and art thou still alive, and art thou come to me?" Sir Tristram said: "Yea, I am still alive nor will I die, God willing, until I have first brought thee out of this wicked castle and into some place of safety. And never again will I entrust thee unto King Mark's hands; for I have great fear that if he have thee in his hands he will work vengeance upon thee so as to strike at my heart through thee. So, dear love, I come to take thee away from this place; and never again right or wrong, shalt thou be without the shelter of my arm."

Then the Lady Belle Isoult smiled very wonderfully upon Sir Tristram so that her face appeared to shine with a great illumination of love. And she said: "Tristram, I will go with thee whithersoever thou wilt. Yea, I would go with thee even to the grave, for I believe that I should be happy even there, so that thou wert lying beside me."

Then Sir Tristram groaned in spirit and he said: "Isoult, what have I done, that I should always bring unhappiness upon thee?" But the Lady Belle Isoult spake very steadily, saying: "Never unhappiness, Tristram, but always happiness; for I have thy love for aye, and thou hast mine in the same measure, and in that is happiness, even in tears and sorrow, and never unhappiness."

With that Sir Tristram kissed Belle Isoult upon the forehead, and then he lifted her up and carried her in his arms down the stairs of the tower and sat her upon her horse. And Bragwaine followed after, and Gouvernail lifted her up upon her horse.

Sir Tristram taketh Belle Isoult away from Tintagel.

Now all they of that castle were amazed beyond measure to find all those knights armed and prepared for battle so suddenly in their midst. And most of all were they filled with terror to find Sir Tristram at the head of these knights. Wherefore when Sir Tristram made demand that they should open the portcullis of the castle and let fall the drawbridge, the porters thereof dared not refuse him, but did as he said.

So Sir Tristram and his knights rode forth with the Lady Belle Isoult and Bragwaine and no one stayed them. And they rode into the forest, betaking their way toward a certain castle of Sir Tristram's, which they reached in the clear dawning of the daytime.

And so Sir Tristram brought the Lady Belle Isoult away from Tintagel and into safety.

JVSTISSIMVS·REX·

King Mark broods mischief.

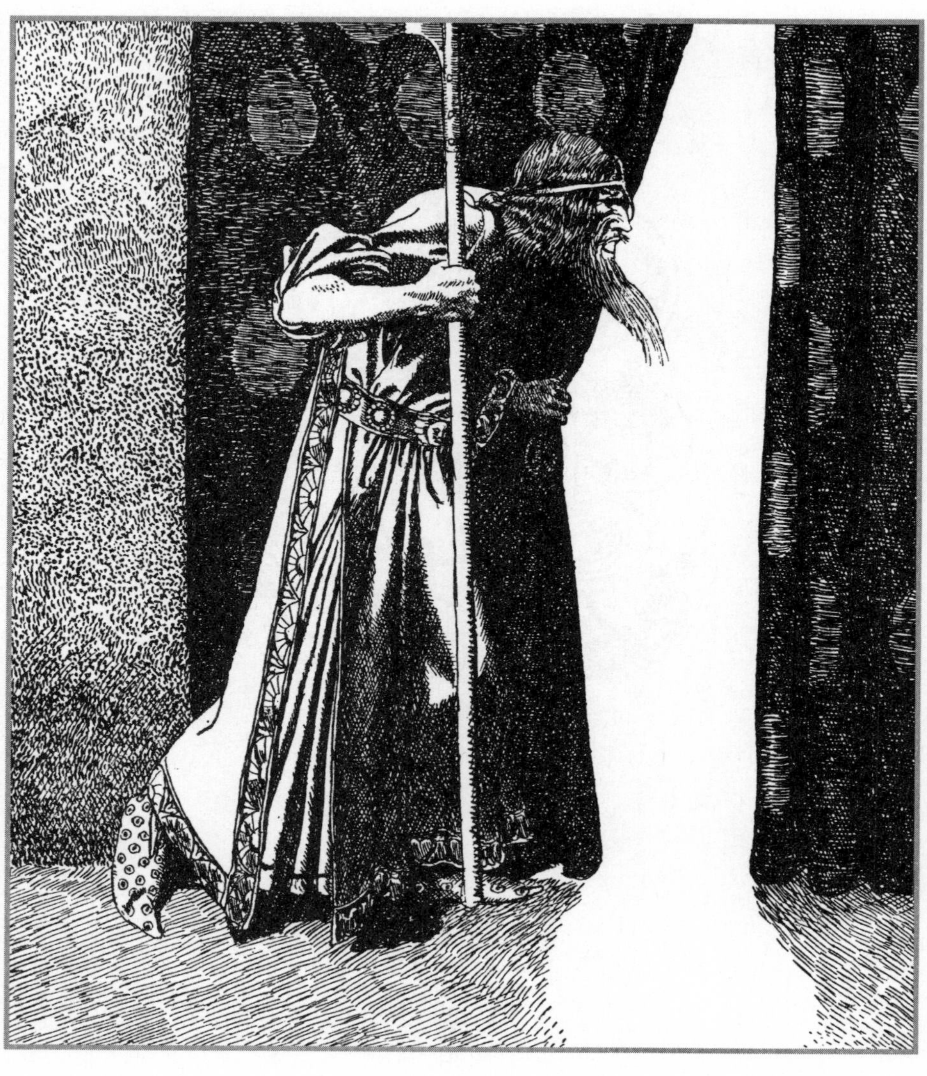

CHAPTER FOURTH

How Sir Tristram and the Lady Belle Isoult Returned to Cornwall, and How They Ended Their Days Together.

AND NOW REMAINETH TO BE TOLD THE REST OF THESE ADVENTURES of Sir Tristram as briefly as may be.

For indeed I thought not, when I began this history, to tell you as much concerning him as I have done. But as I have entered into this history I have come so strongly to perceive how noble and true and loyal was the knighthood of Sir Tristram, that I could not forbear telling you of many things that I had not purposed to speak of.

Yet, as I have said before this, there are a great many adventures that I have not spoken of in this book. For I have told only those things that were necessary for to make you understand how it fared with him in his life.

So now shall be told those last things that concerned him.

Sir Launcelot reproves King Mark.

Now two days after those things aforesaid had come to pass, Sir Launcelot returned unto Tintagel from that quest which he had been upon, and so soon as he came thither he made inquiry of King Mark concerning the welfare of that madman of the forest whom he had left in the care of King Mark. But when he heard that that madman was Sir Tristram, he was astonished beyond all measure; but when he heard how Sir Tristram had been served by King Mark and by the people of the castle under the lead of Sir Andred, he was filled with a great and violent indignation. So he arose and stood before King Mark and said: "Lord King, I have heard much ill said of thee and shameful things concerning thy unknightliness in several courts of chivalry where I have been; and now I know that those things were true; for I have heard from the lips of many people here, how thou didst betray Sir Tristram into bringing the Lady Belle Isoult unto thee; and I have heard from many how thou dost ever do ill and wickedly by him, seeking to take from him both his honor and his life. And yet Sir Tristram hath always been thy true and faithful knight, and hath served thee in all ways thou hast demanded of him. I know that thou hast jealousy for Sir Tristram in thy heart and that thou hast ever imputed wickedness and sin unto him. Yet all the world knoweth that Sir Tristram is a true knight and altogether innocent of any evil. For all the evil which thou hast imputed to him hath no existence saving only in thine own evil heart. Now I give thee and all thy people to know that had ill befallen Sir Tristram at your hands I should have held you accountable therefor and should have punished you in such a way that you would not soon have forgotten it. But of that there is no need, for Sir Tristram himself hath punished you in full measure without any aid from me. So now I will go away from this place and will never come hither again; nor will I acknowledge you should I meet you in court or in field."

So saying, Sir Launcelot turned and went away from that place very proudly and haughtily, leaving them all abashed at his rebuke.

So that day Sir Launcelot went forward through the forest until he reached that castle whereunto Sir Tristram had taken the Lady Belle Isoult, and there he was received by Sir Tristram with all joy and honor. And Sir Launcelot abided at that place for two days, with great pleasure to himself and to Sir Tristram and to Belle Isoult.

Sir Launcelot findeth Sir Tristram and Belle Isoult in the forest.

At the end of that time Sir Launcelot said to Sir Tristram: "Messire, it is not well that you and this dear lady should abide here so nigh to Tintagel. For, certes, King Mark will some time work some grievous ill upon you. So I beseech you to come with me unto my castle of Joyous Gard. There this lady shall reign queen paramount and we shall be her very faithful servants to do her pleasure in all ways. That castle is a very beautiful place, and there she may dwell in peace and safety and tranquillity all the days of her life if she chooses to do so."

Now that saying of Sir Launcelot's seemed good to Sir Tristram and to Belle Isoult; wherefore in three days all they and their court made ready to depart. And they did depart from that castle in the forest unto Joyous Gard, where they were received with great honor and rejoicing.

They depart for Joyous Gard.

So the Lady Belle Isoult abided for three years at Joyous Gard, dwelling there as queen paramount in all truth and innocence of life; and Sir Launcelot and Sir Tristram were her champions and all their courts were her servants. And during those three years there were many famous joustings held at Joyous Gard, and several bel-adventures were performed both by Sir Launcelot and Sir Tristram in her honor.

And indeed I believe that this was the happiest time of all the Lady Belle Isoult's life, for she lived there in peace and love and tranquillity and she suffered neither grief nor misfortune in all that time.

Then one day there came King Arthur to Joyous Gard, and he was received with such joy and celebration as that place had never before beheld. A great feast was set in his honor, and after the feast King Arthur and Sir Tristram and Belle Isoult withdrew to one side and sat together in converse.

King Arthur comes to Joyous Gard.

Then after a while King Arthur said, "Lady, may I ask you a question?" And at that Lady Belle Isoult lifted up her eyes and looked very strangely upon the King, and after a while she said, "Ask thy question, Lord King, and I will answer it if I can." "Lady," said King Arthur, "answer me this question: is it better to dwell in honor with sadness or in dishonor with joy?"

Then Belle Isoult began to pant with great agitation, and by and by she said, "Lord, why ask you me that?" King Arthur said: "Because, lady, I think your heart hath sometimes asked you the selfsame question." Then the Lady Belle Isoult clasped her hands together and cried out: "Yea, yea, my heart hath often asked me that question, but I would not answer it." King Arthur said: "Neither shalt thou answer me, for I am but a weak and erring man as thou art a woman. But answer thou that question to God, dear lady, and then thou shalt answer it in truth."

Therewith King Arthur fell to talking of other things with Sir Tristram, but the lady could not join them in talk, but sat thenceforth in silence, finding it hard to breathe because of the oppression of tears that lay upon her bosom.

And Belle Isoult said no more concerning that question that King Arthur had asked. But three days after that time she came to Sir Tristram and said: "Dear lord, I have bethought me much of what King Arthur said, and this hath come of it, that I must return again unto Cornwall."

Then Sir Tristram turned away his face so that she might not see it, and he said, "Methought it would come to that." And then in a little he went away from that place, leaving her standing there.

So it came about that peace was made betwixt Sir Tristram and King Mark, and Belle Isoult and King Mark, and King Arthur was the peacemaker.

Thereafter Sir Tristram and his court and the Lady Belle Isoult returned unto Cornwall, and there they dwelt for some time in seeming peace. But in that time the Lady Belle Isoult would never see King Mark nor exchange a word with him, but lived entirely apart from him and in her own life in a part of the castle; and at that King Mark was struck

Belle Isoult scorns King Mark.

with such bitterness of despair that he was like to a demon in torment. For he saw, as it were, a treasure very near and yet afar, for he could not come unto it. And the more he suffered that torment, the more he hated Sir Tristram, for in his suffering it appeared to him that Sir Tristram was the cause of that suffering.

So it came about that King Mark set spies to watch Sir Tristram, for in his evil heart he suspected Sir Tristram of treason, and he hoped that his spies might discover Sir Tristram in some act for which he might be punished. So those spies watched Sir Tristram both night and day, but they could find nothing that he did that was amiss.

Now one day Belle Isoult felt such a longing for Sir Tristram that she could not refrain from sending a note to him beseeching him for to come to her so that they might see one another again; and though Sir Tristram misdoubted what he did, yet he went as she desired, even if it should mean the peril of death to him.

Then came those spies to King Mark and told him that Sir Tristram was gone to the bower of the Lady Belle Isoult, and that she had bidden him to come thither.

At that the vitals of King Mark were twisted with such an agony of hatred and despair that he bent him double and cried out, "Woe! Woe! I suffer torments!"

Therewith he arose and went very quickly to that part of the castle where the Lady Belle Isoult inhabited; and he went very softly up by a back way and through a passage to where was a door with curtains hanging before it; and when he had come there he parted the curtains and peeped within. And he beheld that the Lady Belle Isoult and Sir Tristram sat at a game of chess, and he beheld that they played not at the game but that they sat talking together very sadly; and he beheld that Dame Bragwaine sat in a deep window to one side—for Belle Isoult did not wish it to be said that she and Sir Tristram sat alone.

King Mark spies upon Sir Tristram and Isoult.

All this King Mark saw and trembled with a torment of jealousy. So by and by he left that place and went very quietly back into that passageway whence he had come. And when he had come there he perceived a great glaive upon a pole two ells long. This he took into his hand and returned unto that curtained doorway again.

Then being in all ways prepared he parted the curtains silently and stepped very quickly and without noise into the room. And the back of Sir Tristram was toward him.

Then King Mark lifted the glaive on high and he struck; and Sir Tristram sank without a sound.

Yea, I believe that that good knight knew naught of what had happened until he awoke in Paradise to find himself in that realm of happiness and peace.

Then Belle Isoult arose, overturning the table of chessmen as she did so, but she made no outcry nor sound of any sort. But she stood looking down at Sir Tristram for a little space, and then she kneeled down beside his body and touched the face thereof as though to make sure that it was dead. Therewith, as though being assured, she fell down with her body upon his; and King Mark stood there looking down upon them.

Of the passing of Tristram and Isoult.

All this had passed so quickly that Dame Bragwaine hardly knew what had befallen; but now, upon an instant, she suddenly fell to shrieking so piercingly that the whole castle rang with the sound thereof.

Now there were in the outer room several of the knights of the court of Sir Tristram who had come thither with him as witnesses that he performed no treason to the King. These, when Dame Bragwaine shrieked in that wise, came running into the room and therewith beheld what had happened. Then all they stood aghast at that sight.

But there was in the court of Sir Tristram a very young, gallant knight hight Sir Alexander. This knight came to where King Mark stood looking down upon his handiwork as though entranced with what he had done. Then Sir Alexander said to King Mark, "Is this thy work?" And King Mark raised his eyes very heavily and looked at Sir Alexander and he answered, "Ay!" Then Sir Alexander cried out, "Thou hast lived too long!" And therewith drawing his misericordia, he catched King Mark by the left wrist and lifted his arm. And Sir Alexander drave the dagger into the side of King Mark, and King Mark groaned and sank down upon the ground, and in a little while died where he lay.

Sir Alexander slays King Mark.

Then those knights went to where the Lady Belle Isoult lay and lifted her up; but, lo! the soul had left her, and she was dead. For I believe that it was not possible for one of those loving souls to leave its body with out the other quitting its body also, so that they might meet together in Paradise. For there never were two souls in all the history of chivalry that clave to one another so tenderly as did the souls of Tristram and Isoult.

So endeth this story of Sir Tristram, with only this to say, that they two were buried with the graves close together, and that it is said by many who have written of them that there grew a rose-tree up from Sir Tristram's grave, and down upon the grave of Belle Isoult; and it is said that this rose-tree was a miracle, for that upon his grave there grew red roses, and upon her grave there grew pure white roses. For her soul was white like to thrice-carded wool, and so his soul was red with all that was of courage or knightly pride.

And I pray that God may rest the souls of those two as I pray He may rest the souls of all of us who must some time go the way that those two and so many others have travelled before us. Amen.

The Book of Sir Percival

Here beginneth the story of Sir Percival of Gales, who was considered to be one of the three great knights of the Round Table at that time. For, if Sir Launcelot was the chiefest of all the knights who ever came unto King Arthur's court, then it is hard to say whether Sir Tristram of Lyonesse or Sir Percival of Gales was second unto him in renown.

And I pray that it shall be given unto all of ye to live as brave and honorable and pure a life as he did; and that you, upon your part, may claim a like glory and credit in the world in which you dwell by such noble behavior as he exhibited.

Sir Percival of Gales.

Prologue

THE FATHER OF SIR PERCIVAL WAS THAT KING HIGHT PELLINORE WHO fought so terrible a battle with King Arthur as has been told in the Book of King Arthur. For it was after that fight that King Arthur obtained his famous sword Excalibur, as was therein told.

Now, King Pellinore was one of those eleven kings who, in the beginning of King Arthur's reign, were in rebellion against King Arthur as hath been told in the book aforesaid, and he was one of the last of all those kings to yield when he was overcome. So King Arthur drove him from town to town and from place to place until, at last, he was driven away from the habitations of men and into the forests like to a wild beast.

King Pellinore fleeth to the wilderness.

Now, King Pellinore took with him into the wilderness his wife and his four sons; to wit, Lamorack and Aglaval and Dornar and Percival. Of these, Percival was but three years of age; the others, excepting Dornar, being nigh to the estate of manhood. Thereafter that noble family dwelt in the forest like hunted animals, and that was a very great hardship for the lady who had been queen; and, likewise, it was greatly to the peril of the young child, Percival.

Now, Percival was extraordinarily beautiful and his mother loved him above all her other sons. Wherefore she feared lest the young child should die of those hardships in the wilderness.

So one day King Pellinore said: "Dear love, I am now in no wise prepared for to defend thee and this little one. Wherefore, for a while, I shall put ye away from me so that ye may remain in secret hiding until such time as the child shall have grown in years and stature to the estate of manhood and may so defend himself.

"Now of all my one-time possessions I have only two left to me. One of these is a lonely castle in this forest (unto which I am now betaking my way), and the other is a solitary tower at a great distance from this, and in a very desolate part of the world where there are many mountains. Unto that place I shall send ye, for it will not be likely that mine enemies will ever find ye there.

"So my will is this: that if this child groweth in that lonely place to manhood, and if he be weak in body or timid in spirit, thou shalt make of him a clerk of holy orders. But if when he groweth, he shall prove to be strong and lusty of frame and high of spirit, and shall desire to undertake deeds of knighthood, thou then shalt not stay him from his desires, but shall let him go forth into the world as he shall have a mind to do.

"And if a time should come when he desireth to go thus into the world behold! here is a ring set with a very precious ruby; let him bring that ring to me or to any of our sons wheresoever he may find us, and by that ring we shall know that he is my son and their brother, and we will receive him with great gladness."

And King Pellinore's lady said, "It shall be done as thou dost ordain."

So it was that King Pellinore betook himself to that lonely castle where King Arthur found him and fought with him; and Percival's mother betook herself to that dwelling-place in the mountains of which King Pellinore had spoken—which was a single tower that reached up into the sky, like unto a finger of stone.

Percival's mother taketh him to the mountains.

There she abided with Percival for sixteen years, and in all that time Percival knew naught of the world nor of what sort it was, but grew altogether wild and was entirely innocent like to a little child.

In the mean time, during those years, it happened very ill to the house of King Pellinore. For though King Arthur became reconciled to King Pellinore, yet there were in King Arthur's court many who were bitter enemies to that good, worthy knight. So it came about that first King Pellinore was slain by treachery, and then Sir Aglaval and Sir Dornar were slain in the same way, so that Sir Lamorack alone was left of all that noble family.

(And it was said that Sir Gawaine and his brothers were implicated in those murders—they being enemies unto King Pellinore—and great reproach hath always clung to them for the treacherous, unknightly way in which those noble knights of the house of Pellinore were slain.)

Now the news of those several deaths was brought to that lonely tower of the mountain wilderness and to Sir Percival's mother; and when she heard how her husband and two of her sons were dead she gave great outcry of grief, and smote her hands together and wept with great passion. And she cried out: "Mefeareth it will be the time of Lamorack next to be slain. As for Percival; never shall I be willing for him to go out into that cruel world of wicked murderers. For if he should perish also, my heart would surely break."

Percival's mother grieveth for the death of her dear ones.

So she kept Percival always with her and in ignorance of all that concerned the world of knighthood. And though Percival waxed great of body and was beautiful and noble of countenance, yet he dwelt there among those mountains knowing no more of the world that lay beyond that place in which he dwelt than would a little innocent child. Nor did he ever see anyone from the outside world, saving only an old man who was a deaf-mute. And this old man came and went betwixt that tower where Percival and his mother dwelt and the outer world, and from the world he would come back with clothing and provisions loaded upon an old sumpter horse for Percival and his mother and their few attendants. Yet Percival marvelled many times whence those things came, but no one told him and so he lived in entire ignorance of the world.

How Percival dwelt in the mountains.

And Percival's mother would not let him touch any weapon saving only a small Scot's spear which same is a sort of javelin. But with this Percival played every day of his life until he grew so cunning in handling it that he could pierce with it a bird upon the wing in the air.

Now it chanced upon a time when Percival was nineteen years of age that he stood upon a pinnacle of rock and looked down into a certain valley. And it was very early in the spring-time, so that the valley appeared, as it were, to be carpeted all with clear, thin green. There was a shining stream of water that ran down through the midst of the valley, and it was a very fair and peaceful place to behold.

So Percival stood and gazed into that low-land, and lo! a knight rode up through that valley, and the sun shone out from behind a cloud of rain and smote upon his armor so that it appeared to be all ablaze as with pure light, and Percival beheld that knight and wist not what it

Percival beholds a knight-rider.

was he saw. So, after the knight had gone away from the valley, he ran straightway to his mother, all filled with a great wonder, and he said: "Mother! Mother! I have beheld a very wonderful thing." She said, "What was it thou didst see?" Percival said: "I beheld somewhat that was like a man, and he rode upon a horse, and he shone very brightly and with exceeding splendor. Now, I prithee tell me what it was I saw?"

Then Percival's mother knew very well what it was he had seen, and she was greatly troubled at heart, for she wist that if Percival's knightly spirit should be awakened he would no longer be content to dwell in those peaceful solitudes. Wherefore she said to herself: "How is this? Is it to be that this one lamb also shall be taken away from me and nothing left to me of all my flock?" Then she said to Percival: "My son, that which thou didst behold was doubtless an angel." And Percival said, "I would that I too were an angel!" And at that speech the lady, his mother, sighed very deeply.

Now it chanced upon the next day after that that Percival and his mother went down into the forest that lay at the foot of the mountain whereon that tower stood, and they had intent to gather such early flowers of the spring-time as were then abloom. And whilst they were there, lo! there came five knights riding through the forest, and, the leaves being thin like to a mist of green, Percival perceived them a great way off. So he cried out in a loud voice: "Mother! Mother! Behold! Yonder is a whole company of angels such as I saw yesterday! Now I will go and give them greeting."

But his mother said: "How now! How now! Wouldst thou make address unto angels!" And Percival said: "Yea; for they appear to be both mild of face and gentle of mien." So he went forward for to greet those knights.

Now the foremost of that party of knights was Sir Ewaine, who was always both gentle and courteous to everybody. Wherefore, when Sir Ewaine saw Percival nigh at hand, he gave him greeting and said, "Fair youth, what is thy name?" Unto this Percival made reply: "My name is Percival." Sir Ewaine said: "That is a very good name, and thy face likewise is so extraordinarily comely that I take thee to be of some very high lineage. Now tell me, I prithee, who is thy father?" To this Percival said, "I cannot tell thee what is my lineage, for I do not know," and at that Sir Ewaine marvelled a very great deal. Then, after a little while, he said: "I prithee tell me, didst thou see a knight pass this way to-day or yesterday?" And Percival said, "I know not what sort of a thing is a knight." Sir Ewaine said, "A knight is such a sort of man as I am."

Percival holds discourse with five knights.

Upon this Percival understood many things that he did not know before, and he willed with all his soul to know more than those. Wherefore he said: "If thou wilt answer several questions for me, I will gladly answer thine." Upon this Sir Ewaine smiled very cheerfully (for he liked Percival exceedingly), and he said: "Ask what thou wilt and I will answer thee in so far as I am able."

So Percival said, "I prithee tell me what is this thing?" And he laid his hand thereon. And Sir Ewaine said, "That is a saddle." And Percival said, "What is this thing?" And Sir Ewaine said, "That is a sword." And Percival said, "What is this thing?" And Sir Ewaine said, "That is a shield." And so Percival asked him concerning all things that appertained to the accoutrements of a knight, and Sir Ewaine answered all his questions. Then Percival said: "Now I will answer thy question. I saw a knight ride past this way yesterday, and he rode up yonder valley and to the westward."

Upon this Sir Ewaine gave gramercy to Percival and saluted him, and so did the other knights, and they rode their way.

After they had gone Percival returned to his mother, and he beheld that she sat exactly where he had left her, for she was in great travail of soul because she perceived that Percival would not now stay with her very much longer. And when Percival came to where she sat he said to her: "Mother, those were not angels, but very good, excellent knights." And upon this the lady, his mother, burst into a great passion of weeping, so that Percival stood before her all abashed, not knowing why she wept. So by and by he said, "Mother, why dost thou weep?" But she could not answer him for a while, and after a while she said, "Let us return homeward." And so they walked in silence.

Now when they had come to the tower where they dwelt, the lady turned of a sudden unto Percival and she said to him, "Percival, what is in thy heart?" And he said, "Mother, thou knowest very well what is there." She said, "Is it that thou wouldst be a knight also?" And he said, "Thou sayst it." And upon that she said, "Thou shalt have thy will; come with me."

So Percival's mother led him to the stable and to where was that poor pack-horse that brought provisions to that place, and she said: "This is a sorry horse but I have no other for thee. Now let us make a saddle for him." So Percival and his mother twisted sundry cloths and wisps of hay and made a sort of a saddle thereof. And Percival's mother brought him a scrip with bread and cheese for his refreshment and she hung it about his shoulder. And she brought him his javelin which he took in his hand. And then she gave him the ring of King Pellinore with that precious ruby jewel inset into it, and she said: "Take thou this, Percival, and put it upon thy finger, for it is a royal ring. Now when thou leavest me, go unto the court of King Arthur and make diligent inquiry for Sir Lamorack of Gales. And when thou hast found him, show him that ring, and he will see that thou art made a very worthy knight; for, Percival, Sir Lamorack is thy brother. One time thou hadst a father alive, and thou hadst two other brothers. But all they were slain by treachery of our enemies, and only thou and Lamorack are left; so look to it that thou guard thyself when thou art in the world and in the midst of those enemies; for if thou shouldst perish at their hands, I believe my heart would break."

Then she gave Percival advice concerning the duty of one who would make himself worthy of knighthood, and that advice was as follows: "In thy journeying thou art to observe these sundry things: When thou comest to a church or a shrine say a pater-noster unto the glory of God; and if thou hearest a cry of anyone in trouble, hasten to lend thine aid—especially if it be a woman or a child who hath need of it; and if thou meet a lady or a damosel, salute her in seemly fashion; and if thou have to do with a man, be both civil and courageous unto him; and if thou art an-hungered or athirst and findest food and wine, eat and drink enough to satisfy thee, but no more; and if thou findest a treasure or a jewel of price and canst obtain those things without injustice unto another, take that thing for thine own—but give that which thou hast with equal freedom unto others. So, by obeying these precepts, thou shalt become worthy to be a true knight and, haply, be also worthy of thy father, who was a true knight before thee."

Percival's mother giveth him advice.

And Percival said, "All these things will I remember and observe to do."

And Percival's mother said, "But thou wilt not forget me, Percival?" And he said: "Nay, mother; but when I have got me power and fame and wealth, then will I straightway return thitherward and take thee away from this place, and thou shalt be like to a Queen for all the glory that I shall bestow upon thee." Upon this the lady, his mother, both laughed and wept; and Percival stooped and kissed her upon the lips. Then he turned and left her, and he rode away down the mountain and into the forest, and she stood and gazed after him as long as she could see him. And she was very lonely after he had gone.

Percival departs from the mountain.

So I have told you how it came that Percival went out into the world for to become a famous knight.

JUSTISSIMUS·REX·

The Lady Yvette the Fair.

CHAPTER FIRST

How Percival Departed Into the World and How He Found a Fair Damsel in a Pavilion; Likewise How He Came Before Queen Guinevere and How He Undertook His First Adventure.

Now after Percival had ridden upon his way for a very long time, he came at last out of that part of the forest and unto a certain valley where were many osiers growing along beside a stream of water. So he gathered branches of the willow-trees and peeled them and wove them very cunningly into the likeness of armor such as he had seen those knights wear who had come into his forest. And when he had armed himself with wattled osiers he said unto himself, "Now am I accoutred as well as they." Whereupon he rode upon his way with an heart enlarged with joy.

Percival maketh himself armor of willow twigs.

By and by he came out of the forest altogether and unto a considerable village where were many houses thatched with straw. And Percival said to himself: "Ha! how great is the world; I knew not that there were so many people in the world."

But when the folk of that place beheld what sort of a saddle was upon the back of the pack-horse; and when they beheld what sort of armor it was that Percival wore—all woven of osier twigs; and when they beheld how he was armed with a javelin and with no other weapon, they mocked and laughed at him and jeered him. But Percival understood not their mockery, whereupon he said: "Lo! how pleasant and how cheerful is the world. I knew not it was so merry a place." So he laughed and nodded and gave them greeting who mocked him in that manner. And some of them said, "That is a madman." And others said, "Nay, he is a silly fool." And when Percival heard these he said to himself: "I wonder whether there are other sorts of knights that I have not yet heard tell of?"

How Percival rode in the world.

So he rode upon his way very happy, and whenever he met travellers, they would laugh at him; but he would laugh louder than they and give them greeting because of pure pleasure that the great world was so merry and kind.

Now in the declining of the afternoon, he came to a certain pleasant glade, and there he beheld a very noble and stately pavilion in among the trees. And that pavilion was all of yellow satin so that it shone like to gold in the light of the declining sun.

Then Percival said to himself: "Verily, this must be one of those churches concerning which my mother spake to me." So he descended from his horse and went to that pavilion and knelt down and said a pater-noster.

And when he had ended that prayer, he arose and went into the pavilion, and lo! he beheld there a wonderfully beautiful young damsel of sixteen years of age who sat in the pavilion upon a carved bench and upon a cushion of cloth of gold, and who bent over a frame of embroidery, which she was busy weaving in threads of silver and gold. And the hair of that damsel was as black as ebony and her cheeks were like rose leaves for redness, and she wore a fillet of gold around her head, and she was clad in raiment of sky blue silk. And near by was a table spread with meats of divers sorts and likewise with several wines, both white and red. And all the goblets were of silver and all the pattens were of gold, and the table was spread with a napkin embroidered with threads of gold.

Percival enters the golden pavilion.

Now you are to know that the young lady who sat there was the Lady Yvette the Fair, the daughter of King Pecheur.

When Percival came to that pavilion the Lady Yvette looked up and beheld him with great astonishment, and she said to herself: "That must either be a madman or a foolish jester who comes hither clad all in armor of wattled willow twigs." So she said to him, "Sirrah, what dost thou here?" He said, "Lady, is this a church?" Upon that she was angered thinking that he had intended to make a jest and she said: "Begone, fool, for if my father, who is King Pecheur, cometh and findeth thee here, he will punish thee for this jest." But Percival replied, "Nay; I think he will not, lady."

Then the damsel looked at Percival more narrowly and she beheld how noble and beautiful was his countenance and she said to herself: "This is no fool nor a jester, but who he is or what he is I know not."

So she said to Percival, "Whence comest thou?" and he said, "From the mountains and the wilderness." Then he said: "Lady, when I left my mother she told me that whenever I saw good food and drink and was an-hungered, I was to take what I needed. Now I will do so in this case." Whereupon he sat him down to that table and fell to with great appetite.

Percival breaks bread in the golden pavilion.

Then when that damosel beheld what he did she laughed in great measure and clapped her hands together in sport. And she said: "If my father and brothers should return and find thee at this, they would assuredly punish thee very sorely, and thou couldst not make thyself right with them." Percival said, "Why would they do that, lady?" And she said: "Because that is their food and drink, and because my father is a king and my brethren are his sons." Then Percival said, "Certes, they would be uncourteous to begrudge food to a hungry man"; and thereat the damsel laughed again.

Now when Percival had eaten and drunk his fill, he arose from where he sat. And he beheld that the damsel wore a very beautiful ring of carved gold set with a pearl of great price. So he said to her: "Lady, my mother told me that if I beheld a jewel or treasure and desired it for my own, I was to take it if I could do so without offence to anyone. Now I prithee give me that ring upon thy finger, for I desire it a very great deal." At this the maiden regarded Percival very strangely, and she beheld that he was comely beyond any man whom she had ever seen and that his countenance was very noble and exalted and yet exceedingly mild and gentle. So she said to him, speaking very gently, "Why should I give thee my ring?" Whereunto he made reply: "Because thou art the most beautiful lady whom mine eyes ever beheld and I find that I love thee more than I had thought possible to love anyone."

At that the damosel smiled upon him and said, "What is thy name?" And he said, "It is Percival." She said, "That is a good name; who is thy father?" Whereunto he said: "That I cannot tell thee for my mother hath bidden me tell his name to no one yet whiles." She said, "I think he must be some very noble and worthy knight," and Percival said, "He is all that, for he too was a king."

Then the damsel said, "Thou mayst have my ring," and she gave it to him. And when Percival had placed it upon his finger he said: "My mother also told me that I should give freely of what is mine own, wherefore I do give thee this ring of mine in exchange for thine, and I do beseech thee to wear it until I have proved myself worthy of thy kindness. For I hope to win a very famous knighthood and great praise and renown, all of which, if I so accomplish my desires, shall be to thy great glory. I would fain come to thee another time in that wise instead of as I am at this present."

The damsel giveth Percival her ring.

At that the damsel said: "I know not what thou art or whence thou comest who should present thyself in such an extraordinary guise as thou art pleased to do, but, certes, thou must be of some very noble strain. Wherefore I do accept thee for my knight, and I believe that I shall some time have great glory through thee."

Then Percival said: "Lady, my mother said to me that if I met a damosel I was to salute her with all civility. Now have I thy leave to salute thee?" And she said, "Thou hast my leave." So Percival took her by the hand, and kissed her upon the lips (for that was the only manner in which he knew how to salute a woman) and, lo! her face grew all red like to fire. Thereupon Percival quitted that pavilion and mounted his horse and rode away. And it seemed to him that the world was assuredly a very beautiful and wonderful place for to live in.

Percival salutes the damsel of the golden pavilion.

Yet he knew not what the world was really like nor of what a sort it was nor how passing wide, else had he not been so certainly assured that he would win him credit therein, or that he could so easily find that young damsel again after he had thus parted from her.

That night Percival came to a part of the forest where were many huts of folk who made their living by gathering fagots. These people gave him harborage and shelter for the night, for they thought that he was some harmless madman who had wandered afar. And they told him many things he had never known before that time, so that it appeared to him that the world was still more wonderful than he had thought it to be at first.

So he abided there for the night, and when the next morning had come he arose and bathed himself and went his way; and, as he rode upon his poor starved horse, he brake his fast with the bread and cheese that his mother had put into his wallet, and he was very glad at heart and rejoiced exceedingly in the wonderfulness and the beauty of the world in which he found himself to be.

So Percival journeyed on into that forest, and he took such great delight in the beauty of the world in which he travelled that he was at times like to shed tears of pure happiness because of the joy he felt in being alive. For that forest path he travelled led beneath the trees of the woodland; and the trees at that time were in their early tender leaf, so that they appeared to shed showers of golden light everywhere down upon the earth. And the birds of the woodland sang in every bush and thicket; and, anon, the wood pigeon cooed so softly that the heart of Percival yearned with great passion for he knew not what.

How Percival travelled in the forest.

Thus he rode, somewhiles all in a maze of green, and somewhiles out thence into an open glade where the light was wide and bright; and other whiles he came to some forest stream where was a shallow pool of golden gravel, and where the water was so thin and clear that you might not tell where it ended and the pure air began. And therethrough he would drive his horse, splashing with great noise, whilst the little silvery fish would dart away upon all sides, hither and thither, like sparks of light before his coming.

So, because of the beauty of this forest land in its spring-time verdure and pleasantness, the heart of Percival was uplifted with so much joy and delight that he was like to weep for pure pleasure as aforesaid.

Now it chanced at that time that King Arthur and several of his court had come into that forest ahawking; but, the day being warm, the Queen had grown weary of the sport, so she had commanded her attendants to set up a pavilion for her whilst the King continued his hawking. And the pavilion was pitched in an open glade of the forest whereunto Percival came riding.

Then Percival perceived that pavilion set up among the trees, and likewise he saw that the pavilion was of rose colored silk. Also he perceived that not far from him was a young page very gayly and richly clad.

Now when the page beheld Percival and what a singular appearance he presented, he laughed beyond all measure, and Percival, not knowing that he laughed in mockery, laughed also and gave him a very cheerful greeting in return. Then Percival said to the page: "I prithee tell me, fair youth, whose is that pavilion yonder?" And the page said: "It belongeth to Queen Guinevere; for King Arthur is coming hither into the forest with his court."

Percival bespeaketh the Lady Guinevere's page.

At this Percival was very glad, for he deemed that he should now find Sir Lamorack. So he said: "I pray thee tell me, is Sir Lamorack of Gales with the court of the King, for I come hither seeking that good worthy knight?"

Then the page laughed a very great deal, and said: "Who art thou to seek Sir Lamorack? Art thou then a jester?" And Percival said, "What sort of a thing is a jester?" And the page said, "Certes, thou art a silly fool." And Percival said, "What is a fool?"

Upon this the page fell alaughing as though he would never stint his mirth so that Percival began to wax angry for he said to himself: "These people laugh too much and their mirth maketh me weary." So, without more ado, he descended from his horse with intent to enter the Queen's pavilion and to make inquiry there for Sir Lamorack.

Now when that page saw what Percival had a mind to do, he thrust in to prevent him, saying, "Thou shalt not go in!" Upon that Percival said, "Ha! shall I not so?"

And thereupon he smote the page such a buffet that the youth fell down without any motion, as though he had gone dead.

Then Percival straightway entered the Queen's pavilion.

And the first thing he saw was a very beautiful lady surrounded by a court of ladies. And the Queen was eating a mid-day repast whilst a page waited upon her for to serve her, bearing for her refreshment pure wine in a cup of entire gold. And he saw that a noble lord (and the lord was Sir Kay the Seneschal), stood in the midst of that beautiful rosy pavilion directing the Queen's repast; for Sir Kay of all the court had been left in charge of the Queen and her ladies.

Percival beholdeth Queen Guinevere.

Now when Percival entered the tent Sir Kay looked up, and when he perceived what sort of a figure was there, he frowned with great displeasure. "Ha!" he said, "what mad fool is this who cometh hitherward?"

Unto him Percival made reply: "Thou tall man, I prithee tell me, which of these ladies present here is the Queen?" Sir Kay said, "What wouldst thou have with the Queen?" To this Percival said: "I have come hither for to lay my case before King Arthur, and my case is this: I would fain obtain knighthood, and meseems that King Arthur may best help me thereunto."

When the Queen heard the words of Percival she laughed with great merriment. But Sir Kay was still very wroth, and he said: "Sirrah, thou certainly art some silly fool who hath come hither dressed all in armor of willow twigs and without arms or equipment of any sort save only a little Scots spear. Now this is the Queen's court and thou art not fit to be here."

Sir Kay chides Percival.

"Ha," said Percival, "it seems to me that thou art very foolish—thou tall man—to judge of me by my dress and equipment. For, even though I wear such poor apparel as this, yet I may easily be thy superior both in birth and station."

Then Sir Kay was exceedingly wroth and would have made a very bitter answer to Percival, but at that moment something of another sort befell. For, even as Percival ceased speaking, there suddenly entered the pavilion a certain very large and savage knight of an exceedingly terrible appearance; and his countenance was very furious with anger. And this knight was one Sir Boindegardus le Savage, who was held in terror by all that part of King Arthur's realm. For Sir Boindegardus was surnamed the Savage because he dwelt like a wild man in the forest in a lonely dismal castle of the woodland; and because that from this castle he would issue forth at times to rob and pillage the wayfarers who passed by along the forest byways. Many

Sir Boindegardus enters the Queen's pavilion.

knights had gone against Sir Boindegardus, with intent either to slay him or else to make him prisoner; but some of these knights he had overcome, and from others he had escaped, so that he was as yet free to work his evil will as he chose.

So now this savage knight entered that pavilion with his helmet upon his hip and his shield upon his shoulder, and all those ladies who were there were terrified at his coming, for they wist that he came in anger with intent of mischief.

As for Sir Kay (he being clad only in a silken tunic of green color and with scarlet hosen and velvet shoes, fit for the court of a lady) he was afraid, and he wist not how to bear himself in the presence of Sir Boindegardus. Then Sir Boindegardus said, "Where is King Arthur?" And Sir Kay made no reply because of fear. Then one of the Queen's damsels said, "He is hawking out beyond here in the outskirts of the forest." Then Sir Boindegardus said: "I am sorry for that, for I had thought to find him here at this time and to show challenge to him and his entire court, for I fear no one of them. But, as King Arthur is not here, I may, at least, affront his Queen."

Sir Boindegardus affronts the Queen.

With that he smote the elbow of the page who held the goblet for the Queen, and the wine was splashed all in the Queen's face and over her stomacher.

Thereupon the Queen shrieked with terror, and one of her maidens ran to her aid and others came with napkins and wiped her face and her apparel and gave her words of cheer.

Then Sir Kay found courage to say: "Ha! thou art a churlish knight to so affront a lady."

With that Sir Boindegardus turned very fiercely upon him and said: "And thou likest not my behavior, thou mayst follow me hence into a meadow a little distance from this to the eastward where thou mayst avenge that affront upon my person if thou art minded to do so."

Then Sir Kay knew not what to reply for he wist that Sir Boindegardus was a very strong and terrible knight. Wherefore he said, "Thou seest that I am altogether without arms or armor." Upon that Sir Boindegardus laughed in great scorn, and therewith seized the golden goblet from the hands of the page and went out from the pavilion, and mounting his horse rode away bearing that precious chalice with him.

Then the Queen fell aweeping very sorely from fright and shame, and when young Percival beheld her tears, he could not abide the sight thereof. So he cried out

Percival berates Sir Kay.

aloud against Sir Kay, saying: "Thou tall man! that was very ill done of thee; for, certes, with or without armor thou shouldst have taken the quarrel of this lady upon thee. For my mother told me I should take upon me the defence of all such as needed defence, but she did not say that I was to wait for arms or armor to aid me to do what was right. Now, therefore, though I know little of arms or of knighthood, I will take this quarrel upon myself and will do what I may to avenge this lady's affront, if I have her leave to do so."

And Queen Guinevere said: "Thou hast my leave, since Sir Kay does not choose to assume my quarrel."

Now there was a certain very beautiful young damsel of the court of the Queen hight Yelande, surnamed the "Dumb Maiden," because she would hold no commerce with any knight of the court. For in all the year she had been at the court of the King, she had spoken no word to any man, nor had she smiled upon any. This damsel perceiving how comely and noble was the countenance of Percival, came to him and took him by the hand and smiled upon him very kindly. And she said to him: "Fair youth, thou hast a large and noble heart, and I feel very well assured that thou art of a sort altogether different from what thine appearance would lead one to suppose. Now I do affirm that if thou art able to carry this adventure through with thy life, thou wilt some time become one of the greatest knights in all of the world. For never did I hear tell of one who, without arm or armor, would take up a quarrel with a well-approved knight clad in full array. But indeed thy heart is as brave as thy face is comely, and I believe that thou art as noble as thy speech and manner is gentle."

The damsel praises Percival.

Then Sir Kay was very angry with that damsel and he said: "Truly, thou art ill taught to remain for all this year in the court of King Arthur amid the perfect flower of chivalry and yet not to have given to one of those noble and honorable knights a single word or a smile such as thou hast bestowed upon this boor." So saying, he lifted his hand and smote that damsel a box on the ear so that she screamed out aloud with pain and terror.

Sir Kay strikes the damsel.

Upon this Percival came very close to Sir Kay and he said: "Thou discourteous tall man; now I tell thee, except that there are so many ladies here present, and one of these a Queen, I would have to do with thee in such a manner as I do not believe would be at all to thy liking. Now, first of all I shall follow yonder uncivil knight and endeavor to avenge this noble Queen for the affront he hath put upon her, and when I have done with him, then will I hope for the time to come in which I shall have to do with thee for laying hands upon this beautiful young lady who was so kind to me just now. For, in the fulness of time, I will repay the foul blow thou gavest her, and that twenty-fold."

Thereupon Percival straightway went out from that pavilion and mounted upon his sorry horse and rode away in the direction that Sir Boindegardus had taken with the golden goblet.

Now after a long time, he came to another level meadow of grass, and there he beheld Sir Boindegardus riding before him in great state with the golden goblet hanging to the horn of his saddle. And Sir Boindegardus wore his helmet and carried his spear in his right hand and his shield upon his other arm, and he was in all ways prepared for an encounter at arms. And when he perceived Percival come riding out of the forest in pursuit of him, he drew rein and turned. And when Percival had come nigh enough Sir Boindegardus said, "Whence comest thou, fool?" Percival replied, "I come from Queen Guinevere, her pavilion." Then Sir Boindegardus said, "Does that knight who was there follow me hitherward?" Unto which Percival made reply: "Nay, but I have followed thee with intent to punish thee for the affront which thou didst put upon Queen Guinevere."

Percival follows Sir Boindegardus.

Then Sir Boindegardus was very wroth and he said: "Thou fool; I have a very good intention for to slay thee." Therewith he raised his spear and smote Percival with it upon the back of the neck so terrible a blow that he was flung violently down from off his horse. Upon this Percival was so angry that the sky all became like scarlet before his eyes. Wherefore, when he had recovered from the blow he ran unto Sir Boindegardus and catched the spear in his hands and wrestled with such terrible strength that he plucked it away from Sir Boindegardus. And having thus made himself master of that spear, he brake it across his knee and flung it away.

Then Sir Boindegardus was in furious rage, wherefore he drew his bright, shining sword with intent to slay Percival. But when Percival saw what he would be at, he catched up his javelin and, running to a little distance, he turned and threw it at Sir Boindegardus with so cunning an aim that the point of the javelin entered the ocularium of the helmet of Sir Boindegardus and pierced through the eye and the brain and came out of the back of the head. Then Sir Boindegardus pitched down from off his horse all into a heap upon the ground, and Percival ran to him and stooped over him and perceived that he was dead. Then Percival said: "Well, it would seem that I have put an end to a terribly discourteous knight to ladies."

Percival slays Sir Boindegardus.

Now a little after Percival had quitted the pavilion of Queen Guinevere, King Arthur and eleven noble knights of the court returned thither from hawking, and amongst those knights was Sir Launcelot of the Lake and Sir Lamorack of Gales.

King Arthur sends Sir Launcelot and Sir Lamorack in quest of Percival.

Then those who were of the Queen's court told King Arthur what had befallen, and thereat the King felt great displeasure toward Sir Kay. And he said: "Kay, not only hast thou been very discourteous in not assuming this quarrel of the Queen's, but I believe that thou, a well-approved knight, hast in thy fear of Sir Boindegardus been the cause of sending this youth upon an adventure in which he will be subject to such great danger that it may very well be that he shall hardly escape with his life. Now I will that two of you knights shall follow after that youth for to rescue him if it be not too late; and those two shall be Sir Launcelot of the Lake and Sir Lamorack of Gales. So make all haste, Messires, lest some misfortune shall befall this brave, innocent madman."

Thereupon those two knights mounted straightway upon their horses and rode away in that direction whither Percival had gone.

JVSTISSIMVS·REX·

ir Percival & Sir Lamorack ride together.

CHAPTER SECOND

How Sir Percival Was Made Knight by King Arthur; How He Rode Forth With Sir Lamorack and How He Left Sir Lamorack in Quest of Adventure Upon His Own Account; Likewise How a Great Knight Taught Him Craft in Arms.

SO AFTER A CONSIDERABLE TIME THEY CAME TO THAT MEADOW-LAND where Percival had found Sir Boindegardus.

But when they came to that place they perceived a very strange sight. For they beheld one clad all in armor of wattled willow-twigs and that one dragged the body of an armed knight hither and thither upon the ground. So they two rode up to where that affair was toward, and when they had come nigh enough, Sir Launcelot said: "Ha, fair youth, thou art doing a very strange thing. What art thou about?"

How the two knights find Percival in the meadow.

To him Percival said: "Sir, I would get those plates of armor off this knight, and I know not how to do it!"

Then Sir Launcelot laughed, and he said: "Let be for a little while, and I will show thee how to get the plates of armor off." And he said: "How came this knight by his death."

Percival said: "Sir, this knight hath greatly insulted Queen Guinevere (that beautiful lady), and when I followed him thither with intent to take her quarrel upon me, he struck me with his spear. And when I took his spear away from him, and brake it across my knee, he drew his sword and would have slain me, only that I slew him instead."

Then Sir Launcelot was filled with amazement, and he said: "Is not that knight Sir Boindegardus?" And Percival said: "Ay." Then Sir Launcelot said: "Fair youth, know that thou hast slain one of the strongest and most terrible knights in all the world. In this thou hast done a great service unto King Arthur, so if thou wilt come with us to the court of King Arthur, he will doubtless reward thee very bountifully for what thou hast done."

Then Percival looked up into the faces of Sir Launcelot and Sir Lamorack and he perceived that they were very noble. So he smiled upon them and said: "Messires, I pray you tell me who you are and what is your degree." Then Sir Launcelot smiled in return and said: "I am called Sir Launcelot of the Lake, and this, my companion, is called Sir Lamorack of Gales."

Then Percival wist that he stood in the presence of his own brother, and he looked into the countenance of Sir Lamorack and marvelled how noble and exalted it was. And he felt a great passion of love for Sir Lamorack, and a great joy in that love. But he did not tell Sir Lamorack who he was, for he had learned several things since he had come out into the world, and one was that he must not be too hasty in such things. So he said to himself: "I will not as yet tell my brother who I am, lest he shall be ashamed of me. But first I shall win me such credit that he shall not be ashamed of me, and then I will acknowledge to him who I am."

Percival knoweth Sir Lamorack.

Then Sir Launcelot said: "I prithee, fair youth, tell me what is thy name since I have told thee ours, for I find that I have great love for thee so that I would fain know who thou art."

Then Percival said: "My name is Percival."

At that Sir Lamorack cried out: "I knew one whose name was Percival, and he was mine own brother. And if he be alive he must now be just such a youth as thou art."

Then Percival's heart yearned toward Sir Lamorack, so that he looked up and smiled with great love into his face; yet he would not acknowledge to Sir Lamorack who he was, but held his peace for that while.

Then Sir Launcelot said: "Now, fair youth, we will show you how to take the armor off of this dead knight, and after we have done that, we shall take you back to King Arthur, so that he may reward you for what you have done in the way that he may deem best."

So with that Sir Launcelot and Sir Lamorack dismounted from their horses, and they went to that dead knight and unlaced his armor and removed the armor from his body. And when they had done that they aided Percival to remove the armor of wattled osier twigs and they cased him in the armor of Sir Boindegardus; and thereafter they all three rode back to that pavilion where the King and Queen were holding court.

The two knights arm Percival.

But when King Arthur heard that Sir Boindegardus was dead he was filled with great joy; and when he heard how it was that Percival had slain him, he was amazed beyond measure; and he said to Percival: "Surely God is with thee, fair youth, to help thee to perform such a worthy feat of arms as this that thou hast done, for no knight yet hath been able to perform that service." Then he said: "Tell me what it is that thou hast most desire to have, and if it is in my power to give it to thee thou shalt have it."

Then Percival kneeled down before King Arthur, and he said: "Lord, that which I most desire of all things else is to be made knight. So if it is in thy power to do so, I pray thee to make me a knight-royal with thine own hands."

Then King Arthur smiled upon Percival very kindly, and he said: "Percival, it shall be as thou dost desire, and to-morrow I will make thee a knight."

So that night Percival watched his armor in the chapel of a hermit of the forest, and the armor that he watched was the armor that had belonged to Sir Boindegardus (for Percival besought King Arthur that he might wear that armor for his own because it was what he himself had won in battle). And when the next morning had come, Sir Launcelot and Sir Lamorack brought Percival before King Arthur, and King Arthur made him a knight.

King Arthur makes Percival a knight-royal.

After that Sir Percival besought King Arthur that he would give him leave to depart from court so that he might do some worthy deed of arms that might win him worship; and King Arthur gave him that leave he asked for.

Then Sir Percival went to where Sir Kay was sitting, and he said: "Messire, I have not forgot that blow you gave that fair damsel yesterday when she spake so kindly to me. As yet I am too young a knight to handle you; but by and by the time will come when I shall return and repay you that blow tenfold and twentyfold what you gave!" And at these words Sir Kay was in no wise pleased, for he wist that Sir Percival would one day become a very strong and worthy knight.

Sir Percival threatens Sir Kay.

Now all this while the heart of Sir Lamorack yearned very greatly toward Sir Percival, though Sir Lamorack knew not why that should be; so when Sir Percival had obtained permission to go errant, Sir Lamorack asked King Arthur for leave to ride forth so as to be with him; and King Arthur gave Sir Lamorack that leave.

Thus it befell that Sir Lamorack and Sir Percival rode forth together very lovingly and cheerfully. And as they rode upon their way Sir Lamorack told Sir Percival many things concerning the circumstances of knighthood, and to all that he said Sir Percival gave great heed. But Sir Lamorack knew not that he was riding with his own brother or that it was his own brother to whom he was teaching the mysteries of chivalry,

Sir Percival and Sir Lamorack ride together.

and Sir Percival told him nothing thereof. But ever in his heart Sir Percival said to himself: "If God will give me enough of His grace, I will some day do full credit unto thy teaching, O my brother!"

Now, after Sir Percival and Sir Lamorack had travelled a great way, they came at last out of that forest and to an open country where was a well-tilled land and a wide, smooth river flowing down a level plain.

And in the centre of that plain was a town of considerable size, and a very large castle with several tall towers and many roofs and chimneys that stood overlooking the town.

That time they came thitherward the day was declining toward its close, so that all the sky toward the westward shone, like, as it were, to a flame of gold—exceedingly beautiful. And the highway upon which they entered was very broad and smooth, like to a floor for smoothness. And there were all sorts of folk passing along that highway; some afoot and some ahorseback. Also there was a river path beside the river where the horses dragged deep-laden barges down to the town and thence again; and these barges were all painted in bright colors, and the horses were bedight with gay harness and hung with tinkling bells.

All these things Sir Percival beheld with wonder for he had never seen their like before; wherefore he cried out with amazement, saying: "Saints of Glory! How great and wonderful is the world!"

Then Sir Lamorack looked upon him and smiled with great loving-kindness; and he said: "Ha, Percival! This is so small a part of the world that it is but a patch upon it."

Unto this Sir Percival made reply: "Dear Messire, I am so glad that I have come forth into the world that I am hardly able to know whether I am in a vision or am awake."

So, after a considerable while, they came to that town with its castle, and these stood close beside the river—and the town and the castle were hight Cardennan. And the town was of great consideration, being very well famed for its dyed woollen fabrics.

So Sir Percival and Sir Lamorack entered the town. And when Sir Percival beheld all the people in the streets, coming and going upon their businesses; and when he beheld all the gay colors and apparels of fine fabrics that the people wore; and when he beheld the many booths filled with rich wares of divers sorts, he wist not what to think for the wonder that possessed him; wherefore he cried out aloud, as with great passion: "What marvel do I behold! I knew not that a city could be so great as this."

Sir Percival and Sir Lamorack come to Cardennan.

And again Sir Lamorack smiled very kindly upon him and said: "Sayst thou so? Now I tell thee that when one compares this place with Camelot (which is the King's city) it is as a star compared to the full moon in her glory." And at that Sir Percival knew not what to think for wonder.

So they went up the street of the town until they came to the castle of Cardennan and there requested admission. And when the name and the estate of Sir Lamorack were declared, the porter opened the gate with great joy and they entered. Then, by and by, the lord and the lady of the castle came down from a carved wooden gallery and bade them welcome by word of mouth. And after that sundry attendants immediately appeared and assisted Sir Percival and Sir Lamorack to dismount and took their horses to the stable, and sundry other attendants conducted them to certain apartments where they were eased of their armor and bathed in baths of tepid water and given soft raiment for to wear. After that the lord and the lady entertained them with a great feast, where harpers and singers made music, and where certain actors acted a mystery before them.

How the two knights were welcomed by the lord and lady of the castle.

So these two knights and the lord and the lady of the castle ate together and discoursed very pleasantly for a while; but, when the evening was pretty well gone, Sir Lamorack bade good-night, and he and Sir Percival were conducted to a certain very noble apartment where beds of down, spread with flame-colored cloth, had been prepared for their repose.

Thus ended that day which was the first day of the knighthood of Sir Percival of Gales.

Now though Sir Percival had travelled very contentedly with Sir Lamorack for all that while, yet he had determined in his own mind that, as soon as possible, he would leave Sir Lamorack and depart upon his own quest. For he said to himself: "Lo! I am a very green knight as yet, and haply my brother may grow weary of my company and cease to love me. So I will leave him ere he have the chance to tire of me, and I will seek knighthood for myself. After that, if God wills it that I shall win worthy knighthood, then my brother will be glad enough to acknowledge me as his father's son."

So when the next morning had come, Sir Percival arose very softly all in the dawning, and he put on his armor without disturbing Sir Lamorack. Then he stooped and looked into Sir Lamorack's face and beheld that his brother was still enfolded in a deep sleep as in a soft mantle. And as Sir Percival gazed upon Sir Lamorack thus asleep, he loved him with such ardor that he could hardly bear the strength of his love. But he said to himself: "Sleep on, my brother, whilst I go away and leave thee. But when I have earned me great glory, then will I return unto thee and will lay all that I have achieved at thy feet, so that thou shalt be very glad to acknowledge me." So saying to himself, he went away from that place very softly, and Sir Lamorack slept so deeply that he wist not that Sir Percival was gone.

Thereafter Sir Percival went to the courtyard of the castle and he bade certain attendants to prepare his horse for him, and they did so. And he bade certain others for to arm him, and they did so. Thereupon he mounted his horse and left that castle and rode away.

Sir Percival leaves Sir Lamorack.

Now after Sir Percival had left Sir Lamorack still sleeping in the castle as aforetold, he journeyed upon his way, taking great pleasure in all things that he beheld. So he travelled all that morning, and the day was very bright and warm, so that by and by he was an-hungered and athirst. So after a while he came to a certain road that appeared to him to be good for his purpose, so he took that way in great hopes that some adventure would befall him, or else that he would find food and drink.

Then after a while he heard a bell ringing, and after he had followed that bell for some distance, he came to where was the dwelling-place of a hermit and where was a small chapel by the wayside. And Sir Percival beheld that the hermit, who was an old man with a long white beard, rang the bell of that chapel.

So Sir Percival thought that here he might find food and drink; and so he rode forward to where the hermit was ringing the bell. But when Sir Percival came still more nigh he perceived that behind the chapel and to one side there was a very noble knight upon horseback; and he perceived that the knight was clad all in white armor and that his horse (which was white as milk and of very noble strength and proportions) was furnished altogether with furniture of white.

Sir Percival meets his fate at the forest chapel.

This knight, when he perceived Sir Percival, immediately rode up to meet him and saluted Sir Percival very courteously. And the knight said: "Sir, will you not joust a fall with me ere you break your fast? For this is a very fair and level field of green grass and well fitted for such a friendly trial at arms if you have the time for it."

Unto this Sir Percival said: "Messire, I will gladly try a fall with you, though I must tell you that I am a very young green knight, having been knighted only yesterday by King Arthur himself. But though I am unskilled in arms, yet it will pleasure me a great deal to accept so gentle and courteous a challenge as that which you give me."

So with that each knight turned his horse and each took such stand as appeared to him to be best. And when they were in all ways prepared, they drave their horses together with great speed, the one against the other, meeting one another, shield against spear, in the very midst of the course. In that encounter (which was the first that he ever ran) Sir Percival bare himself very well and with great knightliness of endeavor; for he broke his spear upon the white knight into small pieces. But the spear of the white knight held so that Sir Percival was lifted out of his saddle and over the crupper of his horse, and fell upon the ground with great violence and a cloud of dust.

Sir Percival is overthrown by the white knight.

Then the white knight returned from his course and came up to where Sir Percival was. And he inquired of him very courteously: "Sir, art thou hurt?" Thereunto Sir Percival replied: "Nay, sir! I am not hurt, only somewhat shaken by my fall.'"

Then the white knight dismounted from his horse and came to where Sir Percival was. And he lifted up the umbril of his helmet, and Sir Percival perceived that that white knight was Sir Launcelot of the Lake.

And Sir Launcelot said: "Percival, I well knew who you were from the first, but I thought I would see of what mettle you are, and I have found that you are of very good mettle indeed. But you are to know that it is impossible for a young knight such as you, who knoweth naught of the use of knightly weapons, to have to do with a knight well-seasoned in arms as I am, and to have any hope of success in such an encounter. Wherefore you need to be taught the craft of using your weapons perfectly."

To this Sir Percival said: "Messire, tell me, how may I hope to acquire craft at arms such as may serve me in such a stead as this?"

Sir Launcelot said: "I myself will teach thee, imparting to thee such skill as I have at my command. Less than half a day's journey to the southward of this is my castle of Joyous Gard. Thither I was upon my way when I met thee here. Now thou shalt go with me unto Joyous Gard, and there thou shalt abide until thou art in all ways taught the use of arms so that thou mayst uphold that knighthood which I believe God hath endowed thee withal."

So after that Sir Launcelot and Sir Percival went to the dwelling-place of the hermit, and the hermit fed them with the best of that simple fare which he had at his command.

After that, they mounted horse again and rode away to Joyous Gard, and there Sir Percival abided for a year, training himself in all wise so as to prepare himself to uphold that knighthood which in him became so famous. For, during that year Sir Launcelot was his teacher in the art of arms. Likewise he instructed him in all the civilities and the customs of chivalry, so it befell that ere Sir Percival came forth from Joyous

How Sir Percival dwelt at Joyous Gard.

Gard again he was well acquainted with all the ways in which he should comport himself at any time, whether in field or in court.

So when Sir Percival came forth again from Joyous Gard, there was no knight, unless it was Sir Launcelot himself, who could surpass him in skill at arms; nay, not even his own brother, Sir Lamorack; nor was there anybody, even if one were Sir Gawaine or Sir Geraint, who surpassed him in civility of courtliness or nobility of demeanor.

And now I shall tell you of the great adventure that befell Sir Percival after Sir Launcelot had thus taught him at Joyous Gard.

JVSTISSIMVS·REX·

Sir Percival overcometh ye Enchantress Vivien.

CHAPTER THIRD

How Sir Percival Met Two Strange People in the Forest, and How He Succored a Knight Who Was in Very Great Sorrow and Dole.

Now after Sir Percival had left Joyous Gard he rode for several days seeking adventure but meeting none.

Then one day he came to a very dark and wonderful forest which appeared to be so silent and lonely and yet so full of beauty that Sir Percival bethought him that this must surely be some forest of magic. So he entered into that forest with intent to discover if he might find any worthy adventure therein.

(And that forest was a forest of magic; for you are to know that it was the Forest of Arroy, sometimes called the Forest of Adventure, which was several times spoken of in the book of King Arthur. For no one ever entered into that forest but some singular adventure befell him.)

Sir Percival enters the Forest of Arroy.

So Sir Percival rode through this wonderful woodland for a long time very greatly wondering, for everywhere about him was perfect silence, with not so much as a single note of a bird of the woodlands to lighten that stillness. Now, as Sir Percival rode through that silence, he presently became aware of the sound of voices talking together, and shortly thereafter he perceived a knight with a lady riding amid the thin trees that grew there. And the knight rode upon a great white horse, and the lady rode upon a red roan palfrey.

These, when they beheld Sir Percival, waited for him, and as Sir Percival drew nigh to them he perceived that they were of a very singular appearance. For both of them were clad altogether in green, and both of them wore about their necks very wonderful collars of wrought gold inset with opal stones and emeralds. And the face of each was like clear wax for whiteness; and the eyes of each were very bright, like jewels set in ivory. And these two neither laughed nor frowned, but only smiled continually. And that knight whom Sir Percival beheld was Sir Pellias, and the lady was the Lady Nymue of the Lake.

Sir Percival meets two strange people.

Now when Sir Percival beheld these two, he wist that they were fay, wherefore he dismounted very quickly, and kneeled down upon the ground and set his palms together. Then the Lady of the Lake smiled very kindly upon Sir Percival, and she said: "Sir Percival, arise, and tell me what you do in these parts?"

Then Sir Percival arose and he stood before that knight and lady, and he said: "Lady, I wist not how you know who I am, but I believe you are fay and know many things. Touching my purpose in coming here, it is that I am in search of adventure. So if you know of any that I may undertake for your sake, I pray you to tell me of it."

The lady said: "If so be thy desire is of that sort, I may, perchance be able to bring thee unto an adventure that is worthy for any knight to undertake. Go a little distance from this upon the way thou art following and by and by thou wilt behold a bird whose feathers shall shine like to gold for brightness. Follow that bird and it will bring thee to a place where thou shalt find a knight in sore need of thy aid."

And Percival said: "I will do as thou dost advise."

Then the lady said: "Wait a little, I have something for thee." Therewith she took from her neck a small golden amulet pendant from a silken cord very fine and thin. And she said: "Wear this for it will protect thee from all evil enchantments." Therewith saying, she hung the amulet about the neck of Sir Percival, and Sir Percival gave her thanks beyond measure for it.

The Lady of the Lake giveth Sir Percival a charm.

Then the knight and the lady saluted him and he saluted them, and they each went their separate ways.

So Sir Percival travelled that path for some distance as the lady had advised him to do, and by and by he beheld the bird of which she had spoken. And he saw that the plumage of the bird glistered as though it was of gold so that he marvelled at it. And as he drew nigh the bird flew a little distance down the path and then lit upon the ground and he followed it. And when he had come nigh to it again it flew a distance farther and still he followed it. So it flew and he followed for a very great way until by and by the forest grew thin and Sir Percival beheld that there was an open country lying beyond the skirts thereof. And when the bird had brought him thus far it suddenly flew back into the forest again whence it had come, chirping very keenly and shrilly as it flew.

How Percival followed the golden bird.

So Percival came out of the forest into the open country, the like of which he had never before seen, for it was a very desolate barren waste of land. And in the midst of this desolate plain there stood a castle of a very wonderful appearance; for in some parts it

Sir Percival beholds a wonderful castle.

was the color of ultramarine and in other parts it was of crimson; and the ultramarine and the crimson were embellished with very extraordinary devices painted in gold. So because of all those extraordinary colors, that castle shone like a bright rainbow against the sky, wherefore Sir Percival sat his horse for some while and marvelled very greatly thereat.

Then, by and by Sir Percival perceived that the road that led to the castle crossed a bridge of stone, and when he looked at the bridge he saw that midway upon it was a pillar of stone and that a knight clad all in full armor stood chained with iron chains to that stone pillar, and at that sight Sir Percival was very greatly astonished. So he rode very rapidly along that way and so to the bridge and upon the bridge to where the knight was. And when Sir Percival came thus upon the bridge he perceived that the knight who was bound with chains was very noble and haughty of appearance, but that he seemed to be in great pain and suffering because of his being thus bound to that pillar. For the captive knight made continual moan so that it moved the heart of Sir Percival to hear him.

So Sir Percival said: "Sir Knight, this is a sorrowful condition thou art in." And the knight said: "Yea, and I am sorrowful; for I have stood here now for three days and I am in great torment of mind and body."

Sir Percival said, "Maybe I can aid thee," and thereupon he got down from off his horse's back and approached the knight. And he drew his sword so that it flashed in the sun very brightly.

Upon this the knight said: "Messire, what would you be at?" And Sir Percival said: "I would cut the chains that bind thee."

To this the knight said: "How could you do that? For who could cut through chains of iron such as these?"

But Sir Percival said: "I will try what I may do."

Thereupon he lifted up his sword and smote so terribly powerful a blow that the like of it had hardly ever been seen before. For that blow cut through the iron chains and smote the hauberk of the knight so smart a buffet that he fell down to the ground altogether deprived of breath.

Sir Percival sets free the captive knight.

But when Sir Percival saw the knight fall down in that wise, he cried out: "Woe is me! Have I slain this good, gentle knight when I would but do him service?" Thereupon he lifted the knight up upon his knee and eased the armor about his throat. But the knight was not dead, and by and by the breath came back to him again, and he said: "By my faith, that was the most wonderful stroke that ever I beheld any man strike in all of my life."

Thereafter, when the knight had sufficiently recovered, Sir Percival helped him to stand upon his feet; and when he stood thus his strength presently came back to him again in great measure.

And the knight was athirst and craved very vehemently to drink. So Sir Percival helped him to descend a narrow path that led to a stream of water that flowed beneath the bridge; and there the knight stooped and slaked his thirst. And when he had drunk his fill, his strength came altogether back to him again, and he said: "Messire, I have to give thee all thanks that it is possible for me to do, for hadst thou not come unto mine aid, I would else have perished very miserably and at no very distant time from this."

Then Sir Percival said: "I beseech you, Messire, to tell me how you came into that sad plight in which I found you."

The knight telleth his story.

To this the knight said: "I will tell you; it was thus: Two days ago I came thitherward and past yonder castle, and with me were two excellent esquires—for I am a knight of royal blood. Now as we went past that castle there came forth a lady clad all in red and so exceedingly beautiful that she entirely enchanted my heart. And with this lady there came a number of esquires and pages, all of them very beautiful of face, and all clad, as she was, in red. Now when this lady had come nigh to me she spoke me very fair and tempted me with kind words so that I thought I had never fallen upon anyone so courteous as she. But when she had come real close to me, she smote me of a sudden across the shoulders with an ebony staff that she carried in her hand, and at the same time she cried out certain words that I remember not. For immediately a great darkness like to a deep swoon fell upon me and I knew nothing. And when I awakened from that swoon lo! I found myself here, chained fast to this stone pillar. And hadst thou not come hither I would else certainly have died in my torment. And as to what hath become of my esquires, I know not; but as for that lady, methinks she can be none other than a certain enchantress, hight Vivien, who hath wrought such powerful spells upon Merlin as to have removed him from the eyes of all mankind."

Unto all this Sir Percival listened in great wonder, and when the knight had ended his tale he said: "What is thy name?" And the knight said: "My name is Percydes and I am the son of King Pecheur—so called because he is the king of all the fisherfolk who dwell upon the West coast. And now I prithee tell me also thy name and condition, for I find I love thee a very great deal."

And Sir Percival said: "My name is Percival, but I may not at this present tell thee my condition and of whom I am born; for that I must keep secret until I have won me good credit as a knight. But now I have somewhat to do, and that is to deal with this lady Vivien as she shall deserve."

Upon that Sir Percydes cried out: "Go not near to that sorceress, else she will do some great harm to thee with her potent spells as she did to me."

But Sir Percival said: "I have no fear of her."

So Sir Percival arose and crossed the bridge and went toward that wonderful enchanted castle; and Sir Percydes would have gone with him, but Sir Percival said: "Stay where thou art." And so Sir Percydes stayed and Sir Percival went forward alone.

Now as he drew nigh to the castle the gate thereof was opened, and there came forth thence an extraordinarily beautiful lady surrounded by a court of esquires and pages all very beautiful of countenance. And this lady and all of her court were clad in red so that they shone like to several flames of fire. And the lady's hair was as red as gold, and she wore gold ornaments about her neck so that she glistered exceedingly and was very wonderful to behold. And her eyebrows were very black and fine and were joined in the middle like two fine lines drawn together with a pencil, and her eyes were narrow and black, shining like those of a snake.

The Lady Vivien cometh forth to Sir Percival.

Then when Sir Percival beheld this lady how singularly beautiful she was he was altogether enchanted so that he could not forbear to approach her. And, lo! she stood still and smiled upon him so that his heart stirred within his bosom like as though it pulled at the strings that held it. Then she said to Sir Percival, speaking in a very sweet and gentle voice: "Sir Knight, thou art welcome to this place. It would pleasure us very greatly if thou wouldst consider this castle as though it were thine own and would abide within it with me for a while." Therewith speaking she smiled again upon Sir Percival more cunningly than before and reached out her hand toward him.

Then Sir Percival came toward her with intent to take her hand, she smiling upon him all the while so that he could not do otherwise than as she willed.

Now in the other hand this lady held an ebony staff of about an ell in length, and when Sir Percival had come close enough to her, she lifted this staff of a sudden and smote him with it very violently across the shoulders, crying out at the same time, in a voice terribly piercing and shrill: "Be thou a stone!"

Then that charm that the Lady of the Lake had hung around the neck of Sir Percival stood him in good stead, for, excepting for it, he would that instant have been transformed into a stone. But the charm of the sorceress did not work upon him, being prevented by the greater charm of that golden amulet.

But Sir Percival knew very well what the sorceress Vivien had intended to do to him, and he was filled with a great rage of indignation against her because she had meant to transform him into a stone. Therefore he cried out with a loud voice and seized the enchantress by her long golden hair, and drew her so violently forward that she fell down upon her knees. Then he drew his shining sword with intent to sever her long neck, so slender and white like alabaster. But the lady shrieked with great vehemence of terror and besought him mercy. And at that Sir Percival's heart grew soft for pity, for he bethought him that she was a woman and he beheld how smooth and beautiful was her neck, and how her skin was like white satin for smoothness. So when he heard her voice—the voice of a woman beseeching mercy—his heart grew soft, and he could not find strength within him to strike that neck apart with his sword.

Sir Percival draweth sword upon the Lady Vivien.

So he bade her to arise—though he still held her by the hair (all warm, it was, and as soft as silk and very fragrant) and the lady stood up, trembling before him.

Then Sir Percival said to her: "If thou wouldst have thy life I command thee to transform back to their own shape all those people whom thou hast bewitched as thou wouldst have bewitched me."

Then the lady said: "It shall be done." Whereupon she smote her hands very violently together crying out: "All ye who have lost your proper shapes, return thereunto."

Then, lo! upon the instant, a great multitude of round stones that lay scattered about became quick, like to eggs; and they moved and stirred as the life entered into them. And they melted away and, behold! there arose up a great many knights and esquires and several ladies to the number of four score and eight in all. And certain other stones became quickened in like manner, and as Percival looked, lo! there rose up the horses of those people, all caparisoned as though for travel.

The Lady Vivien undoes her enchantment.

Now when those people who had been thus bewitched beheld the Lady Vivien, how Sir Percival held her by the hair of her head, they made great outcry against her for vengeance, saying: "Slay her! Slay her!" And therewith several made at her as though to do as they said and to slay her. But Percival waved his sword before her and said: "Not so! Not so! For this lady is my prisoner and ye shall not harm her unless ye come at her through me."

Thereat they fell silent in a little while, and when he had thus stilled them, he turned to the Lady Vivien and said: "This is my command that I lay upon thee: that thou shalt go into the court of King Arthur and shalt confess thyself to him and that thou shalt fulfil whatever penance he may lay upon thee to perform because of thy transgressions. Now wilt thou do this for to save thy life?"

And the Lady Vivien made reply: "All shall be done according to thy command."

Therewith Sir Percival released his hold upon her and she was free.

Then, finding herself to be thus free, she stepped back a pace or two and looked into Sir Percival his face, and she laughed. And she said: "Thou fool, didst thou think that I would do so mad a thing as that which thou hast made me promise? For what mercy could I expect at the hands of King Arthur seeing that it was I who destroyed the Enchanter Merlin, who was the right adviser of King Arthur! Go to King Arthur thyself and deliver to him thine own messages."

So saying, in an instant, she vanished from the sight of all those who stood there. And with her vanished that castle of crimson and ultramarine and gold—and nothing was left but the bare rocks and the barren plain.

The Lady Vivien escapes.

Then when those who were there recovered from their astonishment, upon beholding that great castle so suddenly disappear, they turned to Sir Percival and gave him worship and thanks without measure, saying to him: "What shall we do in return for saving us from the enchantment of this sorceress?"

And Percival said: "Ye shall do this: ye shall go to the court of King Arthur and tell him how that young knight, Percival, whom he made a knight a year ago, hath liberated you from the enchantment of this sorceress. And you shall seek out Sir Kay and shall say to him that, by and by, I shall return and repay him in full measure, twenty times over, that blow which he gave to the damosel Yelande, the Dumb Maiden because of her kindness to me."

So said Sir Percival, and they said: "It shall be done as thou dost ordain."

Then Sir Percydes said: "Wilt thou not come to my castle and rest thyself there for the night? For thou must be aweary with all thy toil." And Sir Percival said, "I will go with thee." So Sir Percydes and Sir Percival rode away together to the castle of Sir Percydes.

Sir Percydes knoweth the ring that Percival wears.

Now while Sir Percival and Sir Percydes sat at supper in the castle of Sir Percydes, Sir Percival chanced to lay his hand in love upon the sleeve of Sir Percydes's arm, and that moment Sir Percydes saw the ring upon Sir Percival's finger which the young damosel of the pavilion had given unto him in exchange for his ring. When Sir Percydes saw that ring he cried out in great astonishment, "Where didst thou get that ring?"

Sir Percival said, "I will tell thee"; and therewith he told Sir Percydes all that had befallen him when he first came down into the world from the wilderness where he had aforetime dwelt, and how he had entered the yellow pavilion and had discovered the damosel who was now his chosen lady. When Sir Percydes heard that story he laughed in great measure, and then he said: "But how wilt thou find that young damosel again when thou hast a mind for to go to her once more?" To the which Sir Percival made reply: "I know not how I shall find her, nevertheless, I shall assuredly do so. For though the world is much wider and greater than I had thought it to be when I first came down into it, yet I know that I shall find that lady when the fit time cometh for me to seek her."

Then Sir Percydes said: "Dear friend, when thou desireth to find that damosel to whom belongeth the ring, come thou to me and I will tell thee where thou mayst find her; yet I know not why thou dost not go and find her now."

Unto this Sir Percival made reply: "I do not seek her immediately because I am yet so young and so unknown to the world that I could not be of any credit to her should I find her; so first I will seek to obtain credit as a knight, and then I will seek her."

Sir Percydes said: "Well, Percival, I think thou hast great promise of a very wonderful knighthood. Nor do I think thou wilt have difficulty in finding plenty of adventures to undertake. For even to-day I know of an adventure, which if thou couldst perform it successfully, would bring thee such worship that there are very few knights in all the world who will have more worship than thou."

Then Sir Percival said: "I prithee, dear friend, tell me what is that adventure."

Then Sir Percydes told Sir Percival what that adventure was as followeth:

Sir Percydes telleth Sir Percival of Beaurepaire.

"Thou art to know," quoth he, "that somewhat more than a day's journey to the north of this there is a fair plain, very fertile and beautiful to the sight. In the midst of that plain is a small lake of water, and in that lake is an island, and upon the island is a tall castle of very noble size and proportions. That castle is called Beaurepaire, and the lady of that castle is thought to be one of the most beautiful damosels in the world. And the name of the lady is Lady Blanchefleur.

"Now there is a very strong and powerful knight hight Sir Clamadius, otherwise known as the King of the Isles; and he is one of the most famous knights in the world. Sir Clamadius hath for a long while loved the Lady Blanchefleur with such a passion of love that I do not think that the like of that passion is to be found anywhere else in the world. But the Lady Blanchefleur hath no love for Sir Clamadius, but ever turneth away from him with a heart altogether cold of liking.

"But Sir Clamadius is a wonderfully proud and haughty King, wherefore he can ill brook being scorned by any lady. Wherefore he hath now come against the castle of Beaurepaire with an array of knights of his court, and at present layeth siege to that castle aforesaid.

"Now there is not at that castle any knight of sufficient worship to serve as champion thereof, wherefore all they of Beaurepaire stay within the castle walls and Sir Clamadius holds the meadows outside of the castle so that no one enters in or goeth out thereof.

"If thou couldst liberate the Lady Blanchefleur from the duress which Sir Clamadius places upon her, I believe thou wouldst have as great credit in courts of chivalry as it is possible to have. For, since Sir Tristram is gone, Sir Clamadius is believed by many to be the best knight in the world except Sir Launcelot of the Lake; unless it be that Sir Lamorack of Gales is a better knight than he."

Then Sir Percival said: "What thou tellest me gives me great pleasure, for it would be a very good adventure for any young knight to undertake. For if he should lose there would be no shame in losing, and if he should win there would be great glory in winning. So to-morrow I will enter upon that adventure, with intent to discover what fortune I may have therein."

So I have told you how Sir Percival performed his first adventures in the world of chivalry after he had perfected himself in the mysteries of knighthood under the teaching of Sir Launcelot of the Lake, and I have told you how he achieved that adventure with great credit to himself and with great glory to the order of knighthood to which he now truly belonged as a most worthy member.

That night he abided in the castle of Sir Percydes with great comfort and rest to his body, and when the next morning had come he arose, much refreshed and strengthened in spirit. And he descended to the hall where was set a fair and generous breakfast for his further refreshment, and thereat he and Sir Percydes sat themselves down and ate with hearty appetite, discoursing with great amity of spirit as aforetold.

After he had broken his fast he bade farewell to Sir Percydes and mounted his horse and rode away through the bright sunlight toward Beaurepaire and those further adventures that awaited him thereat.

And, as it was with Sir Percival in that first adventure, so may you meet with a like success when you ride forth upon your first undertakings after you have entered into the glory of your knighthood, with your life lying before you and a whole world whereinto ye may freely enter to do your devoirs to the glory of God and your own honor.

So now it shall be told how it fared with Sir Percival in that adventure of the Castle of Beaurepaire.

JVSTISSIMVS·REX·

The Demoiselle
Blanchefleur.

CHAPTER FOURTH

How Sir Percival Undertook the Adventure of the Castle of Beaurepaire and How He Fared Therein after Several Excellent Adventures.

NOW THE WAY THAT SIR PERCIVAL TRAVELLED LED HIM BY THE outskirts of the forest, so that somewhiles he would be in the woodland and somewhiles he would be in the open country. And about noontide he came to a certain cottage of a neatherd that stood all alone in a very pleasant dale. That place a little brook came bickering out from the forest and ran down into the dale and spread out into a small lake, besides which daffadowndillys bloomed in such abundance that it appeared as though all that meadow land was scattered over with an incredible number of yellow stars that had fallen down from out of the sky. And, because of the pleasantness of this place, Sir Percival here dismounted from his horse and sat him down upon a little couch of moss under the shadow of an oak tree that grew nigh to the cottage, there to rest himself for a while with great pleasure. And as he sat there there came a barelegged lass from the cottage and brought him fresh milk to drink; and there came a good, comely housewife and brought him bread and cheese made of cream; and Sir Percival ate and drank with great appetite.

Sir Percival breaks his fast at a forest cottage.

Now whilst Sir Percival sat there resting and refreshing himself in that wise, there appeared of a sudden coming thitherward, a tall and noble knight riding upon a piebald war-horse of Norway strain. So when Sir Percival beheld that knight coming in that wise he quickly put on his helmet and mounted his horse and made him ready for defence in case the knight had a mind to assail him.

Meantime that knight came riding up with great haughtiness of bearing to where Sir Percival was, and when he had come nigh enough he bespake Sir Percival, saying: "Sir Knight, I pray you to tell me your name and whither you go, and upon what quest?"

Sir Percival bespeaketh the strange knight.

Unto this Sir Percival made reply: "Messire, I do not choose to tell you my name, for I am a young knight, very new to adventure, and I know not how I shall succeed in that quest which I have undertaken. So I will wait to try the success of that adventure before I tell my name. But though I may not tell my name I will tell you whither I go and upon what quest. I go for to find a certain castle called Beaurepaire, and I intend to endeavor to liberate the lady of that castle from the duress of a certain knight hight Sir Clamadius, who, I understand, holds her by siege within the walls thereof."

Now, when Sir Percival had ceased speaking, the strange knight said: "Sir, this is a very singular thing: for that adventure of which you speak is the very adventure upon which I myself am bound. Now, as you say, you are a very young knight unused to arms, and as I am in the same degree a knight well seasoned in deeds of arms, it is more fitting that I should undertake this quest than you. For you may know how very well I am used to the service of arms when I tell you that I have had to do in four and twenty battles of various sorts; some of them friendly and some of them otherwise; and that I have had to do in more than four times that many affairs-at-arms with single knights, nearly all of them of great prowess. So now it would seem fitting that you should withdraw you from this affair and let me first essay it. Then, if I fail in my undertaking, you shall assume that adventure."

"Messire," quoth Sir Percival, "I see that you are a knight of much greater experience than I; but, ne'ertheless, I cannot find it in my heart to forego this adventure. So what I have to propose is this: that you and I do combat here in this place, and that he who proveth himself to be the better of us twain shall carry out this undertaking that we are both set upon."

Unto this, that strange knight lent a very willing assent, saying: "Very well, Messire, it shall be as you ask."

So with that each knight turned his horse and rode a little piece away; and each took such stand as pleased him; and each dressed his spear and shield and made him in all wise ready for the encounter. And when they had so prepared themselves, each knight shouted to his horse, and drave spur into its flank and rushed, the one against the other, with such terrible noise and violence that the sound thereof was echoed back from the woods like to a storm of thunder.

Sir Percival doeth battle with the strange knight.

So they met in the midst of the course with such a vehement impact that it was terrible to behold. And in that encounter the spear of each knight was burst all into fragments; and the horse of each fell back upon his haunches and would have been overthrown had not each knight voided his saddle with a very wonderful skill and agility.

Then each knight drew sword and came the one against the other, as furiously as two rams at battle. So they fought for nigh the space of an hour, foining and striking, and tracing hither and tracing thither most furiously; and the noise of the blows they struck might have been heard several furlongs away.

During that battle Sir Percival received several sore wounds so that by and by a great passion of rage seized upon him. So he rushed the battle with might and main, and therewith struck so many furious blows that by and by that other knight held his shield very low for weariness. This Sir Percival perceived, and therewith he smote the other so furious a blow upon the head that the knight sank down upon his knees and could not arise. Then Sir Percival ran to him and catched him by the neck and flung him down violently upon the ground, crying out, "Yield or I slay thee!"

Sir Percival overcometh the strange knight.

Then that knight besought mercy in a very weak voice, saying: "Sir Knight, I beseech thee, spare my life!"

Sir Percival said: "Well, I will spare thee, but tell me, what is thy name?" To this the other said: "I am Sir Lionel, and I am a knight of King Arthur's court and of the Round Table."

Now when Sir Percival heard this he cried out aloud, for he was very greatly grieved, and he said: "Alas, what have I done for to fight against thee in this wise! I am Sir Percival, whom thine own kinsman, Sir Launcelot of the Lake, hath trained in arms. But indeed, I did never think to use that art which he taught me against one so dear to his heart as thou art, Sir Lionel." So with that Sir Percival assisted Sir Lionel to arise to his feet, and Sir Lionel was so weak from that woful battle that he could hardly stand.

Sir Percival giveth aid to Sir Lionel.

Now that stream and lake of water above spoken of was near by, so Sir Percival brought Sir Lionel thither, holding him up as he walked; and there Sir Lionel refreshed himself. Then, when he was revived a little, he turned his eyes very languidly upon Sir Percival, and he said: "Percival, thou hast done to me this day what few knights have ever done before. So all the glory that ever I have won is now thy glory because of this battle. For thou hast overcome me in a fair quarrel and I have yielded myself unto thee, wherefore it is now thy right to command me to thy will."

Then Percival said: "Alas, dear Sir Knight! It is not meet that I should lay command upon such as thou art. But, if thou wilt do so, I beseech thee when thou art come to King Arthur's court that thou wilt tell the King that I, who am his young knight Percival, have borne myself not unbecomingly in my battle with thee. For this is the first battle, knight against knight, that I have undertaken in all of my life. And I beseech thee that thou wilt greet Sir Kay the Seneschal, from me, and that thou wilt say to him that by and by I shall meet him and repay him that buffet which he gave to the damsel Yelande, the Dumb Maiden, in the Queen's pavilion."

Sir Lionel said: "It shall be as thou sayst, and I will do thy bidding. But, touching Sir Kay, I do not believe that he will take very much joy at thy message to him. For he will find small pleasure in the thought of the payment of that buffet that thou hast promised to give him."

Now, as the day by this time was waxing late, Sir Percival abided that night at that neatherd's hut nigh to which this battle had been fought and there had his wounds bathed and dressed; and when the next morning had come he arose early, and saddled his horse, and rode forward upon his way. And as he rode he was very well pleased at the thought of that battle he had fought with Sir Lionel, for he wist that he had obtained great credit to himself in that encounter, and he was aware, now that he had made trial of his strength against such a one as Sir Lionel, he must be one of the greatest knights of the world. So his heart was uplifted with great joy and delight at that thought; that he was now a well-approved knight-champion, worthy of his knighthood. Therefore he rode away for all that day, greatly rejoicing in spirit at the thought of what he had done the day before.

Sir Percival goeth forward upon his adventure.

About the first slant of the afternoon Sir Percival came at last out of the woodlands and into a wide-open plain, very fertile and well tilled, with fields of wheat and rye abounding on all sides. And he saw that in the midst of that plain there was a considerable lake, and that in the midst of that lake there was an island, and that upon the island there stood a fair noble castle, and he wist that that castle must be the castle of Beaurepaire. So he rode down into that valley with some speed.

Now after he had so ridden for a while, he was aware of a knight, very haughty of appearance and bearing, who rode before him upon the same way that he was going. And that knight was clad all in red armor, and he rode upon a horse so black that I believe there was not a single white hair upon him. And all the trappings and the furniture of that horse were of red, so that he presented a very noble appearance. So Sir Percival made haste to overtake that knight, and when he had come nigh he drew rein at a little distance. Thereupon that knight in red bespake Sir Percival very proudly, saying: "Sir Knight, whither ride you, and upon what mission?"

Sir Percival perceives a red knight.

"Messire," quoth Percival, "I ride toward yonder castle, which I take to be the castle of Beaurepaire, and I come hither with intent to succor the Lady Blanchefleur of that castle from a knight, hight Sir Clamadius, who keeps her there a prisoner against her will, so that it behooves any good knight to attempt her rescue."

Upon this the red knight spake very fiercely, saying: "Messire, what business is that of yours? I would have you know that I am a knight of King Clamadius', wherefore I am able to say to you that you shall go no further upon that quest. For I am Sir Engeneron of Grandregarde, and I am Seneschal unto King Clamadius, and I will not have it that thou shalt go any farther upon this way unless you ride over me to go upon it."

"Messire," quoth Sir Percival, "I have no quarrel with you, but if you have a mind to force a quarrel upon me, I will not seek to withdraw myself from an encounter with you. So make yourself ready, and I will make myself ready, and then we shall soon see whether or not I am to pass upon this way."

So therewith each knight turned his horse away to such a place as seemed to him to be fitting; and when they were in all wise prepared they rushed together with an amazing velocity and a noise like to thunder. So they met in the midst of the course. And in that encounter the spear of Sir Engeneron broke into many pieces, but the spear of Sir Percival held, so that he flung Sir Engeneron entirely out of his saddle and over the crupper of his horse and down upon the ground so violently that Sir Engeneron lay there in a swoon.

Sir Percival doeth battle with Sir Engeneron.

Then Sir Percival dismounted from his horse with all speed, and he rushed the helmet of Sir Engeneron off of his head with intent to slay him. But with that Sir Engeneron awoke to his danger, and therewith gat upon his knees and clasped Sir Percival about the thighs, crying out: "Sir, I beseech you upon your knighthood to spare my life."

Sir Engeneron yields himself to Sir Percival.

"Well," said Sir Percival, "since you beseech that upon my knighthood I must needs do as you ask. But I will only do so upon two conditions. The first of these conditions is that you go to the court of King Arthur, and that you surrender yourself as captive to a damsel of that court who is known as the Lady Yelande the Dumb Maiden. And you are to tell that maiden that the young knight who slew Sir Boindegardus greets her and that he tells her that in a little while he will return to repay to Sir Kay that buffet he gave her. This is my first condition." And Sir Engeneron said: "I will perform that condition."

"And my second condition," said Sir Percival, "is this: that you give me your armor for me to use upon this adventure which I have undertaken, and that you take my armor and deposit it with the hermit of a little chapel you shall after a while come to if you return upon the road which brought me hither. After a while I will return and reclaim my armor and will return your armor. This is my second condition."

And Sir Engeneron said: "That condition also I shall fulfil according to your command."

Then Sir Percival said: "Arise." And Sir Engeneron did so. And after that Sir Engeneron put off his armor, and Sir Percival put off his armor. And Sir Percival put on the armor of Sir Engeneron, and Sir Engeneron packed the armor of Sir Percival upon his horse and prepared to depart in obedience to those conditions of Sir Percival. So they parted company, Sir Percival riding upon his way to Beaurepaire, and Sir Engeneron betaking his way to find the chapel of that hermit of whom Sir Percival had spoken.

Sir Percival and Sir Engeneron exchange armor.

So it was that after two adventures, Sir Percival entered upon that undertaking which he had come to perform in behalf of the Lady Blanchefleur.

And now, if it please you to read what follows, you shall hear how it befell with Sir Percival at the castle of Beaurepaire.

After that adventure with Sir Engeneron, Sir Percival rode onward upon his way, and by and by he came to the lake whereon stood the castle and the town of Beaurepaire. And Sir Percival beheld that a long narrow bridge crossed over that part of the lake from the mainland to the island and the town. So Sir Percival rode very boldly forth upon that bridge and across it, and no one stayed him, for all of the knights of Sir Clamadius who beheld him said: "Yonder rides Sir Engeneron." Thus Sir Percival crossed the bridge and rode very boldly forward until he came to the gate of the castle, and those who beheld him said: "Sir Engeneron haply beareth a message to the castle." For no one wist that that knight was not Sir Engeneron, but all thought that it was he because of the armor which he wore.

So Sir Percival came close to the castle, and when he was come there he called very loudly to those within, and by and by there appeared the face of a woman at an upper window and the face was very pale and woe-begone.

Sir Percival cometh to Beaurepaire.

Then Sir Percival said to the woman at the window: "Bid them open the gate and let me in; for I come to bring you succor at this place."

To this the woman said: "I shall not bid them open the gate, for I know from your armor who you are, and that you are Sir Engeneron the Seneschal. And I know that you are one of our bitterest enemies; for you have already slain several of the knights of this castle, and now you seek by guile to enter into the castle itself."

Then Sir Percival said: "I am not Sir Engeneron, but one who hath overthrown Sir Engeneron in battle. I have put on his armor with intent that I might come hither to help defend this place against Sir Clamadius." So said Sir Percival, and therewith he put up the umbril of his helmet, saying: "Look, see; I am not Sir Engeneron." Then the woman at the window saw his face and that it was not the face of Sir Engeneron. And she saw that the face of Sir Percival was mild and gentle, wherefore she ran and told the people of the castle that a knight who was a friend stood without. Therewith they of the castle let fall the drawbridge and opened the gates, and Sir Percival entered into the castle.

Sir Percival entereth Beaurepaire.

Then there came several of the chief people of the castle, and they also were all pale and woe-begone from long fasting, as was the woman whom Sir Percival had first seen; for all were greatly wasted because of the toil and anxiety of that siege. These asked Sir Percival who he was and whence he came and how he came thither; and Sir Percival told them all that it was necessary for them to know. For he told them how he was a young knight trained under the care of Sir Launcelot; and he told them that he had come thither with the hope of serving the Lady Blanchefleur; and he told them what adventures had befallen him in the coming and how he had already overthrown Sir Lionel and Sir Engeneron to get there. Wherefore, from these things, they of the castle perceived that Sir Percival was a very strong, worthy knight, and they gave great joy that he should have come thither to their aid.

So he who was chief of those castle people summoned several attendants, and these came and some took the horse of Sir Percival and led it to the stables, and others relieved Sir Percival of his armor; and others took him to a bath of tepid water, where he bathed himself, and was dried on soft linen towels; and others brought soft garments of gray cloth and clad Sir Percival in them and afterward brought him down into a fair large chamber where there was a table spread as though ready for meat.

Now in a little after Sir Percival was come to that supper-hall the door thereof was opened and there entered several people. With these came a damsel of such extraordinary beauty and gracefulness of figure that Sir Percival stood amazed. For her face was fair beyond words; red upon white, like rose-leaves upon cream; and her eyes

Sir Percival beholds the Lady Blanchefleur.

were bright and glancing like those of a falcon, and her nose was thin and straight, and her lips were very red, like to coral for redness, and her hair was dark and abundant and like to silk for softness. She was clad all in a dress of black, shot with stars of gold, and the dress was lined with ermine and was trimmed with sable at the collar and the cuffs and the hem thereof.

So Sir Percival stood and gazed at that lady with a pleasure beyond words to express, and he wist that this must be the Lady Blanchefleur, for whose sake he had come thither.

And the Lady Blanchefleur looked upon Sir Percival with great kindness, for he appeared to her like to a hero for strength and beauty; wherefore she smiled upon Sir Percival very graciously and came forward and gave him her hand. And Sir Percival took her hand and set it to his lips; and lo! her hand was as soft as silk and very warm, rosy and fragrant, and the fingers thereof glistered with bright golden rings and with gems of divers colors.

Then that beautiful Lady Blanchefleur said: "Messire, this is a very knightly thing for you to do to come hither to this place. And you come in good time, for food groweth very scarce with us so that in a little while we must face starvation. For because of the watch that Sir Clamadius keepeth upon this place, no one can either enter in or go out. Yea, thou art the very first one who hath come hither since he has sat down before Beaurepaire."

The Lady Blanchefleur telleth her sorrows to Sir Percival.

Then presently she ceased smiling and her face clouded over; then bright tears began to drop from the Lady Blanchefleur's eyes; and then she said: "I fear me greatly that Sir Clamadius will at last seize upon this castle, for he hath kept us here prisoner for a long while. Yet though he seize the castle, he shall never seize that which the castle contains. For I keep by me a little casket of silver, and therein is a dagger, very sharp and fine. Therefore the day that Sir Clamadius enters into this castle, I shall thrust that dagger into my heart. For, though Sir Clamadius may seize upon my castle, he shall never possess my soul."

Then Sir Percival was very sorry for the tears he saw shining upon the Lady Blanchefleur's face, wherefore he said: "Lady, I have great hopes that this affair may never reach to that woful extremity thou speakest of." The Lady Blanchefleur said: "I hope not also." And therewith she wiped away her tears and smiled again. Then she said: "See, Sir Percival, the evening has come and it is time to sit at supper, now I beseech thee for to come to table with me, for though we have but little to eat here, yet I assure thee that thou art very welcome to the best that we have."

So therewith Lady Blanchefleur led Sir Percival to the table, and they sat down to such feast as could be had at that place of starvation. For what they had was little enough, being only such fish as they could catch from the lake, and a little bread—but not much—and a very little wine.

Then after they had eaten and drunk what they had, the Lady Blanchefleur took a golden harp into her hand and played thereon, and sang in a voice so clear and high and beautiful that Percival was altogether enchanted and bewitched thereat.

The Lady sings to Sir Percival.

Thus it was that that evening passed with them very pleasantly and cheerfully, so that it was the middle of the night ere Sir Percival withdrew to that couch that had been prepared for his rest.

Now word was brought to Sir Clamadius that Sir Engeneron the Seneschal had been overcome by another knight, wherefore Sir Clamadius wist that that was the knight in Sir Engeneron's armor who had entered into the castle. So Sir Clamadius said: "Certes, this must be a champion of no small prowess who hath undertaken single-handed such a dangerous quest as this, and hath thus entered into the castle, for they appear to make great rejoicings at his coming. Now if he remaineth there it may very well be that they will be encouraged to resist me a great while longer, and so all that I have thus far accomplished shall have been in vain."

Now there was among the counsellors of Sir Clamadius an old knight who was very cunning and far-sighted. He said to the King: "Sire, I think we may be able to devise some plan whereby we may withdraw this knight-champion out of the castle. My plan is this: Let ten of your best knights make parade before that castle tomorrow, and let them give challenge to those within the castle to come forth to battle. Then I believe that this knight will come forth with the other knights from the castle to accept that challenge. Thereafter let it be that our knights withdraw as though in retreat, and so lead this knight and the knights of the castle into an ambushment. There let many fall upon them at once and either slay them or make them prisoners. So the castle shall be deprived of this new champion that hath come to it, and therewith may be so disheartened that it will yield to thee."

The old counsellor giveth advice to Sir Clamadius.

This advice seemed very good to King Clamadius, wherefore, when the next morning had come, he chose him ten knights from among the foremost of all his knights, and he bade them give that challenge in that wise. These did so, and therewith Sir Percival and nine other knights issued out from the castle against them.

But it did not fare as Sir Clamadius had expected; for the attack of Sir Percival and his knights was so fierce and sudden that those ten knights could not withdraw so easily as they intended. For, ere they were able to withdraw, Sir Percival had struck down six of these knights with his own hand and the other four were made prisoners. Thus Sir Percival and his knights did not come into that ambush that had been prepared for them.

Sir Percival doeth great battle.

Then those who were in ambush perceived that their plan had failed, wherefore they broke from cover with intent to do what they could. But Sir Percival and his knights beheld them coming, and so withdrew, defending themselves with great valor. So they came into the castle again in safety.

Thus it was that the plans of King Clamadius and his counsellor failed of effect, whereupon Sir Clamadius was very angry at that wise old knight. So that, when that counsellor came to him again and said: "Sir, I have another plan," King Clamadius cried out very fiercely: "Away with thy plans! They are all of no avail." Then Sir Clamadius said: "When to-morrow comes, I myself will undertake this affair. For I will go and give challenge to this knight, and so I shall hope to decide this quarrel man to man. For unless yonder knight be Sir Launcelot of the Lake or Sir Lamorack of Gales, I do not think he will be my peer in an encounter of man to man."

So when the next morning had come, Sir Clamadius armed himself at all points and straightway betook himself to a fair, smooth meadow beneath the walls of the castle. And when he had come there he cried out: "Sir Red Knight, come forth and speak with me."

Sir Clamadius arms himself for battle.

So after a while Sir Percival appeared at the top of the castle wall, and he said: "Messire, here I am; what is it you would have of me?"

Then Sir Clamadius said: "Messire, are you Sir Launcelot of the Lake?" And Sir Percival said: "Nay, I am not he." Sir Clamadius said: "Art thou then Sir Lamorack of Gales?" And Sir Percival said: "Nay, I am not he." Then Sir Clamadius said: "Who, then, art thou?" Sir Percival said: "I am not any great knight-champion such as those two of whom you speak, but am a young knight who have not fought more than twice or thrice in my life."

At that Sir Clamadius was very glad, for he feared that Sir Percival might be some famous knight well-seasoned in arms. Wherefore when he found that Sir Percival was only a young and untried knight, he thought it would be an easy matter to deal with him. So he said: "Messire, I challenge thee to come forth to battle with me man to man so that thou and I may settle this quarrel betwixt us, for it is a pity to shed more blood than is necessary in this quarrel. So if thou wilt come forth and overthrow me, then I will withdraw my people from this place; but if I overthrow thee, then this castle shall be yielded up to me with all that it contains."

To this Sir Percival said: "Sir Knight, I am very willing to fight with thee upon that issue. But first of all I must obtain the consent of the Lady Blanchefleur to stand her champion."

So Sir Percival went to the Lady Blanchefleur, and he said: "Lady, will you accept me as your champion to fight the issue of this quarrel man to man with Sir Clamadius?"

She said: "Percival, thou art very young to have to do with so old and well-seasoned a knight. Now I greatly fear for your life in such a battle as that."

To this Sir Percival said: "Lady, I know that I am young, but indeed I feel a very big spirit stir within me, so that if thou wilt trust me, I have belief that, with the grace of God, I shall win this battle."

Then the Lady Blanchefleur smiled upon Sir Percival and she said: "Percival, I will gladly entrust my life and safety into thy keeping, for I too have great dependence in thy knighthood."

So straightway Sir Percival armed himself, and when he was in all wise prepared he went forth to that battle with a heart very full of great courage and hope.

There he found Sir Clamadius still parading in that meadow beneath the walls, awaiting the coming of his opponent.

Meanwhile many folk came and stood upon the walls of the castle to behold that encounter, whilst each knight took such stand as appeared good to him. Then, when they were in all wise prepared, each knight drave spurs into his horse and rushed himself against the other with most terrible and fierce violence. Therewith they met in the very midst of the course with an uproar like to thunder that echoed back from the flat walls of the castle.

Sir Percival and Sir Clamadius do battle.

In that encounter the spear of Sir Percival held, but the spear of Sir Clamadius was riven into splinters. And so, Sir Percival riding forward with furious violence, Sir Clamadius was overthrown, horse and man, with such violence that he lay there upon the ground as though he were dead.

Then all those upon the walls shouted aloud with a great noise of rejoicing, whilst those of the party of Sir Clamadius gave lamentation in the same degree.

But Sir Percival voided his saddle in haste, and ran to where Sir Clamadius lay. And Sir Percival rushed the helmet off from the head of Sir Clamadius, and he catched him by the hair of the head, and he raised his sword on high with intent to finish the

Sir Clamadius yields himself.

work he had begun. Therewith Sir Clamadius aroused himself unto his danger, and he cried in a very piercing voice: "Messire, I beseech thee of thy knighthood to spare my life!"

"Well," said Sir Percival, "since you ask me upon my knighthood, I cannot refuse you, for so I was taught by the noble knight, Sir Launcelot, to refuse no boon asked upon my knighthood that I was able to grant. But I will only spare your life upon one condition, and that is this: That you disarm yourself in all wise, and that you go without armor to the court of King Arthur. There you shall deliver yourself as a servant unto a damsel of King Arthur's court, hight Yelande, surnamed the Dumb Maiden. Her you are to tell that the youth who slew Sir Boindegardus hath sent you unto her as a servant. And you are to say to Sir Kay, the Seneschal of King Arthur, that the young knight Percival will in a little while come to repay that buffet he gave to the damoiselle Yelande aforesaid."

So said Sir Percival, and Sir Clamadius said: "It shall be done in all wise as you command, if so be you will spare my life." Then Sir Percival said: "Arise"; and Sir Clamadius arose; and Sir Percival said: "Go hence"; and therewith Sir Clamadius departed as Sir Percival commanded.

So that day Sir Clamadius withdrew from the castle of Beaurepaire with all his array of knights, and after that he went to the court of King Arthur and did in all respects as Sir Percival had commanded him to do.

So it was that Sir Percival fulfilled that quest, and set the Lady Blanchefleur free from duress; and may God grant that you also fulfil all your quests with as great honor and nobility as therein exhibited.

JVSTISSIMVS·REX·

Sir Kay interrupts ye meditations of Sir Percival.

CHAPTER FIFTH

How Sir Percival Repaid Sir Kay the Buffet He One Time Gave Yelande the Dumb Maiden, and How, Thereafter, He Went Forth to Seek His Own Lady of Love.

Now, after these adventures aforesaid, Sir Percival remained for a long while at Beaurepaire, and during that time he was the knight-champion to the Lady Blanchefleur. And the Lady Blanchefleur loved Sir Percival every day with a greater and greater passion, but Sir Percival showed no passion of love for her in return, and thereat Lady Blanchefleur was greatly troubled.

Sir Percival and the Lady Blanchefleur walk together.

Now one day the Lady Blanchefleur and Sir Percival were walking together on a terrace; and it was then come to be the fall of the year, so that the leaves of the trees were showering all down about them like flakes of gold. And that day the Lady Blanchefleur loved Sir Percival so much that her heart was pierced with that love as though with a great agony. But Sir Percival wist not of that.

Then the Lady Blanchefleur said: "Messire, I would that thou wouldst stay here always as our knight-champion."

"Lady," quoth Percival, "that may not be, for in a little while now I must leave you. For, though I shall be sad to go from such a friendly place as this is, yet I am an errant knight, and as I am errant I must fulfil many adventures besides the one I have accomplished here."

"Messire," said the Lady Blanchefleur, "if you will but remain here, this castle shall be yours and all that it contains."

At this Sir Percival was greatly astonished, wherefore he said: "Lady, how may that be? Lo! this castle is yours, and no one can take it away from you, nor can you give it to me for mine own."

Then the Lady Blanchefleur turned away her face and bowed her head, and said in a voice as though it were stifling her for to speak: "Percival, it needs not to take the castle from me; take thou me for thine own, and then the castle and all shall be thine."

At that Sir Percival stood for a space very still as though without breathing. Then by and by he said: "Lady, meseems that no knight could have greater honor paid to him than that which you pay to me. Yet should I accept such a gift as you offer, then I would be doing such dishonor to my knighthood that would make it altogether unworthy of that high honor you pay it. For already I have made my vow to serve a lady, and if I should forswear that vow, I would be a dishonored and unworthy knight."

Sir Percival denies the Lady Blanchefleur.

Then the Lady Blanchefleur cried out in a great voice of suffering: "Say no more, for I am ashamed."

Sir Percival said: "Nay, there is no shame to thee, but great honor to me." But the Lady Blanchefleur would not hear him, but brake away from him in great haste, and left him standing where he was.

So Sir Percival could stay no longer at that place; but as soon as might be, he took horse and rode away. Nor did he see Blanchefleur again after they had thus talked together upon that terrace as aforesaid.

And after Sir Percival had gone, the Lady Blanchefleur abandoned herself to great sorrow, for she wept a long while and a very great deal; nor would she, for a long while, take any joy in living or in the world in which she lived.

So Sir Percival performed that adventure of setting free the duress of the castle of Beaurepaire. And after that and ere the winter came, he performed several other adventures of more or less fame. And during that time, he overthrew eleven knights in various affairs at arms and in all those adventures he met with no mishap himself. And besides such encounters at arms, he performed several very worthy works; for he slew a wild boar that was a terror to all that dwelt nigh to the forest of Umber; and he also slew a very savage wolf that infested the moors of the Dart. Wherefore, because of these several adventures, the name of Sir Percival became very famous in all courts of chivalry, and many said: "Verily, this young knight must be the peer of Sir Launcelot of the Lake himself."

Of the further adventures of Sir Percival.

Now one day toward eventide (and it was a very cold winter day) Sir Percival came to the hut of a hermit in the forest of Usk; and he abode all night at that place.

Now when the morning had come he went out and stood in front of the hut, and he saw that during the night a soft snow had fallen so that all the earth was covered with white. And he saw that it likewise had happened that a hawk had struck a raven in front of the hermit's habitation, and that some of the raven's feathers and some of its blood lay upon the snow.

Now when Sir Percival beheld the blood and the black feathers upon that white snow, he said to himself: "Behold! that snow is not whiter than the brow and the neck of my lady; and that red is not redder than her lips; and that black is not blacker than her hair." Therewith the thought of that lady took great hold upon him and he sighed so deeply that he felt his heart lifted within him because of that sigh. So he stood and gazed upon that white and red and black, and he forgot all things else in the world than his lady-love.

Sir Percival stands in meditation.

Now it befell at that time that there came a party riding through those parts, and that party were Sir Gawaine and Sir Geraint and Sir Kay. And when they saw Sir Percival where he stood leaning against a tree and looking down upon the ground in deep meditation, Sir Kay said: "Who is yonder knight?" (For he wist not that that knight was Sir Percival.) And Sir Kay said further: "I will go and bespeak that knight and ask him who he is."

But Sir Gawaine perceived that Sir Percival was altogether sunk in deep thought, wherefore he said: "Nay, thou wilt do ill to disturb that knight; for either he hath some weighty matter upon his mind, or else he is bethinking him of his lady, and in either case it would be a pity to disturb him until he arouses himself."

But Sir Kay would not heed what Sir Gawaine said, but forthwith he went to where Sir Percival stood; and Sir Percival was altogether unaware of his coming, being so deeply sunk in his thoughts. Then Sir Kay said: "Sir Knight,"—but Sir Percival did not hear him. And Sir Kay said: "Sir Knight, who art thou?" But still Sir Percival did not reply. Then Sir Kay said: "Sir Knight, thou shalt answer me!" And therewith he catched Sir Percival by the arm and shook him very roughly.

Sir Kay shakes the arm of Sir Percival.

Then Sir Percival aroused himself, and he was filled with indignation that anyone should have laid rough hands upon his person. And Sir Percival did not recognize Sir Kay because he was still entangled in that network of thought, but he said very fiercely: "Ha, sirrah! wouldst thou lay hands upon me!" and therewith he raised his fist and smote Sir Kay so terrible a buffet beside the head that Sir Kay instantly fell down as though he were dead and lay without sense of motion upon the ground. Then Sir Percival perceived that there were two other knights standing not far off, and therewith his thoughts of other things came back to him again and he was aware of what he had done in his anger, and was very sorry and ashamed that he should have been so hasty as to have struck that blow.

Sir Percival smites Sir Kay a buffet.

Then Sir Gawaine came to Sir Percival and spake sternly to him saying. "Sir Knight, why didst thou strike my companion so unknightly a blow as that?"

Sir Gawaine chides Sir Percival.

To which Sir Percival said: "Messire, it grieves me sorely that I should have been so hasty, but I was bethinking me of my lady, and this knight disturbed my thoughts; wherefore I smote him in haste."

To this Sir Gawaine made reply: "Sir, I perceive that thou hadst great excuse for thy blow. Ne'theless, I am displeased that thou shouldst have struck that knight. Now I make demand of thee what is thy name and condition?"

And Sir Percival said: "My name is Percival, and I am a knight of King Arthur's making."

At that, when Sir Gawaine and Sir Geraint heard what Sir Percival said, they cried out in great amazement; and Sir Gawaine said: "Ha, Sir Percival! this is indeed well met, for my name is Gawaine and I am a nephew unto King Arthur and am of his court; and this knight is Sir Geraint, and he also is of King Arthur's court and of his Round Table. And we have been in search of thee for this long time for to bring thee unto King Arthur at Camelot. For thy renown is now spread all over this realm, so that they talk of thee in every court of chivalry."

Sir Gawaine and Sir Geraint rejoice over Sir Percival.

And Sir Percival said: "That is good news to me, for I wist not that I had so soon won so much credit. But, touching the matter of returning unto King Arthur's court with you; unto that I crave leave to give my excuses. For, since you tell me that I now have so much credit of knighthood, it behooves me to go immediately unto my lady and to offer my services unto her. For when I parted from her I promised her that I would come to her as soon as I had won me sufficient credit of knighthood. As for this knight whom I have struck, I cannot be sorry for that buffet, even if it was given with my fist and not with my sword as I should have given it. For I have promised Sir Kay by several mouths that I would sometime repay him with just such a buffet as that which he struck the damosel Yelande. So now I have fulfilled my promise and have given him that buffet."

Then Sir Gawaine and Sir Geraint laughed, and Sir Gawaine said: "Well, Sir Percival, thou hast indeed fulfilled thy promise in very good measure. For I make my vow that no one could have been better served with his dessert than was Sir Kay."

Now by this time Sir Kay had recovered from that blow, so that he rose up very ruefully, looking about as though he wist not yet just where he was.

Then Sir Gawaine said to Sir Percival: "As to thy coming unto the court of the King, thou dost right to fulfil thy promise unto thy lady before undertaking any other obligation. For, even though the King himself bid thee come, yet is thy obligation to thy lady superior to the command of the King. So now I bid thee go in quest of thy lady in God's name; only see to it that thou comest to the King's court as soon as thou art able."

Sir Percival will not return to court.

So it was that Sir Percival fulfilled the promise of that buffet unto Sir Kay.

And now you shall hear how he found the Lady Yvette the Fair.

Now after Sir Percival had parted from Sir Gawaine, and Sir Geraint and Sir Kay, he went his way in that direction he wist, and by and by, toward eventide, he came again to the castle of Sir Percydes. And Sir Percydes was at home and he welcomed Sir Percival with great joy and congratulations. For the fame of Sir Percival was now abroad in all the world, so that Sir Percydes welcomed him with great acclaim.

Sir Percival cometh to the castle of Sir Percydes.

So Sir Percival sat down with Sir Percydes and they ate and drank together, and, for the time, Sir Percival said nothing of that which was upon his heart—for he was of a very continent nature and was in no wise hasty in his speech.

But after they had satisfied themselves with food and drink, then Sir Percival spake to Sir Percydes of that which was upon his mind, saying: "Dear friend, thou didst tell me that when I was ready for to come to thee with a certain intent thou wouldst tell me who is the lady whose ring I wear and where I shall find her. Now, I believe that I am a great deal more worthy for to be her knight than I was when I first saw thee; wherefore I am now come to beseech thee to redeem thy promise to me. Now tell me, I beg of thee, who is that lady and where does she dwell?"

Then Sir Percydes said: "Friend, I will declare to thee that which thou dost ask of me. Firstly, that lady is mine own sister, hight Yvette, and she is the daughter of King Pecheur. Secondly, thou shalt find her at the castle of my father, which standeth upon the west coast of this land. Nor shalt thou have any difficulty in finding that castle, for thou mayst easily come to it by inquiring the way of those whom thou mayst meet in that region. But, indeed, it hath been two years since I have seen my father and my sister, and I know not how it is with them."

Sir Percydes declares himself to Sir Percival.

Then Sir Percival came to Sir Percydes and he put his arm about him and kissed him upon either cheek, and he said: "Should I obtain the kind regard of that lady, I know nothing that would more rejoice me than to know that thou art her brother. For, indeed, I entertain a great deal of love for thee."

At that Sir Percydes laughed for joy and he said: "Percival, wilt thou not tell me of what house thou art come?" Percival said: "I will tell thee what thou dost ask:

my father is King Pellinore who was a very good, noble knight of the court of King Arthur and of his Round Table."

Then Sir Percydes cried out with great amazement, saying: "That is very marvellous! I would that I had known this before, for thy mother and my mother were sisters of one father and one mother. So we are cousins german."

Then Sir Percival said: "This is great joy to me!" And his heart was expanded with pleasure at finding that Sir Percydes was of his kindred and that he was no longer alone in that part of the world.

So Sir Percival abided for two days with Sir Percydes and then he betook his way to the westward in pursuance of that adventure. And he was upon the road three days, and upon the morning of the fourth day he came, through diligent inquiry, within sight of the castle of King Pecheur. This castle stood upon a high crag of rock from which it arose against the sky so that it looked to be a part of the crag. And it was a very noble and stately castle, having many tall towers and many buildings within the walls thereof. And a village of white houses of the fisher-folk gathered upon the rocks beneath the castle walls like chicks beneath the shadow of their mother's wings.

Sir Percival departs for the castle of King Pecheur.

And, behold! Percival saw the great sea for the first time in all his life, and was filled with wonder at the huge waves that ran toward the shore and burst upon the rocks, all white like snow. And he was amazed at the multitude of sea fowl that flew about the rocks in such prodigious numbers that they darkened the sky. Likewise he was astonished at the fisher-boats that spread their white sails against the wind, and floated upon the water like swans, for he had never seen their like before. So he sat his horse upon a high rock nigh to the sea and gazed his fill upon those things that were so wonderful to him.

Then after a while Sir Percival went forward to the castle. And as he drew nigh to the castle he became aware that a very reverend man, whose hair and beard were as white as snow, sat upon a cushion of crimson velvet upon a rock that overlooked the sea. Two pages, richly clad in black and silver, stood behind him; and the old man gazed out across the sea, and Sir Percival saw that he neither spake nor moved. But when Sir Percival came near to him the old man arose and went into the castle, and the two pages took up the two crimson velvet cushions and followed him.

But Percival rode up to the castle, and he saw that the gateway of the castle stood open, wherefore he rode into the courtyard of the castle. And when he had come into the courtyard, two attendants immediately appeared and took his horse and assisted him to dismount; but neither of these attendants said aught to him, but both were as silent as deaf-mutes.

Then Percival entered the hall and there he saw the old man whom he had before seen, and the old man sat in a great carved chair beside a fire of large logs of wood. And Sir Percival saw that the eyes of the old man were all red and that his cheeks were channeled with weeping; and Percival was abashed at the sadness of his aspect. Ne'ertheless, he came to where the old man sat and saluted him with great reverence, and he said: "Art thou King Pecheur?" And the old man answered, "Aye, for I am both a fisher and a sinner" (for that word Pecheur meaneth both fisher and sinner).

Sir Percival finds King Pecheur.

Then Sir Percival said: "Sire, I bring thee greetings from thy son, Sir Percydes, who is a very dear friend to me. And likewise I bring thee greeting from myself: for I am Percival, King Pellinore's son, and thy Queen and my mother are sisters. And likewise I come to redeem a pledge, for, behold, here is the ring of thy daughter Yvette, unto whom I am pledged for her true knight. Wherefore, having now achieved a not dishonorable renown in the world of chivalry, I am come to beseech her kindness and to redeem my ring which she hath upon her finger and to give her back her ring again."

Then King Pecheur fell to weeping in great measure and he said: "Percival thy fame hath reached even to this remote place, for every one talketh of thee with great unction. But, touching my daughter Yvette, if thou wilt come with me I will bring thee to her."

So King Pecheur arose and went forth and Sir Percival followed him. And King Pecheur brought Sir Percival to a certain tower; and he brought him up a long and winding stair; and at the top of the stairway was a door. And King Pecheur opened the door and Sir Percival entered the apartment.

The windows of the apartment stood open, and a cold wind came in thereat from off the sea; and there stood a couch in the middle of the room, and it was spread with black velvet; and the Lady Yvette lay reclined upon the couch, and, lo! her face was like to wax for whiteness, and she neither moved nor spake, but only lay there perfectly still; for she was dead.

Sir Percival findeth the Lady Yvette.

Seven waxen candles burned at her head, and seven others at her feet, and the flames of the candles spread and wavered as the cold wind blew upon them. And the hair of her head (as black as those raven feathers that Sir Percival had beheld lying upon the snow) moved like threads of black silk as the wind blew in through the window—but the Lady Yvette moved not nor stirred, but lay like a statue of marble all clad in white.

Then at the first Sir Percival stood very still at the door-way as though he had of a sudden been turned into stone. Then he went forward and stood beside the couch and held his hands very tightly together and gazed at the Lady Yvette where she lay. So he stood for a long while, and he wist not why it was that he felt like as though he had been turned into a stone, without such grief at his heart as he had thought to feel thereat. (For indeed, his spirit was altogether broken though he knew it not.)

Then he spake unto that still figure, and he said: "Dear lady, is it thus I find thee after all this long endeavor of mine? Yet from Paradise, haply, thou mayst perceive all that I have accomplished in thy behalf. So shalt thou be my lady always to the end of my life and I will have none other than thee. Wherefore I herewith give thee thy ring again and take mine own in its stead." Therewith, so speaking, he lifted that hand (all so cold like the snow) and took his ring from off her finger and put her ring back upon it again.

Of the grief of Sir Percival.

Then King Pecheur said, "Percival, hast thou no tears?"

And Percival said, "Nay, I have none." Therewith he turned and left that place, and King Pecheur went with him.

After that Sir Percival abided in that place for three days, and King Pecheur and his lady Queen and their two young sons who dwelt at that place made great pity over him, and wept a great deal. But Sir Percival said but little in reply and wept not at all.

And now I shall tell you of that wonderful vision that came unto Sir Percival at this place upon Christmas day.

For on the third day (which was Christmas day) it chanced that Sir Percival sat alone in the hall of the castle, and he meditated upon the great sorrow that lay upon him. And as he sat thus this very wonderful thing befell him: He suddenly beheld two youths enter that hall. And the faces of the two youths shone with exceeding brightness, and their hair shone like gold, and their raiment was very bright and glistering like to gold. One of these youths bare in his hand a spear of mighty size, and blood dropped from the point of the spear; and the other youth bare in his hand a chalice of pure gold, very wonderful to behold, and he held the chalice in a napkin of fine cambric linen.

Sir Percival beholds the grail.

Then, at first, Sir Percival thought that that which he beheld was a vision conjured up by the deep sorrow that filled his heart, and he was afeard. But the youth who bare the chalice spake in a voice extraordinarily high and clear. And he said: "Percival! Percival! be not afraid! This which thou here beholdest is the Sangreal, and that is the Spear of Sorrow. What then may thy sorrow be in the presence of these holy things that brought with them such great sorrow and affliction of soul that they have become entirely sanctified thereby! Thus, Percival, should thy sorrow so sanctify thy life and not make it bitter to thy taste. For so did this bitter cup become sanctified by the great sorrow that tasted of it."

Percival said: "Are these things real or are they a vision that I behold?"

He who bare the chalice said, "They are real." And he who bare the spear said, "They are real."

Then a great peace and comfort came to Sir Percival's heart and they never left him to the day of his death.

Then they who bare the Sangreal and the Spear went out of the hall, and Sir Percival kneeled there for a while after they had gone and prayed with great devotion and with much comfort and satisfaction.

And this was the first time that any of those knights that were of King Arthur's Round Table ever beheld that holy chalice, the which Sir Percival was one of three to achieve in after-years.

So when Sir Percival came forth from that hall, all those who beheld him were astonished at the great peace and calmness that appeared to emanate from him. But he told no one of that miraculous vision which he had just beheld, and, though it appeareth in the history of these things, yet it was not then made manifest.

Then Sir Percival said to King Pecheur, his uncle and to his aunt and to their sons: "Now, dear friends, the time hath come when I must leave you. For I must now presently go to the court of King Arthur in obedience to his commands and to acknowledge myself unto my brother, Sir Lamorack."

So that day Sir Percival set forth with intent to go to Camelot, where King Arthur was then holding court in great estate of pomp. And Sir Percival reached Camelot upon the fourth day from that time and that was during the feasts of Christmas-tide.

Sir Percival departs for court.

Now King Arthur sat at those feasts and there were six score of very noble company seated with him. And the King's heart was greatly uplifted and expanded with mirth and good cheer. Then, while all were feasting with great concord, there suddenly came into that hall an herald-messenger; the whom, when King Arthur beheld him, he asked: “What message hast thou brought?” Upon this the messenger said: “Lord, there hath come one asking permission to enter here whom you will be very well pleased to see.” The King said, “Who is it?” And the herald-messenger said, “He saith his name is Percival.”

Upon this King Arthur arose from where he sat and all the others uprose with him and there was a great sound of loud voices; for the fame of Sir Percival had waxed very great since he had begun his adventures. So King Arthur and the others went down the hall for to meet Sir Percival.

Then the door opened and Sir Percival came into that place, and his face shone very bright with peace and good-will; and he was exceedingly comely.

King Arthur said, “Art thou Percival?” And Percival said, “I am he.” Thereupon King Arthur took Sir Percival's head into his hands, and he kissed him upon the brow.

Sir Percival is received with joy.

And Sir Percival kissed King Arthur's hand and he kissed the ring of royalty upon the King's finger, and so he became a true knight in fealty unto King Arthur.

Then Sir Percival said: “Lord, have I thy leave to speak?” And King Arthur said, “Say on.” Sir Percival said, “Where is Sir Lamorack?” And King Arthur said, “Yonder he is.” Then Sir Percival perceived where Sir Lamorack stood among the others, and he went to Sir Lamorack and knelt down before him; and Sir Lamorack was very much astonished, and said: “Why dost thou kneel to me, Percival?” Then Sir Percival said, “Dost thou know this ring?”

Then Sir Lamorack knew his father's ring and he cried out in a loud voice: “That is my father's ring; how came ye by it?”

Percival said: “Our mother gave it to me, for I am thy brother.”

Sir Percival declares himself to Sir Lamorack.

Upon this Sir Lamorack cried out with great passion; and he flung his arms about Sir Percival, and he kissed him repeatedly upon the face. And so ardent was the great love and the great passion that moved him that all those who stood about could in no wise contain themselves, but wept at that which they beheld.

Then, after a while, King Arthur said: “Percival, come with me, for I have somewhat to show thee.”

Sir Percival is made Knight of the Round Table.

So King Arthur and Sir Lamorack and Sir Percival and several others went unto that pavilion which was the pavilion of the Round Table, and there King Arthur showed Sir Percival a seat which was immediately upon the right hand of the Seat Perilous.

And upon the back of that seat there was a name emblazoned in letters of gold; and the name was this:

PERCIVAL OF GALES

Then King Arthur said: "Behold, Sir Percival, this is thy seat, for four days ago that name appeared most miraculously, of a sudden, where thou seest it; wherefore that seat is thine."

Then Sir Percival was aware that that name had manifested itself at the time when the Sangreal had appeared unto him in the castle of King Pecheur, and he was moved with a great passion of love and longing for the Lady Yvette; so that, because of the strength of that passion, it took upon it the semblance of a terrible joy. And he said to himself: "If my lady could but have beheld these, how proud would she have been! But, doubtless, she now, looketh down from Paradise and beholdeth us and all that we do." Thereupon he lifted up his eyes as though to behold her, but she was not there, but only the roof of that pavilion.

But he held his peace and said naught to anyone of those thoughts that disturbed him.

With this I conclude for the present the adventures of Sir Percival with only this to say: that thereafter, as soon as might be, he and Sir Lamorack went up into the mountains where their mother dwelt and brought her down thence into the world, and that she was received at the court of King Arthur with great honor and high regard until, after a while, she entered into a nunnery and took the veil.

Likewise it is to be said that Sir Percival lived, as he had vowed to do, a virgin knight for all of his life; for he never paid court to any lady from that time, but ever held within the sanctuary of his mind the image of that dear lady who waited for him in Paradise until he should come unto her in such season as God should see fit.

But you must not think that this is all that there is to tell of that noble, gentle and worthy young knight whose history we have been considering. For after this he performed many glorious services to the great honor of his knighthood and achieved so many notable adventures that the world spoke of him as being second in worship only to Sir Launcelot of the Lake. Yea; there were many who doubted whether Sir Launcelot himself was really a greater knight than Sir Percival; and though I may admit that Sir Launcelot had the greater prowess, yet Sir Percival was, certes, the more pure in heart and transparent of soul of those two.

So, hereafter, if God so wills, I shall tell more of Sir Percival, for I shall have much to write concerning him when I have to tell of the achievement of the Sangreal which he beheld in that vision at the Castle of King Pecheur as aforetold.

So, for this time, no more of these adventures, but fare you well.

Conclusion

THUS ENDETH THE PARTICULAR HISTORY OF THOSE THREE WORTHY, NOBLE, excellent knights-champion—Sir Launcelot of the Lake, Sir Tristram of Lyonesse, and Sir Percival of Gales.

And I do hope that you may have found pleasure in considering their lives and their works as I have done. For as I wrote of their behavior and pondered upon it, meseemed they offered a very high example that anyone might follow to his betterment who lives in this world where so much that is ill needs to be amended.

But though I have told so much, yet, as I have just said, there remain many other things to tell concerning Sir Launcelot and Sir Percival, which may well afford anyone pleasure to read. These I shall recount in another volume at another time, with such particularity as those histories may demand.